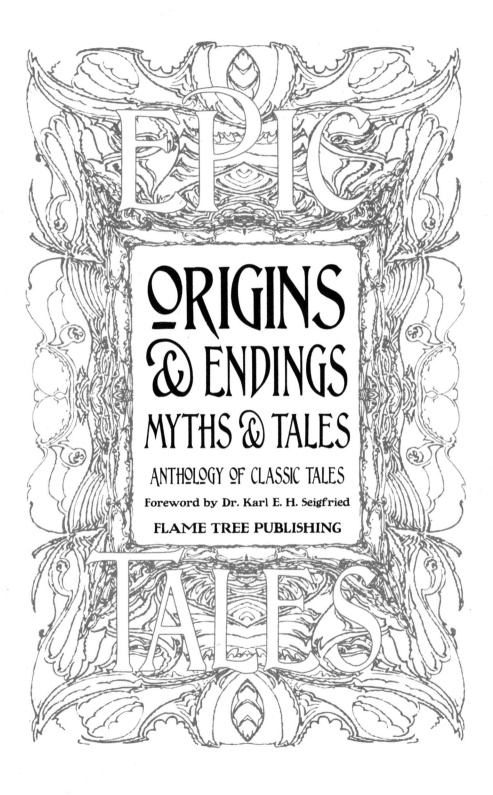

EPIC

ORIGINS & ENDINGS MYTHS & TALES

ANTHOLOGY OF CLASSIC TALES

Foreword by Dr. Karl E. H. Seigfried

FLAME TREE PUBLISHING

TALES

This is a FLAME TREE Book

Publisher & Creative Director: Nick Wells
Editorial Director: Catherine Taylor
Project Editor: Jocelyn Pontes
Special thanks to Michael Kerrigan

FLAME TREE PUBLISHING
6 Melbray Mews, Fulham,
London SW6 3NS, United Kingdom
www.flametreepublishing.com

First published 2025
Copyright © 2025 Flame Tree Publishing Ltd

25 27 29 28 26
1 3 5 7 9 10 8 6 4 2

ISBN: 978-1-83562-291-9
Special ISBN: 978-1-83562-676-4

All rights reserved. No part of this publication may be reproduced, stored in a retrieval system, or transmitted in any form or by any means, electronic, mechanical, photocopying, recording or otherwise, without the prior written permission of the publisher.

The cover image is created by Flame Tree Studio based on artwork by Bourbon-88. Internal decorations are courtesy Shutterstock.com and the following artists: Xenia Artwork, GoodStudio and Anne Mathiasz (story headers).

Due to the historical nature of the original texts, we're aware that there may be some language used which has the potential to cause offence to the modern reader. However, wishing to overall preserve the integrity of the writing, rather than imposing contemporary sensibilities, we have left it largely unaltered.

A copy of the CIP data for this book is available from the British Library.

Printed and bound in China

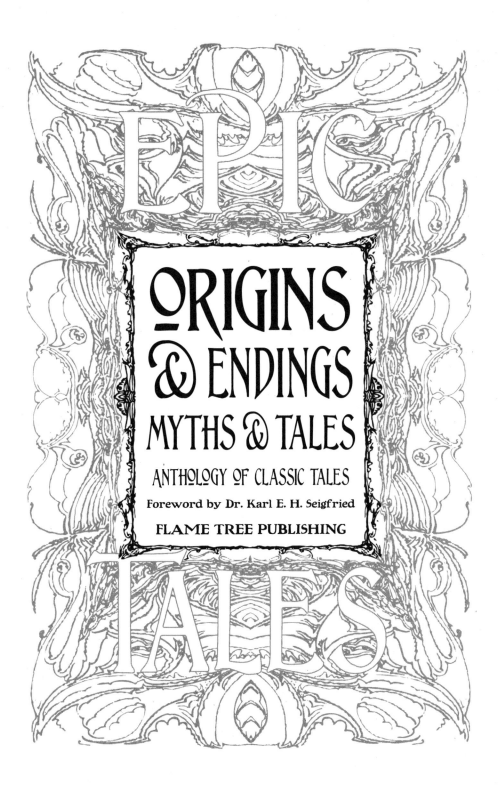

EPIC

ORIGINS & ENDINGS MYTHS & TALES

ANTHOLOGY OF CLASSIC TALES

Foreword by Dr. Karl E. H. Seigfried

FLAME TREE PUBLISHING

TALES

Contents

Foreword 16
Publisher's Note 17

ORIGINS & ENDINGS IN MYTH & FOLKLORE: INTRODUCTION

Thinking Myths 20
Battle of the Sexes 21
The Birth of the Earth 22
The Separation of the Sky 22
Emergent Humanity 23
A Note of Scepticism 23
Deeper Themes 24
Happy Endings? 25
Round and Round We Go 26

CREATION OF THE GODS, THE HEAVENS AND THE EARTH

Introduction 27
Chaos and Nyx 28
   (From Greek mythology)
The Egg Myth 28
   (From Greek mythology)
The Titans 29
   (From Greek mythology)
The Birth of Zeus 30
   (From Greek mythology)
The Giants' War 31
   (From Greek mythology)
Pandora 33
   (From Greek mythology)
The Creation of the Universe 34
   (From the Yoruba people, west Africa)
Olokun's Revenge 36
   (From the Yoruba people, west Africa)

CONTENTS

Agemo Outwits Olokun 37
    (From the Yoruba people, west Africa)

The Gods Descend from the Sky 38
    (From the Dahomean people, west Africa)

God Abandons the Earth 39
    (From Ghana, west Africa)

The Sun and the Moon 40
    (From the Krachi people, west Africa)

Why the Sun and the Moon Live in the Sky 41
    (From southern Nigeria, west Africa)

The Girl of the Early Race, Who Made Stars 42
    (From the San people, southern Africa)

The Creation of the Universe 43
    (From Norse mythology)

The Creation of the Earth 44
    (From Norse mythology)

Night and Day 45
    (From Norse mythology)

Asgard 46
    (From Norse mythology)

The Gods Arrive 47
    (From Irish mythology)

The Rise of the Sun God 49
    (From Irish mythology)

The Creation 53
    (From Turkish mythology)

Pan Gu and the Creation of the Universe 54
    (From Chinese mythology)

How the Five Ancients Became Men 55
    (From Chinese mythology)

Izanagi and Izanami 56
    (From Japanese mythology)

Nasadiya Sukta (The Hymn of Creation) 58
    (From Hindu mythology)

The Birth of Rama 59
    (From Hindu mythology)

Krishna's Birth 60
  (From Hindu mythology)

How the World Was Made 61
  (From the Cherokee people, North America)

The Story of the Creation 63
  (From the Kumeyaay people, North America)

The Mother of the World 64
  (From Native American oral tradition)

The Making of Daylight 67
  (From the Achomawi people, North America)

Creation Myth of the Iroquois 68
  (From the Haudenosaunee people, North America)

Osage Creation Story 71
  (From the Osage people, North America)

Spider's Creation 72
  (From the Zia people, North America)

San Luiseño Creation Myth 73
  (From the Luiseño people, North America)

The Discovery of the Upper World 74
  (From Native American oral tradition)

The Great Deeds of Michabo 76
  (From the Algonquian people, North America)

The Creation of the World 77
  (From the Akimel O'odham people, North America)

The Creation Story of the Four Suns 78
  (From Aztec mythology)

Creation Story of the Mixtecs 79
  (From Mixtec mythology)

The Mayan Creation Story 80
  (From Mayan mythology)

The Creation Story of the Third Book 80
  (From Mayan mythology)

How the World Was Made 82
  (From Philippine mythology)

Tane – The Creation of Nature 84
  (From Polynesian oral tradition)

The Creation of the Stars 85
  (From Polynesian oral tradition)

The Creation of Hawaiki 87
  (From Polynesian oral tradition)

The Human World Emerges

Introduction 91
Prometheus 92
  (From Greek mythology)
Obatala Creates Mankind 93
  (From the Yoruba people, west Africa)
Why Some Men Are White and Others Black 95
  (From the Kongo people, Republic of Congo)
The Punishment of the Inquisitive Man 95
  (From the Boloki people, western Democratic Republic of the Congo)
Mbungi and His Punishment 96
  (From the Boloki people, western Democratic Republic of the Congo)
How the Dog Came to Live with Man 97
  (From the Bushongo people, southern Democratic Republic of the Congo)
Origins of the Ivory Trade 99
  (From the Benga people, Equatorial Guinea and Gabon)
The First Humans 103
  (From Norse mythology)
How the Cymry Land Became Inhabited 104
  (From Welsh mythology)
The Great Red Dragon of Wales 108
  (From Welsh mythology)
The Good King Arthur 112
  (From Welsh mythology)
Why the Sole of Man's Foot Is Flat 113
  (From Serbian mythology)
The Wonderful Alpine Horn 114
  (From Swiss mythology)
The Story of the Fleur-de-Lys 117
  (From Belgian mythology)
The Tradition of the Tea-Plant 119
  (From Chinese mythology)

How Footbinding Started... 124
    (From Chinese mythology)

Prince Sandalwood, the Father of Korea....................... 129
    (From Korean mythology)

The Life of Buddha.. 132
    (From Buddhist mythology)

The Origin of the Three Races................................... 133
    (From Native American oral tradition)

The Origin of Women... 134
    (From Native American oral tradition)

The Old Chippeway.. 136
    (From the Ojibwe people, North America)

The Coyote or Prairie Wolf.. 137
    (From Native American oral tradition)

The First Appearance of Man..................................... 140
    (From the Navajo people, North America)

The Navajo Origin Legend:
    The Story of the Emergence............................... 142
    (From the Navajo people, North America)

The Finding of Fire.. 151
    (From the Yana people, North America)

Omaha Sacred Legend... 153
    (From the Omaha people, North America)

The Legend of the Peace Pipes................................... 154
    (From the Omaha people, North America)

The Raven Myth... 155
    (From the Tlingit people, North America)

Xolotl Creates the
    Parents of Mankind... 161
    (From Aztec mythology)

The Children of Heaven and Earth............................... 162
    (From Polynesian oral tradition)

The Discovery of New Zealand.................................... 166
    (From Polynesian oral tradition)

The Voyage to New Zealand...................................... 168
    (From Polynesian oral tradition)

The First Tui Tonga 176
   (From Polynesian oral tradition)

The Art of Netting Learned by
Kahukura from the Fairies 185
   (From Polynesian oral tradition)

Unmaking & Remaking the World

Introduction 187

The Great Deluge 188
   (From Greek mythology)

The Sack of Troy 189
   (From Greek mythology)

The Giant of the Flood 194
   (From Jewish narrative)

Tales of Ragnarok 197
   (From Norse mythology)

The Decline and Fall of the Gods 205
   (From Irish mythology)

The War Between the Gods of
Fire and Water 207
   (From Chinese mythology)

Nu Wa Repairs the Sky 208
   (From Chinese mythology)

The Flood and the Rainbow 209
   (From the Lenape people, North America)

The Fall of the Lenape 210
   (From the Lenape people, North America)

The Creation of Man and the Flood 213
   (From the Akimel O'odham people, North America)

The Flood 215
   (From the Tlingit people, North America)

The Deluge 216
   (From the Cherokee people, North America)

A Story of the Rise and Fall
of the Toltecs 216
   (From Aztec mythology)

The Mexican Noah 220
   (From Aztec mythology)

Tezcatlipoca, Overthrower
of the Toltecs 220
   (From Aztec mythology)

Tezcatlipoca Deceives the Toltecs 221
   (From Aztec mythology)

EXPLAINING THE NATURAL WORLD

Introduction 224

The Goat, the Lion and the Serpent 225
   (From the Basoko people, Democratic Republic of the Congo)

The City of the Elephants 227
   (From the Basoko people, Democratic Republic of the Congo)

Why the Fowl and Dog Are Abused by the Birds 232
   (From the Boloki people, western Democratic Republic of the Congo)

Why the Fowls Never Shut Their Doors 232
   (From the Lower Congo Basin)

Why the Dog and the Palm-Rat Hate Each Other 233
   (From the Lower Congo Basin)

Why the Congo Robin Has a Red Breast 234
   (From the Lower Congo Basin)

Why the Small-Ants Live in the Houses 235
   (From the Lower Congo Basin)

The Fight Between the Two Fetishes,
Lifuma and Chimpukela 235
   (From the Kongo people, Republic of Congo)

Why the Crocodile Does Not Eat the Hen 236
   (From the Kongo people, Republic of Congo)

Why Mosquitoes Buzz 237
   (From the Mpongwe people, Gabon)

Origin of the Elephant 237
   (From the Benga people, Equatorial Guinea and Gabon)

The Magic Drum 238
   (From the Benga people, Equatorial Guinea and Gabon)

Leopard's Hunting Companions 243
   (From the Benga people, Equatorial Guinea and Gabon)

CONTENTS

Is the Bat a Bird or a Beast?..245
(From the Benga people, Equatorial Guinea and Gabon)

Dog, and His Human Speech...246
(From the Benga people, Equatorial Guinea and Gabon)

The Coming of Darkness...248
(From the Kono people, Sierra Leone)

Why the Moon Waxes and Wanes..248
(From southern Nigeria, west Africa)

Origin of Tiis Lake..249
(From Scandinavian mythology)

Why the Stork Loves Holland..250
(From Dutch mythology)

Assipattle and the Mester Stoorworm.................................253
(From Scottish mythology)

The Five Spirits of the Plague..262
(From Chinese mythology)

The Golden Beetle, or Why the Dog Hates the Cat......262
(From Chinese mythology)

Benten and the Dragon..269
(From Japanese mythology)

The Origin of Corn and Deer..269
(From the Jicarilla Apache people, North America)

The First Fire...272
(From the Cherokee people, North America)

Origin of Strawberries..273
(From the Cherokee people, North America)

Origin of Disease and Medicine..273
(From the Cherokee people, North America)

Origin of the Pleiades and the Pine....................................275
(From the Cherokee people, North America)

Ojeeg Annung, or The Summer Maker..............................276
(From the Ojibwe people, North America)

Peboan and Seegwun..279
(From the Ojibwe people, North America)

Nezhik-e-wä-wä-sun, or The Lone Lightning...............280
(From the Ojibwe people, North America)

Opeechee, or The Origin of the Robin 281
   (From the Ojibwe people, North America)

Mon-daw-min, or The Origin of Indian Corn 282
   (From the Ojibwe people, North America)

The Star Family, or Celestial Sisters 284
   (From the Shawnee people, North America)

The Winning of Halai Auna at the
House of Tuina 286
   (From the Yana people, North America)

Mishemokwa, or The Origin of the
Small Black Bear 291
   (From the Odawa people, North America)

The Origin of Medicine 299
   (From the Haudenosaunee people, North America)

Legend of the Corn 301
   (From the Arikara people, North America)

Origin of the Black Snakes 302
   (From the Passamaquoddy people, North America)

O-wel'-lin the Rock Giant 303
   (From the Miwok people, North America)

The Origin of the Tides 305
   (From the Tsetsaut people, North America)

How Night Came 305
   (From Brazilian mythology)

How the Brazilian Beetles Got
Their Gorgeous Coats 307
   (From Brazilian mythology)

How the Rabbit Lost His Tail 309
   (From Brazilian mythology)

How the Tiger Got His Stripes 310
   (From Brazilian mythology)

Arnomongo and Iput-Iput 312
   (From Philippine mythology)

The Battle of the Crabs 313
   (From Philippine mythology)

The Eagle and the Hen 314
   (From Philippine mythology)

How the Lizards Got Their Markings 315
   (From Philippine mythology)
The Living Head 315
   (From Philippine mythology)
The Meeting of the Plants 316
   (From Philippine mythology)
The Spider and the Fly 316
   (From Philippine mythology)
Why Dogs Wag Their Tails 317
   (From Philippine mythology)
The Monkey and the Turtle 318
   (From Philippine mythology)
Star Tales of the Aboriginal Australians 319
   (From the Euahlayi people, Australia)
The Battle of the Giants 322
   (From Polynesian oral tradition)
The Origin of Kava 324
   (From Polynesian oral tradition)

Death, the Afterlife & the Underworld

Introduction 326
Pluto and the Underworld 327
   (From Greek mythology)
The Visit to the Dead 331
   (From Greek mythology)
The Story of Orpheus and Eurydice 339
   (From Greek mythology)
Death and Burial of the Fjort 341
   (From the Kongo people, Republic of Congo)
The Twin Brothers 343
   (From the Kongo people, Republic of Congo)
Sumerian Stories of the Netherworld 345
   (From Sumerian mythology)
The Adventure of Setne Khamwas
   with the Mummies 356
   (From Egyptian mythology)
The Death of Sigurd 364
   (From Norse mythology)

Frank Martin and the Fairies 366
   (From Irish mythology)

The Talking Head of Donn-Bo 368
   (From Irish mythology)

Departure of the Fairies 370
   (From Scottish mythology)

The Blacksmith's Stool 370
   (From Czech mythology)

Solomon Cursed by His Mother 372
   (From Serbian mythology)

The Voice of Death..373
   (From Romanian mythology)

The Thirty-Three Places Sacred to Kwannon.......................375
   (From Japanese mythology)

Kwannon and the Deer 376
   (From Japanese mythology)

Daikoku's Rat 377
   (From Japanese mythology)

Ta-Hong...377
   (From Korean mythology)

The King of Yom-Na (Hell)..382
   (From Korean mythology)

Hong's Experiences in Hades...384
   (From Korean mythology)

The Daughter of the Sun: Origin of Death.........................386
   (From the Cherokee people, North America)

How Glooskap Left the World 388
   (From the Algonquin people, North America)

The Funeral Fire 390
   (From the Chippewa people, North America)

Retrospection 393
   (From the Blackfoot people, North America)

The Visit to the Dead...394
   (From the Yokut people, North America)

Qalagánguasê, Who Passed to the Land of Ghosts.......395
   (From the Inuit people, North America)

The Land of the Dead...397
   (From the Inuit people, North America)
The Return of the Dead Wife...397
   (From the Tlingit people, North America)
A Journey to Xibalba...399
   (From Mayan mythology)
The Boat that Went to Pulotu..402
   (From Polynesian oral tradition)
The Burial of Te Heu-Heu on Tongariro........................408
   (From Polynesian oral tradition)
How Milu Became the King of Ghosts............................410
   (From Polynesian oral tradition)
Maluae and the Underworld..412
   (From Polynesian oral tradition)
A Visit to the King of Ghosts..415
   (From Hawaiian oral tradition)

BIOGRAPHIES & TEXT SOURCES..419

Foreword

MYTHS, AT A fundamental level, are emanations from and expressions of a given culture. Sometimes, they simply represent a cultural group's sense of humour. Sometimes, they seriously address specific theological issues within the religious life of a cultural unit. A strong focus on the sacrificial rite, for example, can be found in the myths of both Iceland and India, especially in their closely parallel tales of creation through sacrifice and their stories of gods performing sacrifices or becoming sacrifices themselves, sometimes to themselves. Myths can, of course, be enjoyed by readers and listeners of all ages and at all levels of engagement, but there is much to be learned by attempting to – as far as possible – place the myths in their original contexts and within the lives of those living today who still see them as sacred and inspirational texts.

The philosopher Paul Ricœur conceived of myths as symbols interacting in narrative form. When we read seemingly fantastical tales of creation and destruction with details and concepts that may at first seem alien, we should ask what the various characters, objects, and events symbolize – and for whom those symbols had and have meaning. Although the Biblical texts which constitute the myths of Judaism and Christianity are often left out of collections such as this, they can provide a mythology reading guide for those who were raised in those traditions. If the adventures of Moses or Christ are meaningful to the reader, that reader can ask what exactly is meaningful about them, then approach the myths of other faith traditions with a similar sensitivity to embedded meaning. To simply read the myths of other religious traditions as fantasy fiction misses so much.

A basic role of mythology is to address questions about the world and our roles within it. The goal is not necessarily to answer questions but to identify them and struggle with them. Tales of heroes and villains, of gods and monsters, of origins and endings ask us to consider a range of questions. Why is the world like it is? How did it begin? How will it end? Why do things happen? Why do we act as we do? What will become of us? What will become of me? Myths are not wrongheaded answers from primitive peoples, not bad information that science has swept away. If we approach them with honesty and openness, we can find within them ways of seeing the world and ourselves. They may not provide the concrete answers sought by fundamentalists, but – despite their age – they can give us new perspectives on questions we have asked and always will ask.

Mythology, like poetry, can't really be translated. Literal translation can lead to what may have been plain references in the original language becoming bizarre non-sequiturs. Idiomatic translation can lead to a false sense of understanding by feeding the reader metaphors and similes that would have made no sense to the creators of the myths. Older translations have too often been products of outsiders examining the texts of subjugated peoples, sometimes with the specific project of studying in order to better control. Prejudices creep in, such as the common use in translations from decades past of the word *race* for terms meaning *family*, *kindred* and *generation*. There was also a long tradition of European and American translators treating creation and destruction myths as either misunderstandings of Biblical teachings or as signs that the religions were dead ends; *Ragnarök for thee, salvation for me*.

When reading a collection of myths from a wide variety of sources and translations, there is always a danger of mixing up the original culture's value systems, the translator's worldview and our own personal reactions. Without reading the myths in cultural and historical contexts, there is a temptation to genericize into meaninglessly broad and culturally bleached-out categories such as "the hero's journey", to see commonalities that say more about our own conceptions of the world and ourselves than what is expressed in the myths themselves. The challenge to the reader is to approach mythology with both (1) an open mind that avoids hierarchization while being receptive to what may at first seem shockingly different and (2) a critical mind that refuses to see the translator as infallible communicator while supplementing the reading of myths with at least a general understanding of the context in which they were created and continue to be used.

Reading mythology is a lifelong endeavour that never ceases to provide new insights and *aha!* moments. Best wishes on your journey!

Dr. Karl E. H. Seigfried

Publisher's Note

THE POSSIBLE ORIGINS and endings of all things have gripped the human imagination as far back as memory goes. These two subjects form the basis of human curiosity and inquiry into the world around us, driving powerful storytelling through the millennia. In this anthology we have striven to curate a wide range of stories from a variety of cultures around the world, each providing a special insight into two of the greatest and most fundamental questions humanity has attempted to answer: Where did we come from? And where might we be going?

As always, we must remind the reader that, as tales from mythology and folklore are principally derived from an oral storytelling tradition, their written representation depends on the transcription, translation and interpretation by those who heard them and first put them to paper, and also on whether they are recently re-told versions or more directly sourced from original first-hand accounts. The stories in this book are a mixture, and you can learn more about the sources and authors at the back of the book. Due to the historical nature of such texts, we're aware that there may be some language used which has the potential to cause offence to the modern reader. However, wishing to overall preserve the integrity of the writing, rather than imposing contemporary sensibilities, we have left it largely unaltered. For this reason too, please note that spellings may differ between stories depending on their origins.

We also ask the reader to remember that while the myths and tales are timeless, much of the factual information and opinions regarding the nature of countries and their peoples, as well as the style of writing in this anthology, are products of the era during which they were written.

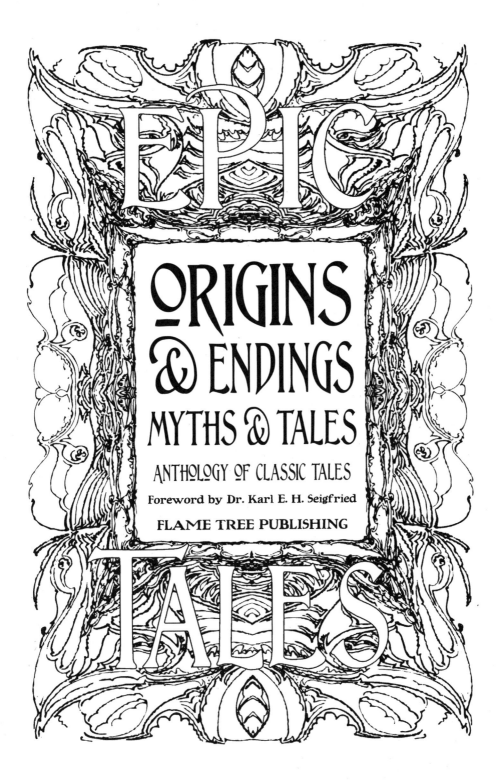

Origins & Endings in Myth & Folklore

Introduction

"THOUSANDS OF YEARS ago," said the Filipino storytellers, "there was no land, nor sun nor moon nor stars, and the world was only a great sea of water, above which stretched the sky" (p.82). The water, they went on, was the kingdom of the god Maguayan, while the sky was ruled by the great god Captan. In time, the tale goes on, Maguayan's daughter Lidagat (the sea itself) and Captan's son Lihangin (the wind) got married. Soon they were having sons and daughters of their own. These children grew up to embody the rocks and metals of the earth as it formed physically and to control the winds that scoured the seas.

If mythologies don't always heed the advice of Lewis Carroll's King of Hearts to "begin at the beginning", they just about invariably end up there at some point. Because where we start holds vital clues to who we are. And the urge to understand this, and account for how our world came to be the way it is, has united men and women across every inhabited continent and in every time – as has the recognition that the comprehension of these things is best to be attained through the kind of concrete examples myths and legends supply, and most easily to be communicated through the compelling power of narratives.

Thinking Myths

This is why the material here takes the form of stories, of compelling narratives: the form has a unique ability to engage a crucial aspect of truth held at the centre of every tale. To take each apart and anatomize its 'content' would diminish it, though it is important at least to get some sense of just how significant and serious that content can be. For the tales collected here tell us how the world was made, how the first plants and trees grew, how the different animal species acquired their distinctive forms. They also, of course, offer accounts of how we humans came into being, how we were first formed, how we went on to acquire familial and social ties and to build wider communities and ethnic groups. Though the tales in this collection have been selected primarily for the insights they offer into human origins and ultimate endings, they have things to say about just about every area of existence.

So much so that it seems mythology itself originated as the way a pre-literate and pre-scientific humanity sought to understand its world, life and death and, ultimately, itself. Mythology made sense of things, at least at some symbolic level, even if it didn't spell out a literalistic history of how those things came to be. In other words, we learned to think in myths.

But the French anthropologist Claude Lévi-Strauss went even further in his famous study *Mythologiques* (1969). So basic were the assumptions myths installed in us, he said, that they actually – and actively – shaped the ways in which we experienced and interpreted our existence. It wasn't just that humans thought in myths, but that myths 'thought' in humans, organizing and structuring their ways of thinking without their even being aware that this was so. Taken together, the stories here suggest something like a road map for human existence as a whole – an articulation, in symbolic terms, of who we are.

This map remains current as it ever was; though rooted in the deepest past, myths are, to all intents and purposes, timeless – no more (nor less) true in the twenty-first century than in the Neolithic. A story only exists in its telling, of course, and every re-telling carries traces of the age and culture in which it was conceived. The versions of the myths we've included here date generally from the late-nineteenth and early-twentieth centuries – a golden age both for folkloric research and for the appreciation of old stories. It was also, of course, an age with its own prejudices. For the most part, though, the great revelation of these tales is twofold: how much we do have in common, at the profoundest level, with much earlier human cultures; and how much they have in common with one another.

Battle of the Sexes

For example, the Filipino creation story continued with the rebellion of the younger deities against the authority of Captan. They set out to take the sky by storm, unleashing torrents and tumults of unimaginable violence and strength.

This tale shares the trope of battling gods with the Greeks, who described the Earth goddess Gaia's sons, the Giants, waging war against the Olympians in the myth of the *Gigantomachia*. The idea of the 'Earth Mother', too, is immediately recognizable as a modern cliché: the ultra-nurturing deity utterly in tune with her maternal role and the mystic rhythms of life more generally. The belief is of deep antiquity, and is readily discernible in many early myths across cultures.

For California's Kumeyaay people, the earth was a woman, and the sky was a man who lay atop her. From their coupling a creation resulted. This account of the earth's origin clearly draws out the sexual symbolism that is only implicit in many other mythologies, like the Greek story of the relation between Zeus' Olympians and Gaia's Earth. This myth, however, is more explicit in spelling out the assumptions of male supremacy which would underlie not just Greek but all subsequent Western cosmologies. Zeus, with his symbolically phallic lightning bolts, was not to support but supplant the reign of Gaia. He stood for order, definition; she for undifferentiated chaos. It wasn't explicitly stated that Zeus's heavenly-based ascendancy was 'better', but it didn't have to be; it marked a progression, a stage in the evolution of the cosmic order.

The point would be summed up succinctly in the fortunes of the French artist Gustave Courbet's 1866 painting *L'Origine du Monde* ('The Origin of the World'). This notorious work had at its centre a close-up view of a woman's vulva, framed by her thighs and abdomen. It was from here, Courbet clearly implied, that we all came. A natural enough assumption, and not in itself a degrading one. This was, some critics have enthused, a work of surpassing artistry, an all but prayerful elevation of the principle of feminine beauty and creative power. Be that as it may, the fact that Courbet's provocative work was received as pornography at the time might give us pause. Even in the earliest myths we find, as in the Greek one, an earthy elementalism (coded feminine) being supplanted by a 'higher' heavenly (and masculine) order.

The Tlicho or 'Dogrib' people of Canada's Northwest Territories tell the story of 'The Mother of the World' – a woman who lives self-sufficiently and completely contented in the wilderness.

She receives a visit from a creature we recognize as a dog and makes him her companion. Then, from above, the godly figure of Manitou descends to see her in her dreams and tells her of her destiny as the mother to a long line of children. She wakes to find her dog transformed into the first man. While she is the maker of humanity, he makes a home for it. Hitherto, the story says, "the world had lain a rude and shapeless mass" (p.66). It is the man who reduces it to order.

He threw the rough and stony crags into the deep valley – he moved the frozen mountain to fill up the boiling chasm. When he had levelled the earth, which before was a thing without form, he marked out with his great walking-staff the lakes, ponds and rivers, and caused them to be filled with water from the interior of the earth, bidding them to be replenished from the rains and melted snows which should fall from the skies, till they should be no more.

Again, we see, the woman makes the substance of the earth, while the man shapes it and gives it form.

The Birth of the Earth

This is not to say that primeval disorder is gendered female in every mythic source. Its embodiment in Norse legend is Ymir, a big, obnoxious – and thoroughly masculine – male, the most massive giant it is possible to imagine. Even so, in some versions of his legend, he gives birth to children through his armpits. We find his symbolism intimately entwined with that of motherhood; the idea is apparently elemental to human understanding of who we are. Ymir lived beside Ginnungagap, the primordial chasm of emptiness. There he subsisted by suckling at the udder of Audhumla, the giant cow – a literally infantilizing way of describing a dreadful giant. He's emotionally impotent as well. We're told how he watched with mounting jealousy as Audhumla licked away at an icy cliff nearby, and the form of a figure – shapely and beautiful, far more appealing than he – slowly took form. Bur, the progenitor of the true gods, was blessed in his looks and accomplishments, but Ymir and his sons would war incessantly with him and his kin. Eventually, Bur's grandson Odin would lead a victorious attack upon Ymir and kill him, the aftermath of which is described in the story 'The Creation of the Earth':

> *Ymir's body was carried by Odin and his brothers to Ginnungagap, where it was placed in the centre. His flesh became the earth, and his skeleton the rocky crags which dipped and soared. From the soil sprang dwarfs, spontaneously, and they would soon be put to work. Ymir's teeth and shards of broken bones became the rocks and pits covering the earth and his blood was cleared to become the seas and waters that flowed across the land. (p.44)*

The Separation of the Sky

How the sky was made was evidently a major challenge to the mythic understanding. One with which we find many different cultures wrestling. Tu-chai-pai, god of the Kumeyaay creation, enlists the advice of his brother Yo-ko-mat-is, who shows him how to rub tobacco into dust, then puff upon it so, slowly but surely, it lifts up the sky. The division between earth and sky seems self-evident to us, even if we may wonder how these first earth-dwellers knew why such a separation might be needed. (We'll often see gods and monsters in these stories having physical forms and occupying places – even fully-formed landscapes, with mountains, rivers and roads – before the universe has ostensibly been created. From a scientific perspective, such situations are plainly nonsense; in the dreamlike logic of myth, though, they scarcely raise an eyebrow.)

We're all products of our environments, after all, even though the advent of urban civilization – many centuries old, but brand-new in the mythic scheme – has transformed the immediate realities of those environments beyond recognition. It seems to have been around 1300 BC that colonists from southeast Asia, travelling in family groups in fragile canoes with all their livestock and possessions, set out across the Pacific on speculative voyages that eventually took them to the islands of Melanesia, Fiji, Tonga and Samoa. The island peoples they became in Polynesia couldn't really imagine the mainland life they'd abandoned so long before. They saw their homeland as Hawaiki, whose legendary creation by J-o, the supreme godhead, was for them the origin of the entire world. J-o's inaugurating innovation was the creation of light, and the separation of day from night, whose continuing alternation would thenceforth be the ordering rhythm of existence. Next, in Tane, the god of trees, he created a force with the strength to push up the sky and separate the heavens from the earth.

In some mythologies this succession was reversed, and heavenly beings looked down from the sky and created the earth. The Japanese Shinto tradition is one example. Here the god Izanagi and his sister-bride Izanami gaze down from heaven to try and detect some sign of solidity and coherence in the shapeless emptiness below. Only when they reach down and stir the waters with a jewelled spear does the liquid congeal to form a tiny island. Small as it is, it's sufficiently substantial to bear their weight; they descend and take up residence there, and, as the days, weeks and months go by, Izanami gives birth to the archipelago that becomes Japan, with all its mountains, forests, rivers, lakes and surrounding seas.

Emergent Humanity

Physical reality is one thing. The 'world' as we think of it is another – more broadly defined to include a human dimension, in its turn encompassing psychological and social planes. We get a sense of that broadening significance from the story told by the Navajo people of what is now the American Southwest, of what they call the 'emergence' of humanity. The First World, in their cosmology, is only one step up from an utter void – little more than an amorphous play of light and darkness, night and day, over an empty waste across which the first rivers run down to vast, dark oceans, to confer some sort of rudimentary shape. Bats, beetles and locusts dwell here in cavities beneath the ground. They undergo a sort of mythohistorical process of evolution which takes them up through slowly-solidifying Second and Third worlds, finally emerging as fully human in the Fifth world, which is our own.

In Western tradition, the story of Prometheus has become emblematic of humanity's striving to better itself. Prometheus was notoriously punished by Zeus for giving people the secret of fire, a discovery which went on to unlock technological progress of every kind. For Alaska's Tlingit, fire was first sighted far out at sea by the Raven – the wisest of the animal-spirits and protector of humanity in its early days. In John R. Swanton's *Tlingit Myths and Texts* (1909), the Raven sends the Chicken Hawk out with some pitch wood tied to his beak, and tells him to hold it to the fire. When he returns, his beak aglow, the Raven puts the fire into the stones on the beach and into the red cedar wood. Henceforth, that is where they should get their fire from, he tells the human tribes.

A Note of Scepticism

Another bird altogether is the focus of the Dutch tale 'Why the Stork Loves Holland'. A fairy deputation to Africa, it seems, invited the stork to migrate north, to deal with a plague of frogs and other vermin. Though unabashedly whimsical, this story does address the question of how the Netherlands came by this iconic bird. The irreverent tone of the tale is actually often to be found in what anthropologists call 'pourquoi stories' (from the French word *pourquoi*, meaning 'why?'). These accounts of how often highly specific things originated appear in mythic storytelling across many cultures. (Readers in English know such tales as 'Just-so stories', from the mock-mythic efforts of Rudyard Kipling, written in 1902 and remaining extremely popular ever since.)

The existence of such stories is a useful corrective to the idea explored above that myths were a way for primitive humanity to fathom the universal mysteries of their reality. Whilst that is clearly true to a point, it's every bit as evident – in myths like this especially – that mythic wisdom may be tongue-in-cheek. Certainly, these stories seem more light-hearted by and large than those grander narratives which describe the creation of the world. And, far from actually explaining the world, their appeal often lies chiefly in their ingenious improbability. In this book, for example, you can read a hilariously roundabout Chinese explanation for how the dog came to hate the cat, a central African explanation for why the crocodile doesn't eat the hen and, from Serbia, the story of how the soles of humans' feet came to be flat.

Deeper Themes

Such stories aren't always trivial in final intent, however wittily they're related. The insights may just be geographical. For instance, Alaska's Tsetsaut tell us all about 'The Origin of the Tides'. But deeper, darker themes are examined too. The Boloki of Africa's Congo Valley offer an intriguing account of how murder came into the world.

Literal darkness is explained by the old Brazilian story of 'How Night Came'. In the earliest days, apparently, the sun shone perpetually and night fell only in the ocean's deepest depths. This all changed when the daughter of the Great Sea Serpent married a son of Man. She enjoyed herself at first, blissfully happy in her marriage, but eventually she grew weary of the endless sunlight of her life ashore. She pined for night, and eventually her husband sent slaves to see her father in the deep. The Great Sea Serpent gave them a sack containing darkness, and all the beasts and birds that went with it. They were to take this back to give to his daughter – her own little personal supply of night. On their journey home, however, spooked by the eerie and unsettling noises coming from inside the sack, they opened it and let night rush upon the world. Since then, night has fallen regularly for everyone.

The Ojibwe of North America's Great Lakes Region describe a poor man who undertakes a fast in hopes that the Great Spirit will be moved to give him guidance on how to feed his starving family. Over several days his body gradually weakens, but when a celestial stranger appears and challenges him to a trial of strength, he agrees to wrestle with him and does his best, though he is no match for his opponent in size or strength. As the days go by, he wrestles with him again, and he grows progressively weaker physically, but he finds he's also charged with ever-greater mental strength. Finally, the stranger throws in the towel and gives him a gift of food: the first known ear of corn. The importance of this staple to a great many Native American peoples is attested by the number of different origin myths there are for it.

Another Ojibwe story, 'Opeechee, or The Origin of the Robin', starts out in a mood of apparent whimsy but ends up in deeper philosophical waters. A young man, Opeechee, finds he's unable to fulfil the warrior's destiny his father evidently wants for him. His metamorphosis into bird form is an allegory for the artist's destiny. 'I shall ever be happy and contented,' Opeechee tells his father, *and although I could not gratify your wishes as a warrior, it will be my daily aim to make you amends for it as a harbinger of peace and joy. I will cheer you by my songs, and strive to inspire in others the joy and lightsomeness I feel in my present state...I am now freed from the cares and pains of human life. My food is spontaneously furnished by the mountains and fields, and my pathway of life is in the bright air. (p.282)*

Happy Endings?

Every story, wrote Aristotle, has a beginning, a middle and an end. Ultimately, only the last of these may matter. As his fellow Athenian Sophocles noted of his tragic protagonist Oedipus, who blinded himself in a fit of shame and guilt on learning he'd killed his father and slept with his mother, "We must call no mortal happy until he has crossed life's border free from pain" (ed. Richard Jebb, *Oedipus Tyrannus*, 1889). Oedipus, after all, had seemed the most fortunate of men until the truth of his existence was accidentally revealed.

We're all heading towards death, of course. In face of its fear we mostly pursue a policy of denial unless, like Oedipus, we're forced to confront the realities of our existence. Few of us manage the philosophical detachment to recognize that death is necessary to life, as the blacksmith in the old Czech story is forced to do. He finds himself in the fortunate position of being able to keep Death prisoner, so he does. Without death, however, he can have no meat; nor hope to control the vermin that soon infest his home and its surroundings. Fish and frogs and other creatures proliferate so limitlessly in the streams that the water in them is no longer drinkable; mosquitoes swarm, and the air fills up with flies. In resignation, he releases death, and, as the story concludes, "made no outcry when she placed her bony fingers on his throat" (p.372).

It's no surprise that storytellers have tried to address the issue of death, as difficult a subject for us to comprehend as to confront. In this book is a Cherokee take on the 'Origin of Disease and Medicine' and the story of how the Sun's daughter introduced death to our existence. A succession of human travellers have meanwhile made their way to the realm of the dead and come back bearing reports. The *katabasis* ('descent') famously made by the Greek hero Odysseus into the Underworld (*Odyssey*, Book XI) was to be emulated in Roman times by Virgil's hero in the *Aeneid*, and in the Christian era by the Italian poet Dante in his *Inferno* (c. 1321). The Greek musician Orpheus very nearly managed to bring his beloved wife Eurydice back from Hades but lost her when, nearing the earth's surface, he looked back.

The Hawaiian hero Ka-ilio-hae, wild dog warrior, sinks into unconsciousness, to all appearances dead, and in that state is ushered into the realm of the King of Ghosts. It seems a place of fun and merriment, and of unimaginably alluring female spirits, one of whom – inevitably – he falls in love with. Fortunately his own sister is on duty as one of the gatekeepers of the kingdom and knows all too well that the delights of Death-land are a trap. She seizes him, dragging him back by force and returning him to his home, where he groggily awakens, better now, to his family's delight.

Such myths clearly consider death in all its solemn mystery and menace. Others show storytellers trying to offer reassurance. The indigenous peoples of Alaska's Lower Yukon tell of the young woman who died, sinking into what seemed a sleep from which she was suddenly awakened by her late grandfather. He led her back through what was apparently the Land of the Dead, across the river of tears shed by mortal mourners for their dead. Her grandmother gave her food and water from her Yukon home, in vessels offered up by the villagers' Festival of the Dead. The Land of the Dead, she found, would be a home from home.

Round and Round We Go

"In my end is my beginning," wrote T.S. Eliot in his *Four Quartets* (1941). Some cultures have seen human existence measuring itself out in cycles of birth, death and regeneration. Mexico's Aztecs, indeed, viewed their history as having consisted of 'Four Suns' – though none of these appears to have brought fine weather. Rather, they had seen civilization thrive for many generations and then be swept away by a succession of cataclysms: flood, famine, tempest and fire. The fifth 'sun' was the present era – at least before it was swept away by one final catastrophe no one could possibly have foreseen: the empire's overthrow by Hernán Cortés and his Conquistadors.

If our beginnings establish who we are and send us out on the course we're going to follow, it takes an ending to confirm what we have been. In focusing on the supposed start and finish of our world, from Creation to Catastrophe, and of our lives from birth to death, this book ends up encompassing just about everything. Hence its awe-inspiring reach, its exhilarating range and its mesmerizing variety. All life, essentially, is here.

Creation of the Gods, the Heavens & the Earth

Introduction

THE YORUBA PEOPLE of West Africa tell of how the world was created as a more or less whimsical initiative of the god Obatala. Once upon a time, there was an endless ocean. Obatala climbed down and poured sand out of a snail shell of miraculously infinite capacity. He then released a white hen, which scratched about, scattering sand to form dry land. Sometimes it fell in larger piles, forming mountain ranges. Digging a hole, Obatala placed a palm nut inside. It quickly grew and propagated itself instantaneously. Quickly, whole forests of palm nuts formed. Obatala made palm wine and, drinking it, was very soon inebriated, hence his incapacity when it came to creating humankind. Wryly witty and unabashedly arbitrary in its account of the creation, this tale exemplifies both the power and the playfulness of the mythic imagination. Mighty as the gods and goddesses are, and seismic as the forces involved may be in theory, myths are human stories; thus their events take place on a human scale. Epic phenomena, recounted as anecdotes: this is the peculiar quality the creation myths possess, and the reason for their very special charm.

Chaos and Nyx

AT FIRST, when all things lay in a great confused mass, the Earth did not exist. Land, sea, and air were mixed up together; so that the earth was not solid, the sea was not fluid, nor the air transparent.

Over this shapeless mass reigned a careless deity called Chaos, whose personal appearance could not be described, as there was no light by which he could be seen. He shared his throne with his wife, the dark goddess of Night, named Nyx or Nox, whose black robes, and still blacker countenance, did not tend to enliven the surrounding gloom.

These two divinities wearied of their power in the course of time, and called their son Erebus (Darkness) to their assistance. His first act was to dethrone and supplant Chaos; and then, thinking he would be happier with a helpmeet, he married his own mother, Nyx. Of course, with our present views, this marriage was a heinous sin; but the ancients, who at first had no fixed laws, did not consider this union unsuitable, and recounted how Erebus and Nyx ruled over the chaotic world together, until their two beautiful children, Aether (Light) and Hemera (Day), acting in concert, dethroned them, and seized the supreme power.

Space, illumined for the first time by their radiance, revealed itself in all its uncouthness. Aether and Hemera carefully examined the confusion, saw its innumerable possibilities, and decided to evolve from it a 'thing of beauty;' but quite conscious of the magnitude of such an undertaking, and feeling that some assistance would be desirable, they summoned Eros (Love), their own child, to their aid. By their combined efforts, Pontus (the Sea) and Gaea (Ge, Tellus, Terra), as the Earth was first called, were created.

In the beginning the Earth did not present the beautiful appearance that it does now. No trees waved their leafy branches on the hillsides; no flowers bloomed in the valleys; no grass grew on the plains; no birds flew through the air. All was silent, bare, and motionless. Eros, the first to perceive these deficiencies, seized his life-giving arrows and pierced the cold bosom of the Earth. Immediately the brown surface was covered with luxuriant verdure; birds of many colours flitted through the foliage of the new-born forest trees; animals of all kinds gamboled over the grassy plains; and swift-darting fishes swam in the limpid streams. All was now life, joy, and motion.

Gaea, roused from her apathy, admired all that had already been done for her embellishment, and, resolving to crown and complete the work so well begun, created Uranus (Heaven).

The Egg Myth

THIS VERSION of the creation of the world, although but one of the many current with the Greeks and Romans, was the one most generally adopted; but another, also very popular, stated that the first divinities, Erebus and Nyx, produced a gigantic egg, from which Eros, the god of love, emerged to create the Earth.

The Earth thus created was supposed by the ancients to be a disk, instead of a sphere as science has proved. The Greeks fancied that their country occupied a central position, and that Mount Olympus, a very high mountain, the mythological abode of their gods, was placed in the exact centre. Their Earth was divided into two equal parts by Pontus (the Sea – equivalent to our Mediterranean and Black Seas); and all around it flowed the great river Oceanus in a 'steady, equable current,' undisturbed by storm, from which the Sea and all the rivers were supposed to derive their waters.

The Greeks also imagined that the portion of the Earth directly north of their country was inhabited by a fortunate race of men, the Hyperboreans, who dwelt in continual bliss, and enjoyed a never-ending springtide. Their homes were said to be 'inaccessible by land or by sea.' They were 'exempt from disease, old age, and death,' and were so virtuous that the gods frequently visited them, and even condescended to share their feasts and games. A people thus favoured could not fail to be happy, and many were the songs in praise of their sunny land.

South of Greece, also near the great river Oceanus, dwelt another nation, just as happy and virtuous as the Hyperboreans – the Ethiopians. They, too, often enjoyed the company of the gods, who shared their innocent pleasures with great delight.

And far away, on the shore of this same marvelous river, according to some mythologists, were the beautiful Isles of the Blest, where mortals who had led virtuous lives, and had thus found favour in the sight of the gods, were transported without tasting of death, and where they enjoyed an eternity of bliss. These islands had sun, moon, and stars of their own, and were never visited by the cold wintry winds that swept down from the north.

The Titans

CHAOS, EREBUS AND NYX were deprived of their power by Aether and Hemera, who did not long enjoy the possession of the sceptre; for Uranus and Gaea, more powerful than their progenitors, soon forced them to depart, and began to reign in their stead. They had not dwelt long on the summit of Mount Olympus, before they found themselves the parents of twelve gigantic children, the Titans, whose strength was such that their father, Uranus, greatly feared them. To prevent their ever making use of it against him, he seized them immediately after their birth, hurled them down into a dark abyss called Tartarus, and there chained them fast.

This chasm was situated far under the earth; and Uranus knew that his six sons (Oceanus, Coeus, Crius, Hyperion, Iapetus, and Cronus), as well as his six daughters, the Titanides (Ilia, Rhea, Themis, Thetis, Mnemosyne, and Phoebe), could not easily escape from its cavernous depths. The Titans did not long remain sole occupants of Tartarus, for one day the brazen doors were again thrown wide open to admit the Cyclopes – Brontes (Thunder), Steropes (Lightning), and Arges (Sheet-lightning) – three later-born children of Uranus and Gaea, who helped the Titans to make the darkness hideous with their incessant clamor for freedom. In due time their number was increased by the three terrible Centimani

(Hundred-handed), Cottus, Briareus, and Gyes, who were sent thither by Uranus to share their fate.

Greatly dissatisfied with the treatment her children had received at their father's hands, Gaea remonstrated, but all in vain. Uranus would not grant her request to set the giants free, and, whenever their muffled cries reached his ear, he trembled for his own safety. Angry beyond all expression, Gaea swore revenge, and descended into Tartarus, where she urged the Titans to conspire against their father, and attempt to wrest the sceptre from his grasp.

All listened attentively to the words of sedition; but none were courageous enough to carry out her plans, except Cronus, the youngest of the Titans, more familiarly known as Saturn or Time, who found confinement and chains peculiarly galling, and who hated his father for his cruelty. Gaea finally induced him to lay violent hands upon his sire, and, after releasing him from his bonds, gave him a scythe, and bade him be of good cheer and return victorious.

Thus armed and admonished, Cronus set forth, came upon his father unawares, defeated him, thanks to his extraordinary weapon, and, after binding him fast, took possession of the vacant throne, intending to rule the universe forever. Enraged at this insult, Uranus cursed his son, and prophesied that a day would come when he, too, would be supplanted by his children, and would suffer just punishment for his rebellion.

Cronus paid no heed to his father's imprecations, but calmly proceeded to release the Titans, his brothers and sisters, who, in their joy and gratitude to escape the dismal realm of Tartarus, expressed their willingness to be ruled by him. Their satisfaction was complete, however, when he chose his own sister Rhea (Cybele, Ops) for his consort, and assigned to each of the others some portion of the world to govern at will. To Oceanus and Thetis, for example, he gave charge over the ocean and all the rivers upon earth; while to Hyperion and Phoebe he entrusted the direction of the sun and moon, which the ancients supposed were daily driven across the sky in brilliant golden chariots.

The Birth of Zeus

PEACE AND SECURITY now reigned on and around Mount Olympus; and Cronus, with great satisfaction, congratulated himself on the result of his enterprise. One fine morning, however, his equanimity was disturbed by the announcement that a son was born to him. The memory of his father's curse then suddenly returned to his mind. Anxious to avert so great a calamity as the loss of his power, he hastened to his wife, determined to devour the child, and thus prevent him from causing further annoyance. Wholly unsuspicious, Rhea heard him enquire for his son. Gladly she placed him in his extended arms; but imagine her surprise and horror when she beheld her husband swallow the babe!

Time passed, and another child was born, but only to meet with the same cruel fate. One infant after another disappeared down the capacious throat of the voracious Cronus – a personification of Time, who creates only to destroy. In vain the bereaved mother besought the life of one little one: the selfish, hard-hearted father would not relent. As her prayers seemed unavailing, Rhea finally resolved to obtain by stratagem the boon her husband denied; and as soon as her youngest son, Zeus, was born, she concealed him.

Cronus, aware of his birth, soon made his appearance, determined to dispose of him in the usual summary manner. For some time Rhea pleaded with him, but at last pretended to yield to his commands. Hastily wrapping a large stone in swaddling clothes, she handed it to Cronus, simulating intense grief. Cronus was evidently not of a very inquiring turn of mind, for he swallowed the whole without investigating the real contents of the shapeless bundle.

Ignorant of the deception practiced upon him, Cronus then took leave, and the overjoyed mother clasped her rescued treasure to her breast. It was not sufficient, however, to have saved young Zeus from imminent death: it was also necessary that his father should remain unconscious of his existence.

To ensure this, Rhea entrusted her babe to the tender care of the Melian nymphs, who bore him off to a cave on Mount Ida. There a goat, Amalthea, was procured to act as nurse, and fulfilled her office so acceptably that she was eventually placed in the heavens as a constellation, a brilliant reward for her kind ministrations. To prevent Zeus' cries being heard in Olympus, the Curetes (Corybantes), Rhea's priests, uttered piercing screams, clashed their weapons, executed fierce dances, and chanted rude war songs.

The real significance of all this unwonted noise and commotion was not at all understood by Cronus, who, in the intervals of his numerous affairs, congratulated himself upon the cunning he had shown to prevent the accomplishment of his father's curse. But all his anxiety and fears were aroused when he suddenly became aware of the fraud practiced upon him, and of young Zeus' continued existence. He immediately tried to devise some plan to get rid of him; but, before he could put it into execution, he found himself attacked, and, after a short but terrible encounter, signally defeated.

Zeus, delighted to have triumphed so quickly, took possession of the supreme power, and aided by Rhea's counsels, and by a nauseous potion prepared by Metis, a daughter of Oceanus, compelled Cronus to produce the unfortunate children he had swallowed; i.e., Poseidon, Hades, Hestia, Demeter and Hera.

Following the example of his predecessor, Zeus gave his brothers and sisters a fair share of his new kingdom. The wisest among the Titans – Mnemosyne, Themis, Oceanus and Hyperion – submitted to the new sovereign without murmur, but the others refused their allegiance; which refusal, of course, occasioned a deadly conflict.

The Giants' War

ZEUS, FROM THE TOP of Mount Olympus, discerned the superior number of his foes, and, quite aware of their might, concluded that reinforcements to his party would not be superfluous. In haste, therefore, he released the Cyclopes from Tartarus, where they had languished so long, stipulating that in exchange for their freedom they should supply him with thunderbolts – weapons which only they knew how to forge. This new engine caused great terror and dismay in the ranks of the enemy, who, nevertheless, soon rallied, and struggled valiantly to overthrow the usurper and win back the sovereignty of the world.

During ten long years the war raged incessantly, neither party wishing to submit to the dominion of the other, but at the end of that time the rebellious Titans were obliged to yield. Some of them were hurled into Tartarus once more, where they were carefully secured by Poseidon, Zeus' brother, while the young conqueror joyfully proclaimed his victory.

The scene of this mighty conflict was supposed to have been in Thessaly, where the country bears the imprint of some great natural convulsion; for the ancients imagined that the gods, making the most of their gigantic strength and stature, hurled huge rocks at each other, and piled mountain upon mountain to reach the abode of Zeus, the Thunderer.

Cronus, the leader and instigator of the revolt, weary at last of bloodshed and strife, withdrew to Italy, or Hesperia, where he founded a prosperous kingdom, and reigned in peace for many long years.

Zeus, having disposed of all the Titans, now fancied he would enjoy the power so unlawfully obtained; but Gaea, to punish him for depriving her children of their birthright, created a terrible monster, called Typhoeus, or Typhon, which she sent to attack him. He was a giant, from whose trunk one hundred dragon heads arose; flames shot from his eyes, nostrils, and mouths; while he incessantly uttered such blood-curdling screams, that the gods, in terror, fled from Mount Olympus and sought refuge in Egypt. In mortal fear lest this terror-inspiring monster would pursue them, the gods there assumed the forms of different animals; and Zeus became a ram, while Hera, his sister and queen, changed herself into a cow.

The king of the gods, however, soon became ashamed of his cowardly flight, and resolved to return to Mount Olympus to slay Typhoeus with his terrible thunderbolts. A long and fierce struggle ensued, at the end of which, Zeus, again victorious, viewed his fallen foe with boundless pride; but his triumph was very short-lived.

Enceladus, another redoubtable giant, also created by Gaea, now appeared to avenge Typhoeus. He too was signally defeated, and bound with adamantine chains in a burning cave under Mount Etna. In early times, before he had become accustomed to his prison, he gave vent to his rage by outcries, imprecations, and groans: sometimes he even breathed forth fire and flames, in hopes of injuring his conqueror. But time, it is said, somewhat cooled his resentment; and now he is content with an occasional change of position, which, owing to his huge size, causes the earth to tremble over a space of many miles, producing what is called an earthquake.

Zeus had now conquered all his foes, asserted his right to the throne, and could at last reign over the world undisturbed; but he knew that it would be no small undertaking to rule well heaven, earth, and sea, and resolved to divide the power with his brothers. To avoid quarrels and recriminations, he portioned the world out into lots, allowing each of his brothers the privilege of drawing his own share.

Poseidon thus obtained control over the sea and all the rivers, and immediately expressed his resolve to wear a symbolic crown, composed exclusively of marine shells and aquatic plants, and to abide within the bounds of his watery realm.

Hades, the most taciturn of the brothers, received for his portion the sceptre of Tartarus and all the Lower World, where no beam of sunlight was ever allowed to find its way; while Zeus reserved for himself the general supervision of his brothers' estates, and the direct management of Heaven and Earth.

Peace now reigned throughout all the world. Not a murmur was heard, except from the Titans, who at length, seeing that further opposition would be useless, grew reconciled to their fate.

In the days of their prosperity, the Titans had intermarried. Cronus had taken Rhea 'for better or for worse;' and Iapetus had seen, loved, and wedded the fair Clymene, one of the ocean nymphs, or Oceanides, daughters of Oceanus. The latter pair became the proud parents of four gigantic sons – Atlas, Menetius, Prometheus (Forethought), and Epimetheus (Afterthought) – who were destined to play prominent parts in Grecian mythology.

Pandora

ONE LOVELY EVENING, while dancing on the green, the gods saw Hermes, Zeus' messenger, coming towards them. His step was slow and weary, his garments dusty and travel-stained, and he seemed almost to stagger beneath the weight of a huge box which rested upon his shoulders. Pandora immediately ceased dancing, to speculate with feminine curiosity upon the contents of the chest. She nudged Epimetheus, and in a whisper begged him to ask Hermes what brought him thither. Epimetheus complied with her request; but Hermes evaded the question, asked permission to deposit his burden in their dwelling for safekeeping, professing himself too weary to convey it to its destination that day, and promised to call for it shortly. The permission was promptly granted. Hermes, with a sigh of relief, placed the box in one corner, and then departed, refusing all hospitable offers of rest and refreshment.

He had scarcely crossed the threshold, when Pandora expressed a strong desire to have a peep at the contents of the mysterious box; but Epimetheus, surprised and shocked, told her that her curiosity was unseemly, and then, to dispel the frown and pout seen for the first time on the fair face of his beloved, he entreated her to come out into the fresh air and join in the merry games of their companions. For the first time, also, Pandora refused to comply with his request. Dismayed, and very much discouraged, Epimetheus sauntered out alone, thinking she would soon join him, and perhaps by some caress atone for her present willfulness.

Left alone with the mysterious casket, Pandora became more and more inquisitive. Stealthily she drew near, and examined it with great interest, for it was curiously wrought of dark wood, and surmounted by a delicately carved head, of such fine workmanship that it seemed to smile and encourage her. Around the box a glittering golden cord was wound, and fastened on top in an intricate knot. Pandora, who prided herself specially on her deft fingers, felt sure she could unfasten it, and, reasoning that it would not be indiscreet to untie it if she did not raise the lid, she set to work. Long she strove, but all in vain. Ever and anon the laughing voices of Epimetheus and his companions, playing in the luxuriant shade, were wafted in on the summer breeze. Repeatedly she heard them call, and beseech her to join them; yet she persisted in her attempt. She was just on the point of giving it up in despair, when suddenly the refractory knot yielded to her fumbling fingers, and the cord, unrolling, dropped on the floor.

Pandora had repeatedly fancied that sounds like whispers issued from the box. The noise now seemed to increase, and she breathlessly applied her ear to the lid to ascertain whether it really proceeded from within. Imagine, therefore, her surprise when she distinctly heard these words, uttered in the most pitiful accents: "Pandora, dear Pandora, have pity upon us! Free us from this gloomy prison! Open, open, we beseech you!"

Pandora's heart beat so fast and loud, that it seemed for a moment to drown all other sounds. Should she open the box? Just then a familiar step outside made her start guiltily. Epimetheus was coming, and she knew he would urge her again to come out, and would prevent the gratification of her curiosity. Precipitately, therefore, she raised the lid to have one little peep before he came in.

Now, Zeus had malignantly crammed into this box all the diseases, sorrows, vices, and crimes that afflict poor humanity; and the box was no sooner opened, than all these ills flew out, in the guise of horrid little brown-winged creatures, closely resembling moths. These little insects fluttered about, alighting, some upon Epimetheus, who had just entered, and some upon Pandora, pricking and stinging them most unmercifully. Then they flew out through the open door and windows, and fastened upon the merrymakers without, whose shouts of joy were soon changed into wails of pain and anguish.

Epimetheus and Pandora had never before experienced the faintest sensation of pain or anger; but, as soon as these winged evil spirits had stung them, they began to weep, and, alas! quarreled for the first time in their lives. Epimetheus reproached his wife in bitterest terms for her thoughtless action; but in the very midst of his vituperation he suddenly heard a sweet little voice entreat for freedom. The sound proceeded from the unfortunate box, whose cover Pandora had dropped again, in the first moment of her surprise and pain. "Open, open, and I will heal your wounds! Please let me out!" it pleaded.

The tearful couple viewed each other inquiringly, and listened again. Once more they heard the same pitiful accents; and Epimetheus bade his wife open the box and set the speaker free, adding very amiably, that she had already done so much harm by her ill-fated curiosity, that it would be difficult to add materially to its evil consequences, and that, perchance, the box contained some good spirit, whose ministrations might prove beneficial.

It was well for Pandora that she opened the box a second time, for the gods, with a sudden impulse of compassion, had concealed among the evil spirits one kindly creature, Hope, whose mission was to heal the wounds inflicted by her fellow-prisoners.

Lightly fluttering hither and thither on her snowy pinions, Hope touched the punctured places on Pandora's and Epimetheus' creamy skin, and relieved their suffering, then quickly flew out of the open window, to perform the same gentle office for the other victims, and cheer their downcast spirits.

Thus, according to the ancients, evil entered into the world, bringing untold misery; but Hope followed closely in its footsteps, to aid struggling humanity, and point to a happier future.

During many centuries, therefore, Hope continued to be revered, although the other divinities had ceased to be worshiped.

According to another version, Pandora was sent down to man, bearing a vase in which the evil spirits were imprisoned, and on the way, seized by a fit of curiosity, raised the cover, and allowed them all to escape.

The Creation of the Universe

BEFORE THE UNIVERSE was created, there existed only a vast expanse of sky above and an endless stretch of water and uninhabited marshland below. Olorun, the wisest of the gods, was supreme ruler of the sky, while Olokun, the most powerful goddess, ruled the seas and marshes.

Both kingdoms were quite separate at that time and there was never any conflict between the two deities. Olorun was more than satisfied with his domain in the sky and hardly noticed what took place below him. Olokun was content with the kingdom she occupied, even though it contained neither living creatures nor vegetation of any kind.

But the young god Obatala was not entirely satisfied with this state of affairs, and one day, as he looked down from the sky upon the dull, grey terrain ruled by Olokun, he thought to himself:

"The kingdom below is a pitiful, barren place. Something must be done to improve its murky appearance. Now if only there were mountains and forests to brighten it up, it would make a perfect home for all sorts of living creatures."

Obatala decided that he must visit Olorun, who was always prepared to listen to him.

"It is a good scheme, but also a very ambitious one," Olorun said to Obatala. "I have no doubt that the hills and valleys you describe would be far better than grey ocean, but who will create this new world, and how will they go about it?"

"If you will give me your blessing," Obatala replied, "I myself will undertake to do this work."

"Then it is settled," said Olorun. "I cannot help you myself, but I will arrange for you to visit my son Orunmila. He will be able to guide you."

Next day, Obatala called upon Orunmila, the eldest son of Olorun, who had been given the power to read the future and to understand the secret of existence. Orunmila produced his divining tray, and when he had placed sixteen palm nuts on it, he shook the tray and cast its contents high into the air. As the nuts dropped to the ground, he read their meaning aloud:

"First, Obatala," he announced, "you must find a chain of gold long enough for you to climb down from the sky to the watery wastes below. Then, as you descend, take with you a snail shell filled with sand, a white hen, a black cat and a palm nut. This is how you should begin your quest."

Obatala listened attentively to his friend's advice and immediately set off to find a goldsmith who would make him the chain he needed to descend from the sky to the surface of the water below.

"I would be happy to make you the chain you ask for," said the goldsmith, "provided you can give me all the gold I need. But I doubt that you will find enough here for me to complete my task."

Obatala would not be dissuaded, however, and having instructed the goldsmith to go ahead with his work, he approached the other sky gods and one by one explained to them his purpose, requesting that they contribute whatever gold they possessed. The response was generous. Some of the gods gave gold dust, others gave rings, bracelets or pendants, and before long a huge, glittering mound had been collected. The goldsmith examined all the gold that was brought before him, but still he complained that there was not enough.

"It is the best I can do," Obatala told him. "I have asked all of the other gods to help out and there is no more gold left in the sky. Make the chain as long as you possibly can and fix a hook to one end. Even if it fails to reach the water below, I am determined to climb down on it."

The goldsmith worked hard to complete the chain and when it was finished, the hook was fastened to the edge of the sky and the chain lowered far below. Orunmila appeared and handed Obatala a bag containing the sand-filled snail's shell, the white hen, the black cat and the palm nut, and as soon as he had slung it over his shoulder, the young god began climbing down the golden chain, lower and lower until he saw that he was leaving the world of light and entering a world of twilight.

Before long, Obatala could feel the damp mists rising up off the surface of the water, but at the same time, he realized that he had just about reached the end of his golden chain.

"I cannot jump from here," he thought. "If I let go of the chain I will fall into the sea and almost certainly drown."

And while he looked around him rather helplessly, he suddenly heard a familiar voice calling to him from up above.

"Make use of the sand I gave you," Orunmila instructed him, "toss it into the water below."

Obatala obeyed, and after he had poured out the sand, he heard Orunmila calling to him a second time:

"Release the white hen," Orunmila cried.

Obatala reached into his bag and pulled out the white hen, dropping her on to the waters beneath where he had sprinkled the sand. As soon as she had landed, the hen began to scratch in the sand, scattering it in all directions. Wherever the grains fell, dry land instantly appeared. The larger heaps of sand became hills, while the smaller heaps became valleys.

Obatala let go of his chain and jumped on to the solid earth. As he walked he smiled with pleasure, for the land now extended a great many miles in all directions. But he was proudest of the spot where his feet had first landed, and decided to name this place Ife. Stooping to the ground, he began digging a hole, and buried his palm nut in the soil. Immediately, a palm tree sprang up from the earth, shedding its seeds as it stretched to its full height so that other trees soon shot up around it. Obatala felled some of these trees and built for himself a sturdy house thatched with palm leaves. And here, in this place, he settled down, separated from the other sky gods, with only his black cat for company.

Olokun's Revenge

AFTER HE HAD lived among the human race for a long period of time, Obatala came to the decision that he had done all he could for his people. The day had arrived for him to retire, he believed, and so he climbed up the golden chain and returned to his home in the sky once more, promising to visit the earth as frequently as possible. The other gods never tired of hearing Obatala describe the kingdom he had created below. Many were so captivated by the image he presented of the newly created human beings, that they decided to depart from the sky and go down to live among them. And as they prepared to leave, Olorun took them aside and counselled them:

"Each of you shall have a special role while you are down there, and I ask that you never forget your duty to the human race. Always listen to the prayers of the people and offer help when they are in need."

One deity, however, was not at all pleased with Obatala's work or the praise he had received from Olorun. The goddess Olokun, ruler of the sea, watched with increasing fury as, one by one, the other gods arrived in her domain and began dividing up the land amongst themselves.

"Obatala has never once consulted me about any of this," she announced angrily, "but he shall pay for the insult to my honour."

The goddess commanded the great waves of her ocean to rise up, for it was her intention to destroy the land Obatala had created and replace it with water once more. The terrible flood began, and soon the fields were completely submerged. Crops were destroyed and thousands of people were swept away by the roaring tide.

Those who survived the deluge fled to the hills and called to Obatala for help, but he could not hear them from his home high above in the sky.

In desperation, the people turned to Eshu, one of the gods recently descended to earth.

"Please return to the sky," they begged, "and tell the great gods of the flood that threatens to destroy everything."

"First you must show that you revere the gods," replied Eshu. "You must offer up a sacrifice and pray hard that you will be saved."

The people went away and returned with a goat which they sacrificed as food for Obatala. But still Eshu refused to carry the message.

"You ask me to perform this great service," he told them, "and yet you do not offer to reward me. If I am to be your messenger, I too deserve a gift."

The people offered up more sacrifices to Eshu and only when he was content that they had shown him appropriate respect did he begin to climb the golden chain back to the sky to deliver his message.

Obatala was deeply upset by the news and extremely anxious for the safety of his people, for he was uncertain how best to deal with so powerful a goddess as Olokun. Once more, he approached Orunmila and asked for advice. Orunmila consulted his divining nuts, and at last he said to Obatala:

"Rest here in the sky while I descend below. I will use my gifts to turn back the water and make the land rise again."

Orunmila went down and, using his special powers, brought the waves under control so that the marshes began to dry up and land became visible again. But although the people greeted the god as their saviour and pleaded with him to act as their protector, Orunmila confessed that he had no desire to remain among them. Before he departed, however, he passed on a great many of his gifts to the people, teaching them how to divine the future and to control the unseen forces of nature. What he taught the people was never lost and it was passed on like a precious heirloom from one generation to another.

Agemo Outwits Olokun

BUT EVEN AFTER Orunmila had returned to his home in the sky, all was not yet settled between Olokun and the other sky gods. More embittered than ever before by her defeat, Olokun began to consider ways in which she might humiliate Olorun, the god who had allowed Obatala to usurp her kingdom.

Now the goddess was a highly skilled weaver, but she was also expert in dyeing the cloths she had woven. And knowing that no other sky god possessed greater knowledge of cloth making, she sent a message to Olorun challenging him to a weaving contest. Olorun received her message rather worriedly and said to himself:

"Olokun knows far more about making cloth that I will ever know, but I cannot allow her to think that she is superior to me in anything. Somehow I must appear to meet her challenge and yet avoid taking part in the contest. But how can I possibly do this?"

He pondered the problem a very long time until, at last, he was struck by a worthwhile thought. Smiling broadly, he summoned Agemo, the chameleon, to his side, and instructed him to carry an important message to Olokun.

Agemo climbed down the golden chain and went in search of Olokun's dwelling.

"The ruler of the sky, Olorun, greets you," he announced. "He says that if your cloth is as magnificent as you say it is, then the ruler of the sky will be happy to compete with you in the contest you have suggested. But he thinks it only fair to see some of your cloth in advance, and has asked me to examine it on his behalf so that I may report to him on its quality."

Olokun was happy to accommodate Olorun's request. She retired to a backroom and having put on a skirt of radiant green cloth, she stood confidently before the chameleon. But as the chameleon looked at the garment, his skin began to change colour until it was exactly the same brilliant shade as the skirt. Next Olokun put on an orange-hued cloth. But again, to her astonishment, the chameleon turned a beautiful shade of bright orange. One by one, the goddess put on skirts of various bright colours, but on each occasion the chameleon perfectly matched the colour of her robe. Finally the goddess thought to herself:

"This person is only a messenger, and if Olorun's servants can reproduce the exact colours of my very finest cloth, what hope will I have in a contest against the supreme god himself?"

The goddess conceded defeat and spoke earnestly to the chameleon:

"Tell your master that the ruler of the seas sends her greetings to the ruler of the sky. Say to him that I acknowledge his supremacy in weaving and in all other things as well."

And so it came to pass that Olorun and Olokun resumed their friendship and that peace was restored to the whole of the universe once more.

The Gods Descend from the Sky

NANA BALUKU, THE mother of all creation, fell pregnant before she finally retired from the universe. Her offspring was androgynous, a being with one body and two faces. The face that resembled a woman was called Mawu and her eyes were the moon. She took control of the night and all territories to the west. The male face was called Lisa and his eyes were the sun. Lisa controlled the east and took charge of the daylight.

At the beginning of the present world, Mawu-Lisa was the only being in existence, but eventually the moon was eclipsed by the sun and many children were conceived. The first fruits of the union were a pair of twins, a male called Da Zodji and a female called Nyohwè Ananu. Another child followed shortly afterwards, a male and female form joined in one body, and this child was named Sogbo. The third birth again produced twins, a male, Agbè, and a female, Naètè. The fourth and fifth children were both male and were named Agè and Gu. Gu's torso was made of stone and a giant sword protruded from the hole in his neck where his head would otherwise have been. The sixth offspring was not made of flesh and blood. He was given the name Djo, meaning air, or atmosphere. Finally, the seventh child born was named Legba, and because he was the youngest, he became Mawu-Lisa's particular favourite.

When these children had grown to adulthood and the appropriate time had arrived to divide up the kingdoms of the universe among them, Mawu-Lisa gathered them together. To their firstborn, the twins Da Zodji and Nyohwè Ananu, the parents gave the earth below and sent them, laden with heavenly riches, down from the sky to inhabit their new home. To Sogbo, who was both man and woman, they gave the sky, commanding him to rule over thunder and lightning. The twins Agbè and Naètè were sent to take command of the waters and the creatures of the deep, while Agè was ordered to live in the bush as a hunter where he could take control of all the birds and beasts of the earth.

To Gu, whom Mawu-Lisa considered their strength, they gave the forests and vast stretches of fertile soil, supplying him also with the tools and weapons mankind would need to cultivate the land. Mawu-Lisa ordered Djo to occupy the space between the earth and the sky and entrusted him with the life-span of human beings. It was also Djo's role to clothe the other sky gods, making them invisible to man.

To each of their offspring, Mawu-Lisa then gave a special language. These are the languages still spoken by the priests and mediums of the gods in their songs and oracles. To Da Zodji and Nyohwè Ananu, Mawu-Lisa gave the language of the earth and took from them all memory of the sky language. They gave to Sogbo, Agbè and Naètè, Agè and Gu the languages they would speak. But to Djo, they gave the language of men.

Then Mawu-Lisa said to Legba: "Because you are my youngest child, I will keep you with me always. Your work will be to visit all the kingdoms ruled over by your brothers and sisters and report to me on their progress."

And that is why Legba knows all the languages of his siblings, and he alone knows the language of Mawu-Lisa. You will find Legba everywhere, because all beings, human and gods, must first approach Legba before Mawu-Lisa, the supreme deity, will answer their prayers.

God Abandons the Earth

IN THE BEGINNING, God was very proud of the human beings he had created and wanted to live as close as possible to them. So he made certain that the sky was low enough for the people to touch and built for himself a home directly above their heads. God was so near that everyone on earth became familiar with his face and every day he would stop to make conversation with the people, offering a helping hand if they were ever in trouble.

This arrangement worked very well at first, but soon God observed that the people had started to take advantage of his closeness. Children began to wipe their greasy hands on the sky when they had finished their meals and often, if a woman was in search of an extra ingredient for dinner, she would simply reach up, tear a piece off the sky and add it to her cooking pot. God remained tolerant through all of this, but he knew his patience would not last forever and hoped that his people would not test its limit much further.

Then one afternoon, just as he had lain down to rest, a group of women gathered underneath the sky to pound the corn they had harvested. One old woman among them had a particularly large wooden bowl and a very long pestle, and as she thumped down on the grains, she knocked violently against the sky. God arose indignantly from his bed and descended below, but as he approached the woman to chastise her, she suddenly jerked back her arm and hit him in the eye with her very long pestle.

God gave a great shout, his voice booming like thunder through the air, and as he shouted, he raised his powerful arms above his head and pushed upwards against the sky with all his strength, flinging it far into the distance.

As soon as they realized that the earth and the sky were separated, the people became angry with the old woman who had injured God and pestered her day and night to bring him back to them. The woman went away and although she was not very clever, she thought long and hard about the problem until she believed she had found the solution. Returning to her village, she ordered her children to collect all the wooden mortars that they could find. These she piled one on top of the other until they had almost bridged the gap between the earth and the heavens. Only one more mortar was needed to complete the job, but although her children searched high and low, they could not find the missing object. In desperation, the old woman told them to remove the lowest mortar from the bottom of the pile and place it on the top. But as soon as they did this, all the mortars came crashing down, killing the old woman, her children and the crowd who had gathered to admire the towering structure.

Ever since that day, God has remained in the heavens where mankind can no longer approach him as easily as before. There are some, however, who say they have caught a glimpse of him and others who offer up sacrifices calling for his forgiveness and asking him to make his home among them once more.

The Sun and the Moon

THE SUN AND the moon fell in love and decided to marry. For a time they were very happy together and produced many children whom they christened "stars". But it was not long before the moon grew weary of her husband and decided to take a lover, refusing to conceal the fact that she greatly enjoyed the variety.

Of course, the sun soon came to hear of his wife's brazen infidelity and the news made him extremely unhappy. He attempted to reason with the moon, but when he saw that his efforts were entirely fruitless, he decided to drive his wife out of his house. Some of the children sided with their mother, while others supported their father. But the sun was never too hard on his wife, in spite of their differences, and saw to it that their possessions were equally divided up.

The moon was always too proud to accept her husband's kindness, however, and even to this day, she continues to make a habit of trespassing on his lands, often taking her children with her and encouraging them to fight the siblings who remain behind with their father.

The constant battles between the star-children of the sun and the star-children of the moon produce great storms of thunder and lightning and it is only when she becomes bored of these confrontations that the moon sends her messenger, the rainbow, into the field, instructing him to wave a cloth of many colours as a signal for her children to retreat.

Sometimes the moon herself is caught by the sun attempting to steal crops from his fields. Whenever this happens, he chases after his estranged wife and if he catches her he begins to flog her or even tries to eat her.

So whenever a man sees an eclipse, he knows that things have come to blows once again between husband and wife up above. At this time, he must be certain to beat his drum and threaten the sun very loudly, for if he does not, the sun might finish the job, and we should certainly lose the moon forever.

Why the Sun and the Moon Live in the Sky

MANY YEARS AGO, the sun and water were great friends, and both lived on the earth together. The sun very often used to visit the water, but the water never returned his visits. At last the sun asked the water why it was that he never came to see him in his house, the water replied that the sun's house was not big enough, and that if he came with his people he would drive the sun out.

He then said, "If you wish me to visit you, you must build a very large compound; but I warn you that it will have to be a tremendous place, as my people are very numerous, and take up a lot of room."

The sun promised to build a very big compound, and soon afterwards he returned home to his wife, the moon, who greeted him with a broad smile when he opened the door. The sun told the moon what he had promised the water, and the next day commenced building a huge compound in which to entertain his friend.

When it was completed, he asked the water to come and visit him the next day. When the water arrived, he called out to the sun, and asked him whether it would be safe for him to enter, and the sun answered, "Yes, come in, my friend." The water then began to flow in, accompanied by the fish and all the water animals.

Very soon the water was knee-deep, so he asked the sun if it was still safe, and the sun again said, "Yes," so more water came in.

When the water was level with the top of a man's head, the water said to the sun, "Do you want more of my people to come?" and the sun and moon both answered, "Yes," not knowing any better, so the water flowed on, until the sun and moon had to perch themselves on the top of the roof.

Again the water addressed the sun, but receiving the same answer, and more of his people rushing in, the water very soon overflowed the top of the roof, and the sun and moon were forced to go up into the sky, where they have remained ever since.

The Girl of the Early Race, Who Made Stars

MY MOTHER WAS the one who told me that the girl arose; she put her hands into the wood ashes; she threw up the wood ashes into the sky. She said to the wood ashes: "The wood ashes which are here, they must altogether become the Milky Way. They must white lie along in the sky, that the stars may stand outside of the Milky Way, while the Milky Way is the Milky Way, while it used to be wood ashes." They (the ashes) altogether become the Milky Way. The Milky Way must go round with the stars; while the Milky Way feels that, the Milky Way lies going round; while the stars sail along; therefore, the Milky Way, lying, goes along with the stars. The Milky Way, when the Milky Way stands upon the earth, the Milky Way turns across in front, while the Milky Way means to wait(?), While the Milky Way feels that the Stars are turning back; while the Stars feel that the Sun is the one who has turned back; he is upon his path; the Stars turn back; while they go to fetch the daybreak; that they may lie nicely, while the Milky Way lies nicely. The Stars shall also stand nicely around.

They shall sail along upon their footprints, which they, always sailing along, are following. While they feel that, they are the Stars which descend.

The Milky Way lying comes to its place, to which the girl threw up the wood ashes, that it may descend nicely; it had lying gone along, while it felt that it lay upon the sky. It had lying gone round, while it felt that the Stars also turned round. They turning round passed over the sky. The sky lies (still); the Stars are those which go along; while they feel that they sail. They had been setting; they had, again, been coming out; they had, sailing along, been following their footprints. They become white, when the Sun comes out. The Sun sets, they stand around above; while they feel that they did turning follow the Sun.

The darkness comes out; they (the Stars) wax red, while they had at first been white. They feel that they stand brightly around; that they may sail along; while they feel that it is night. Then, the people go by night; while they feel that the ground is made light. While they feel that the Stars shine a little. Darkness is upon the ground. The Milky Way gently glows; while it feels that it is wood ashes. Therefore, it gently glows. While it feels that the girl was the one who said that the Milky Way should give a little light for the people, that they might return home by night, in the middle of the night. For, the earth would not have been a little light, had not the Milky Way been there. It and the Stars.

The girl thought that she would throw up (into the air) roots of the *huing* (a scented root eaten by some Bushmen), in order that the *huing* roots should become Stars; therefore, the Stars are red; while they feel that (they) are *huing* roots.

She first gently threw up wood ashes into the sky, that she might presently throw up *huing* roots; while she felt that she was angry with her mother, because her mother had not given her many *huing* roots, that she might eat abundantly; for, she was in the hut. She did not herself go out to seek food; that she might get(?) *huing* for herself; that she might be bringing it (home) for herself; that she might eat; for, she was hungry; while she lay ill in the hut. Her mothers were those who went out. They were those who sought for food. They were bringing home *huing*, that they might eat. She lay in her little hut, which her mother had made for her. Her stick stood there; because she did not yet dig out food. And, she was still in the hut. Her mother was the one who was bringing her food. That she might be eating, lying in the little hut; while her mother thought that she (the girl) did not eat the young men's game (i.e. game killed by them). For, she ate the game of her father, who was an old man. While she thought that the hands of the young men would become cool. Then, the arrow would become cool. The arrow head which is at the top, it would be cold; while the arrow head felt that the bow was cold; while the bow felt that his (the young man's) hands were cold. While the girl thought of her saliva, which, eating, she had put into the springbok meat; this saliva would go into the bow, the inside of the bow would become cool; she, in this manner, thought. Therefore, she feared the young men's game. Her father was the one from whom she alone ate (game). While she felt that she had worked (i.e. treated) her father's hands: she had worked, taking away her saliva (from them).

The Creation of the Universe

IN THE BEGINNING, before there was anything at all, there was a nothingness that stretched as far as there was space. There was no sand, nor sea, no waves nor earth nor heavens. And that space was a void that called to be filled, for its emptiness echoed with a deep and frozen silence. So it was that a land sprung up within that silence, and it took the place of half the universe. It was a land called Filheim, or land of fog, and where it ended sprung another land, where the air burned and blazed. This land was called Muspell. Where the regions met lay a great and profound void, called Ginnungagap, and here a peaceful river flowed, softly spreading into the frosty depths of the void where it froze, layer upon layer, until it formed a fundament. And it was here the heat from Muspell licked at the cold of Filheim until the energy they created spawned the great frost-giant Ymir. Ymir was the greatest and the first of all frost-giants, and his part in the creation of the universe led the frost-giants to believe that they should reign supreme on what he had made.

Filheim had existed for many ages, long before our own earth was created. In the centre was a mighty fountain and it was called Vergelmir, and from that great fountain all the rivers of the universe bubbled and stormed. There was another fountain called Elivagar (although some believe that it is the same fountain with a different name), and from this bubbled up a poisonous mass, which hardened into black ice. Elivagar is the beginning of evil, for goodness can never be black.

Muspell burned with eternal light and her heat was guarded by the flame giant, Surtr, who lashed at the air with his great sabre, filling it with glittering sparks of pure heat. Surtr was the fiercest of the fire giants who would one day make Muspell their home. The word Muspell means 'home of the destroyers of the world' and that description is both frightening and accurate because the fire giants were the most terrifying there were.

On the other side of the slowly filling chasm, Filheim lay in perpetual darkness, bathed in mists which circled and spun until all was masked. Here, between these stark contrasts, Ymir grew, the personification of the frozen ocean, the product of chaos. Fire and ice met here, and it was these profound contrasts that created a phenomenon like no other, and this was life itself. In the chasm another form was created by the frozen river, where the sparks of the Surtr's sabre caused the ice to drip, and to thaw, and then, when they rested, allowed it to freeze once again. This form was Audhumla, a cow who became known as the nourisher. Her udders were swollen with rich, pure milk, and Ymir drank greedily from the four rivers which formed from them.

Audhumla was a vast creature, spreading across the space where the fire met the ice. Her legs were columns, and they held up the corners of space.

Audhumla, the cow, also needed sustenance, and so she licked at the rime-stones which had formed from the crusted ice, and from these stones she drew salt from the depths of the earth. Audhumla licked continuously, and soon there appeared, under her thirsty tongue, the form of a god. On the first day there appeared hair, and on the second, a head. On the third day the whole god was freed from the ice and he stepped forth as Buri, also called the Producer. Buri was beautiful. He had taken the golden flames of the fire, which gave him a warm, gilded glow, and from the frost and ice he had drawn a purity, a freshness that could never be matched.

While Audhumla licked, Ymir slept, sated by the warmth of her milk. Under his arms the perspiration formed a son and a daughter, and his feet produced a giant called Thrudgemir, an evil frost-giant with six heads who went on to bear his own son, the giant Bergelmir. These were the first of the race of frost-giants.

Buri himself had produced a son, called Bor, which is another word for 'born', and as Buri and Bor became aware of the giants, an eternal battle was begun – one which is to this day waged on all parts of earth and heaven.

For giants represent evil in its many forms, and gods represent all that is good, and on that fateful day the fundamental conflict between them began – a cosmic battle which would create the world as we know it.

Buri and Bor fought against the giants, but by the close of each day a stalemate existed. And so it was that Bor married the giantess Bestla, who was the daughter of Bolthorn, or the thorn of evil. Bestla was to give him three fine, strong sons: Odin, Vili and Ve and with the combined forces of these brave boys, Bor was able to destroy the great Ymir. As they slayed him, a tremendous flood burst forth from his body, covering the earth and all the evil beings who inhabited it with his rich red blood.

The Creation of the Earth

YMIR'S BODY WAS carried by Odin and his brothers to Ginnungagap, where it was placed in the centre. His flesh became the earth, and his skeleton the rocky crags which dipped and soared. From the soil sprang dwarfs, spontaneously, and they would soon be put to work. Ymir's teeth and shards of broken bones became the rocks and pits covering the earth and his blood was cleared to become the seas and waters that flowed across the land. The three men worked hard on the body of Ymir; his vast size meant that even a day's work would alter the corpse only slightly.

Ymir's skull became the sky and at each cardinal point of the compass was placed a dwarf whose supreme job it was to support it. These dwarfs were Nordri, Sudri, Austri and Westri and it was from these brave and sturdy dwarfs that the terms North, South, East and West were born. Ymir's hair created trees and bushes.

The brow of Ymir became walls which would protect the gods from all evil creatures, and in the very centre of these brows was Midgard, or 'middle garden', where humans could live safely.

Now almost all of the giants had fallen with the death of Ymir, drowned by his surging blood – all, that is, except Bergelmir, who escaped in a boat with his wife and sought asylum at the edge of the world. Here he created a new world, Jotunheim, or the home of the giants, where he set about the creation of a whole new breed of giants who would carry on his evil deeds.

Odin and his brothers had not yet completed their work. As the earth took on its present form, they slaved at Ymir's corpse to create greater and finer things. Ymir's brains were thrust into the skies to become clouds, and in order to light this new world, they secured the sparks from Surtr's sabre and dotted them among the clouds. The finest sparks were put to one side and they studded the heavenly vault with them; they became like glittering stars in the darkness. The stars were given positions; some were told to pass forward, and then back again in the heavens. This provided seasons, which were duly recorded.

The brightest of the remaining stars were joined together to become the sun and the moon, and they were sent out into the darkness in gleaming gold chariots. The chariots were drawn by Arvakr (the early waker) and Alsvin (the rapid goer), two magnificent white horses under whom were placed balls of cool air which had been trapped in great skins. A shield was placed before the sun so that her rays would not harm the milky hides of the steeds as they travelled into the darkness.

Although the moon and the sun had now been created, and they were sent out on their chariots, there was still no distinction between day and night, and that is a story of its own.

Night and Day

THE CHARIOTS WERE ready, and the steeds were bursting at their harnesses to tend to the prestigious task of setting night and day in place. But who would guide them? The horses would need leadership of some sort, and so it was decided that the beautiful children of the giant Mundilfari – Mani (the moon) and Sol (the sun) would be given the direction of the steeds. And at once, they were launched into the heavens.

Next, Nott (night), who was daughter of one of the giants, Norvi, was provided with a rich black chariot which was drawn by a lustrous stallion called Hrim-faxi (frost mane). From his mane, the frost and dew were sent down to the earth in glimmering baubles. Nott was a goddess, and she had produced three children, each with a different father. From Naglfari, she had a son named Aud; Annar, her second husband, gave her Jord (earth), and with her third husband, the god Dellinger, a son was born and he was called Dag (day).

Dag was the most radiant of her children, and his beauty caused all who saw him to bend down in tears of rapture. He was given his own great chariot, drawn by a perfect white horse called Skin-faxi (shining mane), and as they travelled, wondrous beams of light shot out in every direction, brightening every dark corner of the world and providing much happiness to all.

Many believe that the chariots flew so quickly, and continued their journey round and round the world because they were pursued by wolves: Skoll (repulsion) and Hati (hatred). These evil wolves sought a way to create eternal darkness and like the perpetual battle of good and evil, there could be no end to their chase.

Mani brought along in his chariot Hiuki, who represented the waxing moon, and Bil, who was the waning moon. And so it was that Sun, Moon, Day and Night were in place, with Evening, Midnight, Morning, Forenoon, Noon and Afternoon sent to accompany them. Summer and Winter were rulers of all seasons: Summer was a popular and warm god, a descendant of Svasud. Winter, was an enemy for he represented all that contrasted with Summer, including the icy winds which blew cold and unhappiness over the earth. It was believed that the great frost-giant Hraesvelgr sat on the extreme north of the heavens and that he sent the frozen winds across the land, blighting all with their blasts of icy death.

Asgard

ASGARD IS ANOTHER word for 'enclosure of the gods'. It was a place of great peace, ruled by Odin and built by Odin and his sons on Yggdrasil, above the clouds, and centred over Midgard. Each of the palaces of Asgard was built for pleasure, and only things which were perfect in every way could become part of this wondrous land. The first palace built was Gladsheim, or Joyous home, and it was created to house the twelve thrones of the principal deities. Everything was cast from gold, and it shone in the heavens like the sun itself. A second palace was built for the goddesses, and it was called Vingof, or Friendly Floor. Here, too, everything was made from gold, which is the reason why Asgard's heyday became known as the golden years.

As Asgard was conceived, and built, a council was held, and the rules were set down for gods and goddesses alike. It was decreed at this time that there would be no blood shed within the limits of the realm, and that harmony would reign forever. A forge was built, and all of the weapons and tools required for the construction of the magnificent palaces were made there. The gods held their council at the foot of Yggdrasil, and in order to travel there, a bridge was erected – the rainbow bridge, or Bifrost as it became known. The bridge arched over Midgard, on either side of Filheim, and its colours were so spectacular that one could only gaze in awe upon seeing them for the first time.

The centre of Asgard displayed the plan of Idavale, with hills that dipped and soared with life. Here the great palaces were set in lush green grasses. One was Breibalik, or Broad Gleaming, and there was Glitnir, in which all was made gold and silver. There were palaces clustered in gems, polished and shimmering in the light of the new heavens. And that beauty of Asgard was reflected by the beauteous inhabitants – whose minds and spirits were pure and true. Asgard was the home of all the Aesir, and the setting for most of the legends told here. But there was another family of gods – and they were called the Vanir.

For many years the Vanir lived in their own land, Vanaheim, but the time came when a dispute arose between the two families of gods, and the Aesir waged war against the Vanir. In time, they learned that unity was the only way to move forward, and they put aside their differences and drew strength from their combined forces. In order to ratify their treaty, each side took hostages. So it was that Niord came to dwell in Asgard with Frey and Freyia, and Hoenir went to live in Vanaheim, the ultimate sacrifice by one of the brothers of creation.

The Gods Arrive

THE PEOPLE OF the goddess Danu were not the first divine inhabitants of Ireland. Others had been before them, dwellers in 'the dark backward and abysm of time'. The first of these was called 'The Race of Partholon'. Its head and leader came from the Other World, and landed in Ireland with a retinue of twenty-four males and twenty-four females upon the first of May, the day called "Beltane", sacred to Bilé, the god of death. At this remote time, Ireland consisted of only one treeless, grassless plain, watered by three lakes and nine rivers. But, as the race of Partholon increased, the land stretched, or widened, under them – some said miraculously, and others, by the labours of Partholon's people. At any rate, during the three hundred years they dwelt there, it grew from one plain to four, and acquired seven new lakes, which was fortunate, for the race of Partholon increased from forty-eight members to five thousand, in spite of battles with the Fomors.

These would seem to have been inevitable. Whatever gods ruled, they found themselves in eternal opposition to the not-gods – the powers of darkness, winter, evil, and death. The race of Partholon warred against them with success. At the Plain of Ith, Partholon defeated their leader, a gigantic demon called Cichol the Footless, and dispersed his deformed and monstrous host. After this there was quiet for three hundred years. Then – upon the same fatal first of May – there began a mysterious epidemic, which lasted a week, and destroyed them all. In premonition of their end, they foregathered upon the original, first-created plain – then called *Sen Mag*, or the 'Old Plain' – so that those who survived might the more easily bury those that died.

Following the race of Partholon came the race of Nemed, which carried on the work and traditions of its forerunner. During its time, Ireland again enlarged herself, to the extent of twelve new plains and four more lakes. Like the people of Partholon, the race of Nemed struggled with the Fomors, and defeated them in four consecutive battles. Then Nemed died, with two thousand of his people, from an epidemic, and the remnant, left without their leader, were terribly oppressed by the Fomors. Two Fomorian kings – Morc, son of Dela, and Conann, son of Febar – had built a tower of glass upon Tory Island, always their chief stronghold, and where stories of them still linger, and from this vantage-point they dictated a tax which recalls that paid, in Greek story, to the Cretan Minotaur. Two-thirds of the children born to the race of Nemed during the year were to be delivered up on each day of Samhain. Goaded by this to a last desperate effort, the survivors of Nemed's people attacked the tower and took it, Conann perishing in the struggle. But their triumph was short. Morc, the other king, collected his forces, and inflicted such a slaughter upon the people of Nemed that, out of the sixteen thousand who had assembled for the storming of the tower, only thirty survived. And these returned whence they came, or died.

The enemies alike of Fir Bolg and Fomor, the Tuatha Dé Danann, gods of the Gaels, were the next to arrive, from the sky. They had dwelt in four mythical cities called Findias, Gorias, Murias, and Falias, where they had learned poetry and magic, and whence they had brought to Ireland their four chief treasures. From Findias came Nuada's sword, from whose stroke no one ever escaped or recovered; from Gorias, Lugh's terrible lance; from Murias, the Dagda's cauldron; and from Falias, the Stone of Fál, better known as the "Stone of Destiny", which afterwards fell into the hands of the early kings of Ireland. According to legend, it had the magic property of uttering a human cry when touched by the rightful King of Erin.

The Tuatha Dé Danann landed in a dense cloud upon the coast of Ireland on the mystic first of May without having been opposed, or even noticed by the people, the "Fir Bolgs". That those might still be ignorant of their coming, the Morrígú, helped by Badb and Macha, made use of the magic they had learned in Findias, Gorias, Murias, and Falias. They spread druidically formed showers and fog-sustaining shower-clouds over the country, and caused the air to pour down fire and blood upon the Fir Bolgs, so that they were obliged to shelter themselves for three days and three nights. But the Fir Bolgs had druids of their own, and, in the end, they put a stop to these enchantments by counter-spells, and the air grew clear again.

The Tuatha Dé Danann, advancing westward, had reached a place called the "Plain of the Sea", in Leinster, when the two armies met. Each sent out a warrior to parley. The two adversaries approached each other cautiously, their eyes peeping over the tops of their shields. Then, coming gradually nearer, they spoke to one another, and the desire to examine each other's weapons made them almost friends.

The envoy of the Fir Bolgs looked with wonder at the beautifully shaped, thin, slender, long, sharp-pointed spears of the warrior of the Tuatha Dé Danann, while the ambassador of the tribe of the goddess Danu was not less impressed by the lances of the Fir Bolgs, which were heavy, thick, pointless, but sharply rounded. They agreed to exchange weapons, so that each side might, by an examination of them, be able to come to some opinion as to its opponent's strength. Before parting, the envoy of the Tuatha Dé Danann offered the Fir Bolgs, through their representative, peace, with a division of the country into two equal halves.

The Fir Bolg envoy advised his people to accept this offer. But their king, Eochaid, son of Erc, would not. "If we once give these people half," he said, "they will soon have the whole."

The people of the goddess Danu were, on the other hand, very much impressed by the sight of the Fir Bolgs' weapons. They decided to secure a more advantageous position, and, retreating farther west into Connaught, to a plain then called Nia, but now Moytura, near the present village of Cong, they drew up their line at its extreme end, in front of the pass of Balgatan, which offered a retreat in case of defeat.

The Fir Bolgs followed them and encamped on the nearer side of the plain. Then Nuada, King of the Tuatha Dé Danann, sent an ambassador offering the same terms as before. Again the Fir Bolgs declined them.

"Then when," asked the envoy, "do you intend to give battle?"

"We must have a truce," they said, "for we want time to repair our armour, burnish our helmets, and sharpen our swords. Besides, we must have spears like yours made for us, and you must have spears like ours made for you."

The result of this chivalrous, but, to modern ideas, amazing, parley was that a truce of one hundred and five days was agreed upon.

It was on Midsummer Day that the opposing armies at last met. The people of the goddess Danu appeared in a flaming line, wielding their red-bordered, speckled, and firm shields. Opposite to them were ranged the Fir Bolgs, sparkling, brilliant, and flaming, with their swords, spears, blades, and trowel-spears. The proceedings began with a kind of deadly hurley-match, in which thrice nine of the Tuatha Dé Danann played the same number of the Fir Bolgs, and were defeated and killed. Then followed another parley, to decide how the battle should be carried on, whether there should be fighting every day or only on every second day. Moreover, Nuada obtained from Eochaid an assurance that the battles should always be fought with equal numbers, although this was very disagreeable to the Fir Bolg king, because he had largely the advantage in the numbers of his army. Then warfare recommenced with a series of single combats. At the end of each day the conquerors on both sides went back to their camps, and were refreshed by being bathed in healing baths of medicinal herbs.

So the fight went on for four days, with terrible slaughter upon each side. A Fir Bolg champion called Sreng fought in single combat with Nuada, the King of the Gods, and shore off his hand and half his shield with one terrific blow. Eochaid, the King of the Fir Bolgs, was even less fortunate than Nuada, for he lost his life. Suffering terribly from thirst, he went, with a hundred of his men, to look for water, and was followed, and pursued as far as the strand of Ballysadare, in Sligo. Here he turned to bay, but was killed, his grave being still marked by a tumulus. The Fir Bolgs, reduced at last to three hundred men, demanded single combat until all upon one side were slain. But, sooner than consent to this, the Tuatha Dé Danann offered them a fifth part of Ireland, whichever province they might choose. They agreed, and chose Connaught, ever afterwards their especial home.

The Rise of the Sun God

IT WAS AS a result of the loss of his hand in the battle with the Fir Bolgs that Nuada got his name of *Argetlám*, that is, the 'Silver Handed'. For Diancecht, the physician of the Tuatha Dé Danann, made him an artificial hand of silver, so skilfully that it moved in all its joints, and was as strong and supple as a real one. But, good as it was of its sort, it was a blemish; and, according to Celtic custom, no maimed person could sit upon the throne. Nuada was deposed, and the Tuatha Dé Danann went into council to appoint a new king.

They agreed that it would be a politic thing for them to conciliate the Fomors, the giants of the sea, and make an alliance with them. So they sent a message to Bress, the son of the Fomorian king, Elathan, asking him to come and rule over them. Bress accepted this offer, and they made a marriage between him and Brigit, the daughter of the Dagda. At the same time, Cian, the son of Diancecht, the physician of the Tuatha Dé Danann, married Ethniu, the daughter of the Fomor, Balor. Then Bress was made king, and was endowed with lands and a palace; and he, on his part, gave hostages that he would abdicate if his rule ever became unpleasing to those who had elected him.

But, in spite of all his fair promises, Bress, who belonged in heart to his own fierce people, began to oppress his subjects with excessive taxes. He put a tax upon every hearth, upon every kneading-trough, and upon every quern, as well as a poll-tax of an ounce of gold upon every member of the Tuatha Dé Danann. By a crafty trick, too, he obtained the milk of all their cattle. He asked at first only for the produce of any cows which happened to be brown and hairless, and the people of the goddess Danu granted him this cheerfully. But Bress passed all the cattle in Ireland between two fires, so that their hair was singed off, and thus obtained the monopoly of the main source of food. To earn a livelihood, all the gods, even the greatest, were now forced to labour for him. Ogma, their champion, was sent out to collect firewood, while the Dagda was put to work building forts and castles.

One day, when the Dagda was at his task, his son, Angus, came to him. "You have nearly finished that castle," he said. "What reward do you intend to ask from Bress when it is done?" The Dagda replied that he had not yet thought of it. "Let me give you some advice," said Angus. "Ask Bress to have all the cattle in Ireland gathered together upon a plain, so that you can pick out one for yourself. He will consent to that. Then choose the black-maned heifer called 'Ocean'."

The Dagda finished building the fort, and then went to Bress for his reward. "What will you have?" asked Bress. "I want all the cattle in Ireland gathered together upon a plain, so that I may choose one of them for myself." Bress did this, and the Dagda took the black-maned heifer Angus had told him of. The king, who had expected to be asked very much more, laughed at what he thought was the Dagda's simplicity. But Angus had been wise, as will be seen hereafter.

Meanwhile, Bress was infuriating the people of the goddess Danu by adding avarice to tyranny. It was for kings to be liberal to all-comers, but at the court of Bress no one ever greased his knife with fat, or made his breath smell of ale. Nor were there ever any poets or musicians or jugglers or jesters there to give pleasure to the people, for Bress would distribute no largess. Next, he cut down the very subsistence of the gods. So scanty was his allowance of food that they began to grow weak with famine. Ogma, through feebleness, could only carry one-third of the wood needed for fuel, so that they suffered from cold as well as from hunger.

It was at this crisis that two physicians, Miach, the son, and Airmid, the daughter, of Diancecht, the god of medicine, came to the castle where the dispossessed King Nuada lived. Nuada's porter, blemished, like himself (for he had lost an eye), was sitting at the gate, and on his lap was a cat curled up asleep. The porter asked the strangers who they were. "We are good doctors," they said. "If that is so," he replied, "perhaps you can give me a new eye." "Certainly," they said, "we could take one of the eyes of that cat, and put it in the place where your lost eye used to be." "I should be very pleased if you would do that," answered the porter. So Miach and Airmid removed one of the cat's eyes, and put it in the hollow where the man's eye had been.

This was not wholly a benefit to him, for the eye retained its cat's nature, and, when the man wished to sleep at night, the cat's eye was always looking out for mice, while it could hardly be kept awake during the day. Nevertheless, he was pleased at the time, and went and told Nuada, who commanded that the doctors who had performed this marvellous cure should be brought to him.

As they came in, they heard the king groaning, for Nuada's wrist had festered where the silver hand joined the arm of flesh. Miach asked where Nuada's own hand was, and they told him that it had been buried long ago. But he dug it up and placed it to Nuada's stump; he uttered an incantation over it, saying, "Sinew to sinew, and nerve to nerve be joined!" And in three days and nights the hand had renewed itself and fixed itself to the arm, so that Nuada was whole again.

When Diancecht, Miach's father, heard of this, he was very angry to think that his son should have excelled him in the art of medicine. He sent for him, and struck him upon the head with a sword, cutting the skin, but not wounding the flesh. Miach easily healed this. So Diancecht hit him again, this time to the bone. Again Miach cured himself. The third time his father smote him, the sword went right through the skull to the membrane of the brain, but even this wound Miach was able to leech. At the fourth stroke, however, Diancecht cut the brain in two, and Miach could do nothing for that. He died, and Diancecht buried him. And upon his grave there grew up three hundred and sixty-five stalks of grass, each one a cure for any illness of each of the three hundred and sixty-five nerves in a man's body. Airmid, Miach's sister, plucked all these very carefully, and arranged them on her mantle according to their properties. But her angry and jealous father overturned the cloak and hopelessly confused them. If it had not been for that act, men would know how to cure every illness and would so be immortal.

The healing of Nuada's blemish happened just at the time when all the people of the goddess Danu had at last agreed that the exactions and tyranny of Bress could no longer be borne. It was the insult he put upon Cairpré, son of Ogma the god of literature, that caused things to come to this head. Poets were always held by the Celts in great honour; and when Cairpré, the bard of the Tuatha Dé Danann, went to visit Bress, he expected to be treated with much consideration, and fed at the king's own table. But, instead of doing so, Bress lodged him in a small, dark room where there was no fire, no bed, and no furniture except a mean table on which small cakes of dry bread were put on a little dish for his food. The next morning, Cairpré rose early and left the palace without having spoken to Bress. It was the custom of poets when they left a king's court to utter a panegyric on their host, but Cairpré treated Bress instead to a magical satire. Roughly rendered, it said:

"No meat on the plates,
No milk of the cows;
No shelter for the belated;
No money for the minstrels:
May Bress's cheer be what he gives to others!"

This satire of Cairpré's was so virulent that it caused great red blotches to break out all over Bress's face. This in itself constituted a blemish such as should not be upon a king, and the Tuatha Dé Danann called upon Bress to abdicate and let Nuada take the throne again.

Bress was obliged to do so. He went back to the country of the Fomors, underneath the sea, and complained to his father Elathan, its king, asking him to gather an army to reconquer his throne. The Fomors assembled in council – Elathan, Tethra, Balor, Indech, and all the other warriors and chiefs – and they decided to come with a great host, and take Ireland away, and put it under the sea where the people of the goddess Danu would never be able to find it again.

At the same time, another assembly was also being held at Tara, the capital of the Tuatha Dé Danann. Nuada was celebrating his return to the throne by a feast to his people. While it was at its height, a stranger clothed like a king came to the palace gate. The porter asked him his name and errand.

"I am called Lugh," he said. "I am the grandson of Diancecht by Cian, my father, and the grandson of Balor by Ethniu, my mother."

"But what is your profession?" asked the porter. "For no one is admitted here unless he is a master of some craft."

"I am a carpenter," said Lugh.

"We have no need of a carpenter. We already have a very good one; his name is Luchtainé."

"I am an excellent smith," said Lugh.

"We do not want a smith. We have a very good one; his name is Goibniu."

"I am a professional warrior," said Lugh.

"We have no need of one. Ogma is our champion."

"I am a harpist," said Lugh.

"We have an excellent harpist already."

"I am a warrior renowned for skilfulness rather than for mere strength."

"We already have a man like that."

"I am a poet and tale-teller," said Lugh.

"We have no need of such. We have a most accomplished poet and tale-teller."

"I am a sorcerer," said Lugh.

"We do not want one. We have numberless sorcerers and druids."

"I am a physician," said Lugh.

"Diancecht is our physician."

"I am a cupbearer," said Lugh.

"We already have nine of them."

"I am a worker in bronze."

"We have no need of you. We already have a worker in bronze. His name is Credné."

"Then ask the king," said Lugh, "if he has with him a man who is master of all these crafts at once, for, if he has, there is no need for me to come to Tara."

So the doorkeeper went inside, and told the king that a man had come who called himself Lugh the *Ioldanach*, or the 'Master of all Arts', and that he claimed to know everything.

The king sent out his best chess-player to play against the stranger. Lugh won, inventing a new move called 'Lugh's enclosure'.

Then Nuada invited him in. Lugh entered and sat down upon the chair called the 'sage's seat', kept for the wisest man.

Ogma, the champion, was showing off his strength. Upon the floor was a flagstone so large that fourscore yokes of oxen would have been needed to move it. Ogma pushed it before him along the hall, and out at the door. Then Lugh rose from his chair and pushed it back again. But this stone, huge as it was, was only a portion broken from a still greater rock outside the palace. Lugh picked it up, and put it back into its place.

The Tuatha Dé Danann asked him to play the harp to them. So he played the 'sleep-tune', and the king and all his court fell asleep, and did not wake until the same hour of the following day. Next he played a plaintive air, and they all wept. Lastly, he played a measure which sent them into transports of joy.

When Nuada had seen all these numerous talents of Lugh, he began to wonder whether one so gifted would not be of great help against the Fomors. He took counsel with the others, and, by their advice, lent his throne to Lugh for thirteen days, taking the 'sage's seat' at his side.

Lugh summoned all the Tuatha Dé Danann to a council.

"The Fomors are certainly going to make war on us," he said. "What can each of you do to help?"

Diancecht the Physician said, "I will completely cure everyone who is wounded, provided his head is not cut off, or his brain or spinal marrow hurt."

"I," said Goibniu the Smith, "will replace every broken lance and sword with a new one, even though the war last seven years. And I will make the lances so well that they shall never miss their mark or fail to kill. Dulb, the smith of the Fomors, cannot do as much as that. The fate of the fighting will be decided by my lances."

"And I," said Credné the Bronze-worker, "will furnish all the rivets for the lances, the hilts for the swords, and the rims and bosses for the shields."

"And I," said Luchtainé the Carpenter, "will provide all the shields and lance-shafts."

Ogma the Champion promised to kill the King of the Fomors, with thrice nine of his followers, and to capture one-third of his army.

"And you, O Dagda," said Lugh, "what will you do?"

"I will fight," said the Dagda, "both with force and craft. Wherever the two armies meet, I will crush the bones of the Fomors with my club, till they are like hailstones under a horse's feet."

"And you, O Morrígú?" said Lugh.

"I will pursue them when they flee," she replied. "And I always catch what I chase."

"And you, O Cairpré, son of Etan?" said Lugh to the poet, "what can you do?"

"I will pronounce an immediately effective curse upon them; by one of my satires I will take away all their honour, and, enchanted by me, they shall not be able to stand against our warriors."

"And ye, O sorcerers, what will ye do?"

"We will hurl by our magic arts," replied Mathgan, the head sorcerer, "the twelve mountains of Ireland at the Fomors. These mountains will be Slieve League, Denna Ulad, the Mourne Mountains, Bri Ruri, Slieve Bloom, Slieve Snechta, Slemish, Blai-Sliab, Nephin, Sliab Maccu Belgodon, Segais, and Cruachan Aigle."

Then Lugh asked the cupbearers what they would do.

"We will hide away by magic," they said, "the twelve chief lakes and the twelve chief rivers of Ireland from the Fomors, so that they shall not be able to find any water, however thirsty they may be; those waters will conceal themselves from the Fomors so that they shall not get a drop, while they will give drink to the people of the goddess Danu as long as the war lasts, even if it lasts seven years." And they told Lugh that the twelve chief lakes were Lough Derg, Lough Luimnigh, Lough Corrib, Lough Ree, Lough Mask, Strangford Lough, Lough Laeig, Lough Neagh, Lough Foyle, Lough Gara, Lough Reagh, and Márloch, and that the twelve chief rivers were the Bush, the Boyne, the Bann, the Nem, the Lee, the Shannon, the Moy, the Sligo, the Erne, the Finn, the Liffey, and the Suir.

Finally, the Druid, Figol, son of Mamos, said, "I will send three streams of fire into the faces of the Fomors, and I will take away two-thirds of their valour and strength, but every breath drawn by the people of the goddess Danu will only make them more valourous and strong, so that even if the fighting lasts seven years, they will not be weary of it."

All decided to make ready for a war, and to give the direction of it to Lugh.

The Creation

ALLAH, THE MOST gracious God, whose dwelling place is the seventh heaven, completed the work of creation. Seven planes has the heaven and seven planes also the earth – the abode of evil spirits. In the heavenly ways reside the peris, or good spirits; in the earthly darkness the dews, or evil spirits. The light of heaven is in conflict with the darkness of earth – the peris with the dews. The peris soar to heaven, high above the earth; but the dews sink down into the darkness under the earth. Mountains bar the road to heaven, and only the good spirits can reach the Copper Range, whence the way is open to the Silver Mountains and the Hills of Gold. Evil spirits are blinded by the ineffable radiance of heaven. Their dwelling place is the depths of the earth, the entrance to which is at the spring of waters. There tarry the white and the black sheep, into whose wool the evil spirits penetrate, and are so conveyed to their realm on the seventh plane.

On the white sheep they return to the earth's surface. Peris and dews are powerful, and both were witnesses of the creation of earth's original inhabitant, the First Man.

Allah created the First Man, and appointed him the earth for his dwelling-place. And when the First Mortal appeared upon the earth and the peris rejoiced over Allah's wonderful work, the Father of Evil beheld it, and envy overcame his soul. Straightway he conceived a plan whereby to bring to nought that beneficent work.

He would implant the deadly seed of sin in this favoured creature of the Almighty; and soon the First Man, all unsuspecting, received on his pure body the damnable spittle of the Evil One, who struck him therewith in the region of the stomach. But Allah, the all-merciful, the overcomer of all things, hastened to tear out the contaminated flesh, and flung it to the ground. Thus originated the human navel. The piece of flesh, unclean by reason of the Evil One's spittle having defiled it, obtained new life from the dust, and thus, almost simultaneously with man, was the dog created – half from the human body and half from the Devil's spittle.

Thus it is that no Mahometan will harm a dog, though he refuses to tolerate him in his house. The animal's faithfulness is its human inheritance, its wildness and savagery are from the Evil One. In the Orient the dog does not increase, for while the Moslem is its protector, he is at the same time its implacable enemy.

Pan Gu and the Creation of the Universe

AT THE VERY beginning of time, when only darkness and chaos existed and the heavens and the earth had not yet been properly divided up, the universe resembled the shape of a large egg. And at the centre of this egg, the first living creature one day came into being. After many thousands of years, when he had gathered sufficient strength and energy and had grown to the size of a giant, the creature, who gave himself the name of Pan Gu, awoke fully refreshed from his long rest and stood upright within his shell. He began to yawn very loudly and to stretch his enormous limbs, and as he did so, the walls of the egg were cracked open and separated into two even portions. The lighter, more fragile, part of the egg floated delicately upwards to form the white silken sheet of the sky, while the heavier, more substantial part, dropped downwards to form the earth's crusty surface.

Now when Pan Gu observed this, he was happy and proud to have created some light in place of the darkness and chaos out of which he had emerged. But at the same time, he began to fear that the skies and the earth might fuse once more, and he stood and scratched his huge head, pondering a solution to the problem. And after he had thought things through for quite a while, he decided that the only way to keep the two elements at a safe distance from each other was to place his own great bulk between them. So he took up his position, heaving and pushing upwards against the sky with his hands and pressing downwards into the earth with all the weight of his massive feet until a reasonable gap had been formed.

For the next eighteen thousand years, Pan Gu continued to push the earth and the sky apart, growing taller and taller every day until the gap measured some thirty thousand miles. And when this distance between them had been established, the sky grew firm and solid and the earth became securely fixed far beneath it. Pan Gu then looked around him and seeing that there was no longer any danger of darkness returning to the universe, he felt at last that he could lay down and rest, for his bones ached and he had grown old and frail over the years. Breathing a heavy sigh, he fell into an exhausted sleep from which he never awoke. But as he lay dying, the various parts of his vast body were miraculously transformed to create the world as we mortals know it today.

Pan Gu's head became the mountain ranges; his blood became the rivers and streams; the hairs on his head were changed into colourful and fragrant blossoms and his flesh was restored to become the trees and soil. His left eye was transformed into the sun and his right eye became the moon; his breath was revived in the winds and the clouds and his voice resounded anew as thunder and lightning. Even his sweat and tears were put to good use and were transformed into delicate droplets of rain and sweet-smelling morning dew.

And when people later came to inhabit the earth, they worshipped Pan Gu as a great creator and displayed the utmost respect for all the natural elements, believing them to be his sacred body spread out like a carpet before them beneath the blue arch of the heavens.

How the Five Ancients Became Men

BEFORE THE EARTH was separated from the heavens, all there was was a great ball of watery vapor called chaos. And at that time the spirits of the five elemental powers took shape, and became the five Ancients. The first was called the Yellow Ancient, and he was the ruler of the earth. The second was called the Red Lord, and he was the ruler of the fire. The third was called the Dark Lord, and he was the ruler of the water. The fourth was known as the Wood Prince, and he was the ruler of the wood. The fifth was called the Mother of Metals, and ruled over them. These five Ancients set all their primal spirit into motion, so that water and earth sank down. The heavens floated upward, and the earth grew firm in the depths. Then they allowed the waters to gather into rivers and seas, and hills and plains made their appearance. So the heavens opened and the earth was divided. And there were sun, moon and all the stars, wind, clouds, rain, and dew. The Yellow Ancient set earth's purest power spinning in a circle, and added the effect of fire and water thereto. Then there came forth grasses and trees, birds and beasts, and the tribes of the serpents and insects, fishes and turtles. The Wood Prince and the Mother of Metals combined light and darkness, and thus created the human race as men and women. And thus the world gradually came to be.

At that time there was one who was known as the True Prince of the Jasper Castle. He had acquired the art of sorcery through the cultivation of magic. The five Ancients begged him to rule as the supreme god. He dwelt above the three and thirty heavens, and the Jasper Castle, of white jade with golden gates, was his. Before him stood the stewards of the eight-and-twenty houses of the moon, and the gods of the thunders and the Great Bear, and in addition a class of baneful gods whose influence was evil and deadly. They all aided the True Prince of the Jasper Castle to rule over the thousand tribes under the heavens, and to deal out life and death, fortune and misfortune. The Lord of the Jasper Castle is now known as the Great God, the White Jade Ruler.

The five Ancients withdrew after they had done their work, and thereafter lived in quiet purity. The Red Lord dwells in the south as the god of fire. The Dark Lord dwells in the north, as the mighty master of the sombre polar skies. He lived in a castle of liquid crystal. In later ages, he sent Confucius down upon earth as a saint. Hence, this saint is known as the Son of Crystal. The Wood Prince dwells in the east. He is honoured as the Green Lord, and watches over the coming into being of all creatures. In him lives the power of spring and he is the god of love. The Mother of Metals dwells in the west, by the sea of Jasper, and is also known as the Queen-Mother of the west. She leads the rounds of the fairies, and watches over change and growth. The Yellow Ancient dwells in the middle. He is always going about in the world, in order to save and to help those in any distress. The first time he came to earth he was the Yellow Lord, who taught mankind all sorts of arts. In his later years he fathomed the meaning of the world on the Ethereal Mount, and flew up to the radiant sun. Under the rule of the Dschou dynasty he was born again as Li Oerl, and when he was born his hair and beard were white, for which reason he was called Laotsze, 'Old Child'. He wrote the book of 'Meaning and Life' and spread his teachings through the world. He is honoured as the head of Taoism. At the beginning of the reign of the Han dynasty, he again appeared as the Old Man of the River, (Ho Schang Gung). He spread the teachings of Tao abroad mightily, so that from that time on Taoism flourished greatly. These doctrines are known to this day as the teachings of the Yellow Ancient. There is also a saying, 'First Laotsze was, then the heavens were'. And that must mean that Laotsze was that very same Yellow Ancient of primal days.

Note: This fairy-tale, the first of the legends of the gods, is given in the version current among the people. In it the five elemental spirits of earth, fire, water, wood and metal are brought into connection with a creation myth. 'Prince of the Jasper Castle' or 'The White Jade Ruler', Yu Huang Di, is the popular Chinese synonym for 'the good lord'. The phrase 'White Jade' serves merely to express his dignity. All in all, there are 32 other Yu Huangs, among whom he is the highest. He may be compared to Indra, who dwells in a heaven that also comprises 33 halls. The astronomic relationship between the two is very evident.

Izanagi and Izanami

IZANAGI AND IZANAMI stood on the Floating Bridge of Heaven and looked down into the abyss. They inquired of each other if there were a country far, far below the great Floating Bridge. They were determined to find out. In order to do so they thrust down a jewel-spear, and found the ocean. Raising the spear a little, water dripped from it, coagulated, and became the island of Onogoro-jima ('Spontaneously-congeal-island').

Upon this island the two deities descended. Shortly afterwards they desired to become husband and wife, though as a matter of fact they were brother and sister; but such a relationship in the East has never precluded marriage. These deities accordingly set up a pillar on the island. Izanagi walked round one way, and Izanami the other. When they met, Izanami said: "How delightful! I have met with a lovely youth." One would have thought that this naive remark would have pleased Izanagi; but it made him, extremely angry, and he retorted: "I am a man, and by that right should have spoken first. How is it that on the contrary thou, a woman, shouldst have been the first to speak? This is unlucky. Let us go round again." So it happened that the two deities started afresh. Once again they met, and this time Izanagi remarked: "How delightful! I have met a lovely maiden." Shortly after this very ingenuous proposal Izanagi and Izanami were married.

When Izanami had given birth to islands, seas, rivers, herbs, and trees, she and her lord consulted together, saying: "We have now produced the Great-Eight-Island country, with the mountains, rivers, herbs, and trees. Why should we not produce someone who shall be the Lord of the Universe?"

The wish of these deities was fulfilled, for in due season Amaterasu, the Sun Goddess, was born. She was known as 'Heaven-Illumine-of-Great-Deity', and was so extremely beautiful that her parents determined to send her up the Ladder of Heaven, and in the high sky above to cast for ever her glorious sunshine upon the earth.

Their next child was the Moon God, Tsuki-yumi. His silver radiance was not so fair as the golden effulgence of his sister, the Sun Goddess, but he was, nevertheless, deemed worthy to be her consort. So up the Ladder of Heaven climbed the Moon God. They soon quarrelled, and Amaterasu said: "Thou art a wicked deity. I must not see thee face to face." They were therefore separated by a day and night, and dwelt apart.

The next child of Izanagi and Izanami was Susanoo ('The Impetuous Male'). We shall return to Susanoo and his doings later on, and content ourselves for the present with confining our attention to his parents.

Izanami gave birth to the Fire God, Kagutsuchi. The birth of this child made her extremely ill. Izanagi knelt on the ground, bitterly weeping and lamenting. But his sorrow availed nothing, and Izanami crept away into the Land of Yomi (Hades).

Her lord, however, could not live without her, and he too went into the Land of Yomi. When he discovered her, she said regretfully: "My lord and husband, why is thy coming so late? I have already eaten of the cooking-furnace of Yomi. Nevertheless, I am about to lie down to rest. I pray thee do not look at me."

Izanagi, moved by curiosity, refused to fulfil her wish. It was dark in the Land of Yomi, so he secretly took out his many-toothed comb, broke off a piece, and lighted it. The sight that greeted him was ghastly and horrible in the extreme. His once beautiful wife had now become a swollen and festering creature. Eight varieties of Thunder Gods rested upon her. The Thunder of the Fire, Earth, and Mountain were all there leering upon him, and roaring with their great voices.

Izanagi grew frightened and disgusted, saying: "I have come unawares to a hideous and polluted land." His wife retorted: "Why didst thou not observe that which I charged thee? Now am I put to shame."

Izanami was so angry with her lord for ignoring her wish and breaking in upon her privacy that she sent the Eight Ugly Females of Yomi to pursue him. Izanagi drew his sword and fled down the dark regions of the Underworld. As he ran he took off his headdress, and flung it to the ground. It immediately became a bunch of grapes. When the Ugly Females saw it, they bent down and ate the luscious fruit. Izanami saw them pause, and deemed it wise to pursue her lord herself.

By this time Izanagi had reached the Even Pass of Yomi. Here he placed a huge rock, and eventually came face to face with Izanami. One would scarcely have thought that amid such exciting adventures Izanagi would have solemnly declared a divorce. But this is just what he did do. To this proposal his wife replied: "My dear lord and husband, if thou sayest so, I will strangle to death the people in one day." This plaintive and threatening speech in no way influenced Izanagi, who readily replied that he would cause to be born in one day no less than fifteen hundred.

The above remark must have proved conclusive, for when we next hear of Izanagi he had escaped from the Land of Yomi, from an angry wife, and from the Eight Ugly Females. After his escape he was engaged in copious ablutions, by way of purification, from which numerous deities were born. We read in the *Nihon Shoki*: "After this, Izanagi, his divine task having been accomplished, and his spirit-career about to suffer a change, built himself an abode of gloom in the island of Ahaji, where he dwelt for ever in silence and concealment."

Nasadiya Sukta
(The Hymn of Creation)

THEN WAS NOT non-existent nor existent: there was no realm of air, no sky beyond it.
  What covered it, and where? And what gave shelter? Was water there, unfathomed depth of water?
  Death was not then, nor was there aught immortal: no sign was there, the day's and night's divider.
  That One Thing, breathless, breathed by its own nature: apart from it was nothing whatsoever.
  Darkness there was: at first concealed in darkness this All was indiscriminated chaos.
  All that existed then was void and formless: by the great power of Warmth was born that Unit.
  Thereafter rose Desire in the beginning, Desire, the primal seed and germ of Spirit.
  Sages who searched with their heart's thought discovered the existent's kinship in the non-existent.
  Transversely was their severing line extended: what was above it then, and what below it?
  There were begetters, there were mighty forces, free action here and energy up yonder.
  Who verily knows and who can here declare it, whence it was born and whence comes this creation?
  The Gods are later than this world's production. Who knows then whence it first came into being?
  He, the first origin of this creation, whether he formed it all or did not form it,
  Whose eye controls this world in highest heaven, he verily knows it, or perhaps he knows not.

The Birth of Rama

ONCE, LONG, LONG ago, in the great city of Ayodhya there lived a king. Ayodhya was a prosperous city, one where its citizens were happy, pure of heart and well educated in the teachings of both man and god. Its king was also a good man and happy in almost every respect, for he had many wise counsellors and sages in his family and he had been blessed with a lovely daughter, Santa. This king was called Dasharatha, and he married his sweet daughter to the great sage Rishyasringa, who became a member of his inner circle, advising him on all matters with great wisdom and foresight. Two fine priests – Vashishtha and Vamadeva – were also part of his family, and they were known to all as the most saintly of men.

But Dasharatha had one hole in his glittering life; he longed for a son to carry on his line, a son who would one day be king. For many years he made offerings to the great powers, but to no avail, until such time as he made the most supreme sacrifice, that of a horse. His three wives were overjoyed by the prospect of having a son and when, after one year, the horse returned from the sacrifice, Rishyasringa and Vashishtha prepared the ceremony. With the greatest of respect and joy Rishyasringa was able to announce to Dasharatha that he would father four sons, and they would carry his name into the future.

When any sacrifice is made by man, all of the deities come together to take their portion of what has been offered, and so it was on this occasion that they had assembled to take from the sacrificial horse. There was, however, a dissenter among their ranks, one who was greedy and oppressive, and who caused in his colleagues such dissension that they came forward to Brahma with a request that he be destroyed. The evil rakshasa was called Ravana, and at an early age he had been granted immunity from death by yakshas, rakshasas or gods. His immunity had led him to become selfish and arrogant, and he took great pleasure in flaunting his exemption from the normal fates. Brahma spoke wisely to the gathered deities.

"Ravana is indeed evil," he said quietly, "and he had great foresight in requesting immunity from death by his equals. But," and here Brahma paused. "But," he went on, "he was not wise enough to seek immunity from death by humans – and it is in this way that he must be slain."

The deities were relieved to find that Ravana was not invincible, and as they celebrated amongst themselves, they were quietened by a profound presence who entered their midst. It was the great God Vishnu himself, and he appeared in flowing yellow robes, his eyes sparkling. He carried with him mace, and discus and conch, and he appeared on the back of Garuda, the divine bird attendant of Narayana. The deities fell at his feet, and they begged him to be born as Dasharatha's four sons in order to destroy the deceitful Ravana.

And so it was that Vishnu threw himself into Dasharatha's fire and taking the form of a sacred tiger, spoke to the anxious father-to-be, pronouncing himself the ambassador of God himself. He presented Dasharatha with spiritual food, which he was to share with his wives – two portions to Sumitra, one to Kaikeyi, and one to Kaushalya. And soon, four strong, healthy babies were born to Dasharatha's wives and they were named by Vashishtha, the divine priest. They were Rama, born to Kaushalya, Bharata, born to Kaikeyi, and Lakshman and Satrughna born to Sumitra.

Krishna's Birth

THERE ONCE WAS a king of Mathura, named Ugrasena, who had a beautiful wife. Now his wife was barren, a fact which dismayed them both and caused her to hold her head down in shame. One day, when walking in the wood, she lost her companions and found herself in the company of a demon who assumed her husband's form. Knowing not the difference between this man and the man who was her husband, she allowed him to lie with her and the product of this liaison was a long-awaited son, who they named Kansa.

When Kansa was a child he was cruel and a source of great sorrow to his family and his country. He shunned the religious teachings of the day and taunted his father for his devotion to Rama, the god of his race. His father could only reply, "Rama is my lord, and the dispeller of my grief. If I do not worship him, how shall I cross over the sea of the world?"

The ruthless Kansa laughed heartily at what he considered to be his father's foolishness and immediately usurped his place on the throne. Immediately a proclamation was issued throughout the kingdom, forbidding men to worship Rama and commanding them to pay their devotions to Siva instead.

This arrogance and tyranny went on for many years, and every man and woman throughout the kingdom prayed for relief from the rule of this truly evil man. Finally, the Earth, assuming the form of a cow, went to Indra and complained. And so it was that Brahma listened to the pleas of the Earth and led them to Siva, and then Vishnu. Vishnu had in the past taken on the incarnation of man and they reminded him of that now, begging him to do so in order to afford the destruction of the seemingly invincible Kansa. Each of the gods and goddesses cheered Vishnu in this mission and promised to leave their heavenly homes in order that they could accompany him on earth. Vishnu arranged that Lakshman, Bharata and Sutraghna would accompany him and that Sita, who would take the name of Rukmini, would be his wife.

One day Kansa was carrying the great Vasudeva and his wife Devaki through the sky when a voice set out the following prophecy:

"Kansa, fool that you are, the eighth child of the damsel you are now driving shall take away your life!" And so Kansa drew his sword and was about to take the life of Devaki when Vasudeva intervened, and said:

"Spare her life and I will deliver to you every child she brings forth." Kansa laid down his sword, but he placed a guard with her who stayed by her side for her every living hour. And as child after child was given up to him and slain, he continued in his wretched mission.

But Devaki was a woman with a mind as quick as a tree squirrel, and although Kansa had been advised that the children he had destroyed were her own, this was not the case. The children that had been handed over to him were the children of Hiranyakasipu who had been lodged in the womb of Devaki in order that the cruel Kansa might be fooled. Vishnu said to the goddess Yoganindra, who brought the children from the nether regions:

"Go Yoganindra, go and by my command conduct successively six of their princes to be conceived by Devaki. When these shall have been put to death by Kansa, the seventh conception shall be formed of a portion of Sesha, who is part of me; and you shall transfer before the time of birth to Rohini, another wife of Vasudeva, who resides at Gokula. The report shall run that

Devaki miscarries and I will myself become incarnate in her eighth conception; and you shall take a similar character as the embryo offspring of Yasoda, the wife of a herdsman called Nanda. In the night of the eighth of the dark half of the month Nabhas I shall be born, and you will be born on the ninth. Aided by my power, Vasudeva shall bear me to the bed of Yasoda, and you to the bed of Devaki. Kansa shall take you and hold you up to dash you against a stone, but you shall escape into the sky, where Indra shall meet and do homage to you through reverence of me."

And so it was that when Devaki gave birth to her eighth son, Vasudeva took the child and hurried through the city. When he reached the River Yamuna, which he had to cross, the water rose only to his knees instead of seeking to drown him. And as he reached the house of Nanda, Yasoda had given birth to her child, which Vasudeva seized and, leaving Devaki's child in its place, returned to his wife's bed.

Soon after, the guard heard the cry of a newborn, and summoning himself from the depths of a good sleep, he called for Kansa, who immediately rushed into the home of Devaki and thrust the child against a stone. But as soon as this child touched the ground there was a cry as deep and angry as that of any rakshasa. It rose into the sky and grew into a huge figure with eight arms, each holding a great weapon. It laughed and said to Kansa, "What use is it to you to have hurled me to the ground? He is born that shall kill you, the mighty one amongst the gods."

Kansa collected his ministers and gathered them round. He insisted that every man who was generous in gifts and sacrifices and prayers to the gods must be put to death so that no god shall have subsistence. He said then, "I know now that the tool of my fate is still living. Let therefore active search be made for whatever young children there may be upon earth, and let every boy in whom there are signs of unusual vigour be slain without remorse."

Soon after this Vasudeva and Devaki were released from their confinement, and quickly sought out Nanda, who was still unaware of the change in their children. Vasudeva had brought with him another of his child, by Rohini, who was Balarama, and placed him under the care of Nanda to be brought up as his own child. By this means, as Rama and Lakshman were inseparable companions in previous incarnations, Krishna and Balarama were intimately connected.

Nanda and his family had not been settled long at Gokula before efforts were made to destroy the infant Krishna. A female fiend called Putana, whose breast caused instant death when sucked, had taken the child in her arms and offered him a drink. The infant Krishna seized it with such fervour and sucked with such violence that the horrible fiend roared with pain and met with an instant death.

The birth of Krishna had caused great happiness, despite the evil decrees of Kansa, and throughout the land trees blossomed, flowers bloomed and there was music in the souls of all who lived on earth.

How the World Was Made

THE CHEROKEES BELIEVED the following about how the world was made. The earth is a great floating island in a sea of water. At each of the four corners there is a cord hanging down from the sky. The sky is a solid rock. When the world grows old and worn out, the cords will break, and then the earth will sink down into the ocean. Everything will be water again. All the people will be dead. The Indians are much afraid of this.

In the long time ago, when everything was all water, all the animals lived up above in Galun'lati, beyond the stone arch that made the sky. But it was very much crowded. All the animals wanted more room. The animals began to wonder what was below the water and at last Beaver's grandchild, little Water Beetle, offered to go and find out. Water Beetle darted in every direction over the surface of the water, but it could find no place to rest. There was no land at all. Then Water Beetle dived to the bottom of the water and brought up some soft mud. This began to grow and to spread out on every side until it became the island which we call the earth. Afterwards this earth was fastened to the sky with four cords, but no one remembers who did this.

At first the earth was flat and soft and wet. The animals were anxious to get down, and they sent out different birds to see if it was yet dry, but there was no place to alight; so the birds came back to Galun'lati. Then at last it seemed to be time again, so they sent out Buzzard; they told him to go and make ready for them. This was the Great Buzzard, the father of all the buzzards we see now. He flew all over the earth, low down near the ground, and it was still soft. When he reached the Cherokee country, he was very tired; his wings began to flap and strike the ground. Wherever they struck the earth there was a valley; whenever the wings turned upwards again, there was a mountain. When the animals above saw this, they were afraid that the whole world would be mountains, so they called him back, but the Cherokee country remains full of mountains to this day.

When the earth was dry and the animals came down, it was still dark. Therefore they got the sun and set it in a track to go every day across the island from east to west, just overhead. It was too hot this way. Red Crawfish had his shell scorched a bright red, so that his meat was spoiled. Therefore the Cherokees do not eat it.

Then the medicine men raised the sun a handsbreadth in the air, but it was still too hot. They raised it another time; and then another time; at last they had raised it seven handsbreadths so that it was just under the sky arch. Then it was right and they left it so. That is why the medicine men called the high place 'the seventh height.' Every day the sun goes along under this arch on the under side; it returns at night on the upper side of the arch to its starting place.

There is another world under this earth. It is like this one in every way. The animals, the plants, and the people are the same, but the seasons are different. The streams that come down from the mountains are the trails by which we reach this underworld. The springs at their head are the doorways by which we enter it. But in order to enter the other world, one must fast and then go to the water, and have one of the underground people for a guide. We know that the seasons in the underground world are different, because the water in the spring is always warmer in winter than the air in this world; and in summer the water is cooler.

We do not know who made the first plants and animals. But when they were first made, they were told to watch and keep awake for seven nights. This is the way young men do now when they fast and pray to their medicine. They tried to do this. The first night, nearly all the animals stayed awake. The next night several of them dropped asleep. The third night still more went to sleep. At last, on the seventh night, only the owl, the panther, and one or two more were still awake. Therefore, to these were given the power to see in the dark, to go about as if it were day, and to kill and eat the birds and animals which must sleep during the night.

Even some of the trees went to sleep. Only the cedar, the pine, the spruce, the holly, and the laurel were awake all seven nights. Therefore they are always green. They are also sacred trees. But to the other trees it was said, "Because you did not stay awake, therefore you shall lose your hair every winter."

After the plants and the animals, men began to come to the earth. At first there was only one man and one woman. He hit her with a fish. In seven days a little child came down to the earth. So people came to the earth. They came so rapidly that for a time it seemed as though the earth could not hold them all.

The Story of the Creation

WHEN TU-CHAI-PAI MADE the world, the earth is the woman, the sky is the man. The sky came down upon the earth. The world in the beginning was pure lake covered with tules. Tu-chai-pai and Yo-ko-mat-is, the brother, sat together, stooping far over, bowed down under the weight of the sky.
The Maker said to the brother, "What am I going to do?"
"I do not know," said Yo-ko-mat-is.
"Let us go a little farther," said the Maker.
Then they went a little farther and sat down again.
"Now, what am I going to do? " said Tu-chai-pai.
"I do not know."
All this time Tu-chai-pai knew what he would do, but he was asking the brother.
Then he said, "We-hicht, we-hicht, we-hicht," three times; and he took tobacco in his hand, and rubbed it fine, and blew upon it three times, and every time he blew the heavens rose higher above their heads.
Then the boy did the very same thing, because the Maker told him to do it. The heavens went high, and there was the sky.
Then they did it both together, "We-hicht, we-hicht, we-hicht;" and both took the tobacco, and rubbed it, and puffed upon it, and sent the sky up, so – (into a concave arch).
Then they placed the North, South, East and West. Tu-chai-pai made a line upon the ground.
"Why do you make that line?"
"I am making the line from East to West, and I name them thus, Y-nak, East; A-uk, West. Now you may make it from North to South."
Then Yo-ko-mat-is was thinking very much.
"Why are you thinking?"
"Oh, I must think; but now I have arranged it. I draw a line thus (a crossline), and I name it Ya-wak, South; Ka-tulk, North."
"Why have we done this?"
"I do not know."
"Then I will tell you. Three or four men are coming from the East, and from the West three or four Indians are coming."
The boy asked, "And do four men come from the North, and two or three men come also from the South?"
Then Tu-chai-pai said, "Now I am going to make hills and valleys, and little hollows of water."
"Why are you making all these things?

The Maker said, "After a while, when men come and are walking back and forth in the world, they will need to drink water, or they will die." He had already put the ocean down in its bed, but he made these little waters for the people.

Then he made the forests, and said, "After a while men will die of cold unless I make wood for them to use. What are we going to do now?"

"I do not know."

"We are going to dig in the ground, and take mud, and make the Indians first." And he dug in the ground, and took mud, and made of it first the men, and after that the women. He made the men very well, but he did not make the women very well. It was much trouble to make them, and it took a longtime. He made a beard for the men and boys, but not for the women. After the Indians he made the Mexicans, and he finished all his making. Then he called out very loud, "You can never die, and you can never be tired, but you shall walk all the time." After that he made them so that they could sleep at night, and need not walk around all the time in the darkness. At last he told them that they must travel towards the East, towards the light.

The people walked in darkness till he made the light. Then they came out and searched for the light, and when they found it they were glad. Then be called out to make the moon, and he said to the other, "You may make the moon as I have made the sun. Some time it is going to die. When it grows very small, men may know that it is going to die, and at that time all men, young and old, must run races."

All the pueblos talked about the matter, and they understood that they must run these races, and that Tu-chai-pai was looking at them to see that they did this. After the Maker did all this he did nothing more, but he was thinking many days.

The Mother of the World

IN THE FROZEN regions of the North, beyond the lands which are now the hunting-grounds of the Snakes and Coppermines, there lived, when no other being but herself was, a woman who became the mother of the world. She was a little woman, our fathers told us, not taller than the shoulders of a young maiden of our nation, but she was very beautiful and very wise. Whether she was good-tempered or cross, I cannot tell, for she had no husband, and so there was nothing to vex her, or to try her patience. She had not, as the women of our nation now have, to pound corn, or to fetch home heavy loads of buffalo flesh, or to make snow-sledges, or to wade into the icy rivers to spear salmon, or basket kepling, or to lie concealed among the wet marsh grass and wild rice to snare pelicans, and cranes, and goosanders, while her lazy, good-for-nothing husband lay at home, smoking his pipe, and drinking the pleasant juice of the Nishcaminnick by the warm fire in his cabin. She had only to procure her own food, and this was the berries, and hips, and sorrel, and rock-moss, which, being found plentifully near her cave, were plucked with little trouble. Of these she gathered, in their season, when the sun beamed on the earth like a maiden that loves and is beloved, a great deal to serve her for food when the snows hid the earth from her sight, and the cold winds from the fields of eternal frost obliged her to remain in her rude cavern. Though alone, she was happy. In the summer it was her amusement to watch the juniper and the alders, as they put forth, first their leaves, and then their buds, and when the latter became blossoms, promising to supply the fruit she loved, her observation became more curious and her feelings more interested; then would her heart beat with the rapture of a young mother, whose gaze is fixed on her sleeping child, and her eyes glisten with the dew of joy which wets the cheeks of those who meet long parted friends. Then she would wander forth to search for the little berry whose flower is yellow, and which requires keen eyes to find it in its hiding-place in the grass, and the larger which our white brother eats with his buffalo-meat; and their progress, from the putting forth of the leaf to the ripening of the fruit, was watched by her with eager joy. When tired of gazing upon the pine and stunted poplar, she would lie down in the shade of the creeping birch and dwarf willow, and sink to rest, and dream dreams which were not tinged with the darkness of evil. The sighing of the wind through the branches of the trees, and the murmur of little streams through the thicket, were her music. Throughout the land there was nothing to hurt her, or make her afraid, for there was nothing in it that had life, save herself and the little flower which blooms among thorns. And these two dwelt together like sisters.

One day, when the mother of the world was out gathering berries, and watching the growth of a young pine, which had sprung up near her friend the flower, and threatened, as the flower said, "to take away the beams of the sun from it," she was scared by the sight of a strange creature, which ran upon four legs, and to all her questions answered nothing but "Bow, wow, wow." To every question our mother asked, the creature made the same answer, "bow, wow, wow." So she left off asking him questions, for they were sure to be replied to in three words of a language she could not understand. Did he ask for berries? No, for she offered him a handful of the largest and juiciest which grew in the valley, and he neither took them nor thanked her, unless 'bow' meant 'thank you.' Was he admiring the tall young pines, or the beautiful blossoms of the cranberry, or the graceful bend of the willow, and asking her to join him in his admiration? She knew not, and leaving him to his thoughts, and to utter his strange words with none to reply, she returned to her cave.

Scarcely was she seated on her bed of dried leaves when he came in, and, wagging his tail, and muttering as before, lay down at her feet. Occasionally he would look up into her face very kindly, and then drop his head upon his paws. By and by he was fast asleep, and our mother, who had done no evil action, the remembrance of which should keep her awake, who never stole a beaver-trap, or told a lie, or laughed at a priest, was very soon in the same condition. Then the Manitou of Dreams came to her, and she saw strange things in her sleep. She dreamed that it was night, and the sun had sunk behind the high and broken hills which lay beyond the valley of her dwelling, that the dwarf willow bowed its graceful head still lower with the weight of its tears, which are the evening dew, and the dandelion again imprisoned its leaves within its veil of brown. So far her dreams so closely resembled the reality, that for a time she thought she was awake, and that it was her own world – her cave, her berries, and her flowers, which were before her vision. But an object speedily came to inform her that she dwelt in the paradise of dreams – in the land of departed ideas. At the foot of her couch of leaves, in the place of the dog which she had left there when she slept, stood a being somewhat resembling that she had beheld in the warm season, when bending over the river to lave her bosom with the cooling fluid. It was taller than herself, and there was something on its brow which proclaimed it to be fiercer and bolder, formed to wrestle with rough winds, and to laugh at the coming tempests. For the first time since she was, she turned away to tremble, her soul filled with a new and undefinable feeling, for which she could not account. After shading her eyes a moment from the vision, she looked again, and though her trembling increased, and her brain became giddy, she did not wish the being away, nor did she motion it to go. Why should she? There was a smile upon its lip and brow, and a softness diffused over every feature, which gradually restored her confidence, and gave her the assurance that it would not harm her. She dreamed that the creature came to her arms, and she thought that it passed the season of darkness with its cheek laid on her bosom. To her imagination, the breath which it breathed on her lips was balmy as the juice of the Sweet Gum Tree, or the dew from her little neighbour, the flower. When it spoke, though she could not understand its language, her heart heaved more tumultuously, she knew not why, and when it ceased speaking, her sighs came thick till it spoke again. When she awoke it was gone, the beams of the star of day shone through the fissures of her cavern, and, in the place of the beautiful and loved being lay the strange creature, with the four legs and the old 'bow, wow, wow.'

Four moons passed, and brought no change of scene to the mother of the world. By night, her dreams were ever the same: there was always the same dear and beloved being, each day dearer and more beloved, coming with the shades, and departing with the sun, folding her in its arms, breathing balm on her lips, and pressing her bosom with its downy cheek. By day, the dog was always at her side, whether she went to gather berries or cresses, or to lave her limbs in the stream. Whenever the dog was there, the more beloved being was not; when night came, the dog as surely disappeared, and the other, seen in dreams, supplied his place. But she herself became changed. She took no more joy in the scenes which once pleased her. The pines she had planted throve unnoticed; the creeping birch stifled the willow and the juniper, and she heeded it not; the sweetest berries grew tasteless – she even forgot to visit her pretty sister, the rose. Yet she knew not the cause of her sudden change, nor of the anxiety and apprehension which filled her mind. Why tears bedewed her cheeks till her eyes became blind, why she trembled at times, and grew sick, and feinted, and fell to the earth, she knew not. Her feelings told her of a change, but the relation of its cause, the naming to her startled ear of the mystery of 'the dog by day, and the man by night,' was reserved for a being, who was to prepare the world for the reception of the mighty numbers which were to be the progeny of its mother.

She had wandered forth to a lonely valley – lonely where all was lonely – to weep and sigh over her lost peace, and to think of the dear being with which that loss seemed to her to be in some way connected, when suddenly the sky became darkened, and she saw the form of a being shaped like that which visited her in her sleep, but of immense proportions, coming towards her from the east. The clouds wreathed themselves around his head, his hair swept the mists from the mountain-tops, his eyes were larger than the rising sun when he wears the red flush of anger in the Frog-Moon, and his voice, when he gave it full tone, was louder than the thunder of the Spirit's Bay of Lake Huron. But to the woman he spoke in soft whispers; his terrific accents were reserved for the dog, who quailed beneath them in evident terror, not daring even to utter his only words, 'bow, wow.' The mother of the world related to him her dreams, and asked him why, since she had had them, she was so changed – why she now found no joy in the scenes which once pleased her, but rather wished that she no longer was, her dreams being now all that she loved. The mighty being told her that they were not dreams, but a reality; that the dog which now stood by her side was invested by the Master of Life with power to quit, at the coming in of the shades, the shape of a dog, and to take that of Man, a being who was the counterpart of herself, but formed with strength and resolution, to counteract, by wisdom and sagacity, and to overcome, by strength and valour, the rough difficulties and embarrassments which were to spring up in the path of human life; that he was to be fierce and bold, and she gentle and afraid. He told her that the change she complained of, and which had given her so much grief, wetted her cheek with tears, and filled her bosom with sighs, was the natural result of the intimate connection of two such beings, and was the mode of perpetuating the human race, which had been decreed by the Master of Life; that before the buds now forming should be matured to fruit, she would give birth to two helpless little beings, whom she must feed with her milk, and rear with tender care, for from them would the world be peopled. He had been sent, he said, by the Good Spirit to level and prepare the earth for the reception of the race who were to inhabit it.

Hitherto the world had lain a rude and shapeless mass – the great, man now reduced it to order. He threw the rough and stony crags into the deep valleys – he moved the frozen mountain to fill up the boiling chasm. When he had levelled the earth, which before was a thing without form, he marked out with his great walking-staff the lakes, ponds, and rivers, and caused them to be filled with water from the interior of the earth, bidding them to be replenished from the rains and melted snows which should fall from the skies, till they should be no more.

When he had prepared the earth for the residence of the beings who were to people it, he caught the dog, and, notwithstanding the cries of the mother of the world, and her entreaties to him to spare its life, he tore it in pieces, and distributed it over the earth, and the water, and into air. The entrails he threw into the lakes, ponds, and rivers, commanding them to become fish, and they became fish. These waters, in which no living creature before moved, were now filled with salmon, trout, pike, tittymeg, methy, barble, turbot, and tench, while along the curling waves of the Great Lake the mighty black and white whale, the more sluggish porpoise, and many other finny creatures, sported their gambols. The flesh he dispersed over the land, commanding it to become different kinds of beasts and land-animals, and it obeyed his commands. The heavy moose, and the stupid we-was-kish, came to drink in the Coppermine with the musk-ox, and the deer, and the buffalo. The quiquehatch, and his younger brother, the black bear, and the wolf, that cooks his meat without fire, and the cunning fox, and the wild cat, and the wolverine, were all from the flesh of the dog. The otter was the tail of the dog, the wejack was one of his fore-paws, and the horned horse, and the walrus, were his nose.

Nor did the great man omit to make the skin furnish its proportion of the tribes of living beings. He tore it into many small pieces, and threw it into the air, commanding it to become the different tribes of fowls and birds, and it became the different tribes of fowls and birds. Then first was seen the mighty bird which builds its nest on trees which none can climb, and in the crevices of inaccessible rocks – the eagle, which furnishes the Indians with feathers to their arrows, and steals away the musk-rat and the young beaver as his recompense. Then was the sacred falcon first seen winging his way to the land of long winters; and the bird of alarm, the cunning old owl, and his sister's little son, the cob-a-de-cooch, and the ho-ho. All the birds which skim through the air, or plunge into the water, were formed from the skin of the dog.

When the great man had thus filled the earth with living creatures, he called the mother of the world to him, and gave to her and her offspring the things which he had created, with full power to kill, eat, and never to spare, telling her that he had commanded them to multiply for her use in abundance. When he had finished speaking, he returned to the place whence he came, and has never been heard of since. In due time, the mother of the world was delivered of two children, a son and a daughter, both having the dark visage of the Indian race, and from them proceeded the Dog-ribs, and all the other nations of the earth. The white men were from the same source, but the father of them, having once upon a time been caught stealing a beaver-trap, he become so terrified that he lost his original colour and never regained it, and his children remain with the same pale cheeks to this day.

Brothers, I have told you no lie.

The Making of Daylight

IN THE BEGINNING it was always dark. Darkness was a woman, who had two daughters, and came from the eastward to gamble with Wildcat. She reached Wildcat's house at night, and after supper began to talk about gambling, saying, "I never came here before. I came to gamble." The others present advised Wildcat to play: so all the preparations were made, and, sitting on either side of the fire, they began to play. Darkness bet her two daughters against all the people which Wildcat had. Darkness wanted Wildcat to bet her husband, Chicken-Hawk, but she did not wish to. Finally, on Coyote's advice, she bet him as chief first. Then they began to play, Coyote helping to sing. He thought the game was going favorably, and that Wildcat would win the two girls, and that he would get them for wives. But just as she almost won, Darkness beat her, and, taking Coyote, broke him in two and threw him outside. Darkness then threatened to "stay dark all the time" unless Wildcat would bet her husband, as Darkness wanted him for a husband for her daughters. Wildcat refused, and bet other people in the house. All but three offered themselves to be bet. These were Rabbit, Weasel, and Caterpillar. Finally all were lost to Darkness but these; and then Caterpillar said, "Bet me," and he came near where Wildcat sat. They were gambling with a small slippery thing like ice, instead of the usual gambling-bone. Caterpillar began to sing, and to win. Pretty soon all but one of Darkness' counters were gone, and she began to be afraid. She was afraid of the smooth gambling-stick. Caterpillar told her to sit still, as she was moving about nervously. Suddenly he slid the gambling-stick across at her, and, entering her body, it caused her to burst. Then Caterpillar took her body and threw it outside.

The two girls were sitting there crying. One of them was going to gamble. She told Caterpillar to deal, but he refused. So she began, and won until Caterpillar had only one counter left. Then he began to win, and finally killed her just as he had her mother. He then threw her body outside. Only the youngest sister was left. Caterpillar told her not to cry, as he was not crying, although all his people were lost. They played and played, and, as before, Caterpillar killed her by the same trick. Then Caterpillar said, "In after time, people will say that I was the one who won my people back."

Still, however, it was dark. So Lizard set to work to try to make light. He went over to Big-Lizard's house, and took a light with him. He told Big-Lizard all about what had happened, and told him that he and Caterpillar and Rabbit were the only ones left. Then Lizard put on his cap and began to dance. His cap was made of a grizzly-bear's head. Rabbit was talking, singing, while Lizard was dancing near the house-post. By and by it began to grow light. Lizard made daylight come by dancing. Rabbit said, "That is what people will say; that is what people must say, 'Daylight is coming.'" Lizard's grandmother was sitting there, and she sang, "Daylight is coming, daylight is coming!" Then she made a mistake, and sang about a man. Lizard was angry, and said, "You are always thinking about men." His grandmother answered, "I meant to sing properly, but my teeth are all gone, and so I made a mistake." Lizard then told Rabbit to go out and see where light was coming. He went up and looked, and, looking to the east, saw the dawn and heard the birds singing. He came back and said, "I did not see anything." By and by he went up again, after Lizard had danced some more. This time daylight had come. All over the world people woke up, and made a noise. Then Lizard stopped dancing. He told people to open the doors, to build a fire and go out. It was spring-time, and sunflowers were ripening. All the people came out and talked about Lizard's having made the light.

Creation Myth of the Iroquois

AT THE DAWN of creation, before mankind ever existed, the universe comprised two separate worlds. The lower world was a place of eternal darkness, peopled only by creatures of the water, while the upper world, a kingdom of bright light, was inhabited by the Great Ruler and his family. The goddess Atahensic was daughter of the Great Ruler, and at this time she was heavy with child and very close to her time of confinement. As the hour drew near, her relatives persuaded her to lie down on a soft mattress, wrapping her in a ray of light, so that her weary body would gather strength and refreshment for the task ahead. But as soon as she had closed her eyes, the bed on which she lay began to sink without warning through the thick clouds, plunging rapidly towards the lower world beneath her. Dazzled and alarmed by the descending light, the monsters and creatures of the great water held an emergency council to decide what should be done.

"If the being from above falls on us," said the Water-hen, "it will surely destroy us. We must quickly find a place where it can rest."

"Only the oeh-da, the earth which lies at the very bottom of the water, will be strong enough to hold it," said the Beaver. "I will swim down and bring some back with me.' But the Beaver never returned from his search.

Then the Duck volunteered himself for the same duty, but soon his dead body floated up to the surface. Finally, however, the Muskrat came forward:

"I know the way better than anyone," he told the others, "but the oeh-da is extremely heavy and will grow very fast. Who is prepared to bear its weight when I appear with it?"

The Turtle, who was by far the most capable among them, readily agreed to suffer the load. Shortly afterwards, the Muskrat returned with a small quantity of the oeh-da in his paw which he smoothed on to the turtle's back. It began to spread rapidly, and as soon as it had reached a satisfactory size for the light to rest on, two birds soared into the air and bore the goddess on their outstretched wings down towards the water and safely on to the turtle's back. From that day onwards, the Turtle became known as the Earth Bearer, and whenever the seas rise up in great waves, the people know that it is the Turtle stirring in his bed.

A considerable island of earth now floated on the waves, providing a timely shelter, for soon Atahensic began to hear two voices within her womb, one soft and soothing, the other loud and aggressive, and she knew that her mission to people the island was close at hand. The conflict continued within, as one of her twin infants sought to pass out under the side of his mother's arm, while the other held him back, attempting to spare his mother this unnecessary pain. Both entered into the world in their own individual way, the first bringing trouble and strife, the second bringing freedom and peace. The goddess wisely accepted that it must be so, and named her children Hahgwehdiyu, meaning Good Mind, and Hahgwehdaetgah, meaning Bad Mind. Each went his way, Hahgwehdiyu anxious to bring beauty to the island, Hahgwehdaetgah determined that darkness and evil should prevail.

Not long after she had given birth, Atahensic passed away and the island grew dim in the dawn of its new life. Knowing the goddess would not have wished it this way, Hahgwehdiyu lifted his palm high into the air and began moulding the sky with his fingers. After he had done this, he took his mother's head from her body and placed it firmly in the centre of the firmament:

"You shall be known as the Sun," he announced, "and your face shall light up this new world where you shall rule forever."

But his brother saw all of this good work and set darkness in the west sky, forcing the Sun down behind it. Hahgwehdiyu would not be beaten, however, and removing a portion of his mother's breast, he cast it upwards, creating an orb, inferior to the sun, yet capable of illuminating the darkness. Then he surrounded the orb with numerous spots of light, giving them the name of stars and ordering them to regulate the days, nights, seasons and years. When he had completed this work above, he turned his attention to the soil beneath his feet. To the barren earth he gave the rest of his mother's body from which the seeds of all future life were destined to spring forth.

The Good Mind continued the works of creation, refusing all rest until he had accomplished everything he had set out to do. All over the land he formed creeks and rivers, valleys and hills, luscious pastures and evergreen forests. He created numerous species of animals to inhabit the forests, from the smallest to the greatest, and filled the seas and lakes with fishes and mammals of every variety and colour. He appointed thunder to water the earth and winds to scatter pollen so that, in time, the island became fruitful and productive. But all was not yet complete, for Hahgwehdiyu wisely observed that a greater being was needed to take possession of the Great Island. And so, he began forming two images from the dust of the ground in his own likeness. To these he gave the name of Eagwehowe, meaning the Real People, and by breathing into their nostrils he gave them living souls.

When the earth was created and Hahgwehdiyu had bestowed a protective spirit upon every object of his creation, he went out in search of his brother, hoping to persuade him to abandon his evil and vicious existence. But the Bad Mind was already hard at work, intent on destroying all evidence of Hahgwehdiyu's remarkable labour. Without much effort, he overcame the guardian spirits he encountered and marched throughout the island, bending the rivers, sundering the mountains, gnarling the forests and destroying food crops. He created lethal reptiles to injure mankind, led ferocious monsters into the sea and gathered great hurricanes in the sky. Still dissatisfied with the devastation, however, he began making two images of clay in the form of humans, aiming to create a more superior and destructive race. But he was quickly made to realize that he had not been blessed with the same creative powers as the Good Mind, for as he breathed life into them, his clay figures turned into hideous apes. Infuriated by this discovery, the Bad Mind thundered through the island like a terrible whirlwind, uprooting fruit-trees and wringing the necks of animals and birds. Only one thing would now satisfy his anger, a bloody and ruthless combat to the death, and with this purpose in mind, he hastened towards his twin-brother's dwelling.

Weary of the destruction he had witnessed, the Good Mind willingly submitted himself to the contest that would decide the ruler of the earth. The Bad Mind was keen to discover anything that might help to destroy his brother's temporal life and began to question him rather slyly on the type of weapons they should use.

"Tell me," he said, "what particular instrument would cause you the most injury, so that I may avoid its use, as a gesture of goodwill."

Hahgwehdiyu could see through this evil strategy, however, and falsely informed him that he would certainly be struck down by a lotus arrow.

"There is nothing I fear," the Bad Mind boasted, but Hahgwehdiyu knew this to be untrue, and wisely remembered that ever since childhood the horns of a stag had always induced feelings of terror in his brother.

The battle began and lasted for two days and two nights, causing panic and disruption throughout the earth as mountains shook violently under the strain of the combat and rivers overflowed with the blood of both brothers. At last, however, the Bad Mind could no longer ignore the temptation to shoot the lotus arrow in his brother's direction. The Good Mind responded by charging at him with the stag-horns, impaling him on their sharp points until he screamed in pain and fell to the ground begging for mercy.

Hahgwehdiyu, the supreme ruler of the earth, immediately banished his evil brother to a dark pit beneath the surface of the world, ordering him never to return. Gathering together as many hideous beasts and monsters as he could find, he flung them below so that they might share with their creator a life of eternal doom. Some escaped his grasp, however, and remained on the earth as Servers, half-human and half-beasts, eager to continue the destructive work of the Bad Mind who had now become known as the Evil Spirit.

Hahgwehdiyu, faithful to the wishes of his grandfather, the Great Ruler, carried on with his good work on the floating island, filling the woodlands with game, slaying the monsters, teaching the Indians to make fires and to raise crops, and instructing them in many of the other arts of life until the time had come for him to retire from the earth to his celestial home.

Osage Creation Story

WAY BEYOND, ONCE upon a time, some of the Osages lived in the sky. They did not know where they came from, so they went to Sun. They said, "From where did we come?"

He said, "You are my children."

Then they wandered still further and came to Moon.

Moon said, "I am your mother; Sun is your father. You must go away from here. You must go down to the earth and live there."

So they came to the earth but found it covered with water. They could not return up above. They wept, but no answer came to them. They floated about in the air, seeking help from some god; but they found none.

Now all the animals were with them. Elk was the finest and most stately. They all trusted Elk. So they called to Elk, "Help us."

Then Elk dropped into the water and began to sink. Then he called to the winds. The winds came from all sides and they blew until the waters went upwards, as in a mist. Now before that the winds had traveled in only two directions; they went from north to south and from south to north. But when Elk called to them, they came from the east, from the north, from the west, and from the south. They met at a central place; then they carried the waters upwards.

Now at first the people could see only the rocks. So they traveled on the rocky places. But nothing grew there and there was nothing to eat. Then the waters continued to vanish. At last the people could see the soft earth. When Elk saw the earth, he was so joyous, he rolled over and over on the earth. Then all the loose hairs clung to the soil. So the hairs grew, and from them sprang beans, corn, potatoes, and wild turnips, and at last all the grasses and trees.

Now the people wandered over the land. They found human footsteps. They followed them. They joined with them, and traveled with them in search of food.

The Hoga came down from above, and found the earth covered with water. They flew in every direction. They sought for gods who would help them and drive the water away. They found not one. Then Elk came. He had a loud voice and he shouted to the four corners of the sky. The four winds came in answer. They blew upon the water and it vanished upwards, in a mist. Then the people could see the rocks. Now there was only a little space on the rocks. They knew they must have more room. The people were crowded. So they sent Muskrat down into the water. He did not come back. He was drowned. Then they sent Loon down. He did not come back. He was drowned. Then they sent Beaver down into the water. The water was too deep. Beaver was drowned. Then Crawfish dived into the water. He was gone a long time. When he came up there was a little mud in his claws. Crawfish was so tired he died. But the people took the mud out of his claws and made the land.

Spider's Creation

IN THE BEGINNING, long, long ago, there was but one being in the lower world. This was the spider, Sussistinnako. At that time there were no other insects, no birds, animals, or any other living creature.

The spider drew a line of meal from north to south and then crossed it with another line running east and west. On each side of the first line, north of the second, he placed two small parcels. They were precious but no one knows what was in them except Spider. Then he sat down near the parcels and began to sing. The music was low and sweet and the two parcels accompanied him, by shaking like rattles. Then two women appeared, one from each parcel. In a short time people appeared and began walking around. Then animals, birds, and insects appeared, and the spider continued to sing until his creation was complete.

But there was no light, and as there were many people, they did not pass about much for fear of treading upon each other. The two women first created were the mothers of all. One was named Utset and she as the mother of all Indians. The other was Now-utset, and she was the mother of all other nations. While it was still dark, the spider divided the people into clans, saying to some, "You are of the Corn clan, and you are the first of all." To others he said, "You belong to the Coyote clan." So he divided them into their clans, the clans of the Bear, the Eagle, and other clans.

After Spider had nearly created the earth, Ha-arts, he thought it would be well to have rain to water it, so he created the Cloud People, the Lightning People, the Thunder People, and the Rainbow People, to work for the people of Ha-arts, the earth. He divided this creation into six parts, and each had its home in a spring in the heart of a great mountain upon whose summit was a giant tree. One was in the spruce tree on the Mountain of the North; another in the pine tree on the Mountain of the West; another in the oak tree on the Mountain of the South; and another in the aspen tree on the Mountain of the East; the fifth was on the cedar tree on the Mountain of the Zenith; and the last in an oak on the Mountain of the Nadir.

The spider divided the world into three parts: Ha-arts, the earth; Tinia, the middle plain; and Hu-wa-ka, the upper plain. Then the spider gave to these People of the Clouds and to the rainbow, Tinia, the middle plain.

Now it was still dark, but the people of Ha-arts made houses for themselves by digging in the rocks and the earth. They could not build houses as they do now, because they could not see. In a short time Utset and Now-utset talked much to each other, saying, "We will make light, that our people may see. We cannot tell the people now, but to-morrow will be a good day and the day after to-morrow will be a good day," meaning that their thoughts were good. So they spoke with one tongue. They said, "Now all is covered with darkness, but after a while we will have light."

Then these two mothers, being inspired by Sussistinnako, the spider, made the sun from white shell, turkis, red stone, and abalone shell. After making the sun, they carried him to the east and camped there, since there were no houses. The next morning they climbed to the top of a high mountain and dropped the sun down behind it. After a time he began to ascend. When the people saw the light they were happy.

When the sun was far off, his face was blue; as he came nearer, the face grew brighter. Yet they did not see the sun himself, but only a large mask which covered his whole body.

The people saw that the world was large and the country beautiful. When the two mothers returned to the village, they said to the people, "We are the mothers of all."

The sun lighted the world during the day, but there was no light at night. So the two mothers created the moon from a slightly black stone, many kinds of yellow stone, turkis, and a red stone, that the world might be lighted at night. But the moon travelled slowly and did not always give light. Then the two mothers created the Star People and made their eyes of sparkling white crystal that they might twinkle and brighten the world at night. When the Star People lived in the lower world they were gathered into beautiful groups; they were not scattered about as they are in the upper world.

San Luiseño Creation Myth

IN THE BEGINNING all was empty space. Ké-vish-a-ták-vish was the only being. This period was called Óm-ai-yá-mal signifying emptiness, nobody there. Then came the time called Há-ruh-rúy, upheaval, things coming into shape. Then a time called Chu-tu-taí, the falling of things downward; and after this, Yu-vaí-to-vaí, things working in darkness without the light of sun or moon. Then came the period Tul-múl Pu-shún, signifying that deep down in the heart or core of earth things were working together.

Then came Why-yaí Pee-vaí, a gray glimmering like the whiteness of hoar frost; and then, Mit-aí Kwai-raí, the dimness of twilight. Then came a period of cessation, Na-kaí Ho-wai-yaí, meaning things at a standstill. Then Ké-vish-a-ták-vish made a man, Túk-mit, the Sky; and a woman, To-maí-yo-vit, the Earth. There was no light, but in the darkness these two became conscious of each other.

"Who are you?" asked the man.

"I am To-maí-yo-vit. And you?"

"I am Túk-mit."

"Then you are my brother."

"You are my sister."

By her brother the Sky the Earth conceived and became the Mother of all things. Her first-born children were, in the order of their birth, See-vat and Pá-ve-ut, Ush-la and Pik-la, Ná-na-chel and Patch'-ha-yel, Tópal and Tam'-yush.

Then came forth all other things, people, animals, trees, rocks, and rivers, but not as we see them now. All things then were people.

But at first they were heavy and helpless and could not move about, and they were in darkness, for there was no light. But when the Sun was born he gave a tremendous light which struck the people into unconsciousness, or caused them to roll upon the ground in agony; so that the Earth-Mother, seeing this, caught him up and hid him away for a season; so then there was darkness again.

After the Sun was born there came forth another being called Chung-itch'-nish, a being of power, whose voice sounded as soon as he was born, while all the others rolled helplessly upon the ground, unable to utter a word. The others were so terrified by his appearance that the Earth-Mother hid him away, and ever since he has remained invisible.

The rattlesnake was born at this time, a monster without arms or legs.

When all her children were born, the Earth-Mother left the place and went to Ech'-a-mo Nóy-a-mo. The people rolled, for like newborn babies they could not walk. They began then to crawl on hands and knees, and they talked this way: Chák-o-lá-le, Wá-wa, Tá-ta. This was all that they could say. For food they ate clay. From there they moved to Kak-wé-mai Po-lá-la, then to Po-és-kak Po-lá-lak.

They were growing large now and began to recognize each other. Then the Earth-Mother made the sea so that her children could bathe in it, and so that the breeze from the sea might fill their lungs, for until this time they had not breathed.

Then they moved farther to a place called Na-ché-vo Po-mé-sa-vo, a sort of a cañon which was too small for their abiding-place; so they returned to a place called Tem-ech'-va Tem-eck'-o, and this place people now call Temecula, for the Mexicans changed the Indian name to that.

Here they settled while everything was still in darkness. All this time they had been travelling about without any light.

The Earth-Mother had kept the sun hidden away, but now that the people were grown large enough and could know each other she took the Sun out of his hiding-place, and immediately there was light. They could all see each other; and while the Sun was standing there among them they discussed the matter and decided that he must go east and west and give light all over the world; so all of them raised their arms to the sky three times, and three times cried out 'Cha-cha-cha,' and he rose from among them and went up to his place in the sky.

After this they remained at Temecula, but the world was not big enough for them, and they talked about it and concluded that it must be made larger. So this was done, and they lived there as before.

It was at Temecula that the Earth-Mother taught her children to worship Chung-itch'-nish. Although he could not be seen, he appointed the Raven to be his messenger, flying over the heads of the people to watch for any who had offended against him. Whenever the Raven flew overhead, they would have a big fiesta and dance.

The bear and the rattlesnake were the chosen avengers for Chung-itch'-nish; and any who failed to obey would suffer from their bite. When a man was bitten by a rattlesnake it was known that he had offended Chung-itch'-n ish, and a dance would be performed with religious ceremonies to beg his forgiveness.

The stone bowls, Tam'-yush, were sacred to his worship; so were the toloache and mock-orange plants. All the dances are made for his worship, and all the sacred objects, stone pipes, eagle feathers, tobacco, etc., were used in this connection.

The Discovery of the Upper World

THE MINNATAREES, AND all the other Indians who are not of the stock of the grandfather of nations, were once not of this upper air, but dwelt in the bowels of the earth. The Good Spirit, when he made them, meant, no doubt, at a proper time to put them in enjoyment of all the good things which he had prepared for them upon earth, but he ordered that their first stage of existence should be within it. They all dwelt underground, like moles, in one great cavern. When they emerged it was in different places, but generally near where they now inhabit. At that time few of the Indian tribes wore the human form. Some had the figures or semblances of beasts. The Paukunnawkuts were rabbits, some of the Delawares were ground-hogs, others tortoises, and the Tuscaroras, and a great many others, were rattlesnakes. The Sioux were the hissing-snakes, but the Minnatarees were always men. Their part of the great cavern was situated far towards the mountains of snow.

The great cavern in which the Indians dwelt was indeed a dark and dismal region. In the country of the Minnatarees it was lighted up only by the rays of the sun which strayed through the fissures of the rock and the crevices in the roof of the cavern, while in that of the Mengwe all was dark and sunless. The life of the Indians was a life of misery compared with that they now enjoy, and it was endured only because they were ignorant of a fairer or richer world, or a better or happier state of being.

There were among the Minnatarees two boys, who, from the hour of their birth, showed superior wisdom, sagacity, and cunning. Even while they were children they were wiser than their fathers. They asked their parents whence the light came which streamed through the fissures of the rock and played along the sides of the cavern, and whence and from what descended the roots of the great vine. Their father could not tell them, and their mother only laughed at the question, which appeared to her very foolish. They asked the priest, but he could not tell them; but he said he supposed the light came from the eyes of some great wolf. The boys asked the king tortoise, who sulkily drew his head into his shell, and made no answer. When they asked the chief rattlesnake, he answered that he knew, and would tell them all about it if they would promise to make peace with his tribe, and on no account kill one of his descendants. The boys promised, and the chief rattlesnake then told them that there was a world above them, a beautiful world, peopled by creatures in the shape of beasts, having a pure atmosphere and a soft sky, sweet fruits and mellow water, well-stocked hunting-grounds and well-filled lakes. He told them to ascend by the roots, which were those of a great grape-vine. A while after the boys were missing; nor did they come back till the Minnatarees had celebrated their death, and the lying priest had, as he falsely said, in a vision seen them inhabitants of the land of spirits.

The Indians were surprised by the return of the boys. They came back singing and dancing, and were grown so much, and looked so different from what they did when they left the cavern, that their father and mother scarcely knew them. They were sleek and fat, and when they walked it was with so strong a step that the hollow space rang with the sound of their feet. They were covered with the skins of animals, and had blankets of the skins of racoons and beavers. They described to the Indians the pleasures of the upper world, and the people were delighted with their story. At length they resolved to leave their dull residence underground for the upper regions. All agreed to this except the ground-hog, the badger, and the mole, who said, as they had been put where they were, they would live and die there. The rabbit said he would live sometimes above and sometimes below.

When the Indians had determined to leave their habitations underground, the Minnatarees began, men, women, and children, to clamber up the vine, and one-half of them had already reached the surface of the earth, when a dire mishap involved the remainder in a still more desolate captivity within its bowels.

There was among them a very fat old woman, who was heavier than any six of her nation. Nothing would do but she must go up before some of her neighbours. Away she clambered, but her weight was so great that the vine broke with it, and the opening, to which it afforded the sole means of ascending, closed upon her and the rest of her nation.

The Great Deeds of Michabo

A VERY POWERFUL manitto once visited the earth and, falling in love with its only inhabitant, a beautiful young maiden, he made her his wife. From this union were born four healthy sons, but in giving birth the mother sadly passed away.

The first son was named Michabo and he was destined to become the friend of the human race. Michabo, supreme deity of the Algonquin Indians, is very often represented as an invincible god, endowed with marvellous powers. Sometimes, however, he is given a far more human treatment, and is depicted as a trickster, or troublemaker, as in the story to follow.

The second, Chibiabos, took charge of the dead and ruled the Land of Souls.

The third, Wabassa, immediately fled to the north, transforming himself into a rabbit-spirit, while the fourth, Chokanipok, who was of a fiery temperament, spent his time arguing, especially with his eldest brother.

Michabo, the strongest and most courageous of the four, had always attributed the death of his mother to Chokanipok, and the repeated combats between the two were often fiercely savage.

During one particularly brutal confrontation, Michabo carved huge fragments of flesh from the body of his brother which, as soon as they fell to the ground, were transformed into flintstones. In time, the children of men found a use for these stones and used them to create fire, giving Chokanipok the name of Firestone, or Man of Flint.

After a long and tortuous battle, Chokanipok was finally slain by Michabo who tore out his bowels and changed them into long twining vines from which the earth's vegetation sprung forth.

After this, Michabo journeyed far and wide, carrying with him all manner of tools and equipment which he distributed among men.

He gave them lances and arrow-points; he taught them how to make axes or agukwats; he devised the art of knitting nets to catch fish; he furnished the hunter with charms and signs to use in his chase, and he taught mankind to lay traps and snares.

In the course of his journeys he also killed the ferocious beasts and monsters threatening the human race and cleared the rivers and streams of many of the obstructions which the Evil Spirit had placed there.

When he saw that all this was done, Michabo placed four good spirits at the four cardinal points of the earth, instructing mankind that he should always blow the smoke from his calumet in each of these four directions as a mark of respect during the sacred feasts.

The Spirit of the North, he told them, would always provide snow and ice, enabling man to hunt game. The Spirit of the South would give them melons, maize and tobacco.

The Spirit he had placed in the West would ensure that rain fell upon the crops, and the Spirit of the East would never fail to bring light in place of darkness.

Then, retreating to an immense slab of ice in the Northern Ocean, Michabo kept a watchful eye on mankind, informing them that if ever the day should arrive when their wickedness forced him to depart the earth, his footprints would catch fire and the end of the world would come; for it was he who directed the sun in his daily walks around the earth.

The Creation of the World

IN THE BEGINNING there was nothing at all except darkness. All was darkness and emptiness. For a long, long while, the darkness gathered until it became a great mass. Over this the spirit of Earth Doctor drifted to and fro like a fluffy bit of cotton in the breeze. Then Earth Doctor decided to make for himself an abiding place. So he thought within himself, "Come forth, some kind of plant," and there appeared the creosote bush. He placed this before him and set it upright.

But it at once fell over. He set it upright again; again it fell. So it fell until the fourth time it remained upright.

Then Earth Doctor took from his breast a little dust and flattened it into a cake. When the dust cake was still, he danced upon it, singing a magic song.

Next he created some black insects which made black gum on the creosote bush. Then he made a termite which worked with the small earth cake until it grew very large. As he sang and danced upon it, the flat World stretched out on all sides until it was as large as it is now. Then he made a round sky-cover to fit over it, round like the houses of the Pimas. But the earth shook and stretched, so that it was unsafe. So Earth Doctor made a gray spider which was to spin a web around the edges of the earth and sky, fastening them together. When this was done, the earth grew firm and solid.

Earth Doctor made water, mountains, trees, grass, and weeds – made everything as we see it now. But all was still inky blackness. Then he made a dish, poured water into it, and it became ice. He threw this round block of ice far to the north, and it fell at the place where the earth and sky were woven together. At once the ice began to gleam and shine. We call it now the sun. It rose from the ground in the north up into the sky and then fell back.

Earth Doctor took it and threw it to the west where the earth and sky were sewn together. It rose into the sky and again slid back to the earth.

Then he threw it to the far south, but it slid back again to the flat earth.

Then at last he threw it to the east. It rose higher and higher in the sky until it reached the highest point in the round blue cover and began to slide down on the other side. And so the sun does even yet.

Then Earth Doctor poured more water into the dish and it became ice. He sang a magic song, and threw the round ball of ice to the north where the earth and sky are woven together. It gleamed and shone, but not so brightly as the sun. It became the moon, and it rose in the sky, but fell back again, just as the sun had done. So he threw the ball to the west, and then to the south, but it slid back each time to the earth. Then he threw it to the east, and it rose to the highest point in the sky-cover and began to slide down on the other side. And so it does even to-day, following the sun.

But Earth Doctor saw that when the sun and moon were not in the sky, all was inky darkness. So he sang a magic song, and took some water into his mouth and blew it into the sky, in a spray, to make little stars. Then he took his magic crystal and broke it into pieces and threw them into the sky, to make the larger stars. Next he took his walking stick and placed ashes on the end of it. Then he drew it across the sky to form the Milky Way. So Earth Doctor made all the stars.

The Creation Story of the Four Suns

TONACATECUTLI AND TONACACIUATL dwelt from the beginning in the thirteenth heaven. To them were born, as to an elder generation, four gods – the ruddy Camaxtli (chief divinity of the Tlascalans); the black Tezcatlipoca, wizard of the night; Quetzalcoatl, the wind-god; and the grim Huitzilopochtli, of whom it was said that he was born without flesh, a skeleton.

For six hundred years these deities lived in idleness; then the four brethren assembled, creating first the fire (hearth of the universe) and afterward a half-sun. They formed also Oxomoco and Cipactonal, the first man and first woman, commanding that the former should till the ground, and the latter spin and weave; while to the woman they gave powers of divination and grains of maize that she might work cures. They also divided time into days and inaugurated a year of eighteen twenty-day periods, or three hundred and sixty days. Mictlantecutli and Mictlanciuatl they created to be Lord and Lady of Hell, and they formed the heavens that are below the thirteenth storey of the celestial regions, and the waters of the sea, making in the sea a monster Cipactli, from which they shaped the earth. The gods of the waters, Tlaloctecutli and his wife Chalchiuhtlicue, they created, giving them dominion over the Quarters.

The son of the first pair married a woman formed from a hair of the goddess Xochiquetzal; and the gods, noticing how little was the light given forth by the half-sun, resolved to make another half-sun, whereupon Tezcatlipoca became the sun-bearer – for what we behold traversing the daily heavens is not the sun itself, but only its brightness; the true sun is invisible. The other gods created huge giants, who could uproot trees by brute force, and whose food was acorns. For thirteen times fifty-two years, altogether six hundred and seventy-six, this period lasted – as long as its Sun endured; and it is from this first Sun that time began to be counted, for during the six hundred years of the idleness of the gods, while Huitzilopochtli was in his bones, time was not reckoned.

This Sun came to an end when Quetzalcoatl struck down Tezcatlipoca and became Sun in his place. Tezcatlipoca was metamorphosed into a jaguar (Ursa Major) which is seen by night in the skies wheeling down into the waters whither Quetzalcoatl cast him; and this jaguar devoured the giants of that period.

At the end of six hundred and seventy-six years Quetzalcoatl was treated by his brothers as he had treated Tezcatlipoca, and his Sun came to an end with a great wind which carried away most of the people of that time or transformed them into monkeys.

Then for seven times fifty-two years Tlaloc was Sun; but at the end of this three hundred and sixty-four years Quetzalcoatl rained fire from heaven and made Chalchiuhtlicue Sun in place of her husband, a dignity which she held for three hundred and twelve years (six times fifty-two); and it was in these days that maize began to be used.

Now two thousand six hundred and twenty-eight years had passed since the birth of the gods, and in this year it rained so heavily that the heavens themselves fell, while the people of that time were transformed into fish. When the gods saw this, they created four men, with whose aid Tezcatlipoca and Quetzalcoatl again upreared the heavens, even as they are today; and these two gods becoming lords of the heavens and of the stars, walked therein.

After the deluge and the restoration of the heavens, Tezcatlipoca discovered the art of making fire from sticks and of drawing it from the heart of flint. The first man, Piltzintecutli, and his wife, who had been made of a hair of Xochiquetzal, did not perish in the flood, because they were divine. A son was born to them, and the gods created other people just as they had formerly existed.

But since, except for the fires, all was in darkness, the gods resolved to create a new Sun. This was done by Quetzalcoatl, who cast his own son, by Chalchiuhtlicue, into a great fire, whence he issued as the Sun of our own time; Tlaloc hurled his son into the cinders of the fire, and thence rose the Moon, ever following after the Sun. This Sun, said the gods, should eat hearts and drink blood, and so they established wars that there might be sacrifices of captives to nourish the orbs of light.

Creation Story of the Mixtecs

WHEN THE EARTH had arisen from the primeval waters, one day the deer-god, who bore the surname Puma-Snake, and the beautiful deer-goddess, or Jaguar-Snake, appeared. They had human form, and with their great knowledge (that is, with their magic) they raised a high cliff over the water, and built on it fine palaces for their dwelling. On the summit of this cliff they laid a copper axe with the edge upward, and on this edge the heavens rested. The palaces stood in Upper Mixteca, close to Apoala, and the cliff was called Place where the Heavens Stood.

The gods lived happily together for many centuries, when it chanced that two little boys were born to them, beautiful of form and skilled and experienced in the arts. From the days of their birth they were named Wind-Nine-Snake (Viento de Neuve Culebras) and Wind-Nine-Cave (Viento de Neuve Cavernas).

Much care was given to their education, and they possessed the knowledge of how to change themselves into an eagle or a snake, to make themselves invisible, and even to pass through solid bodies.

After a time these youthful gods decided to make an offering and a sacrifice to their ancestors. Taking incense vessels made of clay, they filled them with tobacco, to which they set fire, allowing it to smoulder. The smoke rose heavenward, and that was the first offering (to the gods). Then they made a garden with shrubs and flowers, trees and fruit-bearing plants, and sweet-scented herbs. Adjoining this they made a grass-grown level place (*un prado*), and equipped it with everything necessary for sacrifice. The pious brothers lived contentedly on this piece of ground, tilled it, burned tobacco, and with prayers, vows, and promises they supplicated their ancestors to let the light appear, to let the water collect in certain places and the earth be freed from its covering (water), for they had no more than that little garden for their subsistence. In order to strengthen their prayer they pierced their ears and their tongues with pointed knives of flint, and sprinkled the blood on the trees and plants with a brush of willow twigs.

The deer-gods had more sons and daughters, but there came a flood in which many of these perished. After the catastrophe was over the god who is called the Creator of All Things formed the heavens and the earth, and restored the human race.

The Mayan Creation Story

WE ARE TOLD that the god Hurakan, the mighty wind, a deity in whom we can discern a Kiche (Mayan from Guatemala) equivalent to Tezcatlipoca, passed over the universe, still wrapped in gloom. He called out "Earth," and the solid land appeared.

Then the chief gods took counsel among themselves as to what should next be made. These were Hurakan, Gucumatz or Quetzalcoatl, and Xpiyacoc and Xmucane, the mother and father gods. They agreed that animals should be created. This was accomplished, and they next turned their attention to the framing of man. They made a number of mannikins carved out of wood. But these were irreverent and angered the gods, who resolved to bring about their downfall.

Then Hurakan (The Heart of Heaven) caused the waters to be swollen, and a mighty flood came upon the mannikins. Also a thick resinous rain descended upon them. The bird Xecotcovach tore out their eyes, the bird Camulatz cut off their heads, the bird Cotzbalam devoured their flesh, the bird Tecumbalam broke their bones and sinews and ground them into powder.

Then all sorts of beings, great and small, abused the mannikins. The household utensils and domestic animals jeered at them, and made game of them in their plight. The dogs and hens said: "Very badly have you treated us and you have bitten us. Now we bite you in turn." The millstones said: "Very much were we tormented by you, and daily, daily, night and day, it was squeak, screech, screech, holi, holi, huqi, huqi, for your sake. Now you shall feel our strength, and we shall grind your flesh and make meal of your bodies." And the dogs growled at the unhappy images because they had not been fed, and tore them with their teeth.

The cups and platters said: "Pain and misery you gave us, smoking our tops and sides, cooking us over the fire, burning and hurting us as if we had no feeling. Now it is your turn, and you shall burn."

The unfortunate mannikins ran hither and thither in their despair. They mounted upon the roofs of the houses, but the houses crumbled beneath their feet; they tried to climb to the tops of the trees, but the trees hurled them down; they were even repulsed by the caves, which closed before them. Thus this ill-starred race was finally destroyed and overthrown, and the only vestiges of them which remain are certain of their progeny, the little monkeys which dwell in the woods.

The Creation Story of the Third Book

THE OPENING OF the third book of the *Popol Vuh* finds the gods once more deliberating as to the creation of man. Four men are evolved as the result of these deliberations. These beings were moulded from a paste of yellow and white maize, and were named Balam-Quitze (Tiger with the Sweet Smile), Balam-Agab (Tiger of the Night), Mahacutah (The Distinguished Name), and Iqi-Balam (Tiger of the Moon).

But the god Hurakan who had formed them was not overpleased with his handiwork, for these beings were too much like the gods themselves. The gods once more took counsel, and agreed that man must be less perfect and possess less knowledge than this new race. He must not become as a god. So Hurakan breathed a cloud over their eyes in order that they might only see a portion of the earth, whereas before they had been able to see the whole round sphere of the world. After this the four men were plunged into a deep sleep, and four women were created, who were given them as wives. These were Caha-Paluma (Falling Water), Choima (Beautiful Water), Tzununiha (House of the Water), and Cakixa (Water of Parrots, or Brilliant Water), who were espoused to the men in the respective order given above.

These eight persons were the ancestors of the Kiche only, after which were created the forerunners of the other peoples. At this time there was no sun, and comparative darkness lay over the face of the earth. Men knew not the art of worship, but blindly lifted their eyes to heaven and prayed the Creator to send them quiet lives and the light of day. But no sun came, and dispeace entered their hearts. So they journeyed to a place called Tulan-Zuiva (The Seven Caves) – practically the same as Chicomoztoc in the Aztec myth – and there gods were vouchsafed to them. The names of these were Tohil, whom Balam-Quitze received; Avilix, whom Balam-Agab received; and Hacavitz, granted to Mahacutah. Iqi-Balam received a god, but as he had no family his worship and knowledge died out.

The Granting of Fire

Grievously did the Kiche feel the want of fire in the sunless world they inhabited, but this the god Tohil (The Rumbler, the Fire-god) quickly provided them with. However, a mighty rain descended and extinguished all the fires in the land. These, however, were always supplied again by the thunder-god Tohil, who had only to strike his feet together to produce fire.

The Kiche Babel

Tulan-Zuiva was a place of great misfortune to the Kiche, for here the race suffered alienation in its different branches by reason of a confounding of their speech, which recalls the story of Babel. Owing to this the first four men were no longer able to comprehend each other, and determined to leave the place of their mischance and to seek the leadership of the god Tohil into another and more fortunate sphere. In this journey they met with innumerable hardships. They had to cross many lofty mountains, and on one occasion had to make a long *detour* across the bed of the ocean, the waters of which were miraculously divided to permit of their passage. At last they arrived at a mountain which they called Hacavitz, after one of their deities, and here they remained, for it had been foretold that here they should see the sun.

At last the luminary appeared. Men and beasts went wild with delight, although his beams were by no means strong, and he appeared more like a reflection in a mirror than the strong sun of later days whose fiery beams speedily sucked up the blood of victims on the altar. As he showed his face the three tribal gods of the Kiche were turned into stone, as were the gods or totems connected with the wild animals. Then arose the first Kiche town, or permanent dwelling-place.

The Last Days of the First Men

Time passed, and the first men of the Kiche race grew old. Visions came to them, in which they were exhorted by the gods to render human sacrifices, and in order to obey the divine injunctions they raided the neighbouring lands, the folk of which made a spirited resistance. But in a great battle the Kiche were miraculously assisted by a horde of wasps and hornets, which flew in the faces of their foes, stinging and blinding them, so that they could not wield weapon nor see to make any effective resistance. After this battle the surrounding races became tributary to them.

Death of the First Men

Now the first men felt that their death-day was nigh, and they called their kin and dependents around them to hear their dying words. In the grief of their souls they chanted the song 'Kamucu,' the song 'We see,' that they had sung so joyfully when they had first seen the light of day. Then they parted from their wives and sons one by one. And of a sudden they were not, and in their place was a great bundle, which was never opened. It was called the 'Majesty Enveloped.' So died the first men of the Kiche.

How the World Was Made

THOUSANDS OF YEARS ago there was no land, nor sun nor moon nor stars, and the world was only a great sea of water, above which stretched the sky. The water was the kingdom of the god Maguayan, and the sky was ruled by the great god Captan.

Maguayan had a daughter called Lidagat, the sea, and Captan had a son known as Lihangin, the wind. The gods agreed to the marriage of their children, so the sea became the bride of the wind.

Three sons and a daughter were born to them. The sons were called Licalibutan, Liadlao and Libulan, and the daughter received the name of Lisuga.

Licalibutan had a body of rock and was strong and brave; Liadlao was formed of gold and was always happy; Libulan was made of copper and was weak and timid; and the beautiful Lisuga had a body of pure silver and was sweet and gentle. Their parents were very fond of them, and nothing was wanting to make them happy.

After a time Lihangin died and left the control of the winds to his eldest son Licalibutan. The faithful wife Lidagat soon followed her husband, and the children, now grown up, were left without father or mother. However, their grandfathers, Captan and Maguayan, took care of them and guarded them from all evil.

After a time, Licalibutan, proud of his power over the winds, resolved to gain more power, and asked his brothers to join him in an attack on Captan in the sky above. At first they refused; but when Licalibutan became angry with them, the amiable Liadlao, not wishing to offend his brother, agreed to help. Then together they induced the timid Libulan to join in the plan.

When all was ready the three brothers rushed at the sky, but they could not beat down the gates of steel that guarded the entrance. Then Licalibutan let loose the strongest winds and blew the bars in every direction. The brothers rushed into the opening, but were met by the angry god Captan. So terrible did he look that they turned and ran in terror; but Captan, furious at the destruction of his gates, sent three bolts of lightning after them.

The first struck the copper Libulan and melted him into a ball. The second struck the golden Liadlao and he too was melted. The third bolt struck Licalibutan and his rocky body broke into many pieces and fell into the sea. So huge was he that parts of his body stuck out above the water and became what is known as land.

In the meantime the gentle Lisuga had missed her brothers and started to look for them. She went towards the sky, but as she approached the broken gates, Captan, blind with anger, struck her too with lightning, and her silver body broke into thousands of pieces.

Captan then came down from the sky and tore the sea apart, calling on Maguayan to come to him and accusing him of ordering the attack on the sky. Soon Maguayan appeared and answered that he knew nothing of the plot as he had been asleep far down in the sea. After a time he succeeded in calming the angry Captan. Together they wept at the loss of their grandchildren, especially the gentle and beautiful Lisuga; but with all their power they could not restore the dead to life. However, they gave to each body a beautiful light that will shine forever.

And so it was that golden Liadlao became the sun and copper Libulan the moon, while the thousands of pieces of silver Lisuga shine as the stars of heaven. To wicked Licalibutan the gods gave no light, but resolved to make his body support a new race of people. So Captan gave Maguayan a seed and he planted it on the land, which, as you will remember, was part of Licalibutan's huge body. Soon a bamboo tree grew up, and from the hollow of one of its branches a man and a woman came out. The man's name was Sicalac, and the woman was called Sicabay. They were the parents of the human race. Their first child was a son whom they called Libo; afterwards they had a daughter who was known as Saman. Pandaguan was a younger son and he had a son called Arion.

Pandaguan was very clever and invented a trap to catch fish. The very first thing he caught was a huge shark. When he brought it to land, it looked so great and fierce that he thought it was surely a god, and he at once ordered his people to worship it. Soon all gathered around and began to sing and pray to the shark. Suddenly the sky and sea opened, and the gods came out and ordered Pandaguan to throw the shark back into the sea and to worship none but them.

All were afraid except Pandaguan. He grew very bold and answered that the shark was as big as the gods, and that since he had been able to overpower it he would also be able to conquer the gods. Then Captan, hearing this, struck Pandaguan with a small thunderbolt, for he did not wish to kill him but merely to teach him a lesson. Then he and Maguayan decided to punish these people by scattering them over the earth, so they carried some to one land and some to another. Many children were afterwards born, and thus the earth became inhabited in all parts.

Pandaguan did not die. After lying on the ground for thirty days he regained his strength, but his body was blackened from the lightning, and all his descendants ever since that day have been black.

His first son, Arion, was taken north, but as he had been born before his father's punishment he did not lose his colour, and all his people therefore are white.

Libo and Saman were carried south, where the hot sun scorched their bodies and caused all their descendants to be of a brown colour.

A son of Saman and a daughter of Sicalac were carried east, where the land at first was so lacking in food that they were compelled to eat clay. On this account their children and their children's children have always been yellow in colour.

And so the world came to be made and peopled. The sun and moon shine in the sky and the beautiful stars light up the night. All over the land, on the body of the envious Licalibutan, the children of Sicalac and Sicabay have grown great in numbers. May they live forever in peace and brotherly love!

Tane – The Creation of Nature

THE GODPOWER OF Tane lifted his father Rangi high above the mountains – oh, high above the mountains, clad in snow he lifted him with the help of the gods who dwelled above the earth.

Ah, bare now was Rangi and naked – oh, he was beautiful and vast, but lonely and bare, and Tane adorned him with the stars; oh, then was Rangi very beautiful indeed!

From his great work Tane was resting upon earth while his eyes were wandering over his mother, and his heart grew sad again, for he beheld that she lay naked under the eyes of Rangi and the gods.

Ah, his love for his mother was great, and he pressed his head to her bosom and spoke: 'Oh, mother, I will not that you sorrow any more over your nakedness for I will adorn you with great beauty; do not sorrow any longer, oh mother, Papa.'

Thereupon he went into the Great Distance, and became the father of the lakes, the Water of the Many Faces; and many of these glittering faces he distributed over Papa. Faces, smiling at Rangi by day, and blushing up to him at every new morning – look my good friend, how the Moana-Rarapa is reflecting the beauty of Mahiku-rangi whilst Rangi is laughing down upon Papa out of his Eye of Day: ah, are they not lovers?

But again Tane wandered into the Great Distance, till he found the Gentle Noise of Air; and taking her to wife, he founded the family of the Multitude of Trees. Their sons were the Totara-tree, the Manuka, the Rimu, and the Kauri-tree: ah, look at the tree under which we are resting; see the majestic beauty of the Kauri, the child of Tane! And their daughters were the Kahiku, and the creeper and the vines.

Whilst the Multitude of Trees were growing up into maturity, Tane rested not till he found the two sisters, the Wanderer in the Sky, and the Wanderer in the Brook, and they gave him his children, the birds.

There, friend, do you hear the sweet sounds? There? – there now; everywhere – ah, it is the black Tui; and there, do you hear the gentle noise and soft clapping of wings over our heads? It is the folk of the Kererus, the wild-doves; ha, listen to their happiness! Come farther into the green shade, my good friend, that your heart may be filled with the beauty of Tane.

Yes, my friend, when Tane had founded these families, then he took them back to her who was still lying lonely and naked, and now he began his great work. Ah, let us wander under the shade of Tane, that your eyes may see how the Multitude of Trees are covering Papa like a beautiful garment, spreading shades and giving happiness to the children of Tiki; perceive in the wonderful garment the great god-power of Tane-mahuta.

Close your eyes, my good friend, that Ngawai may show to your mind the path upon which it may perceive how Tane distributed the multitude of his children over the earth. Ah, – ha, – can you perceive how he puts their feet into the ground? Ha, ha! They will not stand! They lift their heads up to Rangi and cry, and will go whither it pleases them; ha, ha, my friend, they are rebellious, and fight with each other, and run away, for they do not like to stand and grow, and give garment and coolness to Papa, ha, ha!

Ah, can you perceive how Tane looks upon his work of the first day, and sees the rebellion? Can you perceive his rage, the terrible rage of the god? – ha, ha!

Ah, he is wending his way back, tearing his children out of the ground and throwing them down, tearing and throwing, and then, when the sacred colour appeared again at Mahiku-rangi, he began his great work over again! Ha, ha, my friend, ha, ha, can you perceive how he began his work? Listen: he took his children and put them into the ground again, but, ha, ha, oh, he put their heads now into the ground, so that they must stand upright and stretch their feet up to Rangi; ha, ha, could they move now? – and fight? – and run away? Ah – their hair commenced to grow into the earth and took root, and their mouth drank the dew – the tears of Rangi for Papa – and sent it up into the limbs and feet as strength and life, and the feet grew long and branched off and covered themselves with leaves. Ha, my good friend!

Ah, my good friend, when Tane saw his children now, then came joy to his heart, and all over Papa he planted his children, and they grew, and took the earth to their mother.

Oh, beautifully now was Papa dressed in her vast garment, and greater still grew the love of Rangi, and he sent the rays of his Eye of Day down upon her, and created the flowers.

O, my friend, follow Ngawai into the darkness and the pleasures of Tane-mahuta's creation; look, all the life of the forests and all the life in the air is his, ah, he is the great friend of man, he is the god-power of Nature.

Tane, the great son of Rangi.

Tane, who loved Papa.

Tane, the friend of man.'

A soft murmuring was Ngawai's voice, murmuring to the leaves of the trees; murmuring of that what the birds had told her; murmuring to the spirits of the forest, who all are children of Tane-mahuta.

The Creation of the Stars

TE RA, THE DAY-EYE of Rangi is closing, and sends a last glowing look over the peacefully dreaming Moana-rarapa, the Lake of the Glittering Water.

Softly murmurs the lake and reflects the sacred Red with which Tane once adorned the heaven, whilst over his floating colours black swans are drifting like dream-thoughts over a beautiful face. Slowly dying away in blue, deep blue and pure, is the last breath of day silently departing into the heavens.

A canoe is putting off the shore, and voices of children are heard leading it light-hearted with mirth and laughter and splashing of water over the lake, which looks clear and glittering green up to the stars. Softly now breathes the air, and the mirror is gone – the day has departed.

Muttering departs Hupene, our old friend, in dread of the darkness; with his mat he is covering our shoulders and he murmurs these words:

"Remember, while you are watching the stars on the night-mat of Rangi, and know, great is the power of the god Tane-Mahuta, and his are the stars. Remember, his are the stars."

Bright shimmer the stars through the summer night, and the earth breathes freshness and sleep, leading the heart to rest, and it yet filling with longing; but from the heaven descends hope, promising the new day and the future.

Tane once commenced his great wandering to find adornment for his father, the heaven, whom he beheld standing high over Papa, naked by day and lonely and cold by night, and he spoke:

"O, father Rangi, my heart is looking upon you in sorrow, for you are lonely and cold, and I will go in quest for adornments which shall make you beautiful to the eyes of Papa and her children." Thereupon he went on his way, and, whilst he was wandering through the ten heavens, he found Te-Kura, the Red Colour, and that he took back with him upon the earth. Here he rested for seven days and seven nights, and, when his strength was growing again, he commenced his work, and covered the heaven with the beautiful red colour. But behold, when he had finished this great work and descended again to earth, he let his eyes wander over the red sky, which was stretching now over Papa, and he found that this adornment was not worthy of his great father, and full of sorrow he took it away again leaving some of it only at Mahiku-rangi, the End of Heaven. He beheld now, when Rangi was closing his great eye, sending it down into the Po, or when he called for it again in the mornings so that it burst forth out of the Gate of Day, that the beauty of his father at Mahiku-Rangi was wonderful, but ever and ever it disappeared by day and by night.

Seven days and seven nights he was watching the dying away and bursting forth again of Rangi's beauty, and then out of his sorrow he sang these words up to his father: "Oh, Rangi, still you are cold and dark and lonely from the first night, to the second night, to the tenth night, when your daughter Te-marama ascends again out of the Source of Living Water, so that you look down upon Papa silent and sorrowful. What adornment can I find for you, that you may be happy and beautiful, and gladden the heart of Papa, your loved one?"

After he had spoken these words he wandered forth again upon his mighty search, and all over the world he wandered, and farther and farther still he wandered, till he came to Tawhiti-nui, the Great Distance; and farther still, till at last he came to Te-Po, the Lower World. Here he found Hine-a-te-ao, the Daughter of the Light; she is the guardian of the Gates of the Lower World, and, tired from his long journey, he slept in her house.

In the darkness of night he beheld two beautiful stars shining forth; they were the children of Ira, and their names were Lonely South, and Shore of Heaven, the morning star, and his heart was glad over their beauty, so that his eyes could not sleep, and could not but rest upon them all the night.

In the morning he called Hine-a-te-ao, and showed her the two beautiful stars shimmering forth out of the darkness of the Po, and asked for them, for nothing could be more beautiful he thought as an adornment for his Father Rangi. Hine-a-te-ao answered: "Go, son, and take the stars!" And again he pleaded: "Oh, Hine, Daughter of the Light, show me the road that I may go and take the stars." And Hine-a-te-ao answered: "O, son, far is the way indeed! Go to the House of Tupu-renga-o-te-Po, the Growing Night: he is the guardian over the two stars, and his house is standing at Mahiku-rangi. There ask for the two stars, whose names are Toko-meha and Te-pae-tai-o-te-rangi; go and take the stars for your father Rangi."

After Tane had rested, and for seven days and seven nights strengthened himself through powerful incantations and many Karakias, he went on his way to Mahiku-rangi, to the House of the Guardian of the Stars, Tupu.

When at last he had found Tupu, he pictured the sorrows and the nakedness of his father, and asked him to give the beautiful stars to Rangi, and Tupu answered: "Oh, Tane, son of Rangi and Papa, the stars which you behold shimmering yonder are the sacred holders of the world; they are Hira-utu, Fish by the Land, Hira-tai, Fish of the Sea; Parinuku, Cliff by the Earth, and Pari-rangi, Cliff of the Heavens. Yes, it is my wish that you may adorn Rangi with yonder stars." And he gave him the Four Sacred Holders of the World, the stars of the four points of the compass, and then he gave him the five stars, Ao-tahi, Puaka and Tuku-rua, Tama-re-reti and Te-waka-a-tama-rereti.

All these stars Tane took away with him and fastened the four sacred stars in the four corners of Rangi; with the other five he formed a cross in the South.

Many more stars brought Tupu, and Tane distributed them over Rangi from the summit of the mountains whilst still the Sun was standing high in the heavens.

And again sorrow filled his heart when his eyes looked upon his work, for again he found that the adornment was not worthy of his father Rangi.

But at last he had finished his labour and that was about the time when the Sun was again entering the Gate of Night. Resting upon Papa, he watched the beautiful sacred red appear again at Mahiku-rangi, and, when with the departing sun darkness again filled the world, his wandering eyes perceived how star upon star commenced to live and shine forth, till at last Rangi in wonderful beauty was stretching over Papa, and his heart was full of joy and happiness, and he sang: "O, father Rangi, your beauty is indescribable; in truth you are now the ariki of Papa, and all her children will love you!"

Thus had spoken the old friend on the shores of the glittering Moana-rarapa.

The Creation of Hawaiki

"HERE FRIEND," SO speaks Ngawai, "sit beside the old man of my people, and listen to the song of the gods, which is living in the mouth of the blind Matapo, and know that Truth is dwelling upon his lips. Listen to his words!"

These are my words to you, my wanderer, the words of the old Matapo, the oldest of his people, and his eyes are closed and they cannot see you; but they are opened again towards his heart, and what they see your eyes cannot perceive, for upon those who dwell in the womb of night rest his eyes. Listen.

The beginning was J-o, the great atua, the god-power, and the world was filled by Te-po-nui, the Great Darkness – ah! – Te-po-nui filled all the space, from the first space to the hundredth, to the thousandth space.

Ha, my listener, then was it that the Atua commenced his great song of creation, and out of the Darkness sprang forth Life!

And out of the Darkness sprang forth Hine-nui-te-po!

And out of the Darkness sprang forth Te Ao, the Light!

Ha, my listener, Te-Ao – ha! – Te-Ao gave birth to Rangi! Rangi-nui, the great Heaven.

And again sang the atua his great song of creation, and out of Te-po-nui sprang forth Tangaroa, the God of the Oceans!

And out of Te-po-nui sprang forth Papa-tu-a-nuku, the far-stretching Earth.

Ha, the Earth was created! The Earth, and Rangi, the Heaven.

Ah, Rangi-nui, the great Heaven!

Rangi took Hine-nui-te-po for his wife, and their son was Ha-nui-o-rangi, the Great Breath of Heaven. And Ha-nui-o-rangi commenced his great movement, and forth sprang Tawhiri-matea, the father of the winds. And again Ha-nui-o-rangi commenced his great movement, and Te-ata-tuhi sprang forth, the First Glimmer of Light.

Te-ata-tuhi was a woman, and Rangi took her to wife. Her daughter was Te marama, the Moon, and Rangi spoke full of joy:

"O, woman, Te-ata-tuhi, look upon the beauty of Rangi's daughter; ha, she is his daughter for which he was longing," and he made her his eye, his Eye of Night.

Lightening his path, he went in search of his son. He found the woman Te wera-wera, the heat, and his heart went out to her, so that he took her to wife, and Te-Ra was born, Te-Ra, the Sun! Then cried Rangi full of joy, "O, woman, Wera-wera, look upon the beauty of Rangi's son – ha, he is his great son for which he was longing," and he made him his other eye, his Eye of the Day.

Ha, my listener, great now was Rangi's power, Rangi, the Creator! His eyes beheld with admiration Papa-tu-a-nuku, the far-stretching earth, shine forth out of the Darkness, and she was of great beauty.

Ah, she was of great beauty, and Rangi made her his wife that together they might create Hawaiki, and their first son was Rehua. With him were born the rays of light, and he flew high up into the highest heaven, which he made his dwelling-place. He became the god of the highest mountain peak and of the Locks of Heaven, the Sun-rays, when he stands highest on the heaven; and he became the ancestor and the ariki (Lord) over all the spirits and gods in the heavens.

Then Tane was born, and he was the god-power of the masculine sex, and the father of trees and birds. He and his brothers took Papa-tu-a-nuku for their dwelling-place.

The next son of Rangi and Papa – ha, listen my wanderer – was Tiki, our Father, who created Marikoriko, his wife, and became the father of man! Ah! – Rangi and Papa! – Ah! Rangi looked upon the far-stretching Earth out of his Eye of Night and admired her beauty; and he looked upon her out of his Eye of Day and his heart was full of joy, so that he spoke:

"O, woman, Papa, nevermore will I be parted from you; together we will be the world; the parents, Rangi and Papa!"

Then their fourth son was born, Rongo: he was the God-power of Good, and the atua of the Tapu and the sacred incantations; he was the creator of the food for man and the wisdom of cooking and the incantations over the food.

Their fifth son was Tu, the atua of all evil and the god of war. – Ah!

As you have opened your ears to the song of the old man, who is your friend, my listener, so open now your eyes, that they may show you how night presses upon Earth, and darkness has swallowed all, for, know, such was the night and the darkness which reigned between Heaven and Earth, everlasting, from the first time to the hundredth time, to the thousandth time – Ah, know, my friend, when the world was still dwelling in Te-po-nui then was it Tangaroa, the God of the Oceans, who had taken Papa-tu-a-nuku to wife, and their sons were Tinirau, The Many Hundreds, who founded the Family of the waves which encircle the Earth. When Tangaroa had perceived Te-ata-tuhi, the First Glimmer of Light, he wandered forth to find the Gate of Day. Ah, far he wandered, far into the last darknesses, and farther and farther, to the very end of Te-po-nui; but when he came back, then, ha, my listener, then did he find Rangi the ariki over Papa-tu-a-nuku.

Ah, the Heaven was the ariki over the earth!

Full of rage, Tangaroa fell upon Rangi, and wounded him terribly, so that he could not stand and fell upon Papa, and never could lift himself anymore, and no space and no light could come to his sons from this time. Ah, the sons, whose dwelling-place was upon the Earth, they had to live in darkness and night – ah! – ha!; but the sons!, ha, but the sons! Their hearts filled with the longing for the light, that happiness might grow again; and their hearts filled with the longing for space, that the power, living in them, might be born.

Ha, the longing in the hearts of the children of Rangi and Papa became the mother of the great incantations which gave them the power to create space again between Heaven and Earth so that the light could come to them like a wife to all.

And the voice of Tu spoke out of the darkness:

"Listen, all my brothers, together let us overcome Rangi, and let us kill him, for he gives us no room and covers us with blackness! Let us kill Rangi!"

But, my listener, the voice of Tane spoke out of the darkness, and this is what he said:

"Listen, all my brothers, how can we kill Rangi? Is he not our Father? Listen, all my brothers, and this is Tane's word: No, do not let us kill him, but let us search for the incantation to compel our brother Rehua and the host of spirits who dwell outside to help us in our great work, that we may lift our Father upon the highest mountains. Let us hold the Karakia that we may become sacred for our work to lift Rangi from Papa. Let Rangi be far from us, and let us dwell with Papa, our mother."

Ha, these were the words of Tane! – and all the voices out of the darkness spoke their consent, and all the voices together chanted the great incantations to Rehua and the host of gods and spirits calling upon them to come to their aid. Then, my listener, they commenced the sacred Karakia which is held to become strong and unconquerable, all together they chanted this powerful song:

"The night, the night,
The day, the day,
The seeking, the adzing out,
From the seeking the nothing.
Their seeking thought also for their mother,
That man might arise.
Behold this is the word,
The largeness, the length,
The height of their thought,
To free their mother,
That man might live –
This was their counsel."

Ha, Tu now took the sharp-edged stone, and cut the sinews and bands with which Rangi pressed the earth to his breast, and frightful were the cries of the Heaven – ah! Then, calling on Rehua, the strength of the sons grew, and grew, and grew – ah!, my listener, all their strength – but where was the power that could separate the parents? ah – ah! Rangi the powerful could not be separated from Papa; Tu could not find strength enough, and where was the strength of Rongo? And the strength of Tiki? Then came Tane!

Ah, Tane!

Open the eyes of your mind – as you have opened your ears and your eyes. Open the eyes of your mind that they may perceive how Tane separated Heaven and Earth. See how he presses the head of his god-power on the breasts of Papa – see his hair grow and take root – ah – see how his body and his limbs begin to stretch: high, high above, his feet grow into branches and boughs – see how his power grows – oh, how he grows all-powerful into the heaven – ah, see how his power overcomes the strength of Rangi!

Ha, he lifts him!

He lifts the Heaven!

Higher!

Higher! Ha, the heaven is high!

Ah, Heaven and Earth are separated!

Hawaiki is born!

Oh, Tane!

Ah, my listener, Rangi and Papa are separated!

From high above Rangi sent down many words of farewell, so that they sounded all over the far-stretching Earth, and many were his songs of love to Papa. Ah, his tears still fall upon Papa – they are the dew of the mornings. And Papa sang words of farewell, and her sighs flew up to Rangi as white cloud-messengers of love. Ah.

Great was the love of the parents, my listener.

Great was the strength of the children!

Your ear has received the wisdom of the creation of Hawaiki, the home of my people, the Maoris.

The Human World Emerges

Introduction

IN SOUTHERN OREGON'S Klamath Mountains, the Káruk lived contentedly in almost everything, except that – rich as their rivers were in fish, their forests in game – they had no fire. That gift was the exclusive possession of two wicked hags who lived by the Klamath River and refused to share it with anyone else. After many attempts to steal it for themselves, the Káruk turned in desperation to the Coyote. He in turn enlisted the help of his animal friends. Snatching a burning brand from the witches' fire, he had to evade their determined pursuit, handing his prize on to the Cougar, the Bear, the Bat, the Squirrel and, finally, the Frog. After many mesmerizing narrative twists and turns, the Káruk got their precious sparks. This story's anthropomorphized animals provide much colourful entertainment but also remind us how closely our ancestors lived alongside Nature. Human development took place in a wider environmental context. Most of all, though, the story underlines the importance of technological advance in what we may think of as pre-scientific societies. As the millennia passed, those societies grew alike in scale and cultural complexity: these myths show how such changes were experienced.

Prometheus

AT THE TIME of the creation, after covering the new-born Earth with luxuriant vegetation, and peopling it with living creatures of all kinds, Eros perceived that it would be necessary to endow them with instincts which would enable them to preserve and enjoy the life they had received. He therefore called the youngest two sons of Iapetus to his aid, and bade them make a judicious distribution of gifts to all living creatures, and create and endow a superior being, called Man, to rule over all the others.

Prometheus' and Epimetheus' first care was, very naturally, to provide for the beings already created. These they endowed with such reckless generosity, that all their favours were soon dispensed, and none remained for the endowment of man. Although they had not the remotest idea how to overcome this difficulty, they proceeded to fashion man from clay.

They first moulded an image similar in form to the gods; bade Eros breathe into its nostrils the spirit of life, and Athene endow it with a soul; whereupon man lived, and moved, and viewed his new domain.

Justly proud of his handiwork, Prometheus observed man, and longed to bestow upon him some great power, unshared by any other creature of mortal birth, which would raise him far above all other living beings, and bring him nearer to the perfection of the immortal gods. Fire alone, in his estimation, could effect this; but fire was the special possession and prerogative of the gods, and Prometheus knew they would never willingly share it with man, and that, should any one obtain it by stealth, they would never forgive the thief. Long he pondered the matter, and finally determined to obtain fire, or die in the attempt.

One dark night, therefore, he set out for Olympus, entered unperceived into the gods' abode, seized a lighted brand, hid it in his bosom, and departed unseen, exulting in the success of his enterprise. Arrived upon earth once more, he consigned the stolen treasure to the care of man, who immediately adapted it to various purposes, and eloquently expressed his gratitude to the benevolent deity who had risked his own life to obtain it for him.

From his lofty throne on the topmost peak of Mount Olympus Zeus beheld an unusual light down upon earth. Anxious to ascertain its exact nature, he watched it closely, and before long discovered the larceny. His anger then burst forth, terrible to behold; and the gods all quailed when they heard him solemnly vow he would punish the unhappy Prometheus without mercy. To seize the offender in his mighty grasp, bear him off to the Caucasian Mountains, and bind him fast to a great rock, was but a moment's work. There a voracious vulture was summoned to feast upon his liver, the tearing of which from his side by the bird's cruel beak and talons caused the sufferer intense anguish. All day long the vulture gorged himself; but during the cool night, while the bird slept, Prometheus' suffering abated, and the liver grew again, thus prolonging the torture, which bade fair to have no end.

Disheartened by the prospect of long years of unremitting pain, Prometheus at times could not refrain from pitiful complaints; but generation after generation of men lived on earth, and died, blessing him for the gift he had obtained for them at such a terrible cost. After many centuries of woe, Hercules, son of Zeus and Alcmene, found

Prometheus, killed the vulture, broke the adamantine chains, and liberated the long-suffering god.

The first mortals lived on earth in a state of perfect innocence and bliss. The air was pure and balmy; the sun shone brightly all the year; the earth brought forth delicious fruit in abundance; and beautiful, fragrant flowers bloomed everywhere. Man was content. Extreme cold, hunger, sickness, and death were unknown. Zeus, who justly ascribed a good part of this beatific condition to the gift conferred by Prometheus, was greatly displeased, and tried to devise some means to punish mankind for the acceptance of the heavenly fire.

With this purpose in view, he assembled the gods on Mount Olympus, where, in solemn council, they decided to create woman; and, as soon as she had been artfully fashioned, each one endowed her with some special charm, to make her more attractive.

Their united efforts were crowned with the utmost success. Nothing was lacking, except a name for the peerless creature; and the gods, after due consideration, decreed she should be called Pandora. They then bade Hermes take her to Prometheus as a gift from heaven; but he, knowing only too well that nothing good would come to him from the gods, refused to accept her, and cautioned his brother Epimetheus to follow his example. Unfortunately Epimetheus was of a confiding disposition, and when he beheld the maiden he exclaimed, "Surely so beautiful and gentle a being can bring no evil!" and accepted her most joyfully.

The first days of their union were spent in blissful wanderings, hand in hand, under the cool forest shade; in weaving garlands of fragrant flowers; and in refreshing themselves with the luscious fruit, which hung so temptingly within reach.

Obatala Creates Mankind

OBATALA LIVED QUITE contentedly in his new home beneath the skies, quite forgetting that Olorun might wish to know how his plans were progressing. The supreme god soon grew impatient for news and ordered Agemo, the chameleon, to go down the golden chain to investigate. The chameleon descended and when he arrived at Ife, he knocked timidly on Obatala's door.

"Olorun has sent me here," he said, "to discover whether or not you have been successful in your quest."

"Certainly I have," replied Obatala, "look around you and you will see the land I have created and the plants I have raised from the soil. Tell Olorun that it is now a far more pleasant kingdom than it was before, and that I would be more than willing to spend the rest of my time here, except that I am growing increasingly weary of the twilight and long to see brightness once more."

Agemo returned home and reported to Olorun all that he had seen and heard. Olorun smiled, for it pleased him greatly that Obatala had achieved what he had set out to do. The young god, who was among his favourites, had earned a special reward, and so Olorun fashioned with his own hands a dazzling golden orb and tossed it into the sky.

"For you, Obatala, I have created the sun," said Olorun, "it will shed warmth and light on the new world you have brought to life below."

Obatala very gladly received this gift, and as soon as he felt the first rays of the sun shining down on him, his restless spirit grew calmer.

He remained quite satisfied for a time, but then, as the weeks turned to months, he became unsettled once more and began to dream of spending time in the company of other beings, not unlike himself, who could move and speak and with whom he could share his thoughts and feelings.

Obatala sat down and began to claw at the soil as he attempted to picture the little creatures who would keep him company. He found that the clay was soft and pliable, so he began to shape tiny figures in his own image. He laid the first of them in the sun to dry and worked on with great enthusiasm until he had produced several more.

He had been sitting for a long time in the hot sunshine before he realized how tired and thirsty he felt.

"What I need is some palm wine to revive me," he thought to himself, and he stood up and headed off towards the nearest palm tree.

He placed his bowl underneath it and drew off the palm juice, leaving it to ferment in the heat until it had turned to wine. When the wine was ready, Obatala helped himself to a very long drink, and as he gulped down bowl after bowl of the refreshing liquid, he failed to realize that the wine was making him quite drunk.

Obatala had swallowed so much of the wine that his fingers grew clumsy, but he continued to work energetically, too drunk to notice that the clay figures he now produced were no longer perfectly formed. Some had crooked backs or crooked limbs, others had arms and legs of uneven length. Obatala was so pleased with himself he raised his head and called out jubilantly to the skies:

"I have created beings from the soil, but only you, Olorun, can breathe life into them. Grant me this request so that I will always have human beings to keep me company here in Ife."

Olorun heard Obatala's plea and did not hesitate to breathe life into the clay figures, watching with interest as they rose up from the ground and began to obey the commands of their creator. Soon they had built wooden shelters for themselves next to the god's own house, creating the first Yoruba village in Ife where before only one solitary house had stood.

Obatala was filled with admiration and pride, but now, as the effects of the palm wine started to wear off, he began to notice that some of the humans he had created were contorted and misshapen. The sight of the little creatures struggling as they went about their chores filled him with sadness and remorse.

"My drunkenness has caused these people to suffer," he proclaimed solemnly, "and I swear that I will never drink palm wine again. From this day forward, I will be the special protector of all humans who are born with deformities."

Obatala remained faithful to his pledge and dedicated himself to the welfare of the human beings he had created, making sure that he always had a moment to spare for the lame and the blind. He saw to it that the people prospered and, before long, the Yoruba village of Ife had grown into an impressive city. Obatala also made certain that his people had all the tools they needed to clear and cultivate the land.

He presented each man with a copper bush knife and a wooden hoe and taught them to grow millet, yams and a whole variety of other crops, ensuring that mankind had a plentiful supply of food for its survival.

Why Some Men Are White and Others Black

IT WAS IN the beginning, and four men were walking through a wood. They came to a place where there were two rivers. One river was of water, clear as crystal and of great purity; the other was black and foul and horrible to the taste.

And the four men were puzzled as to which river they should cross; for, whereas the dirty river seemed more directly in their way, the clear river was the most pleasant to cross, and perhaps after they had crossed it they might regain the proper path. The men, after some consultation, thought that they ought to cross the black river, and two of them straightway crossed it. The other two, however, scarce touched and tasted the water than they hesitated and returned.

The two that had now nearly crossed the river called to them and urged them to come, but in vain. The other two had determined to leave their companions, and to cross the beautiful and clear river. They crossed it, and were astonished to find that they had become black, except just those parts of them that had touched the black river, namely, their mouths, the soles of their feet and the palms of their hands. The two who had crossed the black river, however, were of a pure white colour.

The two parties now travelled in different directions, and when they had gone some way, the white men were agreeably surprised to come across a large house containing white wives for them to marry; while the black men also found huts, or shimbecs, with black women whom they married. And this is why some people are white and some black.

The Punishment of the Inquisitive Man

MOTU MADE A large garden, and planted it with many bananas and plantain. The garden was in a good position, so the fruit ripened quickly and well. Arriving one day at his garden he found the ripe bunches of bananas and plantain had been cut off and carried away.

After that he did not go once to his garden without finding that some of the fruit had been stolen, so at last he made up his mind to watch the place carefully, and hiding himself he lay in ambush for the thief.

Motu had not been in hiding very long before he saw a number of Cloud-folk descending, who cut down his bananas, and what they could not eat they tied into bundles to carry away. Motu rushed out, and, chasing them, caught one woman whom he took to his house, and after a short time he married her, and gave her a name which meant Favourite.

Although Favourite had come from the Cloud-land she was very intelligent, and went about her housework and farming just like an ordinary woman of the earth. Up to that time neither Motu nor the people of his village had ever seen a fire. They had always eaten their food raw, and on cold, windy, rainy days had sat shivering in their houses because they did not know anything about fire and warmth.

Favourite, however, told some of the Cloud-folk to bring some fire with them next time they came to visit her, which they did. And then she taught the people how to cook food, and how to sit round a fire on cold days.

Motu was very happy with his wife, and the villagers were very glad to have her among them, and, moreover, Favourite persuaded many of the Cloud-folk to settle in her husband's village.

One day Favourite received a covered basket, and putting it on a shelf in the house she said to her husband, "We are now living with much friendship together; but while I am away at the farm you must not open that basket, if you do we shall all leave you."

"All right," replied the husband, "I will never undo it."

Motu was now very glad in his heart, for he had plenty of people, a clever wife, and the villagers treated him as a great man. But he had one trouble: Why did his wife warn him every day not to open the basket? What was in that basket? What was she hiding from him? And foolish-like he decided to open it. Waiting therefore until his wife had gone as usual to the farm he opened the basket, and – there was nothing in it, so laughingly he shut it up and put it in its place.

By and by Favourite returned, and, looking at her husband, she asked him: Why did you open that basket?" And he was speechless at her question.

On the first opportunity, while Motu was away hunting, Favourite gathered her people, and ascended with them to Cloud-land, and never again returned to the earth.

That is how the earth-folk received their fire and a knowledge of cooking; and that is also how Motu through being too inquisitive lost his wife, his people, and his importance as a big man in the village.

Mbungi and His Punishment

MBUNGI ONE DAY said to his wife: "Dig up some cassava, prepare it, and cut down some plantain, for we will go hunting and fishing."

The wife did as she was told, and in a short time everything was ready for the journey. They put their goods into a canoe and paddled away to their hunting and fishing camp.

After resting, the man went and dug a hole and set his traps; and the next morning he found an antelope and a bush pig in the hole. These he took to the camp, cut up, and gave to his wife to cook. By and by when all was cooked she brought the meat to her husband, and as she was taking her portion he said: "Wait, I will ask the forest-folk (or spirits) if you may eat it."

He went and pretended to ask the forest-folk, and brought back a message that if she ate the meat the traps would lose their luck and catch no more animals. In this way the selfish husband had all the meat for himself and his wife went hungry. Mbungi found many animals in his traps, and the woman, because of the prohibition, did not have her share of them.

One day the woman made some fish traps and set them, and on her return to the camp the husband wanted to know where she had been, but she refused to tell him. Next day she went to look at her traps and found many fish in them, which she brought to the camp and cooked. Mbungi, however, returned unsuccessful from his traps; but when he saw his wife's fish he laughed and said: "Bring the fish here for me to eat."

"Wait," answered the woman, "I will ask the forest-folk if you may eat the fish." And she brought back a reply that he was not to eat the fish, for if he did so the fish traps would lose their luck.

It was now Mbungi's turn to be hungry. Days and days passed and he caught no more animals; but his wife always had plenty of fish. He became very thin and angry. One day he drew his large knife, and cutting off the head of his wife he buried the head and the trunk together in the ground, and departed for his town.

Mbungi had not gone very far on his way when he heard a voice shouting: "Mbungi, wait for me, we will go together!" He wondered who was calling him, so he hid himself, and in a little time he saw the head of his wife coming along the road calling after him.

He went, and catching the head he cut it into small pieces and buried it again; but before he had gone far he heard it shouting: "Mbungi, wait for me, we will go together!" He cut and buried it again and again, but it was no use, it continued to follow and call after him.

Mbungi reached his town, and his wife's family asked him: "Where is your wife?" "Oh, she is coming on behind," he replied. They accused him of killing her, but this he strongly denied. While he was denying the charge of murder the head came right into the town; and when the family saw it they immediately tied up Mbungi and killed him.

This was how murder was first introduced into the world.

How the Dog Came to Live with Man

THERE WAS A time, long ago, when the Dog and the Jackal lived together in the wilderness as brothers. Every day they hunted together and every evening they laid out on the grass whatever they had caught, making sure to divide the meal equally between them. But there were evenings when they both returned from a day's hunting empty-handed, and on these occasions, they would curl up side by side under the stars dreaming of the bush calf or the plump zebra they had come so close to killing.

They had never before gone without food for longer than two days, but then, without warning, they suffered a long spell of bad luck and for over a week they could find nothing at all to eat. On the eighth day, although they had both searched everywhere, they returned to their shelter without meat, feeling exhausted and extremely hungry. To add to their misery, a bitterly cold wind blew across the bush, scooping up the leaves they had gathered for warmth, leaving them shivering without any hope of comfort throughout the long night ahead. Curled up together, they attempted to sleep, but the wind continued to howl and they tossed and turned despairingly.

"Jackal," said the Dog after a while. "Isn't it a terrible thing to go to bed hungry after all the effort we have put in today, and isn't it an even worse thing to be both hungry and cold at the same time?"

"Yes, it is brother," replied the Jackal, "but there's very little we can do about it at the moment. Let's just curl up here and try to sleep now. Tomorrow, as soon as the sun rises, we will go out hunting again and with any luck we will be able to find some food to satisfy us."

But even though he snuggled up closer to the Jackal, the Dog could not sleep, for his teeth had begun to chatter and his stomach rumbled more loudly than ever. He lay on the cold earth, his eyes open wide, trying to recall what it was like to be warm and well-fed.

"Jackal," he piped up again, "man has a village quite close to this spot, doesn't he?"

"Yes, that is true," answered the Jackal wearily. "But what difference can that make to us right now?"

"Well," replied the Dog, "most men know how to light a fire and fire would keep us warm if we crept near enough to one."

"If you are suggesting that we take a closer look," said the Jackal, "you can forget about it. I'm not going anywhere near that village. Now go to sleep and leave me in peace."

But the Dog could not let go of the idea and as he thought about it more and more he began to imagine the delicious meal he would make of the scraps and bones left lying around by the villagers.

"Please come with me," he begged the Jackal, "my fur is not as thick as yours and I am dying here from cold and hunger."

"Go there yourself," growled the Jackal, "this was all your idea, I want nothing to do with it."

At last, the Dog could stand it no longer. Forgetting his fear, he jumped up and announced boldly:

"Right, I'm off, nothing can be worse than this. I'm going to that village to sit by the fire and perhaps I'll even come across a tasty bone. If there's any food left over, I'll bring you some. But if I don't return, please come and look for me."

So the Dog started off towards the village, slowing down when he had reached the outskirts and crawling on his belly so that nobody would notice him approach. He could see the red glow of a fire just up ahead and already he felt the warmth of its flames. Very cautiously he slid along the earth and had almost reached his goal when some fowls roosting in a tree overhead began to cackle a loud warning to their master.

At once, a man came rushing out from a nearby hut and lifting his spear high in the air, brought it down within an inch of where the dog lay.

"Please, please don't kill me," whimpered the Dog. "I haven't come here to steal your chickens or to harm you in any way. I am starving and almost frozen to death. I only wanted to lie down by the fire where I could warm myself for a short while."

The man looked at the wretched, shivering creature and could not help feeling a bit sorry for him. It was such a cold night after all, and the Dog's request was not so unreasonable under the circumstances.

"Very well," he said, withdrawing his spear. "You can warm yourself here for a few minutes if you promise to go away again as soon as you feel better."

The Dog crept forward and lay himself down by the fire, thanking the man over and over for his kindness. Soon he felt the blood begin to circulate in his limbs once more. Slowly uncurling himself, he stretched out before the flames and there, just in front of him, he noticed a fat and juicy bone, thrown there by the man at the end of his meal. He sidled up alongside it and began to devour it, feeling happier than he had done for a very long time.

He had just about finished eating when the man suddenly reappeared:

"Aren't you warm enough yet?" he asked, rather anxious to be rid of his visitor from the bush.

"No, not yet," said the Dog, who had spotted another bone he wished to gnaw on.

"Just a few more minutes then," said the man, as he disappeared inside his hut once more.

The Dog grabbed hold of the second bone and began crushing it in his strong jaws, feeling even more contented with himself. But soon the man came out of his hut and asked again:

"When are you going to get up and go? Surely you must be warm enough by now?"

But the Dog, feeling very reluctant to leave the comfort of his surroundings, pleaded with his host:

"Let me stay just a little while longer and I promise to leave you alone after that."

This time the man disappeared and failed to return for several hours, for he had fallen asleep inside his hut, quite forgetting about his guest. But as soon as he awoke, he rushed out of doors to make certain that the Dog had left him as promised. Now he became angry to see the creature snoozing by the fire in exactly the same position as before. Prodding him with his spear, he called for the Dog to get up at once. The Dog rose slowly to his feet and summoning every ounce of his courage, he looked directly into the man's eyes and spoke the following words:

"I know that you want me to go away, but I wish you would let me stay here with you. I could teach you a great many things. I could pass on to you my knowledge of the wild, help you hunt the birds of the forests, keep watch over your house at night and frighten off any intruders. I would never harm your chickens or goats like my brother, the Jackal. I would look after your women and children while you were away. All I ask in return is that you provide me with a warm bed close to your fire and the scraps from your table to satisfy my hunger."

The man now stared back into the Dog's eyes and saw that his expression was honest and trustworthy.

"I will agree to this," he replied. "You may have a home here among the villagers if you perform as you have promised."

And from that day, the Dog has lived with man, guarding his property, protecting his livestock and helping him to hunt in the fields. At night when the Dog settles down to sleep, he hears a cry from the wilderness, "Bo-ah, Bo-ah", and he knows that it is his brother, the Jackal, calling him back home. But he never answers the call, for the Dog is more than content in his new home, enjoying the comforts Jackal was once so happy to ignore.

Origins of the Ivory Trade

UKANAKÂDI LIVED IN his great house, having with him his many wives. One of them bore him a son whom he named Lombolokindi.

As time passed on, the child grew in size, and strength and skill. Because of this, his mother was treated by Ukanakâdi with special favor. This aroused the jealousy of one of the other wives. She took the child one day, and secretly gave him a certain evil medicine, which caused him to be constantly hungry, hungry, hungry. Even when he ate enormously, no amount of food could fill his stomach or satisfy his appetite.

Ukanakâdi finally was angry at the child, and said to the mother, "All the food of my plantations is finished, eaten up by your child. We have no more plantains, no more cassava, no more eddoes, nor anything else in our plantations or in our kitchen gardens. You have brought a curse upon us! Go away to your father's house!" (He said this, not knowing that a Fetish-Medicine had caused all the trouble.)

So the mother went away with her child to her father's house. But there too, the boy ate up all the food of the gardens, until there was none left. Then her father said to her, "All my food is done here; go with your child to your grandfather, and find food there."

So, she went to her grandfather's. But there the same trouble followed.

After she had been there some time, and the child was now a stout lad, and she saw that they were no longer welcome, she said to herself, "Alas! It is so! All my people are weary of me! I will not longer stay at grandfather's. I will go wandering into the forest, and, with the child, will see what I can get."

Taking with her only two ears of corn, she went far off with the lad into the forest. After much wandering, and eating only wild fruits, she selected a spot without having any idea of the locality, and built a shed for a camp in which to stay. At this place, she planted the corn. It quickly sprang up, and bore abundantly. And she planted other gardens. After a time came very many birds; and they began to eat up the corn. She exclaimed, "My son and I alone have come here, and have planted our corn. How is this that all the birds have come so soon to destroy it?" And the son, who by this time had grown to be almost a young man, said to her, "Mother, why do you allow the birds to eat? Why don't you do something?" She replied, "Why do the birds thus destroy the corn? What can I do?" So he came out of the shed into the yard in front of their house and shouted at the birds, "You birds, who have come here to spoil my corn! With this stick I will kill you all!" But the birds jeered at him, saying, "No! Not all! Only one shall die!"

The young man went into the house, took up a magic spearhead he owned, fitted it onto a stick as a shaft; and going out again, he hurled it at the birds. The spear flew at them, pursuing each one, and piercing every one of them in succession. Then it flew on and on, away out into the forest.

The young man took up another medicine charm that he had with him, and, calling to his spear by name, shouted after it, "Tombeseki-o-o! Come back, back, back, here! Again, again, again, return!" The spear heard him, and obeyed, and came back. He laid hold of it, and put it again in the shed. So, he and his mother lived there. She planted a very large garden of plantains, cassava, and many other vegetables, a very large quantity. And her gardens grew, and bore fruit in plenty.

Then there came all kinds of small animals, hogs, antelopes and gazelles, very many; and they spoiled the gardens, eating the fruit, and breaking down the stalks. The mother exclaimed, "My son! The animals have finished all my food of the gardens; everything is lost! Why is this?" He replied, "Yes, it is so! And when they come again tomorrow, I know what I will do to them!"

When they came the next day, he went into the house, took the spear, flung it; and it flew from beast to beast, piercing all of them in succession. Then it went off, flying into the forest, as before. He called after it to return. The spear heard, and obeyed, and came back to the house.

Then he and his mother sat down in the house, complaining of their hunger, and how the animals had spoiled their gardens. So the mother went out, and gathered up what little remained, brought it into the house, and cooked it, leaves and all.

When the mother had planted a third garden, and it had grown, a herd of elephants came to destroy it. She cried out, "Ah! Njâku! What shall I do? You have come to destroy all my gardens! Shall I die with hunger?" The son brought out his spear, and shouting at the elephants, threatened to kill them all. But the herd laughed and said, "When you throw that spear, only one of us shall fall." He threw the spear at the one that spoke. It struck him and all the elephants in succession; and they all died. The spear kept on in its flight into the forest. The young man cried after it, "Spear! Spear! Come back, come back!" And it came to him again.

Each time that the spear had thus gone through the forest, it had mowed down the trees in its path; and thus was made the clearing which the mother had at once utilized for the planting of her successive gardens.

After the elephants, mother and son sat down again in their hunger; they had nothing to eat but leaves. These she cooked; and they ate them all at once.

Then she planted another garden, thinking that now there were no more beasts who would come to ravage. But she did not know that there was still left in the forest one very, very large elephant that had not been in the company of the herd that the son had killed.

There was also, in that forest, one very, very large ox. When the gardens had grown, that ox came, and began to destroy. The young man hurled his spear at the ox. It was wounded, but did not fall; and it went away into the forest with the spear sticking in its side. The young man pursued the ox, following, following, following far away. But he did not overtake it.

On his way, he reached unexpectedly a small, lonely hut, where an old woman was living by herself. When she saw him, she said to him, "Do not follow any longer. That ox was a person like yourself. He is dead; and his people have hung up that spear in their house."

The young man told the old woman that he was very hungry. So she cut down for him an entire bunch of plantains. He was so exceedingly hungry that he could not wait; and before the plantains were entirely cooked, he began to eat of them, and ate them all. The old woman exclaimed, "What sort of a person is this who eats in this way?" In her wisdom, thinking over the matter, she felt sure it was some disease that caused his voracity.

The man, being tired with his journey, fell asleep; and she, by her magic power, caused him to hear or feel nothing. While he was in this state, she cut him open. As she did so, his disease rushed out with a whizzing sound; and she cut away, and removed a tumor, that looked like a stone of glass. That was the thing that had caused his excessive hunger all his life. By her power, she closed the wound.

When he awoke, she cooked food for him, of which he ate, and was satisfied with an ordinary amount like any other person. She then told him what she had done, and said, "As you are now cured, you may pursue that ox. You will reach his town, and you will obtain your spear. But, as you go there, you must make a pretense. You must pretend that you are mourning for the dead. You must cry out in wailing, 'Who killed my uncle-o-o! Who killed my uncle-o-o!'" Thus he went on his way; and finally came to a town where was a crowd of people gathered in and about a house of mourning. Beginning to wail, he went among the mourners. They received him, with the idea that he was some distant relative who had come to attend the funeral. He walked up the street of this town of the Ox-Man, and entering into the house of mourning, said, "Had not the way been so long, my mother also would have come; but, I have come to look at that thing that killed my Uncle." They welcomed him, commended his devotion, and said, "You will not go today. Stay with us. Sleep here tonight; and tomorrow you shall see and take away with you, to show to your mother, that thing."

So, the next day, they gave him the spear, and said, "Go, but do not delay. Return for the closing ceremony (the "Washing") of the mourning." He went away, and came again to the old woman. She said to him, when he showed her the spear, "I told you truly that you would obtain it. But, go with it and this bundle I have made of the tumor of your disease, and show them to your mother."

So he came back to his mother. She rejoiced; and, not knowing that he was cured, she cooked a very large and unusually varied quantity of food, for his unusual hunger, two whole bunches of plantains, and eddoes, and potatoes and yams, etc. Of this he ate only a little, sufficient for an ordinary hunger. As he had not yet told her of his being cured, she cried out in surprise, "What is this? My son will die, for not eating!" And she asked him, "What is the matter?" He replied, "No, I have eaten, and am satisfied. And, mother, this bundle is what I was cured of." Then he told her of what that old woman had done.

On another day, that great elephant that had remained in the forest, came and began to eat in the garden. The son said, "Mother! What shall I do? I thought I had killed all the elephants. I did not know there was this great big one left!" (Nor did he just then know there were left a very great many more.)

Taking his spear, he hurled it, and wounded the elephant. It did not fall, but went away with the spear in its side. The man followed, followed, followed, pursuing the elephant, not, as the other animals had gone, into the forest, but away toward the sea; and it died on the sea beach. There the man found it and his spear.

The sea was new to him; he had not seen it since his childhood. He climbed up on the elephant's body, in order to see all around. As he turned his eyes seaward, he saw a ship coming on the horizon. Also, the people on this ship were looking landward, and they said, "There is something standing on the shore like a person. Let the vessel go there, and see what is ashore."

So, the ship anchored, and a surfboat was launched into the water to go ashore. When the crew landed, they saw the carcass of the elephant, and a person standing with a spear who warned them, "Do not approach near to me!" But they replied, "We do not want you, nor will we hurt you. But we want these tusks of ivory of this elephant. We want elephants." Wondering at this wish, he cut out the tusks, and gave them to the strangers, adding, "Off in the forest are very, very many more tusks, more than I can number. You seem to like them; but they are of no use to me." They earnestly said, "But, bring them, bring them! We will buy them of you with abundance of goods." He agreed, and promised, "I am going now; but, let your ship wait, and I will bring all of those things as many as it is possible for me to carry."

So, he went back to his mother; and he and she carried many, many tusks. They filled the ship full; and the crew of the ship sent ashore an immense quantity of goods. When the vessel went away, it left ashore two carpenters, with direction to build a fine house, and have it completed before the vessel should come again.

The man remained there awhile with the carpenters, after the ship had gone.

One day, looking, on a journey down the coast, at a point of land, he was surprised to recognize his father's town, where he and his mother had lived in his childhood. He said to himself, "That's my father's town! I want them to come to me, and live at my town!" He sent word to them; they removed, and all of them came to live with him. And he married one of their young women. (In the meanwhile, he had brought his mother from the forest.)

While he was living at his new home, one day looking seaward, he saw the promised ship coming to get more ivory, and to give more goods. And he went off to the vessel.

Among the women who were still living of his father's people who had known him as a child, was the one who had given him the evil "medicine" long ago; her object in giving it having been to kill him. After he had gone off to the vessel, this woman came to his wife's home, and, seeing the spear hanging tied from the roof, said, "What is that thing tied there?" His wife replied, "It is a kind of "medicine" of my husband's. It must not be touched." But the woman said, "I know that thing; and what it does." Then she seized it, and put into it its handle the man had removed. She hurled the spear out to sea, and it went on and on, passing over the ship. The man sitting in the saloon, said to the crew, as he recognized the spear in its flight, "I saw something pass over the ship!" He went up on deck, and called after it, "My spear! Come back! Come! Come! Come back!" And he told all the people of the vessel to go below lest they should be injured. The spear turned and came back to him; and he took possession of it. Then said he to the crew, "Come! Escort me ashore!" They landed him ashore, and waited to see what he intended doing.

He called all his father's family, and asked, "Why is it that you have tried to kill me today with this spear! For this, I will this day kill all of you." He summoned all the people to come together. When they had come, he had his mother bring out that tumour bundle, and said, "This is the thing of long ago with which that woman (pointing to the one who in childhood had given him the evil disease) tried to injure me. And, for the same reason, she threw the spear today; thus trying a second time to kill me. None of you have rebuked her. So, I shall kill you all as her associates."

Though they were of his father's family, he attacked and killed them all. The whole town died that day, excepting himself, his wife, his mother and his sister. These four, not liking to remain at that evil place, went off and took passage on the ship.

So, he journeyed, and came to the country of the white people at Manga-Manĕne; and never returned to Africa. But, he kept up a trade in ivory with his native country. But for him, that trade would not have been begun. For, besides his having brought the first elephant to the seacoast, he told the people of Manga-Manĕne beyond the Great Sea, about the tribes of people, and about the elephants that were so abundant, in Africa. And that is all.

The First Humans

ODIN, ALLFATHER, WAS king of all gods, and he travelled across the newly created earth with his brothers Vili and Ve. Vili was now known as Hoenir, and Ve had become Lothur, or Loki. One morning, the three brothers walked together on the shores of the ocean, looking around with pride at the new world around them. Ymir's body had been well distributed, and his blood now ran clear and pure as the ocean, with the fresh new air sparkling above it all. The winds blew padded clouds across a perfect blue sky, and there was happiness all around. But, and there was no mistaking it, there was silence.

The brothers looked at one another, and then looked out across the crisp sands. There lay on the shore two pieces of driftwood which had been flung onto the coast from the sea, and as their eyes caught sight of them, each brother shared the same thought. They raced towards the wood, and Hoenir stood over the first piece, so that his shadow lay across it and the wood appeared at once to have arms and legs. Loki did the same with the second piece of wood, but he moved rather more animatedly, so that the wood appeared to dance in the sunlight. And then Odin bent down and blew a great divine breath across the first piece of wood. There in front of them, the bark, the water-soaked edges of the log began to peel away, and there the body of a pale, naked woman appeared. She lay there, still and not breathing. Odin moved over to the next piece of wood, and he blew once more. Again, the wood curled back to reveal the body of a naked man. He lay as still as the woman.

Odin had given the gift of life to the man and woman, and they had become entities with a soul and a mind. It was now time for Loki to offer his own gifts. He stood at once over the woman and as he bent over her, he transferred the blush of youth, the power of comprehension, and the five senses of touch, smell, sight, hearing and taste. He was rewarded when the woman rose then and smiled unquestioningly at the three gods. She looked around in wonder, and then down at the lifeless body by her side. And Loki leaned across the body of man this time, and gave to him blood, which began to run through his veins. He too received the gifts of understanding, and of the five senses, and he was able to join woman as she stood on the beach.

Hoenir stepped forward then, and offered to both man and woman the power of speech. At this, the two human beings turned and walked together into the new world, their hands held tightly together.

"Stop," said Odin, with great authority.

Turning, the two humans looked at him and nodded. "You are Ash," said Odin to the man, which represented the tree from which he had been created. "And you are Elm," he said to the woman. Then Odin leaned over and draped his cloak around the shoulders of the first human woman and sent her on her way, safe in the care of man, who would continue in that role until the end of time – or so the Vikings said.

How the Cymry Land Became Inhabited

IN ALL BRITAIN today, no wolf roams wild, and the deer are all tame.

Yet in the early ages, when human beings had not yet come into the land, the swamps and forests were full of very savage animals. There were bears and wolves by the thousands, besides lions and the woolly rhinoceros, and tigers with terrible teeth like sabres.

Beavers built their dams over the little rivers, and the great horned oxen were very common. Then, the mountains were higher, and the woods denser. Many of the animals lived in caves, and there were billions of bees and a great many butterflies. In the bogs were ferns of giant size, amid which terrible monsters hid that were always ready for a fight or a frolic.

In so beautiful a land, it seemed a pity that there were no men and women, no boys or girls, and no babies.

Yet the noble race of the Cymry, whom we call the Welsh, were already in Europe and lived in the summer land in the south. A great benefactor was born among them, who grew up to be a wonderfully wise man and taught his people the use of bows and arrows. He made laws, by which the different tribes stopped their continual fighting and quarrels, and united for the common good of all. He persuaded them to take family names. He invented the plow, and showed them how to use it, making furrows in which to plant grain.

When the people found that they could get things to eat right out of the ground, from the seed they had planted, their children were wild with joy.

No people ever loved babies more than these Cymry folk, and it was they who invented the cradle. This saved the hard-working mothers many a burden, for each woman had, besides rearing the children, to work for and wait on her husband.

He was the warrior and hunter, and she did most of the labour, in both the house and the field. When there were many little brats to look after, a cradle was a real help to her. In those days, 'brat' was the general name for little folks. There were good laws about women, especially for their protection. Any rough or brutish fellow was fined heavily, or publicly punished, for striking one of them.

By and by, this great benefactor encouraged his people to the brave adventure, and led them, in crossing the sea to Britain. Men had not yet learned to build boats, with prow or stern, with keels and masts, or with sails, rudders, or oars, or much less to put engines in their bowels, or iron chimneys for smokestacks, by which we see the mighty ships driven across the ocean without regard to wind or tide.

This great benefactor taught his people to make coracles, and on these the whole tribe of thousands of Cymric folk crossed over into Britain, landing in Cornwall. The old name of this shire meant the Horn of Gallia, or Wallia, as the new land was later named. We think of Cornwall as the big toe of the Mother Land. These first comers called it a horn.

It was a funny sight to see these coracles, which they named after their own round bodies. The men went down to the riverside or the seashore, and with their stone hatchets, they chopped down trees. They cut the reeds and osiers, peeled the willow branches, and wove great baskets shaped like bowls. In this work, the women helped the men.

The coracle was made strong by a wooden frame fixed inside round the edge, and by two cross boards, which also served as seats. Then they turned the wicker frame upside down and stretched the hides of animals over the whole frame and bottom. With pitch, gum, or grease, they covered up the cracks or seams. Then they shaped paddles out of wood. When the coracle floated on the water, the whole family, daddy, mammy, kiddies, and any old aunts or uncles, or granddaddies, got into it. They waited for the wind to blow from the south over to the northern land.

At first the coracle spun round and round, but by and by each daddy could, by rowing or paddling, make the thing go straight ahead. So finally, all arrived in the land now called Great Britain.

Though sugar was not then known, or for a thousand years later, the first thing they noticed was the enormous number of bees. When they searched, they found the rock caves and hollow trees full of honey, which had accumulated for generations. Every once in a while the bears, that so like sweet things, found out the hiding place of the bees, and ate up the honey. The children were very happy in sucking the honeycomb, and the mothers made candles out of the beeswax. The newcomers named the country Honey Island.

The brave Cymry men had battles with the darker-skinned people who were already there. When anyone, young or old, died, their friends and relatives sat up all night guarding the body against wild beasts or savage men. This grew to be a settled custom, and such a meeting was called a 'wake'. Everyone present did keep awake, and often in a very lively way.

As the Cymry multiplied, they built many *don*, or towns. All over the land today are names ending in *don*, like London or Croydon, showing where these villages were.

But, while occupied in things for the body, their great ruler did not neglect matters of the mind. He found that some of his people had good voices and loved to sing. Others delighted in making poetry. So he invented or improved the harp, and fixed the rules of verse and song.

Thus ages before writing was known, the Cymry preserved their history and handed down what the wise ones taught.

Men might be born, live and die, come and go, like leaves on the trees, which expand in the springtime and fall in the autumn; but their songs, and poetry, and noble language never die. Even today, the Cymry love the speech of their fathers almost as well as they love their native land.

Yet things were not always lovely in Honey Land, or as sweet as sugar. As the tribes scattered far apart to settle in this or that valley, some had fish, but no salt, and others had plenty of salt, but no fish. Some had all the venison and bear meat they wanted, but no barley or oats. The hill men needed what the men on the seashore could supply. From their sheep and oxen they got wool and leather, and from the wild beasts fur to keep warm in winter. So many of them grew expert in trade. Soon there were among them some very rich men who were the chiefs of the tribes.

In time, hundreds of others learned how to traffic among the tribes and swap, or barter their goods, for as yet there were no coins for money, or bank bills. So they established markets or fairs, to which the girls and boys liked to go and sell their eggs and chickens, for when the wolves and foxes were killed off, sheep and geese multiplied.

But what hindered the peace of the land were the feuds, or quarrels, because the men of one tribe thought they were braver, or better looking, than those in the other tribe. The women were very apt to boast that they wore their clothes – which were made of fox and weasel skins – more gracefully than those in the tribe next to them.

So there was much snarling and quarreling in Cymric Land. The people were too much like naughty children, or when kiddies are not taught good manners, to speak gently and to be kind one to the other.

One of the worst quarrels broke out because in one tribe there were too many maidens and not enough young men for husbands. This was bad for the men, for it spoiled them. They had too many women to wait on them and they grew to be very selfish.

In what might be the next tribe, the trouble was the other way. There were too many boys, a surplus of men, and not nearly enough girls to go round. When any young fellow, moping out his life alone and anxious for a wife, went a-courting in the next tribe, or in their vale, or on their hilltop, he was usually driven off with stones. Then there was a quarrel between the two tribes.

Any young girl who sneaked out at night to meet her young man of another clan, was, when caught, instantly and severely spanked. Then, with her best clothes taken off, she had to stand tied to a post in the market place a whole day. Her hair was pulled down in disorder, and all the dogs were allowed to bark at her. The girls made fun of the poor thing, while they all rubbed one forefinger over the other, pointed at her and cried, "Fie, for shame!" while the boys called her hard names.

If it were known that the young man who wanted a wife had visited a girl in the other tribe, his spear and bow and arrows were taken away from him till the moon was full. The other boys and the girls treated him roughly and called him hard names, but he dare not defend himself and had to suffer patiently. This was all because of the feud between the two tribes.

This went on until the maidens in the valley, who were very many, while yet lovely and attractive, became very lonely and miserable; while the young men, all splendid hunters and warriors, multiplied in the hill country. They were wretched in mind, because not one could get a wife, for all the maidens in their own tribe were already engaged, or had been mated.

One day, news came to the young men on the hilltop that the valley men were all off on a hunting expedition. At once, without waiting a moment, the poor lonely bachelors plucked up their courage. Then, armed with ropes and straps, they marched in a body to the village in the valley below. There, they seized each man a girl, not waiting for any maid to comb her hair, or put on a new frock, or pack up her clothes, or carry anything out of her home, and made off with her, as fast as one pair of legs could move with another pair on top.

At first, this looked like rough treatment – for a lovely girl, thus to be strapped to a brawny big fellow; but after a while, the girls thought it was great fun to be married and each one to have a man to caress, and fondle, and scold, and look for, and boss around; for each wife, inside of her own hut was quite able to rule her husband. Every one of these new wives was delighted to find a man who cared so much for her as to come after her, and risk his life to get her, and each one admired her new, brave husband.

Yet the brides knew too well that their men folks, fathers and brothers, uncles and cousins, would soon come back to attempt their recapture.

And this was just what happened. When a runner brought, to the valley men now far away, the news of the rape of their daughters, the hunters at once ceased chasing the deer and marched quickly back to get the girls and make them come home.

The hill men saw the band of hunters coming after their daughters. They at once took their new wives into a natural rocky fortress, on the top of a precipice, which overlooked the lake.

This stronghold had only one entrance, a sort of gateway of rocks, in front of which was a long steep, narrow path. Here the hill men stood, to resist the attack and hold their prizes.

It was a case of a very few defenders, assaulted by a multitude, and the battle was long and bloody. The hill men scorned to surrender and shot their arrows and hurled their javelins with desperate valour. They battled all day from sunrise until the late afternoon, when shadows began to lengthen. The stars, one by one came out and both parties, after setting sentinels, lay down to rest.

In the morning, again, charge after charge was made. Sword beat against shield and helmet, and clouds of arrows were shot by the archers, who were well posted in favourable situations, on the rocks. Long before noon, the field below was dotted and the narrow pass was choked with dead bodies. In the afternoon, after a short rest and refreshed with food, the valley men, though finding that only four of the hill fighters were alive, stood off at a distance and with their long bows and a shower of arrows left not one to breathe.

Now, thought the victors, we shall get our maidens back again. So, taking their time to wash off the blood and dust, to bind up their wounds, and to eat their supper, they thought it would be an easy job to load up all the girls on their oxcarts and carry them home.

But the valley brides, thus suddenly made widows, were too true to their brave husbands. So, when they had seen the last of their lovers quiet in death, they stripped off all their ornaments and fur robes, until all stood together, each clad in her own innocence, as pure in their purpose as if they were a company of Druid priestesses.

Then, chanting their death song, they marched in procession to the tall cliff, that rose sheer out of the water. One by one, each uttering the name of her beloved, leaped into the waves.

Men at a distance, knowing nothing of the fight, and sailors and fishermen far off on the water, thought that a flock of white birds were swooping down from their eyrie, into the sea to get their food from the fishes. But when none rose up above the waters, they understood, and later heard the whole story of the valour of the men and the devotion of the women.

The solemn silence of night soon brooded over the scene.

The men of the valley stayed only long enough to bury their own dead. Then they marched home and their houses were filled with mourning. Yet they admired the noble sacrifice of their daughters and were proud of them. Afterwards, they raised stone monuments on the field of slaughter.

Today, this water is called the Lake of the Maidens, and the great stones seen near the beach are the memorials marking the place of the slain in battle.

During many centuries, the ancient custom of capturing the bride, with resistance from her male relatives, was vigorously kept up. In the course of time, however, this was turned into a mimic play, with much fun and merriment. Yet, the girls appear to like it, and some even complain if it is not rough enough to seem almost real.

The Great Red Dragon of Wales

EVERY OLD COUNTRY that has won fame in history and built up a civilization of its own, has a national flower. Besides this, some living creature, bird, or beast, or, it may be, a fish is on its flag. In places of honour, it stands as the emblem of the nation; that is, of the people, apart from the land they live on. Besides flag and symbol, it has a motto. That of Wales is, 'Awake: It is light'.

Now, because the glorious stories of Wales, Scotland and Ireland have been nearly lost in that of mighty England, men have at times almost forgotten about the leek, the thistle, and the shamrock, which stand for the other three divisions of the British Isles.

Yet each of these peoples has a history as noble as that of which the rose and the lion are the emblems. Each has also its patron saint and civilizer. So we have Saint George, Saint David, Saint Andrew, and Saint Patrick, all of them white-souled heroes. On the union flag, or standard of the United Kingdom, we see their three crosses.

The lion of England, the harp of Ireland, the thistle of Scotland, and the Red Dragon of Wales represent the four peoples in the British Isles, each with its own speech, traditions, and emblems; yet all in unity and in loyalty, none excelling the Welsh, whose symbol is the Red Dragon. In classic phrase, we talk of Albion, Scotia, Cymry, and Hibernia.

But why red? Almost all the other dragons in the world are white, or yellow, green or purple, blue, or pink. Why a fiery red colour like that of Mars?

Borne on the banners of the Welsh archers, who in old days won the battles of Crecy and Agincourt, and now seen on the crests on the town halls and city flags, in heraldry, and in art, the red dragon is as rampant as when King Arthur sat with His Knights at the Round Table.

The Red Dragon has four three-toed claws, a long, barbed tongue, and tail ending like an arrowhead. With its wide wings unfolded, it guards those ancient liberties, which neither Saxon, nor Norman, nor German, nor kings on the throne, whether foolish or wise, have ever been able to take away. No people on earth combine so handsomely loyal freedom and the larger patriotism, or hold in purer loyalty to the union of hearts and hands in the British Empire, which the sovereign represents, as do the Welsh.

The Welsh are the oldest of the British peoples. They preserve the language of the Druids, bards, and chiefs, of primeval ages which go back and far beyond any royal line in Europe, while most of their fairy tales are pre-ancient and beyond the dating.

Why the Cymric dragon is red, is thus told, from times beyond human record.

It was in those early days, after the Romans in the south had left the island, and the Cymric king, Vortigern, was hard pressed by the Picts and Scots of the north. To his aid, he invited over from beyond the North Sea, or German Ocean, the tribes called the Long Knives, or Saxons, to help him.

But once on the big island, these friends became enemies and would not go back. They wanted to possess all Britain.

Vortigern thought this was treachery. Knowing that the Long Knives would soon attack him, he called his twelve wise men together for their advice. With one voice, they advised him to retreat westward behind the mountains into Cymry. There he must build a strong fortress and there defy his enemies.

So the Saxons, who were Germans, thought they had driven the Cymry beyond the western borders of the country which was later called England, and into what they named the foreign or Welsh parts. Centuries afterwards, this land received the name of Wales.

People in Europe spoke of Galatians, Wallachians, Belgians, Walloons, Alsatians and others as 'Welsh'. They called the new fruit imported from Asia walnuts, but the names 'Wales' and 'Welsh' were unheard of until after the fifth century.

The place chosen for the fortified city of the Cymry was among the mountains. From all over his realm, the king sent for masons and carpenters and collected the materials for building. Then, a solemn invocation was made to the gods by the Druid priests. These grand looking old men were robed in white, with long, snowy beards falling over their breasts, and they had milk-white oxen drawing their chariot. With a silver knife they cut the mistletoe from the tree-branch, hailing it as a sign of favour from God. Then with harp, music and song they dedicated the spot as a stronghold of the Cymric nation.

Then the king set the diggers to work. He promised a rich reward to those men of the pick and shovel who should dig the fastest and throw up the most dirt, so that the masons could, at the earliest moment, begin their part of the work.

But it all turned out differently from what the king expected. Some dragon, or powerful being underground, must have been offended by this invasion of his domain; for, the next morning, they saw that everything in the form of stone, timber, iron or tools, had disappeared during the night. It looked as if an earthquake had swallowed them all up.

Both king and seers, priests and bards, were greatly puzzled at this. However, not being able to account for it, and the Saxons likely to march on them at any time, the sovereign set the diggers at work and again collected more wood and stone.

This time, even the women helped, not only to cook the food, but to drag the logs and stones. They were even ready to cut off their beautiful long hair to make ropes, if necessary.

But in the morning, all had again disappeared, as if swept by a tempest. The ground was bare. Nevertheless, all hands began again, for all hearts were united.

For the third time, the work proceeded. Yet when the sun rose next morning, there was not even a trace of either material or labour.

What was the matter? Had some dragon swallowed everything up?

Vortigern again summoned his twelve wise men, to meet in council, and to inquire concerning the cause of the marvel and to decide what was to be done.

After long deliberation, while all the workmen and people outside waited for their verdict, the wise men agreed upon a remedy.

Now in ancient times, it was a custom all over the world, notably in China and Japan and among our ancestors, that when a new castle or bridge was to be built, they sacrificed a human being. This was done either by walling up the victim while alive, or by mixing his or her blood with the cement used in the walls. Often it was a virgin or a little child thus chosen by lot and made to die, the one for the many.

The idea was not only to ward off the anger of the spirits of the air, or to appease the dragons underground, but also to make the workmen do their best work faithfully, so that the foundation should be sure and the edifice withstand the storm, the wind, and the earthquake shocks.

So, nobody was surprised, or raised his eyebrows, or shook his head, or pursed up his lips, when the king announced that what the wise men declared, must be done and that quickly. Nevertheless, many a mother hugged her darling more closely to her bosom, and fathers feared for their sons or daughters, lest one of these, their own, should be chosen as the victim to be slain.

King Vortigern had the long horn blown for perfect silence, and then he spoke:

"A child must be found who was born without a father. He must be brought here and be solemnly put to death. Then his blood will be sprinkled on the ground and the citadel will be built securely."

Within an hour, swift runners were seen bounding over the Cymric hills. They were dispatched in search of a boy without a father, and a large reward was promised to the young man who found what was wanted. So into every part of the Cymric land, the searchers went.

One messenger noticed some boys playing ball. Two of them were quarrelling. Coming near, he heard one say to the other:

"Oh, you boy without a father, nothing good will ever happen to you."

"This must be the one looked for," said the royal messenger to himself. So he went up to the boy, who had been thus twitted and spoke to him thus:

"Don't mind what he says." Then he prophesied great things, if he would go along with him. The boy was only too glad to go, and the next day the lad was brought before King Vortigern.

The workmen and their wives and children, numbering thousands, had assembled for the solemn ceremony of dedicating the ground by shedding the boy's blood. In strained attention the people held their breath.

The boy asked the king:

"Why have your servants brought me to this place?"

Then the sovereign told him the reason, and the boy asked:

"Who instructed you to do this?"

"My wise men told me so to do, and even the sovereign of the land obeys his wise councillors."

"Order them to come to me, Your Majesty," pleaded the boy.

When the wise men appeared, the boy, in respectful manner, inquired of them thus:

"How was the secret of my life revealed to you? Please speak freely and declare who it was that discovered me to you."

Turning to the king, the boy added:

"Pardon my boldness, Your Majesty. I shall soon reveal the whole matter to you, but I wish first to question your advisers. I want them to tell you what is the real cause, and reveal, if they can, what is hidden here underneath the ground."

But the wise men were confounded. They could not tell and they fully confessed their ignorance.

The boy then said:

"There is a pool of water down below. Please order your men to dig for it."

At once the spades were plied by strong hands, and in a few minutes the workmen saw their faces reflected, as in a looking glass. There was a pool of clear water there.

Turning to the wise men, the boy asked before all:

"Now tell me, what is in the pool?"

As ignorant as before, and now thoroughly ashamed, the wise men were silent.

"Your Majesty, I can tell you, even if these men cannot. There are two vases in the pool."

Two brave men leaped down into the pool. They felt around and brought up two vases, as the boy had said.

Again, the lad put a question to the wise men:

"What is in these vases?"

Once more, those who professed to know the secrets of the world, even to the demanding of the life of a human being, held their tongues.

"There is a tent in them," said the boy. "Separate them, and you will find it so."

By the king's command, a soldier thrust in his hand and found a folded tent.

Again, while all wondered, the boy was in command of the situation. Everything seemed so reasonable, that all were prompt and alert to serve him.

"What a splendid chief and general, he would make, to lead us against our enemies, the 'Long Knives!'" whispered one soldier to another.

"What is in the tent?" asked the boy of the wise men.

Not one of the twelve knew what to say, and there was an almost painful silence.

"I will tell you, Your Majesty, and all here, what is in this tent. There are two serpents, one white and one red. Unfold the tent."

With such a leader, no soldier was afraid, nor did a single person in the crowd draw back. Two stalwart fellows stepped forward to open the tent.

But now, a few of the men and many of the women shrank back while those that had babies, or little folks, snatched up their children, fearing lest the poisonous snakes might wriggle towards them.

The two serpents were coiled up and asleep, but they soon showed signs of waking, and their fiery, lidless eyes glared at the people.

"Now, Your Majesty, and all here, be you the witnesses of what will happen. Let the King and wise men look in the tent."

At this moment, the serpents stretched themselves out at full length, while all fell back, giving them a wide circle to struggle in.

Then they reared their heads. With their glittering eyes flashing fire, they began to struggle with each other. The white one rose up first, threw the red one into the middle of the arena, and then pursued him to the edge of the round space.

Three times did the white serpent gain the victory over the red one.

But while the white serpent seemed to be gloating over the other for a final onset, the red one, gathering strength, erected its head and struck at the other.

The struggle went on for several minutes, but in the end the red serpent overcame the white, driving it first out of the circle, then from the tent, and into the pool, where it disappeared, while the victorious red one moved into the tent again.

When the tent flap was opened for all to see, nothing was visible except a red dragon; for the victorious serpent had turned into this great creature which combined in one new form the body and the powers of bird, beast, reptile and fish. It had wings to fly, the strongest animal strength, and could crawl, swim, and live in either water or air, or on the earth. In its body was the sum total of all life.

Then, in the presence of all the assembly, the youth turned to the wise men to explain the meaning of what had happened. But not a word did they speak. In fact, their faces were full of shame before the great crowd.

"Now, Your Majesty, let me reveal to you the meaning of this mystery."

"Speak on," said the king, gratefully.

"This pool is the emblem of the world, and the tent is that of your kingdom. The two serpents are two dragons. The white serpent is the dragon of the Saxons, who now occupy several of the provinces and districts of Britain and from sea to sea. But when they invade our soil our people will finally drive them back and hold fast forever their beloved Cymric land. But you must choose another site, on which to erect your castle."

After this, whenever a castle was to be built no more human victims were doomed to death. All the twelve men, who had wanted to keep up the old cruel custom, were treated as deceivers of the people. By the king's orders, they were all put to death and buried before all the crowd.

Today, like so many who keep alive old and worn-out notions by means of deception and falsehood, these men are remembered only by the Twelve Mounds, which rise on the surface of the field hard by.

As for the boy, he became a great magician, or, as we in our age would call him, a man of science and wisdom, named Merlin. He lived long on the mountain, but when he went away with a friend, he placed all his treasures in a golden cauldron and hid them in a cave. He rolled a great stone over its mouth. Then with sod and earth he covered it all over so as to hide it from view. His purpose was to leave this his wealth for a leader, who, in some future generation, would use it for the benefit of his country, when most needed.

This special person will be a youth with yellow hair and blue eyes. When he comes to Denas, a bell will ring to invite him into the cave. The moment his foot is over the place, the stone of entrance will open of its own accord. Anyone else will be considered an intruder and it will not be possible for him to carry away the treasure.

The Good King Arthur

PROBABLY EVERYONE KNOWS the story of the great King Arthur who, the legends say, ruled in Britain so many, many years ago and gathered about him at his famous Round Table, knights of splendid courage, tried and proven.

The boy Arthur was really the son of King Uther Pendragon, but few persons knew of his birth. Uther had given him into the care of the enchanter Merlin, who had carried him to the castle of Sir Hector, an old friend of Uther's. Here the young prince lived as a child of the house.

Now Merlin was a very wise man, and when King Uther died several years later, the noblemen asked his advice in choosing a new king.

"Gather together in St. Stephen's Church in London, on Christmas Day," was all the enchanter answered.

So the knights assembled, and when the mass was over and they passed out into the churchyard, there they beheld a large block of stone, upon which rested a heavy anvil. The blade of a jewelled sword was sunk deeply into the anvil.

Wondering, the noblemen drew near. One of them discovered an inscription upon the hilt which said that none but the man who could draw out the sword should ever rule in Uther's place. One by one they tried, but the sword was firmly embedded. No one could draw it forth.

Arthur was only a baby at this time, but some years later Sir Hector travelled up to London, bringing with him his own son, Sir Kay, and his foster son, Arthur. Sir Kay had just reached manhood and was to take part in his first tournament. Imagine his distress, therefore, when, on arriving at the tourney ground, he discovered that he had forgotten to bring his sword.

"I will fetch it for you," cried the young Arthur, anxious to be of service.

He found the apartment of Sir Kay closed and locked; but he was determined to get a sword for his brother, and remembering the huge anvil he had seen in the churchyard, he hurried toward it. Grasping the hilt of the projecting sword, he drew it out easily.

Happy over his good fortune, Arthur returned to the tourney ground and gave the new sword to his foster brother. Sir Hector, who stood near, recognized it.

"Where did you get that sword?" he asked.

"From the great anvil in the churchyard of St. Stephen's I drew it," was the answer.

But Sir Hector still doubted, and when the tournament was over, he and all the principal nobles of the realm rode back to the churchyard.

Arthur replaced the sword in the anvil and stood aside while all present tried to draw it forth. None succeeded. Then Arthur again stepped up, grasped the hilt and pulled out the blade.

"The king, the king!" the people cried; for they knew that at last they had found a worthy successor to the good King Uther.

So Arthur was crowned king and entered upon that wise and kingly rule of which the praises have so often been sung.

Why the Sole of Man's Foot Is Flat

ONCE UPON A time, when the devils turned recreants to God and fled to earth, amongst other things, they took along with them the Sun, which the Tsar of the devils stuck on the point of his lance, and he carried it over his shoulder. But when the Earth complained to God that she would soon be burnt to ashes by the Sun, God sent the Holy Archangel Michael to try by some means or other to take away the Sun from the devil. Now, when the Holy Archangel stepped down to the earth, he made friends with the Tsar of the devils, but the latter saw at once what was Michael's little game, and was always on his guard.

One day the two went together for a walk, and went on and on until they came to the sea. There they made preparations to have a bathe, and the devil stuck his lance into the ground with the Sun still upon it. After they had been bathing for a while, the Holy Archangel said, "Now, let us dive and see who can dive deepest." And the devil said, "Very well!" So the Holy Archangel dived first, and brought up in his mouth some sand from the bottom of the sea. Now it was the devil's turn to dive, but he was afraid that Michael would steal the Sun.

Then he had a fine idea. He spit on the ground, and out of his spittle grew a magpie. He told her to look after the Sun whilst he was diving to get some sand from the bottom of the sea. As soon, however, as the devil dived, the Holy Archangel made the sign of the cross, and instantly the sea was covered with ice nine yards thick. Quickly he seized the Sun, spread out his wings, and flew heavenwards, whilst the magpie croaked for all she was worth. When the devil heard the magpie's voice, he guessed at once what was the matter, and returned as quickly as possible. But when he came near the surface, he found that the sea was frozen up and that he could not get out. Hurriedly he made again for the bottom of the sea, fetched a stone, broke through the ice, and pressed on in pursuit of the Holy Archangel.

The distance between the two grew less and less. Now the Angel had reached the Gate of Heaven and had already put one foot inside, when the devil just caught him by the other foot and tore out of it a large piece of flesh with his claws. And as the Holy Archangel with the regained Sun in his hands stepped before God, he wept and lamented, "What shall I do now, disfigured thus?" Then the Lord God said to him, "Be still and fear not; henceforth shall all men bear a small hollow in the sole of the foot." And as God had said, so it came about that all men received a small hollow in the sole of each foot.

The Wonderful Alpine Horn

WHEN THE LITTLE boys and girls, who read these Swiss fairy tales, grow up to be big and travel in Switzerland, they will enjoy the Alpine horn.

Nearly every shepherd lad in the mountains knows how to blow it. It is made of wood, and is about half as long as an ordinary broom. Its butt, or heavy end, rests on the ground. When a man blows a long blast, the sound, at first, when one is too near, does not seem to be very pleasing; for distance lends enchantment to the sound. But wait a moment, and listen! Far off across the valley, the strains are caught up, and sent back from the tops of the high mountains. Then it sounds as if a great choir of angels had come down from Heaven to sing glory to God, and to bring greetings to all good souls. Nowhere in all the world is there such sweet music made by echoes.

Sometimes there is a double set of echoes, like one rainbow inside of another. Then, it makes one think of a choir of little angels, that sing a second time, after the first heavenly chorus has ceased.

How the Swiss people first received the Alpine horn, as a gift from the fairies, is told in the story of a faithful shepherd's boy, named Perrod. He had to work hard all day in tending the cows that grazed on the high mountain pastures, which the natives call the Alps. But when foreign people speak of 'the Alps,' they mean the ranges of mountains themselves.

In winter, these level stretches of ground are covered with snow and ice, but by the month of June, it is warm enough for the grass and flowers to grow. Then the cowboys and cheese makers go up with their cattle. At night, Perrod, having milked the cows, skimmed the cream off the milk, hung the great cauldron over the fire, and made the cheese.

By this time, that is, well into the late hours, Perrod was almost tired to death. After calling 'good night' to Luquette, his sweetheart, who lived across the valley, and hearing her greeting in answer, he climbed up the ladder into the loft, and lay down on his bed. This was only a pile of straw, but he was asleep almost the very moment he touched it, for he was a healthy lad and the mountain air was better than medicine. It was especially good for sound sleep, and he knew he must get up early, at sunrise, to lead the cows and goats out to pasture. Then the all-day concert of tinkling bells began.

But this night, instead of slumber, without once waking until day dawn, Perrod had closed his eyes for only about three hours when he heard a crackling sound that woke him up. He thought at first the wind was blowing hard enough to rip off some of the bark strips from the roof of the chalet, and was tumbling down some of the heavy stones laid on to keep them in place. But when he saw the reflection on the walls and ceiling of a bright fire, he crawled quietly out of bed. Then he peeped down and through the cracks in the board floor, to see what was going on.

Three men were around the fire. One, the biggest fellow of the three, was hanging up the cauldron on the hooks. The second piled on more wood, while the others warmed their hands in the bright blaze.

The three men were all different in appearance, the one from the other, and an odd-looking lot they were. The tremendously tall man seemed to be a giant, in weight and size. His sleeves were rolled up, showing that his arms were sunburnt until they were very dark. When he lifted up the cauldron, to hang it up or take it down, his muscles stood out like whipcords.

But the man sitting on a milking stool, at the right-hand side of the fireplace, was entirely different, being smaller, and with white skin and golden hair. He had a long horn, which rested on the floor beside him.

The man on the left-hand side of the fireplace appeared to be a woodman or hunter. At least, he seemed to be used to the forest. Though it was pitch-dark night, he knew where the wood lay, piled up under the eaves of the chalet; for, when the fire burned low, he went outdoors and returned with an armload of fagots. Then he piled up the wood, and the fire blazed, and crackled, and roared, until the boy in the loft thought the hut would be burned up, too. Yet, though he trembled at the strange sight, he was brave. He resolved not to be quiet if the big men tried to steal his cheese, which was to be food for the family during the winter.

Just as he was wondering whether his sisters and old daddy would have enough to eat during the long cold winter of eight months that was soon coming, when snow and ice covered the fields, he saw a curious thing happen. Sweet music began, such as had never met his ears since he was in his cradle and his mother sang to him.

It was the man with the golden hair, who seemed to be the real gentleman of the party. He it was who made the music. He first handed something to the giant, who dropped it into the cauldron. Then, with his horn, he disappeared through the door. When outside, he lifted the instrument to his lips and blew a blast.

Perrod was so interested in watching the giant that he paid little attention to the man outside, or to the sound he had made, for he saw the hunter take a bottle out of his pocket and hand it over to the biggest fellow, who stood at the cauldron over the fire. This one poured the liquid, which seemed to be blood red, into the big iron pot. Then, with a ladle as big as a shovel and long as a gun, he stirred vigorously. Then, three beakers, or cups, were set upon the table.

By this time, the golden-haired man outside had finished his blast of music, which seemed to float across the valleys down into the defiles, over the pastures, and through the wood. It grew sweeter and sweeter as it swelled on the gentle night breeze, until all the mountains seemed to have awakened, turned into living angels and lifted up their voices. The sweet strain ended with a prolonged sad note, as if melancholy had fallen on the musicians, and then it ceased.

A strange thing happened. All the cows and goats woke up from their sleep, and one, from all directions, could hear the tinkling of their neck bells, all over the pastures, far and near. The poor creatures thought it was time to get up and be milked, but they were puzzled to find it was yet dark. In fact, they were all still quite sleepy and very slow to move.

Something even far more wonderful happened next. Perrod, after first hearing the horn blow, thought the music had ceased: when, suddenly, it all seemed to come back in vastly greater volume. The sounds were multiplied, as if a thousand echoes had blended into one and all heaven had joined in the melody. Perrod was entranced. He even closed his eyes lest he might, by looking down at the strange men, lose some of what seemed to him a choir of angels singing.

When the last strain had ceased, Perrod opened his eyes. The golden-haired musician had re-entered the chalet and resumed his seat, sitting down again on the milkstool at the right of the fire; while the hunter rearranged three glass goblets, on the rough wooden table from which Perrod ate his meals.

All three of the strangers then solemnly watched the cauldron as the liquid boiled, just as the cream does when cheese is to be made; the big man stirring up with his huge ladle. At a particular moment, the giant lifted the cauldron and emptied out the contents into the three glass vessels. To the amazement of Perrod, there issued, from the same vessel, three very different colours.

In the first glass, filled to the brim, the draught was as red as blood, and it foamed at the top. The drops, flying out on the board, left crimson stains.

Giving a tap on the cauldron, with the big ladle, the tall man let flow, into the second glass, what seemed to be the same liquid; but this time, it was as green as grass, but hissing hot, and bubbling.

Another loud ladle tap on the cauldron, and out flowed a stream as cold as snow water, and as white as the edelweiss flower. The liquid rested in the goblet as quiet as milk, but seemed to be frosty on the top.

Now the giant-like fellow, shaking his huge ladle in his right hand, and putting his left at the side of his mouth, shouted with a voice of thunder:

"Come down, you boy, and make your choice of one of these three. Each has a glorious gift to him who drinks. Come quick, for it will soon be daylight."

Perrod knew he was discovered, but he was a brave boy. If his legs trembled, his heart was big. Moreover, the golden-haired man gave him a nod, and winked his eye, to encourage the lad.

So Perrod at once climbed down and stood before the table, on which were the three chalices.

"Drink, young friend," said the giant, "from any one of these, but know that in the red liquid is a gift to the Swiss men. Drain this cup, and then you will have strength, like me." At that, he bent his arm to show his mighty muscles. "You will be able to conquer the strongest man or fiercest beast. Besides, I shall give you a hundred fat cows, each of which will yield much milk, rich in butter. Drain this cup, and, according to my promise, you will see the kine tomorrow."

Then the hunter spoke: "Better drink from my goblet. After this green draught, you will have all the gold you want, and heaps of coins; and then you can marry, and still easily support your old father and mother." So saying, he tossed handfuls of gold pieces on the floor, piling them up until they reached the lad's knees. Perrod opened his eyes wide in astonishment, for here was not a promise in words, but the actual thing, that he could see for himself.

He was just about to stretch both his hands and drink the green liquid when the golden-haired man, speaking gently to Perrod, said:

"I cannot promise you either cows or coins, but if you drink the liquid in the white goblet, you will be able to use this horn, make music in the mountains and call your cows, as I have done. Thus your flocks and herds also will share with you my gift."

Not a minute did Perrod wait to decide. "I care more for music than for money or strength," he said, and, lifting the glass, he put it to his lips and drained the cup dry.

"What was it, and how did it taste?" do you ask? It was what the cows gave him every day – pure fresh milk, but cold as glacier water.

"Good," cried the man with the golden hair. "Any other choice would have meant death. Here is the horn. Blow it tomorrow, and see what will happen."

As if lifted up on wings to his straw bed, but holding on to his horn, Perrod heard the door shut and bang as the three men went out, two of them scowling. Then the fire cooled to ashes. He fell asleep and dreamed of the time when, in the church, he should lead his bride to the altar, his lovely sweetheart, Luquette, to be married, and the two should have a chateau and home of their own.

Awakening at the first moment when the rosy light of the rising sun made the face of the mountains blush, even while the valleys below were still in darkness, and long before his sisters in the village far away had awakened, he rushed out to the edge of the pasture. Then he drew in a man's breath, filled his lungs and, putting his lips to the mouthpiece of the horn, blew a long blast. He listened eagerly for the far-off echoes. A pleasant double surprise awaited him.

All over the pastures, in the chalets of the high plateau and along the mountain slopes, even down to the valleys, there was heard, at once, the tinkling of goat bells, cow bells, and the sound even of what hung in the metal collars of donkeys and horses, until the chorus of bell music was wonderful.

"Very fine, but is that all?" thought Perrod.

But another surprise! From across the great ravine, or chasm, out rushed his beloved Luquette. Hastily throwing a wrap around her shoulders, she stood in bare feet, threw a kiss to Perrod, and shouted to him her joy.

Now came the crowning wonder. From the high peaks, miles distant, and now rosy red in the dayspring, came back the music, in multiplied echoes, as if all the snow ranges of the Alps were singing. Pure, sweet, prolonged, the boy thought of what he had heard read in the church, that at creation, 'the morning stars sang together.' So it seemed now to him.

Through many centuries, and to this day, to call the cows together, to make the goats look up and turn homeward to seek shelter of the night, for men's evening prayer and chant of thanksgiving, for the signals of defence against enemies, for beginning the festal dance, or, to sound the wedding joy, the Alpine horn is the delight of the Swiss. It is like the carillons of the Belgic folk, the chimes of Normandy, the tower music of Holland, or the bagpipes of the Highlander. In a foreign land, in dreams, in its memories it tells of 'home, sweet home.'

The Story of the Fleur-de-Lys

LONG BEFORE COWS in Belgium wore earrings, to denote their pedigree and good breeding, or sugar was made out of beets, there were wonderful things done by the fairies.

These were so many, that some industrious farmers and their wives got together to see if they could equal or exceed the fairies in doing good things for their country. They wished to outrival the fairies, excel them if possible, and make Belgium great among the nations.

These honest folk used to meet together in the evenings and tell fairy tales, so that they and their little ones, as they grew up in their wooden shoes, might know just what fairies were good for. This was done, because they supposed that everything unusual, or wonderful in nature, was the work of the fairies, and they felt that human beings ought, in other ways, to beat them in a contest of wits.

Some of the inhabitants arranged a meeting to talk with the fairies, who should tell what they had accomplished in the three kingdoms of nature – mineral, vegetable and animal. The meeting was at night, of course, for fairies are never seen in the daytime.

Having already shown what they had done for the animals of Belgium, the fairy-folk proposed to talk about what they had done, with the plants and minerals, to enrich Belgium and make the country great.

The first story the fairies told was 'How the lowly flower got into royal society', and thus the fairy began:

"All the world, as the French say, knows that the fleur-de-lys, the lily of France, has for centuries been their national emblem. In the blazonry of kings and queens, it was sewn on royal robes and embroidered in gold and silver on flags and banners. It was stamped on the coins, and made the symbol of everything glorious in France. All the world has heard of the Bourbon lilies, for that family of kings and rulers made it especially their own emblem.

"But originally the fleur-de-lys was our Belgian flower, that grew in the meadows along our river Lys (or Leye).

"To tell the full story of the Frankish tribes, who made France a kingdom, and especially of the Salic Franks, we must go back, in time, to the early ages. We must travel up into Dutch Gelderland, where the waters of the North Sea or German Ocean, wash the shores, and the waves fling their spray over the land.

"The Salic Franks, that is, the Free men of the Salt, which was born of Heaven's fire and ocean's water, once dwelt by the sea. To get the crystals out of the brine, they cut down the trees of the forest, in which the fairies lived. Then they piled up the logs, and made a great blaze. The tongues of fire leaped higher and higher, for they were trying to get back to Heaven, their old home. Then the forefathers of our nation went down to the sea and drew up the salt water. This they flung on the red-hot logs, praying all the time for the salt to come.

"The fire was put out by this means, and when they looked on the charred wood, they found thousands of shining white spots, which were crystals of pure salt. These, they scraped up, and, after refining, by means of water and evaporation, in the sun's rays, they used the salt on their food and as offerings to the gods.

"The forefathers therefore considered salt as the child born of fire and water, of Heaven and ocean. So they took the name Salis, which means 'of the salt.' Through the changes in the language, the name 'Salians' was used to denote a host. They were very proud of being Franks, or freemen, and were known as the Salic Franks. They became very powerful and even defied the Romans.

"When they found that their enemies were weakening, and food was scarce in the north, they resolved to march south and west, and possess the rich land stretching between the Maas and the Seine rivers, which is now Belgium and France.

"Assembling the entire host, with their chariots, wives and little ones, in the great moot-place, or sand-walled enclosure, a few miles from Nijkerk, they marched in one mighty army into Belgic Land. Reaching the river Lys, when the iris and the lily were in full bloom, each one of the tribesmen plucked a stem and blossom of the plant and stuck it in his cap.

"Then they rushed on, conquering and to conquer, until all the wide area of the country now called 'France,' and named after the Franks, was theirs. The flower of the Lys, or fleur-de-lys, under which they had won victory, was chosen as their emblem. Thus, the once lovely Belgic flower was elevated into royal society.

"Even better, the Franks gave up their cruel pagan rites, and, believing in the Heavenly Father of all mankind, and in his beloved Son, and in the Holy Spirit, the fleur-de-lys was made the emblem of their faith. The missionaries often used it to teach the blessed doctrine of the trinity – three forms of life, proceeding from one common stem and nature.

"Now all Belgians know that our city, Tournai, was for centuries the centre and capital of this great Frankish empire. When Childeric, their emperor, died, he was buried at Tournai, and his tomb was here, in the church of St. Brice. On the robes, which cover his honoured dust, when his coffin was opened, centuries ago, were found three hundred golden bees, models of those that gathered honey from the flowers that grew along the Lys and other rivers of Belgic Land.

"All the world knows, also, how Napoleon, who made himself emperor of the French, had these golden bees embroidered on his coronation robes. Just as the Bourbons had claimed the lily as the particular blazon of their family, so Napoleon made the golden bee his symbol.

"In truth, it has been the fashion, with these royal mortals, to take lowly flowers and humble insects for their heraldry. Did not a common shrub, named by Europeans, the 'broom,' the planta genista, become the proud emblem of the Plantagenets, kings of England?"

At this point, the fairy storyteller stopped and made apology for being so long. She hoped she had not been tedious. She then gave her final word: "Good men and women, Belgians all, would you make your country one of the best, to be always loved and honoured of your children's children, while ever attracting admiring and delighted visitors, to come to see the wonders of Belgic land? Would you? Then, please remember that the universe is full of fairies, though men nowadays call them 'forces', and they are ever ready to help you. Do your best to allure, coax, win, tame and harness them, for your use and benefit.

"Do not count any flower too lowly, or soil too poor; for in each is a secret worth learning and, even more, worth possessing. Believe what a wise man has said, concerning even the plants that you call 'weeds' – these which you uproot, plow under, throw out and burn. Yet each one may possess some secret charm, some virtue, or a message or science to you. For what says the seer?

"He defines a weed as a 'plant, the virtues of which have not yet been discovered'."

Now the storyteller, stepping out of fairy regions into Yankee land, would remind all who read the fairy's message, and especially his American young friends, that the wise man, whom the fairy quoted, was our own Emerson. We forget not, either, that the white silken flags, under which Lafayette and the 'sparkling Bourbonnaires' marched, were embroidered with the fleur-de-lys. These French soldiers of 1780, who kept step with the Continentals, on the way to Yorktown, were under the Bourbon lilies. Let us remember also, that the old moot-place of the Salic Franks is still to be seen near Nijkerk, in Gelderland, the pretty town, whence came 'Corlaer', and Van Rensselaer, and the settlers of New Netherland, out of which grew the four noble states of New York, Pennsylvania, New Jersey, and Delaware.

The Tradition of the Tea-Plant

"**GOOD IS THE** continence of the eye; Good is the continence of the ear; Good is the continence of the nostrils; Good is the continence of the tongue; Good is the continence of the body; Good is the continence of speech; Good is all...."

Again the Vulture of Temptation soared to the highest heaven of his contemplation, bringing his soul down, down, reeling and fluttering, back to the World of Illusion. Again the memory made dizzy his thought, like the perfume of some venomous flower. Yet he had seen the bayadere for an instant only, when passing through Kasi upon his way to China – to the vast empire of souls that thirsted after the refreshment of Buddha's law, as sun-parched fields thirst for the life-giving rain. When she called him, and dropped her little gift into his mendicant's bowl, he had indeed lifted his fan before his face, yet not quickly enough; and the penalty of that fault had followed him a thousand leagues – pursued after him even into the strange land to which he had come to hear the words of the Universal Teacher. Accursed beauty! surely framed by the Tempter of tempters, by Mara himself, for the perdition of the just! Wisely had Bhagavat warned his disciples: "O ye Cramanas, women are not to be looked upon! And if ye chance to meet women, ye must not suffer your eyes to dwell upon them; but, maintaining holy reserve, speak not to them at all. Then fail not to whisper unto your own hearts, 'Lo, we are Cramanas, whose duty it is to remain uncontaminated by the corruptions of this world, even as the Lotos, which suffereth no vileness to cling unto its leaves, though it blossom amid the refuse of the wayside ditch.'" Then also came to his memory, but with a new and terrible meaning, the words of the Twentieth-and-Third of the Admonitions:

"Of all attachments unto objects of desire, the strongest indeed is the attachment to form. Happily, this passion is unique; for were there any other like unto it, then to enter the Perfect Way were impossible."

How, indeed, thus haunted by the illusion of form, was he to fulfil the vow that he had made to pass a night and a day in perfect and unbroken meditation? Already the night was beginning! Assuredly, for sickness of the soul, for fever of the spirit, there was no physic save prayer. The sunset was swiftly fading out. He strove to pray:

"O the Jewel in the Lotos!

"Even as the tortoise withdraweth its extremities into its shell, let me, O Blessed One, withdraw my senses wholly into meditation!

"O the Jewel in the Lotos!

"For even as rain penetrateth the broken roof of a dwelling long uninhabited, so may passion enter the soul uninhabited by meditation.

"O the Jewel in the Lotos!

"Even as still water that hath deposited all its slime, so let my soul, O Tathâgata, be made pure! Give me strong power to rise above the world, O Master, even as the wild bird rises from its marsh to follow the pathway of the Sun!

"O the Jewel in the Lotos!

"By day shineth the sun, by night shineth the moon; shineth also the warrior in harness of war; shineth likewise in meditations the Cramana. But the Buddha at all times, by night or by day, shineth ever the same, illuminating the world.

"O the Jewel in the Lotos!

"Let me cease, O thou Perfectly Awakened, to remain as an Ape in the World-forest, forever ascending and descending in search of the fruits of folly. Swift as the twining of serpents, vast as the growth of lianas in a forest, are the all-encircling growths of the Plant of Desire.

"O the Jewel in the Lotos!"

Vain his prayer, alas! vain also his invocation! The mystic meaning of the holy text – the sense of the Lotos, the sense of the Jewel – had evaporated from the words, and their monotonous utterance now served only to lend more dangerous definition to the memory that tempted and tortured him. O the jewel in her ear! What lotos-bud more dainty than the folded flower of flesh, with its dripping of diamond-fire! Again he saw it, and the curve of the cheek beyond, luscious to look upon as beautiful brown fruit. How true the Two Hundred and Eighty-Fourth verse of the Admonitions! – "So long as a man shall not have torn from his heart even the smallest rootlet of that liana of desire which draweth his thought toward women, even so long shall his soul remain fettered." And there came to his mind also the Three Hundred and Forty-Fifth verse of the same blessed book, regarding fetters:

"In bonds of rope, wise teachers have said, there is no strength; nor in fetters of wood, nor yet in fetters of iron. Much stronger than any of these is the fetter of concern for the jewelled earrings of women."

"Omniscient Gotama!" he cried, "all-seeing Tathagata! How multiform the Consolation of Thy Word! how marvellous Thy understanding of the human heart! Was this also one of Thy temptations? – one of the myriad illusions marshalled before Thee by Mara in that night when the earth rocked as a chariot, and the sacred trembling passed from sun to sun, from system to system, from universe to universe, from eternity to eternity?"

O the jewel in her ear! The vision would not go! Nay, each time it hovered before his thought it seemed to take a warmer life, a fonder look, a fairer form; to develop with his weakness; to gain force from his enervation. He saw the eyes, large, limpid, soft, and black as a deer's; the pearls in the dark hair, and the pearls in the pink mouth; the lips curling to a kiss, a flower-kiss; and a fragrance seemed to float to his senses, sweet, strange, soporific – a perfume of youth, an odor of woman. Rising to his feet, with strong resolve he pronounced again the sacred invocation; and he recited the holy words of the Chapter of Impermanency:

"Gazing upon the heavens and upon the earth ye must say, These are not permanent. Gazing upon the mountains and the rivers, ye must say, These are not permanent. Gazing upon the forms and upon the faces of exterior beings, and beholding their growth and their development, ye must say, These are not permanent."

And nevertheless! how sweet illusion! The illusion of the great sun; the illusion of the shadow-casting hills; the illusion of waters, formless and multiform; the illusion of – Nay, nay I what impious fancy! Accursed girl! yet, yet! why should he curse her? Had she ever done aught to merit the malediction of an ascetic? Never, never! Only her form, the memory of her, the beautiful phantom of her, the accursed phantom of her! What was she? An illusion creating illusions, a mockery, a dream, a shadow, a vanity, a vexation of spirit! The fault, the sin, was in himself, in his rebellious thought, in his untamed memory. Though mobile as water, intangible as vapor, Thought, nevertheless, may be tamed by the Will, may be harnessed to the chariot of Wisdom – must be! – that happiness be found. And he recited the blessed verses of the "Book of the Way of the Law":

"All forms are only temporary." When this great truth is fully comprehended by any one, then is he delivered from all pain. This is the Way of Purification.

"All forms are subject unto pain." When this great truth is fully comprehended by any one, then is he delivered from all pain. This is the Way of Purification.

"All forms are without substantial reality." When this great truth is fully comprehended by any one, then is he delivered from all pain. This is the way of ...

Her form, too, unsubstantial, unreal, an illusion only, though comeliest of illusions? She had given him alms! Was the merit of the giver illusive also, illusive like the grace of the supple fingers that gave? Assuredly there were mysteries in the Abhidharma impenetrable, incomprehensible!... It was a golden coin, stamped with the symbol of an elephant – not more of an illusion, indeed, than the gifts of Kings to the Buddha! Gold upon her bosom also, less fine than the gold of her skin. Naked between the silken sash and the narrow breast-corslet, her young waist curved glossy and pliant as a bow. Richer the silver in her voice than in the hollow pagals that made a moonlight about her ankles! But her smile! – the little teeth like flower-stamens in the perfumed blossom of her mouth!

O weakness! O shame! How had the strong Charioteer of Resolve thus lost his control over the wild team of fancy! Was this languor of the Will a signal of coming peril, the peril of slumber? So strangely vivid those fancies were, so brightly definite, as about to take visible form, to move with factitious life, to play some unholy drama upon the stage of dreams! "O Thou Fully Awakened!" he cried aloud, "help now thy humble disciple to obtain the blessed wakefulness of perfect contemplation! let him find force to fulfil his vow! suffer not Mara to prevail against him!" And he recited the eternal verses of the Chapter of Wakefulness:

"Completely and eternally awake are the disciples of Gotama! Unceasingly, by day and night, their thoughts are fixed upon the Law.
"Completely and eternally awake are the disciples of Gotama! Unceasingly, by day and night, their thoughts are fixed upon the Community.
"Completely and eternally awake are the disciples of Gotama! Unceasingly, by day and night, their thoughts are fixed upon the Body.
"Completely and eternally awake are the disciples of Gotama! Unceasingly, by day and night, their minds know the sweetness of perfect peace.
"Completely and eternally awake are the disciples of Gotama! Unceasingly, by day and night, their minds enjoy the deep peace of meditation."

There came a murmur to his ears; a murmuring of many voices, smothering the utterances of his own, like a tumult of waters. The stars went out before his sight; the heavens darkened their infinities: all things became viewless, became blackness; and the great murmur deepened, like the murmur of a rising tide; and the earth seemed to sink from beneath him. His feet no longer touched the ground; a sense of supernatural buoyancy pervaded every fibre of his body: he felt himself floating in obscurity; then sinking softly, slowly, like a feather dropped from the pinnacle of a temple. Was this death? Nay, for all suddenly, as transported by the Sixth Supernatural Power, he stood again in light – a perfumed, sleepy light, vapory, beautiful – that bathed the marvellous streets of some Indian city. Now the nature of the murmur became manifest to him; for he moved with a mighty throng, a people of pilgrims, a nation of worshippers. But these were not of his faith; they bore upon their foreheads the smeared symbols of obscene gods! Still, he could not escape from their midst; the mile-broad human torrent bore him irresistibly with it, as a leaf is swept by the waters of the Ganges. Rajahs were there with their trains, and princes riding upon elephants, and Brahmins robed in their vestments, and swarms of voluptuous dancing-girls, moving to chant of kabit and damâri. But whither, whither? Out of the city into the sun they passed, between avenues of banyan, down colonnades of palm. But whither, whither?

Blue-distant, a mountain of carven stone appeared before them – the Temple, lifting to heaven its wilderness of chiselled pinnacles, flinging to the sky the golden spray of its decoration. Higher it grew with approach, the blue tones changed to gray, the outlines sharpened in the light. Then each detail became visible: the elephants of the pedestals standing upon tortoises of rock; the great grim faces of the capitals; the serpents and monsters writhing among the friezes; the many-headed gods of basalt in their galleries of fretted niches, tier above tier; the pictured foulnesses, the painted lusts, the divinities of abomination. And, yawning in the sloping precipice of sculpture, beneath a frenzied swarming of gods and Gopia – a beetling pyramid of limbs and bodies interlocked – the Gate, cavernous and shadowy as the mouth of Siva, devoured the living multitude.

The eddy of the throng whirled him with it to the vastness of the interior. None seemed to note his yellow robe, none even to observe his presence. Giant aisles intercrossed their heights above him; myriads of mighty pillars, fantastically carven, filed away to invisibility behind the yellow illumination of torch-fires. Strange images, weirdly sensuous, loomed up through haze of incense. Colossal figures, that at a distance assumed the form of elephants or garuda-birds, changed aspect when approached, and revealed as the secret of their design an interplaiting of the bodies of women; while one divinity rode all the monstrous allegories – one divinity or demon, eternally the same in the repetition of the sculptor, universally visible as though self-multiplied. The huge pillars themselves were symbols, figures, carnalities; the orgiastic spirit of that worship lived and writhed in the contorted bronze of the lamps, the twisted gold of the cups, the chiselled marble of the tanks....

How far had he proceeded? He knew not; the journey among those countless columns, past those armies of petrified gods, down lanes of flickering lights, seemed longer than the voyage of a caravan, longer than his pilgrimage to China! But suddenly, inexplicably, there came a silence as of cemeteries; the living ocean seemed to have ebbed away from about him, to have been engulfed within abysses of subterranean architecture! He found himself alone in some strange crypt before a basin, shell-shaped and shallow, bearing in its centre a rounded column of less than human height, whose smooth and spherical summit was wreathed with flowers. Lamps similarly formed, and fed with oil of palm, hung above it. There was no other graven image, no visible divinity. Flowers of countless varieties lay heaped upon the pavement; they covered its surface like a carpet, thick, soft; they exhaled their ghosts beneath his feet. The perfume seemed to penetrate his brain – a perfume sensuous, intoxicating, unholy; an unconquerable languor mastered his will, and he sank to rest upon the floral offerings.

The sound of a tread, light as a whisper, approached through the heavy stillness, with a drowsy tinkling of pagals, a tintinnabulation of anklets. All suddenly he felt glide about his neck the tepid smoothness of a woman's arm. She, she! his Illusion, his Temptation; but how transformed, transfigured! – preternatural in her loveliness, incomprehensible in her charm! Delicate as a jasmine-petal the cheek that touched his own; deep as night, sweet as summer, the eyes that watched him. "Heart's-thief," her flower-lips whispered, "heart's-thief, how have I sought for thee! How have I found thee! Sweets I bring thee, my beloved; lips and bosom; fruit and blossom. Hast thirst? Drink from the well of mine eyes! Wouldst sacrifice? I am thine altar! Wouldst pray? I am thy God!"

Their lips touched; her kiss seemed to change the cells of his blood to flame. For a moment Illusion triumphed; Mara prevailed!... With a shock of resolve the dreamer awoke in the night – under the stars of the Chinese sky.

Only a mockery of sleep! But the vow had been violated, the sacred purpose unfulfilled! Humiliated, penitent, but resolved, the ascetic drew from his girdle a keen knife, and with unfaltering hands severed his eyelids from his eyes, and flung them from him. "O Thou Perfectly Awakened!" he prayed, "thy disciple hath not been overcome save through the feebleness of the body; and his vow hath been renewed. Here shall he linger, without food or drink, until the moment of its fulfilment." And having assumed the hieratic posture – seated himself with his lower limbs folded beneath him, and the palms of his hands upward, the right upon the left, the left resting upon the sole of his upturned foot – he resumed his meditation.

* * *

Dawn blushed; day brightened. The sun shortened all the shadows of the land, and lengthened them again, and sank at last upon his funeral pyre of crimson-burning cloud. Night came and glittered and passed. But Mara had tempted in vain. This time the vow had been fulfilled, the holy purpose accomplished.

And again the sun arose to fill the World with laughter of light; flowers opened their hearts to him; birds sang their morning hymn of fire worship; the deep forest trembled with delight; and far upon the plain, the eaves of many-storied temples and the peaked caps of the city-towers caught aureate glory. Strong in the holiness of his accomplished vow, the Indian pilgrim arose in the morning glow. He started for amazement as he lifted his hands to his eyes. What! was everything a dream? Impossible! Yet now his eyes felt no pain; neither were they lidless; not even so much as one of their lashes was lacking. What marvel had been wrought? In vain he looked for the severed lids that he had flung upon the ground; they had mysteriously vanished. But lo! there where he had cast them two wondrous shrubs were growing, with dainty leaflets eyelid-shaped, and snowy buds just opening to the East.

Then, by virtue of the supernatural power acquired in that mighty meditation, it was given the holy missionary to know the secret of that newly created plant – the subtle virtue of its leaves. And he named it, in the language of the nation to whom he brought the Lotos of the Good Law, "TE"; and he spake to it, saying:

"Blessed be thou, sweet plant, beneficent, life-giving, formed by the spirit of virtuous resolve! Lo! the fame of thee shall yet spread unto the ends of the earth; and the perfume of thy life be borne unto the uttermost parts by all the winds of heaven! Verily, for all time to come men who drink of thy sap shall find such refreshment that weariness may not overcome them nor languor seize upon them; – neither shall they know the confusion of drowsiness, nor any desire for slumber in the hour of duty or of prayer. Blessed be thou!"

* * *

And still, as a mist of incense, as a smoke of universal sacrifice, perpetually ascends to heaven from all the lands of earth the pleasant vapor of TE, created for the refreshment of mankind by the power of a holy vow, the virtue of a pious atonement.

How Footbinding Started

IN THE VERY beginning of all things, when the gods were creating the world, at last the time came to separate the earth from the heavens. This was hard work, and if it had not been for the coolness and skill of a young goddess all would have failed. This goddess was named Lu-o. She had been idly watching the growth of the planet, when, to her horror, she saw the newly made ball slipping slowly from its place. In another second it would have shot down into the bottomless pit. Quick as a flash Lu-o stopped it with her magic wand and held it firmly until the chief god came dashing up to the rescue.

But this was not all. When men and women were put on the earth Lu-o helped them greatly by setting an example of purity and kindness. Everyone loved her and pointed her out as the one who was always willing to do a good deed. After she had left the world and gone into the land of the gods, beautiful statues of her were set up in many temples to keep her image always before the eyes of sinful people. The greatest of these was in the capital city. Thus, when sorrowful women wished to offer up their prayers to some virtuous goddess they would go to a temple of Lu-o and pour out their hearts before her shrine.

At one time the wicked Chow-sin, last ruler of the Yins, went to pray in the city Temple. There his royal eyes were captivated by the sight of a wonderful face, the beauty of which was so great that he fell in love with it at once, telling his ministers that he wished he might take this goddess, who was no other than Lu-o, for one of his wives.

Now Lu-o was terribly angry that an earthly prince should dare to make such a remark about her. Then and there she determined to punish the Emperor. Calling her assistant spirits, she told them of Chow-sin's insult. Of all her servants the most cunning was one whom we shall call Fox Sprite, because he really belonged to the fox family. Lu-o ordered Fox Sprite to spare himself no trouble in making the wicked ruler suffer for his impudence.

For many days, try as he would, Chow-sin, the great Son of Heaven, could not forget the face he had seen in the temple.

"He is stark mad," laughed his courtiers behind his back, "to fall in love with a statue."

"I must find a woman just like her," said the Emperor, "and take her to wife."

"Why not, most Mighty One," suggested a favourite adviser, "send forth a command throughout the length and breadth of your Empire, that no maiden shall be taken in marriage until you have chosen yourself a wife whose beauty shall equal that of Lu-o?"

Chow-sin was pleased with this suggestion and doubtless would have followed it had not his Prime Minister begged him to postpone issuing the order. "Your Imperial Highness," began the official, "since you have been pleased once or twice to follow my counsel, I beg of you to give ear now to what I say."

"Speak, and your words shall have my best attention," replied Chow-sin, with a gracious wave of the hand.

"Know then, Great One, that in the southern part of your realm there dwells a viceroy whose bravery has made him famous in battle."

"Are you speaking of Su-nan?" questioned Chow-sin, frowning, for this Su-nan had once been a rebel.

"None other, mighty Son of Heaven. Famous is he as a soldier, but his name is now even greater in that he is the father of the most beautiful girl in all China. This lovely flower that has bloomed of late within his household is still unmarried. Why not order her father to bring her to the palace that you may wed her and place her in your royal dwelling?"

"And are you sure of this wondrous beauty you describe so prettily?" asked the ruler, a smile of pleasure lighting up his face.

"So sure that I will stake my head on your being satisfied."

"Enough! I command you at once to summon the viceroy and his daughter. Add the imperial seal to the message."

The Prime Minister smilingly departed to give the order. In his heart he was more than delighted that the Emperor had accepted his suggestion, for Su-nan, the viceroy, had long been his chief enemy, and he planned in this way to overthrow him. The viceroy, as he knew, was a man of iron. He would certainly not feel honoured at the thought of having his daughter enter the Imperial Palace as a secondary wife. Doubtless he would refuse to obey the order and would thus bring about his own immediate downfall.

Nor was the Prime Minister mistaken. When Su-nan received the imperial message his heart was hot with anger against his sovereign. To be robbed of his lovely Ta-ki, even by the throne, was, in his eyes, a terrible disgrace. Could he have been sure that she would be made Empress it might have been different, but with so many others sharing Chow-sin's favour, her promotion to first place in the Great One's household was by no means certain. Besides, she was Su-nan's favourite child, and the old man could not bear the thought of separation from her. Rather would he give up his life than let her go to this cruel ruler.

"No, you shall not do it," said he to Ta-ki, "not though I must die to save you."

The beautiful girl listened to her father's words, in tears. Throwing herself at his feet she thanked him for his mercy and promised to love him more fondly than ever. She told him that her vanity had not been flattered by what most girls might have thought an honour, that she would rather have the love of one good man like her father, than share with others the affections of a king.

After listening to his daughter, the viceroy sent a respectful answer to the palace, thanking the Emperor for his favour, but saying he could not give up Ta-ki. "She is unworthy of the honour you purpose doing her," he said, in conclusion, "for, having been the apple of her father's eye, she would not be happy to share even your most august favour with the many others you have chosen."

When the Emperor learned of Su-nan's reply he could hardly believe his ears. To have his command thus disobeyed was an unheard-of crime. Never before had a subject of the Middle Kingdom offered such an insult to a ruler. Boiling with rage, he ordered his prime minister to send forth an army that would bring the viceroy to his senses. "Tell him if he disobeys that he and his family, together with all they possess, shall be destroyed."

Delighted at the success of his plot against Su-nan, the Prime Minister sent a regiment of soldiers to bring the rebel to terms. In the meantime the friends of the daring viceroy had not been idle. Hearing of the danger threatening their ruler, who had become a general favourite, hundreds of men offered him their aid against the army of Chow-sin. Thus when the Emperor's banners were seen approaching and the war drums were heard rolling in the distance, the rebels, with a great shout, dashed forth to do battle for their leader. In the fight that took place the Imperial soldiers were forced to run.

When the Emperor heard of this defeat he was hot with anger. He called together his advisers and commanded that an army, double the size of the first one, should be sent to Su-nan's country to destroy the fields and villages of the people who had risen up against him. "Spare not one of them," he shouted, "for they are traitors to the Dragon Throne."

Once more the viceroy's friends resolved to support him, even to the death. Ta-ki, his daughter, went apart from the other members of the family, weeping most bitterly that she had brought such sorrow upon them. "Rather would I go into the palace and be the lowest among Chow-sin's women than to be the cause of all this grief," she cried, in desperation.

But her father soothed her, saying, "Be of good cheer, Ta-ki. The Emperor's army, though it be twice as large as mine, shall not overcome us. Right is on our side. The gods of battle will help those who fight for justice."

One week later a second battle was fought, and the struggle was so close that none could foresee the result. The Imperial army was commanded by the oldest nobles in the kingdom, those most skilled in warfare, while the viceroy's men were young and poorly drilled. Moreover, the members of the Dragon Army had been promised double pay if they should accomplish the wishes of their sovereign, while Su-nan's soldiers knew only too well that they would be put to the sword if they should be defeated.

Just as the clash of arms was at its highest, the sound of gongs was heard upon a distant hill. The government troops were amazed at seeing fresh companies marching to the rescue of their foe. With a wild cry of disappointment they turned and fled from the field. These unexpected reinforcements turned out to be women whom Ta-ki had persuaded to dress up as soldiers and go with her for the purpose of frightening the enemy. Thus for a second time was Su-nan victorious.

During the following year several battles occurred that counted for little, except that in each of them many of Su-nan's followers were killed. At last one of the viceroy's best friends came to him, saying, "Noble lord, it is useless to continue the struggle. I fear you must give up the fight. You have lost more than half your supporters; the remaining bowmen are either sick or wounded and can be of little use. The Emperor, moreover, is even now raising a new army from the distant provinces, and will soon send against us a force ten times as great as any we have yet seen. There being no hope of victory, further fighting would be folly. Lead, therefore, your daughter to the palace. Throw yourself upon the mercy of the throne. You must accept cheerfully the fate the gods have suffered you to bear."

Ta-ki, chancing to overhear this conversation, rushed in and begged her father to hold out no longer, but to deliver her up to the greed of the wicked Chow-sin.

With a sigh, the viceroy yielded to their wishes. The next day he despatched a messenger to the Emperor, promising to bring Ta-ki at once to the capital.

Now we must not forget Fox Sprite, the demon, who had been commanded by the good goddess Lu-o to bring a dreadful punishment upon the Emperor. Through all the years of strife between Chow-sin and the rebels, Fox Sprite had been waiting patiently for his chance. He knew well that some day, sooner or later, there would come an hour when Chow-sin would be at his mercy. When the time came, therefore, for Ta-ki to go to the palace, Fox Sprite felt that at last his chance had come. The beautiful maiden for whom Chow-sin had given up so many hundreds of his soldiers, would clearly have great power over the Emperor. She must be made to help in the punishment of her wicked husband. So Fox Sprite made himself invisible and travelled with the viceroy's party as it went from central China to the capital.

On the last night of their journey Su-nan and his daughter stopped for rest and food at a large inn. No sooner had the girl gone to her room for the night than Fox Sprite followed her. Then he made himself visible. At first she was frightened to see so strange a being in her room, but when Fox Sprite told her he was a servant of the great goddess, Lu-o, she was comforted, for she knew that Lu-o was the friend of women and children.

"But how can I help to punish the Emperor?" she faltered, when the sprite told her he wanted her assistance. "I am but a helpless girl," and here she began to cry.

"Dry your tears," he said soothingly. "It will be very easy. Only let me take your form for a little. When I am the Emperor's wife," laughing, "I shall find a way to punish him, for no one can give a man more pain that his wife can, if she desires to do so. You know, I am a servant of Lu-o and can do anything I wish."

"But the Emperor won't have a fox for a wife," she sobbed.

"Though I am still a fox I shall look like the beautiful Ta-ki. Make your heart easy. He will never know."

"Oh, I see," she smiled, "you will put your spirit into my body and you will look just like me, though you really won't be me. But what will become of the real me? Shall I have to be a fox and look like you?"

"No, not unless you want to. I will make you invisible, and you can be ready to go back into your own body when I have got rid of the Emperor."

"Very well," replied the girl, somewhat relieved by his explanation, "but try not to be too long about it, because I don't like the idea of somebody else walking about in my body."

So Fox Sprite caused his own spirit to enter the girl's body, and no one could have told by her outward appearance that any change had taken place. The beautiful girl was now in reality the sly Fox Sprite, but in one way only did she look like a fox. When the fox-spirit entered her body, her feet suddenly shrivelled up and became very similar in shape and size to the feet of the animal who had her in his power. When the fox noticed this, at first he was somewhat annoyed, but, feeling that no one else would know, he did not take the trouble to change the fox feet back to human form.

On the following morning, when the viceroy called his daughter for the last stage of their journey, he greeted Fox Sprite without suspecting that anything unusual had happened since he had last seen Ta-ki. So well did this crafty spirit perform his part that the father was completely deceived, by look, by voice, and by gesture.

The next day the travellers arrived at the capital and Su-nan presented himself before Chow-sin, the Emperor, leading Fox Sprite with him. Of course the crafty fox with all his magic powers was soon able to gain the mastery over the wicked ruler. The Great One pardoned Su-nan, although he had fully intended to put him to death as a rebel.

Now the chance for which Fox Sprite had been waiting had come. He began at once, causing the Emperor to do many deeds of violence. The people had already begun to dislike Chow-sin, and soon he became hateful in their sight. Many of the leading members of the court were put to death unjustly. Horrible tortures were devised for punishing those who did not find favour with the crown. At last there was open talk of a rebellion. Of course, all these things delighted the wily fox, for he saw that, sooner or later, the Son of Heaven would be turned out of the palace, and he knew that then his work for the goddess Lu-o would be finished.

Besides worming his way into the heart of the Emperor, the fox became a general favourite with the ladies of the palace. These women saw in Chow-sin's latest wife the most beautiful woman who had ever lived in the royal harem. One would think that this beauty might have caused them to hate Fox Sprite, but such was not the case. They admired the plumpness of Fox Sprite's body, the fairness of Fox Sprite's complexion, the fire in Fox Sprite's eyes, but most of all they wondered at the smallness of Fox Sprite's feet, for, you remember, the supposed Ta-ki now had fox's feet instead of those of human shape.

Thus small feet became the fashion among women. All the court ladies, old and young, beautiful and ugly, began thinking of plans for making their own feet as tiny as those of Fox Sprite. In this way they thought to increase their chances of finding favour with the Emperor.

Gradually people outside the palace began to hear of this absurd fashion. Mothers bound the feet of their little girls, in such a manner as to stop their growth. The bones of the toes were bent backwards and broken, so eager were the elders to have their daughters grow up into tiny-footed maidens. Thus, for several years of their girlhood the little ones were compelled to endure the most severe tortures. It was not long before the new fashion took firm root in China. It became almost impossible for parents to get husbands for their daughters unless the girls had suffered the severe pains of foot-binding. And even to this day we find that many of the people are still under the influence of Fox Sprite's magic, and believe that a tiny, misshapen foot is more beautiful than a natural one.

But let us return to the story of Fox Sprite and the wicked Emperor. For a number of years matters grew continually worse in the country. At last the people rose in a body against the ruler.

A great battle was fought. The wicked Chow-sin was overthrown and put to death by means of those very instruments of torture he had used so often against his subjects. By this time it had become known to all the lords and noblemen that the Emperor's favourite had been the main cause of their ruler's wickedness; hence they demanded the death of Fox Sprite. But no one wished to kill so lovely a creature. Everyone appointed refused to do the deed.

Finally, a grey-headed member of the court allowed himself to be blindfolded. With a sharp sword he pierced the body of Fox Sprite to the heart. Those standing near covered their eyes with their hands, for they could not bear to see so wonderful a woman die. Suddenly, as they looked up, they saw a sight so strange that all were filled with amazement. Instead of falling to the ground, the graceful form swayed backward and forward for a moment, when all at once there seemed to spring from her side a huge mountain fox. The animal glanced around him, then, with a cry of fear, dashing past officials, courtiers and soldiers, he rushed through the gate of the enclosure.

"A fox!" cried the people, full of wonder.

At that moment Ta-ki fell in a swoon upon the floor. When they picked her up, thinking, of course, that she had died from the sword thrust, they could find no blood on her body, and, on looking more closely, they saw that there was not even the slightest wound.

"Marvel of marvels!" they all shouted. "The gods have shielded her!"

Just then Ta-ki opened her eyes and looked about her. "Where am I?" she asked, in faint voice. "Pray tell me what has happened."

Then they told her what they had seen, and at last it was plain to the beautiful woman that, after all these years, Fox Sprite had left her body. She was herself once more. For a long time she could not make the people believe her story; they all said that she must have lost her mind; that the gods had saved her life, but had punished her for her wickedness by taking away her reason.

But that night, when her maids were undressing her in the palace, they saw her feet, which had once more become their natural size, and then they knew she had been telling the truth.

How Ta-ki became the wife of a good nobleman who had long admired her great beauty is much too long a story to be told here. Of one thing, however, we are certain, that she lived long and was happy ever afterwards.

Prince Sandalwood, the Father of Korea

FOUR LITTLE FOLKS lived in the home of Mr. Kim, two girls and two boys. Their names were Peach Blossom and Pearl, Eight-fold Strength and Dragon. Dragon was the oldest, a boy. Grandma Kim was very fond of telling them stories about the heroes and fairies of their beautiful country.

One evening when Papa Kim came home from his office in the Government buildings, he carried two little books in his hand, which he handed over to Grandma. One was a little almanac looking in its bright cover of red, green and blue as gay as the piles of cakes and confectionery made when people get married; for every one knows how rich in colors are pastry and sweets for the bride's friends at a Korean wedding party.

The second little book contained the direction sent out by the Royal Minister of Ceremonies for the celebration of the festival in honor of the Ancestor-Prince, Old Sandalwood, the Father of Korea. Twice a year in Ping Yang City they made offerings of meat and other food in his honor, but always uncooked.

"Who was old Sandalwood?" asked Peach Blossom, the older of the little girls.

"What did he do?" asked Yongi (Dragon), the older boy.

"Let me tell you," said Grandma, as they cuddled together round her on the oiled-paper carpet over the main flue at the end of the room where it was warmest; for it was early in December and the wind was roaring outside.

"Now I shall tell you, also, why the bear is good and the tiger bad," said Grandma. "Well, to begin—

"Long, long ago, before there were any refined people in the Land of Dawn, and no men but rude savages, a bear and a tiger met together. It was on the southern slope of Old Whitehead Mountain in the forest. These wild animals were not satisfied with the kind of human beings already on the earth, and they wanted better ones. They thought that if they could become human they would be able to improve upon the quality. So these patriotic beasts, the bear and the tiger, agreed to go before Hananim, the Great One of Heaven and Earth, and ask him to change at once their form and nature; or, at least, tell them how it could be done.

"But where to find Him – that was the question. So they put their heads down in token of politeness, stretched out their paws and waited a long while, hoping to get light on the subject.

"Then a Voice spoke out saying, 'Eat a bunch of garlic and stay in a cave for twenty-one days. If you do, you will become human.'

"So into the dark cave they crawled, chewed their garlic and went to sleep.

"It was cold and gloomy in the cave and with nothing to hunt or eat, the tiger got tired. Day after day he moped, snarled, growled and behaved rudely to his companion. But the bear bore the tiger's insults.

"Finally on the eleventh day, the tiger, seeing no signs of losing his stripes or of shedding his hair, claws or tail, and with no prospect of fingers or toes in view, concluded to give up trying to become a man. He bounded out of the cave and at once went hunting in the woods, going back to his old life.

"But the bear, patiently sucking her paw, waited till the twenty-one days had passed. Then her hairy hide and claws dropped off, like an overcoat. Her nose and ears suddenly shortened and she stood upright – a perfect woman.

"Walking out of the cave the new creature sat beside a brook, and in the pure water beheld how lovely she was. There she waited to see what would take place next.

"About this time while these things were going on down in the world matters of interest were happening in the skies. Whanung, the Son of the Great One in the Heavens, asked his father to give him an earthly kingdom to rule over. Pleased with his request, the Lord of Heaven decided to present his son with the Land of the Dragon's Back, which men called Korea.

"Now as everybody knows, this country of ours, the Everlasting Great Land of the Dayspring, rose up on the first morning of creation out of the sea, in the form of a dragon. His spine, loins and tail form the great range of mountains that makes the backbone of our beautiful country, while his head rises skyward in the eternal White Mountain in the North. On its summit amid the snow and ice lies the blue lake of pure water, from which flow out our boundary rivers."

"What is the name of this lake?" asked Yongi the boy.

"The Dragon's Pool," said Grandma Kim, "and during one whole night, ever so long ago, the dragon breathed hard and long until its breath filled the heavens with clouds. This was the way that the Great One in the Skies prepared the way for his son's coming to earth.

"People thought there was an earthquake, but when they woke up in the morning and looked up to the grand mountain, so gloriously white, they saw the cloud rising far up in the sky. As the bright sun shone upon it, the cloud turned into pink, red, yellow and the whole eastern sky looked so lovely that our country then received its name – the Land of Morning Radiance.

"Down out of his cloud of many colors, and borne on the wind, Whanung, the Heavenly Prince, descended first to the mountain top, and then to the lower earth. When he entered the great forest he found a beautiful woman sitting by the brookside. It was the bear that had been transformed into lovely human shape and nature.

"The Heavenly Prince was delighted. He chose her as his bride and, by and by, a little baby boy was born.

"The mother made for her son a cradle of soft moss and reared her child in the forest.

"Now the people who dwelt at the foot of the mountain were in those days very rude and simple. They wore no hats, had no white clothes, lived in huts, and did not know how to warm their houses with flues running under the floors, nor had they any books or writings. Their sacred place was under a sandalwood tree, on a small mountain named Tabak, in Ping Yang province.

"They had seen the cloud rising from the Dragon's Pool so rich in colors, and as they looked they saw it move southward and nearer to them, until it stood over the sacred sandalwood tree; when out stepped a white-robed being, and descending through the air alighted in the forest and on the tree.

"Oh, how beautiful this spirit looked against the blue sky! Yet the tree was far away and long was the journey to it.

"'Let us all go to the sacred tree,' said the leader of the people. So together they hied over hill and valley until they reached the holy ground and ranged themselves in circles about it.

"A lovely sight greeted their eyes. There sat under the tree a youth of grand appearance, arrayed in princely dress. Though young looking and rosy in face, his countenance was august and majestic. Despite his youth, he was wise and venerable.

"'I have come from my ancestors in Heaven to rule over you, my children,' he said, looking at them most kindly.

"At once the people fell on their knees and all bent reverently, shouting:

"'Thou art our king, we acknowledge thee, and will loyally obey only thee.'

"Seeing that they wanted to know what he could tell them, he began to instruct them, even before he gave them laws and rules and taught them how to improve their houses. He told them stories. The first one explained to them why it was that the bear is good and the tiger bad.

"The people wondered at his wisdom, and henceforth the tiger was hated, while people began to like the bear more and more.

"'What name shall we give our King, so that we may properly address him?' asked the people of their elders. 'It is right that we should call him after the place in which we saw him, under our holy tree. Let his title, therefore, be the August and Venerable Sandalwood.' So they saluted him thus and he accepted the honor.

"Seeing that the people were rough and unkempt, Prince Sandalwood showed them how to tie up and dress their hair. He ordained that men should wear their long locks in the form of a topknot. Boys must braid their hair and let it hang down over their backs. No boy could be called a man, until he married a wife. Then he could twist his hair into a knot, put on a hat, have a headdress like an adult and wear a long white coat.

"As for the women, they must plait their tresses and wear them plainly at their neck, except at marriage, or on great occasions of ceremony. Then they might pile up their hair like a pagoda and use long hairpins, jewels, silk and flowers.

"Thus our Korean civilization was begun, and to this day the law of the hat and hair distinguishes us above all people," said Grandma. "We still honor the August and Venerable Prince Sandalwood. Now, good-night, my darlings."

The Life of Buddha

IT WAS IN the fifth century, when Prince Gautama was born in Kapiavastu, the capital of Shakya. The Raja at this time was Suddhodana and he was married to the two daughters of the Raja of the neighbouring tribe, the Koiyans. There are many myths which set out the birth of Buddha, each subsequent version more splendid and divine. Queen Maya, wife of Suddhodana, recounts a dream in which she saw a white elephant lowered from heaven, and how the moon itself fell into her lap, a ball of pure, white light. And when the birth occurred, Buddha was thrust from her side, like the opening of the letter 'B'.

Now the young prince was born into great luxury, and he was cosseted and adored by the household on all sides. When he learned to walk there were arms outstretched in every direction, but the young prince shunned them all and took seven steps to the north, seven steps to the east, seven steps to the south and seven steps to the west, which signalled to all his spiritual conquest of the earth.

The prince was trained in every sport, becoming an expert in all kinds of martial skills. He was well versed in the arts, and he married, at a very early age, Yasodhara, who he won in a contest at the age of only sixteen. It was not long after this marriage that Yasodhara bore him a son, who he named Rahula.

Gautama lived the life of a normal Indian ruler, eating and drinking plenty, and finding great pleasure in the women the place offered. He had concubines and a chariot that took him far and wide. Although he was a wise man, he thought little about the world around him for it had been his oyster for as long as he could remember and he polished his own little pearl daily, enjoying what he saw in his reflection.

One day, as Gautama was out in his chariot with his respected confidante and charioteer Channa, he spied an old man shuffling along the earth and mumbling to himself. He leant heavily on his stick and clearly had some difficulty moving at all. Channa said wisely, "Ah, that shall be the fate of all of us one day."

Several days later Gautama was out once again with Channa, and he saw a man lying poor and ill in the gutter. He expressed some surprise that a man could be in such a state and asked Channa how this had happened.

Channa spoke wisely, "Ah, this shall be the fate of all of us. Suffering comes to us all."

It was on their third such trip that Gautama saw the body of a man who had recently died. He looked puzzled for such occurrences were not the common sight of princes. Any ugliness like illness and death had been swept from his sight until now.

Channa spoke wisely, "Ah, this shall be the fate of us all."

Now Gautama was deeply affected by his three experiences and it caused him to spend many long hours pondering his condition, and the fate that would eventually befall him – and them all. He found no pleasure in his food or drink. He left his women in peace and he decided that there was nothing lasting or true in his life. And so it was decided that he would leave his palaces and all the trappings of his life to live a life of meditation and solitude.

Later that night, by the glow of the silver moon, he ordered Channa to saddle his favourite horse Kanthaka, and they rode away from the palace, silently escaping from a life that Gautama now knew he could not live. The gods had smiled on him and his enlightenment, and they helped quiet the hooves of his horse so that the sound of their clatter on the flagstones would not waken his family. Without a whisper, the men left, Channa accompanying Gautama until they reached the edge of the forest. And there, stripping himself of his finery, the prince said good-bye to his dear companion and to his life. At the age of just twenty-nine, Gautama had left it all.

In the wilds of the Indian countryside, the prince lost himself to the world. For many years he sat in meditation. The gods sent him many temptations, including the daughters of Mara, the goddess of seduction, whose wiry bodies writhed and danced, offering him pleasures for which he had at one time hungered. But he resisted them all, for within Gautama was a new calm. He was on the verge of enlightenment.

Gautama fasted for long periods, until he realized the need for food. Reaching out, he plucked the fruit of the fig tree and in its leafy shade he achieved complete bodhi, or enlightenment.

His philosophy had been worked out in his meditations, and all had become clear. He knew now that desire was the root of evil, of anger and violence. He realized that desire made fools of man, chasing money and women and an afterlife. He realized that a person who cannot control desire goes through chains of existences – birth and then death and then birth again, over and over. This was a wheel which could be stopped; this was a chain which could be broken. By suppressing desire, links of the chain can be removed, and instead of there being rebirth after death, there would be the state of nirvana, where there could be no suffering, no more death, no more births.

And so the supreme Buddha took it upon himself to go back into the world, to preach his new wisdom. He could, then, have given himself over to nirvana but his calling drew him to spread the message, to reach out as a teacher to the people who needed deliverance from the unholy waste that their lives had become.

Buddha walked to Varanasi, where he dressed himself in yellow robes – a personification of the sunlight which flowed through his veins and fed his wisdom. He returned to Kapiavastu, and there he appeared to his own people, joined by his son Rahula. For the next forty-five years, Buddha wandered and preached. Animosity and anger were quietened by his gentle words – even the most ferocious of animals bowed to his touch.

The Origin of the Three Races

HAVING RESOLVED TO create a new species, the Great Spirit took himself off to a place of solitude and began the labour that was to last him several days. He toiled long and hard and at length he produced a being, different from anything else he had ever before created. The figure, whose skin was black as the night, enthralled the Great Spirit, and at first he was deeply satisfied with his work. But soon, he felt that a single example of the new species was not enough and he decided to embark upon a second attempt, hopeful that the result would bring him equal pleasure.

On the next occasion, his creation proved to be a being with a red skin colour. Placing him alongside his brother, the Great Spirit smiled. He was even more pleased with the fruits of his labour, but once again, after only a short time, he became anxious to try his hand a third time.

"This will be my last effort," he told himself, and he wandered off to complete his final creation. The being he produced this time had a white skin colour, far lighter than the other two. It proved to be the Great Spirit's favourite, and so utterly satisfied him that he spent several minutes turning it over in the palm of his hand before releasing it to the company of its two elder brothers.

Calling the three men before him one day soon afterwards, the Great Spirit pointed to three boxes lying in the earth. The first box contained books, papers and quills; the second was filled with bows and arrows, tomahawks and spears; the third held a collection of spades, axes, hoes and hammers. The Great Spirit then addressed his children with these words:

"My sons, what you see before you are the means by which you shall live. Each of you must choose one of the boxes for your future use." And saying this, he beckoned to his favourite, the white man, instructing him to make the first choice.

The youngest brother passed by the working-tools, the axes, hoes and hammers, without paying them any attention whatsoever and moved towards the weapons of war and hunting. Here, he hesitated, lifting a number of them from the box so that he might examine them more closely. The red-skinned brother trembled, for with his whole heart he longed to take possession of these instruments and feared that he was close to losing them. But the white man deliberated only a moment longer and then passed swiftly on to the box of books and writing tools, signalling to the Great Spirit that he had finally reached his decision.

The red-skinned brother came next, and he sprang forward and immediately seized upon the bows and arrows, the tomahawks and spears, delighted with himself that he was now the owner of so valuable a collection.

Last of all, the black man stepped forward, the Great Spirit's first offspring. Having no choice left, he lifted the remaining box filled with tools of the land and humbly carried it all the way back to his dwelling.

It was in this manner, according to ancient Seminole legend, that the three races came into being.

The Origin of Women

THERE WAS A time, when, throughout the Island, neither on land nor in the water, in field or forest, was there a woman to be found. Vain things were plenty – there was the turkey, and the swan, and the blue jay, and the wood-duck, and the wakon bird; and noisy, chattering, singing creatures, such as the daw, and the thrush, and the rook, and the prairie-dog, abounded – indeed there were more of each than was pleasing to the ear – but of women, vain, noisy, laughing, chattering women, there were none. It was, indeed, quite a still world to what it is now. Whether it is better and happier, will depend much upon the opinion men entertain of those, who have changed its character from calm and peaceable to boisterous and noisy. Some will think it is much improved by the circumstance which deprived the Kickapoos of their tails – while others will greatly deplore its occurrence.

At the time of which I am telling my brother, the Kickapoos, and indeed all red men, wherever found – and at that time there were none but red men in the world – were furnished with long tails like horses and buffaloes. It was very handy to have these appendages in a country where flies were numerous and troublesome, as they were in the land of the Kickapoos – tails being much more sudden in their movements than hands, and more conveniently situated, as every body must see, for whisking off the flies which light upon the back. Then they were very beautiful things, these long tails, especially when handsomely painted and ornamented, as their owners used to ornament them, with beads, and shells, and wampum – and being intended as a natural decoration to the creature, the depriving him of it may well have produced, as it did, a great deal of sport and merriment among the other animals, who were not compelled to submit to the deprivation. The fox, who is rather impudent, for a long time after they were chopped off, sent to the Kickapoos every day to enquire "how their tails were;" and the bear shook his fat sides with laughter at the joke, which he thought a very good one, of sending one of his cubs with a request for a "dozen spare tails."

I have said, that throughout the land there were no women. There were men – a plenty, the land was thronged with them – not born, but created of clay – and left to bake in the sun till they received life – and these men were very contented and happy. Wars were very few then, for no one need be told that half the wars which have arisen have grown out of quarrels on account of love of women, and the other half on account of their maintenance. There was universal peace and harmony throughout the land. The Kickapoos ate their deer's flesh with the Potowatomies, hunted the otter with the Osages, and the beaver with the Hurons; and the fierce Iroquois, instead of waking the wild shout of war, went to the land of the Sauks and Ioways to buy wampum, wherewith to decorate their tails. Happy would it have been for the red men if they were still furnished with these appendages, and wanted those which have been supplied in their place – women!

But the consequence which usually attends prosperity happened to the Indians. They became very proud and vain, and forgot their creator and preserver. They no more offered the fattest and choicest of their game upon the memahoppa, or altar-stone, nor evinced any gratitude, nor sung, nor danced in his praise, when he sent his rains to cleanse the earth and his lightnings to cool and purify the air. When their corn grew ripe and tall, they imputed it to their own good conduct and management; when their hunt was successful, to their own skill and perseverance. Reckoning not, as in times past, of the superintendence of the Great Spirit over all things, they banished him altogether from their proud and haughty hearts, teaching them to forget that there was aught greater or more powerful than himself.

Though slow to anger, and waiting long before he remembers the provocations he has received, the Great Spirit, in the end, and when no atonement is made, always inflicts an adequate punishment for every offence. Seeing how wicked the Indians had become, he said to his Manitous: "It is time that the Kickapoos and other red men were punished. They laugh at my thunders, they make mock of my lightnings and hurricanes, they use my bounties without thanking me for them. When their corn grows ripe and tall, instead of imputing its luxuriance to my warm suns and reviving showers, they say, 'We have managed it well;' when their hunt is successful, they place it to account of their own skill and perseverance. Reckoning not, as in times past, of my superintendence over all things, they have banished me altogether from their haughty hearts, and taught themselves to forget that there is aught greater and more powerful than the Indian."

So saying, he bade his chief Manitou repair to the dwelling-places of the red men, and, to punish them for their wickedness, deprive them of that which they most valued, and bestow upon them a scourge and affliction adequate to their offences. The Spirit obeyed his master, and descended to the earth, lighting down upon the lands occupied by the Kickapoos. It was not long before he discovered what it was which that people and the other Indians most valued. He saw, from the pains they took in decorating their tails with gay paints, and beads, and shells, and wampum, that they prized them above every other possession. Calling together all the red men, he acquainted them with the will of his master, and demanded the instant sacrifice of the article upon which they set so much value. It is impossible to describe the sorrow and compunction which filled their bosoms, when they found that the forfeit for their wickedness was to be that beautiful and beloved appendage. But their prayers and entreaties, to be spared the humiliation and sacrifice, were in vain. The Spirit was inexorable, and they were compelled to place their tails on the block and to behold them amputated.

The punishment being in part performed, the Spirit next bethought himself of a gift which should prove to them "a scourge and affliction adequate to their offences." It was to convert the tails thus lopped off into vain, noisy, chattering, laughing creatures, whose faces should he like the sky in the Moon of Plants, and whose hearts should be treacherous, fickle, and inconstant; yet, strange to relate, who should be loved above all other things on the earth or in the skies. For them should life often be hazarded – reputation, fame, and virtue, often forfeited – pain and ignominy incurred. They were to be as a burden placed on the shoulders of an already overloaded man; and yet, a burden he would rather strive to carry than abandon. He further appointed that they should retain the frisky nature of the material from which they were made, and they have retained it to this day.

The Great Spirit, deeming that the trouble wherewith he had provided the red man would not sufficiently vex and punish him, determined to add another infliction, whose sting, though not so potent and irksome, should be without any alleviation whatever. He sent great swarms of mosquitoes. Deprived of tails, by which flies could be brushed away at the pleasure of the wearers, the Indians dragged out for a long time a miserable existence. The mosquitoes stung them, and their tails teased them. The little insects worried them continually, and their frisky companions, the women, were any thing but a cup of composing drink. At length the Great Spirit, seeing how the poor Indians were afflicted, mercifully withdrew the greater part of the mosquitoes, leaving a few as a memorial of the pest which had formerly annoyed them. The Kickapoos petitioned that the women should also be taken away from them, and their old appendages returned – but the Great Spirit answered, that women were a necessary evil, and must remain.

The Old Chippeway

THE OLD MAN Chippeway, the first of men, when he first landed on the earth, near where the present Dogribs have their hunting-grounds, found the world a beautiful world, well stocked with food, and abounding with pleasant things. He found no man, woman, or child upon it; but in time, being lonely, he created children, to whom he gave two kinds of fruit, the black and the white, but he forbade them to eat the black. Having given his commands for the government and guidance of his family, he took leave of them for a time, to go into a far country where the sun dwelt, for the purpose of bringing it to the earth. After a very long journey, and a long absence, he returned, bringing with him the sun, and he was delighted to find that his children had remained obedient, and had eaten only of the white food.

Again he left them to go on another expedition. The sun he had brought lighted up the earth for only a short time, and in the land from which he had brought it he had noticed another body, which served as a lamp in the dark hours. He resolved therefore to journey and bring back with him the moon; so, bidding adieu to his children and his dwelling, he set forth once more. While he had been absent on his first expedition, his children had eaten up all the white food, and now, when he set out, he forgot to provide them with a fresh supply. For a long time they resisted the craving for food, but at last they could hold out no longer, and satisfied their hunger with the black fruit.

The old Chippeway soon returned, bringing with him the moon. He soon discovered that his children had transgressed his command, and had eaten the food of disease and death. He told them what was the consequence of their act – that in future the earth would produce bad fruits, that sickness would come amongst men, that pain would rack them, and their lives be lives of fatigue and danger.

Having brought the sun and moon to the earth, the old man Chippeway rested, and made no more expeditions. He lived an immense number of years, and saw all the troubles he declared would follow the eating of the black food. At last he became tired of life, and his sole desire was to be freed from it.

"Go," said he, to one of his sons, "to the river of the Bear Lake, and fetch me a man of the little wise people (the beavers). Let it be one with a brown ring round the end of the tail, and a white spot on the tip of the nose. Let him be just two seasons old upon the first day of the coming frog-moon, and see that his teeth be sharp."

The man did as he was directed. He went to the river of the Bear Lake, and brought a man of the little wise people. He had a brown ring round the end of his tail, and a white spot on the tip of his nose. He was just two seasons old upon the first day of the frog-moon, and his teeth were very sharp.

"Take the wise four-legged man," said the old Chippeway, "and pull from his jaws seven of his teeth."

The man did as he was directed, and brought the teeth to the old man. Then he bade him call all his people together, and when they were come the old man thus addressed them –

"I am old, and am tired of life, and wish to sleep the sleep of death. I will go hence. Take the seven teeth of the wise little four-legged man and drive them into my body."

They did so, and as the last tooth entered him the old man died.

The Coyote or Prairie Wolf

IN THE BEGINNING, when the Káruks lived on the shores of the Klamath River, beyond the desert of the sage-brush and far from the Rocky mountains, on towards the falling place of the sun, they had many good gifts. Their forests were noble and their deer were stately and fat. The bear was fierce, but his flesh was sweet and life-giving, and the Káruks grew strong by feeding upon it. But they longed for the gift of fire. In the evening when the beautiful red appeared in the sky they looked and looked upon it and wished that they might catch just one spark from the fagots in the heavens.

All the fire in the world at that time was held by two old hags who lived at the mouth of the river and watched it with jealous care. They also held the key of the dam that kept back the shining salmon.

The Káruks hated the old women and sought for some way to deceive them, so that they might loose the salmon, but most of all they wanted the precious fire. They lay and shivered under the thick bear-skin robes, for the nights were long and cold in their country, and the north wind blew in their faces and cut them sharply with his spears of ice and his arrows of snow.

They tried many times to steal the fire. Those rich in wampum offered to buy it, while some who were cunning attempted to wheedle the old hags into giving it to them, but all to no purpose. At last they thought of asking the animals to help them. But who so cunning and so brave as to undertake the task? The bear was too clumsy and growled too much, the elk was too tall and his antlers would strike against the lodge pole of the wigwam; the dog was not wise, and the serpent was never known to do good to the Káruks or to any man.

The council sat and smoked and thought about the matter and at last decided to ask the Coyote, for he was lean and hungry and might be glad to earn some food. Moreover, he would feel proud to have the Káruks ask a favor of him, for even the meanest beast despised him because he had such hard work to get a living.

So they went to see the Coyote. His home was in the deserts halfway to the mountains, where he cowered behind the sage-brush, from whence he kept a sharp lookout for blood spilled by the hunter, the flesh that he threw away, or animals small and weak enough for him to be able to capture. The Coyote must forever go hungry, for when the animals were let loose upon the earth and each sprang upon its prey, the mountain sheep which was given to the Coyote dodged him, and ever since all coyotes blunder in the chase.

The Káruks found him sniffing at the ground for the hunter's trail. He felt flattered when he knew that they had come to see him, but he was far too cunning to show it. They explained their errand, but he would not promise to do anything. He took the food that they offered him, some dog's meat, buffalo steaks, and bear's kidney, dainties that the Káruks gave to an honored guest. Then he could no longer conceal his pleasure, nor refuse to do what they asked of him.

He did not need to hunt that night, so he curled himself up snugly, put his nose under his paws, whisked his tail about to keep his feet warm, and for the first time in his life was really comfortable. He soon fell asleep, but not before he had made up his mind that it would be well to do his best for the Káruks; it was much better than hunting in the desert.

The next morning he set out early to secure help from other animals, for he could not do the thing alone. The smaller ones did not dare to refuse him, and the larger ones felt sorry for the poor creature, and were willing to be of use to him.

The Coyote placed a frog nearest to the camp of the Káruks, then a squirrel, a bat, a bear, and a cougar at certain measured distances, arranged in proportion to their strength and to the roughness of the road. Last of all a Káruk was told to hide in the bushes near the hut where the old hags lived.

Then the Coyote walked slowly up to the door and scratched for admittance. One of the sisters went to see what was wanted and she let him in; they were surely not afraid of a miserable coyote. He walked wearily to the center of the lodge, where he dropped down as if tired out, and shivered so that he shook the very lodge pole.

The two old hags who sat by the fire, cooking salmon turned to look at him, and one of them said: "Come up near the fire if you are cold," and she made room for him directly in front of the blaze.

He dragged himself to it and lay with his head upon his paws. When he grew uncomfortably warm he gave two short barks as a signal to the man outside.

The old hags thought he barked because he enjoyed the fire. "Ha! ha!" they said, "wouldn't the Káruks like this?"

Just then there was a fearful noise of hammering and of stones striking the lodge. The old women rushed out to drive the enemy away.

Instantly the Coyote seized a half-burnt stick of wood and fled like a comet down the trail in the forest. The hags pursued him; but when he heard their shrieks he ran all the faster.

Nearer and nearer they came, now they were almost upon him and his strength was fast giving out. By a great effort he flung the brand from him, just as they put out their hands to catch him.

The Cougar seized it and ran with long bounds down the winding road. The hags followed, but were no match for him and he had no trouble in handing it over to the Bear.

The Bear was very awkward and dropped it several times from his clumsy paws, so that the old women gained upon him rapidly; and had it not been that the Bat seized it and flew high in the air quite unexpectedly, the Káruks would never have got the fire. As for the old Bear, he rolled over against the tree exhausted.

The Bat led the hags a roundabout chase over trees, now flying high, now close to their very heads, until he nearly tired them out.

They took courage when they saw the Squirrel spring forward to catch the stick that the Bat let fall from a great height. "Surely we can catch him," they said; and they gathered their skirts about them and pursued him with furious haste.

All this time the brand was burning and it grew so hot that the Squirrel could hardly hold it. But he was a brave, little fellow and hopped and jumped steadily on through the woods, though his tail was burnt so badly that it curled up over his back and shoulders. He bears the marks of the singeing to this day. Just as he thought he would have to drop it, he caught sight of the Frog. It was such a little piece by this time that the Frog could hardly take it from him, but he caught hold of it and ran on. The smoke blinded him and made his eyes smart, besides choking him so that he lost ground, and soon heard the hags close to him.

He was the last, and only a pond lay between him and the village of the Káruks. His heart thumped against his sides and he dropped the fire in order to take breath before jumping into the water, when the old women pounced upon him.

But he was too quick for them. He dodged them, swallowed the brand and jumped into the lake. They leaped after him, but it was of no use, for they could not swim. So he got away, and they had to turn back and go to their hut at the mouth of the river.

The Káruks were waiting on the edge of the pond, and when the Frog crossed they welcomed him with shouts of joy. But where was the fire? He lost no time in showing them, for he spat out the sparks upon some fagots and they quickly caught alight.

But the Frog lost his tail and it never grew again. Tadpoles still wear tails, but when they become full-grown frogs they cast them off, out of respect to their brave ancestor, who is king of all the animals that inhabit the bogs and marshes of the Klamath country.

After his success in getting the fire, the Coyote was a great favorite with the Káruks and dined off the choicest bits that were brought into the camp.

They were not satisfied even now that they had roasted meat and corn, but must needs coax the Coyote to go and get the salmon. They explained to him that the big, shining fish were all in a great dam at the mouth of the river and that the old hags from whom he had stolen the fire kept the key.

The Coyote was willing, but he said: "Wait a little till my coat changes so that the hags will not know me."

So they waited till his coat grew thin and light in color, and then when he was ready, accompanied him, with song and shouting, to the edge of the village.

He went down the Klamath many days' journey, until he reached the mouth of the river, where he saw the old hags' lodge. He rapped at the door. They were asleep by the fire, but one of them being roused by the noise, growled, "Come in."

Instead of hanging his head, drooping his tail, and looking weary, as he had done when he went to steal the fire, the Coyote held up his head, frisked his tail and grinned at them. He was of much greater importance now, and he was sleek and round from being well fed, so the hags did not know him.

They cooked salmon, but offered him none. He said nothing, for he was not hungry, having dined off food that the Káruks had prepared for him. "Ha!" he thought, "I shall soon have all the salmon I want from the Káruks."

The next morning he pretended to be asleep when the elder sister arose and went to the cupboard to get the key of the dam. She was going for salmon for breakfast. When she had left the lodge he stretched himself lazily and walked slowly towards the door. Once outside he ran after the old woman and flung himself between her feet, so that she fell down and in doing so dropped the key. He seized it, went to the dam and unlocked it.

The green water shining with silvery salmon rushed through it so fast that it broke not only the lock, but the dam itself, and thereafter the Káruks had all the salmon that they wanted.

The Coyote grew proud over his success and was not satisfied with the kindness and honor shown to him by the Káruks. He wanted to dance through heaven. He chose a bright blue Star for a partner and called out to her night after night to dance with him. At last she grew tired of his howling; so one night she told him to go to the highest point of the cliff and she would reach down far enough for him to dance with her.

He had fine sport for a while; but as she lifted him higher and higher he began to feel cold, until his paws became numb and slipped from his partner's wrist, and he fell into the great chasm that is between the sky and the earth at the edge of the world. He went down, down, until every bit of him was lost; for Coyotes could not be permitted to dance with Stars.

The First Appearance of Man

A GREAT MANY years ago the Navajos, Pueblos and the white man all lived beneath the earth's surface as one people at the place known as Cerra Naztarny, on the Rio San Juan. The underground world they lived in had no light, and in those days they survived entirely on the flesh of whatever animal they managed to capture in the darkness. But in spite of every difficulty, their world was a peaceful one. The people shared the same outlook and the same language and even the same dwelling, a large and comfortable cave, where each man lived on equal terms with his neighbour.

Among the Navajos there were two dumb men who were skilled in a great many things, but especially in the art of playing the Indian flute. One evening, the elder of the two, having reached a particularly rousing point in his performance, stood up with his flute, tilting it high in the air. Quite by accident, he cracked the instrument against the roof of the cave, producing a peculiarly hollow sound which excited his curiosity.

Determined to discover what lay above their heads, the dumb man called to a raccoon nearby, requesting his assistance. The raccoon ascended to the roof of the cave using the flute as a ladder and began digging furiously. But after a reasonable length of time, when he became convinced he was not making any progress, the raccoon came back down the ladder allowing the moth-worm to ascend in his place.

It was several hours before the moth-worm succeeded in boring through the roof, but his perseverance was rewarded when at last a tiny stream of light filtered into the cave. Wriggling through the opening he had made, he soon found himself upon a mountain, surrounded by water. He was more than pleased at the sight, and began throwing up a little mound on which to rest.

As he sat there, looking around him more attentively, he noticed four large white swans, placed at the four cardinal points, each carrying an arrow under either wing.

The swan from the north was the first to spot the little visitor, and as soon as he did so he rushed upon him, thrusting both of his arrows through the body of the moth-worm. When he saw that the arrows had drawn blood, the swan withdrew each of them and examined them closely.

"He is of my race," he then called aloud to his three brothers, and they, in turn, came forward and subjected the moth-worm to the same peculiar ceremony. After the ordeal was gone through, each of the swans resumed its former station and began tunnelling in the earth until it had created a great ditch into which the water swiftly flowed, leaving behind a mass of soft, sticky mud.

The worm carefully descended to the dumb man and related to him all that had happened. The raccoon was then sent through the hole in the roof to verify the tiny creature's story, but as soon as he leaped to the ground, he became stuck in the mud almost to his thighs, staining his paws and legs so that the black marks have remained to this day.

After a struggle, the disgruntled raccoon managed to free himself and made his way back down to the cave where the dumb man called upon the wind to come forth and blow upon the mud until it had dried out.

Once this task had been completed, a throng of men and animals gathered at the opening in the roof, anxious to explore the new world for themselves. The larger beasts poured from the cave in a steady stream and scattered directly to the plains.

The birds and smaller animals headed straightaway for the woodlands, while the people, the last to emerge, immediately separated into different groups, each with its own new language.

The Navajos, who were the first to appear, commenced a large painting in the sand. The Pueblos cut their hair and began building houses.

The white man set off towards the point where the sun rises, and was not heard from again for a great many years.

The Navajo Origin Legend: The Story of the Emergence

AT TO'BĬLHASKĬ'DI (in the middle of the first world), white arose in the east, and they regarded it as day there, they say; blue rose in the south, and still it was day to them, and they moved around; yellow rose in the west and showed that evening had come; then dark arose in the north, and they lay down and slept.

At To'bĭlhaskĭ'di water flowed out (from a central source) in different directions; one stream flowed to the east, another to the south, and another to the west. There were dwelling places on the border of the stream that flowed to the east, on that which flowed to the south, and on that which flowed to the west also.

To the east there was a place called Tan (Corn), to the south a place called Nahodoóla, and to the west a place called Lókatsosakád (Standing Reed). Again, to the east there was a place called Essalái (One Pot), to the south a place called To'hádzĭtĭl (They Come Often for Water), and to the west a place called Dsĭllĭtsíbehogán (House Made of the Red Mountain). Then, again, to the east there was a place called Léyahogán (Underground House), to the south a place called Tsĭltsĭ'ntha (Among Aromatic Sumac), and to the west a place called Tse'lĭsíbehogán (House Made of Red Rock).

Holatsí Dĭlyĭ'le (dark ants) lived there. Holatsí Lĭtsí (red ants) lived there. Tanĭlaí (dragon flies) lived there. Tsaltsá (yellow beetles) lived there. Woĭntlĭ'zi (hard beetles) lived there. Tse'yoáli (stone-carrier beetles) lived there. Kĭnlĭ'zĭn (black beetles) lived there. Maitsán (coyote-dung beetles) lived there. Tsápani (bats) lived there. Totsó' (white-faced beetles) lived there. Wonĭstsídi (locusts) lived there. Wonistsídikai (white locusts) lived there. These twelve people started in life there.

To the east extended an ocean, to the south an ocean, to the west an ocean, and to the north an ocean. In the ocean to the east lay Tiéholtsodi; he was chief of the people there. In the ocean to the south lived Thaltláhale (Blue Heron), who was chief of the people there. In the ocean to the west lay Tsal (Frog), who was chief of the people there. In the ocean to the north was Idni'dsĭlkaí (White Mountain Thunder), and he was chief of the people there.

The people quarrelled among themselves, and this is the way it happened. They committed adultery, one people with another. Many of the women were guilty. They tried to stop it, but they could not. Tiéholtsodi, the chief in the east, said, "What shall we do with them? They like not the land they dwell in." In the south Blue Heron spoke to them, and in the west Frog said, "No longer shall you dwell here, I say. I am chief here." To the north White Mountain Lightning said, "Go elsewhere at once. Depart from here!"

When again they sinned and again they quarrelled, Tiéholtsodi, in the east, would not speak to them; Blue Heron, in the south, would not speak to them; Frog, in the west, would say nothing; and White Mountain Thunder, in the north, would not speak to them.

Again, at the end of four nights, the same thing happened. Those who dwelt at the south again committed crime, and again they had contentions. One woman and one man sought to enter in the east (to complain to the chief), but they were driven out. In the south they sought to go in where Blue Heron lay, but again they were driven out. In the west, where Frog was the chief, again they tried to enter; but again they were driven out. To the north again they were driven out. The chief said, "None of you (shall enter here). Go elsewhere and keep on going." That night at Nahodoóla they held a council, but they arrived at no decision. At dawn, Tiéholtsodi began to talk. "You pay no attention to my words. Everywhere you disobey me; you must go to some other place. Not upon this earth shall you remain." Thus he spoke to them.

Among the women, for four nights they talked about it. At the end of the fourth night, in the morning, as they were rising, something white appeared in the east. It appeared also in the south, the west, and the north. It looked like a chain of mountains, without a break, stretching around them. It was water that surrounded them. Water impassable, water insurmountable, flowed all around. All at once they started.

They went in circles upward till they reached the sky. It was smooth. They looked down; but there the water had risen, and there was nothing else but water there. While they were flying around, one, having a blue head, thrust out his head from the sky and called to them, saying, "In here, to the eastward, there is a hole." They entered the hole and went through it up to the surface (of the second world).

The blue one belonged to the Hastsósidĭne', or Swallow People. The Swallow People lived there. A great many of their houses, rough and lumpy, lay scattered all around. Each tapered toward the top, and at that part there was a hole for entrance. A great many people approached and gathered around the strangers, but they said nothing.

The first world was red in colour; the second world, into which the people had now entered, was blue. They sent out two couriers, a Locust and a White Locust, to the east, to explore the land and see if there were in it any people like themselves. At the end of two days the couriers returned, and said that in one day's travel they had reached the edge of the world – the top of a great cliff that arose from an abyss whose bottom they could not see; but that they found in all their journey no people, no animals of any kind, no trees, no grass, no sage-brush, no mountains, nothing but bare, level ground. The same couriers were then dispatched in turn to the south, to the west, and to the north. They were gone on each journey two days, and when they returned related, as before, that they had reached the edge of the world, and discovered nothing but an uninhabited waste. Here, then, the strangers found themselves in the centre of a vast barren plain, where there was neither food nor a kindred people. When the couriers had returned from the north, the Swallows visited the camp of the newly arrived people, and asked them why they had sent out the couriers to the east. "We sent them out," was the reply, "to see what was in the land, and to see if there were any people like ourselves here." "And what did your couriers tell you?" asked the Swallows. "They told us that they came to the edge of the world, yet found no plant and no living thing in all the land." (The same questions were asked and the same answers given for the other points of the compass.) "They spoke the truth," said the Swallow People. "Had you asked us in the beginning what the land contained, we would have told you and saved you all your trouble. Until you came, no one has ever dwelt in all this land but ourselves." The people then said to the Swallows, "You understand our language and are much like us. You have legs, feet, bodies, heads, and wings, as we have: why cannot your people and our people become friends?" "Let it be as you wish," said the Swallows, and both parties began at once to treat each other as members of one tribe; they mingled one among the other, and addressed one another by the terms of relationship, as, my brother, my sister, my father, my son, etc.

They all lived together pleasantly and happily for twenty-three days; but on the twenty-fourth night one of the strangers made too free with the wife of the Swallow chief, and next morning, when the latter found out what had happened, he said to the strangers, "We have treated you as friends, and thus you return our kindness. We doubt not that for such crimes you were driven from the lower world, and now you must leave this. This is our land and we will have you here no longer. Besides, this is a bad land. People are dying here every day, and, even if we spare you, you cannot live here long." The Locusts took the lead on hearing this; they soared upwards; the others followed, and all soared and circled till they reached the sky.

When they reached the sky they found it, like the sky of the first world, smooth and hard with no opening; but while they were circling round under it, they saw a white face peering out at them – it was the face of Ní'ltsi, the Wind. He called to them and told them if they would fly to the south they would find a hole through which they could pass; so off they flew, as bidden, and soon they discovered a slit in the sky which slanted upwards toward the south; through this slit they flew, and soon entered the third world in the south.

The colour of the third world was yellow. Here they found nothing but the Grasshopper People. The latter gathered around the wanderers in great numbers, but said nothing. They lived in holes in the ground along the banks of a great river which flowed through their land to the east. The wanderers sent out the same Locust messengers that they had sent out in the second world to explore the land to the east, to the south, to the west, to the north, to find out what the land contained, and to see if there were any kindred people in it; but the messengers returned from each journey after an absence of two days, saying they had reached the end of the world, and that they had found a barren land with no people in it save the Grasshoppers.

When the couriers returned from their fourth journey, the two great chiefs of the Grasshoppers visited the strangers and asked them why they had sent out the explorers, and the strangers answered that they had sent them out to see what grew in the land, and to find if there were any people like themselves in it. "And what did your couriers find?" said the Grasshopper chiefs. "They found nothing save the bare land and the river, and no people but yourselves." "There is nothing else in the land," said the chiefs. "Long we have lived here, but we have seen no other people but ourselves until you came."

The strangers then spoke to the Grasshoppers, as they had spoken to the Swallows in the second world, and begged that they might join them and become one people with them. The Grasshoppers consented, and the two peoples at once mingled among one another and embraced one another, and called one another by the endearing terms of relationship, as if they were all of the same tribe.

As before, all went well for twenty-three days; but on the twenty-fourth, one of the strangers served a chief of the Grasshoppers, as the chief of the Swallows had been served in the lower world. In the morning, when the wrong was discovered, the chief reviled the strangers and bade them depart. "For such crimes," he said, "I suppose you were chased from the world below: you shall drink no more of our water, you shall breathe no more of our air. Begone!"

Up they all flew again, and circled round and round until they came to the sky above them, and they found it smooth and hard as before. When they had circled round for some time, looking in vain for an entrance, they saw a red head stuck out of the sky, and they heard a voice which told them to fly to the west. It was the head of Red Wind which they saw, and it was his voice that spoke to them. The passage which they found in the west was twisted round like the tendril of a vine; it had thus been made by the wind. They flew up in circles through it and came out in the fourth world. Four of the Grasshoppers came with them; one was white, one blue, one yellow, and one black. We have grasshoppers of these four colours with us to this day.

The surface of the fourth world was mixed black and white. The colours in the sky were the same as in the lower worlds, but they differed in their duration. In the first world, the white, the blue, the yellow, and the black all lasted about an equal length of time every day. In the second world the blue and the black lasted a little longer than the other two colours. In the third world they lasted still longer. In the fourth world there was but little of the white and yellow; the blue and the black lasted most of the time. As yet there was neither sun, moon, nor star.

When they arrived on the surface of the fourth world they saw no living thing; but they observed four great snow-covered peaks sticking up at the horizon – one at the east, one at the south, one at the west, and one at the north.

They sent two couriers to the east. These returned at the end of two days. They related that they had not been able to reach the eastern mountain, and that, though they had travelled far, they had seen no track or trail or sign of life. Two couriers were then sent to the south. When they returned, at the end of two days, they related that they had reached a low range of mountains this side of the great peak; that they had seen no living creature, but had seen two different kinds of tracks, such as they had never seen before, and they described such as the deer and the turkey make now. Two couriers were next sent to the west. In two days these returned, having failed to reach the great peak in the west, and having seen no living thing and no sign of life. At last two couriers were sent to the north. When these got back to their kindred they said they had found a race of strange men, who cut their hair square in front, who lived in houses in the ground and cultivated fields. These people, who were engaged in gathering their harvest, the couriers said, treated them very kindly and gave them food to eat. It was now evident to the wanderers that the fourth world was larger than any of the worlds below.

The day following the return of the couriers who went to the north, two of the newly discovered race – Kisáni (Pueblos) they were called – entered the camp of the exiles and guided the latter to a stream of water. The water was red, and the Kisáni told the wanderers they must not walk through the stream, for if they did the water would injure their feet. The Kisáni showed them a square raft made of four logs – a white pine, a blue spruce, and yellow pine, and a black spruce – on which they might cross; so they went over the stream and visited the homes of the Kisáni.

The Kisáni gave the wanderers corn and pumpkins to eat, and the latter lived for some time on the food given to them daily by their new friends. They held a council among themselves, in which they resolved to mend their manners for the future and do nothing to make the Kisáni angry. The land of the Kisáni had neither rain nor snow; the crops were raised by irrigation.

Late in the autumn they heard in the east the distant sound of a great voice calling. They listened and waited, and soon heard the voice nearer and louder. They listened still and heard the voice a third time, nearer and louder than before. Once more they listened, and soon they heard the voice louder still, and clear like the voice of one near at hand. A moment later four mysterious beings appeared to them. These were: Bĭtsís Lakaí, or White Body, a being like the god of this world whom the Navajos call Hastséyalti; Bĭtsís Dotlí'z, or Blue Body, who was like the present Navajo god Tó'nenīli, or Water Sprinkler; Bĭtsís Lĭtsói, or Yellow Body; and Bĭtsís Lĭzī'n, or Black Body, who was the same as the present Navajo god of fire, Hastsézĭni.

These beings, without speaking, made many signs to the people, as if instructing them; but the latter did not understand them. When the gods had gone, the people long discussed the mysterious visit, and tried to make out what the gods meant by the signs they had made. Thus, the gods visited four days in succession. On the fourth day, when the other three had departed, Black Body remained behind and spoke to the people in their own language. He said, "You do not seem to understand the signs that these gods make you, so I must tell you what they mean. They want to make more people, but in form like themselves. You have bodies like theirs; but you have the teeth, the feet, and the claws of beasts and insects. The new creatures are to have hands and feet like ours. But you are uncleanly, you smell badly. Have yourselves well cleansed when we return; we will come back in twelve days."

On the morning of the twelfth day, the people washed themselves well. The women dried themselves with yellow cornmeal, the men with white cornmeal. Soon after the ablutions were completed they heard the distant call of the approaching gods. It was shouted, as before, four times – nearer and louder at each repetition – and, after the fourth call, the gods appeared. Blue Body and Black Body each carried a sacred buckskin. White Body carried two ears of corn, one yellow, one white, each covered at the end completely with grains.

The gods laid one buckskin on the ground with the head to the west; on this they placed the two ears of corn, with their tips to the east, and over the corn they spread the other buckskin with its head to the east; under the white ear they put the feather of a white eagle, under the yellow ear the feather of a yellow eagle. Then they told the people to stand at a distance and allow the wind to enter. The white wind blew from the east, and the yellow wind blew from the west, between the skins. While the wind was blowing, eight of the Mirage People came and walked around the objects on the ground four times, and as they walked the eagle feathers, whose tips protruded from between the buckskins, were seen to move. When the Mirage People had finished their walk the upper buckskin was lifted – the ears of corn had disappeared; a man and a woman lay there in their stead.

The white ear of corn had been changed into a man, the yellow ear into a woman. It was the wind that gave them life. It is the wind that comes out of our mouths now that gives us life. When this ceases to blow we die. In the skin at the tips of our fingers we see the trail of the wind; it shows us where the wind blew when our ancestors were created.

The pair thus created were First Man and First Woman (Atsé Hastín and Atsé Estsán). The gods directed the people to build an enclosure of brushwood for the pair. When the enclosure was finished, First Man and First Woman entered it, and the gods said to them, "Live together now as husband and wife." At the end of four days hermaphrodite twins were born, and at the end of four days more a boy and a girl were born, who in four days grew to maturity and lived with one another as husband and wife. The primal pair had in all five pairs of twins, the first of which only was barren, being hermaphrodites.

In four days after the last pair of twins was born, the gods came again and took First Man and First Woman away to the eastern mountain where the gods dwelt, and kept them there for four days. When they returned all their children were taken to the eastern mountain and kept there for four days. Soon after they all returned it was observed that they occasionally wore masks, such as Hastséyalti and Hastséhogan wear now, and that when they wore these masks they prayed for all good things – for abundant rain and abundant crops. It is thought, too, that during their visit to the eastern mountain they learned the awful secrets of witchcraft, for the antíhi (witches, wizards) always keep such masks with them and marry those too nearly related to them.

When they returned from the eastern mountain the brothers and sisters separated; and, keeping the fact of their former unlawful marriages secret, the brothers married women of the Mirage People and the sisters married men of the Mirage People. They kept secret, too, all the mysteries they had learned in the eastern mountain. The women, thus married, bore children every four days, and the children grew to maturity in four days, were married, and in their turn had children every four days. This numerous offspring married among the Kisáni, and among those who had come from the lower world, and soon there was a multitude of people in the land.

These descendants of First Man and First Woman made a great farm. They built a dam and dug a wide irrigating ditch. But they feared the Kisáni might injure their dam or their crops; so they put one of the hermaphrodites to watch the dam and the other to watch the lower end of the field. The hermaphrodite who watched at the dam invented pottery. He made first a plate, a bowl, and a dipper, which were greatly admired by the people. The hermaphrodite who lived at the lower end of the farm invented the wicker water-bottle. Others made, from thin split boards of cottonwood, implements which they shoved before them to clear the weeds out of the land. They made also hoes from shoulder-blades of deer and axes of stone. They got their seeds from the Kisáni.

Once, they killed a little deer, and someone among them thought that perhaps they might make, from the skin of the head, a mask, by means of which they could approach other deer and kill them. They tried to make such a mask but failed; they could not make it fit. They debated over the invention and considered it for four days, but did not succeed. On the morning of the fifth day they heard the gods shouting in the distance. As on a previous occasion, they shouted four times, and after the fourth call they made their appearance. They brought with them heads of deer and of antelope. They showed the people how the masks were made and fitted, how the eyeholes were cut, how the motions of the deer were to be imitated, and explained to them all the other mysteries of the deer-hunt. Next day, hunters went out and several deer were killed; from these more masks were made, and with these masks more men went out to hunt; after that time the camp had abundance of meat. The people dressed the deerskins and made garments out of them.

The people from the third world had been in the fourth world eight years when the following incident occurred: One day they saw the sky stooping down and the earth rising up to meet it. For a moment they came in contact, and then there sprang out of the earth, at the point of contact, the Coyote and the Badger. We think now that the Coyote and the Badger are children of the sky. The Coyote rose first, and for this reason we think he is the elder brother of the Badger. At once the Coyote came over to the camp and skulked round among the people, while the Badger went down into the hole that led to the lower world.

First Man told the people the names of the four mountains which rose in the distance. They were named the same as the four mountains that now bound the Navajo land. There was Tsisnadzi'ni in the east, Tsótsil in the south, Dokoslíd in the west, and Depĕ'ntsa in the north, and he told them that a different race of people lived in each mountain.

First Man was the chief of all these people in the fourth world, except the Kisáni. He was a great hunter, and his wife, First Woman, was very corpulent. One day, he brought home from the hunt a fine fat deer. The woman boiled some of it and they had a hearty meal. When they were done, the woman wiped her greasy hands on her dress, and made a remark which greatly enraged her husband; they had a quarrel about this, which First Man ended by jumping across the fire and remaining by himself in silence for the rest of the night.

Next morning First Man went out early and called aloud to the people, "Come hither, all ye men," he said; "I wish to speak to you, but let all the women stay behind; I do not wish to see them." Soon all the males gathered, and he told them what his wife had said the night before. "They believe," he said, "that they can live without us. Let us see if they can hunt game and till the fields without our help. Let us see what sort of a living they can make by themselves. Let us leave them and persuade the Kisáni to come with us. We will cross the stream, and when we are gone over we will keep the raft on the other side." He sent for the hermaphrodites. They came, covered with meal, for they had been grinding corn. "What have you that you have made yourselves?" he asked. "We have each two mealing-stones, and we have cups and bowls and baskets and many other things," they answered. "Then take these all along with you," he ordered, "and join us to cross the stream." Then all the men and the hermaphrodites assembled at the river and crossed to the north side on the raft, and they took over with them their stone axes and farm implements and everything they had made. When they had all crossed they sent the raft down to the Kisáni for them to cross. The latter came over – six gentes of them – but they took their women with them. While some of the young men were crossing the stream they cried at parting with their wives; still they went at the bidding of their chief. The men left the women everything the latter had helped to make or raise.

As soon as they had crossed the river some of the men went out hunting, for the young boys needed food, and some set to work to chop down willows and build huts. They had themselves all sheltered in four days.

That winter the women had abundance of food, and they feasted, sang, and had a merry time. They often came down to the bank of the river and called across to the men and taunted and reviled them. Next year, the men prepared a few small fields and raised a little corn; but they did not have much corn to eat, and lived a good deal by hunting. The women planted all of the old farm, but they did not work it very well; so in the winter they had a small crop, and they did not sing and make merry as in the previous winter. In the second spring the women planted less, while the men planted more, cleared more land, and increased the size of their farm. Each year the fields and crops of the men increased, while those of the women diminished and they began to suffer for want of food. Some went out and gathered the seeds of wild plants to eat. In the autumn of the third year of separation many women jumped into the river and tried to swim over; but they were carried under the surface of the water and were never seen again. In the fourth year the men had more food than they could eat; corn and pumpkins lay untouched in the fields, while the women were starving.

First Man at length began to think what the effect of his course might be. He saw that if he continued to keep the men and the women apart the race might die out, so he called the men and spoke his thoughts to them. Some said, "Surely our race will perish," and others said, "What good is our abundance to us? We think so much of our poor women starving in our sight that we cannot eat." Then he sent a man to the shore to call across the stream to find if First Woman were still there, and to bid her come down to the bank if she were. She came to the bank, and First Man called to her and asked if she still thought she could live alone. "No," she replied, "we cannot live without our husbands." The men and the women were then told to assemble at the shores of the stream; the raft was sent over and the women were ferried across. They were made to bathe their bodies and dry them with meal. They were put in a corral and kept there until night, when they were let out to join the men in their feasts.

When they were let out of the corral, it was found that three were missing. After dark, voices were heard calling from the other side of the river; they were the voices of the missing ones – a mother and her two daughters. They begged to be ferried over, but the men told them it was too dark, that they must wait until morning. Hearing this, they jumped into the stream and tried to swim over. The mother succeeded in reaching the opposite bank and finding her husband. The daughters were seized by Tiéholtsodi, the water monster, and dragged down under the water.

For three nights and three days, the people heard nothing about the young women and supposed them lost forever. On the morning of the fourth day, the call of the gods was heard – four times as usual – and after the fourth call White Body made his appearance, holding up two fingers and pointing to the river. The people supposed that these signs had reference to the lost girls. Some of the men crossed the stream on the raft and looked for the tracks of the lost ones; they traced the tracks to the edge of the water, but no farther. White Body went away, but soon returned, accompanied by Blue Body. White Body carried a large bowl of white shell, and Blue Body a large bowl of blue shell. They asked for a man and a woman to accompany them, and they went down to the river. They put both the bowls on the surface of the water and caused them to spin around. Beneath the spinning bowls the water opened, for it was hollow, and gave entrance to a large house of four rooms. The room in the east was made of the dark waters, the room in the south of the blue waters, the room in the west of the yellow waters, and the room in the north of waters of all colours.

The man and the woman descended and Coyote followed them. They went first into the east room, but there they found nothing; then they went into the south room, but there they found nothing; next they went into the west room, where again they found nothing; at last they went into the north room, and there they beheld the water monster Tiéholtsodi, with the two girls he had stolen and two children of his own. The man and the woman demanded the children, and as he said nothing in reply they took them and walked away. But as they went out Coyote, unperceived by all, took the two children of Tiéholtsodi and carried them off under his robe. Coyote always wore his robe folded close around him and always slept with it thus folded, so no one was surprised to see that he still wore his robe in this way when he came up from the waters, and no one suspected that he had stolen the children of Tiéholtsodi.

Next day, the people were surprised to see deer, turkey and antelope running past from east to west, and to see animals of six different kinds (two kinds of Hawks, two kinds of Squirrels, the Hummingbird and the Bat) come into their camp as if for refuge. The game animals ran past in increasing numbers during the three days following. On the morning of the fourth day, when the white light rose, the people observed in the east a strange white gleam along the horizon, and they sent out the Locust couriers to see what caused this unusual appearance. The Locusts returned before sunset, and told the people that a vast flood of waters was fast approaching from the east. On hearing this, the people all assembled together, the Kisáni with the others, in a great multitude, and they wailed and wept over the approaching catastrophe. They wept and moaned all night and could not sleep.

When the white light arose in the east, next morning, the waters were seen high as mountains encircling the whole horizon, except in the west, and rolling on rapidly. The people packed up all their goods as fast as they could and ran up on a high hill nearby for temporary safety. Here they held a council. Someone suggested that perhaps the two Squirrels (Hazáitso and Hazáistozi) might help them. "We will try what we can do," said the Squirrels. One planted a piñon seed, the other a juniper seed, and they grew so very fast that the people hoped that they would soon grow so tall that the flood could not reach their tops, and that all might find shelter there. But after the trees grew a little way, they began to branch out and grew no higher. Then the frightened people called on the Weasels (Glo'dsĭlkái and Glo'dsĭlzĭ'ni). One of these planted a spruce seed and one a pine seed. The trees sprouted at once and grew fast, and again the people began to hope; but soon the trees commenced to branch, and they dwindled to slender points at the top and ceased to grow higher. Now they were in the depths of despair, for the waters were coming nearer every moment, when they saw two men approaching the hill on which they were gathered.

One of the approaching men was old and grey-haired; the other, who was young, walked in advance. They ascended the hill and passed through the crowd, speaking to no one. The young man sat down on the summit, the old man sat down behind him, and the Locust sat down behind the old man – all facing the east. The elder took out seven bags from under his robe and opened them. Each contained a small quantity of earth. He told the people that in these bags he had earth from the seven sacred mountains. There were in the fourth world seven sacred mountains, named and placed like the sacred mountains of the present Navajo land. "Ah! Perhaps our father can do something for us," said the people. "I cannot, but my son may be able to help you," said the old man. Then they bade the son to help them, and he said he would if they all moved away from where he stood, faced to the west, and looked not around until he called them; for no one should see him at his work. They did as he desired, and in a few moments he called them to come to him. When they came, they saw that he had spread the sacred earth on the ground and planted in it thirty-two reeds, each of which had thirty-two joints. As they gazed they beheld the roots of the reeds striking out into the soil and growing rapidly downward. A moment later all the reeds joined together and became one reed of great size, with a hole in its eastern side. He bade them enter the hollow of the reed through this hole. When they were all safely inside, the opening closed, and none too soon, for scarcely had it closed when they heard the loud noise of the surging waters outside, saying, "Yin, yin, yin."

The waters rose fast, but the reed grew faster, and soon it grew so high that it began to sway, and the people inside were in great fear lest, with their weight, it might break and topple over into the water. White Body, Blue Body and Black Body were along. Black Body blew a great breath out through a hole in the top of the reed; a heavy dark cloud formed around the reed and kept it steady. But the reed grew higher and higher; again it began to sway, and again the people within were in great fear, whereat he blew and made another cloud to steady the reed. By sunset it had grown up close to the sky, but it swayed and waved so much that they could not secure it to the sky until Black Body, who was uppermost, took the plume out of his headband and stuck it out through the top of the cane against the sky, and this is why the reed (Phragmites communis) always carries a plume on its head now.

Seeing no hole in the sky, they sent up the Great Hawk, Giní′tso, to see what he could do. He flew up and began to scratch in the sky with his claws, and he scratched and scratched till he was lost to sight. After a while he came back, and said that he scratched to where he could see light, but that he did not get through the sky. Next, they sent up a Locust. He was gone a long time, and when he came back he had this story to tell: He had gotten through to the upper world, and came out on a little island in the centre of a lake. When he got out, he saw approaching him from the east a black Grebe, and from the west a yellow Grebe. One of them said to him, "Who are you and whence come you?"

But he made no reply. The other then said, "We own half of this world – I in the east, my brother in the west. We give you a challenge. If you can do as we do, we shall give you one half of the world; if you cannot, you must die." Each had an arrow made of the black wind. He passed the arrow from side to side through his heart and flung it down to Wonístsídi, the Locust. The latter picked up one of the arrows, ran it from side to side through his heart, as he had seen the Grebes do, and threw it down. The Grebes swam away, one to the east and one to the west, and troubled him no more. When they had gone, two more Grebes appeared, a blue one from the south and a shining one from the north. They spoke to him as the other Grebes had spoken, and gave him the same challenge. Again he passed the arrow through his heart and the Grebes departed, leaving the land to the locust. To this day we see in every locust's sides the holes made by the arrows. But the hole the Locust made in ascending was too small for many of the people, so they sent Badger up to make it larger. When Badger came back his legs were stained black with the mud, and the legs of all badgers have been black ever since. Then, First Man and First Woman led the way and all the others followed them, and they climbed up through the hole to the surface of this – the fifth – world.

The Finding of Fire

THE YANAS HAVE their own story about first finding fire. Names in brackets in the story below signify the creature or thing into which the personage was changed subsequently.

In the beginning Au Mujaupa (master of fire) had fire very far down south on the other side of a big river. The people in this country had no real fire; they had a kind of fire, but it wasn't good. It just warmed a little; it wouldn't cook like the fire which we have now. People killed deer and fished, but they had to eat fish and venison raw.

In the west people had fire, but it wouldn't cook. In the north there were many people, and in the east; but they had no fire that would cook.

"There must be fire in some place," said the people at Pawi; "how can we find it?"

"I will go out to-night to look," said Ahalamila (grey wolf).

That night he went to look for fire. He went to the top of Wahkanopa, looked east and west, saw no fire in either place. Next he looked north; no fire in the north. He looked south; saw no fire anywhere.

Ahalamila came home and talked to the chief and people. "I saw no fire," said he; "I could not see any, but I will go to a better place the next time and take some one with me. I will go to-morrow night to the top of Wahkalu. Who here has a good head, who a sharp eye to see fire? I want to look for fire to-morrow night from the top of Wahkalu; from that place I will look all around the whole world to find fire."

"We have a man here," said the chief, "who can see through a tree, who can see down through the earth to bed rock, who can see through a mountain. You can take him to-morrow night with you. He is Siwegi (a small bird)."

Ahalamila went to Siwegi. "Will you go to-morrow night to look for fire?" asked he.

"I will go if the way is not too long."

"Oh," said Ahalamila, "it will not be long. I will shorten it."

Siwegi agreed to go; and when the time came, they started. Ahalamila doubled up the trail and made it short; in an hour they were on the top of Wahkalu, both ready now to look for fire. The night is very dark; they can see the smallest fire easily.

They look to the east, look with great care, look a good while, see no fire; they look to the north in the same way, see no fire; they look to the west, no fire there. Now Ahalamila looks south, looks a long time, and sees nothing: he looks half an hour to the south, sees a little glimmer like a light very far away.

"Siwegi," said he, "I see a small light down south; it seems like fire far away. I think it is fire."

"Look again," said Siwegi, "look sharply. Maybe it is fire."

"I have looked enough, I think it is fire," said Ahalamila; "but I want you to see it, I want you to look now."

Siwegi looked a little while. "Yes, that is fire," said he.

"Well," said Ahalamila, "we see fire, we know that it is far off in the south."

Ahalamila made the road short, and they were back at Pawi in an hour. "We have found fire," said Ahalamila to the chief and the people. "We know where fire is, we can have fire now."

"We must have that fire," said the people.

"There is no way to get the fire but to go for it," said Ahalamila.

"Well," said the chief, "since Ahalamila saw the fire he will go for it; but the road is long. Who will go and help him? Who will go for fire with Ahalamila?"

About fifty men offered to go, and they started next morning. The journey was long and very hard. Soon two or three men were tired and went home; not long after more were tired, and when they had gone far down to a great river, just north of where the fire was, of the fifty who started only three were left – Ahalamila, Metsi (coyote), and old Shushu Marimi (dog woman).

Just south of the great river Au Mujaupa had a very big village, and in the village a large sweat-house.

In that house he kept the fire, and had a great crowd of people living in the country outside who served him, and kept every one in the world from stealing his fire. These people were Patcha (snow), Chil Wareko (big rain), Chil Daiauna (big hail), Sabil Keyu (small hail), Juhauju (west wind), Juwaju (south wind), Jukami (north wind), Jukilauju (east wind).

The three, Ahalamila, Metsi, and old Shushu Marimi, were at the northern end of the bridge, and sat there watching till all at the sweat-house was quiet. The bridge was very narrow and slippery; so Ahalamila put pitch on his feet and hands, and on Metsi's and Shushu's feet and hands. All three crossed without slipping, and found every one asleep in the sweat-house.

The old chief, Au Mujaupa, had covered the fire well with ashes. All was silent within and without. Ahalamila, Metsi, and Shushu crept onto the sweat-house quietly, and looked in. All were asleep.

"I will go down first," said Metsi.

"No, I will go first," said Ahalamila. "I will get the fire and reach it to you; you take it and run very fast."

Ahalamila slipped down. Metsi and Shushu remained on the roof. Ahalamila opened the fire carefully, took out a good piece and handed it to the old woman. She put it in her ear. He handed her another; she put it in her other ear, slipped down from the top of the sweat-house, ran across the bridge, and hurried away.

Ahalamila gave Metsi two pieces. He put them in his two ears and started. Ahalamila filled his own ears and followed.

The three had run over two mountains when Au Mujaupa woke up and saw that the ashes had been opened, and that fire had been taken, that a coal had fallen near the central pillar. He sprang up, went to the top of the sweat-house, shouted, called to all his people:

"Fire has been stolen! Fire has been stolen! Go, you, and follow!"

Now Patcha, Chil Wareko, Chil Daiauna, Sabil Keyu, and all the wind people rose up and followed, raced and stormed in every direction. So much rain came that the whole country was covered with water.

Now Juwaju was ahead of all Au Mujaupa's people chasing the three robbers. Chil Wareko came too, and fell upon the three furiously; he drenched and chilled them. Next came Jukami and Patcha, who nearly froze them.

Metsi was almost dead; the fire went out in both his ears. Ahalamila lost his fire, too. Chil Wareko, Juwaju, and Patcha quenched it, and then he let it fall.

Old Shushu was behind a good way, but she ran all the time. She kept her hand on one ear as she ran. She lost the fire out of her other ear, and when the piece fell out it broke in two and fell apart. Chil Wareko picked up the fire and took it back; he found six pieces, thought that he had all. He and the others stopped following.

Ahalamila and Metsi ran ahead, left old Shushu to get on the best she could, and reached home first. They were wet, very cold, and tired.

"Where is your fire?" asked the chief.

"I have none; Chil Wareko took my fire," said Ahalamila.

"Where is your fire?" asked the chief.

"Chil Wareko took it," said Metsi.

The chief was very sorry, and all the people were sorry. The old woman did not come, and the people said, "She must be frozen dead."

At sundown old Shushu came back; she came very slowly, was terribly tired, but courageous. She reached the sweat-house, came in, said nothing, lay down wet and cold.

"Where is the fire?" asked she; "did not Ahalamila and Metsi bring fire? They are young and strong, and had plenty of fire."

After a while she stood up, drew some wood-dust together, then sat down, opened her ear and held it over the dust; a big piece of fire came out. Wood was brought quickly, and soon the whole sweat-house was warm. The people who were cold before were warm now and glad.

"Bring meat and we will try how it tastes when 'tis roasted," said the chief.

He cut some venison and roasted it. One and another tasted the meat. "It is very good," said they; a third one said, "I'll try it," and Gagi (crow) took a taste. "Oh, it is sweet, very good," said Gagi.

Each one roasted meat and ate heartily. Next day all went to hunt, and had a great feast in the evening. A chief from another place came to the feast and got fire, took it home with him. Soon all people had fire; every one had fire in all parts of the country.

Omaha Sacred Legend

IN THE BEGINNING the people were in water. They opened their eyes, but they could see nothing. As the people came out of the water, they first saw the daylight. They had no clothing. Then they took weeds and grasses and from them wove clothing.

The people lived near a large body of water; it was in a wooded country where there was game. The men hunted the deer with clubs; they did not know the use of the bow. The people wandered about the shores of the great water. They were poor and cold. The people thought, "What shall we do to help ourselves?" So they began chipping stones. They found a bluish stone that was easily flaked and chipped; so they made knives and arrowheads out of it. But they were still poor and cold. They thought, "What shall we do?"

Then a man found an elm root that was very dry. He dug a hole in it and put a stick in and rubbed it. Then smoke came. He smelled it. Then the people smelled it and came near. Others helped him to rub. At last a spark came. They blew this into a flame. Thus fire came to warm the people and to cook their food.

After this the people built grass houses; they cut the grass with the shoulder blade of a deer. Now the people had fire and ate their meat roasted. Then they grew tired of roast meat. They thought, "How shall we cook our meat differently?"

A man found a piece of clay that stuck well together. Then he brought sand to mix with it. Then he moulded it as a pot. Then he gathered grass until he had a large heap of it; he put the clay pot into the midst of the grass and set it on fire. This made the clay hard. After a time he put water into the pot; the water did not leak out. This was good. So he put water into it and then meat into it, and put the pot over the fire. Thus the people had boiled meat to eat.

Now their grass coverings would grow fuzzy and drop off. It was hard to gather and keep these coverings. The people were not satisfied. Again they thought, "What can we do to have something different to wear?"

Before this, they had been throwing away the hides from the game which they killed. But now they took their stone knives to scrape down the hides and make them thin. They rubbed the hides with grass and with their hands to make them soft. Then they used the hides for clothing. Now they had clothing and were warm.

Now the women had to break the dry wood to keep up the fires. They had no tools. So the men made a stone ax with a groove. Then they put a handle on the grooved stone and fastened it with rawhide. This was used. Then they wanted something better to break the wood. So they made wedges of stone.

Now the grass shelter came to pieces easily. Then the people thought, "What shall we do? How can we get something that will not come to pieces?" Then they tried putting skins on poles.

First they tried deerskins. But they were too small. They tried elk skins. But they became hard and stiff in the rain and sun. Then they did not try skins longer. They used bark to cover the poles of their tepees.

But the bark houses were not warm. Then the people took the leg bone of the deer and splintered it So they made sharp pieces for awls. Then they took buffalo skins and sinews, and with the awl they fastened the skins together. So they made comfortable covers for their tepees.

Then a man wandered around a long time. One day he found some small pieces of something which were white, and red, and blue. He thought they must be something of great value, so he hid them in a mound of earth. Now one day he went to see if they were safe. Behold! When he came to the mound, green stalks were growing out of it. And on the stalks were small kernels of white, and red, and blue. Behold! It was corn. Then the man took the corn, and gave it to the people. They tried it for food. They found it good, and have ever since called it their life.

Now when the people found the corn good, they thought to hide it in mounds as the first man had done. So they took the shoulder blade of an elk and made mounds. Then they hid the corn in it. So the corn grew and the people had food.

Now as the people wandered around, they came to a forest where the birch trees grew. There was a great lake there. Then they made canoes of birch bark. They traveled in them on the water. Then a man found two young animals. He carried them home. He fed them so they grew bigger. Then he made a harness which he placed upon them and fastened it to poles. So these animals became burden bearers. Before that, every burden had to be carried on the back. Now the dogs helped the people.

The Legend of the Peace Pipes

THE PEOPLE CAME across a great water on logs tied together. They pitched their tents on the shore. Then they thought to make for themselves certain bounds within which they were to live and rules which should govern them. They cleared a space of grass and weeds so they could see each other's faces. They sat down and there was no obstruction between them.

While they were holding a council, an owl hooted in the trees near by. The leader said, "That bird is to take part in our council. He calls to us. He offers us his aid."

Immediately afterward they heard a woodpecker. He knocked against the trees. The leader said, "That bird calls to us. He offers us his aid. He will take part in our council."

Then the chief appointed a man as servant. He said, "Go into the woods and get an ash sapling." The servant came back with a sapling having a rough bark.

"We do not want that," said the leader. "Go again and get a sapling with a smooth bark, bluish in colour at the joint where a branch comes." So the servant went out, and came back with a sapling of the kind described.

When the leader took up the sapling, an eagle came and soared about the council which was sitting in the grass. He dropped a downy feather; it fell. It fell in the centre of the cleared space. Now this was the white eagle. The chief said, "This is not what we want," so the white eagle passed on.

Then the bald eagle came swooping down, as though attacking its prey. It balanced itself on its wings directly over the cleared space. It uttered fierce cries, and dropped one of its downy feathers, which stood on the ground as the other eagle's feather had done. The chief said, "This is not what we want." So the bald eagle passed on.

Then came the spotted eagle, and soared over the council, and dropped its feather as the others had done. The chief said, "This is not what we want," and the spotted eagle passed on.

Then the imperial eagle, the eagle with the fantail, came, and soared over the people. It dropped a downy feather which stood upright in the centre of the cleared space. The chief said, "This is what we want."

So the feathers of this eagle were used in making the peace pipes, together with the feathers of the owl and woodpecker, and with other things. These peace pipes were to be used in forming friendly relations with other tribes.

When the peace pipes were made, seven other pipes were made for keeping peace within the tribe. One pipe was to prevent revenge. If one man should kill another, the chief took this pipe to the relatives and offered it to them. If the relatives of the dead man refused to accept it, it was offered again.

It was offered four times. If it was refused four times, the chief said, "Well, you must take the consequences. We will do nothing, and you cannot now ask to see the pipes." He meant if they took revenge and any trouble came to them, they could not ask for help or for mercy.

Each band had its own pipe.

The Raven Myth

IT WAS IN the time when there were no people on the earth plain. The first man, for four days, lay coiled up in the pod of the beach pea. On the fifth day, he stretched out his feet and burst the pod. He fell to the ground and when he stood up he was a full-grown man. Man looked all around him and then at himself. He moved his hands and arms, his neck and legs. When he looked back he saw, still hanging to the vine, the pod of the beach pea, with a hole in the lower end out of which he had dropped. When he looked about him again, he saw that he was getting farther from his starting place. The ground seemed to move up and down under his feet, and it was very soft. After a while, he had a strange feeling in his stomach, so he stooped down to drink some water from a small pool at his feet. Then he felt better.

When Man looked up again he saw coming toward him, with a fluttering motion, something dark. He watched the dark thing until it stopped just in front of him. It was Raven.

As soon as Raven stopped, he raised one of his wings and pushed up his beak, as though it were a mask, to the top of his head. Thus Raven changed at once into a man. Raven stared hard at Man, moving from side to side to see him better.

Raven said, "What are you? Where did you come from? I have never seen anything like you."

Raven still stared at Man, surprised to find this new thing so much like himself. He made Man walk around a little, while he perked his head from side to side to see him better. Then Raven said again, in astonishment, "Where did you come from? I have never seen anything like you before."

Man said, "I came from the pea pod." He pointed to the plant from which he came.

"Ah, I made that vine," said Raven. "But I did not know that anything like you would come from it. Come with me to the high ground over there; it is thicker and harder. This ground I made later and it is soft and thin."

So Man and Raven walked to the higher ground which was firm and hard. Raven asked Man if he had eaten anything. Man said he had taken some of the soft stuff from one of the pools.

"Ah, you drank some water," said Raven. "Now wait for me here."

Raven drew down his beak, as though it were a mask, over his face. He at once became a bird and flew far up into the sky – far out of sight. Man waited until the fourth day. Then Raven returned bringing four berries in his claws. He pushed up his beak and so became a man again. Then he gave to Man two salmon berries and two heath berries, saying, "Here is something I made for you to eat. I wish them to be plentiful on the earth. Eat them."

Man put the berries into his mouth, one after the other, and ate them. Then he felt better. Raven left Man near a small creek while he went to the edge of the water. He took two pieces of clay at the water's edge, and shaped them like a pair of mountain sheep. He held them in his hand until they were dry, and then he called Man to come and see them. Man said they were pretty, so Raven told him to close his eyes. Man closed his eyes tightly. Then Raven pulled down his beak-mask, and waved his wings four times over the pieces of clay. At once they bounded away as full-grown mountain sheep. Raven told Man to look.

Man was so much pleased that Raven said, "If these animals are plentiful, perhaps people will try to kill them."

Man said, "Yes."

Then Raven said, "Well, it will be better for them to live among the steep rocks so everyone cannot kill them. There only shall they be found."

Raven took two more pieces of clay and shaped them like tame reindeer. He held them in his hand until they were partly dry, then told Man to look at them. Raven again drew down his beak-mask and waved his wings four times over them. Thus they became alive, but as they were only dry in spots while Raven held them, therefore they remained brown and white, with mottled coat. Raven told Man these tame reindeer would be very few in number.

Again, Raven took two pieces of clay and shaped them like the caribou or wild reindeer. But he held them in his hands only a little while so that only the bellies of the reindeer became dry and white. Then Raven drew down his beak-mask, and waved his wings over them, and they bounded away. But because only their bellies were dry and white while Raven held them, therefore the wild reindeer is brown except its white belly.

Raven said to Man, "These animals will be very common. People will kill many of them."

Thus Raven began to create the animals.

Raven said one day to Man, "You are lonely by yourself. I will make you a companion." He went to some white clay at a spot distant from the clay of which he had made animals, and made of the clay a figure almost like Man. Raven kept looking at Man while he shaped the figure. Then he took fine water grass from the creek and fastened it on the back of the head for hair. When the clay was shaped, Raven drew down his beak-mask and waved his wings over it. The clay became a beautiful girl. The girl was white and fair because Raven let the clay dry entirely before he waved his wings over it.

Raven took the girl to Man. "There is a companion for you," he said.

Now, in the days of the first people on the earth plain, there were no mountains far or near. No rain ever fell and there were no winds. The sun shone always very brightly.

Then Raven showed the first people on the earth plain how to sleep warmly in the dry moss when they were tired. Raven himself drew down his beak-mask and went to sleep like a bird.

When Raven awakened, he went back to the creek. Here he made two sticklebacks, two greylings, and two blackfish. When these were swimming about in the water, he called Man to see them. Man raised his hand in surprise and the sticklebacks darted away. Raven told him the greylings would be found in clear mountain streams, while the sticklebacks would live along the coast, and that both would be good for food.

Raven next made the shrewmouse. He said, "The shrewmouse will not be good for food. It will prevent the earth plain from looking bare and cheerless."

In this way Raven was busy several days, making birds and fishes and animals. He showed each of them to Man and explained what they were good for. Then Raven flew into the sky, far, far away, and was gone four days. When he came back he brought a salmon to Man.

But Raven noticed that the ponds and lakes were silent and lonely, so he made water bugs to flit upon the surface of the water. He also made the beaver and the muskrat to live around the borders of the ponds. Raven told Man that the beavers would live along the streams and build strong houses, so Man must build a strong house also. Raven said the beavers would be very cunning and only good hunters could catch them. He also told Man how to catch the muskrat and how to use its skin for clothing.

Raven also made flies and mosquitoes and other insects to make the earth plain more cheerful. At first mosquitoes were like flies; they did not bite. One day Man killed a deer. After he had cut it up and placed the fat on a bush, he fell asleep. When he awoke he found the mosquitoes had eaten all of it. Then Man was very angry and scolded the mosquitoes. He said, "Never eat meat again. Eat men." Before that mosquitoes never bit people.

When the first baby came on the earth plain, Raven rubbed it all over with white clay. He told Man it would grow into a man like himself. The next morning the baby was a big boy. He ran around pulling up grass and flowers that Raven had planted. By the third day the baby was a full-grown man.

Then another baby was born on the earth plain. She was rubbed over with the white clay. The next day the baby was a big girl, walking around. On the third day she was a full-grown woman.

Now Raven began to be afraid that men would kill all the creatures he had made. He was afraid they would kill them for food and clothing. Therefore, Raven went to a creek nearby. He took white clay and shaped it like a bear. Then he waved his wings over it, and the clay became a bear. But Raven jumped very quickly to one side when the bear became alive because it looked fiercely around and growled. Then Raven showed the bear to Man and told him to be careful. He said the bear was very fierce and would tear him to pieces if he disturbed it.

Then Raven made the seals, and taught Man how to catch them. He also taught Man how to make strong lines from sealskin, and snares for the deer.

Then Raven went away to the place of the pea vine.

When he reached the pea vine, he found three other men had just fallen from the same pod that Man had fallen from. These men were looking about them in wonder. Raven led them away from the pea vine, but in a different direction from the first man. He brought them close to the sea. Raven stayed with these three men a long time. He taught them how to take wood from the bushes and small trees he planted in hollows and sheltered places, and to make a fire drill, and also a bow. He made many more plants and birds which like the seacoast, but he did not make so many as in the land where Man lived. He taught these men how to make bows and arrows, spears and nets, and how to use them; and also how to capture the seals, which were now plentiful in the sea. Then he taught them how to make kayaks, and how to build houses of drift logs and of bushes, covered with earth. Then he made wives for these men, and went back to Man.

When Raven reached the land where Man lived, he thought the earth plain still looked bare. So, while the others slept, Raven planted birch and spruce and cottonwood trees to grow in the low places. Then he woke up the people, who were pleased with the trees.

Then Raven taught Man how to make fire with the fire drill, and to place the spark of tinder in a bunch of dry grass and to wave it about until it blazed, and then to put dry wood upon it. He showed them how to roast fish on a stick, and how to make fish traps of splints and willow bark, and how to dry salmon for winter use.

Where Man lived there was now a large village because the people did everything as Raven told them, and therefore all the babies grew up in three days. One day, Raven came back and sat down by Man by the creek and they talked of many things. Man asked Raven about the skyland. Man wanted to see the skyland which Raven had made. Therefore, Raven took Man to the land in the sky.

Man found that the skyland was a very beautiful country, and that it had a much better climate than his land. But the people who lived there were very small. Their heads did not reach to Man's hips. The people wore fur clothing, with beautiful patterns, such as people on earth now wear, because Man showed his people how to make them. In the lakes were strange animals which would have killed Man if he had tried to drink of the water. In a dry lakebed, thickly covered with tall grass, Man saw a wonderful animal resting upon the tips of the grasses. It had a long head and six legs. It had fine, thick hair, and on the back of the head were two thick, short horns which bent forward and then curved back at the tips. Raven told Man it took many people to kill this animal.

Then they came to a round hole in the sky and around the edge of the hole was short grass, glowing like fire. Raven said, "This is the star called the moon-dog." Some of the grass had been pulled up. Raven said he had taken some to start the first fire on earth.

Then Raven said to Man, "Shut your eyes. I will take you to another country." Man climbed upon Raven's back and they dropped down through the star hole. They floated a long, long time through the air, then they floated through something else. When they stopped, Raven saw he was at the bottom of the sea. Man could breathe there, but it seemed foggy. Raven said that was the appearance of the water. Then Raven said, "I want to make some new animals here; but you must not walk about. You lie down and if you get tired, turn over on the other side."

Man went to sleep lying on one side, and slept a long while. When he waked up, he wanted to turn over, but he could not. Then Man thought, "I wish I could turn over," and at once he turned. As he turned, he was surprised to see that his body was covered with long, white hairs; and his fingers were long claws. Then he went to sleep again. This he did three times more. Then when he woke up, Raven stood by him. Raven said, "I have changed you into a white bear. How do you like it?" Man could not make a sound until Raven waved his wings over him. Then he said he did not like it; if he was a bear he would have to live on the sea, while his son lived on land; so Man should feel badly. Then Raven struck the white skin with his wings and it fell off. So Man became himself again. But Raven took the empty bearskin, and placed one of his own tail feathers inside it for a spine. Then he waved his wing over it, and a white bear arose. Ever since then, white bears have been found on the frozen sea.

Raven said, "How many times did you turn over?"

Man said, "Four."

Raven said, "You slept just four years."

Then Raven made other animals. He made the a-mi-kuk, a large, slimy animal, with thick skin, and with four long, wide-spreading arms. This is a fierce animal and lives in the sea. It wraps its four long arms around a man or a kayak and drags it under the water. A man cannot escape it. If he climbs out of his kayak on the ice, the a-mi-kuk will dart underneath and break the ice. If Man runs away on shore, the a-mi-kuk pursues him by burrowing through the earth. No man can escape from it when once it pursues him.

Then Raven showed Man the walrus, and the dog walrus, with head and teeth like a dog. It always swam with large herds of walrus and with a stroke of its tail could kill a man. He showed him whales and the grampus. Raven told Man that only good hunters could kill a whale, but when one was killed an entire village could feast on it. He showed him also the sea fox, which is so fierce it kills men; and the sea otter, which is like the land otter but has finer fur, tipped with white, and other fishes and animals as they rose to the surface of the water.

Then Raven said, "Close your eyes. Hold fast to me."

Then Man found himself on the shore near his home. The village was very large. His wife was very old and his son was an old man. The people gave him place of honour in the kashim, and made him their headsman. So Man taught the young men many things.

Now Man wanted again to see the skyland, so Raven and Man went up among the dwarf people and lived there a long time. But on earth the village grew very large; the men killed many animals.

Now in those days, the sun shone always very brightly. No rain ever fell and no winds blew.

Man and Raven were angry because the people killed many animals. They took a long line and a grass basket, one night, and caught ten reindeer which they put into the basket. Now in those days reindeer had sharp teeth, like dogs. The next night, Raven took the reindeer and let them down on the earth close to Man's village. Raven said, "Break down the first house you see and kill the people. Men are becoming too many." The reindeer did as Raven commanded. They stamped on the house and broke it down. They ate up the people with their sharp, wolf-like teeth. The next night, Raven let the reindeer down; again they broke down a house and ate up the people with their sharp teeth.

The village people were much frightened. The third night they covered the third house with a mixture of deer fat and berries. On the third night when the reindeer began to tear down the third house, their mouths were filled with the fat and sour berries. Then the reindeer ran away, shaking their heads so violently that all their long, sharp teeth fell out. Ever since then reindeer have had small teeth and cannot harm people.

After the reindeer ran away, Raven and Man returned to the skyland. Man said, "If the people do not stop killing so many animals, they will kill everything you have made. It would be better to take the sun away from them. Then it will be dark and people will die."

Raven said, "That is right. You stay here. I will go and take away the sun."

So Raven went away and took the sun out of the sky. He put it in a skin bag and carried it far away, to a distant part of the skyland. Then it became dark on earth.

The people on earth were frightened when the sun vanished. They offered Raven presents of food and furs if he would bring back the sun. Raven said, "No." After a while Raven felt sorry for them, so he let them have a little light. He held up the sun in one hand for two days so people could hunt and secure food. Then he put the sun in the skin bag again and the earth was dark. Then, after a long time, when the people made him many gifts, he would let them have a little light again.

Now Raven had a brother living in the village. He was sorry for the earth people. So Raven's brother thought a long time. Then he died. The people put him in a grave box and had a burial feast. Then they left the grave box. At once Raven's brother slipped out of the box and went away from the village. He hid his raven mask and coat in a tree. Soon Raven's wife came for water. When she took up a dipperful to drink, Raven's brother, by magic, became a small leaf. He fell into the water and Raven's wife swallowed him...

When Raven-Boy was born he grew very rapidly. He was running about when he was only a few days old. He cried for the sun which was in the skin bag, hanging on the rafters. Raven was fond of the boy so he let him play with the sun; yet he was afraid Raven-Boy would lose the sun, so he watched him.

When Raven-Boy began to play out of doors, he cried and begged for the sun. Raven said, "No." Then Raven-Boy cried more than ever. At last Raven gave him the sun in the house. Raven-Boy played with it a long while.

When no one was looking, he ran quickly out of the house. He ran to the tree, put on his raven mask and coat, and flew far away with the sun in the skin bag.

When Raven-Boy was far up in the sky, he heard Raven call, "Do not hide the sun. Let it out of the bag. Do not keep it always dark."

Raven thought the boy had stolen it for himself.

Raven-Boy flew to the place where the sun belonged. He tore off the skin covering and put the sun in its place. Then he saw a broad path leading far away. He followed it to the side of a hole fringed with short, bright grass. He remembered that Raven had said, "Do not keep it always dark," therefore he made the sky turn, with all the stars and the sun. Thus it is now sometimes dark and sometimes light.

Raven-Boy picked some of the short, bright grass by the edge of the sky hole and stuck it into the sky. This is the morning star.

Raven-Boy went down to the earth. The people were glad to see him. They said, "What has become of Man who went into the skyland with Raven?" Now this was the first time that Raven-Boy had heard of Man. He started to fly up into the sky, but he could get only a small distance above the earth. When he found he could not get back to the sky, Raven-Boy wandered to the second village, where lived the men who had come from the pod of the beach pea. Raven-Boy there married a wife and he had many children. But the children could not fly to the sky. They had lost the magic power. Therefore, the ravens now flutter over the tundras like other birds.

Xolotl Creates the Parents of Mankind

ALL PROVINCES WERE agreed that in heaven were a god and goddess, Citlallatonac and Citlalicue, and that the goddess gave birth to a stone knife (*tecpatl*), to the amazement and horror of her other sons which were in heaven.

The stone hurled forth by these outraged sons and falling to Chicomoxtoc ('Seven Caves'), was shattered, and from its fragments arose sixteen hundred earth-godlings. These sent Tlotli, the Hawk, heavenward to demand of their mother the privilege of creating men to be their servants; and she replied that they should send to Mictlantecutli, Lord of Hell, for a bone or ashes of the dead, from which a man and woman would be born.

Xolotl was dispatched as messenger, secured the bone, and fled with it; but being pursued by the Lord of Hell, he stumbled, and the bone broke. With such fragments as he could secure he reached the earth, and the bones, placed in a vessel, were sprinkled with blood drawn from the bodies of the gods. On the fourth day a boy emerged from the mixture; on the eighth, a girl; and these were reared by Xolotl to become parents of mankind.

Men differ in size because the bone broke into unequal fragments; and as human beings multiplied, they were assigned as servants to the several gods.

Now, the Sun had not been shining for a long time, and the deities assembled at Teotiuacan to consider the matter.

Having built a great fire, they announced that that one among their devotees who should first hurl himself into it should have the honour of becoming the Sun, and when one had courageously entered the flames, they awaited the sunrise, wagering as to the quarter in which he would appear; but they guessed wrong, and for this they were condemned to be sacrificed, as they were soon to learn.

When the Sun appeared, he remained ominously motionless; and although Tlotli was sent to demand that he continue his journey, he refused, saying that he should remain where he was until they were all destroyed. Citli ('Hare') in anger shot the Sun with an arrow, but the latter hurled it back, piercing the forehead of his antagonist.

The gods then recognized their inferiority and allowed themselves to be sacrificed, their hearts being torn out by Xolotl, who slew himself last of all. Before departing, however, each divinity gave to his followers, as a sacred bundle, his vesture wrapped about a green gem which was to serve as a heart.

Tezcatlipoca was one of the departed deities, but one day he appeared to a mourning follower whom he commanded to journey to the House of the Sun beyond the waters and to bring thence singers and musical instruments to make a feast for him. This the messenger did, singing as he went.

The Sun warned his people not to harken to the stranger, but the music was irresistible, and some of them were lured to follow him back to earth, where they instituted the musical rites.

The Children of Heaven and Earth
Ko Nga Tama A Rangi – A Tradition Relating to the Origin of the Human Race

MEN HAD BUT one pair of primitive ancestors; they sprang from the vast heaven that exists above us, and from the earth which lies beneath us. According to the traditions of our race, Rangi and Papa, or Heaven and Earth, were the source from which, in the beginning, all things originated. Darkness then rested upon the heaven and upon the earth, and they still both clave together, for they had not yet been rent apart; and the children they had begotten were ever thinking amongst themselves what might be the difference between darkness and light; they knew that beings had multiplied and increased, and yet light had never broken upon them, but it ever continued dark. Hence these sayings are found in our ancient religious services: 'There was darkness from the first division of time, unto the tenth, to the hundredth, to the thousandth', that is, for a vast space of time; and these divisions of times were considered as beings, and were each termed a Po; and on their account there was as yet no world with its bright light, but darkness only for the beings which existed.

At last the beings who had been begotten by Heaven and Earth, worn out by the continued darkness, consulted amongst themselves, saying: "Let us now determine what we should do with Rangi and Papa, whether it would be better to slay them or to rend them apart." Then spoke Tu-matauenga, the fiercest of the children of Heaven and Earth: "It is well, let us slay them."

Then spake Tane-mahuta, the father of forests and of all things that inhabit them, or that are constructed from trees: "Nay, not so. It is better to rend them apart, and to let the heaven stand far above us, and the earth lie under out feet. Let the sky become as a stranger to us, but the earth remain close to us as our nursing mother."

The brothers all consented to this proposal, with the exception of Tawhiri-ma-tea, the father of winds and storms, and he, fearing that his kingdom was about to be overthrown, grieved greatly at the thought of his parents being torn apart. Five of the brothers willingly consented to the separation of their parents, but one of them would not agree to it.

Hence, also, these sayings of old are found in our prayers: 'Darkness, darkness, light, light, the seeking, the searching, in chaos, in chaos'; these signified the way in which the offspring of heaven and earth sought for some mode of dealing with their parents, so that human beings might increase and live.

So, also, these sayings of old time. 'The multitude, the length', signified the multitude of the thoughts of the children of Heaven and Earth, and the length of time they considered whether they should slay their parents, that human beings might be called into existence; for it was in this manner that they talked and consulted amongst themselves.

But at length their plans having been agreed on, lo, Rongo-ma-tane, the god and father of the cultivated food of man, rises up, that he may rend apart the heavens and the earth; he struggles, but he rends them not apart. Lo, next, Tangaroa, the god and father of fish and reptiles, rises up, that he may rend apart the heavens and the earth; he also struggles, but he rends them not apart. Lo, next, Haumia-tikitiki, the god and father of the food of man which springs without cultivation, rises up and struggles, but ineffectually. Lo, then, Tu-matauenga, the god and father of fierce human beings, rises up and struggles, but he, too, fails in his efforts. Then, at last, slowly uprises Tane-mahuta, the god and father of forests, of birds, and of insects, and he struggles with his parents; in vain he strives to rend them apart with his hands and arms. Lo, he pauses; his head is now firmly planted on his mother the earth, his feet he raises up and rests against his father the skies, he strains his back and limbs with mighty effort. Now are rent apart Rangi and Papa, and with cries and groans of woe they shriek aloud: 'Wherefore slay you thus your parents? Why commit you so dreadful a crime as to slay us, as to rend your parents apart?' But Tane-mahuta pauses not, he regards not their shrieks and cries; far, far beneath him he presses down the earth; far, far above him he thrusts up the sky.

Hence these sayings of olden time: 'It was the fierce thrusting of Tane which tore the heaven from the earth, so that they were rent apart, and darkness was made manifest, and so was the light.'

No sooner was heaven rent from earth than the multitude of human beings were discovered whom they had begotten, and who had hitherto lain concealed between the bodies of Rangi and Papa.

Then, also, there arose in the breast of Tawhiri-ma-tea, the god and father of winds and storms, a fierce desire to wage war with his brothers, because they had rent apart their common parents. He from the first had refused to consent to his mother being torn from her lord and children; it was his brothers alone that wished for this separation, and desired that Papa-tu-a-nuku, or the Earth alone, should be left as a parent for them.

The god of hurricanes and storms dreads also that the world should become too fair and beautiful, so he rises, follows his father to the realm above, and hurries to the sheltered hollows in the boundless skies; there he hides and clings, and nestling in this place of rest he consults long with his parent, and as the vast Heaven listens to the suggestions of Tawhiri-ma-tea, thoughts and plans are formed in his breast, and Tawhiri-ma-tea also understands what he should do. Then by himself and the vast Heaven were begotten his numerous brood, and they rapidly increased and grew. Ta-whiri-ma-tea despatches one of them to the westward, and one to the southward, and one to the eastward, and one to the northward; and he gives corresponding names to himself and to his progeny the mighty winds.

He next sends forth fierce squalls, whirlwinds, dense clouds, massy clouds, dark clouds, gloomy thick clouds, fiery clouds, clouds which precede hurricanes, clouds of fiery black, clouds reflecting glowing red light, clouds wildly drifting from all quarters and wildly bursting, clouds of thunder storms, and clouds hurriedly flying. In the midst of these Tawhiri-ma-tea himself sweeps wildly on. Alas! alas! then rages the fierce hurricane; and whilst Tane-mahuta and his gigantic forests still stand, unconscious and unsuspecting, the blast of the breath of the mouth of Tawhiri-ma-tea smites them, the gigantic trees are snapt off right in the middle; alas! alas! they are rent to atoms, dashed to the earth, with boughs and branches torn and scattered, and lying on the earth, trees and branches all alike left for the insect, for the grub, and for loathsome rottenness.

From the forests and their inhabitants Tawhiri-ma-tea next swoops down upon the seas, and lashes in his wrath the ocean. Ah! ah! waves steep as cliffs arise, whose summits are so lofty that to look from them would make the beholder giddy; these soon eddy in whirlpools, and Tangaroa, the god of ocean, and father of all that dwell therein, flies affrighted through his seas; but before he fled, his children consulted together how they might secure their safety, for Tangaroa had begotten Punga, and he had begotten two children, Ika-tere, the father of fish, and Tu-te-wehiwehi, or Tu-te-wanawana, the father of reptiles.

When Tangaroa fled for safety to the ocean, then Tu-te-wehiwehi and Ika-tere, and their children, disputed together as to what they should do to escape from the storms, and Tu-te-wehiwehi and his party cried aloud: "Let us fly inland"; but Ika-tere and his party cried aloud: "Let us fly to the sea." Some would not obey one order, some would not obey the other, and they escaped in two parties: the party of Tu-te-wehiwehi, or the reptiles, hid themselves ashore; the party of Punga rushed to the sea. This is what, in our ancient religious services, is called the separation of Ta-whiri-ma-tea.

Hence these traditions have been handed down:

Ika-tere, the father of things which inhabit water, cried aloud to Tu-te-wehiwehi: "Ho, ho, let us all escape to the sea."

But Tu-te-wehiwehi shouted in answer: "Nay, nay, let us rather fly inland."

Then Ika-tere warned him, saying: "Fly inland, then; and the fate of you and your race will be, that when they catch you, before you are cooked, they will 6inge off your scales over a lighted wisp of dry fern."

But Tu-te-wehiwehi answered him, saying: "Seek safety, then, in the sea; and the future fate of your race will be, that when they serve out little baskets of cooked vegetable food to each person you will be laid upon the top of the food to give a relish to it."

Then without delay these two races of beings separated. The fish fled in confusion to the sea, the reptiles sought safety in the forests and scrubs.'

Tangaroa, enraged at some of his children deserting him, and, being sheltered by the god of the forests on dry land, has ever since waged war on his brother Tane, who, in return, has waged war against him.

Hence Tane supplies the offspring of his brother Tu-matauenga with canoes, with spears and with fish-hooks made from his trees, and with nets woven from his fibrous plants, that they may destroy the offspring of Tangaroa; whilst Tangaroa, in return, swallows up the offspring of Tane, overwhelming canoes with the surges of his sea, swallowing up the lands, trees, and houses that are swept off by floods, and ever wastes away, with his lapping waves, the shores that confine him, that the giants of the forests may be washed down and swept out into his boundless ocean, that he may then swallow up the insects, the young birds, and the various animals which inhabit them – all which things are recorded in the prayers which were offered to these gods.

Tawhiri-ma-tea next rushed on to attack his brothers Rongo-ma-tane and Haumia-tikitiki, the gods and progenitors of cultivated and uncultivated food; but Papa, to save these for her other children, caught them up, and hid them in a place of safety; and so well were these children of hers concealed by their mother Earth, that Tawhiri-ma-tea sought for them in vain.

Tawhiri-ma-tea having thus vanquished all his other brothers, next rushed against Tu-matauenga, to try his strength against his; he exerted all his force against him, but he could neither shake him nor prevail against him. What did Tu-matauenga care for his brother's wrath? he was the only one of the whole party of brothers who had planned the destruction of their parents, and had shown himself brave and fierce in war; his brothers had yielded at once before the tremendous assaults of Tawhiri-ma-tea and his progeny – Tane-mahuta and his offspring had been broken and torn in pieces – Tangaroa and his children had fled to the depths of the ocean or the recesses of the shore – Rongo-ma-tane and Haumia-tikitiki had been hidden from him in the earth – but Tu-matauenga, or man, still stood erect and unshaken upon the breast of his mother Earth; and now at length the hearts of Heaven and of the god of storms became tranquil, and their passions were assuaged.

Tu-matauenga, or fierce man, having thus successfully resisted his brother, the god of hurricanes and storms, next took thought how he could turn upon his brothers and slay them, because they had not assisted him or fought bravely when Tawhiri-ma-tea had attacked them to avenge the separation of their parents, and because they had left him alone to show his prowess in the fight. As yet death had no power over man. It was not until the birth of the children of Taranga and of Makea-tu-tara, of Maui-taha, of Maui-roto, of Maui-pae, of Maui-waho, and of Maui-tikitiki-o-Taranga, the demi-god who tried to drain Hine-nui-te-po, that death had power over men. If that goddess had not been deceived by Maui-tikitiki, men would not have died, but would in that case have lived for ever; it was from his deceiving Hine-nui-te-po that death obtained power over mankind, and penetrated to every part of the earth.

Tu-matauenga continued to reflect upon the cowardly manner in which his brothers had acted, in leaving him to show his courage alone, and he first sought some means of injuring Tane-mahuta, because he had not come to aid him in his combat with Tawhiri-ma-tea, and partly because he was aware that Tane had had a numerous progeny, who were rapidly increasing, and might at last prove hostile to him, and injure him, so he began to collect leaves of the whanake tree, and twisted them into nooses, and when his work was ended, he went to the forest to put up his snares, and hung them up – ha! ha! the children of Tane fell before him, none of them could any longer fly or move in safety.

Then he next determined to take revenge on his brother Tangaroa, who had also deserted him in the combat; so he sought for his offspring, and found them leaping or swimming in the water; then he cut many leaves from the flax-plant, and netted nets with the flax, and dragged these, and hauled the children of Tangaroa ashore.

After that, he determined also to be revenged upon his brothers Rongo-ma-tane and Haumia-tikitiki; he soon found them by their peculiar leaves, and he scraped into shape a wooden hoe, and plaited a basket, and dug in the earth and pulled up all kinds of plants with edible roots, and the plants which had been dug up withered in the sun.

Thus Tu-matauenga devoured all his brothers, and consumed the whole of them, in revenge for their having deserted him and left him to fight alone against Tawhiri-ma-tea and Rangi.

When his brothers had all thus been overcome by Tu, he assumed several names, namely, Tu-ka-riri, Tu-ka-nguha, Tu-ka-taua, Tu-whaka-heke-tan-gata, Tu-mata-wha-iti, and Tu-matauenga; he assumed one name for each of his attributes displayed in the victories over his brothers. Four of his brothers were entirely deposed by him, and became his food; but one of them, Tawhiri-ma-tea, he could not vanquish or make common, by eating him for food, so he, the last born child of Heaven and Earth, was left as an enemy for man, and still, with a rage equal to that of Man, this elder brother ever attacks him in storms and hurricanes, endeavouring to destroy him alike by sea and land.

Now, the meanings of these names of the children of the Heaven and Earth are as follows:

Tangaroa signifies fish of every kind; Rongo-ma-tane signifies the sweet potato, and all vegetables cultivated as food; Haumia-tikitiki signifies fern root, and all kinds of food which grow wild; Tane-mahuta signifies forests, the birds and insects which inhabit them, and all things fashioned from wood; Tawhiri-ma-tea signifies winds and storms; and Tu-matauenga signifies man.

Four of his brothers having, as before stated, been made common, or articles of food, by Tu-matauenga, he assigned for each of them fitting incanta–tions, that they might be abundant, and that he might easily obtain them.

Some incantations were proper to Tane-mahuta, they were called Tane.

Some incantations were for Tangaroa, they were called Tangaroa.

Some were for Rongo-ma-tane, they were called Rongo-ma-tane.

Some were for Haumia-tikitiki, they were called Haumia.

The reason that he sought out these incantations was, that his brothers might be made common by him, and serve for his food. There were also incantations for Tawhiri-ma-tea to cause favourable winds, and prayers to the vast Heaven for fair weather, as also for mother Earth that she might produce all things abundantly. But it was the great God that taught these prayers to man. There were also many prayers and incantations composed for man, suited to the different times and circumstances of his life – prayers at the baptism of an infant; prayers for abundance of food, for wealth; prayers in illness; prayers to spirits, and for many other things.

The bursting forth of the wrathful fury of Ta-whiri-ma-tea against his brothers, was the cause of the disappearance of a great part of the dry land; during that contest a great part of mother Earth was submerged. The names of those beings of ancient days who submerged so large a portion of the earth were – Terrible-rain, Long-continued-rain, Fierce-hail-storms; and their progeny were, Mist, Heavy-dew, and Light-dew, and these together submerged the greater part of the earth, so that only a small portion of dry land projected above the sea.

From that time clear light increased upon the earth, and all the beings which were hidden between Rangi and Papa before they were separated, now multiplied upon the earth. The first beings begotten by Rangi and Papa were not like human beings; but Tu-matauenga bore the likeness of a man, as did all his brothers, as also did a Po, a Ao, a Kore, te Kimihanga and Runuku, and thus it continued until the times of Ngainui and his generation, and of Whiro-te-tupua and his generation, and of Tiki-tawhito-ariki and his generation, and it has so continued to this day.

The children of Tu-matauenga were begotten on this earth, and they increased, and continued to multiply, until we reach at last the generation of Maui-taha, and of his brothers Maui-roto, Maui–waho, Maui-pae, and Maui-tikitiki-o-Taranga.

Up to this time the vast Heaven has still ever remained separated from his spouse the Earth. Yet their mutual love still continues – the soft warm sighs of her loving bosom still ever rise up to him, ascending from the woody mountains and valleys, and men call these mists; and the vast Heaven, as he mourns through the long nights his separation from his beloved, drops frequent tears upon her bosom, and men seeing these, term them dew-drops.

The Discovery of New Zealand
The Legend of Poutini and Whaiapi

NOW PAY ATTENTION to the cause of the contention which arose between Poutini and Whaiapu, which led them to emigrate to New Zealand. For a long time they both rested in the same place, and Hine-tu–a-hoanga, to whom the stone Whaiapu belonged, became excessively enraged with Ngahue, and with his stone Poutini.

At last she drove Ngahue out and forced him to leave the place, and Ngahue departed and went to a strange land, taking his jasper. When Heni-tu-a-hoanga saw that he was departing with his precious stone, she followed after them, and Ngahue arrived at Tuhua with his stone, and Hine-tu-a-hoanga arrived and landed there at the same time with him, and began to drive him away again. Then Ngahue went to seek a place where his jasper stones might remain in peace, and he found in the sea this island Aotearoa (the northern island of New Zealand), and he thought he would land there.

Then he thought again, lest he and his enemy should be too close to one another, and should quarrel again, that it would be better for him to go farther off with his jasper, a very long way off. So he carried it off with him, and they coasted along, and at length arrived at Arahura (on the west coast of the middle island), and he made that an everlasting resting-piace for his jasper; then he broke off a portion of his jasper, and took it with him and returned, and as he coasted along he at length reached Wairere (believed to be upon the east coast of the northern island), and he visited Whangaparoa and Tauranga, and from thence he returned direct to Hawaiki, and reported that he had discovered a new country which produced the moa and jasper in abundance. He now manufactured sharp axes from his jasper; two axes were made from it, Tutauru and Hau-hau-te-rangi. He manufactured some portions of one piece of it into images for neck ornaments, and some portions into ear ornaments; the name of one of these ear ornaments was Kaukaumatua, which was recently in the possession of Te Heuheu, and was only lost in 1846, when he was killed with so many of his tribe by a landslip. The axe Tutauru was only lately lost by Purahokura and his brother Reretai, who were descended from Tama-ihu-toroa. When Ngahue returning, arrived again in Hawaiki, he found them all engaged in war, and when they heard his description of the beauty of this country of Aotea, some of them determined to come here.

Construction of Canoes to Emigrate to New Zealand

They then felled a totara tree in Rarotonga, which lies on the other side of Hawaiki, that they might build the Arawa from it. The tree was felled, and thus the canoe was hewn out from it and finished. The names of the men who built this canoe were, Rata, Wahie-roa, Ngahue, Parata, and some other skilful men, who helped to hew out the Arawa and to finish it.

Preparations to Emigrate

A chief of the name of Hotu-roa, hearing that the Arawa was built, and wishing to accompany them, came to Tama-te-kapua and asked him to lend him his workmen to hew out some canoes for him too, and they went and built and finished the Tainui and some other canoes.

The workmen above mentioned are those who built the canoes in which our forefathers crossed the ocean to this island, to Aotea-roa. The names of the canoes were as follows: the Arawa was first completed, then Tainui, then Matatua, and Takitumu, and Kura-hau-po, and Toko-maru, and Matawhaorua. These are the names of the canoes in which our forefathers departed from Hawaiki, and crossed to this island. When they had lashed the topsides on to the Tainui, Rata slew the son of Manaia, and hid his body in the chips and shavings of the canoes. The names of the axes with which they hewed out these canoes were Hauhau-te-Rangi, and Tutauru. Tutauru was the axe with which they cut off the head of Uenuku.

All these axes were made from the block of green stone brought back by Ngahue to Hawaiki, which was called ' The fish of Ngahue.' He had previously come to these islands from Hawaiki, when he was driven out from thence by Hine-tu-a-hoanga, whose fish or stone was Obsidian. From that cause Ngahue came to these islands; the canoes which afterwards arrived here came in consequence of his discovery.

The Voyage to New Zealand

WHEN THE CANOES were built and ready for sea, they were dragged afloat, the separate lading of each canoe was collected and put on board, with all the crews. Tama-te-kapua then remembered that he had no skilful priest on board his canoe, and he thought the best thing he could do was to outwit Ngatoro-i-rangi, the chief who had com–mand of the Tainui. So just as his canoe shoved off, he called out to Ngatoro: "I say, Ngatoro, just come on board my canoe, and perform the necessary religious rites for me." Then the priest Ngatoro came on board, and Tama-te-kapua said to him: "You had better also call your wife, Kearoa on board, that she may make the canoe clean or common, with an offering of sea-weed to be laid in the canoe instead of an offering of fish, for you know the second fish caught in a canoe, or seaweed, or some substitute, ought to be offered for the females, the first for the males; then my canoe will be quite common, for all the ceremonies will have been observed, which should be followed with canoes made by priests." Ngatoro assented to all this, and called his wife, and they both go into Tama's canoe. The very moment they were on board, Tama' called out to the men on board his canoe: "Heave up the anchors and make sail"; and he carried off with him Ngatoro and his wife, that he might have a priest and wise man on board his canoe. Then they up with the fore-sail, the main-sail, and the mizen, and away shot the canoe. Up then came Ngatoro from below, and said:

"Shorten sail, that we may go more slowly, lest I miss my own canoe." And Tama' replied: "Oh, no, no; wait a little, and your canoe will follow after us." For a short time it kept near them, but soon dropped more and more astern, and when darkness overtook them, on they sailed, each canoe proceeding on its own course.

Two thefts were upon this occasion perpetrated by Tama-te-kapua; he carried off the wife of Ruaeo, and Ngatoro and his wife, on board the Arawa. He made a fool of Ruaeo too, for he said to him: "Oh, Rua', you, like a good fellow, just run back to the village and fetch me my axe Tutauru, I pushed it in under the sill of the window of my house." And Rua' was foolish enough to run back to the house. Then off went Tama' with the canoe, and when Rua' came back again, the canoe was so far off that its sails did not look much bigger than little flies. So he fell to weeping for all his goods on board the canoe, and for his wife Whakaoti-rangi, whom Tama-te-kapua had carried off as a wife for himself. Tama-te-kapua committed these two great thefts when he sailed for these islands. Hence this proverb: 'A descendant of Tama-te-kapua will steal anything he can'.

When evening came on, Rua' threw himself into the water, as a preparation for his incantations to recover his wife, and he then changed the stars of evening into the stars of morning, and those of the morning into the stars of the evening, and this was accomplished. In the meantime the Arawa scudded away far out on the ocean, and Ngatoro thought to himself: "What a rate this canoe goes at – what a vast space we have already traversed. I know what I'll do, I'll climb up upon the roof of the house which is built on the platform joining the two canoes, and try to get a glimpse of the land in the horizon, and ascertain whether we are near it, or very far off." But in the first place he felt some suspicions about his wife, lest Tama-te-kapua should steal her too, for he had found out what a treacherous person he was. So ho took a string and tied one end of it to his wife's hair, and kept the other end of the string in his hand, and then he climbed up on the roof. He had hardly got on the top of the roof when Tama' laid hold of his wife, and he cunningly untied the end of the string which Ngatoro had fastened to her hair, and made it fast to one of the beams of the canoe, and Ngatoro feeling it tight thought his wife had not moved, and that it was still fast to her. At last Ngatoro came down again, and Tama-te-kapua heard the noise of his steps as he was coming, but he had not time to get the string tied fast to the hair of Kearoa's head again, but he jumped as fast as he could into his own berth, which was next to that of Ngatoro, and Ngatoro, to his surprise, found one end of the string tied fast to the beam of the canoe.

Then he knew that his wife had been disturbed by Tama', and he asked her, saying: "Oh, wife, has not some one disturbed you?" Then his wife replied to him: "Cannot you tell that from the string being fastened to the beam of the canoe?" And then he asked her: "Who was it?" And she said: "Who was it, indeed? Could it be any one else but Tama-te-kapua?" Then her husband said to her: "You are a noble woman indeed thus to confess this; you have gladdened my heart by this confession; I thought after Tama' had carried us both off in this way, that he would have acted generously, and not loosely in this manner; but, since he has dealt in this way, I will now have my revenge on him."

Then that priest again went forth upon the roof of the house and stood there, and he called aloud to the heavens, in the same way that Rua' did, and he changed the stars of the evening into those of morning, and he raised the winds that they should blow upon the prow of the canoe, and drive it astern, and the crew of the canoe were at their wits' end, and quite forgot their skill as seamen, and the canoe drew straight into the whirlpool, called 'The throat of Te Parata', and dashed right into that whirlpool.

The canoe became engulphed by the whirlpool, and its prow disappeared in it. In a moment the waters reached the first bailing place in the bows, in another second they reached the second bailing place in the centre, and the canoe now appeared to be going down into the whirlpool head foremost; then up started Hei, but before he could rise they had already sunk far into the whirlpool. Next the rush of waters was heard by Ihenga, who slept forward, and he shouted out: "Oh, Ngatoro, oh, we are settling down head first. The pillow of your wife Kearoa has already fallen from under her head!" Ngatoro sat astern listening; the same cries of distress reached him a second time. Then up sprang Tama-te-kapua, and he in despair shouted out: "Oh, Ngatoro, Ngatoro, aloft there! Do you hear? The canoe is gone down so much by the bow, that Kearoa's pillow has rolled from under her head." The priest heard them, but neither moved nor answered until he heard the goods rolling from the decks and splashing into the water; the crew meanwhile held on to the canoe with their hands with great difficulty, some of them having already fallen into the sea.

When these things all took place, the heart of Ngatoro was moved with pity, for he heard, too, the shrieks and cries of the men, and the weeping of the women and children. Then up stood that mighty man again, and by his incantations changed the aspect of the heavens, so that the storm ceased, and he repeated another incantation to draw the canoe back out of the whirlpool, that is, to lift it up again.

Lo, the canoe rose up from the whirlpool, floating rightly; but, although the canoe itself thus floated out of the whirlpool, a great part of its lading had been thrown out into the water, a few things only were saved, and remained in the canoe. A great part of their provisions were lost as the canoe was sinking into the whirlpool. Thence comes the native proverb, if they can give a stranger but little food, or only make a present of a small basket of food: 'Oh, it is the half-filled basket of Whakaoti-rangi, for she only managed to save a very small part of her provisions. Then they sailed on, and landed at Whanga-Paraoa, in Aotea here. As they drew near to land, they saw with surprise some pohutu–kawa trees of the sea-coast, covered with beautiful red flowers, and the still water reflected back the redness of the trees.

Then one of the chiefs of the canoe cried out to his messmates: "See there, red ornaments for the head are much more plentiful in this country than in Hawaiki, so I'll throw my red head ornaments into the water"; and, so saying, he threw them into the sea. The name of that man was Tauninihi; the name of the red head ornament he threw into the sea was Taiwhakaea. The moment they got on shore they run to gather the pohutukawa flowers, but no sooner did they touch them than the flowers fell to pieces; then they found out that these red head ornaments were nothing but flowers. All the chiefs on board the Arawa were then troubled that they should have been so foolish as to throw away their red head ornaments into the sea. Very shortly afterwards the ornaments of Tauninihi were found by Mahina on the beach of Mabiti. As soon as Tauninihi heard they had been picked up, he ran to Mahina to get them again, but Mahina would not give them up to him; thence this proverb for anything which has been lost and is found by another person: "I will not give it up, 'tis the red head ornament which Mahina found."

As soon as the party landed at Whanga-Paraoa, they planted sweet potatoes, that they might grow there; and they are still to be found growing on the cliffs at that place.

Then the crew, wearied from the voyage, wandered idly along the shore, and there they found the fresh carcase of a sperm whale stranded upon the beach. The Tainui had already arrived in the same neighbourhood, although they did not at first see that canoe nor the people who had come in it; when, however, they met, they began to dispute as to who had landed first and first found the dead whale, and as to which canoe it consequently belonged; so, to settle the question, they agreed to examine the sacred place which each party had set up to return thanks in to the gods for their safe arrival, that they might see which had been longest built; and, doing so, they found that the posts of the sacred place put up by the Arawa were quite green, whilst the posts of the sacred place set up by the Tainui had evidently been carefully dried over the fire before they had been fixed in the ground. The people who had come in the Tainui also showed part of a rope which they had made fast to its jawbone. When these things were seen, it was admitted that the whale belonged to the people who came in the Tainui, and it was surrendered to them. And the people in the Arawa, determining to separate from those in the Tainui, selected some of their crew to explore the country in a north-west direction, following the coast line. The canoe then coasted along, the land party following it along the shore; this was made up of 140 men, whose chief was Taikehu, and these gave to a place the name of Te Ranga of Taikehu.

The Tainui left Whanga-Paraoa shortly after the Arawa, and, proceeding nearly in the same direction as the Arawa, made the Gulf of Hauraki, and then coasted along to Rakau-mangamanga, or Cape Brett, and to the island with an arched passage through it, called Motukokako, which lies off the cape; thence they ran along the coast to Whiwhia, and to Te Aukanapanapa, and to Muri-whenua, or the country near the North Cape. Finding that the land ended there, they returned again along the coast until they reached the Tamaki, and landed there, and afterwards proceeded up the creek to Tau-oma, or the portage, where they were surprised to see flocks of sea-gulls and oyster-catchers passing over from the westward; so they went off to explore the country in that direction, and to their great surprise found a large sheet of water lying immediately behind them, so they determined to drag their canoes over the portage at a place they named Otahuhu, and to launch them again on the vast sheet of salt-water which they had found.

The first canoe which they hauled across was the Toko-maru – that they got across without difficulty. They next began to drag the Tainui over the isthmus; they hauled away at it in vain, they could not stir it; for one of the wives of Hoturoa, named Marama-kiko-hura, who was unwilling that the tired crews should proceed further on this new expedition, had by her enchantments fixed it so firmly to the earth that no human strength could stir it; so they hauled, they hauled, they excited themselves with cries and cheers, but they hauled in vain, they cried aloud in vain, they could not move it. When their strength was quite exhausted by these efforts, then another of the wives of Hoturoa, more learned in magic and incantations than Marama-kiko-hura, grieved at seeing the exhaustion and distress of her people, rose up, and chanted forth an incantation far more powerful than that of Marama-kiko-hura; then at once the canoe glided easily over the carefully-laid skids, and it soon floated securely upon the harbour of Manuka. The willing crews urged on the canoes with their paddles; they soon discovered the mouth of the harbour upon the west coast, and passed out through it into the open sea; they coasted along the western coast to the southwards, and discovering the small port of Kawhia, they entered it, and, hauling up their canoe, fixed themselves there for the time, whilst the Arawa was left at Maketu.

We now return to the Arawa. We left the people of it at Tauranga. That canoe next floated at Motiti; they named that place after a spot in Ha–waiki (because there was no firewood there). Next Tia, to commemorate his name, called the place now known by the name of Rangiuru, Takapu-o-tapui-ika-nui-a-Tia. Then Hei stood up and called out: "I name that place Takapu-o-wai-tahanui-a-Hei"; the name of that place is now Otawa. Then stood up Tama-te-kapua, and pointing to the place now called the Heads of Maketu, he called out: "I name that place Te Kuraetanga-o-te-ihu-o-Tama-te-kapua." Next Kahu called a place, after his name, Motiti-nui-a-Kahu.

Ruaeo, who had already arrived at Maketu, started up. He was the first to arrive there in his canoe – the Pukeatea-wai-nui – for he had been left behind by the Arawa, and his wife Whakaoti-rangi had been carried off by Tama-te-kapua, and after the Arawa had left he had sailed in his own canoe for these islands, and landed at Maketu, and his canoe reached land the first; well, he started up, cast his line into the sea, with the hooks attached to it, and they got fast in one of the beams of the Arawa, and it was pulled ashore by him (whilst the crew were asleep), and the hundred and forty men who had accompanied him stood upon the beach of Maketu, with skids all ready laid, and the Arawa was by them dragged upon the shore in the night, and left there; and Ruaeo seated himself under the side of the Arawa, and played upon his flute, and the music woke his wife, and she said: "Dear me, that's Rua'!" – and when she looked, there he was sitting under the side of the canoe, and they passed the night together.

At last Rua' said: "O mother of my children, go back now to your new husband, and presently I'll play upon the flute and putorino, so that both you and Tama-te-kapua may hear. Then do you say to Tama-te-kapua 'O! la, I had a dream in the night that I heard Rua playing a tune upon his flute', and that will make him so jealous that he will give you a blow, and then you can run away from him again, as if you were in a rage and hurt, and you can come to me."

Then Whakaoti-rangi returned, and lay down by Tama-te-kapua, and she did everything exactly as Rua' had told her, and Tama' began to beat her (and she ran away from him). Early in the morning Rua' performed incantations, by which he kept all the people in the canoe in a profound sleep, and whilst they still slept from his enchantments, the sun rose, and mounted high up in the heavens. In the forenoon, Rua' gave the canoe a heavy blow with his club; they all started up; it was almost noon, and when they looked down over the edge of their canoe, there were the hundred and forty men of Rua' sitting under them, all beautifully dressed with feathers, as if they had been living on the Gannet Island, in the channel of Karewa, where feathers are so abundant; and when the crew of the Arawa heard this, they all rushed upon deck, and saw Rua' standing in the midst of his one hundred and forty warriors.

Then Rua' shouted out as he stood: "Come here, Tama-te-kapua; let us two fight the battle, you and I alone. If you are stronger than I am, well and good, let it be so; if I am stronger than you are, I'll dash you to the earth."

Up sprang then the hero Tama-te-kapua; he held a carved two-handed sword, a sword the handle of which was decked with red feathers. Rua' held a similar weapon. Tama' first struck a fierce blow at Rua'. Rua' parried it, and it glanced harmlessly off; then Rua' threw away his sword, and seized both the arms of Tama-te-kapua; he held his arms and his sword, and dashed him to the earth. Tama' half rose, and was again dashed down; once more he almost rose, and was thrown again. Still Tama' fiercely struggled to rise and renew the fight. For the fourth time he almost rose up, then Rua', overcome with rage, took a heap of vermin (this he had prepared for the purpose, to cover Tama' with insult and shame), and rubbed them on Tama-te-kapua's head and ear, and they adhered so fast that Tama' tried in vain to get them out.

Then Rua' said: "There, I've beaten you; now keep the woman, as a payment for the insults I've heaped upon you, and for having been beaten by me." But Tama' did not hear a word he said; he was almost driven mad with the pain and itching, and could do nothing but stand scratching and rubbing his head; whilst Rua' departed with his hundred and forty men to seek some other dwelling-place for themselves; if they had turned against Tama' and his people to fight against them, they would have slain them all.

These men were giants – Tama-te-kapua was nine feet high, Rua' was eleven feet high; there have been no men since that time so tall as those heroes.

The only man of these later times who was as tall as these was Tu-hou-rangi: he was nine feet high; he was six feet up to the armpits. This generation have seen his bones, they used to be always set up by the priests in the sacred places when they were made high places for the sacred sacrifices of the natives, at the times the potatoes and sweet potatoes were dug up, and when the fishing season commenced, and when they attacked an enemy; then might be seen the people collecting, in their best garments, and with their ornaments, on the days when the priests exposed Tu-hou-rangi's bones to their view. At the time that the island Mokoia, in the lake of Roto-rua, was stormed and taken by the Nga-Puhi, they probably carried those bones off, for they have not since been seen.

After the dispute between Tama-te-kapua and Rua' took place, Tama' and his party dwelt at Maketu, and their descendants after a little time spread to other places. Ngatoro-i-rangi went, however, about the country, and where he found dry valleys, stamped on the earth, and brought forth springs of water; he also visited the mountains, and placed Patupaiarehe, or fairies, there, and then returned to Maketu and dwelt there.

After this a dispute arose between Tama-te-kapua and Kahu-mata-momoe, and in consequence of that disturbance, Tama' and Ngatoro removed to Tauranga, and found Taikehu living there, and collecting food for them (by fishing), and that place was called by them Te Bang a-a-Taikehu; it lies beyond Motu-hoa; then they departed from Tauranga, and stopped at Kati-kati, where they ate food. Tama's men devoured the food very fast, whilst he kept on only nibbling his, therefore they applied this circumstance as a name for the place, and called it: 'Kati-kati-o-Tama-te-kapua', the nibbling of Tama-te kapua; then they halted at Whakahau, so called because they here ordered food to be cooked, which they did not stop to eat, but went right on with Ngatoro, and this circumstance gave its name to the place; and they went on from place to place till they arrived at Whitianga, which they so called from their crossing the river there, and they continued going from one place to another till they came to Tangiaro, and Ngatoro stuck up a stone and left it there, and they dwelt in Moehau and Hau-raki.

They occupied those places as a permanent residence, and Tama-te-kapua died, and was buried there. When he was dying, he ordered his children to return to Maketu, to visit his relations; and they assented, and went back. If the children of Tama-te-kapua had remained at Hau-raki, that place would now have been left to them as a possession.

Tama-te-kapua, when dying, told his children where the precious ear-drop Kaukau-matua was, which he had hidden under the window of his house; and his children returned with Ngatoro to Maketu, and dwelt there; and as soon as Ngatoro arrived, he went to the waters to bathe himself, as he had come there in a state of tapu, upon account of his having buried Tama-te-kapua, and having bathed, he then became free from the tapu and clean.

Ngatoro then took the daughter of Ihenga to wife, and he went and searched for the precious ear-drop Kaukau-matua, and found it, as Tama-te-kapua had told him. After this the wife of Kahu-mata-momoe conceived a child.

At this time Ihenga, taking some dogs with him to catch kiwis with, went to Paritangi by way of Hakomiti, and kiwi was chased by one of his dogs, and caught in a lake, and the dog ate some of the fish and shellfish in the lake, after diving in the water to get them, and returned to its master carrying the captured kiwi in its mouth, and on reaching its master, it dropped the kiwi, and vomited up the raw fish and shell-fish which it had eaten.

When Ihenga saw his dog wet all over, and the fish it had vomited up, he knew there was a lake there, and was extremely glad, and returned joyfully to Maketu, and there he had the usual religious ceremonies which follow the birth of a child performed over his wife and the child she had given birth to; and when this had been done, he went to explore the coimtry which he had previously visited with his dog.

To his great surprise he discovered a lake; it was Lake Roto-iti; he left a mark there to show that he claimed it as his own. He went farther and discovered Lake Roto-rua; he saw that its waters were running; he left there also a mark to show that he claimed the lake as his own. As he went along the side of the lake; he found a man occupying the ground; then he thought to himself that he would endeavour to gain possession of it by craft, so he looked out for a spot fit for a sacred place, where men could offer up their prayers, and for another spot fit for a sacred place, where nets could be hung up, and he found fit spots; then he took suitable stones to surround the sacred place with, and old pieces of seaweed, looking as if they had years ago been employed as offerings, and he went into the middle of the shrubbery, thick with boughs of the taha shrub, of the koromuka, and of the karamu; there he stuck up the posts of the sacred place in the midst of the shrubs, and tied bunches of fiax-leaves on the posts, and having done this, he went to visit the village of the people who lived there.

They saw someone approaching and cried out:

"A stranger, a stranger, is coming here!" As soon as Ihenga heard these cries, he sat down upon the ground, and then, without waiting for the people of the place to begin the speeches, he jumped up, and commenced to speak thus: "What theft is this, what theft is this of the people here, that they are taking away my land?" – for he saw that they had their store-houses full of prepared fern-roots and of dried fish, and shell-fish, and their heaps of fishing-nets, so as he spoke, he appeared to swell with rage, and his throat appeared to grow large from passion as he talked: "Who authorized you to come here, and take possession of my place? Be off, be off, be off! leave alone the place of the man who speaks to you, to whom it has belonged for a very long time, for a very long time indeed."

Then Maru-punga-nui, the son of Tua-Roto-rua, the man to whom the place really belonged, said to Ihenga: "It is not your place, it belongs to me; if it belongs to you, where is your village, where is your sacred place, where is your net, where are your cultivations and gardens?"

Ihenga answered him: "Come here and see them." So they went together, and ascended a hill, and Ihenga said: "See there, there is my net hanging up against the ricks; but it was no such thing, it was only a mark like a net hanging up, caused by part of a cliff having slipped away; and there are the posts of the pine round my village; but there was really nothing but some old stumps of trees; look there too at my sacred place a little beyond yours; and now come with me, and see my sacred place, if you are quite sure you see my village, and my fishing-net – come along." So they went together, and there he saw the sacred place standing in the shrubbery, until at last he believed Ihenga, and the place was all given up to Ihenga, and he took possession of it and lived there, and the descendants of Tua-Roto-rua departed from that place, and a portion of them, under the chiefs Kawa-arero and Mata-aho, occupied the island of Mokoia, in Lake Roto-rua.

At this time Ngatoro again went to stamp on the earth, and to bring forth springs in places where there was no water, and came out on the great central plains which surround Lake Taupo, where a piece of large cloak made of kiekie-leaves was stripped off by the bushes, and the strips took root, and became large trees, nearly as large as the Kahikatea tree (they are called Painanga, and many of them are growing there still).

Whenever he ascended a hill, he left marks there, to show that he claimed it; the marks he left were fairies. Some of the generation now living have seen these spirits; they are malicious spirits. If you take embers from an oven in which food has been cooked, and use them for a fire in a house, these spirits become offended; although there be many people sleeping in that house, not one of them could escape (the fairies would, whilst they slept, press the whole of them to death).

Ngatoro went straight on and rested at Taupo, and he beheld that the summit of Mount Tongariro was covered with snow, and he was seized with a longing to ascend it, and he climbed up, saying to his companions who remained below at their encampment: "Remember now, do not you, who I am going to leave behind, taste food from the time I leave you until I return, when we will all feast together." Then he began to ascend the mountain, but he had not quite got to the summit when those he had left behind began to eat food, and he therefore found the greatest difficulty in reacliing the summit of the mountain, and the hero nearly perished in the attempt.

At last he gathered strength, and thought he could save himself, if he prayed aloud to the gods of Hawaiki to send fire to him, and to produce a volcano upon the mountain; (and his prayer was answered,) and fire was given to him, and the mountain became a volcano, and it came by the way of Whakaari, or White Island, of Mau-tohora, of Okakaru, of Roto-ehu, of Roto-iti, of Roto-rua, of Tara-wera, of Pae-roa, of Orakeikorako, and of Taupo; it came right underneath the earth, spouting up at all the above-mentioned places, and ascended right up Tongariro, to him who was sitting upon the top of the mountain, and thence the hero was revived again, and descended, and returned to Maketu, and dwelt there.

The Arawa had been laid up by its crew at Maketu, where they landed, and the people who had arrived with the party in the Arawa spread themselves over the country, examining it, some penetrating to Roto-rua, some to Taupo, some to Whanganui, some to Ruatahuna, and no one was left at Maketu but Hei' and his son, and Tia and his son, and the usual place of residence of Ngatoro-i-rangi was on the island of Motiti. The people who came with the Tainui were still in Kawhia, where they had landed.

One of their chiefs, named Raumati, heard that the Arawa was laid up at Maketu, so he started with all his own immediate dependants, and reaching Tauranga, halted there, and in the evening again pressed on towards Maketu, and reached the bank of the river, opposite that on which the Arawa was lying, thatched over with reeds and dried branches and leaves; then he slung a dart, the point of which was bound round with combustible materials, over to the other side of the river; the point of the dart was lighted, and it stuck right in the dry thatch of the roof over the Arawa, and the shed of dry stuff taking fire, the canoe was entirely destroyed.

On the night that the Arawa was burnt by Raumati, there was not a person left at Maketu; they were all scattered in the forests, at Tapu-ika, and at Waitaha, and Ngatoro-i-rangi was at that moment at his residence on the island of Motiti. The pa, or fortified village at Maketu, was left quite empty, without a soul in it. The canoe was lying alone, with none to watch it; they had all gone to collect food of different kinds – it happened to be a season in which food was very abundant, and from that cause the people were all scattered in small parties about the country, fishing, fowling, and collecting food.

As soon as the next morning dawned, Raumati could see that the fortified village of Maketu was empty, and not a person left in it, so he and his armed followers at once passed over the river and entered the village, which they found entirely deserted.

At night, as the Arawa burnt, the people, who were scattered about in the various parts of the country, saw the fire, for the bright glare of the gleaming flames was reflected in the sky, lighting up the heavens, and they all thought that it was the village at Maketu that had been burnt; but those persons who were near Waitaha and close to the sea-shore near where the Arawa was, at once said: "That must be the Arawa which is burning; it must have been accidentally set on fire by some of our friends who have come to visit us." The next day they went to see what had taken place, and when they reached the place where the Arawa had been lying, they found it had been burnt by an enemy, and that nothing but the ashes of it were left them. Then a messenger started to all the places where the people were scattered about, to warn them of what had taken place, and they then first heard the bad news.

The children of Hou, as they discussed in their house of assembly the burning of the Arawa, remembered the proverb of their father, which he spake to them as they were on the point of leaving Hawaiki, and when he bid them farewell.

He then said to them: "My children, Mako, O Tia, O Hei, hearken to these my words: There was but one great chief in Hawaiki, and that was Whakatauihu. Now do you, my dear children, depart in peace, and when you reach the place you are going to, do not follow after the deeds of Tu, the god of war; if you do you will perish, as if swept off by the winds, but rather follow quiet and useful occupations, then you will die tranquilly a natural death. Depart, and dwell in peace with all, leave war and strife behind you here. Depart, and dwell in peace. It is war and its evils which are driving you from hence; dwell in peace where you are going, conduct yourselves like men, let there be no quarrelling amongst you, but build up a great people."

These were the last words which Houmai-ta-whiti addressed to his children, and they ever kept these sayings of their father firmly fixed in their hearts. "Depart in peace to explore new homes for yourselves."

Uenuku perhaps gave no such parting words of advice to his children, when they left him for this country, because they brought war and its evils with them from the other side of the ocean to New Zealand. But, of course, when Raumati burnt the Arawa, the descendants of Houmai-ta-whiti could not help continually considering what they ought to do, whether they should declare war upon account of the destruction of their canoe, or whether they should let this act pass by without notice. They kept these thoughts always close in mind, and impatient feelings kept ever rising up in their hearts. They could not help saying to one another: 'It was upon account of war and its consequences, that we deserted our own country, that we left our fathers, our homes, and our people, and war and evil are following after us here. Yet we cannot remain patient under such an injury, every feeling urges us to revenge this wrong.'

At last they made an end of deliberation, and unanimously agreed that they would declare war, to obtain compensation for the evil act of Raumati in burning the Arawa; and then commenced the great war which was waged between those who arrived in the Arawa and those who arrived in the Tainui.

The First Tui Tonga

THERE FIRST APPEARED on the earth the human offspring of a worm or grub, and the head of the worm became Tui Tonga. His name was Kohai and he was the first Tui Tonga in the world. The descendants of the worm became very numerous.

A large casuarina tree grew on the island of Toonangakava, between the islands of Mataaho and Talakite in the lagoon of Tongatabu. This great casuarina tree reached to the sky, and a god came down from the sky by this great tree. This god was Tangaloa Eitumatupua.

When he came down there was a woman fishing. Her name was Ilaheva and also Vaepopua. The god from the sky came to her and caught her, and they cohabited. Their sleeping place was called Mohenga.

The god ascended to the sky by the big casuarina, but again returned to the woman. They went and slept on the island of Talakite. They overslept and the day dawned. There flew by a tern, called tala, and found them. The tern cried and the god Eitumatupua awoke. He called the woman Ilaheva: "Wake! it is day. The tern has seen us, because we overslept. Wake! It is day." So that island was called Talakite (Tern-saw) in commemoration of the tern finding them. Another island was called Mataaho (Eye-of-day).

The god returned to the sky, but came back to the woman and they co-habited. The woman Ilaheva became pregnant and gave birth to a male child. The woman tended the child on earth, but the god dwelt in the sky. After a time the god returned and asked the woman about their child.

"Ilaheva, what is our child?" Ilaheva answered: "A male child." Then said the god: "His name shall be Ahoeitu (Day-has-dawned)." Moreover, the god asked the woman: "Is the soil of your land clay or sand?" The woman replied: "My place is sandy." Then said the god: "Wait until I throw down a piece of clay from the sky, to make a garden for the boy Ahoeitu, and also a yam for the garden of our child."

So the god poured down the mount (near Maufanga, Tongatabu) called Holohiufi (Pour-the-yam), and brought down the yam from the sky. The name of the yam was *heketala* (slip-tern). That was the garden he brought down.

The god returned to the sky, while the woman and child remained on earth, on their land called Popua (the land to the east of Maufanga in Tongatabu, on which rises the hill Holohiufi). The mother and son lived together until the child Ahoeitu was big. Ahoeitu asked his mother: "Vaepopua, who is my father? Tell me so that I may go some time and see him." And the mother told him that his father was in the sky. "What is his name?" the boy asked. "It is Eitumatupua," replied the mother.

The boy grew big and one day he told his mother: "I want to go to the sky, so that I can see my father, but there is nothing for me to go in." His mother instructed him: "Go and climb the great casuarina, for that is the road to the sky; and see you father." She gave him a tapa loin cloth and anointed his head with oil. When he was ready, he asked: "How will I know my father, as I am not acquainted with his dwelling place in the sky?" His mother replied: "You will go to the sky and proceed along the big wide road. You will see you father catching pigeons on the mound by the road."

Ahoeitu climbed the great casuarina tree and reached the sky. He went along the road as his mother had directed, found the mound, and saw his father catching pigeons. When his father saw him approaching, he sat down because he was overpowered at seeing his son. Ahoeitu spoke when he saw his father sit down, as if paying respect to him, his own son. That is why he spoke at once to his father, saying: "Lord, stand up. Do not sit down."

The lad went to his father and they pressed noses and cried. Then the father asked him: "Where have you come from?" "I have come from earth, sent by Ilaheva, my mother, to seek you, my father Eitumatupua." His father responded: "Here am I," and he put forth his hand and drew his son's head to him and again they pressed noses and cried. The god was overpowered at the realization that here was his son. Leaving the pigeon catching, they went to Eitumatupua's residence, to the house of Ahoeitu's father. There they had kava and food.

That day the celestial sons of Eitumatupua were having an entertainment. They were playing the game called *sikaulutoa* (played with a reed throwing-stick with a head of toa or casuarina wood). The god sent Ahoeitu to his brothers, saying: "You had better go to the entertainment of your brothers, which they are having on the road in the green (*malae*)." So Ahoeitu went and looked on at the game of throwing reeds at the casuarina trunk. The people saw the lad and all gazed at him with one accord. They liked him, because he was very handsome and well formed. All of the people at the entertainment wondered who he was and whence he had come. His brothers were immediately jealous of him.

Some of the people said that they knew that he was the son of Eituma-tupua, who has just come to the sky from the earth. Then all the people of the entertainment knew, and also his brothers knew that this lad was their brother. The brothers were very angry and jealous that it should be said that this strange lad was the son of their father. They, therefore, sprang upon and tore him to pieces, then cooked and ate him. (Some accounts say his flesh was eaten uncooked.) His head was left over, so they threw it among the plants called hoi. This caused one kind of hoi to become bitter. There is another kind that is sweet. The bitter kind became so because Ahoeitu's head was thrown into it. That kind of *hoi* is not eaten, because it is poisonous.

After a little while Ahoeitu's father, Eitumatupua, said to a woman: "Go, woman, and seek the lad at the entertainment, so that he may eat, lest he become hungry." The woman went at once to the entertainment and asked: "Where is Ahoeitu? The lad is wanted to come and eat." The people answered: "He was here walking around and observing the sika game." They searched, but could not find him at the entertainment. So the woman returned to Eitumatupua and reported: "The lad is not to be found."

Eitumatupua suspected that Ahoeitu's brothers had killed the lad. Therefore, he sent a message for them to come. He asked them: "Where is the lad?" and they lied, saying: "We do not know." Then their father said: "Come and vomit." A big wooden bowl was brought. They were told to tickle their throats, so that they would vomit up the flesh of the lad and also the blood; in fact, all the parts they had eaten. They all had their throats tickled and they vomited, filling the wooden bowl.

They were then asked: "Where is his head?" The murderers replied: "We threw it into the bush, into the *hoi* bush." Then the god Eitumatupua sent a messenger to seek the head of Ahoeitu.

They also collected his bones and put them together with his head into the bowl and poured water on to the flesh and blood. Then were plucked and brought the leaves of the *nonufiafia* tree. The leaves of this tree placed on a sick person possess the virtue of bringing immediate recovery, even if the person is nigh unto death. So the *nonufiafia*, or the Malay apple (*Eugenia malaccensis*), leaves were covered over the remains of Ahoeitu, and the bowl containing them was taken and put behind the house. They visited the bowl continually and, after a time, poured out the water. The flesh of his body had become compact. They visited the bowl again and again and at last found him sitting up in it.

Then they told Eitumatupua that Ahoeitu was alive, for he was sitting up. They were told to bring him into the house, into the presence of his father. Then Eitumatupua spoke, ordering that the brothers of Ahoeitu, who ate him, be brought. Their father then addressed them.

"You have killed Ahoeitu. He shall descend as the ruler of Tonga, while you, his brothers, remain here." But the brothers loved Ahoeitu, as they had just realized that he was their real brother and had one father with them. Therefore, they pleaded with their father to be allowed to accompany Ahoeitu, a plea which was finally granted.

Ahoeitu returned to earth and became Tui Tonga, the first (divine) Tui Tonga of the world. The Tui Tonga who originated from the offspring of the worm were displaced.

Ahoeitu's brothers followed and joined him. They were Talafale, Matakehe, Maliepo, Tui Loloko, and Tui Folaha. Eitumatupua told Talafale that he was to go to the earth, but that he would not be Tui Tonga, as he was a murderer. He was, however, to be called Tui Faleua. Eitumatupua said that Maliepo and Matakehe were to go to guard the Tui Tonga. Tui Loloko and Tui Folaha were to govern. Should a Tui Tonga die, they were to have charge of all funerary arrangements, just as though it were the funeral of the Tui Langi (King of the Sky), Eitumatupua.

It is the descendants of Ahoeitu, he who was murdered in the sky, who have successively been Tui Tonga. The descendants of Talafale are the Tui Pelehake. The descendants of Matakehe are not known, having become extinct. The descendants of Maliepo are called Lauaki. The descendants of Tui Loloko are still called Tui Loloko.

The Tui Tonga and their families are of the highest rank, because Ahoeitu came originally from the sky. He was the first chief appointed from the sky, the Tui Tonga of all the world of brown people as far as Uea (Wallis island), the ruler of the world. His divine origin makes his descendants real chiefs. In fact, it became customary to ask of one who is proud or thinks himself a chief: "Is he a chief? Did he descend from the sky?"

The son of Ahoeitu was Lolofakangalo, and he became Tui Tonga when Ahoeitu died; and the son of Lolofakangalo was Fangaoneone and he became the third Tui Tonga. The son of Fangaoneone was Lihau, and he was the fourth Tui Tonga. The son of Lihau was Kofutu; he was the fifth Tui Tonga. Kaloa, the son of Kofutu, was the sixth Tui Tonga. His son Mauhau was the seventh Tui Tonga. Then followed Apuanea, Afulunga, Momo, and Tuitatui. It was Tuitatui who erected the Haamonga-a-Maui, or Burden-of-Maui (the well-known trilithon of Tongatabu).

The following account concerns the Tui Tonga Tuitatui and what he did on the raised platform house (*fale fatataki*). His sister went to him. Her name was Latutama and she was female Tui Tonga. Her attendant followed her to Tuitatui's house. After his sister arrived Tuitatui ascended to his platform and then he began his lies, for, behold, he had desire for his sister to go up to the platform, so that they might have sexual intercourse. From above he said to his sister below: "Here is a vessel coming, a vessel from Haapai very likely; a very large vessel."

And Latutama answered: "Oh, it is your lies." "It is not my lies," retorted Tuitatui. "Come up and see the vessel yourself." Then his sister climbed up and sat with him on the platform, while her attendant remained below, and Tuitatui and his sister had sexual intercourse. That was the way of that Tui Tonga, and it was known to the attendant.

They dwelt together at their place of abode in Hahake (eastern Tonga–tabu), the name of which was Heketa (near the modern village of Niutoua). The trilithon called the Burden-of-Maui and Tuitatui's terraced stone tomb are situated there. There was also there the Olotele (or dwelling-place of the Tui Tonga) and the course for the game played by the Tui Tonga with the sikaulutoa (a reed throwing-stick with a head of toa, or casuarina wood).

The sons of Tuitatui were Talaatama and Talaihaapepe. When Tuitatui died, his son Talaatama succeeded him.

Then Talaatama spoke to his brother Talaihaapepe concerning the undesirability of Heketa as a place of residence. Said he: "Let us move and leave this dwelling place, because of our love for our two vessels; lest here they go aground and be broken to pieces, for this is a very bad anchorage." His brother Talaihaapepe replied: "It is true, but where will we go?" And Talaatama answered: "To Fangalongonoa (*fanga*, shore; *longonoa*, quiet), lest our vessels get wrecked." That is the reason why they moved their vessels to Fangalongonoa and made their dwelling near by. The place where they dwelt was called Mua. They took their two vessels with them. The name of one vessel was 'Akiheuho', and the name of the other vessel was 'Tongafuesia'.

That is the reason why Laufilitonga dwells at Mua. It is the dwelling place prepared by Talaatama and Talaihaapepe. It was they who first moved from Hahake (referring to Heketa on the northeast coast of Tong-atabu) and it was they who prepared Mua. And all of the Tui Tonga who have succeeded them have dwelt there, even unto Laufilitonga, the present Tui Tonga.

When Talaatama died, he was succeeded by Tui Tonga Nui Tama Tou. This was not a person, but a piece of *tou* (*Cordia aspera*) wood which Talai-haapepe caused to be set up as Tui Tonga, for he did not himself wish to become Tui Tonga immediately after his brother Talaatama. It being Talaihaapepe's desire that a dummy Tui Tonga be enthroned, the piece of tou wood was dressed in tapa and fine mats and duly appointed. A royal wife (*moheofo*), too, was appointed for the Tama Tou. After it had been three years Tui Tonga, the vault stones were cut for the tomb and the Tama Tou was buried in the vault. Then it was pretended that his wife was pregnant, so that she might give birth to a Tui Tonga. The fictitious child was none other than the wily Talaihaapepe, the brother of Talaatama, who was then proclaimed Tui Tonga. A proclamation was made to the people of the land that the Tui Tonga's wife (the moheofo) had given birth to a son whose father was the recently deceased Tui Tonga Tama Tou. The truth of the matter was that it was really Talaihaapepe, who was at once proclaimed Tui Tonga.

These are the things that those three Tui Tonga, Tuitatui, Talaatama and Talaihaapepe, did.

Then followed in succession the Tui Tonga Talakaifaiki, Talafapite, Tui Tonga Maakatoe, Tui Tonga i Puipui, and Havea.

Havea was assassinated. He died and his body was cut in two and his head and chest floated on shore. He was murdered while having his bath, and the name of the expanse of water where he bathed is Tolopona. It is by the roadside at a place called Alakifonua (modern village of Alaki, Tongatabu island). After his head and chest floated on shore, a gallinule (*Porphyrio vitiensis*) called *kalae* came and pecked the face of the dead chief. In consequence that beach was called Houmakalae. When Lufe, the chief of the dead Tui Tonga's mother's family, learned of the king's death, he said: 'The Tui Tonga is dead. He has died a bad death, for he is cut in two. Come and kill me and join my buttocks and legs to the Tui Tonga's trunk, so that the corpse may be complete.' His relatives obeyed him. They slew him to make the Tui Tonga's body complete and then buried the remains. Thus it was done for the Tui Tonga Havea who was slain.

Another Tui Tonga was Tatafueikimeimua; another was Lomiaetupua; another Tui Tonga was Havea (II.), who was shot by a Fijian man called Tuluvota; he was shot through the head and he died.

Another Tui Tonga was Takalaua. His wife was a woman called Vae. When she was born, she had a head like a pigeon's head, and her parents deserted her. Her father's name was Leasinga and her mother's name was Leamata. They left her at the island of Ata (near Tongatabu), while they sailed to Haapai.

Ahe, the chief of the island of Ata, went down to look at the place where the boat had been beached, and he said, "Perhaps the canoe went last night." He walked about near the place where the canoe landed, and he saw something moving. It was covered with a piece of tapa. Behold, a woman had given birth to a girl child and deserted her, because she and her husband disliked the infant and were afraid of their child. Her parents were Leasinga and Leamata. Because she had a head like a pigeon's, they decided to abandon her. The chief of Ata went and unwrapped the moving bundle, and said: "It is a girl with a pigeon's head."

He took her, did the chief of the island, and fed and cared for her, and adopted her as his daughter, and called her Vae. She lived and grew big, and the beak of the bird was shed, and her head, like a pigeon's, was changed. She grew very beautiful, and she was brought to Mua as a wife for the Tui Tonga Takalaua. The woman who was born with the pigeon's head bore children to Takalaua, the Tui Tonga. Her first son was Kauulufonuafekai, and her second son was Moungamotua, and the third was Melinoatonga, and the fourth was Lotauai, and the fifth was Latutoevave; that child talked from his mother's womb. Those were all Vaelaveamata's children to the Tui Tonga Takalaua.

Vae had five male children, some were grown up and some were still young when their father Takalaua the Tui Tonga was murdered. His children, Kauulufonuafekai, Moungamotua, and his other sons, were very angry over their father's murder, and they said: 'Let us go and seek the two murderers.'

They made war on Tongatabu and conquered it, and the two murderers fled to Eua. And Kauulufonuafekai and his people entered a vessel and pursued the two murderers, whose names were Tamasia and Malofafa, to Eua. They fought the people of Eua, and conquered them, and the two fugitives fled to Haapai. Kauulufonuafekai and his brothers sailed in pursuit to Haapai. Haapai was waiting ready for war with the avengers, and they fought and Haapai was conquered. The two murderers then fled to Vavau, and Kauulufonuafekai pursued, and conquered Vavau. Again the two murderers fled, this time to Niuatoputapu. Kauulufonuafekai pursued, and fought and conquered Niuatoputapu. Thence the two murderers fled to Niuafoou. Still they were pursued. Kauulufonuafekai fought and conquered Niuafoou also. The two murderers again fled, but whither? Kauulufonuafekai went to Futuna to seek them, and fought and conquered Futuna.

Kauulufonuafekai had spoken in the vessel to his brothers and warriors: "Do you think my bravery is my own, or is it a god (*faahikehe*) that blesses me and makes me brave?" And his brothers, warriors, and people in the vessel all answered: "What man in the world is strong in his own body, and brave in his own mind, if not blessed by a god? You are brave and strong, because a god blesses you. That is the reason why you are strong and brave." Kauulufonuafekai replied: "I am not brave because of the help of a god. My bravery is the bravery of a man." Then his brothers said to him: "It is not. You are brave and strong from a god." Kauulufonuafekai replied: "I will divide my body into two parts when we go and fight at Futuna. I will leave my back for the god to bless and protect, while I guard my front myself, and if I am wounded in front, it will be a sign that I am brave and strong because a god blesses me; but should I be wounded' in my back, it will be a sign that it is my own bravery, and that a god has nothing to do with it."

They went and fought the Futunans, who attempted to drive the Tongan vessel away. Then the Tongans in turn chased the Futunans on the sea and drove their warriors inland. But they were fighting for nothing, for the murderers were not at Futuna; they were at Uea. Thus Futuna was fought for nought, as it was thought that the murderers were there. They fought Futuna and the warriors from the vessel of Kauulufonuafekai, chased the people of Futuna, and caused them to flee. Kauulufonuafekai ran up the road in pursuit. A man in ambush speared Kauulufonuafekai through his back into his chest. The chief turned and clubbed the man who had speared him. And Kauulufonuafekai, returning, said: "I told you. Don't you say that I am brave through a god. Here I am wounded in the place that was left for the god to guard. I am not wounded from my front. My wound came from my back, which I left for him to guard; therefore I am not brave and strong from any god. It is my own bravery and the strength of this world. Come and we will go on board the vessel."

They went on board and sailed, but one of their brothers, Lotauai, was left behind at Futuna, for the people of Futuna had captured him. They did not kill him, but they let him live.

The vessel of Kauulufonuafekai sailed, and after voyaging for five days Kauulufonuafekai said: "Let us return to Futuna, because I have love for my brother, who is detained there; and my wound is itching, because it wants to fight." So they returned and Futuna saw the vessel coming, and the Futunans spoke to the lad, the brother of the chief, whom they had taken and they called his name: "Lotauai! the vessel is returning; the brave chief is coming again." And Lotauai, the lad that they held, said: "I told you that the chief would return with his warriors. It is for love of me, because you hold me prisoner. Had the chief and his warriors come for love of me, and come and found me dead, you having killed me, Futuna would indeed have died (been exterminated). But I am alive, so no one will be killed and you will not he punished."

Then the people of Futuna said to the lad: "Lotauai, what can we do to live!" They were afraid that the chief would come and kill them.

The chief's brother said: "Come and put on fine mats (*ngafingafi*), and pluck leaves from the chestnut (*ifi*) tree and put them round your neck. That is the thing to do to live, for it is the recognized Tongan way of begging mercy. Come and sit with bowed head at my back, while I sit in front, so that the chief that you are afraid of will see that I am still alive. That is the means by which you will live. Also prepare for his reception; cook food, and bring kava. After we have pacified the chief by sueing for mercy, then bring the kava and food, then we (Tongans) will drink it and g-o away." The vessel arrived and the people of the land came with loin mats (*ngafingafi*) round them, and chestnut leaves around their necks. And came the brave chief, and found his young brother still alive. And his young brother told the chief: "The people of the land are sueing for mercy, to live, because they are afraid." Kauulufonuafekai replied: "They live, and I am thankful that my brother still lives."

Then the kava and food were brought by the people of Futuna. They had kava with the chief and made friends. Then Kauulufonuafekai gave a Tongan boat to the people of Futuna, and said: "I have no wealth (tapa and mats) to give you, but here is a present for you, that I give you: Any vessel coming from Tonga is yours, but do not kill its people. All goods that are brought in it from Tonga are to be your present. That is my payment to you, because you allowed my brother, whom you took, to live, and I received a wound from you in the fight. That is why I give you the goods from the Tongan vessels." Hence comes the meaning of the expression: "Vete fakafutuna, to seize like the Futunans."

Then the vessel left to go and seek the murderers in Fiji. Kauulufonuafekai went and fought the different islands of Fiji, but the two murderers were not found in Fiji. They returned from Fiji and went to Uea, and fought and conquered Uea.

The two murderers were not able to flee from Uea, but were overtaken there, for they were prisoners held for sacrifice. When the Uea people came to sue for mercy, after they were conquered in the fight, the two murderers came with them. Kauulufonuafekai did not know the faces of the two murderers, but he knew their names. When the Uea people came to sue for pardon they all had long hair; but the two murderers, wlho came with them, had short hair which was just beginning to grow, their heads having been shaven. The chief knew them by their short hair, as all the Ueans had long hair. The chief called: "Tamasia!" for that was the name of one. He answered: "I am here." Then the chief called out the name of the other one: "Malofafa!" and he answered: "I am here." The chief then said: "What a long time you have been. Thanks to the god that you fled and that you are still alive. Come, you two Tongan men, we will sail for Tonga."

The vessel conveyed the two men to Tonga. There Kauulufonuafekai commanded that the two murderers should be brought and cut up alive as food for Takalaua's funeral kava. They were brought and cut up, and after they were cut up, their pieces were collected and burned in the fire.

It is said that Kauulufonuafekai had had their teeth pulled out at Uea, and then he had thrown them a string of dry kava, that he had worn round his neck most of the time since he had left Tonga. Upon throwing the dry kava to them, he told them to chew it. They tried to chew, with their bleeding gums, but were not able in the least to chew. After a very long, long time of thus giving them pain, from the morning of one day to the next day, Kauulufonuafekai told them to enter the vessel for them to leave for Tonga.

Takalaua, the Tui Tonga that was murdered, was buried, and Kauulufonuafekai was appointed Tui Tonga. He, the child of the woman with the pigeon's head, was Tui Tonga. The brother of Kauulufonuafekai, Moungamotua, was appointed Tui Haatakalaua (*tui*, king; *haa*, family; Takalaua, his father's name) and he went and lived at 'Kauhalalalo' in Fonuamotu near Loamanu (at Mua, Tongatabu), in order to rule from there the land. And he was to be called Tui Haatakalaua. Moungamotua was the first Tui Haatakalaua, the brother of Kauulufonuafekai, the Tui Tonga.

Kauulufonuafekai was the first to arrange that the apaapa, or master of ceremonies in the kava ring, should sit at a distance, not near to him, because he was afraid of being murdered, as his father, the Tui Tonga Takalaua, was murdered. Therefore the kava ring was formed so that the people in it sat at a distance from the chief. He instructed some of his brothers to sit at his back to guard him lest he should be murdered. The name given to those brothers that sat behind him, was *huhueiki* (*huhu*, to suspect; eiki, chief).

Another Tui Tonga was Vakafuhu; another was Puipuifatu; another was called Kauulufonua; another Tui Tonga was Tapuosi I., and another Tui Tonga was Uluakimata I., (Telea). His vessel was called Lomipeau (*lomi*, keep under; *peau*, waves). That was the ship that often went to Uea to cut and load stones for the terraces (*paepae*) of the royal tombs. Paepae o Telea is the name of the graveyard of the Tui Tonga Telea. Fatafehi he was the son of Telea; his mother was Mataukipa. Another Tui Tonga was Tapuosi II., and another Tui Tonga was Uluakimata II. His sons were the Tui Tonga Tui Pulotu I. and his brother, Tokemoana. The latter was appointed Tui Haauluakimata (tui, ruler; haa, family; Uluaki-mata, his father's name). Their sister Sinaitakala, was the female Tui Tonga; Fatani was their brother, also Faleafu, all of one father.

The son of Tui Pulotu was Fakanaanaa and he was Tui Tonga; another Tui Tonga was Tui Pulotu II.; and another Tui Tonga was Maulupekotofa. The son of Pau was Fatafehi Fuanunuiava, and the son of Fuanu-nuiava was Laufilitonga, the Tui Tonga that is alive in the world. That is the end of the Tui Tonga. The old Tui Tonga, the offspring of the Worm, are gone. The list of female Tui Tonga is not given, but only the list of the male Tui Tonga.

Here are their names in order: (1) Ahoeitu, (2) Lolofakangalo, (3) Fangaoneone, (4) Lihau, (5) Kofutu, (6) Kaloa, (7) Mauhau, (8) Apuanea, (9) Afulunga, (10) Momo, (11) Tuitatui, (12) Talaatama, (13) Tui Tonga Nui Tama Tou, (14) Talaihaapepe, (15) Talakaifaiki, (16) Talafapite, (17) Tui Tonga Maakatoe, (18) Tui Tonga i Puipui, (19) Havea I., (20) Tatafueikimeimua, (21) Lomiaetupua, (22) Havea II., (23) Takalaua, (24) Kauulufonuafekai, (25) Vakafuhu, (26) Puipuifatu, (27) Kauulufonua, (28) Tapuosi I., (29) Uluakimata I. (Telea), (30) Fatafehi, (31) Tapuosi II., (32) Uluakimata II., (33) Tui Pulotu I., (34) Fakanaanaa, (35) Tui Pulotu II., (36), Pau, (37) Maulupekotofa, (38) Fatafehi Fuanunuiava, (39) Laufilitonga.

The Tui Tonga Uluakimata, he who was called Telea, had many wives. One of his wives was Talafaiva. She was said, by the people of Mua who saw her, to be the most beautiful of women, for there was not another woman in the world so beautiful as she – she was unsurpassed. She was also a very great chief, for both her parents were chiefs. There was not another woman of such high rank, or so beautiful, or so well formed. She was the only woman called by all the world *fakatouato* (chief by both parents). Talafaiva brought fifty other wives (*fokonofo*) to Telea. The second wife of Telea was Nanasilapaha, and she brought fifty other wives to Telea. The third wife of Telea was Mataukipa and she brought one hundred other wives to Telea.

Mataukipa was the wife that always received the tail of the fish, and rump of the pig every day. "Why is the head of the fish, and the head of the pig, and the middle cut of the fish, and back of the pig always taken to Talafaiva and Nanasilapaha?" This was the question which troubled Mataukipa, so she decided to confer with her father. "I will go to my father, Kauulufonuahuo (head-of-the-land-cultivators), and ask him if it is good or bad this thing that the Tui Tonga is doing to me." So she carried her child on her back and went to the place called Mataliku, where Kauulufonuahuo dwelt. He was an industrious gardener, growing yams, bananas, *kape* (a root like the taro), taro, *ufilei* (a small sweet yam), *hoi* (fruit tree), and large bread fruit trees.

Her father saw his daughter coming, and went to greet her. "You have come. Who is with you?" His daughter, Mataukipa, answered: "Only we two." Then the father asked: "Why was there no one to come with you? Why only you two? Are you angry?" and Mataukipa replied: "No!" Her father said: "You stay here while I go and prepare some food, then I will take you back to Mua."

They had their kava prepared twice. Then the people went and prepared the oven and baked yams and a pig. Afterwards the daughter spoke to her father: "Why are the Tui Tonga's wishes like that?" she asked, and her father inquired: "How?" His daughter replied: "When our fish and pig is brought, the two women always eat the head and back of the pig, and the head and middle part of the fish, and I always get the tail of the fish and the rump of the pig."

The father of the woman laughed, and made this reply to the woman: "And are you grieved at it?" The woman answered: "I am grieved at it."

The father replied to the woman: "Don't be grieved. Your portion is the rump of the pig and the tail of the fish, because the land will come eventually to your children. They will be rulers."

The woman's mind was at peace after her father's explanation as to why she always was given the tail of the fish and rump of the pig, but before that she was jealous of the two women, and thought: "The chief loves the two women more than me." Consequently she was jealous.

They returned to her place and the woman was content, because of the explanation of her father, and they all lived together. When the Tui Tonga Telea died, the woman Mataukipa had a son called Fatafehi, and a daughter called Sinaitakala-i-langi-leka. Fatafehi was appointed Tui Tonga and Sinaitakala became female Tui Tonga. Thus what Mataukipa's father had told her came true; her son became Tui Tonga and her daughter female Tui Tonga and her descendants were Tui Tonga, the last being Laufili-tonga.

The Tui Tonga Telea dwelt in the bush, because he preferred it, and was more at home there, especially on the weather shore of Vavau. Each of his dwelling places and sleeping places at the weather shore of Vavau has a name, and each place is named after the thing he did at that place.

Telea and his wife Talafaiva came and dwelt on the island of Euakafa. Their house was built on the top of the mountain, and a reed fence was erected round the place. There was a big tree called *foui* growing there, and Talafaiva told Telea: "It is not a nice tree. You had better have it cut down." But Telea answered: "Oh, leave it. It is all right."

They had dwelt there for some time, when a man called Lolomanaia came from a place called Makave (in Vavau island). His vessel landed at the place where Telea dwelt, because Lolomanaia was in love with Talafaiva. He ascended and waited till it was dark. When it was dark he went to the place of Telea. He pushed the gate to see if it was closed or open. When he pushed it he found that it was closed, and he tried and tried to find some way to get inside the fence. He went round outside of the fence and found the big tree that Talafaiva had told Telea to cut down. He climbed the tree and thereby gained access to the enclosure. He slept with the woman Talafaiva, the wife of Tui Tonga Telea. After they had slept he tattooed a black mark on her abdomen, to annoy Telea, for him (Telea) to know that he (Lolomanaia) had committed adultery with his wife.

Telea slept with Talafaiva in the day, and he saw what had been done to his wife's abdomen. Telea asked her: "Who, Talafaiva, has tattooed your stomach?" Talafaiva replied: "It is true! Chief, will you pardon me? It was Lolomanaia, who came to me. Don't you be angry, because you know I told you, on the day that the fence was made for our enclosure, to cut down the big foui tree, because the tree was badly placed, and you said to leave it. The man climbed up it and came to me. His name was Lolomanaia." Telea was very wroth and arose and went out. He called his man servant by name. "Uka! come here, for me to tell you. Go and beat Talafaiva. She has had intercourse with a man."

Uka took a club, and went with it to her. Telea did not know that he was really going to kill Talafaiva. He only meant that he should beat her. After Telea's wrath cooled, he found that Uka had really killed Talafaiva, and that she was dead. The beautiful and well formed woman was dead. Uka came to report to Telea, and Telea asked: "Have you beaten Tala-faiva?" and Uka, the man servant, answered: "I have beaten her." The chief asked: "And how is she?" Uka replied: "She is dead," and Telea asked: "Is she quite dead?" and Uka replied: "She is quite dead." Again Telea asked: "Is she quite dead, my wife Talafaiva?" and Uka made reply: "She is quite dead."

Telea was grief stricken: "Oh! oh! my misplaced confidence! I did not mean that you should really go and kill her. I only meant for you to beat her a little because I was angry. I really loved my wife, whom you have killed. You are an old fool!" Telea went and wept over Talafaiva, who was really dead, for a night and a day.

Then Telea the Tui Tonga said: "We will go and cut stones for a vault for Talafaiva." So they went and cut the stones for the vault, and made the vault. Then Talafaiva was buried in the vault. The grave yard with the vault standing in it is on Euakafa island. The big casuarina tree at the graveyard is called Talafaiva. That is all about Talafaiva, the wife of Telea, about her ways and the meaning of what we hear about her. After Talafaiva's death Telea went to Tonga (Tongatabu) and lived there and died there.

The stones for the vault of this Tui Tonga Telea were cut at Uea, and the terrace stones were cut there also. This is the Tui Tonga that owned the vessel called Lomipeau, and this is the vessel that brought the stones for his vault and the terrace round it.

The Art of Netting Learned by Kahukura from the Fairies
(Ko Te Korero Mo Nga Patupaiarehe)

ONCE UPON A time, a man of the name of Kahukura wished to pay a visit to Rangiaowhia, a place lying far to the northward, near the country of the tribe called Te Rarawa. Whilst he lived at his own village, he was continually haunted by a desire to visit that place. At length he started on his journey, and reached Rangiaowhia, and as he was on his road, he passed a place where some people had been cleaning mackerel, and he saw the inside of the fish lying all about the sand on the seashore. Surprised at this, he looked about at the marks, and said to himself: "Oh, this must have been done by some of the people of the district." But when he came to look a little more narrowly at the footmarks, he saw that the people who had been fishing had made them in the night-time, not that morning, nor in the day; and he said to himself: "These are no mortals who have been fishing here – spirits must have done this; had they been men, some of the reeds and grass which they sat on in their canoe would have been lying about." He felt quite sure from several circumstances, that spirits or fairies had been there; and after observing everything well, he returned to the house where he was stopping. He, however, held fast in his heart what he had seen, as something very striking to tell all his friends in every direction, and as likely to be the means of gaining knowledge which might enable him to find out something new.

So that night he returned to the place where he had observed all these things, and just as he reached the spot, back had come the fairies too, to haul their net for mackerel; and some of them were shouting out: "The net here! the net here!" Then a canoe paddled off to fetch the other in which the net was laid, and as they dropped the net into the water, they began to cry out: "Drop the net in the sea at Rangiaowliia, and haul it at Mamaku." These words were sung out by the fairies, as an encouragement in their work, and from the joy of their hearts at their sport in fishing.

As the fairies were dragging the net to the shore, Kahukura managed to mix amongst them, and hauled away at the rope; he happened to be a very fair man, so that his skin was almost as white as that of these fairies, and from that cause he was not observed by them. As the net came close in to the shore, the fairies began to cheer and shout: "Go out into the sea some of you, in front of the rock, lest the nets should be entangled in Tawatawauia a Teweteweuia", for that was the name of a rugged rock standing out from the sandy shore; the main body of the fairies kept hauling at the net, and Kahukura pulled away in the midst of them.

When the first fish reached the shore, thrown up in the ripples driven before the net as they hauled it in, the fairies had not yet remarked Kahukura, for he was almost as fair as they were. It was just at the very first peep of dawn that the fish were all landed, and the fairies ran hastily to pick them up from the sand, and to haul the net up on the beach. They did not act with their fish as men do, dividing them into separate loads for each, but every one took up what fish he liked, and ran a twig through their gills, and as they strung the fish, they continued calling out: 'Make haste, run here, all of you, and finish the work before the sun rises.'

Kahukura kept on stringing his fish with the rest of them. He had only a very short string, and, making a slip-knot at the end of it, when he had covered the string with fish, he lifted them up, but had hardly raised them from the ground when the slip-knot gave way from the weight of the fish, and off they fell; then some of the fairies ran good-naturedly to help him to string his fish again, and one of them tied the knot at the end of the string for him, but the fairy had hardty gone after knotting it, before Kahukura had unfastened it, and again tied a slip-knot at the end; then he began stringing his fish again, and when he had got a great many on, up he lifted them, and off they slipped as before. This trick he repeated several times, and delayed the fairies in their work by getting them to knot his string for him, and put his fish on it. At last full daylight broke, so that there was light enough to distinguish a man's face, and the fairies saw that Kahukura was a man; then they dispersed in confusion, leaving their fish and their net, and abandoning their canoes, which were nothing but stems of the flax. In a moment the fairies started for their own abodes; in their hurry, as has just been said, they abandoned their net, which was made of rushes; and off the good people fled as fast as they could go. Now was first discovered the stitch for netting a net, for they left theirs with Kahukura, and it became a pattern for him. He thus taught his children to make nets, and by them the Maori race were made acquainted with that art, which they have now known from very remote times.

Unmaking & Remaking the World

Introduction

THE DRAGON IN Chinese myth was associated more with water than with fire. His phallic serpent-shape suggested fertility, which in turn meant rain. So it was appropriate that, when the greatest of the dragons, the water-god Gong Gong, went careering into a Mountain, he unleashed a dreadful flood upon the earth. For the mountain, it turned out, was a vital pillar holding up the heavens, and without it the roof of the earth started sagging and letting in water. Chaos ensued, and the situation was only sorted out when Gong Gong's mother, Nu Wa, collected coloured stones and heated them to melting in a fire to patch the hole. That these two stories constitute half of Chinese tradition's Four Great Myths is an indication of how important natural disasters have been for an always-vulnerable humankind. They remain so still, of course, as we're being reminded in the context of global climate change, but our forebears didn't have the defences that we do. The most powerful empire, the greatest city, was just a plague, a famine or a flood away from being brought low, and potentially destroyed completely – a great endeavour brought abruptly to a premature ending.

The Great Deluge

LITTLE BY LITTLE the world was peopled; and the first years of man's existence upon earth were, as we have seen, years of unalloyed happiness. There was no occasion for labour, for the earth brought forth spontaneously all that was necessary for man's subsistence. 'Innocence, virtue, and truth prevailed; neither were there any laws to restrict men, nor judges to punish.' This time of bliss has justly borne the title of Golden Age, and the people in Italy then throve under the wise rule of good old Saturn, or Cronus.

Unfortunately, nothing in this world is lasting; and the Golden Age was followed by another, not quite so prosperous, hence called the Silver Age, when the year was first divided into seasons, and men were obliged to toil for their daily bread.

Yet, in spite of these few hardships, the people were happy, far happier than their descendants during the Age of Brass, which speedily followed, when strife became customary, and differences were settled by blows. But by far the worst of all was the Iron Age, when men's passions knew no bounds, and they even dared refuse all homage to the immortal gods. War was waged incessantly; the earth was saturated with blood; the rights of hospitality were openly violated; and murder, rape, and theft were committed on all sides.

Zeus had kept a close watch over men's actions during all these years; and this evil conduct aroused his wrath to such a point, that he vowed he would annihilate the human race. But the modes of destruction were manifold, and, as he could not decide which would eventually prove most efficacious, he summoned the gods to deliberate and aid him by their counsels. The first suggestion offered, was to destroy the world by fire, kindled by Zeus' much-dreaded thunderbolts; and the king of gods was about to put it into instant execution, when his arm was stayed by the objection that the rising flames might set fire to his own abode, and reduce its magnificence to unsightly ashes. He therefore rejected the plan as impracticable, and bade the gods devise other means of destruction.

After much delay and discussion, the immortals agreed to wash mankind off the face of the earth by a mighty deluge. The winds were instructed to gather together the rain clouds over the earth. Poseidon let loose the waves of the sea, bidding them rise, overflow, and deluge the land. No sooner had the gods spoken, than the elements obeyed: the winds blew; the rain fell in torrents; lakes, seas, rivers, and oceans broke their bonds; and terrified mortals, forgetting their petty quarrels in a common impulse to flee from the death which threatened them, climbed the highest mountains, clung to uprooted trees, and even took refuge in the light skiffs they had constructed in happier days. Their efforts were all in vain, however; for the waters rose higher and higher, overtook them one after another in their ineffectual efforts to escape, closed over the homes where they might have been so happy, and drowned their last despairing cries in their seething depths.

The rain continued to fall, until, after many days, the waves covered all the surface of the earth except the summit of Mount Parnassus, the highest peak in Greece. On this mountain, surrounded by the ever-rising flood, stood the son of Prometheus, Deucalion, with his faithful wife Pyrrha, a daughter of Epimetheus and Pandora. From thence they, the sole survivors, viewed the universal desolation with tear-dimmed eyes.

In spite of the general depravity, the lives of this couple had always been pure and virtuous; and when Zeus saw them there alone, and remembered their piety, he decided not to include them in the general destruction, but to save their lives. He therefore bade the winds return to their cave, and the rain to cease. Poseidon, in accordance with his decree, blew a resounding blast upon his conch shell to recall the wandering waves, which immediately returned within their usual bounds.

Deucalion and Pyrrha followed the receding waves step by step down the steep mountain side, wondering how they should re-people the desolate earth. As they talked, they came to the shrine of Delphi, which alone had been able to resist the force of the waves.

There they entered to consult the wishes of the gods. Their surprise and horror were unbounded, however, when a voice exclaimed, "Depart from hence with veiled heads, and cast your mother's bones behind you!"

To obey such a command seemed sacrilegious in the extreme; for the dead had always been held in deep veneration by the Greeks, and the desecration of a grave was considered a heinous crime, and punished accordingly. But, they reasoned, the gods' oracles can seldom be accepted in a literal sense; and Deucalion, after due thought, explained to Pyrrha what he conceived to be the meaning of this mysterious command.

"The Earth," said he, "is the mother of all, and the stones may be considered her bones." Husband and wife speedily decided to act upon this premise, and continued their descent, casting stones behind them. All those thrown by Deucalion were immediately changed into men, while those cast by Pyrrha became women.

Thus the earth was peopled for the second time with a blameless race of men, sent to replace the wicked beings slain by Zeus. Deucalion and Pyrrha shortly after became the happy parents of a son named Hellen, who gave his name to all the Hellenic or Greek race; while his sons Aeolus and Dorus, and grandsons Ion and Achaeus, became the ancestors of the Aeolian, Dorian, Ionian, and Achaian nations.

Other mythologists, in treating of the deluvian myths, state that Deucalion and Pyrrha took refuge in an ark, which, after sailing about for many days, was stranded on the top of Mount Parnassus. This version was far less popular with the Greeks, although it betrays still more plainly the common source whence all these myths are derived.

The Sack of Troy

FOR TEN YEARS, King Agamemnon and the men of Greece laid siege to Troy. But though sentence had gone forth against the city, yet the day of its fall tarried, because certain of the gods loved it well and defended it, as Apollo and Mars, the god of war, and Father Jupiter himself. Wherefore Minerva put it into the heart of Epeius, Lord of the Isles, that he should make a cunning device wherewith to take the city. Now the device was this: he made a great horse of wood, feigning it to be a peace-offering to Minerva, that the Greeks might have a safe return to their homes. In the belly of this there hid themselves certain of the bravest of the chiefs, as Menelaus, and Ulysses, and Thoas the Aetolian, and Machaon the great physician, and Pyrrhus, son of Achilles (but Achilles himself was dead, slain by Paris, Apollo helping, even as he was about to take the city), and others also, and with them Epeius himself. But the rest of the people made as if they had departed to their homes; only they went not further than Tenedos, which was an island near to the coast.

Great joy was there in Troy when it was noised abroad that the men of Greece had departed. The gates were opened, and the people went forth to see the plain and the camp. And one said to another as they went, "Here they set the battle in array, and there were the tents of the fierce Achilles, and there lay the ships." And some stood and marvelled at the great peace-offering to Minerva, even the horse of wood. And Thymoetes, who was one of the elders of the city, was the first who advised that it should be brought within the walls and set in the citadel. Now whether he gave this counsel out of a false heart or because the gods would have it so, no man knows. But Capys, and others with him, said that it should be drowned in water or burned with fire, or that men should pierce it and see whether there were aught within. And the people were divided, some crying one thing and some another. Then came forward the priest Laocoön, and a great company with him, crying, "What madness is this? Think ye that the men of Greece are indeed departed or that there is any profit in their gifts? Surely there are armed men in this mighty horse; or haply they have made it that they may look down upon our walls. Touch it not, for as for these men of Greece, I fear them, even though they bring gifts in their hands."

And as he spake he cast his great spear at the horse, so that it sounded again. But the gods would not that Troy should be saved.

Meanwhile, there came certain shepherds dragging with them one whose hands were bound behind his back. He had come forth to them, they said, of his own accord when they were in the field. And first the young men gathered about him mocking him, but when he cried aloud, "What place is left for me, for the Greeks suffer me not to live and the men of Troy cry for vengeance upon me?" they rather pitied him, and bade him speak and say whence he came and what he had to tell.

Then the man spake, turning to King Priam, "I will speak the truth, whatever befall me. My name is Sinon and I deny not that I am a Greek. Haply thou hast heard the name of Palamedes, whom the Greeks slew, but now, being dead, lament; and the cause was that because he counselled peace, men falsely accused him of treason. Now, of this Palamedes I was a poor kinsman and followed him to Troy. And when he was dead, through the false witness of Ulysses, I lived in great grief and trouble, nor could I hold my peace, but sware that if ever I came back to Argos I would avenge me of him that had done this deed. Then did Ulysses seek occasion against me, whispering evil things, nor rested till at the last, Calchas the soothsayer helping him – but what profit it that I should tell these things? For doubtless ye hold one Greek to be even as another. Wherefore slay me and doubtless ye will do a pleasure to Ulysses and the sons of Atreus."

Then they bade him tell on, and he said:

"Often would the Greeks have fled to their homes, being weary of the war, but still the stormy sea hindered them. And when this horse that ye see had been built, most of all did the dreadful thunder roll from the one end of the heaven to the other. Then the Greeks sent one who should inquire of Apollo; and Apollo answered them thus: 'Men of Greece, even as ye appeased the winds with blood when ye came to Troy, so must ye appease them with blood now that ye would go from thence.' Then did men tremble to think on whom the doom should fall, and Ulysses, with much clamour, drew forth Calchas the soothsayer into the midst, and bade him say who it was that the gods would have as a sacrifice. Then did many forbode evil for me. Ten days did the soothsayer keep silence, saying that he would not give any man to death. But then, for in truth the two had planned the matter beforehand, he spake, appointing me to die. And to this thing they all agreed, each being glad to turn to another that which he feared for himself. But when the day was come and all things were ready, the salted meal for the sacrifice and the garlands, lo! I burst my bonds and fled and hid myself in the sedges of a pool, waiting till they should have set sail, if haply that might be. But never shall I see country or father or children again. For doubtless on these will they take vengeance for my flight. Only do thou, O King, have pity on me, who have suffered many things, not having harmed any man."

And King Priam had pity on him, and bade them loose his bonds, saying, "Whoever thou art, forget now thy country. Henceforth thou art one of us. But tell me true: why made they this huge horse? Who contrived it? What seek they by it – to please the gods or to further their siege?"

Then said Sinon, and as he spake he stretched his hands to the sky, "I call you to witness, ye everlasting fires of heaven, that with good right I now break my oath of fealty and reveal the secrets of my countrymen. Listen then, O King. All our hope has ever been in the help of Minerva. But from the day when Diomed and Ulysses dared, having bloody hands, to snatch her image from her holy place in Troy, her face was turned from us. Well do I remember how the eyes of the image, well-nigh before they had set it in the camp, blazed with wrath, and how the salt sweat stood upon its limbs, aye, and how it thrice leapt from the ground, shaking shield and spear. Then Calchas told us that we must cross the seas again and seek at home fresh omens for our war. And this, indeed, they are doing even now, and will return anon. Also the soothsayer said, 'Meanwhile ye must make the likeness of a horse, to be a peace-offering to Minerva. And take heed that ye make it huge of bulk, so that the men of Troy may not receive it into their gates, nor bring it within their walls and get safety for themselves thereby. For if,' he said, 'the men of Troy harm this image at all, they shall surely perish; but if they bring it into their city, then shall Asia lay siege hereafter to the city of Pelops, and our children shall suffer the doom which we would fain have brought on Troy.'"

These words wrought much on the men of Troy, and as they pondered on them, lo! the gods sent another marvel to deceive them. For while Laocoön, the priest of Neptune, was slaying a bull at the altar of his god, there came two serpents across the sea from Tenedos, whose heads and necks, whereon were thick manes of hair, were high above the waves, and many scaly coils trailed behind in the waters. And when they reached the land they still sped forward. Their eyes were red as blood and blazed with fire and their forked tongues hissed loud for rage. Then all the men of Troy grew pale with fear and fled away, but these turned not aside this way or that, seeking Laocoön where he stood. And first they wrapped themselves about his little sons, one serpent about each, and began to devour them. And when the father would have given help to his children, having a sword in his hand, they seized upon himself and bound him fast with their folds. Twice they compassed him about his body, and twice about his neck, lifting their heads far above him. And all the while he strove to tear them away with his hands, his priest's garlands dripping with blood. Nor did he cease to cry horribly aloud, even as a bull bellows when after an ill stroke of the axe it flees from the altar.

But when their work was done, the two glided to the citadel of Minerva and hid themselves beneath the feet and the shield of the goddess. And men said one to another, "Lo! the priest Laocoön has been judged according to his deeds; for he cast his spear against this holy thing, and now the gods have slain him." Then all cried out together that the horse of wood must be drawn to the citadel. Whereupon they opened the Scaean Gate and pulled down the wall that was thereby, and put rollers under the feet of the horse and joined ropes thereto. So in much joy they drew it into the city, youths and maidens singing about it the while and laying their hands to the ropes with great gladness.

And yet there wanted no signs and tokens of evil to come. Four times it halted on the threshold of the gate, and men might have heard a clashing of arms within. Cassandra also opened her mouth, prophesying evil; but no man heeded her, for that was ever the doom upon her, not to be believed, though speaking truth. So the men of Troy drew the horse into the city. And that night they kept a feast to all the gods with great joy, not knowing that the last day of the great city had come.

But when night was now fully come and the men of Troy lay asleep, lo! from the ship of King Agamemnon there rose up a flame for a signal to the Greeks; and these straightway manned their ships and made across the sea from Tenedos, there being a great calm and the moon also giving them light. Sinon likewise opened a secret door that was in the great horse and the chiefs issued forth therefrom and opened the gates of the city, slaying those that kept watch.

Meanwhile, there came a vision to Aeneas, who now, Hector being dead, was the chief hope and stay of the men of Troy. It was Hector's self that he seemed to see, but not such as he had seen him coming back rejoicing with the arms of Achilles or setting fire to the ships, but even as he lay after that Achilles dragged him at his chariot wheels, covered with dust, and blood, his feet swollen and pierced through with thongs. To him said Aeneas, not knowing what he said, "Why hast thou tarried so long? Much have we suffered waiting for thee! And what grief hath marked thy face, and whence these wounds?"

But to this the spirit answered nothing, but said, groaning the while, "Fly, son of Venus, fly and save thee from these flames. The enemy is in the walls and Troy hath utterly perished. If any hand could have saved our city, this hand had done so. Thou art now the hope of Troy. Take then her gods and flee with them for company, seeking the city that thou shalt one day build across the sea."

And now the alarm of battle came nearer and nearer, and Aeneas, waking from sleep, climbed upon the roof and looked on the city. As a shepherd stands and sees a fierce flame sweeping before the south wind over the cornfields or a flood rushing down from the mountains, so he stood. And as he looked, the great palace of Deiphobus sank down in the fire and the house of Ucalegon, which was hard by, blazed forth, till the sea by Sigeum shone with the light. Then, scarce knowing what he sought, he girded on his armour, thinking perchance that he might yet win some place of vantage or at the least might avenge himself on the enemy or find honour in his death. But as he passed from out of his house there met him Panthus, the priest of Apollo that was on the citadel, who cried to him, "O Aeneas, the glory is departed from Troy and the Greeks have the mastery in the city; for armed men are coming forth from the great horse of wood and thousands also swarm in at the gates, which Sinon hath treacherously opened." And as he spake others came up under the light of the moon, as Hypanis and Dymas and young Coroebus, who had but newly come to Troy, seeking Cassandra to be his wife. To whom Aeneas spake, "If ye are minded, my brethren, to follow me to the death, come on. For how things fare this night ye see. The gods who were the stay of this city have departed from it; nor is aught remaining to which we may bring succor. Yet can we die as brave men in battle. And haply he that counts his life to be lost may yet save it." Then, even as ravening wolves hasten through the mist seeking for prey, so they went through the city, doing dreadful deeds. And for a while the men of Greece fled before them.

First of all there met them Androgeos with a great company following him, who, thinking them to be friends, said, "Haste, comrades; why are ye so late? We are spoiling this city of Troy and ye are but newly come from the ships." But forthwith, for they answered him not as he had looked for, he knew that he had fallen among enemies. Then even as one who treads upon a snake unawares among thorns and flies from it when it rises angrily against him with swelling neck, so Androgeos would have fled. But the men of Troy rushed on and, seeing that they knew all the place and that great fear was upon the Greeks, slew many men. Then said Coroebus, "We have good luck in this matter, my friends. Come now, let us change our shields and put upon us the armour of these Greeks. For whether we deal with our enemy by craft or by force, who will ask?" Then he took to himself the helmet and shield of Androgeos and also girded the sword upon him. In like manner did the others, and thus, going disguised among the Greeks, slew many, so that some again fled to the ships and some were fain to climb into the horse of wood. But lo! men came dragging by the hair from the temple of Minerva the virgin Cassandra, whom when Coroebus beheld, and how she lifted up her eyes to heaven (but as for her hands, they were bound with iron), he endured not the sight, but threw himself upon those that dragged her, the others following him. Then did a grievous mischance befall them, for the men of Troy that stood upon the roof of the temple cast spears against them, judging them to be enemies. The Greeks also, being wroth that the virgin should be taken from them, fought the more fiercely, and many who had before been put to flight in the city came against them and prevailed, being indeed many against few. Then first of all fell Coroebus, being slain by Peneleus the Boeotian, and Rhipeus also, the most righteous of all the sons of Troy. But the gods dealt not with him after his righteousness. Hypanis also was slain and Dymas and Panthus escaped not for all that more than other men he feared the gods and was also the priest of Apollo.

Then was Aeneas severed from the rest, having with him two only, Iphitus and Pelias, Iphitus being an old man and Pelias sorely wounded by Ulysses. And these, hearing a great shouting, hastened to the palace of King Priam, where the battle was fiercer than in any place beside. For some of the Greeks were seeking to climb the walls, laying ladders thereto, whereon they stood, holding forth their shields with their left hands and with their right grasping the roofs. And the men of Troy, on the other hand, being in the last extremity, tore down the battlements and the gilded beams wherewith the men of old had adorned the palace. Then Aeneas, knowing of a secret door whereby the unhappy Andromache in past days had been wont to enter, bringing her son Astyanax to his grandfather, climbed on to the roof and joined himself to those that fought therefrom. Now upon this roof there was a tower, whence all Troy could be seen and the camp of the Greeks and the ships. This the men of Troy loosened from its foundations with bars of iron, and thrust it over, so that it fell upon the enemy, slaying many of them. But not the less did others press forward, casting all the while stones and javelins and all that came to their hands.

Meanwhile, others sought to break down the gates of the palace, Pyrrhus, son of Achilles, being foremost among them, clad in shining armour of bronze. Like to a serpent was he, which sleeps indeed during the winter, but in the spring comes forth into the light, full fed on evil herbs, and, having cast his skin and renewed his youth, lifts his head into the light of the sun and hisses with forked tongue. And with Pyrrhus were tall Periphas and Automedon, who had been armour-bearer to his father Achilles, and following them the youth of Scyros, which was the kingdom of his grandfather, Lycomedes. With a great battle-axe he hewed through the doors, breaking down also the doorposts, though they were plated with bronze, making, as it were, a great window, through which a man might see the palace within, the hall of King Priam and of the kings who had reigned aforetime in Troy. But when they that were within perceived it, there arose a great cry of women wailing aloud and clinging to the doors and kissing them. But ever Pyrrhus pressed on, fierce and strong as ever was his father Achilles, nor could aught stand against him, either the doors or they that guarded them. Then, as a river bursts its banks and overflows the plain, so did the sons of Greece rush into the palace.

But old Priam, when he saw the enemy in his hall, girded on him his armour, which now by reason of old age he had long laid aside, and took a spear in his hand and would have gone against the adversary, only Queen Hecuba called to him from where she sat. For she and her daughters had fled to the great altar of the household gods and sat crowded about it like unto doves that are driven by a storm. Now the altar stood in an open court that was in the midst of the palace, with a great bay tree above it. So when she saw Priam, how he had girded himself with armour as a youth, she cried to him and said, "What hath bewitched thee, that thou girdest thyself with armour? It is not the sword that shall help us this day; no, not though my own Hector were here, but rather the gods and their altars. Come hither to us, for here thou wilt be safe, or at the least wilt die with us."

So she made the old man sit down in the midst. But lo! there came flying through the palace, Polites, his son, wounded to death by the spear of Pyrrhus, and Pyrrhus close behind him. And he, even as he came into the sight of his father and his mother, fell dead upon the ground. But when King Priam saw it he contained not himself, but cried aloud, "Now may the gods, if there be any justice in heaven, recompense thee for this wickedness, seeing that thou hast not spared to slay the son before his father's eyes. Great Achilles, whom thou falsely callest thy sire, did not thus to Priam, though he was an enemy, but reverenced right and truth and gave the body of Hector for burial and sent me back to my city."

And as he spake the old man cast a spear, but aimless and without force, which pierced not even the boss of the shield. Then said the son of Achilles, "Go thou and tell my father of his unworthy son and all these evils deeds. And that thou mayest tell him die!" And as he spake he caught in his left hand the old man's white hair and dragged him, slipping the while in the blood of his own son, to the altar, and then, lifting his sword high for a blow, drove it to the hilt in the old man's side. So King Priam, who had ruled mightily over many peoples and countries in the land of Asia, was slain that night, having first seen Troy burning about him and his citadel laid even with the ground. So was his carcass cast out upon the earth, headless and without a name.

The Giant of the Flood

JUST BEFORE THE world was drowned all the animals gathered in front of the Ark and Father Noah carefully inspected them.

"All ye that lie down shall enter and be saved from the deluge that is about to destroy the world," he said. "Ye that stand cannot enter."

Then the various creatures began to march forward into the Ark. Father Noah watched them closely. He seemed troubled.

"I wonder," he said to himself, "how I shall obtain a unicorn, and how I shall get it into the Ark."

"I can bring thee a unicorn, Father Noah," he heard in a voice of thunder, and turning round he saw the giant, Og. "But thou must agree to save me, too, from the flood."

"Begone," cried Noah. "Thou art a demon, not a human being. I can have no dealings with thee."

"Pity me," whined the giant. "See how my figure is shrinking. Once I was so tall that I could drink water from the clouds and toast fish at the sun. I fear not that I shall be drowned, but that all the food will be destroyed and that I shall perish of hunger."

Noah, however, only smiled; but he grew serious again when Og brought a unicorn. It was as big as a mountain, although the giant said it was the smallest he could find. It lay down in front of the Ark and Noah saw by that action that he must save it. For some time he was puzzled what to do, but at last a bright idea struck him. He attached the huge beast to the Ark by a rope fastened to its horn so that it could swim alongside and be fed.

Og seated himself on a mountain near at hand and watched the rain pouring down. Faster and faster it fell in torrents until the rivers overflowed and the waters began to rise rapidly on the land and sweep all things away. Father Noah stood gloomily before the door of the Ark until the water reached his neck. Then it swept him inside. The door closed with a bang, and the Ark rose gallantly on the flood and began to move along. The unicorn swam alongside, and as it passed Og, the giant jumped on to its back.

"See, Father Noah," he cried, with a huge chuckle, "you will have to save me after all. I will snatch all the food you put through the window for the unicorn."

Noah saw that it was useless to argue with Og, who might, indeed, sink the Ark with his tremendous strength.

"I will make a bargain with thee," he shouted from a window. "I will feed thee, but thou must promise to be a servant to my descendants."

Og was very hungry, so he accepted the conditions and devoured his first breakfast.

The rain continued to fall in great big sheets that shut out the light of day. Inside the Ark, however, all was bright and cheerful, for Noah had collected the most precious of the stones of the earth and had used them for the windows. Their radiance illumined the whole of the three storeys in the Ark. Some of the animals were troublesome and Noah got no sleep at all.

The lion had a bad attack of fever. In a corner a bird slept the whole of the time. This was the phoenix.

"Wake up," said Noah, one day. "It is feeding time."

"Thank you," returned the bird. "I saw thou wert busy, Father Noah, so I would not trouble thee."

Thou art a good bird," said Noah, much touched, "therefore thou shalt never die."

One day the rain ceased, the clouds rolled away and the sun shone brilliantly again. How strange the world looked! It was like a vast ocean. Nothing but water could be seen anywhere, and only one or two of the highest mountain tops peeped above the flood.

All the world was drowned, and Noah gazed on the desolate scene from one of the windows with tears in his eyes. Og, riding gaily on the unicorn behind the Ark, was quite happy.

"Ha, ha!" he laughed gleefully. "I shall be able to eat and drink just as much as I like now and shall never be troubled by those tiny little creatures, the mortals."

"Be not so sure," said Noah. "Those tiny mortals shall be thy masters and shall outlive thee and the whole race of giants and demons."

The giant did not relish this prospect. He knew that whatever Noah prophesied would come true, and he was so sad that he ate no food for two days and began to grow smaller and thinner. He became more and more unhappy as day by day the water subsided and the mountains began to appear. At last the Ark rested on Mount Ararat, and Og's long ride came to an end.

"I will soon leave thee, Father Noah," he said. "I shall wander round the world to see what is left of it."

"Thou canst not go until I permit thee," said Noah. "Hast thou forgotten our compact so soon? Thou must be my servant. I have work for thee."

Giants are not fond of work, and Og, who was the father of all the giants, was particularly lazy. He cared only to eat and sleep, but he knew he was in Noah's power, and he shed bitter tears when he saw the land appear again.

"Stop," commanded Noah. "Dost thou wish to drown the world once more with thy big tears?"

So Og sat on a mountain and rocked from side to side, weeping silently to himself. He watched the animals leave the Ark and had to do all the hard work when Noah's children built houses. Daily he complained that he was shrinking to the size of the mortals, for Noah said there was not too much food.

One day Noah said to him, "Come with me, Og. I am going around the world. I am commanded to plant fruit and flowers to make the earth beautiful. I need thy help."

For many days they wandered all over the earth, and Og was compelled to carry the heavy bag of seeds. The last thing Noah planted was the grape vine.

"What is this – food, or drink?" asked Og.

"Both," replied Noah. "It can be eaten, or its juice made into wine," and as he planted it, he blessed the grape. "Be thou," he said, "a plant pleasing to the eye, bear fruit that will be food for the hungry and a health-giving drink to the thirsty and sick."

Og grunted.

"I will offer up sacrifice to this wonderful fruit," he said. "May I not do so now that our labours are over?"

Noah agreed, and the giant brought a sheep, a lion, a pig and a monkey. First, he slaughtered the sheep, then the lion.

"When a man shall taste but a few drops of the wine," he said, "he shall be as harmless as a sheep. When he takes a little more he shall be as strong as a lion."

Then Og began to dance around the plant, and he killed the pig and the monkey. Noah was very much surprised.

"I am giving thy descendants two extra blessings," said Og, chuckling.

He rolled over and over on the ground in great glee and then said:

"When a man shall drink too much of the juice of the wine, then shall he become a beast like the pig, and if then he still continues to drink, he shall behave foolishly like a monkey."

And that is why, unto this day, too much wine makes a man silly.

Og himself often drank too much, and many years afterward, when he was a servant to the patriarch Abraham, the latter scolded him until he became so frightened that he dropped a tooth. Abraham made an ivory chair for himself from this tooth. Afterwards Og became King of Bashan, but he forgot his compact with Noah and instead of helping the Israelites to obtain Canaan he opposed them.

"I will kill them all with one blow," he declared.

Exerting all his enormous strength he uprooted a mountain, and raising it high above his head he prepared to drop it on the camp of the Israelites and crush it.

But a wonderful thing happened. The mountain was full of grasshoppers and ants who had bored millions of tiny holes in it. When King Og raised the great mass it crumbled in his hands and fell over his head and round his neck like a collar. He tried to pull it off, but his teeth became entangled in the mass. As he danced about in rage and pain, Moses, the leader of the Israelites, approached him.

Moses was a tiny man compared with Og. He was only ten ells high, and he carried with him a sword of the same length. With a mighty effort he jumped ten ells into the air, and raising the sword, he managed to strike the giant on the ankle and wound him mortally.

Thus, after many years, did the terrible giant of the flood perish for breaking his word to Father Noah.

Tales of Ragnarok

Baldur's Doom

IN ASGARD THERE were two places that meant strength and joy to the Aesir and the Vanir: one was the garden where grew the apples that Iduna gathered, and the other was the Peace Stead, where, in a palace called Breidablik, Baldur the Well-Beloved dwelt.

In the Peace Stead no crime had ever been committed, no blood had ever been shed, no falseness had ever been spoken. Contentment came into the minds of all in Asgard when they thought upon this place. Ah! Were it not that the Peace Stead was there, happy with Baldur's presence, the minds of the Aesir and the Vanir might have become gloomy and stern from thinking on the direful things that were arrayed against them.

Baldur was beautiful. So beautiful was he that all the white blossoms on the earth were called by his name. Baldur was happy. So happy was he that all the birds on the earth sang his name. So just and so wise was Baldur that the judgment he pronounced might never be altered. Nothing foul or unclean had ever come near where he had his dwelling:

> *'Tis Breidablik called,*
> *Where Baldur the Fair*
> *Hath built him a bower,*
> *In the land where I know*
> *Least loathliness lies.*

Healing things were done in Baldur's Stead. Tyr's wrist was healed of the wounds that Fenrir's fangs had made. And there Frey's mind became less troubled with the foreboding that Loki had filled it with when he railed at him about the bartering of his sword.

Now, after Fenrir had been bound to the rock in the faraway island, the Aesir and the Vanir knew a while of contentment. They passed bright days in Baldur's Stead, listening to the birds that made music there. And it was there that Bragi the Poet wove into his never-ending story the tale of Thor's adventures amongst the Giants.

But even into Baldur's Stead foreboding came. One day, little Hnossa, the child of Freya and the lost Odur, was brought there in such sorrow that no one outside could comfort her. Nanna, Baldur's gentle wife, took the child upon her lap and found ways of soothing her. Then Hnossa told of a dream that had filled her with fright.

She had dreamt of Hela, the Queen that is half living woman and half corpse. In her dream Hela had come into Asgard saying, "A lord of the Aesir I must have to dwell with me in my realm beneath the earth." Hnossa had such fear from this dream that she had fallen into a deep sorrow.

A silence fell upon all when the dream of Hnossa was told. Nanna looked wistfully at Odin All-Father. And Odin, looking at Frigga, saw that a fear had entered her breast.

He left the Peace Stead and went to his watchtower Hlidskjalf. He waited there till Hugin and Munin should come to him. Every day his two ravens flew through the world, and coming back to him told him of all that was happening. And now they might tell him of happenings that would let him guess if Hela had indeed turned her thoughts toward Asgard, or if she had the power to draw one down to her dismal abode.

The ravens flew to him, and lighting one on each of his shoulders, told him of things that were being said up and down Ygdrassil, the World Tree. Ratatösk the Squirrel was saying them. And Ratatösk had heard them from the brood of serpents that with Nidhögg, the great dragon, gnawed ever at the root of Ygdrassil. He told it to the Eagle that sat ever on the topmost bough, that in Hela's habitation a bed was spread and a chair was left empty for some lordly comer.

And hearing this, Odin thought that it were better that Fenrir the Wolf should range ravenously through Asgard than that Hela should win one from amongst them to fill that chair and lie in that bed.

He mounted Sleipner, his eight-legged steed, and rode down toward the abodes of the Dead. For three days and three nights of silence and darkness he journeyed on. Once, one of the hounds of Helheim broke loose and bayed upon Sleipner's tracks. For a day and a night Garm, the hound, pursued them, and Odin smelled the blood that dripped from his monstrous jaws.

At last he came to where, wrapped in their shrouds, a field of the Dead lay. He dismounted from Sleipner and called upon one to rise and speak with him. It was on Volva, a dead prophetess, he called. And when he pronounced her name he uttered a rune that had the power to break the sleep of the Dead.

There was a groaning in the middle of where the shrouded ones lay. Then Odin cried, out, "Arise, Volva, prophetess." There was a stir in the middle of where the shrouded ones lay, and a head and shoulders were thrust up from amongst the Dead.

"Who calls on Volva the Prophetess? The rains have drenched my flesh and the storms have shaken my bones for more seasons than the living know. No living voice has a right to call me from my sleep with the Dead."

"It is Vegtam the Wanderer who calls. For whom is the bed prepared and the seat left empty in Hela's habitation?"

"For Baldur, Odin's son, is the bed prepared and the seat left empty. Now let me go back to my sleep with the Dead."

But now Odin saw beyond Volva's prophecy. "Who is it," he cried out, "that stands with unbowed head and that will not lament for Baldur? Answer, Volva, prophetess!"

"Thou seest far, but thou canst not see clearly. Thou art Odin. I can see clearly but I cannot see far. Now let me go back to my sleep with the Dead."

"Volva, prophetess!" Odin cried out again.

But the voice from amongst the shrouded ones said, "Thou canst not wake me anymore until the fires of Muspelheim blaze above my head."

Then there was silence in the field of the Dead, and Odin turned Sleipner, his steed, and for four days, through the gloom and silence, he journeyed back to Asgard.

Frigga had felt the fear that Odin had felt. She looked toward Baldur, and the shade of Hela came between her and her son. But then she heard the birds sing in the Peace Stead and she knew that none of all the things in the world would injure Baldur.

And to make it sure she went to all the things that could hurt him and from each of them she took an oath that it would not injure Baldur, the Well-Beloved. She took an oath from fire and from water, from iron and from all metals, from earths and stones and great trees, from birds and beasts and creeping things, from poisons and diseases. Very readily they all gave the oath that they would work no injury on Baldur.

Then when Frigga went back and told what she had accomplished, the gloom that had lain on Asgard lifted. Baldur would be spared to them. Hela might have a place prepared in her dark habitation, but neither fire nor water, nor iron nor any metals, nor earths nor stones nor great woods, nor birds nor beasts nor creeping things, nor poisons nor diseases, would help her to bring him down. "Hela has no arms to draw you to her," the Aesir and the Vanir cried to Baldur.

Hope was renewed for them and they made games to honour Baldur. They had him stand in the Peace Stead and they brought against him all the things that had sworn to leave him hurtless. And neither the battle-axe flung full at him, nor the stone out of the sling, nor the burning brand, nor the deluge of water would injure the beloved of Asgard. The Aesir and the Vanir laughed joyously to see these things fall harmlessly from him while a throng came to join them in the games; Dwarfs and friendly Giants.

But Loki the Hater came in with that throng. He watched the games from afar. He saw the missiles and the weapons being flung and he saw Baldur stand smiling and happy under the strokes of metal and stones and great woods. He wondered at the sight, but he knew that he might not ask the meaning of it from the ones who knew him.

He changed his shape into that of an old woman and he went amongst those who were making sport for Baldur. He spoke to Dwarfs and friendly Giants. "Go to Frigga and ask. Go to Frigga and ask," was all the answer Loki got from any of them.

Then to Fensalir, Frigga's mansion, Loki went. He told those in the mansion that he was Groa, the old Enchantress who was drawing out of Thor's head the fragments of a grindstone that a Giant's throw had embedded in it. Frigga knew about Groa and she praised the Enchantress for what she had done.

"Many fragments of the great grindstone have I taken out of Thor's head by the charms I know," said the pretended Groa. "Thor was so grateful that he brought back to me the husband that he once had carried off to the end of the earth. So overjoyed was I to find my husband restored that I forgot the rest of the charms. And I left some fragments of the stone in Thor's head."

So Loki said, repeating a story that was true. "Now I remember the rest of the charm," he said, "and I can draw out the fragments of the stone that are left. But will you not tell me, O Queen, what is the meaning of the extraordinary things I saw the Aesir and the Vanir doing?"

"I will tell you," said Frigga, looking kindly and happily at the pretended old woman. "They are hurling all manner of heavy and dangerous things at Baldur, my beloved son. And all Asgard cheers to see that neither metal nor stone nor great wood will hurt him."

"But why will they not hurt him?" said the pretended Enchantress.

"Because I have drawn an oath from all dangerous and threatening things to leave Baldur hurtless," said Frigga.

"From all things, lady? Is there no thing in all the world that has not taken an oath to leave Baldur hurtless?"

"Well, indeed, there is one thing that has not taken the oath. But that thing is so small and weak that I passed it by without taking thought of it."

"What can it be, lady?"

"The Mistletoe that is without root or strength. It grows on the eastern side of Valhalla. I passed it by without drawing an oath from it."

"Surely you were not wrong to pass it by. What could the Mistletoe – the rootless Mistletoe – do against Baldur?"

Saying this the pretended Enchantress hobbled off.

But not far did the pretender go hobbling. He changed his gait and hurried to the eastern side of Valhalla. There a great oak tree flourished and out of a branch of it a little bush of Mistletoe grew. Loki broke off a spray and with it in his hand he went to where the Aesir and the Vanir were still playing games to honour Baldur.

All were laughing as Loki drew near, for the Giants and the Dwarfs, the Asyniur and the Vana, were all casting missiles. The Giants threw too far and the Dwarfs could not throw far enough, while the Asyniur and the Vana threw far and wide of the mark. In the midst of all that glee and gamesomeness it was strange to see one standing joyless. But one stood so, and he was of the Aesir – Hödur, Baldur's blind brother.

"Why do you not enter the game?" said Loki to him in his changed voice.

"I have no missile to throw at Baldur," Hödur said.

"Take this and throw it," said Loki. "It is a twig of the Mistletoe."

"I cannot see to throw it," said Hödur.

"I will guide your hand," said Loki. He put the twig of Mistletoe in Hödur's hand and he guided the hand for the throw. The twig flew toward Baldur. It struck him on the breast and it pierced him. Then Baldur fell down with a deep groan.

The Aesir and the Vanir, the Dwarfs and the friendly Giants, stood still in doubt and fear and amazement. Loki slipped away. And blind Hödur, from whose hand the twig of Mistletoe had gone, stood quiet, not knowing that his throw had bereft Baldur of life.

Then a wailing rose around the Peace Stead. It was from the Asyniur and the Vana. Baldur was dead, and they began to lament him. And while they were lamenting him, the beloved of Asgard, Odin came amongst them.

"Hela has won our Baldur from us," Odin said to Frigga as they both bent over the body of their beloved son.

"Nay, I will not say it," Frigga said.

When the Aesir and the Vanir had won their senses back the mother of Baldur went amongst them. "Who amongst you would win my love and goodwill?" she said. "Whoever would let him ride down to Hela's dark realm and ask the Queen to take ransom for Baldur. It may be she will take it and let Baldur come back to us. Who amongst you will go? Odin's steed is ready for the journey."

Then forth stepped Hermod the Nimble, the brother of Baldur. He mounted Sleipner and turned the eight-legged steed down toward Hela's dark realm.

For nine days and nine nights Hermod rode on. His way was through rugged glens, one deeper and darker than the other. He came to the river that is called Giöll and to the bridge across it that is all glittering with gold. The pale maid who guards the bridge spoke to him.

"The hue of life is still on thee," said Modgudur, the pale maid. "Why dost thou journey down to Hela's deathly realm?"

"I am Hermod," he said, "and I go to see if Hela will take ransom for Baldur."

"Fearful is Hela's habitation for one to come to," said Modgudur, the pale maid. "All round it is a steep wall that even thy steed might hardly leap. Its threshold is Precipice. The bed therein is Care, the table is Hunger, the hanging of the chamber is Burning Anguish."

"It may be that Hela will take ransom for Baldur."

"If all things in the world still lament for Baldur, Hela will have to take ransom and let him go from her," said Modgudur, the pale maid that guards the glittering bridge.

"It is well, then, for all things lament Baldur. I will go to her and make her take ransom."

"Thou mayst not pass until it is of a surety that all things still lament him. Go back to the world and make sure. If thou dost come to this glittering bridge and tell me that all things still lament Baldur, I will let thee pass and Hela will have to hearken to thee."

"I will come back to thee, and thou, Modgudur, pale maid, wilt have to let me pass."

"Then I will let thee pass," said Modgudur.

Joyously, Hermod turned Sleipner and rode back through the rugged glens, each one less gloomy than the other. He reached the upper world, and saw that all things were still lamenting for Baldur. Joyously, Hermod rode onward. He met the Vanir in the middle of the world and he told them the happy tidings.

Then Hermod and the Vanir went through the world seeking out each thing and finding that each thing still wept for Baldur. But one day, Hermod came upon a crow that was sitting on the dead branch of a tree. The crow made no lament as he came near. She rose up and flew away and Hermod followed her to make sure that she lamented for Baldur.

He lost sight of her near a cave. And then before the cave he saw a hag with blackened teeth who raised no voice of lament. "If thou art the crow that came flying here, make lament for Baldur," Hermod said.

"I, Thaukt, will make no lament for Baldur," the hag said, "let Hela keep what she holds."

"All things weep tears for Baldur," Hermod said.

"I will weep dry tears for him," said the hag.

She hobbled into her cave, and as Hermod followed a crow fluttered out. He knew that this was Thaukt, the evil hag, transformed. He followed her, and she went through the world croaking, "Let Hela keep what she holds. Let Hela keep what she holds."

Then Hermod knew that he might not ride to Hela's habitation. All things knew that there was one thing in the world that would not lament for Baldur. The Vanir came back to him, and with head bowed over Sleipner's mane, Hermod rode into Asgard.

Now the Aesir and the Vanir, knowing that no ransom would be taken for Baldur and that the joy and content of Asgard were gone indeed, made ready his body for the burning. First they covered Baldur's body with a rich robe, and each left beside it his most precious possession. Then they all took leave of him, kissing him upon the brow. But Nanna, his gentle wife, flung herself on his dead breast and her heart broke and she died of her grief. Then did the Aesir and the Vanir weep afresh. And they took the body of Nanna and they placed it side by side with Baldur's.

On his own great ship, Ringhorn, would Baldur be placed with Nanna beside him. Then the ship would be launched on the water and all would be burned with fire.

But it was found that none of the Aesir or the Vanir were able to launch Baldur's great ship. Hyrroken, a Giantess, was sent for. She came mounted on a great wolf with twisted serpents for a bridle. Four Giants held fast the wolf when she alighted. She came to the ship and with a single push she sent it into the sea. The rollers struck out fire as the ship dashed across them.

Then when it rode the water fires mounted on the ship. And in the blaze of the fires one was seen bending over the body of Baldur and whispering into his ear. It was Odin All-Father. Then he went down off the ship and all the fires rose into a mighty burning. Speechlessly, the Aesir and the Vanir watched with tears streaming down their faces while all things lamented, crying, "Baldur the Beautiful is dead, is dead."

And what was it that Odin All-Father whispered to Baldur as he bent above him with the flames of the burning ship around? He whispered of a heaven above Asgard that Surtur's flames might not reach, and of a life that would come to beauty again after the World of Men and the World of the Gods had been searched through and through with fire.

Loki's Punishment

The crow went flying toward the north, croaking as she flew, "Let Hela keep what she holds. Let Hela keep what she holds." That crow was the hag Thaukt transformed, and the hag Thaukt was Loki.

He flew to the north and came into the wastes of Jötunheim. As a crow he lived there, hiding himself from the wrath of the Gods. He told the Giants that the time had come for them to build the ship Naglfar, the ship that was to be built out of the nails of dead men, and that was to sail to Asgard on the day of Ragnarök with the Giant Hrymer steering it. And harkening to what he said the Giants then and there began to build Naglfar, the ship that Gods and men wished to remain unbuilt for long.

Then Loki, tiring of the wastes of Jötunheim, flew to the burning south. As a lizard he lived amongst the rocks of Muspelheim, and he made the Fire Giants rejoice when he told them of the loss of Frey's sword and of Tyr's right hand.

But still in Asgard there was one who wept for Loki – Siguna, his wife. Although he had left her and had shown his hatred for her, Siguna wept for her evil husband.

He left Muspelheim as he had left Jötunheim and he came to live in the World of Men. He knew that he had now come into a place where the wrath of the Gods might find him, and so he made plans to be ever ready for escape. He had come to the River where, ages before, he had slain the otter that was the son of the Enchanter, and on the very rock where the otter had eaten the salmon on the day of his killing, Loki built his house. He made four doors to it so that he might see in every direction. And the power that he kept for himself was the power of transforming himself into a salmon.

Often as a salmon he swam in the River. But even for the fishes that swam beside him Loki had hatred. Out of flax and yarn he wove a net that men might have the means of taking them out of the water.

The wrath that the Gods had against Loki did not pass away. It was he who, as Thaukt, the Hag, had given Hela the power to keep Baldur unransomed. It was he who had put into Hödur's hand the sprig of Mistletoe that had bereft Baldur of life. Empty was Asgard now that Baldur lived no more in the Peace Stead, and stern and gloomy grew the minds of the Aesir and the Vanir with thinking on the direful things that were arrayed against them. Odin in his hall of Valhalla thought only of the ways by which he could bring heroes to him to be his help in defending Asgard.

The Gods searched through the world and they found at last the place where Loki had made his dwelling. He was weaving the net to take fishes when he saw them coming from four directions. He threw the net into the fire so that it was burnt, and he sprang into the River and transformed himself into a salmon. When the Gods entered his dwelling they found only the burnt-out fire.

But there was one amongst them who could understand all that he saw. In the ashes were the marks of the burnt net and he knew that these were the tracing of something to catch fishes. And from the marks left in the ashes he made a net that was the same as the one Loki had burnt.

With it in their hands the Gods went down the River, dragging the net through the water. Loki was affrighted to find the thing of his own weaving brought against him. He lay between two stones at the bottom of the River, and the net passed over him.

But the Gods knew that the net had touched something at the bottom. They fastened weights to it and they dragged the net through the River again. Loki knew that he might not escape it this time and he rose in the water and swam toward the sea. The Gods caught sight of him as he leaped over a waterfall. They followed him, dragging the net. Thor waded behind, ready to seize him should he turn back.

Loki came out at the mouth of the River and behold! There was a great eagle hovering over the waves of the sea and ready to swoop down on fishes. He turned back in the River. He made a leap that took him over the net that the Gods were dragging. But Thor was behind the net and he caught the salmon in his powerful hands and he held him for all the struggle that Loki made. No fish had ever struggled so before. Loki got himself free all but his tail, but Thor held to the tail and brought him amongst the rocks and forced him to take on his proper form.

He was in the hands of those whose wrath was strong against him. They brought him to a cavern and they bound him to three sharp-pointed rocks. With cords that were made of the sinews of wolves they bound him, and they transformed the cords into iron bands. There they would have left Loki bound and helpless. But Skadi, with her fierce Giant blood, was not content that he should be left untormented. She found a serpent that had deadly venom and she hung this serpent above Loki's head. The drops of venom fell upon him, bringing him anguish drop by drop, minute by minute. So Loki's torture went on.

But Siguna with the pitying heart came to his relief. She exiled herself from Asgard, and endured the darkness and the cold of the cavern, that she might take some of the torment away from him who was her husband. Over Loki Siguna stood, holding in her hands a cup into which fell the serpent's venom, thus sparing him from the full measure of anguish. Now and then Siguna had to turn aside to spill out the flowing cup, and then the drops of venom fell upon Loki and he screamed in agony, twisting in his bonds. It was then that men felt the earthquake. There in his bonds Loki stayed until the coming of Ragnarök, the Twilight of the Gods.

The Twilight of the Gods

Snow fell on the four quarters of the world; icy winds blew from every side; the sun and the moon were hidden by storms. It was the Fimbul Winter: no spring came and no summer; no autumn brought harvest or fruit, and winter grew into winter again.

There was three years' winter. The first was called the Winter of Winds: storms blew and snows drove down and frosts were mighty. The children of men might hardly keep alive in that dread winter.

The second winter was called the Winter of the Sword: those who were left alive amongst men robbed and slew for what was left to feed on; brother fell on brother and slew him, and over all the world there were mighty battles.

And the third winter was called the Winter of the Wolf. Then the ancient witch who lived in Jarnvid, the Iron Wood, fed the Wolf Managarm on unburied men and on the corpses of those who fell in battle. Mightily grew and flourished the Wolf that was to be the devourer of Mani, the Moon. The Champions in Valhalla would find their seats splashed with the blood that Managarm dashed from his jaws; this was a sign to the Gods that the time of the last battle was approaching.

A cock crew; far down in the bowels of the earth he was and beside Hela's habitation: the rusty-red cock of Hel crew, and his crowing made a stir in the lower worlds. In Jötunheim a cock crew, Fialar, the crimson cock, and at his crowing the Giants aroused themselves. High up in Asgard a cock crew, the golden cock Gullinkambir, and at his crowing the Champions in Valhalla bestirred themselves.

A dog barked; deep down in the earth a dog barked; it was Garm, the hound with bloody mouth, barking in Gnipa's Cave. The Dwarfs who heard groaned before their doors of stone. The tree Ygdrassil moaned in all its branches. There was a rending noise as the Giants moved their ship; there was a trampling sound as the hosts of Muspelheim gathered their horses.

But Jötunheim and Muspelheim and Hel waited tremblingly; it might be that Fenrir the Wolf might not burst the bonds wherewith the Gods had bound him. Without his being loosed the Gods might not be destroyed. And then was heard the rending of the rock as Fenrir broke loose. For the second time the Hound Garm barked in Gnipa's Cave.

Then was heard the galloping of the horses of the riders of Muspelheim; then was heard the laughter of Loki; then was heard the blowing of Heimdall's horn; then was heard the opening of Valhalla's five hundred and forty doors, as eight hundred Champions made ready to pass through each door.

Odin took council with Mimir's head. Up from the waters of the Well of Wisdom he drew it, and by the power of the runes he knew he made the head speak to him. Where best might the Aesir and the Vanir and the Einherjar, who were the Champions of Midgard, meet, and how best might they strive with the forces of Muspelheim and Jötunheim and Hel? The head of Mimir counseled Odin to meet them on Vigard Plain and to wage there such war that the powers of evil would be destroyed forever, even though his own world should be destroyed with them.

The riders of Muspelheim reached Bifröst, the Rainbow Bridge. Now would they storm the City of the Gods and fill it with flame. But Bifröst broke under the weight of the riders of Muspelheim, and they came not to the City of the Gods.

Jörmungand, the serpent that encircles the world, reared itself up from the sea. The waters flooded the lands, and the remnant of the world's inhabitants was swept away. That mighty flood floated Naglfar, the Ship of Nails that the Giants were so long building, and floated the ship of Hel also. With Hrymer the Giant steering it, Naglfar sailed against the Gods, with all the powers of Jötunheim aboard. And Loki steered the ship of Hel with the Wolf Fenrir upon it for the place of the last battle.

Since Bifröst was broken, the Aesir and the Vanir, the Asyniur and the Vana, the Einherjar and the Valkyries rode downward to Vigard through the waters of Thund. Odin rode at the head of his Champions. His helmet was of gold and in his hand was his spear Gungnir. Thor and Tyr were in his company.

In Mirkvid, the Dark Forest, the Vanir stood against the host of Muspelheim. From the broken end of the Rainbow Bridge the riders came, all flashing and flaming, with fire before them and after them. Niörd was there with Skadi, his Giant wife, fierce in her wardress; Freya was there also, and Frey had Gerda beside him as a battle-maiden. Terribly bright flashed Surtur's sword. No sword ever owned was as bright as his except the sword that Frey had given to Skirnir. Frey and Surtur fought; he perished, Frey perished in that battle, but he would not have perished if he had had in his hand his own magic sword.

And now, for the third time, Garm, the hound with blood upon his jaws, barked. He had broken loose on the world, and with fierce bounds he rushed toward Vigard Plain, where the Gods had assembled their powers. Loud barked Garm. The Eagle Hraesvelgur screamed on the edge of heaven. Then the skies were cloven, and the tree Ygdrassil was shaken in all its roots.

To the place where the Gods had drawn up their ranks came the ship of Jötunheim and the ship of Hel, came the riders of Muspelheim, and Garm, the hound with blood upon his jaws. And out of the sea that now surrounded the plain of Vigard the serpent Jörmungand came.

What said Odin to the Gods and to the Champions who surrounded him? "We will give our lives and let our world be destroyed, but we will battle so that these evil powers will not live after us." Out of Hel's ship sprang Fenrir the Wolf. His mouth gaped; his lower jaw hung against the earth, and his upper jaw scraped the sky. Against the Wolf Odin All-Father fought. Thor might not aid him, for Thor had now to encounter Jörmungand, the monstrous serpent.

By Fenrir the Wolf Odin was slain. But the younger Gods were now advancing to the battle; and Vidar, the Silent God, came face to face with Fenrir. He laid his foot on the Wolf's lower jaw, that foot that had on the sandal made of all the scraps of leather that shoemakers had laid by for him, and with his hands he seized the upper jaw and tore his gullet. Thus died Fenrir, the fiercest of all the enemies of the Gods.

Jörmungand, the monstrous serpent, would have overwhelmed all with the venom he was ready to pour forth. But Thor sprang forward and crushed him with a stroke of his hammer Miölnir. Then Thor stepped back nine paces. But the serpent blew his venom over him, and blinded and choked and burnt, Thor, the World's Defender, perished.

Loki sprang from his ship and strove with Heimdall, the Warder of the Rainbow Bridge and the Watcher for the Gods. Loki slew Heimdall and was slain by him.

Bravely fought Tyr, the God who had sacrificed his sword hand for the binding of the Wolf. Bravely he fought, and many of the powers of evil perished by his strong left hand. But Garm, the hound with bloody jaws, slew Tyr.

And now the riders of Muspelheim came down on the field. Bright and gleaming were all their weapons. Before them and behind them went wasting fires. Surtur cast fire upon the earth; the tree Ygdrassil took fire and burned in all its great branches; the World Tree was wasted in the blaze. But the fearful fire that Surtur brought on the earth destroyed him and all his host.

The Wolf Hati caught up on Sol, the Sun; the Wolf Managarm seized on Mani, the Moon; they devoured them; stars fell, and darkness came down on the world.

The seas flowed over the burnt and wasted earth and the skies were dark above the sea, for Sol and Mani were no more. But at last the seas drew back and earth appeared again, green and beautiful. A new Sun and a new Moon appeared in the heavens, one a daughter of Sol and the other a daughter of Mani. No grim wolves kept them in pursuit.

Four of the younger Gods stood on the highest of the world's peaks; they were Vidar and Vali, the sons of Odin, and Modi and Magni, the sons of Thor. Modi and Magni found Miölnir, Thor's hammer, and with it they slew the monsters that still raged through the world, the Hound Garm and the Wolf Managarm.

Vidar and Vali found in the grass the golden tablets on which were inscribed the runes of wisdom of the elder Gods. The runes told them of a heaven that was above Asgard, of Gimli, that was untouched by Surtur's fire. Vili and Ve, Will and Holiness, ruled in it. Baldur and Hödur came from Hela's habitation, and the Gods sat on the peak together and held speech with each other, calling to mind the secrets and the happenings they had known before Ragnarök, the Twilight of the Gods.

Deep in a wood, two of human kind were left; the fire of Surtur did not touch them; they slept, and when they wakened the world was green and beautiful again. These two fed on the dews of the morning; a woman and a man they were. Lif and Lifthrasir. They walked abroad in the world, and from them and from their children came the men and women who spread themselves over the earth.

The Decline and Fall of the Gods

GOBHAN THE ARCHITECT and his son, young Gobhan, were sent for by Balor of the Blows to build him a palace. They built it so well that Balor decided never to let them leave his kingdom alive, for fear they should build another one equally good for someone else. He therefore had all the scaffolding removed from round the palace while they were still on the top, with the intention of leaving them up there to die of hunger. But, when they discovered this, they began to destroy the roof, so that Balor was obliged to let them come down.

He nonetheless refused to allow them to return to Ireland. The crafty Gobhan, however, had his plan ready. He told Balor that the injury that had been done to the palace roof could not be repaired without special tools, which he had left behind him at home. Balor declined to let either old Gobhan or young Gobhan go back to fetch them; but he offered to send his own son. Gobhan gave Balor's son directions for the journey. He was to travel until he came to a house with a stack of corn at the door. Entering it, he would find a woman with one hand and a child with one eye.

Balor's son found the house and asked the woman for the tools. She expected him; for it had been arranged between Gobhan and his wife what should be done if Balor refused to let him return. She took Balor's son to a huge chest, and told him that the tools were at the bottom of it, so far down that she could not reach them, and that he must get into the chest, and pick them up himself. But, as soon as he was safely inside, she shut the lid on him, telling him that he would have to stay there until his father allowed old Gobhan and young Gobhan to come home with their pay. And she sent the same message to Balor himself.

There was an exchange of prisoners, Balor giving the two Gobhans their pay and a ship to take them home, and Gobhan's wife releasing Balor's son. But, before the two builders went, Balor asked them whom he should now employ to repair his palace. Old Gobhan told him that, next to himself, there was no workman in Ireland better than one Gavidjeen Go.

When Gobhan got back to Ireland, he sent Gavidjeen Go to Balor. But he gave him a piece of advice – to accept as pay only one thing: Balor's grey cow, which would fill twenty barrels at one milking. Balor agreed to this, but, when he gave the cow to Gavidjeen Go to take back with him to Ireland, he omitted to include her byre-rope, which was the only thing that would keep her from returning to her original owner.

The grey cow gave so much trouble to Gavidjeen Go by her straying, that he was obliged to hire military champions to watch her during the day and bring her safely home at night. The bargain made was that Gavidjeen Go should forge the champion a sword for his pay, but that, if he lost the cow, his life was to be forfeited.

At last, a certain warrior called Cian was unlucky enough to let the cow escape. He followed her tracks down to the seashore and right to the edge of the waves, and there he lost them altogether. He was tearing his hair in his perplexity, when he saw a man rowing a coracle. The man, who was no other than Manannán son of Lêr, came in close to the shore, and asked what was the matter.

Cian told him.

"What would you give to anyone who would take you to the place where the grey cow is?" asked Manannán.

"I have nothing to give," replied Cian.

"All I ask," said Manannán, "is half of whatever you gain before you come back."

Cian agreed to that willingly enough, and Manannán told him to get into the coracle. In the wink of an eye, he had landed him in Balor's kingdom, the realm of the cold, where they roast no meat, but eat their food raw. Cian was not used to this diet, so he lit himself a fire, and began to cook some food. Balor saw the fire, and came down to it, and he was so pleased that he appointed Cian to be his fire-maker and cook.

Now Balor had a daughter, of whom a druid had prophesied that she would, some day, bear a son who would kill his grandfather. Therefore, like Acrisius, in Greek legend, he shut her up in a tower, guarded by women, and allowed her to see no man but himself. One day, Cian saw Balor go to the tower. He waited until he had come back, and then went to explore. He had the gift of opening locked doors and shutting them again after him. When he got inside, he lit a fire, and this novelty so delighted Balor's daughter that she invited him to visit her again. After this – in the Achill islander's quaint phrase – 'he was ever coming there, until a child happened to her'. Balor's daughter gave the baby to Cian to take away. She also gave him the byre-rope which belonged to the grey cow.

Cian was in great danger now, for Balor had found out about the child. He led the grey cow away with the rope to the seashore, and waited for Manannán. The Son of Lêr had told Cian that, when he was in any difficulty, he was to think of him, and he would at once appear. Cian thought of him now, and, in a moment, Manannán appeared with his coracle. Cian got into the boat, with the baby and the grey cow, just as Balor, in hot pursuit, came down to the beach.

Balor, by his incantations, raised a great storm to drown them; but Manannán, whose druidism was greater, stilled it. Then Balor turned the sea into fire, to burn them; but Manannán put it out with a stone.

When they were safe back in Ireland, Manannán asked Cian for his promised reward.

"I have gained nothing but the boy, and I cannot cut him in two, so I will give him to you whole," he replied.

"That is what I was wanting all the time," said Manannán; "when he grows up, there will be no champion equal to him."

So Manannán baptized the boy, calling him 'the Dul-Dauna'. This name, meaning 'Blind-Stubborn', is certainly a curious corruption of the original *Ioldanach* 'Master of all Knowledge'. When the boy had grown up, he went one day to the seashore. A ship came past, in which was a man. The traditions of Donnybrook Fair are evidently prehistoric, for the boy, without troubling to ask who the stranger was, took a dart 'out of his pocket', hurled it, and hit him. The man in the boat happened to be Balor. Thus, in accordance with the prophecy, he was slain by his grandson, who, though the folktale does not name him, was obviously Lugh.

The War Between the Gods of Fire and Water

FOR A GREAT many years after Nu Wa had created human beings, the earth remained a peaceful and joyous place and it was not until the final years of the Goddess's reign that mankind first encountered pain and suffering. For Nu Wa was extremely protective of the race she had created and considered it her supreme duty to shelter it from all harm and evil. People depended on Nu Wa for her guardianship and she, in turn, enabled them to live in comfort and security.

One day, however, two of the Gods who dwelt in the heavens, known as Gong Gong and Zhurong, became entangled in a fierce and bitter dispute. No one knew precisely why the two

Gods began to shout and threaten one another, but before long they were resolved to do battle against each other and to remain fighting to the bitter end. Gong Gong, who was the God of Water, was well known as a violent and ambitious character and his bright red wavy hair perfectly mirrored his fiery and riotous spirit. Zhurong, the God of Fire, was equally belligerent when provoked and his great height and bulk rendered him no less terrifying in appearance.

Several days of fierce fighting ensued between the two of them during which the skies buckled and shifted under the strain of the combat. An end to this savage battle seemed to be nowhere in sight, as each God thrust and lunged with increasing fury and rage, determined to prove himself more powerful than the other. But on the fourth day, Gong Gong began to weary and Zhurong gained the upper hand, felling his opponent to the ground and causing him to tumble right out of the heavens.

Crashing to the earth with a loud bang, Gong Gong soon became acutely aware of the shame and disgrace of his defeat and decided that he would never again have the courage to face any of his fellow Gods. He was now resolved to end his own life and looked around him for some means by which he might perform this task honourably and successfully. And seeing a large mountain range in the distance rising in the shape of a giant pillar to the skies, Gong Gong ran towards it with all the speed he could muster and rammed his head violently against its base.

As soon as he had done this, a terrifying noise erupted from within the mountain, and gazing upwards, Gong Gong saw that a great wedge of rock had broken away from the peak, leaving behind a large gaping hole in the sky. Without the support of the mountain, the sky began to collapse and plummet towards the earth's surface, causing great crevasses to appear on impact. Many of these crevasses released intensely hot flames which instantly engulfed the earth's vegetation, while others spouted streams of filthy water which merged to form a great ocean. And as the flood and destruction spread throughout the entire world, Nu Wa's people no longer knew where to turn to for help. Thousands of them drowned, while others wandered the earth in terror and fear, their homes consumed by the raging flames and their crops destroyed by the swift-flowing water.

Nu Wa witnessed all of this in great distress and could not bear to see the race she had created suffer such appalling misery and deprivation. Though she was now old and looking forward to her time of rest, she decided that she must quickly take action to save her people, and it seemed that the only way for her to do this was to repair the heavens as soon as she possibly could with her very own hands.

Nu Wa Repairs the Sky

NU WA RAPIDLY set about gathering the materials she needed to mend the great hole in the sky. One of the first places she visited in her search was the river Yangtze where she stooped down and gathered up as many pebbles as she could hold in both arms. These were carefully chosen in a variety of colours and carried to a forge in the heavens where they were melted down into a thick, gravel-like paste. Once she had returned to earth, Nu Wa began to repair the damage, anxiously filling the gaping hole with the paste and smoothing whatever remained of it into the surrounding cracks in the firmament. Then she hurried once more to the river bank and, collecting together the tallest reeds, she built a large, smouldering fire and burnt the reeds until they formed a huge mound of ashes. With these ashes Nu Wa sealed the crevasses of the earth, so that water no longer gushed out from beneath its surface and the swollen rivers gradually began to subside.

After she had done this, Nu Wa surveyed her work, yet she was still not convinced that she had done enough to prevent the heavens collapsing again in the future. So she went out and captured one of the giant immortal tortoises which were known to swim among the jagged rocks at the deepest point of the ocean and brought it ashore to slaughter it. And when she had killed the creature, she chopped off its four sturdy legs and stood them upright at the four points of the compass as extra support for the heavens. Only now was the Goddess satisfied and she began to gather round her some of her frightened people in an attempt to reassure them that order had finally been restored.

To help them forget the terrible experiences they had been put through, Nu Wa made a flute for them out of thirteen sticks of bamboo and with it she began to play the sweetest, most soothing music. All who heard it grew calmer almost at once and the earth slowly began to emerge from the chaos and destruction to which it had been subjected. From that day forth, Nu Wa's people honoured her by calling her 'Goddess of music' and many among them took great pride in learning the instrument she had introduced them to.

But even though the heavens had been repaired, the earth was never quite the same again. Gong Gong's damage to the mountain had caused the skies to tilt permanently towards the north-west so that the Pole Star, around which the heavens revolved, was dislodged from its position directly overhead. The sun and the moon were also tilted, this time in the direction of the west, leaving a great depression in the south-east. And not only that, but the peak of the mountain which had crashed to the earth had left a huge hollow where it landed in the east into which the rivers and streams of the world flowed incessantly.

Nu Wa had done all she could to salvage the earth and shortly afterwards, she died. Her body was transformed into a thousand fairies who watched over the human race on her behalf. Her people believe that the reason China's rivers flow eastwards was because of Gong Gong's foolish collision with the mountain, a belief that is still shared by their ancestors today.

The Flood and the Rainbow

THE LENNI-LENAPI ARE the First People, so that they know this story is true. After the Creation of the earth, the Mysterious One covered it with a blue roof. Sometimes the roof was very black. Then the Manitou of Waters became uneasy. He feared the rain would no longer be able to pour down upon the earth through this dark roof. Therefore the Manitou of Waters prayed to the Mysterious One that the waters from above be not cut off.

At once the Mysterious One commanded to blow the Spirit of the Wind, who dwells in the Darkening Land. At once thick clouds arose. They covered all the earth, so that the dark roof could no longer be seen.

Then the voice of the Mysterious One was heard amongst the clouds. The voice was deep and heavy, like the sound of falling rivers.

Then the Spirit of Rain, the brother of the Spirit of Waters and the Spirit of the Winds, poured down water from above. The waters fell for a long time. They fell until all the earth was covered. Then the birds took refuge in the branches of the highest trees. The animals followed the trails to the mountain peaks.

Then the Manitou of Waters feared no longer. Therefore the Mysterious One ordered the rain to cease and the clouds to disappear. Then Sin-go-wi-chi-na-xa, the rainbow, was seen in the sky.

Therefore the Lenni-Lenapi watch for the rainbow, because it means that the Mysterious One is no longer angry.

The Fall of the Lenape

THE DELAWARES ARE the grandfather of nations, the parent stock from which have proceeded the many tribes who roam over the woods of this vast island. From them are descended the red men of the east and the west, of the shores of the Great Sea and of the northern lakes. Among these the Mengwe was a favoured grandchild. In the days that are gone, the Delawares fought his battles, his war was theirs; and the hostile shout that woke in his woods was answered by the defiance of the sons of the Leni Lenape.

But the Mengwe was ungrateful, and forgot these benefits; he was treacherous, and raised his hand against his benefactors and former friends. His hostile bands invaded the lands of his grandfather, but they were defeated, and fled howling to their wilderness. The Mengwe, by their cunning and duplicity, had brought all the tribes of the land upon the Lenape, whose sons nevertheless continued in possession of their hunting-grounds, for they were very brave. Still their enemy continued his arts. He first sought to raise quarrels and disturbances, which in the end might lead to wars between the Lenape and the distant tribes who were friendly to them, for which purpose they privately murdered people on one or the other side, seeking to make the injured party believe that some particular nation or individual had been the aggressor. They left a war-club painted as the Lenape paints his in the country of the Cherokees, where they purposely committed a murder, and that people, deceived by appearances, fell suddenly on the Lenape, and a bloody and devastating war ensued between the two nations. They frequently stole into the country of the Lenape and their associates, committing murders and making off with plunder. Their treachery having at length been discovered, the Lenape marched with a powerful force into their country to destroy them. Finding that they were no match for the brave Delawares, Thannawage, an aged and wise Mohawk, called the different tribes of the Mengwe to the great council-fire. "You see," said he, "how easily the sons of our grandfather overcome us in battle. Their pole is strung full of the scalps of our nation, while ours has but here one and there one. This must not be; the last man of the Mengwe is not yet prepared to die. We must become united, the Mohawks, the Oneidas, the Onondagos, the Cayugas, and the Senecas, must become one people; they must move together in the conflict, they must smoke in one pipe, and eat their meat in one lodge." The people listened to the words of Thannawage, and the five nations became one people.

Still, though united they did not prevail over the Lenape and their connexions; the latter were most usually victorious. While these wars were at their greatest height, and when neither could decidedly pronounce themselves conquerors, the Bigknives arrived in Canada, and a war commenced between them and the confederated Iroquois. Thus placed between two fires, and in danger of being exterminated, they resorted to their old cunning and knavery. They sent a deputation of their principal warriors, with the sacred calumet and the belt of peace, to the sons of their grandfather. But they appeared not to wish for peace, but to be guided by wisdom and compassion alone, and to be fearful only of being considered as cowards. "A warrior," said they, "with the bloody weapon in his hand should never intimate, a desire for peace, or hold pacific language to his enemies. He should show throughout a determined courage, and appear as ready and willing to fight as at the beginning of the contest. Will a man who would not be thought a liar threaten and sue in the same breath; will he hold the peace-belt in one hand, and smoke the unpainted calumet, while his other hand grasps a tomahawk? Will he strike his breast, and say 'I am brave and fearless,' yet show that he is a mocking-bird? No, men's actions should be of a piece with their words, whether good or bad; good cannot come out of evil, neither can the brave man feel faint-hearted, or the fawn become a tiger. The Mengwe were brave: they would not abase themselves in the eyes of the Lenape by admitting that they were vanquished, or proposing peace. They made use of their women to soften the hearts of our nation. They said to their wives and the wives of the Lenape, Are you tired of the fathers of your children? – to the mothers, Does the Lenape hate her sons? – to our young women, Do the eyes of the maidens turn with aversion from the youths of your nation? If the wife is tired of her husband, if the mother hate her sons, if the dark-eyed maiden feels no grief when the Lenape youth goes forth to battle and certain death, nor sheds a tear when he paints his face, and dresses his hair, and fills his quiver with arrows, then let them remain silent, and the messengers of the Mengwe will return to their nation."

The women to whom they spoke were moved by the eloquence of the treacherous Iroquois, and they persuaded the enraged combatants to bury their hatchets, and make the tree of peace grow tall and firm-rooted. They lamented, with great feeling and many tears, the loss which their country had sustained in these wars: there was not a woman among them who had not lost a son, or a brother, or a father, or a husband. They described the sorrows of bereaved mothers and widowed wives; the pains mothers endured ere they were permitted to behold their offspring; the anxieties attending the progress of their sons from infancy to manhood, from the cradle to the hour when they chewed the bitter root, and put on new mocassins; these unavoidable evils they had borne: but, after all these trials, how cruel it was, they said, to see those promising youths reared with so much care, and so tenderly beloved, fall victims to the insatiable rage of war, and a prey to the relentless cruelty of their enemies. "See them slaughtered," cried they, with tears and groans, "on the field of battle. See them put to death as prisoners by a protracted torture, and in the midst of lingering torments. Hark, the death-cries! 'Tis the Iroquois, 'tis the Delawares, 'tis the Delawares returning from battle! I see the beautiful young warriors among them, crowned with flowers, their faces painted black, and their arms tied with cords. Hark! they are singing their death-song. 'I am brave and intrepid, I do not fear death, I care not for tortures. Those who fear them are less than women. I was bred a warrior; my father never knew fear, and I am his son.' Then we behold them surrounded with flames, their flesh torn from their bones, the skin of their head peeled off, coals heaped thereon, and sharp thorns driven into their flesh.

The thought of such scenes makes us curse our own existence, and shudder at the thought of bringing children into the world."

Again they gave utterance to loud lamentation and wailing for the unavoidable separation they were doomed to experience from their husbands. The men they had selected for their partners, who were to protect and feed them, to cherish and make them happy, left them exposed to hunger and a thousand enemies, while they courted dangers in distant regions. Or, if they followed their husbands, they were exposed in a greater degree than those husbands themselves to the risks attending the perilous warfare.

Then the young maidens took up the song, and painted the share of sorrows which fell to them. Often, when beloved by a youthful hunter, their hearts were doomed to wither in the pang of an eternal separation. The eyes they so loved to look upon were soon to be deprived of their lustre – the step so noble, fearless, and commanding led them but to death. They called passionately upon their countrymen and upon the Iroquois to put a stop to war. They conjured them, by every thing that was dear to them, to take pity on the sufferings of their wives and helpless infants, their weeping mothers, and beloved maidens; to turn their faces once more towards their homes, families, and friends; to forgive the wrongs each nation had suffered from the other, lay aside their weapons, and smoke together in the pipe of peace and amity. They had each given sufficient proofs of courage; the contending nations were alike high-minded and brave: why should they not embrace as friends who had been respected as enemies?

Thus spoke the women, at the prompting of the artful Mengwe; it is not necessary to say that they were listened to. The Delawares at length came to believe that it would be an honour to a powerful nation, who could not be suspected of wanting either courage or strength, with arms in their hands and recent victory perched on the staff of their nation, to assume that station by which they would be the means, and the only means, of saving the Indian race from utter extirpation.

To the voice of the women the artful Mengwe added many arguments, which were of weight with the unsuspecting Delawares, and many pleas addressed to their generosity. There remained, they said, no resource for them but that some magnanimous nation should assume the part and situation of the woman.

It could not be given to a weak and contemptible tribe; such would not be listened to: it must be given to a valiant and honoured tribe, and such were the Delawares – one who should command influence and respect. As men, they had been justly dreaded; as women, they would be respected and honoured; none would be so daring or base as to attack or insult them; as women, they would have a right to interfere in all the quarrels of other nations, and to stop or prevent the effusion of Indian blood. They entreated them, therefore, to become the woman in name and in fact; to lay down their arms and all the insignia of warriors; to devote themselves to planting corn and other pacific pursuits, and thus become the means of preserving peace and harmony among the nations.

Unhappily, our nation listened to this croaking of a raven; and forgot how many times it had been heard before disturbing their slumbers and ringing its echoes in the hollow night. They knew it was true that the Indian nations, excited by their own wild passions, were in the way of total extirpation by each other's hand. And, foolish men! they believed, notwithstanding all past experience, that the Mengwe were sincere, and only wished the preservation of the Indian race. As if the panther could forget its nature, or the rattlesnake cease to remember its means of defence; as if the Mengwe had forgotten the blood of their race, which had been shed by the sons of the Lenape, and could think of forgiveness while their defeats were the subject of every dream.

In a luckless hour, the Delawares gave their consent, and agreed to become women. Then the Iroquois appointed a great feast, and invited the Delaware nation to it. They came at the bidding of their treacherous foes, and were declared by them, in the following words, to be no longer men and warriors, but women and peace-makers. "We dress you," said the orator, "in a woman's long habit, reaching down to your feet, and we adorn your ears with rings," meaning that they should no more take up arms. "We hang a calabash, filled with oil and medicines, upon your arm. With the oil you shall cleanse the ears of other nations, that they may attend to good and not to bad words; and with the medicine you shall heal those who are walking in foolish ways, that they may return to their senses, and incline their hearts to peace. And we deliver into your hands a plant of Indian corn and a hoe, which shall be the emblems of your future calling and pursuits." So the great peace-belt, the chain of friendship, was laid upon the shoulders of the new mediator, who became a woman, buried the tomahawk, planted the corn, and forgot the glories which Areskoui confers upon the successful and dauntless warrior.

Before this, no Mengwe had been permitted, even when at peace, to visit the country of the Delawares. Whenever such had appeared, whenever the blue feather of an Iroquois was seen in a glade of the Lenape wihittuck, its possessor was hunted down as one hunts a wolf or a bear. But, now the woman had voluntarily abandoned her bow and her spear, what had she to do with weapons of war? The former warrior needed now no paints, unless to attract the eye of a maiden; the Mengwe needed not to fear the Lenape women. Then the pleasant glades of the Lenape wihittuck became thronged with curious eyes and false hearts; hostile feet threaded the mazes of her forest; hostile hands were laid upon the most fertile spots of her territory. To-day, came a few Iroquois; they wished for but a little piece of land – they had it. To-morrow, came another band; they wanted permission to kill a very few deer – it was granted them, and the cry of the hunter of the lakes was heard from the sea to the mountains. One remained, that the seeds of peace might not wither; another, to protect, oh changed times! the woman, who was the peace-maker, from the tomahawks of hostile tribes. But, while they were amusing the Lenape with flattering tales and the songs of mocking-birds, they were concerting measures to destroy them. They left war-clubs, such as the Delawares used, in the lands of the Cherokees, to incite them to fall upon us. Why delays my tongue to finish its tale? The fatal unmanning of our tribe wrought our ruin. The white people encroached upon us, because we were women and could not resent; the men of our own colour were not more just or generous. The Delawares stand abased by the children of their grandchild, overthrown by men defeated in a hundred battles. They are no longer warriors, but women.

Brothers, I would weep, were I not a man, for the downfall of my nation.

The Creation of Man and the Flood

AFTER THE WORLD was ready, Earth Doctor made all kinds of animals and creeping things. Then he made images of clay, and told them to be people. After a while there were so many people that there was not food and water enough for all. They were never sick and none died. At last there grew to be so many they were obliged to eat each other. Then Earth Doctor, because he could not give them food and water enough, killed them all. He caught the hook of his staff into the sky and pulled it down so that it crushed all the people and all the animals, until there was nothing living on the earth. Earth Doctor made a hole through the earth with his stick, and through that he went, coming out safe, but alone, on the other side.

He called upon the sun and moon to come out of the wreck of the world and sky, and they did so. But there was no sky for them to travel through, no stars, and no Milky Way. So Earth Doctor made these all over again. Then he created another race of men and animals.

Then Coyote was born. Moon was his mother. When Coyote was large and strong he came to the land where the Pima Indians lived.

Then Elder Brother was born. Earth was his mother, and Sky his father. He was so powerful that he spoke roughly to Earth Doctor, who trembled before him. The people began to increase in numbers, just as they had done before, but Elder Brother shortened their lives, so the earth did not become so crowded. But Elder Brother did not like the people created by Earth Doctor, so he planned to destroy them again. So Elder Brother planned to create a magic baby...

The screams of the baby shook the earth. They could be heard for a great distance. Then Earth Doctor called all the people together, and told them there would be a great flood. He sang a magic song and then bored a hole through the flat earth-plain through to the other side. Some of the people went into the hole to escape the flood that was coming, but not very many got through. Some of the people asked Elder Brother to help them, but he did not answer. Only Coyote he answered. He told Coyote to find a big log and sit on it, so that he would float on the surface of the water with the driftwood. Elder Brother got into a big olla which he had made, and closed it tight. So he rolled along on the ground under the olla. He sang a magic song as he climbed into his olla.

A young man went to the place where the baby was screaming. Its tears were a great torrent which cut gorges in the earth before it. The water was rising all over the earth. He bent over the child to pick it up, and immediately both became birds and flew above the flood. Only five birds were saved from the flood. One was a flicker and one a vulture. They clung by their beaks to the sky to keep themselves above the waters, but the tail of the flicker was washed by the waves and that is why it is stiff to this day. At last a god took pity on them and gave them power to make 'nests of down' from their own breasts on which they floated on the water. One of these birds was the vipisimal, and if any one injures it to this day, the flood may come again.

Now South Doctor called his people to him and told them that a flood was coming. He sang a magic song and he bored a hole in the ground with a cane so that people might go through to the other side. Others he sent to Earth Doctor, but Earth Doctor told them they were too late. So they sent the people to the top of a high mountain called Crooked Mountain. South Doctor sang a magic song and traced his cane around the mountain, but that held back the waters only for a short time. Four times he sang and traced a line around the mountain, yet the flood rose again each time. There was only one thing more to do.

He held his magic crystals in his left hand and sang a song. Then he struck it with his cane. A thunder peal rang through the mountains. He threw his staff into the water and it cracked with a loud noise. Turning, he saw a dog near him. He said, "How high is the tide?" The dog said, "It is very near the top." He looked at the people as he said it. When they heard his voice they all turned to stone. They stood just as they were, and they are there to this day in groups: some of the men talking, some of the women cooking, and some crying.

But Earth Doctor escaped by enclosing himself in his reed staff, which floated upon the water. Elder Brother rolled along in his olla until he came near the mouth of the Colorado River. The olla is now called Black Mountain. After the flood he came out and visited all parts of the land.

When he met Coyote and Earth Doctor, each claimed to have been the first to appear after the flood, but at last they admitted Elder Brother was the first, so he became ruler of the world.

The Flood

LONG, LONG AGO, in the days of the animal people, Raven-at-the-head-of-Nass became angry. He said, "Let rain pour down all over the world. Let people die of starvation." At once it became so stormy people could not get food, so they began to starve. Their canoes were also broken up, their houses fell in upon them, and they suffered very much. Then Nas-ca-ki-yel, Raven-at-the-head-of-Nass, asked for his jointed dance hat. When he put it on water began pouring out of the top of it. It is from Raven that the Indians obtained this kind of a hat.

When the water rose to the house floor, Raven and his mother climbed upon the lowest retaining timber. This house we are speaking of, although it looked like a house to them, was really part of the world. It had eight rows of retaining timbers.

When Raven and his mother climbed to a higher timber, the people of the world were climbing into the hills. Then Raven and his mother climbed to the fourth timber; by that time the water was halfway up the mountains. When the house was nearly full of water, Raven's mother got into the skin of a cax. To this very day, Tlingits do not eat the cax because it was Raven's mother. Then Raven got into the skin of a white bird with a copper-coloured bill. Now the cax is a diver and stayed upon the surface of the water. But Raven flew to the very highest cloud and hung there by his bill. But his tail was in the water.

After Raven had hung in the cloud for days and days – nobody knows how long – he pulled his bill out and prayed to fall on a piece of kelp. He thought the water had gone down. When Raven fell upon the kelp and flew away, he found the waters just halfway down the mountains.

Raven flew around until he met a shark, which had been swimming around with a long stick. Raven took the stick and climbed down it as a ladder to the bottom of the ocean. But Raven had set Eagle to watch the tide.

Raven wandered around the bottom of the ocean until he came to an old woman. He said to her, "How cold I am after eating those sea urchins." He repeated this over and over again.

At last the woman said, "What low tide is this Raven talking about?" Raven did not answer. The woman kept repeating, "What low tide are you talking about?"

Then Raven became angry. He said, "I will stick these sea urchins into you if you don't keep quiet." At last he did so.

Then the woman began singing, "Don't, Raven! The tide will go down if you don't stop."

But the water was receding, as Raven had told it to, in his magic words. Raven asked Eagle, who was watching the tide, "How far down is the tide now?"

"The tide is as far down as half a man."

"How far down is the tide?" he asked again.

"The tide is very low," said Eagle.

Then the old woman started her magic song again.

Raven said, "Let it get dry all around the world."

After a while, Eagle said, "The tide is very low now. You can hardly see any water."

Raven said, "Let it get still drier."

At last everything was dry. This is the lowest tide there ever was. All the salmon, and whales and seals lay on the sands because the water was so low. Then the people killed them for food. They had enough food to last them a long time.

When the tide began to rise again, the people were frightened. They feared there would be another flood, so they carried their food back a long distance.

Afterward, Raven returned to Nass River and found that people there had not changed their ways. They were dancing and feasting. They asked Raven to join them.

The Deluge

A LONG TIME ago a man had a dog, which began to go down to the river every day and look at the water and howl. At last the man was angry and scolded the dog, which then spoke to him and said, "Very soon there is going to be a great freshet and the water will come so high that everybody will be drowned; but if you will make a raft to get upon when the rain comes you can be saved, but you must first throw me into the water." The man did not believe it, and the dog said, "If you want a sign that I speak the truth, look at the back of my neck." He looked and saw that the dog's neck had the skin worn off so that the bones stuck out.

Then he believed the dog, and began to build a raft. Soon the rain came and he took his family, with plenty of provisions, and they all got upon it. It rained for a long time, and the water rose until the mountains were covered and all the people in the world were drowned. Then the rain stopped and the waters went down again, until at last it was safe to come off the raft. Now there was no one alive but the man and his family, but one day they heard a sound of dancing and shouting on the other side of the ridge. The man climbed to the top and looked over; everything was still, but all along the valley he saw great piles of bones of the people who had been drowned, and then he knew that the ghosts had been dancing.

A Story of the Rise and Fall of the Toltecs

THE TOLTECS, IXTLILXOCHITL says, founded the magnificent city of Tollan in the year 566 of the Incarnation. This city, the site of which is now occupied by the modern town of Tula, was situated north-west of the mountains which bound the Mexican valley. Thither were the Toltecs guided by the powerful necromancer Hueymatzin (Great Hand), and under his direction they decided to build a city upon the site of what had been their place of bivouac.

For six years they toiled at the building of Tollan, and magnificent edifices, palaces, and temples arose, the whole forming a capital of a splendour unparalleled in the New World. The valley wherein it stood was known as the 'Place of Fruits,' in allusion to its great fertility. The surrounding rivers teemed with fish, and the hills which encircled this delectable site sheltered large herds of game. But as yet the Toltecs were without a ruler, and in the seventh year of their occupation of the city the assembled chieftains took counsel together, and resolved to surrender their power into the hands of a monarch whom the people might elect. The choice fell upon Chalchiuh Tlatonac (Shining Precious Stone), who reigned for fifty-two years.

Legends of Toltec Artistry

Happily settled in their new country, and ruled over by a king whom they could regard with reverence, the Toltecs made rapid progress in the various arts, and their city began to be celebrated far and wide for the excellence of its craftsmen and the beauty of its architecture and pottery. The name of 'Toltec,' in fact, came to be regarded by the surrounding peoples as synonymous with 'artist,' and as a kind of hall-mark which guaranteed the superiority of any article of Toltec workmanship. Everything in and about the city was eloquent of the taste and artistry of its founders. The very walls were encrusted with rare stones, and their masonry was so beautifully chiselled and laid as to resemble the choicest mosaic. One of the edifices of which the inhabitants of Tollan were most justly proud was the temple wherein their high-priest officiated. This building was a very gem of architectural art and mural decoration. It contained four apartments. The walls of the first were inlaid with gold, the second with precious stones of every description, the third with beautiful sea-shells of all conceivable hues and of the most brilliant and tender shades encrusted in bricks of silver, which sparkled in the sun in such a manner as to dazzle the eyes of beholders. The fourth apartment was formed of a brilliant red stone, ornamented with shells.

The House of Feathers

Still more fantastic and weirdly beautiful was another edifice, 'The House of Feathers.' This also possessed four apartments, one decorated with feathers of a brilliant yellow, another with the radiant and sparkling hues of the Blue Bird. These were woven into a kind of tapestry, and placed against the walls in graceful hangings. An apartment described as of entrancing beauty was that in which the decorative scheme consisted of plumage of the purest and most dazzling white. The remaining chamber was hung with feathers of a brilliant red.

Huemac the Wicked

A succession of more or less able kings succeeded the founder of the Toltec monarchy, until in 994 CE Huemac II ascended the throne of Tollan. He ruled first with wisdom, and paid great attention to the duties of the state and religion. But later he fell from the high place he had made for himself in the regard of the people by his faithless deception of them and his intemperate and licentious habits. The provinces rose in revolt, and many signs and gloomy omens foretold the downfall of the city. Toveyo, a cunning sorcerer, collected a great concourse of people near Tollan, and by dint of beating upon a magic drum until the darkest hours of the night, forced them to dance to its sound until, exhausted by their efforts, they fell headlong over a dizzy precipice into a deep ravine, where they were turned into stone. Toveyo also maliciously destroyed a stone bridge, so that thousands of people fell into the river beneath and were drowned. The neighbouring volcanoes burst into eruption, presenting a frightful aspect, and grisly apparitions could be seen among the flames threatening the city with terrible gestures of menace.

The rulers of Tollan resolved to lose no time in placating the gods, whom they decided from the portents must have conceived the most violent wrath against their capital. They therefore ordained a great sacrifice of war-captives. But upon the first of the victims being placed upon the altar a still more terrible catastrophe occurred. In the method of sacrifice common to the Nahua race the breast of a youth was opened for the purpose of extracting the heart, but no such organ could the officiating priest perceive. Moreover the veins of the victim were bloodless. Such a deadly odour was exhaled from the corpse that a terrible pestilence arose, which caused the death of thousands of Toltecs. Huemac, the unrighteous monarch who had brought all this suffering upon his folk, was confronted in the forest by the Tlalocs, or gods of moisture, and humbly petitioned these deities to spare him, and not to take from him his wealth and rank. But the gods were disgusted at the callous selfishness displayed in his desires, and departed, threatening the Toltec race with six years of plagues.

The Plagues of the Toltecs

In the next winter such a severe frost visited the land that all crops and plants were killed. A summer of torrid heat followed, so intense in its suffocating fierceness that the streams were dried up and the very rocks were melted. Then heavy rain-storms descended, which flooded the streets and ways, and terrible tempests swept through the land. Vast numbers of loathsome toads invaded the valley, consuming the refuse left by the destructive frost and heat, and entering the very houses of the people. In the following year a terrible drought caused the death of thousands from starvation, and the ensuing winter was again a marvel of severity. Locusts descended in cloud-like swarms, and hail- and thunder-storms completed the wreck. During these visitations nine-tenths of the people perished, and all artistic endeavour ceased because of the awful struggle for food.

King Acxitl

With the cessation of these inflictions the wicked Huemac resolved upon a more upright course of life, and became most assiduous for the welfare and proper government of his people. But he had announced that Acxitl, his illegitimate son, should succeed him, and had further resolved to abdicate at once in favour of this youth. With the Toltecs, as with most primitive peoples, the early kings were regarded as divine, and the attempt to place on the throne one who was not of the royal blood was looked upon as a serious offence against the gods. A revolt ensued, but its two principal leaders were bought over by promises of preferment. Acxitl ascended the throne, and for a time ruled wisely. But he soon, like his father, gave way to a life of dissipation, and succeeded in setting a bad example to the members of his court and to the priesthood, the vicious spirit communicating itself to all classes of his subjects and permeating every rank of society. The iniquities of the people of the capital and the enormities practised by the royal favourites caused such scandal in the outlying provinces that at length they broke into open revolt, and Huehuetzin, chief of an eastern viceroyalty, joined to himself two other malcontent lords and marched upon the city of Tollan at the head of a strong force. Acxitl could not muster an army sufficiently powerful to repel the rebels, and was forced to resort to the expedient of buying them off with rich presents, thus patching up a truce. But the fate of Tollan was in the balance. Hordes of rude Chichimec savages, profiting by the civil broils in the Toltec state, invaded the lake region of Anahuac, or Mexico, and settled upon its fruitful soil. The end was in sight!

A Terrible Visitation

The wrath of the gods increased instead of diminishing, and in order to appease them a great convention of the wise men of the realm met at Teotihuacan, the sacred city of the Toltecs. But during their deliberations a giant of immense proportions rushed into their midst, and, seizing upon them by scores with his bony hands, hurled them to the ground, dashing their brains out. In this manner he slew great numbers, and when the panic-stricken folk imagined themselves delivered from him he returned in a different guise and slew many more. Again the grisly monster appeared, this time taking the form of a beautiful child. The people, fascinated by its loveliness, ran to observe it more closely, only to discover that its head was a mass of corruption, the stench from which was so fatal that many were killed outright. The fiend who had thus plagued the Toltecs at length designed to inform them that the gods would listen no longer to their prayers, but had fully resolved to destroy them root and branch, and he further counselled them to seek safety in flight.

Fall of the Toltec State

By this time the principal families of Tollan had deserted the country, taking refuge in neighbouring states. Once more Huehuetzin menaced Tollan, and by dint of almost superhuman efforts old King Huemac, who had left his retirement, raised a force sufficient to face the enemy. Acxitl's mother enlisted the services of the women of the city, and formed them into a regiment of Amazons. At the head of all was Acxitl, who divided his forces, despatching one portion to the front under his commander-in-chief, and forming the other into a reserve under his own leadership. During three years the king defended Tollan against the combined forces of the rebels and the semi-savage Chichimecs. At length the Toltecs, almost decimated, fled after a final desperate battle into the marshes of Lake Tezcuco and the fastnesses of the mountains. Their other cities were given over to destruction, and the Toltec empire was at an end.

The Chichimec Exodus

Meanwhile the rude Chichimecs of the north, who had for many years carried on a constant warfare with the Toltecs, were surprised that their enemies sought their borders no more, a practice which they had engaged in principally for the purpose of obtaining captives for sacrifice. In order to discover the reason for this suspicious quiet they sent out spies into Toltec territory, who returned with the amazing news that the Toltec domain for a distance of six hundred miles from the Chichimec frontier was a desert, the towns ruined and empty and their inhabitants scattered. Xolotl, the Chichimec king, summoned his chieftains to his capital, and, acquainting them with what the spies had said, proposed an expedition for the purpose of annexing the abandoned land. No less than 3,202,000 people composed this migration, and only 1,600,000 remained in the Chichimec territory.

The Chichimecs occupied most of the ruined cities, many of which they rebuilt. Those Toltecs who remained became peaceful subjects, and through their knowledge of commerce and handicrafts amassed considerable wealth. A tribute was, however, demanded from them, which was peremptorily refused by Nauhyotl, the Toltec ruler of Colhuacan; but he was defeated and slain, and the Chichimec rule was at last supreme.

The Disappearance of the Toltecs

The transmitters of this legendary account give it as their belief, which is shared by some authorities of standing, that the Toltecs, fleeing from the civil broils of their city and the inroads of the Chichimecs, passed into Central America, where they became the founders of the civilization of that country, and the architects of the many wonderful cities the ruins of which now litter its plains and are encountered in its forests.

The Mexican Noah

AND THIS YEAR was that of Ce-calli, and on the first day all was lost. The mountain itself was submerged in the water, and the water remained tranquil for fifty-two springs.

Now toward the close of the year Titlacahuan had forewarned the man named Nata and his wife Nena, saying, "Make no more *pulque*, but straightway hollow out a large cypress, and enter it when in the month Tozoztli the water shall approach the sky." They entered it, and when Titlacahuan had closed the door he said, "Thou shalt eat but a single ear of maize, and thy wife but one also."

As soon as they had finished eating, they went forth, and the water was tranquil; for the log did not move any more; and opening it they saw many fish.

Then they built a fire, rubbing together pieces of wood, and they roasted fish. The gods Citallinicue and Citallatonac, looking below, exclaimed, "Divine Lord, what means that fire below? Why do they thus smoke the heavens?"

Straightway descended Titlacahuan-Tezcatlipoca, and commenced to scold, saying, "What is this fire doing here?" And seizing the fishes (or in other versions, Nata and Nena themselves) he moulded their hinder parts and changed their heads, and they were at once transformed into dogs.

Tezcatlipoca, Overthrower of the Toltecs

IN THE DAYS of Quetzalcoatl there was abundance of everything necessary for subsistence. The maize was plentiful, the calabashes were as thick as one's arm, and cotton grew in all colours without having to be dyed. A variety of birds of rich plumage filled the air with their songs, and gold, silver, and precious stones were abundant. In the reign of Quetzalcoatl there was peace and plenty for all men.

But this blissful state was too fortunate, too happy to endure. Envious of the calm enjoyment of the god and his people the Toltecs, three wicked 'necromancers' plotted their downfall. The reference is of course to the gods of the invading Nahua tribes, the deities Huitzilopochtli, Titlacahuan or Tezcatlipoca, and Tlacahuepan. These laid evil enchantments upon the city of Tollan, and Tezcatlipoca in particular took the lead in these envious conspiracies. Disguised as an aged man with white hair, he presented himself at the palace of Quetzalcoatl, where he said to the pages-in-waiting: "Pray present me to your master the king. I desire to speak with him."

The pages advised him to retire, as Quetzalcoatl was indisposed and could see no one. He requested them, however, to tell the god that he was waiting outside. They did so, and procured his admittance.

On entering the chamber of Quetzalcoatl the wily Tezcatlipoca simulated much sympathy with the suffering god-king. "How are you, my son?" he asked. "I have brought you a drug which you should drink, and which will put an end to the course of your malady."

"You are welcome, old man," replied Quetzalcoatl. "I have known for many days that you would come. I am exceedingly indisposed. The malady affects my entire system, and I can use neither my hands nor feet."

Tezcatlipoca assured him that if he partook of the medicine which he had brought him he would immediately experience a great improvement in health. Quetzalcoatl drank the potion, and at once felt much revived. The cunning Tezcatlipoca pressed another and still another cup of the potion upon him, and as it was nothing but *pulque*, the wine of the country, he speedily became intoxicated, and was as wax in the hands of his adversary.

Tezcatlipoca Deceives the Toltecs

TEZCATLIPOCA, IN PURSUANCE of his policy inimical to the Toltec state, took the form of an Indian of the name of Toueyo (Toveyo), and bent his steps to the palace of Uemac, chief of the Toltecs in temporal matters. This worthy had a daughter so fair that she was desired in marriage by many of the Toltecs, but all to no purpose, as her father refused her hand to one and all. The princess, beholding the false Toueyo passing her father's palace, fell deeply in love with him, and so tumultuous was her passion that she became seriously ill because of her longing for him. Uemac, hearing of her indisposition, bent his steps to her apartments, and inquired of her women the cause of her illness. They told him that it was occasioned by the sudden passion which had seized her for the Indian who had recently come that way. Uemac at once gave orders for the arrest of Toueyo, and he was haled before the temporal chief of Tollan.

"Whence come you?" inquired Uemac of his prisoner, who was very scantily attired.

"Lord, I am a stranger, and I have come to these parts to sell green paint," replied Tezcatlipoca.

"Why are you dressed in this fashion? Why do you not wear a cloak?" asked the chief.

"My lord, I follow the custom of my country," replied Tezcatlipoca.

"You have inspired a passion in the breast of my daughter," said Uemac. "What should be done to you for thus disgracing me?"

"Slay me; I care not," said the cunning Tezcatlipoca.

"Nay," replied Uemac, "for if I slay you my daughter will perish. Go to her and say that she may wed you and be happy."

Now the marriage of Toueyo to the daughter of Uemac aroused much discontent among the Toltecs; and they murmured among themselves, and said: "Wherefore did Uemac give his daughter to this Toueyo?" Uemac, having got wind of these murmurings, resolved to distract the attention of the Toltecs by making war upon the neighbouring state of Coatepec. The Toltecs assembled armed for the fray, and having arrived at the country of the men of Coatepec they placed Toueyo in ambush with his body-servants, hoping that he would be slain by their adversaries. But Toueyo and his men killed a large number of the enemy and put them to flight. His triumph was celebrated by Uemac with much pomp. The knightly plumes were placed upon his head, and his body was painted with red and yellow – an honour reserved for those who distinguished themselves in battle.

Tezcatlipoca's next step was to announce a great feast in Tollan, to which all the people for miles around were invited. Great crowds assembled, and danced and sang in the city to the sound of the drum. Tezcatlipoca sang to them and forced them to accompany the rhythm of his song with their feet. Faster and faster the people danced, until the pace became so furious that they were driven to madness, lost their footing, and tumbled pell-mell down a deep ravine, where they were changed into rocks. Others in attempting to cross a stone bridge precipitated themselves into the water below, and were changed into stones.

On another occasion Tezcatlipoca presented himself as a valiant warrior named Tequiua, and invited all the inhabitants of Tollan and its environs to come to the flower-garden called Xochitla. When assembled there he attacked them with a hoe, and slew a great number, and others in panic crushed their comrades to death.

Tezcatlipoca and Tlacahuepan on another occasion repaired to the market-place of Tollan, the former displaying upon the palm of his hand a small infant whom he caused to dance and to cut the most amusing capers. This infant was in reality Huitzilopochtli, the Nahua god of war. At this sight the Toltecs crowded upon one another for the purpose of getting a better view, and their eagerness resulted in many being crushed to death. So enraged were the Toltecs at this that upon the advice of Tlacahuepan they slew both Tezcatlipoca and Huitzilopochtli. When this had been done the bodies of the slain gods gave forth such a pernicious effluvia that thousands of the Toltecs died of the pestilence. The god Tlacahuepan then advised them to cast out the bodies lest worse befell them, but on their attempting to do so they discovered their weight to be so great that they could not move them. Hundreds wound cords round the corpses, but the strands broke, and those who pulled upon them fell and died suddenly, tumbling one upon the other, and suffocating those upon whom they collapsed.

The Toltecs were so tormented by the enchantments of Tezcatlipoca that it was soon apparent to them that their fortunes were on the wane and that the end of their empire was at hand. Quetzalcoatl, chagrined at the turn things had taken, resolved to quit Tollan and go to the country of Tlapallan, whence he had come on his civilizing mission to Mexico. He burned all the houses which he had built, and buried his treasure of gold and precious stones in the deep valleys between the mountains. He changed the cacao-trees into mezquites, and he ordered all the birds of rich plumage and song to quit the valley of Anahuac and to follow him to a distance of more than a hundred leagues. On the road from Tollan he discovered a great tree at a point called Quauhtitlan. There he rested, and requested his pages to hand him a mirror.

Regarding himself in the polished surface, he exclaimed, "I am old," and from that circumstance the spot was named Huehuequauhtitlan (Old Quauhtitlan). Proceeding on his way accompanied by musicians who played the flute, he walked until fatigue arrested his steps, and he seated himself upon a stone, on which he left the imprint of his hands. This place is called Temacpalco (The Impress of the Hands). At Coaapan he was met by the Nahua gods, who were inimical to him and to the Toltecs.

"Where do you go?" they asked him. "Why do you leave your capital?"

"I go to Tlapallan," replied Quetzalcoatl, "whence I came."

"For what reason?" persisted the enchanters.

"My father the Sun has called me thence," replied Quetzalcoatl.

"Go, then, happily," they said, "but leave us the secret of your art, the secret of founding in silver, of working in precious stones and woods, of painting, and of feather-working, and other matters."

But Quetzalcoatl refused, and cast all his treasures into the fountain of Cozcaapa (Water of Precious Stones). At Cochtan he was met by another enchanter, who asked him whither he was bound, and on learning his destination proffered him a draught of wine. On tasting the vintage Quetzalcoatl was overcome with sleep. Continuing his journey in the morning, the god passed between a volcano and the Sierra Nevada (Mountain of Snow), where all the pages who accompanied him died of cold. He regretted this misfortune exceedingly, and wept, lamenting their fate with most bitter tears and mournful songs. On reaching the summit of Mount Poyauhtecatl he slid to the base. Arriving at the sea-shore, he embarked upon a raft of serpents, and was wafted away toward the land of Tlapallan.

Explaining the Natural World

Introduction

THOUGH A BOY, the youngest of seven sons, Assipattle was a sort of Scottish Cinderella, even down to his name, which means 'one who grovels among the ashes'. Despised by his family, he was made to work at all the dirtiest, most onerous tasks. Yet it was he who stepped up when the Stoorworm came to attack his community. Every Saturday, seven maidens had to be sacrificed to this dreadful sea monster. The villagers watched in horror from the nearby clifftops as the beast devoured their daughters. Assipattle protested at their passivity, but the men of the village responded with derision. Who was he to criticize, weakling that he was? But what Assipattle lacked in strength, he made up for in courage and resourcefulness, and at last he found a way of killing the cruel sea serpent. Its teeth, scattered in the seas, became the Orkney Islands – and an engaging yarn became a geographical origin story. Just about every culture has found whimsical ways of explaining the world, its topography, its natural features and its flora and fauna. Mythology has always been the key. Why dogs wag their tails, how lizards got their markings, why the moon waxes and wanes, how the tiger got his stripes, why night is dark… There are explanations to be had for all these things.

The Goat, the Lion and the Serpent

A GOAT AND a lion were travelling together one day on the outskirts of a forest, at the end of which there was a community of mankind comfortably hutted within a village, which was fenced round with tall and pointed stakes. The Goat said to the Lion:

"Well, now, my friend, where do you come from this day?"

"I have come from a feast that I have given many friends of mine – to the leopard, hyena, wolf, jackal, wild cat, buffalo, zebra and many more. The long-necked giraffe and dew-lapped eland were also there, as well as the springing antelope."

"That is grand company you keep, indeed," said the Goat, with a sigh. "As for poor me, I am alone. No one cares for me very much, but I find abundance of grass and sweet leafage, and when I am full, I seek a soft spot under a tree, and chew my cud, dreamily and contentedly. And of other sorrows, save an occasional pang of hunger, in my wanderings I know of none."

"Do you mean to say that you do not envy me my regal dignity and strength?"

"I do not indeed, because as yet I have been ignorant of them."

"What? Know you not that I am the strongest of all who dwell in the forest or wilderness? that when I roar all who hear me bow down their heads, and shrink in fear?"

"Indeed, I do not know all this, nor am I very sure that you are not deceiving yourself, because I know many whose offensive powers are much more dangerous, my friend, than yours. True, your teeth are large, and your claws are sharp, and your roar is loud enough, and your appearance is imposing. Still, I know a tiny thing in these woods that is much more to be dreaded than you are; and I think if you matched yourself against it in a contest, that same tiny thing would become victor."

"Bah!" said the Lion, impatiently, "you anger me. Why, even today all who were at the feast acknowledged that they were but feeble creatures compared with me: and you will own that if I but clawed you once there would be no life left in you."

"What you say in regard to me is true enough, and, as I said before, I do not pretend to the possession of strength. But this tiny thing that I know of is not likely to have been at your feast."

"What may this tiny thing be that is so dreadful?" asked the Lion, sneeringly.

"The Serpent," answered the Goat, chewing his cud with an indifferent air.

"The Serpent!" said the Lion, astounded. "What, that crawling reptile, which feeds on mice and sleeping birds – that soft, vine-like, creeping thing that coils itself in tufts of grass, and branches of bush?"

"Yes, that is its name and character clearly."

"Why, my weight alone would tread it until it became flat like a smashed egg."

"I would not try to do so if I were you. Its fangs are sharper than your great corner teeth or claws."

"Will you match it against my strength?"

"Yes."

"And if you lose, what will be the forfeit?"

"If you survive the fight, I will be your slave, and you may command me for any purpose you please. But what will you give me if you lose?"

"What you please."

"Well, then, I will take one hundred bunches of bananas; and you had better bring them here alongside of me, before you begin."

"Where is this Serpent that will fight with me?"

"Close by. When you have brought the bananas he will be here, waiting for you."

The Lion stalked proudly away to procure the bananas, and the Goat proceeded into the bush, where he saw Serpent drowsily coiled in many coils on a slender branch.

"Serpent," said the Goat, "wake up. Lion is raging for a fight with you. He has made a bet of a hundred bunches of bananas that he will be the victor, and I have pledged my life that you will be the strong one; and, hark you, obey my hints, and my life is safe, and I shall be provided with food for at least three moons."

"Well," said Serpent, languidly, "what is it that you wish me to do?"

"Take position on a bush about three cubits high, that stands near the scene where the fight is to take place, and when Lion is ready, raise your crest high and boldly, and ask him to advance near you that you may see him well, because you are short-sighted, you know. And he, full of his conceit and despising your slight form, will advance towards you, unwitting of your mode of attack. Then fasten your fangs in his eyebrows, and coil yourself round his neck. If there is any virtue left in your venom, poor Lion will lie stark before long."

"And if I do this, what will you do for me?"

"I am thy servant and friend for all time."

"It is well," answered the Serpent. "Lead the way."

Accordingly Goat led Serpent to the scene of the combat, and the latter coiled itself in position, as Goat had advised, on the leafy top of a young bush.

Presently Lion came, with a long line of servile animals, bearing 100 bunches of bananas; and, after dismissing them, he turned to the Goat, and said:

"Well, Goatee, where is your friend who is stronger than I am? I feel curious to see him."

"Are you Lion?" asked a sibilant voice from the top of a bush.

"Yes, I am; and who are you that do not know me?"

"I am Serpent, friend Lion, and short of sight and slow of movement. Advance nearer to me, for I see you not."

Lion uttered a loud roaring laugh, and went confidently near the Serpent – who had raised his crest and arched his neck – so near that his breath seemed to blow the slender form to a tremulous movement.

"You shake already," said Lion, mockingly.

"Yes, I shake but to strike the better, my friend," said Serpent, as he darted forward and fixed his fangs in the right eyebrow of Lion, and at the same moment its body glided round the neck of Lion, and became buried out of sight in the copious mane.

Like the pain of fire the deadly venom was felt quickly in the head and body. When it reached the heart, Lion fell down and lay still and dead.

"Well done," cried Goat, as he danced around the pile of bananas. "Provisions for three moons have I, and this doughty roarer is of no more value than a dead goat."

Goat and Serpent then vowed friendship for one another, after which Serpent said:

"Now follow me, and obey. I have a little work for you."

"Work! What work, O Serpent?"

"It is light and agreeable. If you follow that path, you will find a village of mankind. You will there proclaim to the people what I have done, and show this carcase to them. In return for this they will make much of you, and you will find abundance of food in their gardens – tender leaves of manioc and peanut, mellow bananas and plenty of rich greens daily. True, when you are fat and a feast is to be made, they will kill you and eat you; but, for all your kind, comfort, plenty and warm, dry housing is more agreeable than the cold, damp jungle, and destruction by the feral beasts."

"Nay, neither the work nor the fate is grievous, and I thank you, O Serpent; but for you there can be no other home than the bush and the tuft of grass, and you will always be a dreaded enemy of all who come near your resting place."

Then they parted. The Goat went along the path, and came to the gardens of a village, where a woman was chopping fuel. Looking up she saw a creature with grand horns coming near to her, bleating. Her first impulse was to run away, but seeing, as it bleated, that it was a fodder-eating animal, with no means of offence, she plucked some manioc greens and coaxed it to her, upon which the Goat came and spoke to her.

"Follow me, for I have a strange thing to show you a little distance off."

The woman, wondering that a four-footed animal could address her in intelligible speech, followed; and the Goat trotted gently before her to where Lion lay dead. The woman, upon seeing the body, stopped and asked, "What is the meaning of this?"

The Goat answered, "This was once the king of beasts; the fear of him was upon all that lived in the woods and in the wilderness. But he too often boasted of his might, and became too proud. I therefore dared him to fight a tiny creature of the bush, and lo! The boaster was slain."

"And how do you name the victor?"

"The Serpent."

"Ah! You say true. Serpent is king over all, except man," answered the woman.

"You are of a wise kind," answered the Goat. "Serpent confessed to me that man was his superior, and sent me to you that I might become man's creature. Henceforth man shall feed me with greens, tender tops of plants, and house and protect me; but when the feast day comes, man shall kill me, and eat of my flesh. These are the words of Serpent."

The woman hearkened to all Goat's words, and retained them in her memory. Then she unrobed the Lion of his furry spoil, and conveyed it to the village, where she astonished her folk with all that had happened to her. From that day to this the goat kind has remained with the families of man, and people are grateful to the Serpent for his gift to them; for had not the Serpent commanded it to seek their presence, the Goat had remained forever wild like the antelope, its brother.

The City of the Elephants

A BUNGANDU MAN named Dudu, and his wife Salimba, were one day seeking in the forest a long way from the town for a proper redwood tree, out of which they could make a wooden mortar wherein they could pound their manioc. They saw several trees of this kind as they proceeded, but after examining one, and then another, they would appear to be dissatisfied, and say, "Perhaps if we went a little further we might find a still better tree for our purpose."

And so Dudu and Salimba proceeded further and further into the tall and thick woods, and ever before them there appeared to be still finer trees which would after all be unsuited for their purpose, being too soft, or too hard, or hollow, or too old, or of another kind than the useful redwood. They strayed in this manner very far. In the forest where there is no path or track, it is not easy to tell which direction one came from, and as they had walked round many trees, they were too confused to know which way they ought to turn homeward. When Dudu said he was sure that his course was the right one for home, Salimba was as sure that the opposite was the true way. They agreed to walk in the direction Dudu wished, and after a long time spent on it, they gave it up and tried another, but neither took them any nearer home.

The night overtook them and they slept at the foot of a tree. The next day they wandered still farther from their town, and they became anxious and hungry. As one cannot see many yards off on any side in the forest, an animal hears the coming step long before the hunter gets a chance to use his weapon. Therefore, though they heard the rustle of the flying antelope, or wild pig as it rushed away, it only served to make their anxiety greater. And the second day passed, and when night came upon them they were still hungrier.

Towards the middle of the third day, they came into an open place by a pool frequented by Kiboko (hippo), and there was a margin of grass round about it, and as they came in view of it, both, at the same time, sighted a grazing buffalo.

Dudu bade his wife stand behind a tree while he chose two of his best and sharpest arrows, and after a careful look at his bowstring, he crept up to the buffalo, and drove an arrow home as far as the guiding leaf, which nearly buried it in the body. While the beast looked around and started from the twinge within, Dudu shot his second arrow into his windpipe, and it fell to the ground quite choked. Now here was water to drink and food to eat, and after cutting a load of meat they chose a thick bush-clump a little distance from the pool, made a fire, and, after satisfying their hunger, slept in content. The fourth day they stopped and roasted a meat provision that would last many days, because they knew that luck is not constant in the woods.

On the fifth they travelled, and for three days more they wandered. They then met a young lion who, at the sight of them, boldly advanced, but Dudu sighted his bow, and sent an arrow into his chest which sickened him of the fight, and he turned and fled.

A few days afterwards, Dudu saw an elephant standing close to them behind a high bush, and whispered to his wife:

"Ah, now, we have a chance to get meat enough for a month."

"But," said Salimba, "why should you wish to kill him, when we have enough meat still with us? Do not hurt him. Ah, what a fine back he has, and how strong he is. Perhaps he would carry us home."

"How could an elephant understand our wishes?" asked Dudu.

"Talk to him anyhow, perhaps he will be clever enough to understand what we want."

Dudu laughed at his wife's simplicity, but to please her he said, "Elephant, we have lost our way; will you carry us and take us home, and we shall be your friends forever."

The Elephant ceased waving his trunk, and nodding to himself, and turning to them said:

"If you come near to me and take hold of my ears, you may get on my back, and I will carry you safely."

When the Elephant spoke, Dudu fell back from surprise, and looked at him as though he had not heard aright, but Salimba advanced with all confidence, and laid hold of one of his ears, and pulled herself up on to his back. When she was seated, she cried out, "Come, Dudu, what are you looking at? Did you not hear him say he would carry you?"

Seeing his wife smiling and comfortable on the Elephant's back, Dudu became a little braver and moved forward slowly, when the Elephant spoke again, "Come, Dudu, be not afraid. Follow your wife, and do as she did, and then I will travel home with you quickly."

Dudu then put aside his fears, and his surprise, and seizing the Elephant's ear, he ascended and seated himself by his wife on the Elephant's back.

Without another word the Elephant moved on rapidly, and the motion seemed to Dudu and Salimba most delightful. Whenever any overhanging branch was in the way, the Elephant wrenched it off, or bent it and passed on. No creek, stream, gulley, or river stopped him, he seemed to know exactly the way he should go, as if the road he was travelling was well known to him.

When it was getting dark he stopped and asked his friends if they would not like to rest for the night, and finding that they so wished it, he stopped at a nice place by the side of the river, and they slid to the ground, Dudu first, and Salimba last. He then broke dead branches for them, out of which they made a fire, and the Elephant stayed by them, as though he was their slave.

Hearing their talk, he understood that they would like to have something better than dried meat to eat, and he said to them, "I am glad to know your wishes, for I think I can help you. Bide here a little, and I will go and search."

About the middle of the night he returned to them with something white in his trunk, and a young antelope in front of him. The white thing was a great manioc root, which he dropped into Salimba's lap.

"There, Salimba," he said, "there is food for you, eat your fill and sleep in peace, for I will watch over you."

Dudu and Salimba had seen many strange things that day, but they were both still more astonished at the kindly and intelligent care which their friend the Elephant took of them. While they roasted their fresh meat over the flame, and the manioc root was baking under the heap of hot embers, the Elephant dug with his tusks for the juicy roots of his favourite trees round about their camp, and munched away contentedly.

The next morning, all three, after a bathe in the river, set out on their journey more familiar with one another, and in a happier mood.

About noon, while they were resting during the heat of the day, two lions came near to roar at them, but when Dudu was drawing his bow at one of them, the Elephant said:

"You leave them to me; I will make them run pretty quick," saying which he tore off a great bough of a tree, and nourishing this with his trunk, he trotted on the double quick towards them, and used it so heartily that they both skurried away with their bellies to the ground, and their hides shrinking and quivering out of fear of the great rod.

In the afternoon the Elephant and his human friends set off again, and sometime after they came to a wide and deep river. He begged his friends to descend while he tried to find out the shallowest part. It took him some time to do this; but, having discovered a ford where the water was not quite over his back, he returned to them, and urged them to mount him as he wished to reach home before dark.

As the Elephant was about to enter the river, he said to Dudu, "I see some hunters of your own kind creeping up towards us. Perhaps they are your kinsmen. Talk to them, and let us see whether they be friends or foes."

Dudu hailed them, but they gave no answer, and, as they approached nearer, they were seen to prepare to cast their spears, so the Elephant said, "I see that they are not your friends; therefore, as I cross the river, do you look out for them, and keep them at a distance. If they come to the other side of the river, I shall know how to deal with them."

They got to the opposite bank safely; but, as they were landing, Dudu and Salimba noticed that their pursuers had discovered a canoe, and that they were pulling hard after them. But the Elephant soon after landing came to a broad path smoothed by much travel, over which he took them at a quick pace, so fast, indeed, that the pursuers had to run to be able to keep up with them. Dudu, every now and then let fly an arrow at the hunters, which kept them at a safe distance.

Towards night they came to the City of the Elephants, which was very large and fit to shelter such a multitude as they now saw. Their elephant did not linger, however, but took his friends at the same quick pace until they came to a mighty elephant that was much larger than any other, and his ivories were gleaming white and curled up, and exceedingly long. Before him Dudu and Salimba were told by their friend to descend and salaam, and he told his lord how he had found them lost in the woods, and how for the sake of the kindly words of the woman he had befriended them, and assisted them to the city of his tribe. When the King Elephant heard all this he was much pleased, and said to Dudu and Salimba that they were welcome to his city, and how they should not want for anything, as long as they would be pleased to stay with them, but as for the hunters who had dared to chase them, he would give orders at once. Accordingly he gave a signal, and ten active young elephants dashed out of the city, and in a short time not one of the hunters was left alive, though one of them had leaped into the river, thinking that he could escape in that manner. But then you know that an elephant is as much at home in a river as a Kiboko (a hippopotamus), so that the last man was soon caught and was drowned.

Dudu and Salimba, however, on account of Salimba's kind heart in preventing her husband wounding the elephant, were made free of the place, and their friend took them with him to many families, and the big pa's and ma's told their little babies all about them and their habits, and said that, though most of the human kind were very stupid and wicked, Dudu and Salimba were very good, and putting their trunks into their ears they whispered that Salimba was the better of the two. Then the little elephants gathered about them and trotted by their side and around them and diverted them with their antics, their races, their wrestlings and other trials of strength, but when they became familiar and somewhat rude in their rough play, their elephant friend would admonish them, and if that did not suffice, he would switch them soundly.

The City of the Elephants was a spacious and well-trodden glade in the midst of a thick forest, and as it was entered one saw how wisely the elephant families had arranged their manner of life. For without, the trees stood as thick as water reeds, and the bush or underwood was like an old hedge of milkweed knitted together by thorny vines and snaky climbers into which the human hunter might not even poke his nose without hurt. Well, the burly elephants had, by much uprooting, created deep hollows, or recesses, wherein a family of two and more might snugly rest, and not even a dart of sunshine might reach them.

Round about the great glade the dark leafy arches ran, and Dudu and his wife saw that the elephant families were numerous – for by one sweeping look they could tell that there were more elephants than there are human beings in a goodly village. In some of the recesses there was a row of six and more elephants; in another the parents stood head to head, and their children, big and little, clung close to their parents' sides; in another a family stood with heads turned towards the entrance, and so on all around – while under a big tree in the middle there was quite a gathering of big fellows, as though they were holding a serious palaver; under another tree one seemed to be on the outlook; another paced slowly from side to side; another plucked at this branch or at that; another appeared to be heaving a tree, or sharpening a blunted ivory; others seemed appointed to uproot the sprouts, lest the glade might become choked with underwood.

Near the entrance on both sides were a brave company of them, faces turned outward, swinging their trunks, napping their ears, rubbing against each other, or who with pate against pate seemed to be drowsily considering something. There was a continual coming in and a going out, singly, or in small companies. The roads that ran through the glade were like a network, clean and smooth, while that which went towards the king's place was so wide that twenty men might walk abreast. At the far end the king stood under his own tree, with his family under the arches behind him.

This was the City of the Elephants as Dudu and Salimba saw it. I ought to say that the outlets of it were many. One went straight through the woods in a line up river, at the other end it ran in a line following the river downward; one went to a lakelet, where juicy plants and reeds throve like corn in a man's fields, and where the elephants rejoiced in its cool water, and washed themselves and infants; another went to an ancient clearing where the plantain and manioc grew wild, and wherein more than two human tribes might find food for countless seasons.

Then said their friend to Dudu and Salimba: "Now that I have shown you our manner of life, it is for you to ease your longing for a while and rest with us. When you yearn for home, go tell our king, and he will send you with credit to your kindred."

Then Dudu and his wife resolved to stay, and eat, and they stayed a whole season, not only unhurt, but tenderly cared for, with never a hungry hour or uneasy night. But at last Salimba's heart remembered her children, and kinfolk and her own warm house and village pleasures, and on hinting of these memories to her husband, he said that after all there was no place like Bungandu. He remembered his long pipe, and the talk-house, the stool-making, shaft-polishing, bow-fitting and the little tinkering jobs, the wine trough and the merry drinking bouts, and he wept softly as he thought of them.

They thus agreed that it was time for them to travel homeward, and together they sought the elephant king, and frankly told him of their state.

"My friends," he replied, "be no longer sad, but haste to depart. With the morning's dawn guides shall take you to Bungandu with such gifts as shall make you welcome to your folk. And when you come to them, say to them that the elephant king desires lasting peace and friendship with them. On our side we shall not injure their plantations, neither a plantain, nor a manioc root belonging to them; and on your side dig no pits for our unwary youngsters, nor hang the barbed iron aloft, nor plant the poisoned stake in the path, so we shall escape hurt and be unprovoked." And Dudu put his hand on the king's trunk as the pledge of good faith.

In the morning, four elephants, as bearers of the gifts from the king – bales of bark cloth, and showy mats and soft hides and other things – and two fighting elephants besides their old friend, stood by the entrance to the city, and when the king elephant came up he lifted Salimba first on the back of her old companion, and then placed Dudu by her side, and at a parting wave the company moved on.

In ten days they reached the edge of the plantation of Bungandu, and the leader halted. The bales were set down on the ground, and then their friend asked of Dudu and his wife:

"Know you where you are?"

"We do," they answered.

"Is this Bungandu?" he asked.

"This is Bungandu," they replied.

"Then here we part, that we may not alarm your friends. Go now your way, and we go our way. Go tell your folk how the elephants treat their friends, and let there be peace forever between us."

The elephants turned away, and Dudu and Salimba, after hiding their wealth in the underwood, went arm in arm into the village of Bungandu. When their friends saw them, they greeted them as we would greet our friends whom we have long believed to be dead, but who come back smiling and rejoicing to us. When the people heard their story they greatly wondered and doubted, but when Dudu and Salimba took them to the place of parting and showed them the hoof prints of seven elephants on the road, and the bales that they had hidden in the underwood, they believed their story. And they made it a rule from that day that no man of the tribe ever should lift a spear, or draw a bow, or dig a pit, or plant the poisoned stake in the path, or hang the barbed iron aloft, to do hurt to an elephant. And as a proof that I have but told the truth go ask the Bungandu, and they will say why none of their race will ever seek to hurt the elephant, and it will be the same as I have told you. That is my story.

Why the Fowl and Dog Are Abused by the Birds

THERE WAS A time when all the birds and animals lived in the sky. One day it was very rainy and cold – so cold that they were all shivering. The birds said to the Dog: "Go down and fetch us some fire to warm ourselves."

The Dog descended, but seeing plenty of bones and pieces of fish lying about on the ground he forgot to take the fire to the shivering birds.

The birds and animals waited, and the Dog not returning they sent the Fowl to hasten him with the fire.

The Fowl, however, on arriving below, beheld plenty of palm nuts, pea nuts, maize and other good things, so he did not tell the Dog to take up the fire, and did not take any himself.

This is the reason why you can hear of an evening a bird that sings with notes like this, "*Nsusu akende bombo! Nsusu akende bombo!*" which means, The Fowl has become a slave! The Fowl has become a slave!

And the Heron sometimes sits on a tree near a village and cries, "*Mbwa owa! Mbwa owa!*" – Dog, you die! Dog, you die!

This is why you hear these birds jeer at and abuse the Fowl and Dog, because they left their friends to shiver in the cold while they enjoyed themselves in warmth and plenty.

Why the Fowls Never Shut Their Doors

THERE LIVED ONCE a chief who owned a large number of Fowls. On arising early one morning he found that the door of their house had been left open all night. He thereupon woke up the Head Cock and asked why he had not shut the door.

The Cock replied: "We did not go to sleep very early last night, as we quarrelled over who should shut the door. I told one to do it, and he told another, and at last we became so angry with each other that no one would shut the door, so we went to sleep leaving it open."

The owner snapped his fingers in speechless surprise at the Fowl's excuse, and walked away.

Another day the chief went to see his wives' farms and found them all clean and well weeded, but the road leading to the farms, which was nobody's work, was choked with tall grass and weeds. That evening the chief called out loudly so that all the town could hear: "You women, I went to your farms today, and found the road covered with tall grass and weeds. Truly you are near relatives of the fowls, who sleep with open door because each tells the other to shut it. Tomorrow all of you go and clear the road."

When the Fowls heard these remarks they were very vexed, and the Cock said: "You have heard what our owner has shouted out to the whole town. He has held us up as a bad example to all in the place, yet when I went to a neighbouring town the day before yesterday I saw a buffalo rotting by the roadside."

"Why was it rotting there?" asked the Black Hen of her husband.

The Cock replied: "When I reached the town the other day I heard that Don't-care, who is the son of Peter Pay-if-you-like, went outside his house and saw a buffalo; he aroused his companions and told them to go and shoot it; but they said: 'Go and shoot it yourself.' 'What?! Am I to see the buffalo and shoot it also?' he asked. Thereupon Wise-man fired at the buffalo, and told another to go and see if it were killed. He came back and said it was wounded; so another went and killed it; but he would not cut it up; and another went and cut it into pieces. Then each thought that the other should carry the flesh into the town; consequently it was left in the bush, and that was why the buffalo meat rotted at the roadside."

The Black Hen said: "Indeed, is that so?" But the Speckled Hen observed: "That it would be better for human beings if they looked better after their own business, instead of poking their noses into affairs belonging to Fowls, and holding them up as a bad example to their women."

The Head Cock said: "That from that day neither he, nor his children, nor his grandchildren should ever shut the doors of their houses, no matter how cold it might be, or what risks they might run of being eaten by wild animals." Thus it is that Fowls never shut their doors at night. They are angry that human beings, who conduct their own affairs so badly, should find fault with the way in which Fowls look after theirs.

Why the Dog and the Palm-Rat Hate Each Other

ONE DAY THE Dog, the Palm-rat, the Hawk, and the Eagle arranged to take a journey together, but before starting they agreed not to thwart each other in any matter.

They had not gone very far when the Eagle saw a bunch of unripe palm nuts, and said: "When these palm nuts are ripe, and I have eaten them, then we will proceed on our way."

They waited many days until the palm nuts ripened and were eaten by the Eagle, then they started again, and by and by the Hawk espied the bush (a great space covered with tall grass, canes and stunted trees), and said: "When this bush is burnt, and I have eaten the locusts, and drunk in the smoke from the fire, then we will go."

So they waited while the bush dried, and was burnt, and the Hawk ate his locusts, and drank in the smoke from the burning grass, then they were ready to start again; but when the Palm-rat saw the bush was burnt, he said: "We remain here until the grass and canes have grown again, so that I may eat the young canes, for remember we agreed not to thwart or oppose each other on this journey."

They waited there some months until the canes grew again, and the Palm-rat had eaten them.

Once more they started on their travels, and on reaching a large forest the Dog said: "Now I will dry my nose."

His companions answered: "All right, we will go for firewood."

The Palm-rat and the Hawk fetched the wood, and the Eagle went for the fire. The Dog put his nose near the fire, but every time it dried he made it wet again by licking it. They remained a long time in the forest, but the Dog's nose never became properly dry: it was an endless job.

His companions became vexed, and the Hawk and the Eagle flew away, leaving the Palm-rat and the Dog alone. At last the patience of the Palm-rat was exhausted, and he, too, ran away; but the Dog chased him to kill him, and this is the reason why the Dog and the Palm-rat hate each other. He would not wait until the Dog's nose was dry.

Why the Congo Robin Has a Red Breast

"KINSIDIKITI" IS A small bird with red round its mouth and red spots on its breast. The female has no red spots on the breast, and the following is the legend accounting for the difference:

One day the Robin and his wife found that they had no red-camwood powder with which to beautify themselves, so the husband made preparations for a journey to Stanley Pool to buy some redwood from those who brought it from the Upper Congo towns to sell at the Pool markets.

He was a long time on the road, but at last reached the place only to find that all the redwood for making the powder had been sold to others, who were before him. He tried one trader after another with no success, for all had sold out, but one said: "I have none to sell, but I can give you a small piece, enough for yourself."

He gave him a small piece, and for safety the Robin put it in his throat, as he wanted to take it home to his wife. As he travelled homeward the redwood melted in his mouth and throat, and came out round his beak and through his chest to his feathers, and ever since then he has had a red mouth and breast.

Why the Small-Ants Live in the Houses

THERE ARE MANY species of ants in Congo, but there are two kinds – the Small-ant and the Driver-ant – that have most to do with the people; the former are to be found in the houses, and it is difficult to keep food free of them, and the latter are the scavengers that scour the country in search of carrion; their bite is fierce and tenacious, and is dreaded by all who come into contact with them. The characteristics of the two species of ants are turned to account in the story.

One day, the Driver-ants and the Small-ants were assembled together, and the former said, "We will govern the country as chiefs." But the Small-ants objected to this arrangement, and asserted that they were quite able to rule the land. The Driver-ants laughed at them for having no strength, and while they were discussing the matter an Elder came along and inquired into the matter, and on being told the whole affair, he said, "You Driver-ants, and you Small-ants, go, and the first who brings a piece of the skin of a man shall rule over the country."

The Driver-ants went off and waited at a crossroad, and directly they saw a person coming they crowded out and bit his legs. When the man felt the bites he ran off a little way and pulled the Driver-ants off his legs and killed them, and consequently they were not able to procure a piece of skin, although many died in the attempt.

The Small-ants went into a person's house and sat there quietly waiting; and by and by a man arrived who, while returning from his work, had hit his foot against a stone and raised the skin. He took a knife from the wall and sat down and cut off the loose skin, which he threw away. The watching Ants soon found the piece of skin, and carried it to the place where they had held the discussion with the Driver-ants, and gave it to the Elder as a proof of their wisdom and strength. The Elder gave the decision in their favour, and told them that they were the rulers of the land. This is the reason why the Small-ants live in houses, while the Driver-ants have to live in the bush.

The Fight Between the Two Fetishes, Lifuma and Chimpukela

NOW THIS IS a sad but true story, for it is of recent occurrence, and many living witnesses can vouch for its truth.

Poor King Jack, late of Cabinda, now retired a little into the interior of KaCongo, known to all who visit this part of Africa, either in whaler, steamer, or man of war, owns the fetish called Lifuma. Lifuma had all his life sniffed the fresh sea breezes, and rejoiced with his people when they returned from the deep sea in their canoes laden with fish. But now circumstances (namely, the occupation of Cabinda by the Portuguese) forced him to retire to the interior, behind the coastline between Futilla and Cabinda.

How he longed to see his people happy yet again is proved by the trouble he put himself to in trying to gain possession of a part of the seabeach that he thought should belong to his 'hinterland'. He left the sweet waters of Lake Chinganga Miyengela (waters that have travelled even to the white man's country, and returned without being corrupted) and quietly travelled down to the seabeach, near to a place called Kaia. Once there, he picked up a few shells and pebbles, and filled a pint mug with salt water, meaning to carry them back to his sweetwater home, and to place them on the holy ground beside him as a sign of his ownership of the seabeach, and as a means whereby his people might once more play on the seabeach by the salt water, and once again occupy themselves in fishing in the deep blue sea.

Peaceful and benevolent was indeed his mission, and perhaps, as he passed the town of Kaia and Subantanu unmolested, he at last thought that his object was secured. Alas! The bird Ngundu espied him, and rushed to town to acquaint the Kaia people's fetish, called Chimpukela. Then Chimpukela, ran after Lifuma, and caught him up, and roughly asked him what he had there, bidden under his cloth.

"Go away," cried the anxious Lifuma, as he pushed Chimpukela aside.

Chimpukela stumbled over an ant hill and fell, so that when he got up again he was very angry with Lifuma, and knocked him down. Poor Lifuma fell upon a thorn of the Minyundu tree and broke his leg. The mug of salt water was also spilt, and Chimpukela took from him all the relics he had gathered upon his seabeach.

Then Chimpukela swore that ant hills should no longer exist in his country, and that is why you never see one there now as you travel through his country.

And Lifuma cursed the bird Ngundu, and the tree Minyundu, and canoes, and salt water and everything pertaining to the beach. And that is why all these things do not now exist in his country, or on his sweetwater lake.

Why the Crocodile Does Not Eat the Hen

THERE WAS A certain hen; and she used to go down to the river's edge daily to pick up bits of food. One day a crocodile came near to her and threatened to eat her, and she cried: "Oh, brother, don't!"

And the crocodile was so surprised and troubled by this cry that he went away, thinking how he could be her brother. He returned again to the river another day, fully determined to make a meal of the hen.

But she again cried out: "Oh, brother, don't

"Bother the hen!" the crocodile growled, as she once more turned away. "How can I be her brother? She lives in a town on land; I live in mine in the water."

Then the crocodile determined to see Nzambi about the question, and get her to settle it; and so he went his way. He had not gone very far when he met his friend Mbambi (a very large kind of lizard). "Oh, Mbambi!" he said, "I am sorely troubled. A nice fat hen comes daily to the river to feed; and each day, as I am about to catch her, and take her to my home and feed on her, she startles me by calling me 'brother'. I can't stand it any longer; and I am now off to Nzambi, to hold a palaver about it."

"Silly idiot!" said the Mbambi, do nothing of the sort, or you will only lose the palaver and show your ignorance. Don't you know, dear crocodile, that the duck lives in the water and lays eggs? the turtle does the same; and I also lay eggs. The hen does the same; and so do you, my silly friend. Therefore we are all brothers in a sense." And for this reason the crocodile now does not eat the hen.

Why Mosquitoes Buzz

IN THE TIME of Long-ago, in Njambi's Town, Mosquito and Ear went out to take a bath together. After taking her bath, Ear began to rub an oily substance over herself, while Mosquito did not. So Ear said to Mosquito, "Why do you leave your skin so rough? It is better to rub on a little oil." Mosquito replied, "I have none." So Ear said, "Indeed! I did not know that. I will give you part of mine, as I have plenty." Mosquito had to wait the while that Ear was rubbing the soft wax over herself. But, as soon as Ear had finished, she put back the wax into her ear where she usually kept it, and did not fulfil her promise to Mosquito.

When Mosquito saw this, that the wax was put away, he came near to the door, and said, "I want the oil you promised for rubbing on my body." But Ear took no notice of him, except to call on Hands to drive Mosquito away.

So, to this day, Mosquito is not willing to cease making his claim for the unfulfilled promise; and is always coming to our ears, and buzzing and crying. Always Mosquito comes and says, "I want my oil, Bz-z-z-z." But Ear remains silent, and gives no answer. And Mosquito keeps on grumbling and complaining, and gets angry and bites.

Origin of the Elephant

UHÂDWE, BOKUME AND Njâku were human beings, all three born of one mother. (Afterwards Bokume was called "Njâpĕ.")

As time went on, Uhâdwe called his brethren, Bokume and Njâku, and said, "My brothers! Let us separate; myself, I am going to the Great Sea; you, Bokume go to the Forest; you, Njâku, also go to the Forest."

Bokume went to the forest and grew up there, and became the valuable mahogany tree (Okume).

Njâku departed; but he went in anger, saying, "I will not remain in the forest, I am going to build with the townspeople." He came striding back to the town. As he emerged there from the forest, his feet swelled and swelled, and became elephant feet. His ear extended halfway down. His teeth spreading, this one grew to a tusk, and that one grew to a tusk. The townspeople began to hoot at him. And he turned back to the forest. But, as he went, he said to them, "In my going now to the Forest, I and whatever plants you shall plant in the forest shall journey together," (i.e., that their plantations should be destroyed by him). So Njâku went; and their food went.

When Uhâdwe had gone thence and emerged at the Sea, from the place where he emerged there grew the stem of "bush-rope" (the Calamus palm); and the staff he held became a mangrove forest. The footprints where he and his dog trod are there on the beach of Corisco Bay until this day. He created a sandbank from where he stood, extending through the ocean, by which he crossed over to the Land of the Great Sea. When he reached that Land, he prepared a ship. He put into it every production by which white people obtain wealth, and he said to the crew, "Go ye and take for me my brother."

The ship came to Africa and put down anchor; but, for four days the crew did not find any person coming from shore to set foot on the ship, or to go from the ship to set foot ashore, the natives being destitute of canoes.

Finally, Uhâdwe came and appeared to the townspeople in a dream, and said, "Go ye to the forest and cut down Njâpĕ, dig out a canoe, and go alongside the ship."

Early next morning they went to the forest, and came to the Okume trees; they cut one down, and hacked it into shape. They launched it on the sea, and said to their young men, "Go!" Four young men went into the canoe to go alongside the ship. When they had nearly reached it, looking hither and thither they feared, and they stopped and ceased paddling. The white men on the ship made repeated signs to them. Then the young men, having come close, spoke to the white men in the native language. A white man answered also in the same language. That white man said, "I have come to buy the tusks of the beast which is here in the forest with big feet and tusks and great ears, that is called Njâku." They said, "Yes! A good thing!" When they were about leaving, the white man advancing to them, deposited with them four bunches of tobacco, four bales of prints, four caps and other things.

When they reached the shore, they told the others, "The white men want Njâku's tusks; and also they have things by which to kill his tribe."

The next morning, they went to the white men; they were trusted with guns and bullets and powder; they went to the forest, and fought with the elephants. In two days the ship was loaded, and it departed.

This continues to happen so until this day, in the Ivory Trade.

The Magic Drum

IN THE ANCIENT days, there were Mankind and all the Tribes of the Animals living together in one country. They built their towns, and they dwelt together in one place. In the country of

King Maseni, Tortoise and Leopard occupied the same town; the one at one end of the street, and the other at the other.

Leopard married two women; Tortoise also his two.

It happened that a time of famine came, and a very great hunger fell on the Tribes covering that whole region of country. So, King Maseni issued a law, thus: "Any person who shall be found having a piece of food, he shall he brought to me." (That is, for the equal distribution of that food.) And he appointed police as watchmen to look after that whole region.

The famine increased. People sat down hopelessly and died of hunger. Just as, even today, it destroys the poor; not only of Africa, but also in the lands of Manga-Manĕne (White Man's Land). And, as the days passed, people continued sitting in their hopelessness.

One day, Tortoise went out early, going, going and entering into the jungles, to seek for his special food, mushrooms. He had said to his wife, "I am going to stroll on the beach off down toward the south." As he journeyed and journeyed, he came to a river. It was a large one, several hundred feet in width. There he saw a coconut tree growing on the riverbank. When he reached the foot of the tree, and looked up at its top, he discovered that it was full of very many nuts. He said to himself, "I'm going up there, to gather nuts; for, hunger has seized me." He laid aside his travelling-bag, leaving it on the ground, and at once climbed the tree, expecting to gather many of the nuts. He plucked two, and threw them to the ground. Plucking another, and attempting to throw it, it slipped from his hand, and fell into the stream running below.

Then he exclaimed, "I've come here in hunger; and does my coconut fall into the water to be lost?" He said to himself, "I'll leave here, and drop into the water, and follow the nut." So, he plunged down, *splash!* into the water. He dove down to where the nut had sunk, to get it. And he was carried away by the current. Following the nut where the current had carried it, he came to the landing-place of a strange Town, where was a large House. People were there in it. And other people were outside, playing. They called to him. From the House, he heard a Voice, saying, "Take me! take me! take me!" (It was a Drum that spoke.)

At the landing-place was a woman washing a child. The woman said to him, "What is it that brought you here? And, Kudu, where are you going?" He replied, "There is great hunger in our town. So, on my way, I came seeking for my mushrooms. Then it was that I saw a coco tree; and I climbed it; for, I am hungry and have nothing to eat. I threw down the nuts. One fell into the river. I followed it; and I came hither." Then the woman said, "Now then, you are saved." And she added, "Kudu! go to that House over there. You will see a Thing there. That Thing is a Drum. Start, and go at once to where the Drums are."

Others of those people called out to him, "There are many such Things there. But, the kind that you will see which says, 'Take me! take me!' do not take it. But, the Drum which is silent and does not speak, but only echoes, 'wo-wo-wo,' without any real words, you must take it. Carry it with you, and tie it to that coco tree. Then you must say to the Drum, 'Ngâmâ! speak as they told to you!'" So, Tortoise went on, and on, to the House, and took the Drum, and, carrying it, came back to the riverbank where the Woman was. She said to him, "You must first try to learn how to use it. Beat it!" He beat it. And a table appeared with all kinds of food! And when he had eaten, he said to the Drum, "Put it back!" And the table disappeared.

He carried the Drum with him clear back to the foot of the coco tree. He tied it with a rattan to the tree, and then said to the Drum, "Ngâmâ! do as they said!" Instantly, the Drum set out a long table, and put on all sorts of food. Tortoise felt very glad and happy for the abundance of food. So he ate and ate, and was satisfied. Again he said, "Ngâmâ! do as they said!" And Drum took back the table and the food to itself up the tree, leaving a little food at the foot; and then came back to the hand of Tortoise.

He put this little food in his travelling-bag, and gathered from the ground the coconuts he had left lying there in the morning, and started to go back to his town. He stopped at a spot a short distance in the rear of the town. So delighted was he with his Drum that he tested it again. He stood it up, and with the palm of his hand struck it, *tomu!* A table at once stood there, with all kinds of food. Again he ate, and also filled his travelling-bag. Then he said to a tree that was standing nearby, "Bend down!" It bowed; and he tied the Drum to its branch; and went off into the town. The coconuts and the mushrooms he handed to his women and children. After he had entered his house, his chief wife said to him, "Where have you been all this long while since the morning?" He replied evasively, "I went wandering clear down to the beach to gather coconuts. And, this day I saw a very fine thing. You, my wife, shall see it!" Then he drew out the food from the bag, potatoes, and rice, and beef. And he said, "The while that we eat this food, no one must show any of it to Njâ." So, they two, and his other wife and their family of children ate.

Soon day darkened; and they all went to go to sleep. And soon another day began to break. At daybreak, Tortoise started to go off to the place where was the Drum. Arriving there, he went to the tree, and said to the Drum, "Ngâmâ! do as they said!" The Drum came rapidly down to the ground, and put out the table all covered with food. Tortoise took a part, and ate, and was satisfied. Then he also filled the bag. Then said he to the Drum, "Do as you did!" And Drum took back the things, and went up the tree. On another day, at daybreak, he went to the tree and did the same way.

On another day, as he was going, his eldest son, curious to find out where his father obtained so much food, secretly followed him. Tortoise went to where the Drum was. The child hid himself, and stood still. He heard his father say to the tree, "Bend!" And its top bent down. The child saw the whole process, as Tortoise took the Drum, stood it up, and with the palm of his hand, struck it, *vĕ!* saying, "Do as you have been told to do!" At once a table stood prepared, at which Tortoise sat down and ate. And then, when he had finished, saying, "Tree! bend down," it bent over for Drum to be tied to it. He returned Drum to the branch; and the tree stood erect.

On other days, Tortoise came to the tree, and did the same way, eating; and returning to his house; on all such occasions, bringing food for his family. One day, the son, who had seen how to do all those things, came to the tree, and said to it, "Bow down." It bowed; and he did as his father had done. So Drum spread the table. The child ate, and finished eating. Then said he to Drum, "Put them away!" And the table disappeared. Then he took up the Drum, instead of fastening it to the tree, and secretly carried it to town to his own house. He went to call privately his brothers, and his father's women, and other members of the family. When they had come together in his house, at his command, the Drum did as usual; and they ate. And when he said to the Drum, "Put away the things!" it put them away.

Tortoise came that day from the forest where he had been searching for the loved mushrooms for his family. He said to himself, "Before going into the town, I will first go to the tree to eat." As he approached the tree, when only a short distance from it, the tree was standing as usual, but the Drum was not there! He exclaimed, "Truly, now, what is this joke of the tree?" As he neared the foot of the tree, still there was no Drum to be seen! He said to the tree, "Bow down!" There was no response! He passed on to the town, took his axe, and returned at once to the tree, in anger saying, "Lest I cut you down, bend!" The tree stood still. Tortoise began at once with his axe chopping, *ko! ko!* The tree fell, toppling to the ground, *tomu!* He said to it, "You! produce the Drum, lest I cut you in pieces!" He split the tree all into pieces; but he did not see the Drum. He returned to the town; and, as he went, he walked anxiously, saying to himself, "Who has done this thing?" When he reached his house, he was so displeased that he declined to speak. Then his eldest son came to him, and said, "O! my father! why is it that you are silent and do not speak?

What have you done in the forest? What is it?" He replied, "I don't want to talk." The son said, "Ah! my father! You were satisfied when you used to come and eat, and you brought us mushrooms. I am the one who took the Drum." Tortoise said to him, "My child, now bring out to us the Drum." He brought it out of an inner room. Then Tortoise and the son called together all their people privately, and assembled them in the house. They commanded the Drum. It did as it usually did. They ate. Their little children took their scraps of potatoes and meat of wild animals, and, in their excitement, forgot orders, and went out eating their food in the open street. Other children saw them, and begged of them. They gave to them. Among them were children of Leopard, who went and showed the meat to their father.

All suddenly, Leopard came to the house of Tortoise, and found him and his family feasting. Leopard said, "Ah! Chum! you have done me evil. You are eating; and I and my family are dying with hunger!" Tortoise replied, "Yes, not today, but tomorrow you shall eat." So, Leopard returned to his house.

After that, the day darkened. And they all went to lie down in sleep. Then, the next day broke.

Early in the morning, Tortoise, out in the street, announced, "From my house to Njâ's there will be no strolling into the forest today. Today, only food."

Tortoise then went off by himself to the coco tree (whither he had secretly during the night carried the Drum). Arriving at the foot of the tree, he desired to test whether its power had been lost by the use of it in his town. So, he gave the usual orders; and they were, as usual, obeyed. Tortoise then went off with the Drum, carrying it openly on his shoulder, into the town, and directly to the house of Leopard, and said to him, "Call all your people! Let them come!" They all came into the house; and the people of Tortoise also. He gave the usual commands. At once, Drum produced an abundance of food, and a table for it. So, they all ate, and were satisfied. And Drum took back the table to itself. Drum remained in the house of Leopard for about two weeks. It ended its supply of food, being displeased at Leopard's rough usage of itself; and there was no more food. Leopard went to Tortoise, and told him, "Drum has no more food. Go, and get another." Tortoise was provoked at the abuse of his Drum, but he took it, and hung it up in his house.

At this time, the watchmen heard of the supply of food at Leopard's house, and they asked him about it. He denied having any. They asked him, "Where then did you get this food which we saw your children eating?" He said, "From the children of Kudu." The officers went at once to King Maseni, and reported, "We saw a person who has food." He inquired, "Who is he?" They replied, "Kudu." The King ordered, "Go ye, and summon Kudu." They went and told Tortoise, "The King summons you." Tortoise asked, "What have I done to the King? Since the King and I have been living in this country, he has not summoned me." Nevertheless, he obeyed and journeyed to the King's house. The King said to him, "You are keeping food, while all the Tribes are dying of hunger? You! bring all those foods!" Tortoise replied, "Please excuse me! I will not come again today with them. But, tomorrow, you must call for all the tribes."

The next morning, the King had his bell rung, and an order announced, "Any person whatever, old or young, come to eat!" The whole community assembled at the King's house. Tortoise also came from his town, holding his Drum in his hand. The distant members of that Tribe, (not knowing and not having heard what that Drum had been doing) twitted him, "Is it for a dance?"

Entering into the King's house, Tortoise stood up the Drum; with his palm he struck it, *vĕ!* saying, "Let every kind of food appear!" It appeared. The town was like a table, covered with every variety of food. The entire community ate, and were satisfied; and they dispersed. Tortoise took the Drum, and journeyed back to his town. He spoke to his hungry family, "Come ye!" They came. They struck the Drum; it was motionless; and nothing came from it! They struck it again.

Silent! (It was indignant at having been used by other hands than those of Tortoise.) So, they sat down with hunger.

The next day, Tortoise went rapidly off to the coco tree, climbed it, gathered two nuts, threw one into the river, dropped into the stream, and followed the nut as he had done before. He came as before to that landing-place, and to the Woman, and told her about the failure of the Drum. She told him that she knew of it, and directed him to go and take another. He went on to that House, and to those People. And they, as before, asked him, "Kudu! whither goest thou?" He replied, "You know I have come to take my coconut." But they said, "No! leave the nut, and take a Drum." And, as before, they advised him to take a silent one. So, he came to the House of Drums. These called to him, "Take me! take me!" Then, he thought to himself, "Yes! I'll take one of those Drums that talk. Perhaps they will have even better things than the other." So, he took one, and came out of the House, and told those People, "I have taken. And, now, for my journey."

He started from the landing-place, and on up the river, to the foot of the coco tree. He tied the Drum to the tree with a cord, as before, set it up, and gave it a slap, *vĕ!* And a table stood there! He said, "Ngâmâ! do as you usually do!" Instantly, there were thrown down on the table, *mbwâ!* whips instead of food. Tortoise, surprised, said, "As usual!" The Drum picked up one of the whips, and beat Tortoise, *vĕ!* He cried out with pain, and said to the Drum, "But, now do also as you do. Take these things away." And Drum returned the table and whips to itself. Tortoise regretfully said to himself, "Those People told me not to take a Drum that talked; but my heart deceived me."

However, a plan occurred to him by which to obtain a revenge on Leopard and the King for the trouble he had been put to.

So, taking up the Drum, he came to his own town, and went at once to the house of Leopard, to whom he said, "Tomorrow come with your people and mine to the town of King Maseni." Leopard rejoiced at the thought: "This is the Drum of food!"

Then Tortoise journeyed to the King's town, and said, "I have found food, according to your order. Call the people tomorrow."

In the morning, the King's bell was rung, and his people, accompanied by those of Tortoise and Leopard, came to his house. Tortoise privately spoke to his own people, "No one of you must follow me into the house. Remain outside of the window."

Tortoise said to the King, "The food of today must be eaten only inside of your house." So, the King's people, with those of Leopard, entered into the house. There, Tortoise said, "We shall eat this food only if all the doors and windows are fastened." So, they were fastened (excepting one which Tortoise kept open near himself). Then, the Drum was sounded, and Tortoise commanded it, "Do as you have said." And the tables appeared. But, instead of food, were whips. The people wondered, "Ah! what do these mean? Where do they come from?" Tortoise stationed himself by the open window, and commanded the Drum, "As usual!" Instantly the whips flew about the room, lashing everybody, even the King, and especially Leopard. The thrashing was great, and Leopard and his people were crying with pain. Their bodies were injured, being covered with cuts.

But Tortoise had promptly jumped out of the window. And, standing outside, he ordered, "Ngâmâ! do as you do!" And the whips and tables returned to it, and the whipping ceased. But Tortoise knew that the angry crowd would try to seize and kill him. So, taking advantage of the confusion in the house, he and his people fled to the water of the river, and scattered, hiding among the logs and roots in the stream. As he was disappearing, Leopard shouted after him, "You and I shall not see each other! If we do, it will be you who will be killed!"

Leopard's Hunting Companions

LEOPARD AND OTHER Beasts, with a son of Leopard's sister, were residing in the same town. One day, Leopard said to the others, "I have here a word to say." They replied, "Tell it." "We must go to kill Beasts (not of our company) for our food, at a place which I will show you a number of miles away." And they made their arrangements.

After two days, he said, "Now, for the journey!" So they finished their preparations. And Leopard said to his nephew, "You stay in the town. I and the others will go to our work."

They began their journey, and had gone only a part of the way, when Leopard exclaimed, "I forgot my spear! Wait for me while I go back to the town." There he found his nephew sitting down, waiting. Leopard said to him, "I have come to tell you that, every day, while we are away, you must come early to where we are killing the animals; and secretly you must take away the meat and bring it here to my house." The nephew heard and promised.

Leopard returned to the others who were awaiting him on the road, and told them to come on. They went, and they arrived at the spot which he had chosen. There they hastily built a small house for their camp. The next day they said, "Now, let us go and make our snares for the animals." They began making snares, and set their traps early in the afternoon. A few hours later, they returned to the camp. Later still, before sunset, they said, "Let us go to examine our snares." They found they had caught an Igwana. They killed it and put it on the drying-frame over the fire in the house.

Then the day darkened. And they went to their sleep.

And then the day broke.

And Leopard said, "While we go to the snares, who shall remain to take care of this house?" They agreed, "Let Etoli stay at the camp." House-Rat assented, "All right." So the others went away together.

The camp had been made near a small stream. At that same hour, Leopard's nephew came to the camp, according to his uncle's directions. He had in his hands a plate and a drum. He came near to the house cautiously. With the plate he twice swept the surface of the water, as if bailing out a canoe. Rat heard the swish of the water, and called out, "Who is splashing water there? Who is dabbling in this water?" The nephew responded, "It is I, a friend." And Rat said, "Well, then come."

The nephew came to the house. After a little conversation, he said to Rat, "I have here a drum, and, while I beat it, you dance for me." Rat was pleased, and said, "Very well." So, the nephew beat the drum, and Rat danced. After a while, the nephew said to Rat, "Go you, out into the front, and dance there, while I beat the drum here." As Rat went out, the nephew snatched the dried meat and ran away with it, suddenly disappearing around a corner of the house. He came to the town, and placed the meat in his own house.

Rat waited a while in the front, and, not hearing the drum, came back into the house, and called out, "Chum! where are you?" He looked about, and his eyes falling on the drying-frame, he saw that the dried meat was not there. He began to mourn, "Ah! Leopard will kill me today, because of the loss of his meat."

While he was thus speaking, the company of trappers, together with Leopard, came back from their morning's work. Leopard told Rat all that had occurred to them in the forest at their traps and snares; and then said, "Now, tell me what you have been doing, and the happenings of this camp." Rat told him, "Someone has come and taken away the dried meat, but I did not see who it was." Leopard said, "You are full of falsehood. Yourself have eaten it while we were away in the forest." So, Leopard gave him a heavy flogging. Then they put on the drying-frame the animal they had trapped that day.

The next day they went again to the forest; and Wild-Rat was left in charge of the camp. The nephew came, as on the day before, with his plate and drum, and did in the same way at the water. And he deceived the Wild-Rat with his drumming, in the same way as he had done to House-Rat.

When Leopard and the others came back from the forest, Wild-Rat told him of the loss of the meat; and said that he had seen no one, and did not know who took it. Leopard said to him, "You, Ko, have eaten the meat, just as your relative Etoli ate his yesterday."

Thus Leopard and his company went each day to the traps. On the third day, Porcupine was caught; on the fourth, Gazelle; on the fifth, Ox; on the sixth, Elephant. Beast after beast was caught, killed and dried; and, day by day, the meat of all was stolen. The last to be thus caught and stolen was Tortoise.

The nephew in Leopard's town looked with satisfaction on the pile of dried meat that had been collected in his own house. He said to himself, "My uncle told me to gather them; and I have done so. But, I will not put them in Uncle's house."

In the camp, there was left only one animal of Leopard's companions that had not been placed on guard. It was a Bird, a water Wag-tail. It said to Leopard one day, "While you all go on your errand today, I will remain as keeper of the house." Leopard replied, "No! my friend, I don't wish you to remain." (For, Leopard knew that that Bird was very cautious and wise, more so than some other animals.) Nevertheless, they went, leaving the Bird in charge of the house.

The nephew came, as usual, with his plate and drum. He splashed the water of the stream as usual, to see whether there was anyone in the house to respond. And the Bird asked, "Who are you?" The nephew answered, in a humble voice, "I." He came on through the stream, on his way, catching two crayfish. He entered the house, and he said to the Bird, "Get me some salt, and a leaf in which to tie and roast these crayfish." When the Bird gave him the leaf, he tied them in it, and laid the small bundle on the coals on the fireplace. But he at once took up the bundle, opened it, and ate the fish, before they were really cooked. The Bird said to him, "Those fish were not yet cooked. Your stomach is like your Uncle Njâ's. Both you and your Uncle like to eat things raw."

The Bird at once suspected that the nephew was the thief. When the nephew said, "I have here a drum," Bird at once, as if very willing, replied, "Drum! I want to dance." The nephew was standing in the front with his drum, and he said to Bird, "Come and dance out here; for, the drum sounds much better outside." But the Bird said, "I will not dance in the same place with you." The nephew then said, "Well, then; change places; you come here, and I go into the house." But the Bird refused, "No! I stay in the house."

Most of the morning was thus spent by the nephew trying to deceive the Bird and get into the house alone. Finally, the nephew wearied, and gave up the effort and left.

Soon the company of trappers, with Leopard, returned from the forest. He told the Bird all the news of their forest work. Looking at the drying-frames, Leopard saw that the dried meat was still there. He thought in his heart, "My nephew has not come today to get this meat."

The Bird then told Leopard all the news of the camp, and how the nephew had been acting. At the last, he exclaimed, "So! it is your nephew who has been coming here every day to take away the dried meat!" And all the animals agreed, "So! so! that's so!" But Leopard replied, "I don't believe it. But, let us adjourn and examine." (He supposed the meat was hidden in his own house, and would not be discovered.)

They all scattered, and hastened to their town. There they entered the nephew's house; and there they found a great pile of dried meat. They proved the theft on Leopard himself, pointing out, "Here is the very meat in the house of one of your own family. We are sure that you yourself made the conspiracy with your nephew for him to do the stealing for you." And they all denounced him, "You are a thief and a liar! You shall not join with us anymore in the same town."

Leopard went away in wrath saying, "Do you prove it on me? Well then! all you beasts, whenever and wherever I shall meet you, it will be only to eat you!"

So, leopards are always enemies to all other animals, and they kill them whenever they are able.

Is the Bat a Bird or a Beast?

BAT LIVED AT a place by itself, with only its mother. Shortly after their settling there, the mother became sick, very near to death. Bat called for Antelope, and said to him, "Make medicine for my mother." Antelope looked steadily at her to discern her disease. Then he told Bat, "There is no one who can make the medicine that will cure your mother, except Joba." Having given this information, Antelope returned to his own place.

On another day, early in the morning, Bat arose to go to call Sun. He did not start until about seven o'clock. He met Sun on the road about eleven o'clock. And he said to Sun, "My journey was on the way to see you." Sun told him, "If you have a word to say, speak!" So Bat requested, "Come! Make Medicine for my mother. She is sick." But Sun replied, "I can't go to make medicine unless you meet me in my house; not here on the road. Go back; and come to me at my house tomorrow." So Bat went back to his town.

And the day darkened. And they all slept their sleep.

And the next day broke. At six o'clock, Bat started to go to call Sun. About nine o'clock, he met Sun on the path; and he told Sun what he was come for. But Sun said to him, "Whenever I emerge from my house, I do not go back, but I keep on to the end of my journey. Go back, for another day." Bat returned to his town.

He made other journeys in order to see Sun at his house, five successive days; and every day he was late, and met Sun already on the way of his own journey for his own business.

Finally, on the seventh day, Bat's mother died. Then Bat, in his grief, said, "It is Joba who has killed my mother! Had he made medicine for me, she would have recovered."

Very many people came together that day in a crowd, at the Kwedi (mourning) for the dead. The wailing was held from six o'clock in the morning until eleven o'clock of the next day. At that hour, Bat announced, "Let her be taken to the grave." He called other Beasts to go into the house together with him, in order to carry the corpse. They took up the body, and carried it on the way to the grave.

On their arrival at the grave, these Beasts said to Bat, "We have a rule that, before we bury a person, we must first look upon the face." (To identify it). So, they opened the coffin. When they had looked on the face, they said, "No! We can't bury this person; for, it is not our relative, it does not belong to us Beasts. This person indeed resembles us in having teeth like us. And it also has a head like us. But, that it has wings, makes it look like a bird. It is a bird. Call for the Birds! We will disperse." So, they dispersed.

Then Bat called the Birds to come. They came, big and little; Pelicans, Eagles, Herons and all the others. When they all had come together, they said to Bat, "Show us the dead body." He told them, "Here it is! Come! Look upon it!" They looked and examined carefully. Then they said, "Yes! It resembles us; for, it has wings as we. But, about the teeth, no! We birds, none of us, have any teeth. This person does not resemble us with those teeth. It does not belong to us." And all the Birds stepped aside.

During the while that the talking had been going on, Ants had come and laid hold of the body, and could not be driven away. Then one of the Birds said to Bat, "I told you, you ought not to delay the burial, for, many things might happen." The Ants had eaten the body and there was no burial. And all the birds and beasts went away.

Bat, left alone, said to himself, "All the fault of all this trouble is because of Joba. If he had made medicine, my mother would not be dead. So I, Ndemi and Joba shall not look on each other. We shall have no friendship. If he emerges, I shall hide myself. I won't meet him or look at him." And he added, "I shall mourn for my mother always. I will make no visits. I will walk about only at night, not in the daytime, lest I meet Joba or other people."

Dog, and His Human Speech

DOG AND HIS mother were the only inhabitants of their hamlet. He had the power to speak both as a beast and as a human being.

One day the mother said to the son, "You are now a strong man; go, and seek a marriage. Go, and marry Eyâle, the daughter of Njambo." And he said to his mother, "I will go tomorrow."

That day darkened. And they both went to lie down in their places for sleep.

Then soon, another day began to break.

Dog said to his mother, "This is the time of my journey." It was about sunrise in the morning. And he began his journey. He went the distance of about eight miles; and arrived at the journey's end before the middle of the morning.

He entered the house of Njambo, the father of Eyâle. Njambo and his wife saluted him, "Mbolo!" and he responded, "Ai! Mbolo!" Njambo asked him, "My friend! What is the cause of your journey?" Dog, with his animal language, answered, "I have come to marry your daughter Eyâle." Njambo consented; and the mother of the girl also agreed. They called their daughter, and asked her; and she also replied, "Yes! With all my heart." This young woman was of very fine appearance in face and body. So, all the parties agreed to the marriage.

After that, about sunset in the evening, when they sat down at supper, the son-in-law, Dog, was not able to eat for some unknown reason.

That day darkened; and they went to their sleep.

And, then, the next daylight broke. But, by an hour after sunrise in the morning, Dog had not risen; he was still asleep.

The mother of the woman said to her, "Get some water ready for the washing of your husband's face, whenever he shall awake." She also said to her daughter, "I am going to go into the forest to the plantation to get food for your husband; for, since his coming, he has not eaten. Also, here is a chicken; the lads may kill and prepare it. But, you yourself must split ngândâ (gourd seeds, whose oily kernels are mashed into a pudding)." She handed Eyâle the dish of gourd seeds, and went off into the forest. Njambo also went away on an errand with his wife. The daughter took the dish of seeds, and, sitting down, began to shell them. As she shelled, she threw the kernels on the ground, but the shells she put on a plate.

Shortly after the mother had gone, Dog woke from sleep. He rose from his bed, and came out to the room where his wife was, and stood near her, watching her working at the seeds. He stood silent, looking closely, and observed that she was still throwing away the kernels, the good part, and saving the shells on the plate. He spoke to her with his human voice, "No! Woman! Not so! Do you throw the good parts, to the ground, and the worthless husks onto the plate?"

While he was thus speaking to his wife, she suddenly fell to the ground. And at once she died. He laid hold of her to lift her up. But, behold! She was a corpse.

Soon afterwards, the father and the mother came, having returned from their errands. They found their child a corpse; and they said to Dog, "Mbwa! What is this?" He, with his own language replied, "I cannot tell." But they insisted, "Tell us the reason!"

So Dog spoke with his human voice, "You, Woman, went to the forest while I was asleep. You, Man, you also went in company of your wife, while I was asleep. When I rose from sleep, I found my wife was cracking ngândâ. She was taking the good kernels to throw on the ground, and was keeping the shells for the plate. And I spoke and told her, 'The good kernels which you are throwing on the ground are to be eaten, not the husks.'"

While he was telling them this, they too, also fell to the ground, and died, apparently without cause.

When the people of the town heard about all this, they said, "This person carries an evil Medicine for killing people. Let him be seized and killed!"

So Dog fled away rapidly into the forest; and he finally reached the hamlet of his mother. His body was scratched and torn by the branches and thorns of the bushes of the forest, in his hasty flight. His mother exclaimed, "Mbwa! What's the matter? Such haste! And your body so disordered!" He replied, using their own language, "No! I won't tell you. I won't speak." But, his mother begged him, "Please! My child! Tell me!" So, finally, he spoke, using his strange voice, and said, "My mother! I tell you! Njambo and his wife liked me for the marriage; and the woman consented entirely. I was at that time asleep, when the Man and his wife went to the forest. When I rose from my sleep, I found the woman Eyâle cracking ngândâ, and throwing away the kernels and keeping the husks. And I told her, 'The good ones which you are throwing away are the ones to be eaten.' And, at once she died."

While he was speaking thus to his mother, she also fell dead on the ground. The news was carried to the town of Dog's mother's brother, and very many people came to the Mourning. His Uncle came to Dog, and said, "Mbwa! What is the reason of all this?" But Dog would not answer. He only said, "No! I won't speak." Then they all begged him, "Tell us the reason." But he replied only, "No! I won't speak."

Finally, as they urged him, he chose two of them, and said to the company, "The rest of you remain here, and watch while I go and speak to these two." Then Dog spoke to those two men with the same voice as he had to his mother. And at once they died, as she had died. Then he exclaimed, "Ah! No! If I speak so, people will come to an end!" And all the people agreed, "Yes, Mbwa! It is so. Your human speech kills us people. Don't speak any more."

And he went away to live with Mankind.

The Coming of Darkness

WHEN GOD FIRST made the world, there was never any darkness or cold. The sun always shone brightly during the day, and at night, the moon bathed the earth in a softer light, ensuring that everything could still be seen quite clearly.

But one day God sent for the Bat and handed him a mysterious parcel to take to the moon. He told the Bat it contained darkness, but as he did not have the time to explain precisely what darkness was, the Bat went on his way without fully realizing the importance of his mission.

He flew at a leisurely pace with the parcel strapped on his back until he began to feel rather tired and hungry. He was in no great hurry he decided, and so he put down his load by the roadside and wandered off in search of something to eat.

But while he was away, a group of mischievous animals approached the spot where he had paused to rest and, seeing the parcel, began to open it, thinking there might be something of value inside of it. The Bat returned just as they were untying the last piece of string and rushed forward to stop them. But too late! The darkness forced its way through the opening and rose up into the sky before anyone had a chance to catch it.

Quickly the Bat gave chase, flying about everywhere, trying to grab hold of the darkness and return it to the parcel before God discovered what had happened. But the harder he tried, the more the darkness eluded him, so that eventually he fell into an exhausted sleep lasting several hours.

When the Bat awoke, he found himself in a strange twilight world and once again, he began chasing about in every direction, hoping he would succeed where he had failed before.

But the Bat has never managed to catch the darkness, although you will see him every evening just after the sun has set, trying to trap it and deliver it safely to the moon as God first commanded him.

Why the Moon Waxes and Wanes

THERE WAS ONCE an old woman who was very poor, and lived in a small mud hut thatched with mats made from the leaves of the tombo palm in the bush. She was often very hungry, as there was no one to look after her.

EXPLAINING THE NATURAL WORLD

In the olden days, the moon used often to come down to the earth, although she lived most of the time in the sky. The moon was a fat woman with a skin of hide, and she was full of fat meat. She was quite round, and in the night used to give plenty of light. The moon was sorry for the poor starving old woman, so she came to her and said, "You may cut some of my meat away for your food." This the old woman did every evening, and the moon got smaller and smaller until you could scarcely see her at all. Of course this made her give very little light, and all the people began to grumble in consequence, and to ask why it was that the moon was getting so thin.

At last the people went to the old woman's house where there happened to be a little girl sleeping. She had been there for some little time, and had seen the moon come down every evening, and the old woman go out with her knife and carve her daily supply of meat out of the moon. As she was very frightened, she told the people all about it, so they determined to set a watch on the movements of the old woman.

That very night the moon came down as usual, and the old woman went out with her knife and basket to get her food; but before she could carve any meat all the people rushed out shouting, and the moon was so frightened that she went back again into the sky, and never came down again to the earth. The old woman was left to starve in the bush.

Ever since that time the moon has hidden herself most of the day, as she was so frightened, and she still gets very thin once a month, but later on she gets fat again, and when she is quite fat she gives plenty of light all the night; but this does not last very long, and she begins to get thinner and thinner, in the same way as she did when the old woman was carving her meat from her.

Origin of Tiis Lake

A TROLL HAD once taken up his abode near the village of Kund, in the high bank on which the church now stands; but when the people about there had become pious, and went constantly to church, the Troll was dreadfully annoyed by their almost incessant ringing of bells in the steeple of the church. He was at last obliged, in consequence of it, to take his departure; for nothing has more contributed to the emigration of the Troll-folk out of the country than the increasing piety of the people, and their taking to bell-ringing. The Troll of Kund accordingly quitted the country, and went over to Funen, where he lived for some time in peace and quiet.

Now it chanced that a man who had lately settled in the town of Kund, coming to Funen on business, met on the road with this same Troll. "Where do you live?" said the Troll to him. Now there was nothing whatever about the Troll unlike a man, so he answered him, as was the truth, "I am from the town of Kund." "So?" said the Troll. "I don't know you, then! And yet I think I know every man in Kund. Will you, however," continued he, "just be so kind to take a letter from me back with you to Kund?" The man said, of course, he had no objection. The Troll then thrust the letter into his pocket, and charged him strictly not to take it out till he came to Kund church, and then to throw it over the churchyard wall, and the person for whom it was intended would get it.

The Troll then went away in great haste, and with him the letter went entirely out of the man's mind. But when he was come back to Zealand he sat down by the meadow where Tiis Lake now is, and suddenly recollected the Troll's letter. He felt a great desire to look at it at least. So he took it out of his pocket, and sat a while with it in his hands, when suddenly there began to dribble a little water out of the seal. The letter now unfolded itself, and the water came out faster and faster, and it was with the utmost difficulty that the poor man was enabled to save his life; for the malicious Troll had enclosed an entire lake in the letter. The Troll, it is plain, had thought to avenge himself on Kund church by destroying it in this manner; but God ordered it so that the lake chanced to run out in the great meadow where it now flows.

Why the Stork Loves Holland

ABOVE ALL COUNTRIES in Europe, this bird, wise in the head and long in the legs, loves Holland. Flying all the way from Africa, the stork is at home among dykes and windmills.

Storks are seen by the thousands in Holland and Friesland. Sometimes they strut in the streets, not in the least frightened or disturbed. They make their nests among the tiles and chimneys, on the red roofs of the houses, and they rear their young even on the church towers.

If a man sets an old cart wheel flat on a treetop, the storks accept this as an invitation to come and stay. At once they proceed, first of all, to arrange their toilet, after their long flight. They do this even before they build their nest. You can see them, by the hour, preening their feathers and combing their plumage, with their long bills. Then, as solemnly as a boss mason, they set about gathering sticks and hay for their houses. They never seem to be in a hurry.

A stork lays on a bit of wood, and then goes at his toilet again, looking around to see that other folks are busy. Year after year, a pair of storks will use the same nest, rebuilding, or repairing it, each springtime. The stork is a steady citizen and does not like to change. Once treated well in one place by the landlord, Mr. and Mrs. Stork keep the same apartments and watch over the family cradle inside the house, to see that it is always occupied by a baby. The return of the stork is, in Holland, a household celebration.

Out in the fields, Mr. Stork is happy indeed, for Holland is the paradise of frogs; so the gentleman of the red legs finds plenty to eat. He takes his time for going to dinner, and rarely rushes for quick lunch. After business hours in the morning, he lays his long beak among his thick breast feathers, until it is quite hidden. Then, perched up in the air on one long leg, like a stilt, he takes a nap, often for hours.

With the other leg crossed, he seems to be resting on the figure four.

Towards evening, he shakes out his wings, flaps them once or twice, and takes a walk, but he is never in haste. Beginning his hunt, he soon has enough frogs, mice, grubs, worms or insects to make a good meal. It is because this bird feels so much at home, in town and country, making part of the landscape, that we so associate together Holland and the stork, as we usually do.

The Dutch proverb pictures the scene, which is so common. "In the same field, the cow eats grass; the greyhound hunts the hare; and the stork helps himself to the frogs." Indeed, if it were not for the stork, Holland would, like old Egypt in the time of Moses, be overrun with frogs.

The Dutch call the stork by the sweet name "Ooijevaar," or the treasure-bringer. Every springtime, the boys and girls, fathers and mothers, shout welcome to the white bird from Egypt.

"What do you bring me?" is their question or thought.

If the bird deserts its old home on their roof, the family is in grief, thinking it has lost its luck; but if Daddy Stork, with Mrs. Stork's approval, chooses a new place for their nest, there is more rejoicing in that house, than if money had been found. 'Where there are nestlings on the roof, there will be babies in the house,' is what the Dutch say; for both are welcome.

To tell why the stork loves Holland, we must go back to the Africa of a million years ago. Then, we shall ask the Dutch fairies how they succeeded in making the new land, in the west, so popular in the stork world. For what reason did the wise birds emigrate to the cold country a thousand miles away? They were so regular and punctual, that a great prophet wrote:

"Yea, the stork in the heaven knoweth her appointed times."

Ages ago, there were camels and caravans in Africa, but there was no Holland, for the land was still under the waves. In India, also, the stork was an old bird, that waded in the pools and kept the frogs from croaking in terms of the multiplication table. Sometimes the stork population increased too fast and some went hungry for food; for, the proverb tells us that a stork 'died while waiting for the ocean to dry, hoping to get a supply of dried fish'.

When on the coast of the North Sea, the Land of a Million Islands was made, the frog emigrants were there first. They poured in so fast, that it seemed a question as to who should own the country – frogs or men. Some were very big, as if ambitious to be bulls. They croaked so loud, that they drowned out the fairy music, and made the night hideous with their noises. The snakes spoiled the country for the little birds, while the toads seemed to think that the salt ocean had been kept out, and the land made, especially for them.

The Dutch fairies were disgusted at the way these reptiles behaved, for they could not enjoy themselves, as in the old days. If they went to dance in the meadow, on moonlit nights, they always found a big bullfrog sitting in their ring, mocking them with its bellowing. So when they heard about the storks in Africa, and what hearty appetites they had, for the various wrigglers, crawlers, jumpers and splashers in the waters, they resolved to invite them, in a body, to Holland.

The Dutch fairies knew nothing of the habits of the bird and scarcely imagined how such a creature might look, but they heard many pleasant things about the stork's good character. The wise bird had an excellent reputation, not only for being kind to its young, but also for attending to the wants of its parents, when they were old. It was even said that in some countries the stork was the symbol for filial piety.

So the fairies of all the Netherlands despatched a delegation to Egypt and a congress of storks was called to consider this invitation to go west. Messengers were at once sent to all the red-legged birds, among the bulrushes of the Nile, or that lived on the roofs of the temples, or that perched on the pyramids, or dwelt on the top of old columns, or that stood in rows along the eaves of the town houses. The town birds gained their living by acting as street cleaners, but the river birds made their meals chiefly on fish, frogs and mice.

The invitation was discussed in stork meeting, and it was unanimously accepted; except by some old grannies and grandpops that feared in the strange land they would not be well fed. On a second motion, it was agreed that only the strongest birds should attempt the flight. Those afraid, or too weak to go, must stay behind and attend to the old folks. Such a rattle of mandibles was never heard in Egypt before, as when this stork meeting adjourned.

Now when storks travel, they go in flocks. Thousands of them left Egypt together. High in the air, with their broad wings spread and their long legs stretched out behind them, they covered Europe in a few hours. Then they scattered all over the marshy lands of the new country. It was agreed that each pair was to find its own home. When the cold autumn should come, they were to assemble again for flight to Egypt.

It was a new sight for the fairies, the frogs and the men, to look over the landscape and see these snow-white strangers. They were so pretty to look at, while promenading over the meadows, wading in the ponds and ditches, or standing silently by the riverbanks. Soon, however, these foreign birds were very unpopular in bullfrog land, and as for the snakes, they thought that Holland would be ruined by these hungry strangers. On the other hand, it was good news, in fairyland, that all fairies could dance safely on their meadow rings, for the bullfrogs were now afraid to venture in the grass, lest they should be gobbled up, for the frogs could not hide from the storks. The new birds could poke their big bills so far into the mud-holes, that no frog, or snake, big or little, was safe. The stork's red legs were so long, and the birds could wade in such deep water, that hundreds of frogs were soon eaten up, and there were many widows and orphans in the ponds and puddles.

When the fairies got more acquainted with their new guests, and saw how they behaved, they nearly died of laughing. They were not surprised at their diet, or eating habits, but they soon discovered that the storks were not songbirds. Instead of having voices, they seemed to talk to each other by clattering their long jaws, or snapping their mandibles together. Their snowy plumage – all being white but their wing feathers – was admired, was envied, and their long, bright coloured legs were a wonder. At first the fairies thought their guests wore red stockings and they thought how heavy must be the laundry work on wash days; for in Holland, everything must be clean.

Of all creatures on earth, as the fairies thought, the funniest was seen when Mr. Stork was in love. To attract and please his lady love, he made the most grotesque gestures. He would leap up from the ground and move with a hop, skip and jump. Then he spread out his wings, as if to hug his beloved. Then he danced around her, as if he were filled with wine. All the time he made the best music he knew how, by clattering his mandibles together. He intended this performance for a sort of love ditty, or serenade. The whole program was more amusing than anything that an ape, goat or donkey could get up. How the fairies did laugh!

Yet the fairies were very grateful to the storks for ridding their meadows of so much vermin. How these delicate looking, snow white and graceful creatures could put so many snails, snakes, tadpoles, and toads into their stomachs and turn them into snow white feathers, wonderful wings and long legs, as red as a rose, was a mystery to them. It seemed more wonderful than anything which they could do, but as fairies have no stomachs and do not eat, this whole matter of digestion was a mystery to them.

Besides the terror and gloom in the frog world, every reptile winced and squirmed, when he heard of this new enemy. All crawlers, creepers, and jumpers had so long imagined that the land was theirs and had been made solely for their benefit! Nor did they know how to conquer the storks. The frog daddies could do nothing, and the frog mothers were every moment afraid to let either the tadpoles or froggies go out of their sight. They worried lest they should see their babies caught up in a pair of long, bony jaws, as sharp as scissors, there to wriggle and crow, until their darlings disappeared within the monster.

One anecdote of the many that were long told in the old Dutch frog ponds was this: showing into what clangers curiosity may lead youngsters. We put it in quotation marks to show that it was told as a true story, and not printed in a book, or made up.

"A tadpole often teased its froggy mother to let it go and see a red pole, of which it had heard from a traveller. Mrs. Frog would not at first let her son go, but promised that as soon as the tadpole lost his tail, and his flippers had turned into forelegs, and his hindquarters had properly sprouted, so that he could hop out of danger, he might then venture on his travels. She warned him, however, not to go too near to that curious red pole, of which he had heard. Nobody as yet found out just what this red thing, standing in the water, was; but danger was suspected by old heads, and all little froggies were warned to be careful and keep away. In reality, the red stick was the leg of a stork, sound asleep, for it was taking its usual afternoon nap. The frogs on the bank, and those in the pool that held their noses above water, to get their breath, had never before seen anything like this red stilt, or its cross pole; for no bird of this sort had ever before flown into their neighbourhood. They never suspected that it was a stork, with its legs shaped like the figure four. Indeed, they knew nothing of its long bill, that could open and shut like a trap, catching a frog or snake, and swallowing it in a moment.

"Unfortunately for this uneducated young frog, that had never travelled from home, it now went too near the red pole, and, to show how brave it was, rubbed its nose against the queer thing. Suddenly the horrible creature, that had only been asleep, woke up and snapped its jaws. In a moment, a wriggling froggy disappeared from sight into the stomach of a monster, that had two red legs, instead of one. At the sight of such gluttony, there was an awful splash, for a whole row of frogs had jumped from the bank into the pool. After this, it was evident that Holland was not to belong entirely to the frogs."

As for the human beings, they were so happy over the war with the vermin and the victory of the storks, that they made this bird their pride and joy. They heaped honours upon the stork as the saviour of their country. They placed boxes on the roofs of their houses for these birds to nest in. All the old cart wheels in the land were hunted up. They sawed off the willow trees a few feet above the ground, and set the wheels in flat, which the storks used as their parlours and dressing rooms.

As for the knights, they placed the figure of the stork on their shields, banners, and coats of arms, while citizens made this bird prominent on their city seals. The capital of the country, The Hague, was dedicated to this bird, and, for all time, a pond was dug within the city limits, where storks were fed and cared for at the public expense. Even today, many a good story, illustrating the tender affection of The Hague storks for their young, is told and enjoyed as an example to Dutch mothers to be the best in the world.

Out in the country at large, in any of the eleven provinces, whenever they drained a swamp, or pumped out a pond to make a village, it was not looked upon as a part of Holland, unless there were storks. Even in the new wild places they planted stakes on the pumped out dry land, called polders. On the top of these, sticks were laid as invitations for the stork families to come and live with the people. Along the roads, they stuck posts for storks' nests. It became a custom with farmers, when the storks came back, to kill the fatted calf, or lamb, and leave the refuse meat out in the fields for a feast to these bird visitors. A score of Dutch proverbs exist, all of them complimentary to the bird that loves babies and cradles.

Last of all, the Dutch children, even in the reign of Queen Wilhelmina, made letter carriers of their friends the treasure-bringers. Tying tiny slips of paper to their red legs, they sent messages, in autumn, to the boys and girls in the old land of the sphinx and pyramids, of Moses, and the children of Israel. In the springtime, the children's return messages were received in the country which bids eternal welcome to the bird named the Bringer of Blessings.

This is why the storks love Holland.

Assipattle and the Mester Stoorworm

IN FAR BYGONE days, in the north, there lived a well-to-do farmer, who had seven sons and one daughter. And the youngest of these seven sons bore a very curious name; for men called him Assipattle, which means, 'He who grovels among the ashes.'

Perhaps Assipattle deserved his name, for he was rather a lazy boy, who never did any work on the farm as his brothers did, but ran about the doors with ragged clothes and unkempt hair, and whose mind was ever filled with wondrous stories of Trolls and Giants, Elves and Goblins.

When the sun was hot in the long summer afternoons, when the bees droned drowsily and even the tiny insects seemed almost asleep, the boy was content to throw himself down on the ash-heap amongst the ashes, and lie there, lazily letting them run through his fingers, as one might play with sand on the seashore, basking in the sunshine and telling stories to himself.

And his brothers, working hard in the fields, would point to him with mocking fingers, and laugh, and say to each other how well the name suited him, and of how little use he was in the world.

And when they came home from their work, they would push him about and tease him, and even his mother would make him sweep the floor, and draw water from the well, and fetch peats from the peat-stack, and do all the little odd jobs that nobody else would do.

So poor Assipattle had rather a hard life of it, and he would often have been very miserable had it not been for his sister, who loved him dearly, and who would listen quite patiently to all the stories that he had to tell; who never laughed at him or told him that he was telling lies, as his brothers did.

But one day a very sad thing happened – at least, it was a sad thing for poor Assipattle.

For it chanced that the King of these parts had one only daughter, the Princess Gemdelovely, whom he loved dearly, and to whom he denied nothing. And Princess Gemdelovely was in want of a waiting-maid, and as she had seen Assipattle's sister standing by the garden gate as she was riding by one day, and had taken a fancy to her, she asked her father if she might ask her to come and live at the Castle and serve her.

Her father agreed at once, as he always did agree to any of her wishes; and sent a messenger in haste to the farmer's house to ask if his daughter would come to the Castle to be the Princess's waiting-maid.

And, of course, the farmer was very pleased at the piece of good fortune which had befallen the girl, and so was her mother, and so were her six brothers, all except poor Assipattle, who looked with wistful eyes after his sister as she rode away, proud of her new clothes and of the rivlins which her father had made her out of cowhide, which she was to wear in the Palace when she waited on the Princess, for at home she always ran barefoot.

Time passed, and one day a rider rode in hot haste through the country bearing the most terrible tidings. For the evening before, some fishermen, out in their boats, had caught sight of the Mester Stoorworm, which, as everyone knows, was the largest, and the first, and the greatest of all Sea-Serpents. It was that beast which, in the Good Book, is called the Leviathan, and if it had been measured in our day, its tail would have touched Iceland, while its snout rested on the North Cape.

And the fishermen had noticed that this fearsome Monster had its head turned towards the mainland, and that it opened its mouth and yawned horribly, as if to show that it was hungry, and that, if it were not fed, it would kill every living thing upon the land, both man and beast, bird and creeping thing.

For 'twas well known that its breath was so poisonous that it consumed as with a burning fire everything that it lighted on. So that, if it pleased the awful creature to lift its head and put forth its breath, like noxious vapour, over the country, in a few weeks the fair land would be turned into a region of desolation.

As you may imagine, everyone was almost paralyzed with terror at this awful calamity which threatened them; and the King called a solemn meeting of all his Counsellors, and asked them if they could devise any way of warding off the danger.

And for three whole days they sat in Council, these grave, bearded men, and many were the suggestions which were made, and many the words of wisdom which were spoken; but, alas! no one was wise enough to think of a way by which the Mester Stoorworm might be driven back.

At last, at the end of the third day, when everyone had given up hope of finding a remedy, the door of the Council Chamber opened and the Queen appeared.

Now the Queen was the King's second wife, and she was not a favourite in the Kingdom, for she was a proud, insolent woman, who did not behave kindly to her step-daughter, the Princess Gemdelovely, and who spent much more of her time in the company of a great Sorcerer, whom everyone feared and dreaded, than she did in that of the King, her husband.

So the sober Counsellors looked at her disapprovingly as she came boldly into the Council Chamber and stood up beside the King's Chair of State, and, speaking in a loud, clear voice, addressed them thus:

"Ye think that ye are brave men and strong, oh, ye Elders, and fit to be the Protectors of the People. And so it may be, when it is mortals that ye are called on to face. But ye be no match for the foe that now threatens our land. Before him your weapons be but as straw. 'Tis not through strength of arm, but through sorcery, that he will be overcome. So listen to my words, even though they be but those of a woman, and take counsel with the great Sorcerer, from whom nothing is hid, but who knoweth all the mysteries of the earth, and of the air, and of the sea."

Now the King and his Counsellors liked not this advice, for they hated the Sorcerer, who had, as they thought, too much influence with the Queen; but they were at their wits' end, and knew not to whom to turn for help, so they were fain to do as she said and summon the Wizard before them.

And when he obeyed the summons and appeared in their midst, they liked him none the better for his looks. For he was long, and thin, and awesome, with a beard that came down to his knee, and hair that wrapped him about like a mantle, and his face was the colour of mortar, as if he had always lived in darkness, and had been afraid to look on the sun.

But there was no help to be found in any other man, so they laid the case before him, and asked him what they should do. And he answered coldly that he would think over the matter, and come again to the Assembly the following day and give them his advice.

And his advice, when they heard it, was like to turn their hair white with horror.

For he said that the only way to satisfy the Monster, and to make it spare the land, was to feed it every Saturday with seven young maidens, who must be the fairest who could be found; and if, after this remedy had been tried once or twice, it did not succeed in mollifying the Stoorworm and inducing him to depart, there was but one other measure that he could suggest, but that was so horrible and dreadful that he would not rend their hearts by mentioning it in the meantime.

And as, although they hated him, they feared him also, the Council had e'en to abide by his words, and pronounced the awful doom.

And so it came about that, every Saturday, seven bonnie, innocent maidens were bound hand and foot and laid on a rock which ran into the sea, and the Monster stretched out his long, jagged tongue, and swept them into his mouth; while all the rest of the folk looked on from the top of a high hill – or, at least, the men looked – with cold, set faces, while the women hid theirs in their aprons and wept aloud.

"Is there no other way," they cried, "no other way than this, to save the land?"

But the men only groaned and shook their heads. "No other way," they answered; "no other way."

Then suddenly a boy's indignant voice rang out among the crowd. "Is there no grown man who would fight that Monster, and kill him, and save the lassies alive? I would do it; I am not feared for the Mester Stoorworm."

It was the boy Assipattle who spoke, and everyone looked at him in amazement as he stood staring at the great Sea-Serpent, his fingers twitching with rage, and his great blue eyes glowing with pity and indignation.

"The poor bairn's mad; the sight hath turned his head," they whispered one to another; and they would have crowded round him to pet and comfort him, but his elder brother came and gave him a heavy clout on the side of his head.

"Thou fight the Stoorworm!" he cried contemptuously. "A likely story! Go home to thy ash-pit, and stop speaking havers"; and, taking his arm, he drew him to the place where his other brothers were waiting, and they all went home together.

But all the time Assipattle kept on saying that he meant to kill the Stoorworm; and at last his brothers became so angry at what they thought was mere bragging, that they picked up stones and pelted him so hard with them that at last he took to his heels and ran away from them.

That evening the six brothers were threshing corn in the barn, and Assipattle, as usual, was lying among the ashes thinking his own thoughts, when his mother came out and bade him run and tell the others to come in for their supper.

The boy did as he was bid, for he was a willing enough little fellow; but when he entered the barn his brothers, in revenge for his having run away from them in the afternoon, set on him and pulled him down, and piled so much straw on top of him that, had his father not come from the house to see what they were all waiting for, he would, of a surety, have been smothered.

But when, at supper-time, his mother was quarrelling with the other lads for what they had done, and saying to them that it was only cowards who set on bairns littler and younger than themselves, Assipattle looked up from the bicker of porridge which he was supping.

"Vex not thyself, Mother," he said, "for I could have fought them all if I liked; ay, and beaten them, too."

"Why didst thou not essay it then?" cried everybody at once.

"Because I knew that I would need all my strength when I go to fight the Giant Stoorworm," replied Assipattle gravely.

And, as you may fancy, the others laughed louder than before.

Time passed, and every Saturday seven lassies were thrown to the Stoorworm, until at last it was felt that this state of things could not be allowed to go on any longer; for if it did, there would soon be no maidens at all left in the country.

So the Elders met once more, and, after long consultation, it was agreed that the Sorcerer should be summoned, and asked what his other remedy was. "For, by our troth," said they, "it cannot be worse than that which we are practicing now."

But had they known it, the new remedy was even more dreadful than the old. For the cruel Queen hated her step-daughter, Gemdelovely, and the wicked Sorcerer knew that she did, and that she would not be sorry to get rid of her, and, things being as they were, he thought that he saw a way to please the Queen. So he stood up in the Council, and, pretending to be very sorry, said that the only other thing that could be done was to give the Princess Gemdelovely to the Stoorworm, then would it of a surety depart.

When they heard this sentence a terrible stillness fell upon the Council, and everyone covered his face with his hands, for no man dare look at the King.

But although his dear daughter was as the apple of his eye, he was a just and righteous Monarch, and he felt that it was not right that other fathers should have been forced to part with their daughters, in order to try and save the country, if his child was to be spared.

So, after he had had speech with the Princess, he stood up before the Elders, and declared, with trembling voice, that both he and she were ready to make the sacrifice.

"She is my only child," he said, "and the last of her race. Yet it seemeth good to both of us that she should lay down her life, if by so doing she may save the land that she loves so well."

Salt tears ran down the faces of the great bearded men as they heard their King's words, for they all knew how dear the Princess Gemdelovely was to him. But it was felt that what he said was wise and true, and that the thing was just and right; for 'twere better, surely, that one maiden should die, even although she were of Royal blood, than that bands of other maidens should go to their death week by week, and all to no purpose.

So, amid heavy sobs, the aged Lawman – he who was the chief man of the Council – rose up to pronounce the Princess's doom. But, ere he did so, the King's Kemper – or Fighting-man – stepped forward.

"Nature teaches us that it is fitting that each beast hath a tail," he said, "and this Doom, which our Lawman is about to pronounce, is in very sooth a venomous beast. And, if I had my way, the tail which it would bear after it is this, that if the Mester Stoorworm doth not depart, and that right speedily, after he have devoured the Princess, the next thing that is offered to him be no tender young maiden, but that tough, lean old Sorcerer."

And at his words there was such a great shout of approval that the wicked Sorcerer seemed to shrink within himself, and his pale face grew paler than it was before.

Now, three weeks were allowed between the time that the Doom was pronounced upon the Princess and the time that it was carried out, so that the King might send Ambassadors to all the neighbouring Kingdoms to issue proclamations that, if any Champion would come forward who was able to drive away the Stoorworm and save the Princess, he should have her for his wife.

And with her he should have the Kingdom, as well as a very famous sword that was now in the King's possession, but which had belonged to the great god Odin, with which he had fought and vanquished all his foes.

The sword bore the name of Sickersnapper, and no man had any power against it.

The news of all these things spread over the length and breadth of the land, and everyone mourned for the fate that was like to befall the Princess Gemdelovely. And the farmer, and his wife, and their six sons mourned also; – all but Assipattle, who sat amongst the ashes and said nothing.

When the King's Proclamation was made known throughout the neighbouring Kingdoms, there was a fine stir among all the young Gallants, for it seemed but a little thing to slay a Sea-Monster; and a beautiful wife, a fertile Kingdom, and a trusty sword are not to be won every day.

So six-and-thirty Champions arrived at the King's Palace, each hoping to gain the prize.

But the King sent them all out to look at the Giant Stoorworm lying in the sea with its enormous mouth open, and when they saw it, twelve of them were seized with sudden illness, and twelve of them were so afraid that they took to their heels and ran, and never stopped till they reached their own countries; and so only twelve returned to the King's Palace, and as for them, they were so downcast at the thought of the task that they had undertaken that they had no spirit left in them at all.

And none of them dare try to kill the Stoorworm; so the three weeks passed slowly by, until the night before the day on which the Princess was to be sacrificed. On that night the King, feeling that he must do something to entertain his guests, made a great supper for them.

But, as you may think, it was a dreary feast, for everyone was thinking so much about the terrible thing that was to happen on the morrow, that no one could eat or drink.

And when it was all over, and everybody had retired to rest, save the King and his old Kemperman, the King returned to the great hall, and went slowly up to his Chair of State, high up on the dais. It was not like the Chairs of State that we know nowadays; it was nothing but a massive Kist, in which he kept all the things which he treasured most.

The old Monarch undid the iron bolts with trembling fingers, and lifted the lid, and took out the wondrous sword Sickersnapper, which had belonged to the great god Odin.

His trusty Kemperman, who had stood by him in a hundred fights, watched him with pitying eyes.

"Why lift ye out the sword," he said softly, "when thy fighting days are done? Right nobly hast thou fought thy battles in the past, oh, my Lord! when thine arm was strong and sure. But when folk's years number four score and sixteen, as thine do, 'tis time to leave such work to other and younger men."

The old King turned on him angrily, with something of the old fire in his eyes. "Wheest," he cried, "else will I turn this sword on thee. Dost thou think that I can see my only bairn devoured by a Monster, and not lift a finger to try and save her when no other man will? I tell thee – and I will swear it with my two thumbs crossed on Sickersnapper – that both the sword and I will be destroyed before so much as one of her hairs be touched. So go, an' thou love me, my old comrade, and order my boat to be ready, with the sail set and the prow pointed out to sea. I will go myself and fight the Stoorworm; and if I do not return, I will lay it on thee to guard my cherished daughter. Peradventure, my life may redeem hers."

Now that night everybody at the farm went to bed betimes, for next morning the whole family was to set out early, to go to the top of the hill near the sea, to see the Princess eaten by the Stoorworm. All except Assipattle, who was to be left at home to herd the geese.

The lad was so vexed at this – for he had great schemes in his head – that he could not sleep. And as he lay tossing and tumbling about in his corner among the ashes, he heard his father and mother talking in the great box-bed. And, as he listened, he found that they were having an argument.

"'Tis such a long way to the hill overlooking the sea, I fear me I shall never walk it," said his mother. "I think I had better bide at home."

"Nay," replied her husband, "that would be a bonny-like thing, when all the country-side is to be there. Thou shalt ride behind me on my good mare Go-Swift."

"I do not care to trouble thee to take me behind thee," said his wife, "for methinks thou dost not love me as thou wert wont to do."

"The woman's havering," cried the Goodman of the house impatiently. "What makes thee think that I have ceased to love thee?"

"Because thou wilt no longer tell me thy secrets," answered his wife. "To go no further, think of this very horse, Go-Swift. For five long years I have been begging thee to tell me how it is that, when thou ridest her, she flies faster than the wind, while if any other man mount her, she hirples along like a broken-down nag."

The Goodman laughed. "'Twas not for lack of love, Goodwife," he said, "though it might be lack of trust. For women's tongues wag but loosely; and I did not want other folk to ken my secret. But since my silence hath vexed thy heart, I will e'en tell it thee.

"When I want Go-Swift to stand, I give her one clap on the left shoulder. When I would have her go like any other horse, I give her two claps on the right. But when I want her to fly like the wind, I whistle through the windpipe of a goose. And, as I never ken when I want her to gallop like that, I aye keep the bird's thrapple in the left-hand pocket of my coat."

"So that is how thou managest the beast," said the farmer's wife, in a satisfied tone; "and that is what becomes of all my goose thrapples. Oh! but thou art a clever fellow, Goodman; and now that I ken the way of it I may go to sleep."

Assipattle was not tumbling about in the ashes now; he was sitting up in the darkness, with glowing cheeks and sparkling eyes.

His opportunity had come at last, and he knew it.

He waited patiently till their heavy breathing told him that his parents were asleep; then he crept over to where his father's clothes were, and took the goose's windpipe out of the pocket of his coat, and slipped noiselessly out of the house. Once he was out of it, he ran like lightning to the stable. He saddled and bridled Go-Swift, and threw a halter round her neck, and led her to the stable door.

The good mare, unaccustomed to her new groom, pranced, and reared, and plunged; but Assipattle, knowing his father's secret, clapped her once on the left shoulder, and she stood as still as a stone. Then he mounted her, and gave her two claps on the right shoulder, and the good horse trotted off briskly, giving a loud neigh as she did so.

The unwonted sound, ringing out in the stillness of the night, roused the household, and the Goodman and his six sons came tumbling down the wooden stairs, shouting to one another in confusion that someone was stealing Go-Swift.

The farmer was the first to reach the door; and when he saw, in the starlight, the vanishing form of his favourite steed, he cried at the top of his voice:

"Stop thief, ho!
Go-Swift, whoa!"

And when Go-Swift heard that she pulled up in a moment. All seemed lost, for the farmer and his sons could run very fast indeed, and it seemed to Assipattle, sitting motionless on Go-Swift's back, that they would very soon make up on him.

But, luckily, he remembered the goose's thrapple, and he pulled it out of his pocket and whistled through it. In an instant the good mare bounded forward, swift as the wind, and was over the hill and out of reach of its pursuers before they had taken ten steps more.

Day was dawning when the lad came within sight of the sea; and there, in front of him, in the water, lay the enormous Monster whom he had come so far to slay. Anyone would have said that he was mad even to dream of making such an attempt, for he was but a slim, unarmed youth, and the Mester Stoorworm was so big that men said it would reach the fourth part round the world. And its tongue was jagged at the end like a fork, and with this fork it could sweep whatever it chose into its mouth, and devour it at its leisure.

For all this, Assipattle was not afraid, for he had the heart of a hero underneath his tattered garments. "I must be cautious," he said to himself, "and do by my wits what I cannot do by my strength."

He climbed down from his seat on Go-Swift's back, and tethered the good steed to a tree, and walked on, looking well about him, till he came to a little cottage on the edge of a wood.

The door was not locked, so he entered, and found its occupant, an old woman, fast asleep in bed. He did not disturb her, but he took down an iron pot from the shelf, and examined it closely.

"This will serve my purpose," he said, "and surely the old dame would not grudge it if she knew 'twas to save the Princess's life."

Then he lifted a live peat from the smouldering fire, and went his way.

Down at the water's edge he found the King's boat lying, guarded by a single boatman, with its sails set and its prow turned in the direction of the Mester Stoorworm.

"It's a cold morning," said Assipattle. "Art thou not well-nigh frozen sitting there? If thou wilt come on shore, and run about, and warm thyself, I will get into the boat and guard it till thou returnest."

"A likely story," replied the man. "And what would the King say if he were to come, as I expect every moment he will do, and find me playing myself on the sand, and his good boat left to a smatchet like thee? 'Twould be as much as my head is worth."

"As thou wilt," answered Assipattle carelessly, beginning to search among the rocks. "In the meantime, I must be looking for a wheen mussels to roast for my breakfast." And after he had gathered the mussels, he began to make a hole in the sand to put the live peat in. The boatman watched him curiously, for he, too, was beginning to feel hungry.

Presently the lad gave a wild shriek, and jumped high in the air. "Gold, gold!" he cried. "By the name of Thor, who would have looked to find gold here?"

This was too much for the boatman. Forgetting all about his head and the King, he jumped out of the boat, and, pushing Assipattle aside, began to scrape among the sand with all his might.

While he was doing so, Assipattle seized his pot, jumped into the boat, pushed her off, and was half a mile out to sea before the outwitted man, who, needless to say, could find no gold, noticed what he was about.

And, of course, he was very angry, and the old King was more angry still when he came down to the shore, attended by his Nobles and carrying the great sword Sickersnapper, in the vain hope that he, poor feeble old man that he was, might be able in some way to defeat the Monster and save his daughter.

But to make such an attempt was beyond his power now that his boat was gone. So he could only stand on the shore, along with the fast assembling crowd of his subjects, and watch what would befall.

And this was what befell!

Assipattle, sailing slowly over the sea, and watching the Mester Stoorworm intently, noticed that the terrible Monster yawned occasionally, as if longing for his weekly feast. And as it yawned a great flood of sea-water went down its throat, and came out again at its huge gills.

So the brave lad took down his sail, and pointed the prow of his boat straight at the Monster's mouth, and the next time it yawned he and his boat were sucked right in, and, like Jonah, went straight down its throat into the dark regions inside its body. On and on the boat floated; but as it went the water grew less, pouring out of the Stoorworm's gills, till at last it stuck, as it were, on dry land. And Assipattle jumped out, his pot in his hand, and began to explore.

Presently he came to the huge creature's liver, and having heard that the liver of a fish is full of oil, he made a hole in it and put in the live peat.

Woe's me! but there was a conflagration! And Assipattle just got back to his boat in time; for the Mester Stoorworm, in its convulsions, threw the boat right out of its mouth again, and it was flung up, high and dry, on the bare land.

The commotion in the sea was so terrible that the King and his daughter – who by this time had come down to the shore dressed like a bride, in white, ready to be thrown to the Monster – and all his Courtiers, and all the country-folk, were fain to take refuge on the hill top, out of harm's way, and stand and see what happened next.

And this was what happened next.

The poor, distressed creature – for it was now to be pitied, even although it was a great, cruel, awful Mester Stoorworm – tossed itself to and fro, twisting and writhing.

And as it tossed its awful head out of the water its tongue fell out, and struck the earth with such force that it made a great dent in it, into which the sea rushed. And that dent formed the crooked Straits which now divide Denmark from Norway and Sweden.

Then some of its teeth fell out and rested in the sea, and became the Islands that we now call the Orkney Isles; and a little afterwards some more teeth dropped out, and they became what we now call the Shetland Isles.

After that the creature twisted itself into a great lump and died; and this lump became the Island of Iceland; and the fire which Assipattle had kindled with his live peat still burns on underneath it, and that is why there are mountains which throw out fire in that chilly land.

When at last it was plainly seen that the Mester Stoorworm was dead, the King could scarce contain himself with joy. He put his arms round Assipattle's neck, and kissed him, and called him his son. And he took off his own Royal Mantle and put it on the lad, and girded his good sword Sickersnapper round his waist. And he called his daughter, the Princess Gemdelovely, to him, and put her hand in his, and declared that when the right time came she should be his wife, and that he should be ruler over all the Kingdom.

Then the whole company mounted their horses again, and Assipattle rode on Go-Swift by the Princess's side; and so they returned, with great joy, to the King's Palace.

But as they were nearing the gate Assipattle's sister, she who was the Princess's maid, ran out to meet him, and signed to the Princess to lout down, and whispered something in her ear.

The Princess's face grew dark, and she turned her horse's head and rode back to where her father was, with his Nobles. She told him the words that the maiden had spoken; and when he heard them his face, too, grew as black as thunder.

For the matter was this: The cruel Queen, full of joy at the thought that she was to be rid, once for all, of her step-daughter, had been making love to the wicked Sorcerer all the morning in the old King's absence.

"He shall be killed at once," cried the Monarch. "Such behaviour cannot be overlooked."

"Thou wilt have much ado to find him, Your Majesty," said the girl, "for 'tis more than an hour since he and the Queen fled together on the fleetest horses that they could find in the stables."

"But I can find him," cried Assipattle; and he went off like the wind on his good horse Go-Swift.

It was not long before he came within sight of the fugitives, and he drew his sword and shouted to them to stop.

They heard the shout, and turned round, and they both laughed aloud in derision when they saw that it was only the boy who grovelled in the ashes who pursued them.

"The insolent brat! I will cut off his head for him! I will teach him a lesson!" cried the Sorcerer; and he rode boldly back to meet Assipattle. For although he was no fighter, he knew that no ordinary weapon could harm his enchanted body; therefore he was not afraid.

But he did not count on Assipattle having the Sword of the great god Odin, with which he had slain all his enemies; and before this magic weapon he was powerless. And, at one thrust, the young lad ran it through his body as easily as if he had been any ordinary man, and he fell from his horse, dead.

Then the Courtiers of the King, who had also set off in pursuit, but whose steeds were less fleet of foot than Go-Swift, came up, and seized the bridle of the Queen's horse, and led it and its rider back to the Palace.

She was brought before the Council, and judged, and condemned to be shut up in a high tower for the remainder of her life. Which thing surely came to pass.

As for Assipattle, when the proper time came he was married to the Princess Gemdelovely, with great feasting and rejoicing. And when the old King died they ruled the Kingdom for many a long year.

The Five Spirits of the Plague

WITH REGARD TO the Ministry of Seasonal Epidemics, it is told that in the sixth moon of the eleventh year of the reign of Kao Tsu, founder of the Sui dynasty, five men appeared in the air, clothed in robes of five colours, each carrying different objects in his hands: the first a spoon and earthenware vase, the second a leather bag and sword, the third a fan, the fourth a club, the fifth a jug of fire.

The Emperor asked his Grand Historiographer who these were and if they were benevolent or evil spirits. The official answered: "These are the five powers of the five directions. Their appearance indicates the imminence of epidemics, which will last throughout the four seasons of the year." "What remedy is there, and how am I to protect the people?" inquired the Emperor. "There is no remedy," replied the official, "for epidemics are sent by Heaven." During that year the mortality was very great. The Emperor built a temple to the five men and granted them the title of Marshals to the Five Spirits of the Plague. During that and the following dynasty sacrifices were offered to them on the fifth day of the fifth moon.

The Golden Beetle, or Why the Dog Hates the Cat

"**WHAT WE SHALL** eat tomorrow, I haven't the slightest idea!" said Widow Wang to her eldest son, as he started out one morning in search of work.

"Oh, the gods will provide. I'll find a few coppers somewhere," replied the boy, trying to speak cheerfully, although in his heart he also had not the slightest idea in which direction to turn.

The winter had been a hard one: extreme cold, deep snow, and violent winds. The Wang house had suffered greatly. The roof had fallen in, weighed down by heavy snow. Then a hurricane had blown a wall over, and Ming-li, the son, up all night and exposed to a bitter cold wind, had caught pneumonia. Long days of illness followed, with the spending of extra money for medicine. All their scant savings had soon melted away, and at the shop where Ming-li had been employed his place was filled by another. When at last he arose from his sick-bed he was too weak for hard labour and there seemed to be no work in the neighbouring villages for him to do. Night after night he came home, trying not to be discouraged, but in his heart feeling the deep pangs of sorrow that come to the good son who sees his mother suffering for want of food and clothing.

"Bless his good heart!" said the poor widow after he had gone. "No mother ever had a better boy. I hope he is right in saying the gods will provide. It has been getting so much worse these past few weeks that it seems now as if my stomach were as empty as a rich man's brain. Why, even the rats have deserted our cottage, and there's nothing left for poor Tabby, while old Blackfoot is nearly dead from starvation."

When the old woman referred to the sorrows of her pets, her remarks were answered by a pitiful mewing and woebegone barking from the corner where the two unfed creatures were curled up together trying to keep warm.

Just then there was a loud knocking at the gate. When the widow Wang called out, "Come in!" she was surprised to see an old bald-headed priest standing in the doorway. "Sorry, but we have nothing," she went on, feeling sure the visitor had come in search of food. "We have fed on scraps these two weeks – on scraps and scrapings – and now we are living on the memories of what we used to have when my son's father was living. Our cat was so fat she couldn't climb to the roof. Now look at her. You can hardly see her, she's so thin. No, I'm sorry we can't help you, friend priest, but you see how it is."

"I didn't come for alms," cried the clean-shaven one, looking at her kindly, "but only to see what I could do to help you. The gods have listened long to the prayers of your devoted son. They honour him because he has not waited till you die to do sacrifice for you. They have seen how faithfully he has served you ever since his illness, and now, when he is worn out and unable to work, they are resolved to reward him for his virtue. You likewise have been a good mother and shall receive the gift I am now bringing."

"What do you mean?" faltered Mrs. Wang, hardly believing her ears at hearing a priest speak of bestowing mercies. "Have you come here to laugh at our misfortunes?"

"By no means. Here in my hand I hold a tiny golden beetle which you will find has a magic power greater than any you ever dreamed of. I will leave this precious thing with you, a present from the god of filial conduct."

"Yes, it will sell for a good sum," murmured the other, looking closely at the trinket, "and will give us millet for several days. Thanks, good priest, for your kindness."

"But you must by no means sell this golden beetle, for it has the power to fill your stomachs as long as you live."

The widow stared in open-mouthed wonder at the priest's surprising words.

"Yes, you must not doubt me, but listen carefully to what I tell you. Whenever you wish food, you have only to place this ornament in a kettle of boiling water, saying over and over again the names of what you want to eat. In three minutes take off the lid, and there will be your dinner, smoking hot, and cooked more perfectly than any food you have ever eaten."

"May I try it now?" she asked eagerly.

"As soon as I am gone."

When the door was shut, the old woman hurriedly kindled a fire, boiled some water, and then dropped in the golden beetle, repeating these words again and again:

"Dumplings, dumplings, come to me,
I am thin as thin can be.
Dumplings, dumplings, smoking hot,
Dumplings, dumplings, fill the pot."

Would those three minutes never pass? Could the priest have told the truth? Her old head was nearly wild with excitement as clouds of steam rose from the kettle. Off came the lid! She could wait no longer. Wonder of wonders! There before her unbelieving eyes was a pot, full to the brim of pork dumplings, dancing up and down in the bubbling water, the best, the most delicious dumplings she had ever tasted. She ate and ate till there was no room left in her greedy stomach, and then she feasted the cat and the dog until they were ready to burst.

"Good fortune has come at last," whispered Blackfoot, the dog, to Whitehead, the cat, as they lay down to sun themselves outside. "I fear I couldn't have held out another week without running away to look for food. I don't know just what's happened, but there's no use questioning the gods."

Mrs. Wang fairly danced for joy at the thought of her son's return and of how she would feast him.

"Poor boy, how surprised he will be at our fortune – and it's all on account of his goodness to his old mother."

When Ming-li came, with a dark cloud overhanging his brow, the widow saw plainly that disappointment was written there.

"Come, come, lad!" she cried cheerily, "clear up your face and smile, for the gods have been good to us and I shall soon show you how richly your devotion has been rewarded." So saying, she dropped the golden beetle into the boiling water and stirred up the fire.

Thinking his mother had gone stark mad for want of food, Ming-li stared solemnly at her. Anything was preferable to this misery. Should he sell his last outer garment for a few pennies and buy millet for her? Blackfoot licked his hand comfortingly, as if to say, "Cheer up, master, fortune has turned in our favour." Whitehead leaped upon a bench, purring like a sawmill.

Ming-li did not have long to wait. Almost in the twinkling of an eye he heard his mother crying out,

"Sit down at the table, son, and eat these dumplings while they are smoking hot."

Could he have heard correctly? Did his ears deceive him? No, there on the table was a huge platter full of the delicious pork dumplings he liked better than anything else in all the world, except, of course, his mother.

"Eat and ask no questions," counselled the Widow Wang. "When you are satisfied I will tell you everything."

Wise advice! Very soon the young man's chopsticks were twinkling like a little star in the verses. He ate long and happily, while his good mother watched him, her heart overflowing with joy at seeing him at last able to satisfy his hunger. But still the old woman could hardly wait for him to finish, she was so anxious to tell him her wonderful secret.

"Here, son!" she cried at last, as he began to pause between mouthfuls, "look at my treasure!" And she held out to him the golden beetle.

"First tell me what good fairy of a rich man has been filling our hands with silver?"

"That's just what I am trying to tell you," she laughed, "for there was a fairy here this afternoon sure enough, only he was dressed like a bald priest. That golden beetle is all he gave me, but with it comes a secret worth thousands of cash to us."

The youth fingered the trinket idly, still doubting his senses, and waiting impatiently for the secret of his delicious dinner. "But, mother, what has this brass bauble to do with the dumplings, these wonderful pork dumplings, the finest I ever ate?"

"Baubles indeed! Brass! Fie, fie, my boy! You little know what you are saying. Only listen and you shall hear a tale that will open your eyes."

She then told him what had happened, and ended by setting all of the left-over dumplings upon the floor for Blackfoot and Whitehead, a thing her son had never seen her do before, for they had been miserably poor and had had to save every scrap for the next meal.

Now began a long period of perfect happiness. Mother, son, dog and cat – all enjoyed themselves to their hearts' content. All manner of new foods such as they had never tasted were called forth from the pot by the wonderful little beetle. Bird-nest soup, shark's fins, and a hundred other delicacies were theirs for the asking, and soon Ming-li regained all his strength, but, I fear, at the same time grew somewhat lazy, for it was no longer necessary for him to work. As for the two animals, they became fat and sleek and their hair grew long and glossy.

But alas! according to a Chinese proverb, pride invites sorrow. The little family became so proud of their good fortune that they began to ask friends and relatives to dinner that they might show off their good meals. One day a Mr. and Mrs. Chu came from a distant village. They were much astonished at seeing the high style in which the Wangs lived. They had expected a beggar's meal, but went away with full stomachs.

"It's the best stuff I ever ate," said Mr. Chu, as they entered their own tumble-down house.

"Yes, and I know where it came from," exclaimed his wife. "I saw Widow Wang take a little gold ornament out of the pot and hide it in a cupboard. It must be some sort of charm, for I heard her mumbling to herself about pork and dumplings just as she was stirring up the fire."

"A charm, eh? Why is it that other people have all the luck? It looks as if we were doomed forever to be poor."

"Why not borrow Mrs. Wang's charm for a few days until we can pick up a little flesh to keep our bones from clattering? Turn about's fair play. Of course, we'll return it sooner or later."

"Doubtless they keep very close watch over it. When would you find them away from home, now that they don't have to work any more? As their house only contains one room, and that no bigger than ours, it would be difficult to borrow this golden trinket. It is harder, for more reasons than one, to steal from a beggar than from a king."

"Luck is surely with us," cried Mrs. Chu, clapping her hands. "They are going this very day to the Temple fair. I overheard Mrs. Wang tell her son that he must not forget he was to take her about the middle of the afternoon. I will slip back then and borrow the little charm from the box in which she hid it."

"Aren't you afraid of Blackfoot?"

"Pooh! he's so fat he can do nothing but roll. If the widow comes back suddenly, I'll tell her I came to look for my big hair-pin, that I lost it while I was at dinner."

"All right, go ahead, only of course we must remember we're borrowing the thing, not stealing it, for the Wangs have always been good friends to us, and then, too, we have just dined with them."

So skilfully did this crafty woman carry out her plans that within an hour she was back in her own house, gleefully showing the priest's charm to her husband. Not a soul had seen her enter the Wang house. The dog had made no noise, and the cat had only blinked her surprise at seeing a stranger and had gone to sleep again on the floor.

Great was the clamour and weeping when, on returning from the fair in expectation of a hot supper, the widow found her treasure missing. It was long before she could grasp the truth. She went back to the little box in the cupboard ten times before she could believe it was empty, and the room looked as if a cyclone had struck it, so long and carefully did the two unfortunates hunt for the lost beetle.

Then came days of hunger which were all the harder to bear since the recent period of good food and plenty. Oh, if they had only not got used to such dainties! How hard it was to go back to scraps and scrapings!

But if the widow and her son were sad over the loss of the good meals, the two pets were even more so. They were reduced to beggary and had to go forth daily upon the streets in search of stray bones and refuse that decent dogs and cats turned up their noses at.

One day, after this period of starvation had been going on for some time, Whitehead began suddenly to frisk about in great excitement.

"Whatever is the matter with you?" growled Blackfoot. "Are you mad from hunger, or have you caught another flea?"

"I was just thinking over our affairs, and now I know the cause of all our trouble."

"Do you indeed?" sneered Blackfoot.

"Yes, I do indeed, and you'd better think twice before you mock me, for I hold your future in my paw, as you will very soon see."

"Well, you needn't get angry about nothing. What wonderful discovery have you made – that every rat has one tail?"

"First of all, are you willing to help me bring good fortune back to our family?"

"Of course I am. Don't be silly," barked the dog, wagging his tail joyfully at the thought of another good dinner. "Surely! surely! I will do anything you like if it will bring Dame Fortune back again."

"All right. Here is the plan. There has been a thief in the house who has stolen our mistress's golden beetle. You remember all our big dinners that came from the pot? Well, every day I saw our mistress take a little golden beetle out of the black box and put it into the pot. One day she held it up before me, saying, 'Look, puss, there is the cause of all our happiness. Don't you wish it was yours?' Then she laughed and put it back into the box that stays in the cupboard."

"Is that true?" questioned Blackfoot. "Why didn't you say something about it before?"

"You remember the day Mr. and Mrs. Chu were here, and how Mrs. Chu returned in the afternoon after master and mistress had gone to the fair? I saw her, out of the tail of my eye, go to that very black box and take out the golden beetle. I thought it curious, but never dreamed she was a thief. Alas! I was wrong! She took the beetle, and if I am not mistaken, she and her husband are now enjoying the feasts that belong to us."

"Let's claw them," growled Blackfoot, gnashing his teeth.

"That would do no good," counselled the other, "for they would be sure to come out best in the end. We want the beetle back – that's the main thing. We'll leave revenge to human beings; it is none of our business."

"What do you suggest?" said Blackfoot. "I am with you through thick and thin."

"Let's go to the Chu house and make off with the beetle."

"Alas, that I am not a cat!" moaned Blackfoot. "If we go there I couldn't get inside, for robbers always keep their gates well locked. If I were like you I could scale the wall. It is the first time in all my life I ever envied a cat."

"We will go together," continued Whitehead. "I will ride on your back when we are fording the river, and you can protect me from strange animals. When we get to the Chu house, I will climb over the wall and manage the rest of the business myself. Only you must wait outside to help me to get home with the prize."

No sooner arranged than done. The companions set out that very night on their adventure. They crossed the river as the cat had suggested, and Blackfoot really enjoyed the swim, for, as he said, it took him back to his puppyhood, while the cat did not get a single drop of water on her face. It was midnight when they reached the Chu house.

"Just wait till I return," purred Whitehead in Blackfoot's ear.

With a mighty spring she reached the top of the mud wall, and then jumped down to the inside court. While she was resting in the shadow, trying to decide just how to go about her work, a slight rustling attracted her attention, and pop! one giant spring, one stretch-out of the claws, and she had caught a rat that had just come out of his hole for a drink and a midnight walk.

Now, Whitehead was so hungry that she would have made short work of this tempting prey if the rat had not opened its mouth and, to her amazement, begun to talk in good cat dialect.

"Pray, good puss, not so fast with your sharp teeth! Kindly be careful with your claws! Don't you know it is the custom now to put prisoners on their honour? I will promise not to run away."

"Pooh! what honour has a rat?"

"Most of us haven't much, I grant you, but my family was brought up under the roof of Confucius, and there we picked up so many crumbs of wisdom that we are exceptions to the rule. If you will spare me, I will obey you for life, in fact, will be your humble slave." Then, with a quick jerk, freeing itself, "See, I am loose now, but honour holds me as if I were tied, and so I make no further attempt to get away."

"Much good it would do you," purred Whitehead, her fur crackling noisily, and her mouth watering for a taste of rat steak. "However, I am quite willing to put you to the test. First, answer a few polite questions and I will see if you're a truthful fellow. What kind of food is your master eating now, that you should be so round and plump when I am thin and scrawny?"

"Oh, we have been in luck lately, I can tell you. Master and mistress feed on the fat of the land, and of course we hangers-on get the crumbs."

"But this is a poor tumble-down house. How can they afford such eating?"

"That is a great secret, but as I am in honour bound to tell you, here goes. My mistress has just obtained in some manner or other, a fairy's charm—"

"She stole it from our place," hissed the cat, "I will claw her eyes out if I get the chance. Why, we've been fairly starving for want of that beetle. She stole it from us just after she had been an invited guest! What do you think of that for honour, Sir Rat? Were your mistress's ancestors followers of the sage?"

"Oh, oh, oh! Why, that explains everything!" wailed the rat. "I have often wondered how they got the golden beetle, and yet of course I dared not ask any questions."

"No, certainly not! But hark you, friend rat – you get that golden trinket back for me, and I will set you free at once of all obligations. Do you know where she hides it?"

"Yes, in a crevice where the wall is broken. I will bring it to you in a jiffy, but how shall we exist when our charm is gone? There will be a season of scanty food, I fear; beggars' fare for all of us."

"Live on the memory of your good deed," purred the cat. "It is splendid, you know, to be an honest beggar. Now scoot! I trust you completely, since your people lived in the home of Confucius. I will wait here for your return. Ah!" laughed Whitehead to herself, "luck seems to be coming our way again!"

Five minutes later the rat appeared, bearing the trinket in its mouth. It passed the beetle over to the cat, and then with a whisk was off for ever. Its honour was safe, but it was afraid of Whitehead. It had seen the gleam of desire in her green eyes, and the cat might have broken her word if she had not been so anxious to get back home where her mistress could command the wonderful kettle once more to bring forth food.

The two adventurers reached the river just as the sun was rising above the eastern hills.

"Be careful," cautioned Blackfoot, as the cat leaped upon his back for her ride across the stream, "be careful not to forget the treasure. In short, remember that even though you are a female, it is necessary to keep your mouth closed till we reach the other side."

"Thanks, but I don't think I need your advice," replied Whitehead, picking up the beetle and leaping on to the dog's back.

But alas! just as they were nearing the farther shore, the excited cat forgot her wisdom for a moment. A fish suddenly leaped out of the water directly under her nose. It was too great a temptation. Snap! went her jaws in a vain effort to land the scaly treasure, and the golden beetle sank to the bottom of the river.

"There!" said the dog angrily, "what did I tell you? Now all our trouble has been in vain – all on account of your stupidity."

For a time there was a bitter dispute, and the companions called each other some very bad names – such as turtle and rabbit. Just as they were starting away from the river, disappointed and discouraged, a friendly frog who had by chance heard their conversation offered to fetch the treasure from the bottom of the stream. No sooner said than done, and after thanking this accommodating animal profusely, they turned homeward once more.

When they reached the cottage the door was shut, and, bark as he would, Blackfoot could not persuade his master to open it. There was the sound of loud wailing inside.

"Mistress is broken-hearted," whispered the cat, "I will go to her and make her happy."

So saying, she sprang lightly through a hole in the paper window, which, alas! was too small and too far from the ground for the faithful dog to enter.

A sad sight greeted the gaze of Whitehead. The son was lying on the bed unconscious, almost dead for want of food, while his mother, in despair, was rocking backwards and forwards wringing her wrinkled hands and crying at the top of her voice for someone to come and save them.

"Here I am, mistress," cried Whitehead, "and here is the treasure you are weeping for. I have rescued it and brought it back to you."

The widow, wild with joy at sight of the beetle, seized the cat in her scrawny arms and hugged the pet tightly to her bosom.

"Breakfast, son, breakfast! Wake up from your swoon! Fortune has come again. We are saved from starvation!"

Soon a steaming hot meal was ready, and you may well imagine how the old woman and her son, heaping praises upon Whitehead, filled the beast's platter with good things, but never a word did they say of the faithful dog, who remained outside sniffing the fragrant odours and waiting in sad wonder, for all this time the artful cat had said nothing of Blackfoot's part in the rescue of the golden beetle.

At last, when breakfast was over, slipping away from the others, Whitehead jumped out through the hole in the window.

"Oh, my dear Blackfoot," she began laughingly, "you should have been inside to see what a feast they gave me! Mistress was so delighted at my bringing back her treasure that she could not give me enough to eat, nor say enough kind things about me. Too bad, old fellow, that you are hungry. You'd better run out into the street and hunt up a bone."

Maddened by the shameful treachery of his companion, the enraged dog sprang upon the cat and in a few seconds had shaken her to death.

"So dies the one who forgets a friend and who loses honour," he cried sadly, as he stood over the body of his companion.

Rushing out into the street, he proclaimed the treachery of Whitehead to the members of his tribe, at the same time advising that all self-respecting dogs should from that time onwards make war upon the feline race.

And that is why the descendants of old Blackfoot, whether in China or in the great countries of the West, have waged continual war upon the children and grandchildren of Whitehead, for a thousand generations of dogs have fought them and hated them with a great and lasting hatred.

Benten and the Dragon

IN A CERTAIN cave there lived a formidable dragon, which devoured the children of the village of Koshigoe. In the sixth century Benten was determined to put a stop to this monster's unseemly behaviour, and having caused a great earthquake she hovered in the clouds over the cave where the dread dragon had taken up his abode. Benten then descended from the clouds, entered the cavern, married the dragon, and was thus able, through her good influence, to put an end to the slaughter of little children. With the coming of Benten there arose from the sea the famous Island of Enoshima, which has remained to this day sacred to the Goddess of the Sea.

The Origin of Corn and Deer

ONCE THERE WAS a man who went around with a little turkey. The man lost all he had in gambling. His people brought together more things for him and again he gambled them all away. Then they agreed they would kill him if he lost again. They tied some things to his tipi poles for him. He came back and looked at them. "Now I will play the hoop and pole game again," he said. His turkey went around in front of him and said, "My father, why is it that you have such a poor mind? If you lose all this again, they are going to kill you."

He started away and came to the side of a river. A pretty tree was standing there. He commenced to chop it with a stone ax. At sunset, only a little part of it remained to be chopped. He went home and came again in the morning. The tree stood as it had when he first saw it. He commenced chopping at it again. At sunset there was only a little more to be chopped. He went home. He came back the next morning and commenced chopping. When only a little more remained to be chopped it was night and he went home. He came back the next day and the tree stood as if it had never been cut.

Right by the tree there was a cliff. TcactcîyaLkîdn, the talking god, stood there and spoke to him, "My friend," he said, "why are you always bothering my tree?" "I have use for this, my friend," the other replied, "that is why I bother it." "What will you do with it?" asked the god. "I am going down the river by means of it," he said. The god made motions four times and felled it. He cut off a length just long enough for a man to lie in. He put back the remainder of the tree on the stump and it came together again as if it had never been cut.

"My friend, get all the birds that peck trees to hollow it out for you." Then all the birds came together and pecked at the inside of it, going through the tree. The man tried to get inside but it was not yet big enough. The birds went through it four times again in each direction. The hole was now large enough to receive his body. Then he distributed the beads among the birds that had worked for him.

Then the god came again to help him. He used the foam on the water to smooth the log. Spider closed both ends of the log for him. "It's ready, my child," said the god. "There are four bad places in succession," he told him. Making motions four times the god put the log with the man inside of it into the water. It floated down stream with him. It came down to the place where the whirlpool is and the log began to spin around. It went on down stream from there with him until it came to the waterfall where it stuck. The god got it loose for him and it floated down to a place where the Pueblo Indians were pulling out driftwood. They pulled the log out but the god put it back. It went on down until it came where there was much driftwood floating. It floated down with him from there. When it landed he tried in vain to get out. After a while, he succeeded.

As he walked along beside the river he began to wish he had something to plant. He caught a lot of ducks, and pulled out their feathers which he used for a bed. He ate the birds but saved the sinew from their legs and used it for making arrows. When he had been there four days and the sun was setting he saw his turkey silhouetted against the sky. He came toward him. They walked together along the river. As they walked along he said he wished he had seeds to plant.

"My father," said the turkey, "clear a piece of ground." He cleared it. Then the turkey stood with his wings outstretched, facing in each direction. When he walked from the east, black corn lay in a row; he walked from the south, blue corn lay in a row; he walked from the west, yellow corn lay in a row; he walked from the north, and corn of different colors lay in a row. "Now plant this," he said.

He planted all the different kinds of corn. When it had been planted one day, it commenced to come up. After the second day, the corn had two leaves. On the third day, it was quite high. On the fourth day, it had brown tassels. The turkey went around gobbling.

The man lay down in the feathers and slept. On the other side, to the east, stood a rocky ridge. He saw a fire over there. In the morning he went where the fire had been but there was no fire nor any tracks. That evening there was a fire there again. He stood up a forked stick and placed himself sitting on his heels so that the fire appeared In a line with the fork of the stick. The next day, getting his bearings in this way, he went again to the place where he had seen the fire. There were no tracks there. He went home again. When the sun went down he sat in the same place and saw the fire again. The next morning he went where the fire had been. There were no tracks there. He went back home.

The corn and the tobacco were now ripe. He rolled a cigarette and tied it to his belt. The third day, at sunset, there was a fire there again. When he went to the place a girl was sitting where the stream flowed out from the mountains. She was rubbing a deerskin. The man stood by her but she could not see him. The cicada had loaned him its flute. He stood there and blew upon it. As the girl was working at the buckskin she pushed her hand down and turned her head to listen. She looked under the grass but could not find the cicada. She sat down again and began to rub the buckskin. The man blew again upon the flute. Again, she looked for it without finding it. He stood on this side of her and blew on the flute again. She got up and started toward her home.

He followed behind her and then she saw him. Causing the solid rock to open she went in. He went in behind her but left his arrows lying by the door. When he got inside a very old woman who was sitting there jumped up and ran out. (She was afraid of her son-in-law).

Then the old man came home. He immediately took up his tobacco and filled his pipe. When he was ready he blew some smoke and said to the young man, "Will you smoke with me?" "No," he said. "Where do you come from, I have looked everywhere in this country. Where have people come into existence?" He took up another sack of tobacco and filled another pipe. He smoked and blew the smoke. "Do you want to smoke?" he asked. "No," replied the man. Then he took up another pipe and another sack of tobacco, filled the pipe again, and blew smoke. "Do you want to smoke?" he asked. "No," he answered.

Then the man began to smoke the cigarette he had tied to his belt. The old man smelled the smoke and said, "I wish it was my turn to smoke." He gave him the cigarette and the old man inhaled the smoke. His legs straightened out. The young man blew smoke against the soles of his feet and the palms of his hands. He commenced to get up. "That was something good," he was saying as he stood up. "I wish you would bring me much of it from the place where you got it." "That is all there is," the young man said.

They placed a dish of food before him and he swallowed it at one mouthful. He took up his arrows and started home. Outside, only one footprint was to be seen. He came where his turkey was. Then they tracked him to the place where the corn was growing. When he came to the turkey, it was afraid of him. When it was evening he made two cigarettes and tied them to his clothes. He went again where the others were living. He gave the old man the cigarettes to smoke again and then went home the next morning. This time, there were two tracks outside. "I do not think, he is a human being," the old man said. The next evening he went there again. He carried with him a cigarette which he had made. When the old man had smoked it, he said, "That is good." He went into the tipi.

The turkey was going around a little way off, he was afraid of him. That evening the man went back again carrying four cigarettes. The old man smoked them, saying they were good. The next morning the woman went back with him. They both walked across the river on top of the water. They gathered much corn and tobacco. The woman started home. When she came to the river, she took off her moccasins and waded through. She brought the corn to her people. "It is good," he said, "to eat with deer meat." He gave his father-in-law the corn. The father-in-law, in return, gave him the deer which he possessed.

The old man's name was DînîdeyîniLt'anne, 'Game he raised.' The other man who came to him was named AtdiLdeyeseLdli, 'He floated down.' Then the deer all ran out. The man and woman moved their camp away. The woman made a brush house but the deer came and ate off all the leaves. She made another brush shelter. The deer ate it again. The woman took up the fire poker and hitting the deer with it, said, "Deer will have a sense of smell." Then they went off a little way from her. The next day they went farther away where they could not be seen.

"Turkeys shall live in the mountains and people will live upon them," she said. Then the woman was hungry and she went to the east saying "What has become of my children, all having the same kind of horns?" Then she went to the south and shouted, "Where have you gone, you that have bodies alike? Come back here." Then she went west. "My children, where have you gone, you that have tails alike, come back here." Then she went to the north, "My children, where have you gone, you that have ears alike, come back here."

From that direction, from the north, they came running back. They ran and surrounded her. From the west also they came and surrounded her. She killed a large number of them. "Now you may go and live in the mountains. People will live upon you. You shall have a sense of smell. People will live upon you." Then the corn was all that belonged to them.

The First Fire

IN THE BEGINNING there was no fire and the world was cold. Then the Thunders, who lived up in Galun'lati, sent their lightning and put fire into the bottom of a hollow sycamore tree which grew on an island. The animals knew it was there because they could see the smoke coming out at the top, but they could not get to it on account of the water, so they held a council to decide what to do. This was a long, long time ago.

Every animal was anxious to go after the fire. Raven offered. He was large and strong, so he was sent first. He flew high and far across the water, and lighted on the sycamore tree. There he perched, wondering what to do next. Then he looked at himself. The heat had scorched his feathers black. Raven was so frightened he flew back across the water without any fire.

Then little Wa-hu-hu, the Screech Owl, offered to go. He flew high and far across the water and perched upon a hollow tree. As he sat there looking into the hollow tree, wondering what to do, a blast of hot air came up and hurt his eyes. Screech Owl was frightened. He flew back as best he could, because he could hardly see. That is why his eyes are red even to this day.

Then Hooting Owl and the Horned Owl went, but by the time they reached the hollow tree, the fire was blazing so fiercely that the smoke nearly blinded them. The ashes carried up by the breeze made white rings around their eyes. So they had to come home without fire. Therefore they have white rings around their eyes.

None of the rest of the birds would go to the fire. Then Uk-su-hi, the racer snake, said he would go through the water and bring back fire. He swam to the island and crawled through the grass to the tree. Then he went into the tree by a small hole at the bottom. But the heat and smoke were dreadful. The ground at the bottom of the tree was covered with hot ashes. The racer darted back and forth trying to get off the ashes, and at last managed to escape through the same hole by which he had entered. But his body had been burned black. Therefore he is now the black racer. And that is why the black racer darts around and doubles on his track as if trying to escape.

Then great Blacksnake, 'The Climber,' offered to go for fire. He was much larger than the black racer. Blacksnake swam over to the island and climbed up the tree on the outside, as the blacksnake always does, but when he put his head down into the hole the smoke choked him so that he fell into the burning stump. Before he could climb out, he, too, was burned black.

So the birds, and the animals, and the snakes held another council. The world was still very cold. There was no fire. But all the birds, and the snakes, and all the four-footed animals refused to go for fire. They were all afraid of the burning sycamore.

Then Water Spider said she would go. This is not the water spider that looks like a mosquito, but the other one – the one with black downy hair and red stripes on her body. She could run on top of the water, or dive to the bottom.

The animals said, "How can you bring back fire?"

But Water Spider spun a thread from her body and wove it into a tusti bowl which she fastened on her back. Then she swam over to the island and through the grass to the fire. Water Spider put one little coal of fire into her bowl, and then swam back with it.

That is how fire came to the world. And that is why Water Spider has a tusti bowl on her back.

Origin of Strawberries

THE FOLLOWING IS a Cherokee story about the first strawberries. When the world was new, there was one man and one woman. They were happy; then they quarreled. At last the woman left the man and began to walk away toward the Sunland, the Eastland. The man followed. He felt sorry, but the woman walked straight on. She did not look back.

Then Sun, the great Apportioner, was sorry for the man. He said:

"Are you still angry with your wife?"

The man said, "No."

Sun said, "Would you like to have her come back to you?"

"Yes," said the man.

So Sun made a great patch of huckleberries which he placed in front of the woman's trail. She passed them without paying any attention to them. Then Sun made a clump of blackberry bushes and put those in front of her trail. The woman walked on. Then Sun created beautiful service-berry bushes which stood beside the trail. Still the woman walked on.

So Sun made other fruits and berries. But the woman did not look at them.

Then Sun created a patch of beautiful ripe strawberries. They were the first strawberries. When the woman saw those, she stopped to gather a few. As she gathered them, she turned her face toward the west. Then she remembered the man. She turned to the Sunland but could not go on. She could not go any further.

Then the woman picked some of the strawberries and started back on her trail, away from the Sunland. So her husband met her, and they went back together.

Origin of Disease and Medicine

IN THE OLD days the beasts, birds, fishes, insects and plants could all talk, and they and the people lived together in peace and friendship. But as time went on, the people increased so rapidly that their settlements spread over the whole earth, and the poor animals found themselves beginning to be cramped for room. This was bad enough, but to make it worse Man invented bows, knives, blowguns, spears and hooks, and began to slaughter the larger animals, birds, and fishes for their flesh or their skins, while the smaller creatures, such as the frogs and worms, were crushed and trodden upon without thought, out of pure carelessness or contempt. So the animals resolved to consult upon measures for their common safety.

The Bears were the first to meet in council in their townhouse under Kuwâ'hĭ mountain, the 'Mulberry place', and the old White Bear chief presided. After each in turn had complained of the way in which Man killed their friends, ate their flesh, and used their skins for his own purposes, it was decided to begin war at once against him. Someone asked what weapons Man used to destroy them. "Bows and arrows, of course," cried all the Bears in chorus. "And what are they made of?" was the next question. "The bow of wood, and the string of our entrails," replied one of the Bears. It was then proposed that they make a bow and some arrows and see if they could not use the same weapons against Man himself. So one Bear got a nice piece of locust wood and another sacrificed himself for the good of the rest in order to furnish a piece of his entrails for the string. But when everything was ready and the first Bear stepped up to make the trial, it was found that in letting the arrow fly after drawing back the bow, his long claws caught the string and spoiled the shot. This was annoying, but someone suggested that they might trim his claws, which was accordingly done, and on a second trial it was found that the arrow went straight to the mark. But here the chief, the old White Bear, objected, saying it was necessary that they should have long claws in order to be able to climb trees. "One of us has already died to furnish the bowstring, and if we now cut off our claws we must all starve together. It is better to trust to the teeth and claws that nature gave us, for it is plain that man's weapons were not intended for us."

No one could think of any better plan, so the old chief dismissed the council and the Bears dispersed to the woods and thickets without having concerted any way to prevent the increase of the human race. Had the result of the council been otherwise, we should now be at war with the Bears, but as it is, the hunter does not even ask the Bear's pardon when he kills one.

The Deer next held a council under their chief, the Little Deer, and after some talk decided to send rheumatism to every hunter who should kill one of them unless he took care to ask their pardon for the offense. They sent notice of their decision to the nearest settlement of Indians and told them at the same time what to do when necessity forced them to kill one of the Deer tribe. Now, whenever the hunter shoots a Deer, the Little Deer, who is swift as the wind and cannot be wounded, runs quickly up to the spot and, bending over the blood-stains, asks the spirit of the Deer if it has heard the prayer of the hunter for pardon. If the reply be "Yes," all is well, and the Little Deer goes on his way; but if the reply be "No," he follows on the trail of the hunter, guided by the drops of blood on the ground, until he arrives at his cabin in the settlement, when the Little Deer enters invisibly and strikes the hunter with rheumatism, so that he becomes at once a helpless cripple. No hunter who has regard for his health ever fails to ask pardon of the Deer for killing it, although some hunters who have not learned the prayer may try to turn aside the Little Deer from his pursuit by building a fire behind them in the trail.

Next came the Fishes and Reptiles, who had their own complaints against Man. They held their council together and determined to make their victims dream of snakes twining about them in slimy folds and blowing foul breath in their faces, or to make them dream of eating raw or decaying fish, so that they would lose appetite, sicken, and die. This is why people dream about snakes and fish.

Finally the Birds, Insects, and smaller animals came together for the same purpose, and the Grubworm was chief of the council. It was decided that each in turn should give an opinion, and then they would vote on the question as to whether or not Man was guilty. Seven votes should be enough to condemn him. One after another denounced Man's cruelty and injustice toward the other animals and voted in favour of his death. The Frog spoke first, saying, "We must do something to check the increase of the race, or people will become so numerous that we shall be crowded from off the earth. See how they have kicked me about because I'm ugly, as they say, until my back is covered with sores," and here he showed the spots on his skin. Next came the Bird – no one remembers now which one it was – who condemned Man, "because he burns my feet off," meaning the way in which the hunter barbecues birds by impaling them on a stick set over the fire, so that their feathers and tender feet are singed off. Others followed in the same strain. The Ground-squirrel alone ventured to say a good word for Man, who seldom hurt him because he was so small, but this made the others so angry that they fell upon the Ground-squirrel and tore him with their claws, and the stripes are on his back to this day.

They began then to devise and name so many new diseases, one after another, that had not their invention at last failed them, no one of the human race would have been able to survive. The Grubworm grew constantly more pleased as the name of each disease was called off, until at last they reached the end of the list, when someone proposed to make menstruation sometimes fatal to women. On this he rose up in his place and cried, "*Wadâñ'!* (Thanks!) I'm glad some more of them will die, for they are getting so thick that they tread on me." The thought fairly made him shake with joy, so that he fell over backward and could not get on his feet again, but had to wriggle off on his back, as the Grubworm has done ever since.

When the Plants, who were friendly to Man, heard what had been done by the animals, they determined to defeat the latters' evil designs. Each Tree, Shrub and Herb, down even to the Grasses and Mosses, agreed to furnish a cure for some one of the diseases named, and each said, "I shall appear to help Man when he calls upon me in his need." Thus came medicine; and the plants, every one of which has its use if we only knew it, furnish the remedy to counteract the evil wrought by the revengeful animals. Even weeds were made for some good purpose, which we must find out for ourselves. When the doctor does not know what medicine to use for a sick man, the spirit of the plant tells him.

Origin of the Pleiades and the Pine

LONG AGO, WHEN the world was new, there were seven boys who used to spend all their time down by the townhouse playing the gatayû'stĭ game, rolling a stone wheel along the ground and sliding a curved stick after it to strike it. Their mothers scolded, but it did no good, so one day they collected some gatayû'stĭ stones and boiled them in the pot with the corn for dinner. When the boys came home hungry their mothers dipped out the stones and said, "Since you like the gatayû'stĭ better than the cornfield, take the stones now for your dinner."

The boys were very angry, and went down to the townhouse, saying, "As our mothers treat us this way, let us go where we shall never trouble them anymore." They began a dance – some say it was the Feather Dance – and went round and round the townhouse, praying to the spirits to help them. At last, their mothers were afraid something was wrong and went out to look for them. They saw the boys still dancing around the townhouse, and as they watched they noticed that their feet were off the earth, and that with every round they rose higher and higher in the air. They ran to get their children, but it was too late, for they were already above the roof of the townhouse – all but one, whose mother managed to pull him down with the gatayû′stĭ pole, but he struck the ground with such force that he sank into it and the earth closed over him.

The other six circled higher and higher until they went up to the sky, where we see them now as the Pleiades, which the Cherokee still call Ani′tsutsă (The Boys). The people grieved long after them, but the mother whose boy had gone into the ground came every morning and every evening to cry over the spot until the earth was damp with her tears. At last a little green shoot sprouted up and grew day by day until it became the tall tree that we call now the pine, and the pine is of the same nature as the stars and holds in itself the same bright light.

Ojeeg Annung, or The Summer Maker

THERE LIVED A celebrated hunter on the southern shores of Lake Superior, who was considered a Manito by some, for there was nothing but what he could accomplish. He lived off the path, in a wild, lonesome, place, with a wife whom he loved, and they were blessed with a son, who had attained his thirteenth year. The hunter's name was Ojeeg, or the Fisher, which is the name of an expert, sprightly little animal common to the region. He was so successful in the chase, that he seldom returned without bringing his wife and son a plentiful supply of venison, or other dainties of the woods. As hunting formed his constant occupation, his son began early to emulate his father in the same employment, and would take his bow and arrows, and exert his skill in trying to kill birds and squirrels. The greatest impediment he met with, was the coldness and severity of the climate. He often returned home, his little fingers benumbed with cold, and crying with vexation at his disappointment. Days, and months, and years passed away, but still the same perpetual depth of snow was seen, covering all the country as with a white cloak.

One day, after a fruitless trial of his forest skill, the little boy was returning homeward with a heavy heart, when he saw a small red squirrel gnawing the top of a pine bur. He had approached within a proper distance to shoot, when the squirrel sat up on its hind legs and thus addressed him:

"My grandchild, put up your arrows, and listen to what I have to tell you." The boy complied rather reluctantly, when the squirrel continued: "My son, I see you pass frequently, with your fingers benumbed with cold, and crying with vexation for not having killed any birds. Now, if you will follow my advice, we will see if you cannot accomplish your wishes. If you will strictly pursue my advice, we will have perpetual summer, and you will then have the pleasure of killing as many birds as you please; and I will also have something to eat, as I am now myself on the point of starvation.

"Listen to me. As soon as you get home you must commence crying. You must throw away your bow and arrows in discontent. If your mother asks you what is the matter, you must not answer her, but continue crying and sobbing. If she offers you anything to eat, you must push it away with apparent discontent, and continue crying. In the evening, when your father returns from hunting, he will inquire of your mother what is the matter with you. She will answer that you came home crying, and would not so much as mention the cause to her. All this while you must not leave off sobbing. At last your father will say, 'My son, why is this unnecessary grief? Tell me the cause. You know I am a spirit, and that nothing is impossible for me to perform.' You must then answer him, and say that you are sorry to see the snow continually on the ground, and ask him if he could not cause it to melt, so that we might have perpetual summer. Say it in a supplicating way, and tell him this is the cause of your grief. Your father will reply, 'It is very hard to accomplish your request, but for your sake, and for my love for you, I will use my utmost endeavors.' He will tell you to be still, and cease crying. He will try to bring summer with all its loveliness. You must then be quiet, and eat that which is set before you."

The squirrel ceased. The boy promised obedience to his advice, and departed. When he reached home, he did as he had been instructed, and all was exactly fulfilled, as it had been predicted by the squirrel.

Ojeeg told him that it was a great undertaking. He must first make a feast, and invite some of his friends to accompany him on a journey. Next day he had a bear roasted whole. All who had been invited to the feast came punctually to the appointment. There were the Otter, Beaver, Lynx, Badger, and Wolverine. After the feast, they arranged it among themselves to set out on the contemplated journey in three days. When the time arrived, the Fisher took leave of his wife and son, as he foresaw that it was for the last time. He and his companions travelled in company day after day, meeting with nothing but the ordinary incidents. On the twentieth day they arrived at the foot of a high mountain, where they saw the tracks of some person who had recently killed an animal, which they knew by the blood that marked the way. The Fisher told his friends that they ought to follow the track, and see if they could not procure something to eat. They followed it for some time; at last they arrived at a lodge, which had been hidden from their view by a hollow in the mountain. Ojeeg told his friends to be very sedate, and not to laugh on any account. The first object that they saw was a man standing at the door of the lodge, but of so deformed a shape that they could not possibly make out who or what sort of a man it could be. His head was enormously large; he had such a queer set of teeth, and no arms. They wondered how he could kill animals. But the secret was soon revealed. He was a great Manito. He invited them to pass the night, to which they consented.

He boiled his meat in a hollow vessel made of wood, and took it out of this singular kettle in some way unknown to his guests. He carefully gave each their portion to eat, but made so many odd movements that the Otter could not refrain from laughing, for he is the only one who is spoken of as a jester. The Manito looked at him with a terrible look, and then made a spring at him, and got on him to smother him, for that was his mode of killing animals. But the Otter, when he felt him on his neck, slipped his head back and made for the door, which he passed in safety; but went out with the curse of the Manito. The others passed the night, and they conversed on different subjects. The Manito told the Fisher that he would accomplish his object, but that it would probably cost him his life. He gave them his advice, directed them how to act, and described a certain road which they must follow, and they would thereby be led to the place of action.

They set off in the morning, and met their friend, the Otter, shivering with cold; but Ojeeg had taken care to bring along some of the meat that had been given him, which he presented to his friend. They pursued their way, and travelled twenty days more before they got to the place which the Manito had told them of. It was a most lofty mountain. They rested on its highest peak to fill their pipes and refresh themselves. Before smoking, they made the customary ceremony, pointing to the heavens, the four winds, the earth, and the zenith; in the mean time, speaking in a loud voice, addressed the Great Spirit, hoping that their object would be accomplished. They then commenced smoking.

They gazed on the sky in silent admiration and astonishment, for they were on so elevated a point, that it appeared to be only a short distance above their heads. After they had finished smoking, they prepared themselves. Ojeeg told the Otter to make the first attempt to try and make a hole in the sky. He consented with a grin. He made a leap, but fell down the hill stunned by the force of his fall; and the snow being moist, and falling on his back, he slid with velocity down the side of the mountain. When he found himself at the bottom, he thought to himself, it is the last time I make such another jump, so I will make the best of my way home. Then it was the turn of the Beaver, who made the attempt, but fell down senseless; then of the Lynx and Badger, who had no better success.

"Now," says Fisher to the Wolverine, "try your skill; your ancestors were celebrated for their activity, hardihood, and perseverance, and I depend on you for success. Now make the attempt." He did so, but also without success. He leaped the second time, but now they could see that the sky was giving way to their repeated attempts. Mustering strength, he made the third leap, and went in. The Fisher nimbly followed him.

They found themselves in a beautiful plain, extending as far as the eye could reach, covered with flowers of a thousand different hues and fragrance. Here and there were clusters of tall, shady trees, separated by innumerable streams of the purest water, which wound around their courses under the cooling shades, and filled the plain with countless beautiful lakes, whose banks and bosom were covered with water-fowl, basking and sporting in the sun. The trees were alive with birds of different plumage, warbling their sweet notes, and delighted with perpetual spring.

The Fisher and his friend beheld very long lodges, and the celestial inhabitants amusing themselves at a distance. Words cannot express the beauty and charms of the place. The lodges were empty of inhabitants, but they saw them lined with mocuks of different sizes, filled with birds and fowls of different plumage. Ojeeg thought of his son, and immediately commenced cutting open the mocuks and letting out the birds, who descended in whole flocks through the opening which they had made. The warm air of those regions also rushed down through the opening, and spread its genial influence over the north.

When the celestial inhabitants saw the birds let loose, and the warm gales descending, they raised a shout like thunder, and ran for their lodges. But it was too late. Spring, summer, and autumn had gone; even perpetual summer had almost all gone; but they separated it with a blow, and only a part descended; but the ends were so mangled, that, wherever it prevails among the lower inhabitants, it is always sickly.

When the Wolverine heard the noise, he made for the opening and safely descended. Not so the Fisher. Anxious to fulfil his son's wishes, he continued to break open the mocuks. He was, at last, obliged to run also, but the opening was now closed by the inhabitants. He ran with all his might over the plains of heaven, and, it would appear, took a northerly direction. He saw his pursuers so close that he had to climb the first large tree he came to. They commenced shooting at him with their arrows, but without effect, for all his body was invulnerable except the space of about an inch near the tip of his tail. At last one of the arrows hit the spot, for he had in this chase assumed the shape of the Fisher after whom he was named.

He looked down from the tree, and saw some among his assailants with the totems of his ancestors. He claimed relationship, and told them to desist, which they only did at the approach of night. He then came down to try and find an opening in the celestial plain, by which he might descend to the earth. But he could find none. At last, becoming faint from the loss of blood from the wound on his tail, he laid himself down towards the north of the plain, and, stretching out his limbs, said, "I have fulfilled my promise to my son, though it has cost me my life; but I die satisfied in the idea that I have done so much good, not only for him, but for my fellow-beings. Hereafter I will be a sign to the inhabitants below for ages to come, who will venerate my name for having succeeded in procuring the varying seasons. They will now have from eight to ten moons without snow."

He was found dead next morning, but they left him as they found him, with the arrow sticking in his tail, as it can be plainly seen, at this time, in the heavens.

Peboan and Seegwun

AN OLD MAN was sitting in his lodge, by the side of a frozen stream. It was the close of winter, and his fire was almost out. He appeared very old and very desolate. His locks were white with age, and he trembled in every joint. Day after day passed in solitude, and he heard nothing but the sounds of the tempest, sweeping before it the new-fallen snow.

One day, as his fire was just dying, a handsome young man approached and entered his dwelling. His cheeks were red with the blood of youth, his eyes sparkled with animation, and a smile played upon his lips. He walked with a light and quick step. His forehead was bound with a wreath of sweet grass, in place of a warrior's frontlet, and he carried a bunch of flowers in his hand.

"Ah, my son," said the old man, "I am happy to see you. Come in. Come, tell me of your adventures, and what strange lands you have been to see. Let us pass the night together. I will tell you of my prowess and exploits, and what I can perform. You shall do the same, and we will amuse ourselves."

He then drew from his sack a curiously-wrought antique pipe, and having filled it with tobacco, rendered mild by an admixture of certain leaves, handed it to his guest. When this ceremony was concluded they began to speak.

"I blow my breath," said the old man, "and the streams stand still. The water becomes stiff and hard as clear stone."

"I breathe," said the young man, "and flowers spring up all over the plains."

"I shake my locks," retorted the old man, "and snow covers the land. The leaves fall from the trees at my command, and my breath blows them away. The birds get up from the water, and fly to a distant land. The animals hide themselves from my breath, and the very ground becomes as hard as flint."

"I shake my ringlets," rejoined the young man, "and warm showers of soft rain fall upon the earth. The plants lift up their heads out of the earth, like the eyes of children glistening with delight. My voice recalls the birds. The warmth of my breath unlocks the streams. Music fills the groves wherever I walk, and all nature rejoices."

At length the sun began to rise. A gentle warmth came over the place. The tongue of the old man became silent. The robin and bluebird began to sing on the top of the lodge. The stream began to murmur by the door, and the fragrance of growing herbs and flowers came softly on the vernal breeze.

Daylight fully revealed to the young man the character of his entertainer. When he looked upon him, he had the icy visage of Peboan. Streams began to flow from his eyes. As the sun increased, he grew less and less in stature, and anon had melted completely away. Nothing remained on the place of his lodge fire but the miskodeed, a small white flower, with a pink border, which is one of the earliest species of northern plants.

Nezhik-e-wä-wä-sun, or The Lone Lightning

A LITTLE ORPHAN boy who had no one to care for him, was once living with his uncle, who treated him very badly, making him do hard things and giving him very little to eat; so that the boy pined away, he never grew much, and became, through hard usage, very thin and light. At last the uncle felt ashamed of this treatment, and determined to make amends for it, by fattening him up, but his real object was, to kill him by over-feeding. He told his wife to give the boy plenty of bear's meat, and let him have the fat, which is thought to be the best part. They were both very assiduous in cramming him, and one day came near choking him to death, by forcing the fat down his throat. The boy escaped and fled from the lodge. He knew not where to go, but wandered about. When night came on, he was afraid the wild beasts would eat him, so he climbed up into the forks of a high pine tree, and there he fell asleep in the branches, and had an aupoway, or ominous dream.

A person appeared to him from the upper sky, and said, "My poor little lad, I pity you, and the bad usage you have received from your uncle has led me to visit you: follow me, and step in my tracks." Immediately his sleep left him, and he rose up and followed his guide, mounting up higher and higher into the air, until he reached the upper sky. Here twelve arrows were put into his hands, and he was told that there were a great many manitoes in the northern sky, against whom he must go to war, and try to waylay and shoot them. Accordingly he went to that part of the sky, and, at long intervals, shot arrow after arrow, until he had expended eleven, in vain attempt to kill the manitoes. At the flight of each arrow, there was a long and solitary streak of lightning in the sky – then all was clear again, and not a cloud or spot could be seen. The twelfth arrow he held a long time in his hands, and looked around keenly on every side to spy the manitoes he was after. But these manitoes were very cunning, and could change their form in a moment. All they feared was the boy's arrows, for these were magic arrows, which had been given to him by a good spirit, and had power to kill them, if aimed aright. At length, the boy drew up his last arrow, settled in his aim, and let fly, as he thought, into the very heart of the chief of the manitoes; but before the arrow reached him, the manito changed himself into a rock. Into this rock, the head of the arrow sank deep and stuck fast.

"Now your gifts are all expended," cried the enraged manito, "and I will make an example of your audacity and pride of heart, for lifting your bow against me" – and so saying, he transformed the boy into the Nezhik-e-wä wä sun, or Lone Lightning, which may be observed in the northern sky, to this day.

Opeechee, or The Origin of the Robin

AN OLD MAN had an only son named Opeechee, who had come to that age which is thought to be most proper to make the long and final fast, that is to secure through life a guardian genius or spirit. In the influence of this choice, it is well known, our people have relied for their prosperity in after life; it was, therefore, an event of deep importance.

The old man was ambitious that his son should surpass all others in whatever was deemed most wise and great among his tribe; and, to fulfil his wishes, he thought it necessary that he should fast a much longer time than any of those persons, renowned for their prowess or wisdom, whose fame he coveted. He therefore directed his son to prepare, with great ceremony, for the important event. After he had been in the sweating lodge and bath several times, he ordered him to lie down upon a clean mat, in a little lodge expressly prepared for him; telling him, at the same time, to endure his fast like a man, and that, at the expiration of twelve days, he should receive food and the blessing of his father.

The lad carefully observed this injunction, lying with perfect composure, with his face covered, awaiting those mystic visitations which were to seal his good or evil fortune. His father visited him regularly every morning, to encourage him to perseverance, expatiating at length on the honor and renown that would attend him through life if he accomplished the full term prescribed. To these admonitions and encouragements the boy never replied, but lay, without the least sign of discontent or murmuring, until the ninth day, when he addressed his father as follows:

"My father, my dreams forebode evil. May I break my fast now, and at a more propitious time make a new fast?" The father answered:

"My son, you know not what you ask. If you get up now, all your glory will depart. Wait patiently a little longer. You have but three days yet to accomplish your desire. You know it is for your own good, and I encourage you to persevere."

The son assented; and, covering himself closer, he lay till the eleventh day, when he repeated his request. Very nearly the same answer was given him by his father, who added that the next day he would himself prepare his first meal, and bring it to him. The boy remained silent, but lay as motionless as a corpse. No one would have known he was living but by the gentle heaving of his breast.

The next morning, the father, elated at having gained his end, prepared a repast for his son, and hastened to set it before him. On coming to the door, he was surprised to hear his son talking to himself. He stooped to listen; and, looking through a small aperture, was more astonished when he beheld his son painted with vermilion over all his breast, and in the act of finishing his work by laying on the paint as far back on his shoulders as he could reach with his hands, saying, at the same time, to himself, "My father has destroyed my fortune as a man. He would not listen to my requests. He will be the loser. I shall be forever happy in my new state, for I have been obedient to my parent; he alone will be the sufferer, for my guardian spirit is a just one; though not propitious to me in the manner I desired, he has shown me pity in another way; he has given me another shape; and now I must go."

At this moment the old man broke in, exclaiming, "My son! my son! I pray you leave me not." But the young man, with the quickness of a bird, had flown to the top of the lodge, and perched himself on the highest pole, having been changed into a beautiful robin redbreast.

He looked down upon his father with pity beaming in his eyes, and addressed him as follows: "Regret not, my father, the change you behold. I shall be happier in my present state than I could have been as a man. I shall always be the friend of men, and keep near their dwellings. I shall ever be happy and contented; and although I could not gratify your wishes as a warrior, it will be my daily aim to make you amends for it as a harbinger of peace and joy. I will cheer you by my songs, and strive to inspire in others the joy and lightsomeness I feel in my present state. This will be some compensation to you for the loss of the glory you expected. I am now free from the cares and pains of human life. My food is spontaneously furnished by the mountains and fields, and my pathway of life is in the bright air." Then stretching himself on his toes, as if delighted with the gift of wings, he carolled one of his sweetest songs, and flew away into a neighboring grove.

Mon-daw-min, or The Origin of Indian Corn

IN TIMES PAST, a poor Indian was living with his wife and children in a beautiful part of the country. He was not only poor, but inexpert in procuring food for his family, and his children were all too young to give him assistance. Although poor, he was a man of a kind and contented disposition. He was always thankful to the Great Spirit for everything he received. The same disposition was inherited by his eldest son, who had now arrived at the proper age to undertake the ceremony of the Ke-ig-uish-im-o-win, or fast, to see what kind of a spirit would be his guide and guardian through life. Wunzh, for this was his name, had been an obedient boy from his infancy, and was of a pensive, thoughtful, and mild disposition, so that he was beloved by the whole family. As soon as the first indications of spring appeared, they built him the customary little lodge at a retired spot, some distance from their own, where he would not be disturbed during this solemn rite. In the mean time he prepared himself, and immediately went into it, and commenced his fast. The first few days, he amused himself, in the mornings, by walking in the woods and over the mountains, examining the early plants and flowers, and in this way prepared himself to enjoy his sleep, and, at the same time, stored his mind with pleasant ideas for his dreams. While he rambled through the woods, he felt a strong desire to know how the plants, herbs, and berries grew, without any aid from man, and why it was that some species were good to eat, and others possessed medicinal or poisonous juices. He recalled these thoughts to mind after he became too languid to walk about, and had confined himself strictly to the lodge; he wished he could dream of something that would prove a benefit to his father and family, and to all others. "True!" he thought, "the Great Spirit made all things, and it is to him that we owe our lives. But could he not make it easier for us to get our food, than by hunting animals and taking fish? I must try to find out this in my visions."

On the third day he became weak and faint, and kept his bed. He fancied, while thus lying, that he saw a handsome young man coming down from the sky and advancing towards him. He was richly and gayly dressed, having on a great many garments of green and yellow colors, but differing in their deeper or lighter shades. He had a plume of waving feathers on his head, and all his motions were graceful.

"I am sent to you, my friend," said the celestial visitor, "by that Great Spirit who made all things in the sky and on the earth. He has seen and knows your motives in fasting. He sees that it is from a kind and benevolent wish to do good to your people, and to procure a benefit for them, and that you do not seek for strength in war or the praise of warriors. I am sent to instruct you, and show you how you can do your kindred good." He then told the young man to arise, and prepare to wrestle with him, as it was only by this means that he could hope to succeed in his wishes. Wunzh knew he was weak from fasting, but he felt his courage rising in his heart, and immediately got up, determined to die rather than fail. He commenced the trial, and after a protracted effort, was almost exhausted, when the beautiful stranger said, "My friend, it is enough for once; I will come again to try you;" and, smiling on him, he ascended in the air in the same direction from which he came. The next day the celestial visitor reappeared at the same hour and renewed the trial. Wunzh felt that his strength was even less than the day before, but the courage of his mind seemed to increase in proportion as his body became weaker. Seeing this, the stranger again spoke to him in the same words he used before, adding, "Tomorrow will be your last trial. Be strong, my friend, for this is the only way you can overcome me, and obtain the boon you seek." On the third day he again appeared at the same time and renewed the struggle. The poor youth was very faint in body, but grew stronger in mind at every contest, and was determined to prevail or perish in the attempt. He exerted his utmost powers, and after the contest had been continued the usual time, the stranger ceased his efforts and declared himself conquered. For the first time he entered the lodge, and sitting down beside the youth, he began to deliver his instructions to him, telling him in what manner he should proceed to take advantage of his victory.

"You have won your desires of the Great Spirit," said the stranger. "You have wrestled manfully. To-morrow will be the seventh day of your fasting. Your father will give you food to strengthen you, and as it is the last day of trial, you will prevail. I know this, and now tell you what you must do to benefit your family and your tribe. To-morrow," he repeated, "I shall meet you and wrestle with you for the last time; and, as soon as you have prevailed against me, you will strip off my garments and throw me down, clean the earth of roots and weeds, make it soft, and bury me in the spot. When you have done this, leave my body in the earth, and do not disturb it, but come occasionally to visit the place, to see whether I have come to life, and be careful never to let the grass or weeds grow on my grave. Once a month cover me with fresh earth. If you follow my instructions, you will accomplish your object of doing good to your fellow-creatures by teaching them the knowledge I now teach you." He then shook him by the hand and disappeared.

In the morning the youth's father came with some slight refreshments, saying, "My son, you have fasted long enough. If the Great Spirit will favor you, he will do it now. It is seven days since you have tasted food, and you must not sacrifice your life. The Master of Life does not require that." "My father," replied the youth, "wait till the sun goes down. I have a particular reason for extending my fast to that hour." "Very well," said the old man, "I shall wait till the hour arrives, and you feel inclined to eat."

At the usual hour of the day the sky-visitor returned, and the trial of strength was renewed. Although the youth had not availed himself of his father's offer of food, he felt that new strength had been given to him, and that exertion had renewed his strength and fortified his courage.

He grasped his angelic antagonist with supernatural strength, threw him down, took from him his beautiful garments and plume, and finding him dead, immediately buried him on the spot, taking all the precautions he had been told of, and being very confident, at the same time, that his friend would again come to life. He then returned to his father's lodge, and partook sparingly of the meal that had been prepared for him. But he never for a moment forgot the grave of his friend. He carefully visited it throughout the spring, and weeded out the grass, and kept the ground in a soft and pliant state. Very soon he saw the tops of the green plumes coming through the ground; and the more careful he was to obey his instructions in keeping the ground in order, the faster they grew. He was, however, careful to conceal the exploit from his father. Days and weeks had passed in this way. The summer was now drawing towards a close, when one day, after a long absence in hunting, Wunzh invited his father to follow him to the quiet and lonesome spot of his former fast. The lodge had been removed, and the weeds kept from growing on the circle where it stood, but in its place stood a tall and graceful plant, with bright-colored silken hair, surmounted with nodding plumes and stately leaves, and golden clusters on each side. "It is my friend," shouted the lad; "it is the friend of all mankind. It is Mondawmin. We need no longer rely on hunting alone; for, as long as this gift is cherished and taken care of, the ground itself will give us a living." He then pulled an ear. "See, my father," said he, "this is what I fasted for. The great Spirit has listened to my voice, and sent us something new, and henceforth our people will not alone depend upon the chase or upon the waters."

He then communicated to his father the instructions given him by the stranger. He told him that the broad husks must be torn away, as he had pulled off the garments in his wrestling; and having done this, directed him how the ear must be held before the fire till the outer skin became brown, while all the milk was retained in the grain. The whole family then united in a feast on the newly-grown ears, expressing gratitude to the Merciful Spirit who gave it. So corn came into the world.

The Star Family, or Celestial Sisters

WAUPEE, OR THE White Hawk, lived in a remote part of the forest, where animals and birds were abundant. Every day he returned from the chase with the reward of his toil, for he was one of the most skilful and celebrated hunters of his tribe. With a tall, manly form, and the fire of youth beaming from his eye, there was no forest too gloomy for him to penetrate, and no track made by the numerous kinds of birds and beasts which he could not follow.

One day he penetrated beyond any point which he had before visited. He travelled through an open forest, which enabled him to see a great distance. At length he beheld a light breaking through the foliage, which made him sure that he was on the borders of a prairie. It was a wide plain covered with grass and flowers. After walking some time without a path, he suddenly came to a ring worn through the sod, as if it had been made by footsteps following a circle. But what excited his surprise was, that there was no path leading to or from it. Not the least trace of footsteps could be found, even in a crushed leaf or broken twig. He thought he would hide himself, and lie in wait to see what this circle meant. Presently he heard the faint sounds of music in the air. He looked up in the direction they came from, and saw a small object descending from above. At first it looked like a mere speck, but rapidly increased, and, as it came down, the music became plainer and sweeter. It assumed the form of a basket, and was filled with twelve sisters of the most lovely forms and enchanting beauty. As soon as the basket touched the ground, they leaped out, and began to dance round the magic ring, striking, as they did so, a shining ball as we strike the drum. Waupee gazed upon their graceful forms and motions from his place of concealment. He admired them all, but was most pleased with the youngest. Unable longer to restrain his admiration, he rushed out and endeavored to seize her. But the sisters, with the quickness of birds, the moment they descried the form of a man, leaped back into the basket and were drawn up into the sky.

Regretting his ill luck and indiscretion, he gazed till he saw them disappear, and then said, "They are gone, and I shall see them no more." He returned to his solitary lodge, but found no relief to his mind. Next day he went back to the prairie, and took his station near the ring; but in order to deceive the sisters, he assumed the form of an opossum. He had not waited long, when he saw the wicker car descend, and heard the same sweet music. They commenced the same sportive dance, and seemed even more beautiful and graceful than before. He crept slowly towards the ring, but the instant the sisters saw him they were startled, and sprang into their car. It rose but a short distance, when one of the elder sisters spoke. "Perhaps," said she, "it is come to show us how the game is played by mortals." "Oh no!" the youngest replied; "quick, let us ascend." And all joining in a chant, they rose out of sight.

Waupee returned to his own form again, and walked sorrowfully back to his lodge. But the night seemed a very long one, and he went back betimes the next day. He reflected upon the sort of plan to follow to secure success. He found an old stump near by, in which there were a number of mice. He thought their small form would not create alarm, and accordingly assumed it. He brought the stump and sat it up near the ring. The sisters came down and resumed their sport. "But see," cried the younger sister, "that stump was not there before." She ran affrighted towards the car. They only smiled, and gathering round the stump, struck it in jest, when out ran the mice, and Waupee among the rest. They killed them all but one, which was pursued by the youngest sister; but just as she had raised her stick to kill it, the form of Waupee arose, and he clasped his prize in his arms. The other eleven sprang to their basket and were drawn up to the skies.

He exerted all his skill to please his bride and win her affections. He wiped the tears from her eyes. He related his adventures in the chase. He dwelt upon the charms of life on the earth. He was incessant in his attentions, and picked out the way for her to walk as he led her gently towards his lodge. He felt his heart glow with joy as she entered it, and from that moment he was one of the happiest of men. Winter and summer passed rapidly away, and their happiness was increased by the addition of a beautiful boy to their lodge. She was a daughter of one the stars, and as the scenes of earth began to pall her sight, she sighed to revisit her father. But she was obliged to hide these feelings from her husband. She remembered the charm that would carry her up, and took occasion, while Waupee was engaged in the chase, to construct a wicker basket, which she kept concealed. In the mean time she collected such rarities from the earth as she thought would please her father, as well as the most dainty kinds of food. When all was in readiness, she went out one day, while Waupee was absent, to the charmed ring, taking her little son with her. As soon as they got into the car, she commenced her song and the basket rose. As the song was wafted by the wind, it caught her husband's ear. It was a voice which he well knew, and he instantly ran to the prairie. But he could not reach the ring before he saw his wife and child ascend. He lifted up his voice in loud appeals, but they were unavailing. The basket still went up. He watched it till it became a small speck, and finally it vanished in the sky. He then bent his head down to the ground, and was miserable.

Waupee bewailed his loss through a long winter and a long summer. But he found no relief. He mourned his wife's loss sorely, but his son's still more. In the mean time his wife had reached her home in the stars, and almost forgot, in the blissful employments there, that she had left a husband on the earth. She was reminded of this by the presence of her son, who, as he grew up, became anxious to visit the scene of his birth. His grandfather said to his daughter one day, "Go, my child, and take your son down to his father, and ask him to come up and live with us. But tell him to bring along a specimen of each kind of bird and animal he kills in the chase." She accordingly took the boy and descended. Waupee, who was ever near the enchanted spot, heard her voice as she came down the sky. His heart beat with impatience as he saw her form and that of his son, and they were soon clasped in his arms.

He heard the message of the Star, and began to hunt with the greatest activity, that he might collect the present. He spent whole nights, as well as days, in searching for every curious and beautiful bird or animal. He only preserved a tail, foot, or wing of each, to identify the species; and, when all was ready, they went to the circle and were carried up.

Great joy was manifested on their arrival at the starry plains. The Star Chief invited all his people to a feast, and, when they had assembled, he proclaimed aloud, that each one might take of the earthly gifts such as he liked best. A very strange confusion immediately arose. Some chose a foot, some a wing, some a tail, and some a claw. Those who selected tails or claws were changed into animals, and ran off; the others assumed the form of birds, and flew away. Waupee chose a white hawk's feather. His wife and son followed his example, when each one became a white hawk. Pleased with his transformation, and new vitality, the chief spread out gracefully his white wings, and followed by his wife and son, descended to the earth, where the species are still to be found.

The Winning of Halai Auna at the House of Tuina

OLD PUL MIAUNA had a son, Pun Miaupa, a wife, and two daughters.

Pun Miaupa had a quarrel with his father and made up his mind to leave him. "I am going away," said he to his father and mother one day.

"I am tired of living here."

The mother began to cry.

"Which way are you going?" asked the father.

Pun Miaupa gave no answer; wouldn't tell his father where he was going. The father stood up and walked out of the house. The mother stopped crying and said:

"I want you to go straight to my brother, your uncle Igupa Topa. Tell him where you are going. Do not go without seeing him."

Pun Miaupa left his mother, went to his uncle's, stood on the roof of the sweat-house. The old man was very busy throwing out grass that day. A great many people had gambled at his house a day earlier; they had left much grass in it.

"Uncle, are you alive?" asked Pun Miaupa.

The old uncle looked up and saw his nephew, who said:

"Uncle, I am full grown. I am going on a very long journey, I am going far away. My mother told me to come here and see you."

"Where are you going, my nephew?"

"To the north."

"I thought so," said the old man, who knew that his nephew would go to get Wakara's youngest daughter.

Wakara took all his daughter's suitors to Tuina's sweat-house, and they were killed there. Igupa Topa knew this and said, "Wait a little, nephew, I will go with you."

"Uncle," said Pun Miaupa, "you are too old. I don't want you to go; the journey would kill you. I want to travel very fast on this journey."

"I will go at my own pace, I will go as I like," said the uncle.

"Well, come with me if you can go fast."

Igupa Topa dressed, took a staff, and looked very old. "Go on, I am ready," said he.

Pun Miaupa started. He turned around to look at his uncle, and saw the old man; saw him fall while coming out of the sweat-house. Pun Miaupa stopped, held down his head, and thought, "He will not go, even as far as Wajami."

The uncle rose and followed on.

"You are too old, uncle; you cannot walk well. Stay at home; that is better for you."

"Go ahead," said the old man; "walk fast. I will come as I can."

Pun Miaupa went on; his uncle followed. Igupa Topa stumbled every few steps, fell, hurt himself, tore his skin. Pun Miaupa looked back very often. The uncle was always tumbling. "He must be bruised and broken from these falls," thought the nephew.

Pun Miaupa was on a hill beyond Chichipana. He sat down and smoked. His uncle came up while he was sitting there.

"Let me smoke; then I want to see you jump to that mountain over there," said the old man, pointing to it.

"I shall leave you behind if I do that."

"Leave me to myself," said the old man.

Pun Miaupa put on deerskin leggings and a beaded shirt – a splendid dress. He went then with one spring to the top of the opposite mountain and looked back to see his uncle; but old Igupa Topa had jumped too. He was just passing Pun Miaupa and went far beyond him.

"I thought you were too old to jump," said Pun Miaupa, coming up to him.

They jumped again, jumped to a second mountain, and the uncle was ahead the second time. After that they walked on. The old man fell very often, but Pun Miaupa did not pity him any longer; he laughed when his uncle fell. They travelled a good while, travelled fast, and when both reached Wajami Mountain, they sat down to rest there.

"I want Wakara to send out his youngest daughter for wood," said Pun Miaupa in his mind; and the next minute Wakara, who was far away in his own sweat-house, told his youngest daughter to take a basket and go for wood. This daughter was Halai Auna.

At that moment, too, Wakara's wife, Ochul Marimi, said to the girl: "Why do you lie asleep all the time and not help me? I want you to get me leaves for acorn bread."

Halai Auna took the basket and went upon the mountain side to find wood and leaves. Pun Miaupa saw the girl filling her basket.

"That is Wakara's daughter," said he to his uncle.

"Stop! Be careful!" said Igupa Topa.

The uncle put himself into his nephew's heart now to strengthen him. There was only one person to be seen. Igupa Topa went into his nephew, went in because he knew that Tuina killed all men who tried to get Halai Auna, and he wished to save his sister's son, Pun Miaupa.

When the girl had her basket full and turned to place it on her back, she saw Pun Miaupa behind her; she could not move, she was so frightened.

"Why are you afraid? Am I so ugly?" asked Pun Miaupa.

He pleased her; but she said not a word, just ran, hurried home with the basket, and threw it down at the door.

"What is your trouble?" asked the mother. "You don't like to work, I think."

"What is the matter?" asked Wakara. "You are frightened."

"I saw a man on the mountain, a man with woodpecker scalps on his head."

"The southern people wear woodpecker scalps," said Wakara; "that must be one of the southern people."

Pun Miaupa sprang through the air, came down in front of Wakara's sweat-house, went in and sat near Halai Auna on a bear-skin. Nice food was brought for all, and when they had finished eating, Wakara said:

"Now, my daughters, and you, my wife, Ochul Marima, make ready; let us go. I wish to see my brother, Tuina, and hear what he says of Halai Auna's new husband."

They dressed, put on beads, and put red paint on their faces. Halai Auna said nothing. She sat with her head down; she was sorry; she liked Pun Miaupa, she felt sure that they would kill him.

When all were ready, Wakara took his wife's hand and danced around the fire with her. He had two unmarried daughters besides Halai Auna; one of these took her father's hand, the other took Halai Auna's, and all danced around the fire and circled about Pun Miaupa. They put him in the middle and danced in a circle; they began to sing, and rose in the air then and danced right up out of the sweat-house, went through the smoke-hole and moved westward, singing as they went:

"I-nó, i-nó, i-nó, no-má
I-nó, i-nó, i-nó, no-má."

They moved faster as they went, and danced all the time. It was dark when they danced up through the roof of the sweat-house; no one saw them, though there were many people round about. Old Wakara's sons-in-law lived in that place; all the stars were his daughters, and his daughters were married, except Halai Auna and the two who danced around the fire. Wakara went without being seen. He would let no one have Halai Auna unless one whom Tuina could not kill.

Now, a little before daylight they reached Tuina's house. Wakara stood on the roof of the sweat-house and called, "My brother, I want you to spring out of bed."

Tuina was asleep in the sweat-house. He had three daughters and no son. The daughters were called Wediko, and his wife was Utjamhji. Wakara went down into the sweat-house and sat at the side of Tuina. Tuina took a bear-skin and put it down at his other hand, and told Halai Auna and her husband to sit on it. Tuina took up a big sack of tobacco and a large pipe cut out of maple wood. The tobacco was made of his own hair, rolled and cut fine. He put this in the pipe and gave it to Pun Miaupa. Wakara and Tuina watched now, and looked at him. The young man smoked all the tobacco and gave back the pipe.

Tuina filled the pipe now with a different, a stronger tobacco. He used to rub his skin often, and what he rubbed off he dried and made fine. This was his tobacco of the second kind. He had a sackful of this stored away, and he filled his pipe now with it.

Pun Miaupa smoked, seemed to swallow the smoke. It was not he who was smoking, though, but the uncle in his heart. He emptied the pipe and returned it. Tuina took now tobacco of a third kind – his own flesh dried and rubbed fine. He filled the pipe, gave it to Pun Miaupa, and waited to see him fall dead at the second if not at the first whiff.

The country outside the sweat-house was full of dead people, all killed by Tuina's tobacco. Some of the bodies were fresh, others decayed; some were sound skeletons, others a few old bones.

Pun Miaupa smoked out this pipe, gave it back empty. Tuina handed him a fourth pipe. The tobacco was made of his own brains, dried and rubbed fine. Pun Miaupa smoked this and gave the empty pipe back to Tuina.

Tuina now tried the fifth pipe. He filled it with marrow from his own bones, gave it to Halai Auna's husband. Wakara, and Tuina watched now, waiting to see him fall. Pun Miaupa swallowed all and gave the pipe back.

Tuina had no other kind of tobacco and could do no more. He dropped his head. "I don't know what kind of person this is," thought he. All at once he remembered old Igupa Topa, and thought:

"This may be a young one of that kind. I can do nothing with him, he has beaten me."

Halai Auna was very glad to have such a husband. This was the first man of all who had come to see her who had not been killed by Tuina. She laughed all this time in her mind.

Pun Miaupa went out, killed five deer, and brought them in. The women cooked a great deal that day. Wakara and Tuina sat in the house, talked and ate Pun Miaupa's fresh venison. The next night all slept. Igupa Topa went out of Pun Miaupa's heart, went about midnight, and sat north of the pillar in the side of the house, sat without saying a word. He had a white-feather in his head, and looked very angry and greatly dissatisfied.

Early next morning Tuina and Wakara were up and saw the old man sitting there with that big feather in his head, and they looked at him.

"Oh," said Tuina. "I know now why Halai Auna's husband can smoke my tobacco. I know that old Igupa Topa this long time. I know what that old fellow can do."

They put plenty of food before Igupa Topa, but he would eat none of it. Pun Miaupa killed five deer that morning and brought them in. The two old men were glad to see such nice venison, and see so much of it. Igupa Topa sat by himself, and ate nothing.

"Uncle, why do you not eat?" asked Pun Miaupa.

He made no answer, but watched till all were asleep; then he stood up and ate, ate the whole night through, ate all the acorn bread, all the roots, ate all that there was in the house, except venison. That was not his kind of food; he would not touch it. He sat down on the north side of the central pillar when he had finished eating.

"You must work hard to cook food enough," said Tuina next morning to the women. "Some one in this house must be very hungry."

The women worked hard all that day; in the evening the house was full of good food again. Pun Miaupa's uncle would not eat a morsel placed before him, but when night came he ate everything there was except venison.

"There must be some one in this house who is very hungry," said Tuina, when he rose the next morning. "Make ready more food to-day, work hard, my daughters."

"We will not work to-day; that nasty old fellow eats everything in the night time. We will not carry wood and water all day and have nothing to eat the next morning."

"I don't like him, either," said Tuina; "he will go very soon, I hope."

Igupa Topa heard these words and remembered them. Tuina's wife and Wakara's wife, both old women, had to work that day without assistance. In the middle of the forenoon a great cloud rose in the south. Pun Miaupa's uncle raised it. "Let rain come, thick heavy rain," said he in his mind. "I want darkness, I want a big storm and cold rain."

The cloud was black; it covered all the sky; every one came in, and soon the rain began. It rained in streams, in rivers; it filled the valleys, filled all places. The water reached Tuina's sweat-house, rushed in, and filled the whole place; all had to stand in water; and the rain was very cold.

Old Tuina and Wakara were shivering; their teeth knocked together; their wives and daughters were crying. Igupa Topa had taken his nephew and Halai Auna up to his place on the north side, near the roof of his sweat-house, where they were dry.

The sweat-house was nearly full of water. All were crying now. Some time before daylight one of Tuina's daughters was drowned, and then the other two, and Wakara's two daughters. About dawn Tuina and Wakara with their two wives were drowned. All were dead in the sweat-house except Igupa Topa, his nephew, and Halai Auna. At daylight the rain stopped, the water began to go down, and all the bodies floated out through the doorway. The place was dry. Pun Miaupa made a fire. Halai Auna came to the fire and began to cry for her father, her mother and sisters.

"You must not cry," said Pun Miaupa; "my uncle did this. He will bring all to life again quickly."

But Halai Auna was afraid, and she cried for some time.

Just after midday Igupa Topa went outside, saw the dead bodies, and said: "Why sleep all day? It is time to be up, you two old men and you five young girls!"

Tuina and Wakara sprang up, went to the creek, and swam. "No one but Igupa Topa could have done this to us," said they.

All the women rose up as if they had been only sleeping.

"My brother, I shall go home to-morrow," said Wakara. "It is time for me."

Very early next morning Wakara and his wife began to dance, then the two daughters, then Halai Auna and her husband. They danced out by the smoke-hole, rose through the air, sang, and danced themselves home.

Wakara had been five days away, and all his daughters' husbands were saying: "Where is our father-in-law? He may have been killed." All were very glad when they saw old Wakara in the sweat-house next morning.

Before leaving Tuina's sweat-house Igupa Topa had gone into his nephew's heart again. When Wakara came home, he took his new son-in-law to try a sport which he had. The old man had made a great pole out of deer sinews. This pole was fixed in the ground and was taller than the highest tree. Wakara played in this way: A man climbed the pole, a second bent it down and brought the top as near the foot as possible. He let the top go then, and it shot into the air. If the man on the pole held firmly, he was safe; if he lost his grip he was hurled up high, then fell and was killed.

"Come, my son-in-law," said Wakara one day, "I will show you the place where I play sometimes pleasantly."

They went to the place. The old man climbed first, grasped the pole near the top. Pun Miaupa pulled it down; his uncle was in his heart, and he was very strong. He brought the top toward the ground, did not draw very hard, and let the pole fly back again. It sprang into the air. Wakara was not hurled away; he held firmly. Pun Miaupa brought down the pole a second time, he brought it down rather softly, and let it go. Wakara held his place yet. He tried a third time. Wakara was unshaken.

"That will do for me," said Wakara. "Go up now; it is your time."

Pun Miaupa went on the pole and held with his uncle's power. It was not he who held the pole, but Igupa Topa. "I will end you this time," thought Wakara. He bent the pole close to the ground and let go. Wakara looked sharply to see his son-in-law shoot through the air – looked a good while, did not see him. "My son-in-law has gone very high," thought he. He looked a while yet in the sky; at last he looked at the pole, and there was his son-in-law.

He bent the pole a second time, bent it lower than before; then let it fly. This time Wakara looked at the pole, and Pun Miaupa was on the top of it.

Wakara was angry. He bent the pole to the ground, bent angrily, and let it go. "He will fly away this time, surely," thought he, and looked to the sky to see Pun Miaupa, did not see him; looked at the pole, he was on it. "What kind of person is my son-in-law?" thought Wakara.

It was Wakara's turn now to go on the pole, and he climbed it. Pun Miaupa gave his father-in-law a harder pull this time, but he held his place. The second time Pun Miaupa spoke to Wakara in his own mind: "You don't like me, I don't like you; you want to kill me. I will send you high now."

He bent the pole, brought the top almost to the foot of it, and let it fly. He looked to the top, Wakara was gone. He had been hurled up to the sky, and he stayed there.

Pun Miaupa laughed. "Now, my father-in-law," said he, "you will never come down here to live again; you will stay where you are now forever, you will become small and die, then you will come to life and grow large. You will be that way always, growing old and becoming young again."

Pun Miaupa went home alone.

Wakara's daughters waited for their father, and when he didn't come back they began to cry. At last, when it was dark and they saw their father far up in the sky, they cried very bitterly.

Next morning Pun Miaupa took Halai Auna, his wife, and his uncle, and went to his father's house.

Chuhna, the greatest spinner in the world, lived among Wakara's daughters. All day those women cried and lamented.

"What shall we do?" said they; "we want to go and live near our father. Who can take us up to him?"

"I will take you up to him," said Chuhna, the spinner, who had a great rope fastened to the sky.

Chuhna made an immense basket, put in all the daughters with their husbands, and drew them up till they reached the sky; and Wakara's daughters, the stars, are there on the sky yet.

Mishemokwa, or The Origin of the Small Black Bear

IN A REMOTE part of the north lived a great magician called Iamo, and his only sister, who had never seen a human being. Seldom, if ever, had the man any cause to go from home; for, as his wants demanded food, he had only to go a little distance from the lodge, and there, in some particular spot, place his arrows, with their barbs in the ground. Telling his sister where they had been placed, every morning she would go in search, and never fail of finding each struck through the heart of a deer. She had then only to drag them into the lodge and prepare their food. Thus she lived till she attained womanhood, when one day her brother said to her, "Sister, the time is near at hand when you will be ill. Listen to my advice. If you do not, it will probably be the cause of my death. Take the implements with which we kindle our fires. Go some distance from our lodge, and build a separate fire. When you are in want of food, I will tell you where to find it. You must cook for yourself, and I will for myself. When you are ill, do not attempt to come near the lodge, or bring any of the utensils you use. Be sure always to fasten to your belt the implements you need, for you do not know when the time will come. As for myself, I must do the best I can." His sister promised to obey him in all he had said.

Shortly after, her brother had cause to go from home. She was alone in her lodge, combing her hair. She had just untied the belt to which the implements were fastened, when suddenly the event, to which her brother had alluded, occurred. She ran out of the lodge, but in her haste forgot the belt. Afraid to return, she stood for some time thinking. Finally she decided to enter the lodge and get it. For, thought she, my brother is not at home, and I will stay but a moment to catch hold of it. She went back. Running in suddenly, she caught hold of it, and was coming out when her brother came in sight. He knew what was the matter. "Oh," he said, "did I not tell you to take care? But now you have killed me." She was going on her way, but her brother said to her, "What can you do there now? the accident has happened. Go in, and stay where you have always stayed. And what will become of you? You have killed me."

He then laid aside his hunting dress and accoutrements, and soon after both his feet began to inflame and turn black, so that he could not move. Still he directed his sister where to place the arrows, that she might always have food. The inflammation continued to increase, and had now reached his first rib; and he said, "Sister, my end is near. You must do as I tell you. You see my medicine-sack, and my war-club tied to it. It contains all my medicines, and my war-plumes, and my paints of all colors. As soon as the inflammation reaches my breast, you will take my war-club. It has a sharp point, and you will cut off my head. When it is free from my body, take it, place its neck in the sack, which you must open at one end. Then hang it up in its former place. Do not forget my bow and arrows. One of the last you will take to procure food. The remainder tie to my sack, and then hang it up, so that I can look towards the door. Now and then I will speak to you, but not often." His sister again promised to obey.

In a little time his breast was affected. "Now," said he, "take the club and strike off my head." She was afraid, but he told her to muster courage. "Strike," said he, and a smile was on his face. Mustering all her courage, she gave the blow and cut off the head. "Now," said the head, "place me where I told you." And fearfully she obeyed it in all its commands. Retaining its animation, it looked around the lodge as usual, and it would command its sister to go to such places as it thought would procure for her the flesh of different animals she needed. One day the head said, "The time is not distant when I shall be freed from this situation, but I shall have to undergo many sore evils. So the Superior Manito decrees, and I must bear all patiently." In this situation we must leave the head.

In a certain part of the country was a village inhabited by a numerous and warlike band of Indians. In this village was a family of ten young men – brothers. It was in the spring of the year that the youngest of these blackened his face and fasted. His dreams were propitious. Having ended his fast, he sent secretly for his brothers at night, so that none in the village could overhear or find out the direction they intended to go. Though their drum was heard, yet that was a common occurrence. Having ended the usual formalities, he told them how favorable his dreams were, and that he had called them together to know if they would accompany him in a war excursion. They all answered they would. The third brother from the eldest, noted for his oddities, coming up with his war-club when his brother had ceased speaking, jumped up, "Yes," said he, "I will go, and this will be the way I will treat those we are going to fight;" and he struck the post in the centre of the lodge, and gave a yell. The others spoke to him, saying, "Slow, slow, Mudjikewis, when you are in other people's lodges." So he sat down. Then, in turn, they took the drum, and sang their songs, and closed with a feast. The youngest told them not to whisper their intention even to their wives, but secretly to prepare for their journey. They all promised obedience, and Mudjikewis was the first to say so.

The time for their departure drew near. Word was given to assemble on a certain night, when they would depart immediately. Mudjikewis was loud in his demands for his moccasins. Several times his wife asked him the reason. "Besides," said she, "you have a good pair on." "Quick, quick," he said, "since you must know, we are going on a war excursion. So be quick." He thus revealed the secret. That night they met and started. The snow was on the ground, and they travelled all night, lest others should follow them. When it was daylight, the leader took snow and made a ball of it; then tossing it into the air, he said, "It was in this way I saw snow fall in my dream, so that I could not be tracked." And he told them to keep close to each other for fear of losing themselves, as the snow began to fall in very large flakes. Near as they walked, it was with difficulty they could see each other. The snow continued falling all that day and the following night. So it was impossible to track them.

They had now walked for several days, and Mudjikewis was always in the rear. One day, running suddenly forward, he gave the Saw-saw-quan, and struck a tree with his war-club, which broke into pieces as if struck with lightning. "Brothers," said he, "this will be the way I will serve those whom we are going to fight." The leader answered, "Slow, slow, Mudjikewis. The one I lead you to is not to be thought of so lightly." Again he fell back and thought to himself, "What, what: Who can this be he is leading us to?" He felt fearful, and was silent. Day after day they travelled on, till they came to an extensive plain, on the borders of which human bones were bleaching in the sun. The leader spoke. "They are the bones of those who have gone before us. None has ever yet returned to tell the sad tale of their fate." Again Mudjikewis became restless, and, running forward, gave the accustomed yell. Advancing to a large rock which stood above the ground, he struck it, and it fell to pieces. "See, brothers," said he, "thus will I treat those whom we are going to fight." "Still, still," once more said the leader; "he to whom I am leading you is not to be compared to that rock."

Mudjikewis fell back quite thoughtful, saying to himself, "I wonder who this can be that he is going to attack." And he was afraid. Still they continued to see the remains of former warriors, who had been to the place where they were now going, some of whom had retreated as far back as the place where they first saw the bones, beyond which no one had ever escaped. At last they came to a piece of rising ground, from which they plainly distinguished, sleeping on a distant mountain, a mammoth bear.

The distance between them was great, but the size of the animal caused him plainly to be seen. "There," said the leader, "it is he to whom I am leading you; here our troubles only will commence, for he is a Mishemokwa and a Manito. It is he who has that we prize so dearly (i.e., wampum), to obtain which, the warriors whose bones we saw sacrificed their lives. You must not be fearful. Be manly. We shall find him asleep." They advanced boldly till they came near, when they stopped to view him more closely. He was asleep. Then the leader went forward and touched the belt around the animal's neck. "This," he said, "is what we must get. It contains the wampum." They then requested the eldest to try and slip the belt over the bear's head, who appeared to be fast asleep, as he was not in the least disturbed by the attempt to obtain it. All their efforts were in vain, till it came to the one next the youngest. He tried, and the belt moved nearly over the monster's head, but he could get it no further. Then the youngest one and leader made his attempt, and succeeded. Placing it on the back of the oldest, he said, "Now we must run," and off they started. When one became fatigued with its weight, another would relieve him. Thus they ran till they had passed the bones of all former warriors, and were some distance beyond, when, looking back, they saw the monster slowly rising. He stood some time before he missed his wampum. Soon they heard his tremendous howl, like distant thunder, slowly filling all the sky; and then they heard him speak and say, "Who can it be that has dared to steal my wampum? Earth is not so large but that I can find them." And he descended from the hill in pursuit. As if convulsed, the earth shook with every jump he made. Very soon he approached the party. They however kept the belt, exchanging it from one to another, and encouraging each other. But he gained on them fast. "Brothers," said the leader, "has never any one of you, when fasting, dreamed of some friendly spirit who would aid you as a guardian?" A dead silence followed. "Well," said he, "fasting, I dreamed of being in danger of instant death, when I saw a small lodge, with smoke curling from its top. An old man lived in it, and I dreamed he helped me. And may it be verified soon," he said, running forward and giving the peculiar yell, and a howl as if the sounds came from the depths of his stomach, and which is called Checau-dum. Getting upon a piece of rising ground, behold! a lodge, with smoke curling from its top, appeared. This gave them all new strength, and they ran forward and entered it. The leader spoke to the old man who sat in the lodge saying, "Nemesho, help us. We claim your protection, for the great bear will kill us." "Sit down and eat, my grandchildren," said the old man. "Who is a great Manito?" said he, "there is none but me; but let me look," and he opened the door of the lodge, when lo! at a little distance he saw the enraged animal coming on, with slow but powerful leaps. He closed the door. "Yes," said he, "he is indeed a great Manito. My grandchildren, you will be the cause of my losing my life. You asked my protection, and I granted it; so now come what may, I will protect you. When the bear arrives at the door, you must run out of the other end of the lodge." Then putting his hand to the side of the lodge where he sat, he brought out a bag, which he opened. Taking out two small black dogs, he placed them before him. "These are the ones I use when I fight," said he; and he commenced patting, with both hands, the sides of one of them, and they began to swell out, so that he soon filled the lodge by his bulk. And he had great strong teeth. When he attained his full size he growled, and from that moment, as from instinct, he jumped out at the door and met the bear, who in another leap would have reached the lodge. A terrible combat ensued. The skies rang with the howls of the fierce monsters. The remaining dog soon took the field. The brothers, at the onset, took the advice of the old man, and escaped through the opposite side of the lodge. They had not proceeded far before they heard the dying cry of one of the dogs, and soon after of the other. "Well," said the leader, "the old man will share their fate; so run, run, he will soon be after us." They started with fresh vigor, for they had received food from the old man; but very soon the bear came in sight, and again was fast gaining upon them. Again the leader asked the brothers if they could do nothing for their safety. All were silent. The leader, running forward, did as before. "I dreamed," he cried, "that, being in great trouble, an old man helped me who was a Manito. We shall soon see his lodge." Taking courage, they still went on. After going a short distance they saw the lodge of the old Manito. They entered immediately and claimed his protection, telling him a Manito was after them. The old man, setting meat before them, said, "Eat. Who is a Manito? there is no Manito but me. There is none whom I fear." And the earth trembled as the monster advanced. The old man opened the door and saw him coming. He shut it slowly, and said, "Yes, my grandchildren, you have brought trouble upon me." Procuring his medicine sack, he took out his small war-clubs of black stone, and told the young men to run through the other side of the lodge. As he handled the clubs they became very large, and the old man stepped out just as the bear reached the door. Then striking him with one of the clubs, it broke in pieces. The bear stumbled. Renewing the attempt with the other war-club, that also was broken, but the bear fell senseless. Each blow the old man gave him sounded like a clap of thunder, and the howls of the bear ran along till they filled the heavens.

The young men had now ran some distance, when they looked back. They could see that the bear was recovering from the blows. First he moved his paws, and soon they saw him rise on his feet. The old man shared the fate of the first, for they now heard his cries as he was torn in pieces. Again the monster was in pursuit, and fast overtaking them. Not yet discouraged, the young men kept on their way; but the bear was now so close, that the leader once more applied to his brothers, but they could do nothing. "Well," said he, "my dreams will soon be exhausted. After this I have but one more." He advanced, invoking his guardian spirit to aid him. "Once," said he, "I dreamed that, being sorely pressed, I came to a large lake, on the shore of which was a canoe, partly out of water, having ten paddles all in readiness. Do not fear," he cried, "we shall soon get to it." And so it was, even as he had said. Coming to the lake, they saw the canoe with ten paddles, and immediately they embarked. Scarcely had they reached the centre of the lake, when they saw the bear arrive at its borders. Lifting himself on his hind legs, he looked all around. Then he waded into the water; then losing his footing, he turned back, and commenced making the circuit of the lake. Meanwhile, the party remained stationary in the centre to watch his movements. He travelled around, till at last he came to the place from whence he started. Then he commenced drinking up the water, and they saw the current fast setting in towards his open mouth. The leader encouraged them to paddle hard for the opposite shore. When only a short distance from land, the current had increased so much, that they were drawn back by it, and all their efforts to reach it were vain.

Then the leader again spoke, telling them to meet their fates manfully. "Now is the time, Mudjikewis," said he, "to show your prowess. Take courage, and sit in the bow of the canoe; and when it approaches his mouth, try what effect your club will have on his head." He obeyed, and stood ready to give the blow; while the leader, who steered, directed the canoe for the open mouth of the monster.

Rapidly advancing, they were just about to enter his mouth, when Mudjikewis struck him a tremendous blow on the head, and gave the saw-saw-quan. The bear's limbs doubled under him, and he fell stunned by the blow. But before Mudjikewis could renew it the monster disgorged all the water he had drank, with a force which sent the canoe with great velocity to the opposite shore. Instantly leaving the canoe, again they fled, and on they went till they were completely exhausted. The earth again shook, and soon they saw the monster hard after them. Their spirits drooped, and they felt discouraged. The leader exerted himself, by actions and words, to cheer them up; and once more he asked them if they thought of nothing, or could do nothing for their rescue; and, as before, all were silent. "Then," he said, "this is the last time I can apply to my guardian spirit. Now if we do not succeed, our fates are decided." He ran forward, invoking his spirit with great earnestness, and gave the yell. "We shall soon arrive," said he to his brothers, "to the place where my last guardian spirit dwells. In him I place great confidence. Do not, do not be afraid, or your limbs will be fear-bound. We shall soon reach his lodge. Run, run," he cried.

They were now in sight of the lodge of Iamo, the magician of the undying head – of that great magician whose life had been the forfeit of the kind of necromantic leprosy caused by the careless steps of the fatal curse of uncleanliness in his sister. This lodge was the sacred spot of expected relief to which they had been fleeing, from the furious rage of the giant Bear, who had been robbed of her precious boon, the magis-sauniqua. For it had been the design of many previous war parties to obtain this boon.

In the mean time, the undying head of Iamo had remained in the medicine sack, suspended on the sides of his wigwam, where his sister had placed it, with its mystic charms, and feathers, and arrows. This head retained all life and vitality, keeping its eyes open, and directing its sister, in order to procure food, where to place the magic arrows, and speaking at long intervals. One day the sister saw the eyes of the head brighten, as if through pleasure. At last it spoke. "Oh! sister," it said, "in what a pitiful situation you have been the cause of placing me. Soon, very soon, a party of young men will arrive and apply to me for aid; but, alas! how can I give what I would have done with so much pleasure. Nevertheless, take two arrows, and place them where you have been in the habit of placing the others, and have meat prepared and cooked before they arrive. When you hear them coming and calling on my name, go out and say, 'Alas! it is long ago that an accident befell him; I was the cause of it.' If they still come near, ask them in and set meat before them. And now you must follow my directions strictly. When the bear is near, go out and meet him. You will take my medicine sack, bows and arrows, and my head. You must then untie the sack, and spread out before you my paints of all colors, my war eagle feathers, my tufts of dried hair, and whatever else it contains. As the bear approaches, you will take all these articles, one by one, and say to him, 'This is my deceased brother's paint,' and so on with all the other articles, throwing each of them as far from you as you can. The virtues contained in them will cause him to totter; and, to complete his destruction, you will take my head, and that too you will cast as far off as you can, crying aloud, 'See, this is my deceased brother's head.' He will then fall senseless. By this time the young men will have eaten, and you will call them to your assistance. You must then cut the carcass into pieces, yes, into small pieces, and scatter them to the four winds; for, unless you do this, he will again revive." She promised that all should be done as he said. She had only time to prepare the meat, when the voice of the leader was heard calling upon Iamo for aid. The woman went out and invited them in as her brother had directed. But the war party, being closely pursued, came promptly up to the lodge. She invited them in, and placed the meat before them. While they were eating they heard the bear approaching. Untying the medicine sack and taking the head, she had all in readiness for his approach. When he came up, she did as she had been told. "Behold, Mishemokwa," she cried, "this is the meda sack of Iamo. These are war eagle's feathers of Iamo (casting them aside). These are magic arrows of Iamo (casting them down). These are the sacred paints and magic charms of Iamo. These are dried tufts of the hair of furious beasts. And this (swinging it with all her might) is his undying head." The monster began to totter, as she cast one thing after the other on the ground, but still recovering strength, came close up to the woman till she flung the head. As it rolled along the ground, the blood, excited by the feelings of the head in this terrible scene, gushed from the nose and mouth. The bear, tottering, soon fell with a tremendous noise. Then she cried for help, and the young men came rushing out, having partially regained their strength and spirits.

Mudjikewis, stepping up, gave a yell, and struck the monster a blow upon the head. This he repeated till it seemed like a mass of brains; while the others, as quick as possible, cut him into very small pieces, which they then scattered in every direction. While thus employed, happening to look around where they had thrown the meat, wonderful to behold! they saw, starting up and running off in every direction, small black bears, such as are seen at the present day. The country was soon overspread with these black animals. And it was from this monster that the present race of bears, the mukwahs, derived their origin.

Having thus overcome their pursuer, they returned to the lodge. In the mean time, the woman, gathering the implements she had scattered, and the head, placed them again in the sack. But the head did not speak again.

The war party were now triumphant, but they did not know what use to make of their triumph. Having spent so much time, and traversed so vast a country in their flight, the young men gave up the idea of ever returning to their own country, and game being plenty, they determined to remain where they now were, and make this their home. One day they moved off some distance from the lodge for the purpose of hunting, having left the wampum captured with the woman. They were very successful, and amused themselves, as all young men do when alone, by talking and jesting with each other. One of them spoke and said, "We have all this sport to ourselves; let us go and ask our sister if she will not let us bring the head to this place, as it is still alive. It may be pleased to hear us talk and be in our company. In the mean time, we will take food to our sister." They went, and requested the head. She told them to take it, and they took it to their hunting-grounds, and tried to amuse it, but only at times did they see its eyes beam with pleasure. One day, while busy in their encampment, they were unexpectedly attacked by unknown Indians. The skirmish was long contested and bloody. Many of their foes were slain, but still they were thirty to one. The young men fought desperately till they were all killed. The attacking party then retreated to a height of ground, to muster their men, and to count the number of missing and slain. One of their young men had strayed away, and, in endeavoring to overtake them, came to the place where the undying head was hung up. Seeing that alone retain animation, he eyed it for some time with fear and surprise. However, he took it down and opened the sack, and was much pleased to see the beautiful feathers, one of which he placed on his head.

Starting off, it waved gracefully over him till he reached his party, when he threw down the head and sack, and told them how he had found it, and that the sack was full of paints and feathers. They all looked at the head and made sport of it. Numbers of the young men took up the paint and painted themselves, and one of the party took the head by the hair and said, "Look, you ugly thing, and see your paints on the faces of warriors." But the feathers were so beautiful, that numbers of them also placed them on their heads. Then again they used all kinds of indignity to the head, for which they were in turn repaid by the death of those who had used the feathers. Then the chief commanded them to throw all away except the head. "We will see," said he, "when we get home, what we can do to it. We will try to make it shut its eyes."

When they reached their homes they took it to the council lodge, and hung it up before the fire, fastening it with raw hide soaked, which would shrink and become tightened by the action of the fire. "We will then see," they said, "if we cannot make it shut its eyes."

Meanwhile, for several days, the sister of Iamo had been waiting for the young men to bring back the head; till at last, getting impatient, she went in search of it. The young men she found lying within short distances of each other, dead, and covered with wounds. Various other bodies lay scattered in different directions around them. She searched for the head and sack, but they were nowhere to be found. She raised her voice and wept, and blackened her face. Then she walked in different directions, till she came to the place from whence the head had been taken. There she found the magic bow and arrows, where the young men, ignorant of their qualities, had left them. She thought to herself that she would find her brother's head, and came to a piece of rising ground, and there saw some of his paints and feathers. These she carefully put up, and hung upon the branch of a tree till her return.

At dusk she arrived at the first lodge of the enemy, in a very extensive village. Here she used a charm, common among Indians when they wish to meet with a kind reception. On applying to the old man and woman of the lodge, she was kindly received. She made known her errand.

The old man promised to aid her, and told her that the head was hung up before the council fire, and that the chiefs of the village, with their young men, kept watch over it continually. The former are considered as Manitoes. She said she only wished to see it, and would be satisfied if she could only get to the door of the lodge. She knew she had not sufficient power to take it by force. "Come with me," said the Indian, "I will take you there." They went, and they took their seats near the door. The council lodge was filled with warriors, amusing themselves with games, and constantly keeping up a fire to smoke the head, as they said, to make dry meat. They saw the eyes move, and not knowing what to make of it, one spoke and said, "Ha! ha! it is beginning to feel the effects of the smoke." The sister looked up from the door, and as her eyes met those of her brother, tears rolled down the cheeks of the undying head. "Well," said the chief, "I thought we would make you do something at last. Look! look at it – shedding tears," said he to those around him; and they all laughed and passed their jokes upon it. The chief, looking around and observing the woman, after some time said to the old man who came with her, "Who have you got there? I have never seen that woman before in our village." "Yes," replied the man, "you have seen her; she is a relation of mine, and seldom goes out. She stays in my lodge, and asked me to allow her to come with me to this place." In the centre of the lodge sat one of those vain young men who are always forward, and fond of boasting and displaying themselves before others. "Why," said he, "I have seen her often, and it is to his lodge I go almost every night to court her." All the others laughed and continued their games. The young man did not know he was telling a lie to the woman's advantage, who by that means escaped scrutiny.

She returned to the old man's lodge, and immediately set out for her own country. Coming to the spot where the bodies of her adopted brothers lay, she placed them together, their feet toward the east. Then taking an axe which she had, she cast it up into the air, crying out, "Brothers, get up from under it, or it will fall on you." This she repeated three times, and the third time the brothers all arose and stood on their feet.

Mudjikewis commenced rubbing his eyes and stretching himself. "Why," said he, "I have overslept myself." "No, indeed," said one of the others, "do you not know we were all killed, and that is our sister who has brought us to life?" The young men took the bodies of their enemies and burned them. Soon after, the woman went to procure wives for them, in a distant country, they knew not where; but she returned with ten young females, which she gave to the young men, beginning with the eldest. Mudjikewis stepped to and fro, uneasy lest he should not get the one he liked. But he was not disappointed, for she fell to his lot. And they were well matched, for she was a female magician. They then all moved into a very large lodge, and their sister Iamoqua told them that the women must now take turns in going to her brother's head every night, trying to untie it. They all said they would do so with pleasure. The eldest made the first attempt, and with a rushing noise she fled through the air.

Towards daylight she returned. She had been unsuccessful, as she succeeded in untying only one of the knots. All took their turns regularly, and each one succeeded in untying only one knot each time. But when the youngest went, she commenced the work as soon as she reached the lodge; although it had always been occupied, still the Indians never could see any one, for they all possessed invisibility. For ten nights now, the smoke had not ascended, but filled the lodge and drove them out. This last night they were all driven out, and the young woman carried off the head.

The young people and the sister heard the young woman coming high through the air, and they heard her saying, "Prepare the body of our brother." And as soon as they heard it, they went to a small lodge where the black body of Iamo lay. His sister commenced cutting the neck part, from which the head had been severed. She cut so deep as to cause it to bleed;

and the others who were present, by rubbing the body and applying medicines, expelled the blackness. In the mean time, the one who brought it, by cutting the neck of the head, caused that also to bleed.

As soon as she arrived, they placed that close to the body, and by the aid of medicines and various other means, succeeded in restoring Iamo to all his former beauty and manliness. All rejoiced in the happy termination of their troubles, and they had spent some time joyfully together, when Iamo said, "Now I will divide the wampum;" and getting the belt which contained it, he commenced with the eldest, giving it in equal proportions. But the youngest got the most splendid and beautiful, as the bottom of the belt held the richest and rarest.

They were told that, since they had all once died, and were restored to life, they were no longer mortals, but spirits, and they were assigned different stations in the invisible world. Only Mudjikewis's place was, however, named. He was to direct the west wind, hence generally called Kabeyun, the father of Manabozho, there to remain forever. They were commanded, as they had it in their power, to do good to the inhabitants of the earth; and forgetting their sufferings in procuring the wampum, to give all things with a liberal hand. And they were also commanded that it should also be held by them sacred; those grains or shells of the pale hue to be emblematic of peace, while those of the darker hue would lead to evil and to war.

The spirits, then, amid songs and shouts, took their flight to their respective abodes on high; while Iamo, with his sister Iamoqua, descended into the depths below.

The Origin of Medicine

IN THE OLD days, there was peace throughout the earth and mankind lived in friendship and harmony with the great beasts of creation. But as time progressed, the human race multiplied rapidly and became so large that the animals were forced to surrender their settlements and seek out new homes in the forests and deserts. Although cramped and unhappy, they did not complain too vociferously, but embraced these changes with an open mind, hoping that mankind would now remain satisfied. Sadly, however, this was not the case, and within a short time, man began to equip himself with a variety of weapons – bows, arrows, axes, spears and hooks – which he used to attack the beasts of the forests, slaughtering them for their flesh and valuable skins. The animals, at first incredulous, soon became enraged by this show of bloodthirsty contempt and began to consider measures that would guarantee them their survival and safety. The bear tribe was the first to meet in council under Kuwahi mountain, presided over by White Bear, their chief. One after another, members of the tribe stood up and reported the appalling atrocities their families had suffered. Mankind had mutilated their bodies, devoured their flesh, skinned them to make superfluous clothing and displayed their severed heads on wooden stakes as trophies. There was only one way to deal with such hostility, it was unanimously agreed, and it involved wholesale war.

The bears sat down to deliberate their strategy more seriously, but as soon as someone asked about weapons, they all fell silent, knowing that humans had one distinct advantage over them in this respect.

"We should turn man's own instruments upon him," announced one of the elder bears. "Let us go and find one of these bows, together with some arrows, and copy their design." A messenger returned shortly afterwards with these objects and the group gathered round to examine them carefully. A strong piece of locust wood was called for by the chief and with this he constructed a bow. Then, one of the younger bears provided a piece of his gut for the string and soon the weapon was completed, ready for its first testing.

The strongest, most agile bear volunteered his services. He had little trouble drawing back the bow, but as soon as he attempted to let the arrow fly, his long claws became entangled in the string and the shot was ruined. He quickly realized that he would have to trim his claws, and when he had done this, he let a second arrow fly which hit its target successfully. Delighted with himself, he turned to face the chief, but White Bear did not appear at all pleased by the result.

"We need our claws to climb trees," he wisely proclaimed. "If we cut off our claws we will not be able to climb or hunt down prey and soon we would all starve together." And saying this, he ordered the group to scatter amongst the woods, instructing them to reappear before him when they had found a better solution.

The deer also held a similar council under their chief, Little Deer. After they had aired their grievances and lamented the death of their comrades, they came to a decision that if any human hunter should attempt to slay one of them without first asking suitable pardon, he would be struck down by rheumatism. Notice of this decision was sent out to all the Indian villages nearby and the people were instructed what to do if ever necessity demanded that they kill one of the deer tribe.

So now, whenever a deer is hit by an arrow, Little Deer, who moves faster than the wind and can never be wounded, runs to the spot where the victim has fallen and, bending over the pool of blood, asks the spirit of the deer whether or not he has heard the hunter's plea for pardon. If the reply is 'yes,' the hunter remains fit and well, but if the answer is 'no,' then Little Deer tracks him to his cabin and strikes him down with rheumatism, transforming him into a helpless cripple.

The fishes and reptiles were the next to gather together to determine an appropriate punishment for their aggressors. They held a council which lasted only a few minutes, where it was quickly decided that those who tortured or killed any of their species would be tormented by nightmarish visions of slimy serpents with foul breath twining around their limbs and throats, very slowly choking them to death. Or else, these brutal attackers would dream, day and night, of eating raw, decaying fish, causing them to refuse all food and to sicken and die as a result.

Finally, the birds, insects and smaller animals held their own meeting, presided over by a grub-worm. Each creature, he announced, should come forward and state his point of view and if the consensus was against mankind, the entire race should be put to death by the most cruel and painful means.

Frog was the first to leap forward and he delivered his tirade in a loud and angry voice:

"Something will have to be done to stop the spread of this human menace," he thundered. "See how they have kicked me and beaten me with sticks because they think I'm ugly. Now my back is covered with sores that will never disappear." And he pointed to the spots on his skin for everyone around him to examine.

Next a group of birds hopped forward and began to condemn mankind for the way in which he ruthlessly set out to burn their feet, impaling them on a stick over a fire as soon as he had trapped them, and turning them slowly until their claws and feathers were singed black.

Others then followed with a string of complaints and criticisms, so that apart from the ground-squirrel, who had seldom been a victim because of his tiny size, there was not one among the gathering who showed any restraint or compassion towards the human species. Hurriedly, they began to devise and name various lethal diseases to be released among the human population. As the list grew longer, the grub-worm shook with laughter and glee, until he suddenly fell over backwards and could not rise to his feet again, but had to wriggle off on his back, as he has done ever since that day.

Only the plants remained friendly towards man, and before long every tree, shrub and herb, down even to the wild grasses and mosses, agreed to provide some remedy for the diseases now hanging thick in the air.

"We will help mankind in his hour of need," each plant affirmed. "Every one of us shall assist in the struggle against sickness and disease and hope that in return, the earth will be restored to order."

Even the weeds in the fields were endowed with healing properties and, in time, every tribe boasted a shaman, a great healer, capable of hearing the spirit-voices of the plants speaking to him whenever he was in doubt about a cure.

It was in this way that the very first medicine came into being, ensuring the survival of a human race which had come so perilously close to destruction.

Legend of the Corn

THE ARIKARA WERE the first to find the maize. A young man went out hunting. He came to a high hill. Looking down a valley, he saw a buffalo bull near where two rivers joined. When the young man looked to see how he could kill the buffalo, he saw how beautiful the country was. The banks of the two rivers were low, with many trees. The buffalo faced the north; therefore he could not get within bowshot of him. He thought he should wait until the buffalo moved close to the banks of one of the rivers, or to a ravine where there were bushes and shrubs. So the young man waited. The sun went down before the buffalo moved.

Nearly all night the hunter lay awake. He had little food. He felt sorry he could not reach the buffalo. Before the sun rose, he hurried to the top of the hill. The buffalo stood just where it had, but it faced the east. Again he waited for it to move. He waited all day. When the sun went down, the buffalo still stood in the same place.

Nearly all night the young man lay awake. He had very little food indeed. The next morning he rose early, and came to the top of the hill, just as the sun came up. The buffalo was still standing in the same place; but now it faced the south. He waited all day. Then the sun went down.

Now the next morning, when he arose early, the buffalo stood in the same place; this time it faced the west. All day the young man waited, but the buffalo did not move.

Now the young man thought, "Why does not the buffalo move?" He saw it did not drink, did not eat, did not sleep. He thought some power must be influencing it.

Now the next morning, the young man hurried to the top of the hill. The sun had risen and everything was light. The buffalo was gone. Then he saw where the buffalo had stood there was a strange bush.

He went to the place; then he saw it was a plant. He looked for the tracks of the buffalo. He saw where it had turned to the east and to the south and to the west. In the centre there was one track; out of it the small plant had grown. There was no track to show where the buffalo had left the place.

Then the hunter hurried to his village. He told the chiefs and the people of the strange buffalo and the plant. So all the chiefs and the people came to the place. They saw the tracks of the buffalo as he had stood, but there were no tracks of his coming or going.

So all the people knew that Wahkoda had given this strange plant to the people. They knew of other plants they might eat. They knew there was a time when each plant was ripe. So they watched the strange plant; they guarded it and protected it.

Then a flower appeared on the plant. Afterwards, at one of the joints, a new part of the plant pushed out. It had hair. At first the hair was green; then it was brown. Then the people thought, "Perhaps this fruit is ripe." But they did not dare touch it. They met together. They looked at the plant.

Then a young man said, "My life has not been good. If any evil comes to me, it will not matter."

So the people were willing, and the young man put his hand on the plant and then on its fruit. He grasped the fruit boldly. He said to the people, "It is solid. It is ripe." Then he pulled apart the husks, and said, "It is red."

He took a few of the grains and showed them to the people. He ate some. He did not die. So the people knew Wahkoda had sent this plant to them for food.

Now in the fall, when the prairie grass turned brown, the leaves of this plant turned brown also. Then the fruit was plucked, and put away. After the winter was over, the kernels were divided. There were four to each family.

Then the people moved the lodges to the place where the plant had grown. When the hills became green, they planted the seed of the strange plant. But first they built little mounds like the one out of which it grew. So the fruit grew and ripened. It had many colours; red, and yellow, and white, and blue.

Then the next year there were many plants and many ears of corn. So they sent to other tribes. They invited them to visit them and gave them of the new food. Thus the Omahas came to have corn.

Origin of the Black Snakes

FAR AWAY, VERY far in the north, there dwelt by the border of a great lake a man and his wife. They had no children, and the woman was very beautiful and passionate.

The lake was frozen over during the greater part of the year. One day when the woman cut away the ice, she saw in the water a bright pair of large eyes looking steadily at her. They charmed her so that she could not move. Then she distinguished a handsome face; it was that of a fine slender young man. He came out of the water. His eyes seemed brighter and more fascinating than ever; he glittered from head to foot; on his breast was a large shining silvery plate.

The woman learned that this was At-o-sis, the Serpent, but she returned his embraces and held conversation with him, and was so charmed with her lover that she not only met him more than once every day, but even went forth to see him in the night.

Her husband, noticing these frequent absences, asked her why she went forth so frequently. She replied, "To get the fresh air."

The weather grew warmer; the ice left the lake; grass and leaves were growing. Then the woman waited till her husband slept, and stole out from the man whom she kissed no more, to the lover whom she fondled and kissed more than ever.

At last the husband's suspicions being fairly aroused, he resolved to watch her. To do this he said that he would be absent for three days. But he returned at the end of the first day, and found that she was absent. As she came in he observed something like silvery scales on the logs. He asked what they were. She replied, Brooches.

He was still dissatisfied, and said that he would be gone for one day. He went to the top of a hill not far distant, whence he watched her. She went to the shore, and sat there. By and by there rose up out of the lake, at a distance, what seemed to be a brightly shining piece of ice. It came to the strand and rose from the water. It was a very tall and very handsome man, dressed in silver. His wife clasped the bright stranger in her arms, kissing him again and again.

The husband was awed by this strange event. He went home, and tried to persuade his wife to leave the place and to return to her people. This she refused to do. He departed; he left her forever. But her father and mother came to find her. They found her there; they dwelt with her. Every day she brought to them furs and meat.

hey asked her whence she got them. "I have another husband," she replied; "one who suits me. The one I had was bad, and did not use me well. This one brings all the animals to me." Then she sent them away with many presents, Otelling them not to return until the ice had formed; that was in the autumn.

When they returned she had become white. She was with young, and soon gave birth to her offspring. It consisted of many serpents. The parents went home. As they departed she said to them, "When you come again you may see me, but you will not know me."

Years after some hunters, roaming that way, remembered the tale, and looked for the wigwam. It was there, but no one was in it. But all the woods about the place were full of great black snakes, which would rise up like a human being and look one in the face, then glide away without doing any harm.

O-wel'-lin the Rock Giant

THERE WAS A great Giant who lived in the north. His name was Oo-wel'-lin, and he was as big as a pine tree. When he saw the country full of people he said they looked good to eat, and came and carried them off and ate them. He could catch ten men at a time and hold them between his fingers, and put more in a net on his back, and carry them off.

He would visit a village and after eating all the people would move on to another, going southward from his home in the north.

When he had gone to the south end of the world and had visited all the villages and eaten nearly all the people – not quite all, for a few had escaped – he turned back toward the north. He crossed the Wah-kal'-mut-ta (Merced River) at a narrow place in the canyon about six miles above Op'-lah (Merced Falls, where his huge footprints may still be seen in the rocks) showing the exact place where he stepped from Ang-e'-sa-w'-pah on the south side to Hik-ka'-nah on the north side. When night came he went into a cave in the side of a round-topped hill over the ridge from Se-saw-che (a little south of the present town of Coulterville).

The people who had escaped found his sleeping place in the cave and shot their arrows at him but were not able to hurt him, for he was a rock giant.

When he awoke he was hungry and took the trail to go hunting. Then the people said to Oo'-choom the Fly: "Go follow Oo-wel'-lin and when he is hot bite him all over, on his head, on his eyes and ears, and all over his body, everywhere, all the way down to the bottoms of his feet, and find out where he can be hurt.

"All right," answered Oo'-choom the Fly, and he did as he was told. He followed Oo-wel'-lin and bit him everywhere from the top of his head, all the way down to his feet without hurting him, till finally he bit him under the heel. This made Oo-wel'-lin kick. Oo'-choom waited, and when the giant had fallen asleep bit him under the heel of the other foot, and he kicked again. Then Oo'-choom told the people.

When the people heard this they took sharp sticks and long sharp splinters of stone and set them up firmly in the trail, and hid nearby and watched. After a while Oo-wel'-lin came back and stepped on the sharp points till the bottoms of his feet were stuck full of them. This hurt him dreadfully, and he fell down and died.

When he was dead the people asked, "Now he is dead, what are we to do with him?"

And they all answered that they did not know.

But a wise man said, "We will pack wood and make a big fire and burn him."

Then everyone said, "All right, let's burn him," and they brought a great quantity of dry wood and made a big fire and burned Oo-wel'-lin the Giant. When he began to burn, the wise man told everybody to watch closely all the time to see if any part should fly off to live again, and particularly to watch the whites of his eyes. So all the people watched closely all the time he was burning. His flesh did not fly off; his feet did not fly off; his hands did not fly off; but by and by the whites of his eyes flew off quickly – so quickly indeed that no one but Chik'-chik saw them go. Chik'-chik was a small bird whose eyes looked sore, but his sight was keen and quick.

He was watching from a branch about twenty feet above the Giant's head and saw the whites of the eyes fly out. He saw them fly out and saw where they went and quickly darted after them and brought them back and put them in the fire again, and put on more wood and burnt them until they were completely consumed.

The people now made a hole and put Oo-wel'-lin's ashes in it and piled rocks on the place and watched for two or three days. But Oo-wel'-lin was dead and never came out.

Then the wise man asked each person what he would like to be, and called their names. Each answered what animal he would be, and forthwith turned into that animal and has remained the same to this day.

This was the beginning of the animals as they are now – the deer, the ground squirrel, the bear, and other furry animals; the bluejay, the quail, and other birds of all kinds, and snakes and frogs and the yellowjacket wasp and so on.

Before that they were Hoi-ah'-ko – the first people.

The Origin of the Tides

A LONG TIME ago, a man wandered down the Nass River. Wherever he camped, he made rocks of curious shapes. Now his name was Qa, the Raven. The Tlingit call him Yel.

Qa wandered all over the world. At last, he travelled westward. Now at that time the sea was always high.

In the middle of the world Qa discovered a rock in the sea. He built a house under the rock. Then he made a hole through it and through the earth and fitted a lid to it. Raven put a man in charge of the hole. Twice a day he opens the lid and twice each day he closes it. When the hole is open, the water rushes down through it into the depths; then it is ebb tide. When he closes the lid, the water rises again; then it is flood tide.

Once upon a time, Tael, a Tlingit chief, while hunting sea otters was carried out to Qa's rock by the tide. The current was so strong he could not escape. When Tael was drawn toward the rock, he saw a few small trees growing on it. Tael threw his canoe line over one of the trees. Thus he escaped being carried down by the water into the hole under the rock. After some time he heard a noise. The man was putting the lid on the hole. Then the water began to rise. Tael paddled rapidly away. He paddled away until the tide began to ebb again. Then he fastened his canoe to a large stone nearby, and waited until flood tide came again. Thus Tael escaped.

How Night Came

YEARS AND YEARS ago, at the very beginning of time, when the world had just been made, there was no night. It was day all the time. No one had ever heard of sunrise or sunset, starlight or moonbeams. There were no night birds, nor night beasts, nor night flowers. There were no lengthening shadows, nor soft night air, heavy with perfume.

In those days, the daughter of the Great Sea Serpent, who dwelt in the depths of the seas, married one of the sons of the great earth race known as Man. She left her home among the shades of the deep seas and came to dwell with her husband in the land of daylight. Her eyes grew weary of the bright sunlight and her beauty faded. Her husband watched her with sad eyes, but he did not know what to do to help her.

"O, if night would only come," she moaned as she tossed about wearily on her couch. "Here it is always day, but in my father's kingdom there are many shadows. O, for a little of the darkness of night!"

Her husband listened to her moanings. "What is night?" he asked her. "Tell me about it and perhaps I can get a little of it for you."

"Night," said the daughter of the Great Sea Serpent, "is the name we give to the heavy shadows which darken my father's kingdom in the depths of the seas. I love the sunlight of your earth land, but I grow very weary of it. If we could have only a little of the darkness of my father's kingdom to rest our eyes part of the time."

Her husband at once called his three most faithful slaves. "I am about to send you on a journey," he told them. "You are to go to the kingdom of the Great Sea Serpent who dwells in the depths of the seas and ask him to give you some of the darkness of night that his daughter may not die here amid the sunlight of our earth land."

The three slaves set forth for the kingdom of the Great Sea Serpent. After a long, dangerous journey they arrived at his home in the depths of the seas and asked him to give them some of the shadows of night to carry back to the earth land. The Great Sea Serpent gave them a big bagful at once. It was securely fastened and the Great Sea Serpent warned them not to open it until they were once more in the presence of his daughter, their mistress.

The three slaves started out, bearing the big bag full of night upon their heads. Soon they heard strange sounds within the bag. It was the sound of the voices of all the night beasts, all the night birds, and all the night insects. If you have ever heard the night chorus from the jungles on the banks of the rivers, you will know how it sounded. The three slaves had never heard sounds like those in all their lives. They were terribly frightened.

"Let us drop the bag full of night right here where we are and run away as fast as we can," said the first slave.

"We shall perish. We shall perish, anyway, whatever we do," cried the second slave.

"Whether we perish or not I am going to open the bag and see what makes all those terrible sounds," said the third slave.

Accordingly, they laid the bag on the ground and opened it. Out rushed all the night beasts and all the night birds and all the night insects and out rushed the great black cloud of night. The slaves were more frightened than ever at the darkness and escaped to the jungle.

The daughter of the Great Sea Serpent was waiting anxiously for the return of the slaves with the bag full of night. Ever since they had started out on their journey she had looked for their return, shading her eyes with her hand and gazing away off at the horizon, hoping with all her heart that they would hasten to bring the night. In that position she was standing under a royal palm tree, when the three slaves opened the bag and let night escape. "Night comes. Night comes at last," she cried, as she saw the clouds of night upon the horizon. Then she closed her eyes and went to sleep there under the royal palm tree.

When she awoke she felt greatly refreshed. She was once more the happy princess who had left her father's kingdom in the depths of the great seas to come to the earth land. She was now ready to see the day again. She looked up at the bright star shining above the royal palm tree and said, "O, bright beautiful star, henceforth you shall be called the morning star and you shall herald the approach of day. You shall reign queen of the sky at this hour."

Then she called all the birds about her and said to them, "O, wonderful, sweet singing birds, henceforth I command you to sing your sweetest songs at this hour to herald the approach of day." The cock was standing by her side. "You," she said to him, "shall be appointed the watchman of the night. Your voice shall mark the watches of the night and shall warn the others that the *madrugada* comes." To this very day in Brazil we call the early morning the *madrugada*. The cock announces its approach to the waiting birds. The birds sing their sweetest songs at that hour and the morning star reigns in the sky as queen of the *madrugada*.

When it was daylight again the three slaves crept home through the forests and jungles with their empty bag.

"O, faithless slaves," said their master, "why did you not obey the voice of the Great Sea Serpent and open the bag only in the presence of his daughter, your mistress? Because of your disobedience I shall change you into monkeys. Henceforth, you shall live in the trees. Your lips shall always bear the mark of the sealing wax which sealed the bag full of night."

To this very day, one sees the mark upon the monkeys' lips where they bit off the wax which sealed the bag; and in Brazil night leaps out quickly upon the earth just as it leapt quickly out of the bag in those days at the beginning of time. And all the night beasts and night birds and night insects give a sunset chorus in the jungles at nightfall.

How the Brazilian Beetles Got Their Gorgeous Coats

IN BRAZIL, THE beetles have such beautifully coloured, hard-shelled coats upon their backs that they are often set in pins and necklaces like precious stones. Once upon a time, years and years ago, they had ordinary plain brown coats. This is how it happened that the Brazilian beetle earned a new coat.

One day, a little brown beetle was crawling along a wall when a big grey rat ran out of a hole in the wall and looked down scornfully at the little beetle. "O ho!" he said to the beetle, "how slowly you crawl along. You'll never get anywhere in the world. Just look at me and see how fast I can run."

The big grey rat ran to the end of the wall, wheeled around, and came back to the place where the little beetle was slowly crawling along at only a tiny distance from where the rat had left her.

"Don't you wish that you could run like that?" said the big grey rat to the little brown beetle.

"You are surely a fast runner," replied the little brown beetle politely. Her mother had taught her always to be polite and had often said to her that a really polite beetle never boasts about her own accomplishments. The little brown beetle never boasted a single boast about the things she could do. She just went on slowly crawling along the wall.

A bright green and gold parrot in the mango tree over the wall had heard the conversation. "How would you like to race with the beetle?" he asked the big grey rat. "I live next door to the tailor bird," he added, "and just to make the race exciting I'll offer a bright coloured coat as a prize to the one who wins the race. You may choose for it any colour you like and I'll have it made to order."

"I'd like a yellow coat with stripes like the tiger's," said the big grey rat, looking over his shoulder at his gaunt grey sides as if he were already admiring his new coat.

"I'd like a beautiful, bright coloured new coat, too," said the little brown beetle.

The big grey rat laughed long and loud until his gaunt grey sides were shaking. "Why, you talk just as if you thought you had a chance to win the race," he said, when he could speak.

The bright green and gold parrot set the royal palm tree at the top of the cliff as the goal of the race. He gave the signal to start and then he flew away to the royal palm tree to watch for the end of the race.

The big grey rat ran as fast as he could. Then he thought how very tired he was getting. "What's the use of hurrying?" he said to himself. "The little brown beetle cannot possibly win. If I were racing with somebody who could really run it would be very different." Then he started to run more slowly, but every time his heart beat it said, "Hurry up! Hurry up!" The big grey rat decided that it was best to obey the little voice in his heart, so he hurried just as fast as he could.

When he reached the royal palm tree at the top of the cliff he could hardly believe his eyes. He thought he must be having a bad dream. There was the little brown beetle sitting quietly beside the bright green and gold parrot. The big grey rat had never been so surprised in all his life. "How did you ever manage to run fast enough to get here so soon?" he asked the little brown beetle as soon as he could catch his breath.

The little brown beetle drew out the tiny wings from her sides. "Nobody said anything about having to run to win the race," she replied, "so I flew instead."

"I did not know that you could fly," said the big grey rat in a subdued little voice.

"After this," said the bright green and gold parrot, "never judge anyone by his looks alone. You never can tell how often or where you may find concealed wings. You have lost the prize."

Until this day, even in Brazil where the flowers and birds and beasts and insects have such gorgeous colouring, the rat wears a plain dull grey coat.

Then the parrot turned to the little brown beetle who was waiting quietly at his side. "What colour do you want your new coat to be?" he asked.

The little brown beetle looked up at the bright green and gold parrot, at the green and gold palm trees above their heads, at the green mangoes with golden flushes on their cheeks lying on the ground under the mango trees, at the golden sunshine upon the distant green hills. "I choose a coat of green and gold," she said.

From that day to this, the Brazilian beetle has worn a coat of green with golden lights upon it.

For years and years, the Brazilian beetles were all very proud to wear green and gold coats like that of the beetle who raced with the rat.

Then, once upon a time, it happened that there was a little beetle who grew discontented with her coat of green and gold. She looked up at the blue sky and out at the blue sea and wished that she had a blue coat instead. She talked about it so much that finally her mother took her to the parrot who lived next to the tailor bird.

"You may change your coat for a blue one," said the parrot, "but if you change you'll have to give up something."

"Oh, I'll gladly give up anything if only I may have a blue coat instead of a green and gold one," said the discontented little beetle.

When she received her new coat she thought it was very beautiful. It was a lovely shade of blue and it had silvery white lights upon it like the light of the stars. When she put it on, however, she discovered that it was not hard like the green and gold one. From that day to this, the blue beetles' coats have not been hard and firm. That is the reason why the jewellers have difficulty in using them in pins and necklaces like other beetles.

From the moment that the little beetle put on her new blue coat she never grew again. From that day to this the blue beetles have been much smaller than the green and gold ones.

When the Brazilians made their flag, they took for it a square of green the colour of the green beetle's coat. Within this square they placed a diamond of gold like the golden lights which play upon the green beetle's back. Then, within the diamond, they drew a circle to represent the round earth and they coloured it blue like the coat of the blue beetle. Upon the blue circle they placed stars of silvery white like the silvery white lights on the back of the blue beetle. About the blue circle of the earth which they thus pictured, they drew a band of white, and upon this band they wrote the motto of their country, "*Ordem e Progresso*" (order and progress).

How the Rabbit Lost His Tail

ONCE UPON A time, ages and ages ago, the rabbit had a long tail, but the cat had none. She looked with envious eyes at the one which the rabbit had. It was exactly the sort of a tail she longed to have.

The rabbit was always a thoughtless, careless little beast. One day, he went to sleep with his beautiful long tail hanging straight out behind him. Along came Mistress Puss carrying a sharp knife, and with one blow she cut off Mr. Rabbit's tail. Mistress Puss was very spry and she had the tail nearly sewed on to her own body before Mr. Rabbit saw what she was doing.

"Don't you think it looks better on me than it did on you?" asked Mistress Puss.

"It surely is very becoming to you," replied the generous, unselfish rabbit. "It was a little too long for me anyway and I'll tell you what I'll do. I'll let you keep it if you will give me that sharp knife in exchange for it."

The cat gave Mr. Rabbit the knife and he started out into the deep forest with it. "I've lost my tail but I've gained a knife," said he. "I'll get a new tail or something else just as good."

Mr. Rabbit hopped along through the forest for a long time and at last he came to a little old man who was busily engaged in making baskets. He was making the baskets out of rushes and he was biting them off with his teeth. He looked up and spied Mr. Rabbit with the knife in his mouth.

"O, please, Mr. Rabbit," said he, "will you not be so kind as to let me borrow that sharp knife you are carrying? It is very hard work to bite the rushes off with my teeth."

Mr. Rabbit let him take the knife. He started to cut off the rushes with it, when *snap* went the knife! It broke into halves.

"O, dear! O, dear!" cried Mr. Rabbit. "What shall I do! What shall I do! You have broken my nice new knife."

The little old man said that he was very sorry and that he did not mean to do it.

Then Mr. Rabbit said, "A broken knife is of no use to me but perhaps you can use it, even if it is broken. I'll tell you what I'll do. I'll let you keep the knife if you will give me one of your baskets in exchange for it."

The little old man gave Mr. Rabbit a basket and he started on through the deep forest with it. "I lost my tail but I gained a knife. I've lost my knife but I've gained a basket," said he. "I'll get a new tail or something else just as good."

Mr. Rabbit hopped along through the deep forest for a long time, until at last he came to a clearing. Here there was an old woman busily engaged in picking lettuce. When she had gathered it she put it into her apron. She looked up and spied Mr. Rabbit hopping along with his basket.

"O, please, Mr. Rabbit," said she, "will you not be so kind as to let me borrow that nice basket you are carrying?"

Mr. Rabbit let her take the basket. She began to put her lettuce into it when out fell the bottom of the basket.

"O, dear! O, dear!" cried Mr. Rabbit. "What shall I do! What shall I do! You have broken the bottom out of my nice new basket."

The old woman said that she was very sorry and that she did not mean to do it.

Then said Mr. Rabbit, "I'll tell you what I'll do. I'll let you keep that broken basket if you will give me some of your lettuce."

The old woman gave Mr. Rabbit some lettuce and he hopped along with it, saying, "I lost my tail but I gained a knife. I lost my knife but I gained a basket. I lost my basket but I gained some lettuce."

The rabbit was getting very hungry and how nice the lettuce smelled! He took a bite. It was just the very best thing he had ever tasted in all his life. "I don't care if I did lose my tail," said he, "I've found something I like very much better."

From that day to this, no rabbit has ever had a tail. Neither has there ever been a rabbit who cared because he had no tail. From that time to this there has never been a rabbit who did not like lettuce to eat and who was not perfectly happy and contented if there was plenty of it.

How the Tiger Got His Stripes

ONCE UPON A time, ages and ages ago, so long ago that the tiger had no stripes upon his back and the rabbit still had his tail, there was a tiger who had a farm. The farm was very much overgrown with underbrush and the owner sought a workman to clear the ground for him to plant.

The tiger called all the beasts together and said to them when they had assembled, "I need a good workman at once to clear my farm of the underbrush. To the one of you who will do this work I offer an ox in payment."

The monkey was the first one to step forward and apply for the position. The tiger tried him for a little while but he was not a good workman at all. He did not work steadily enough to accomplish anything. The tiger discharged him very soon and he did not pay him.

Then, the tiger hired the goat to do the work. The goat worked faithfully enough but he did not have the brains to do the work well. He would clear a little of the farm in one place and then he would go away and work on another part of it. He never finished anything neatly. The tiger discharged him very soon without paying him.

Next, the tiger tried the armadillo. The armadillo was very strong and he did the work well. The trouble with him was that he had such an appetite. There were a great many ants about the place and the armadillo could never pass by a sweet, tender, juicy ant without stopping to eat it. It was lunch time all day long with him. The tiger discharged him and sent him away without paying him anything.

At last, the rabbit applied for the position. The tiger laughed at him and said, "Why, little rabbit, you are too small to do the work. The monkey, the goat and the armadillo have all failed to give satisfaction. Of course a little beast like you will fail too."

However, there were no other beasts who applied for the position, so the tiger sent for the rabbit and told him that he would try him for a little while.

The rabbit worked faithfully and well, and soon he had cleared a large portion of the ground. The next day, he worked just as well. The tiger thought that he had been very lucky to hire the rabbit. He got tired staying around to watch the rabbit work. The rabbit seemed to know just how to do the work anyway, without orders, so the tiger decided to go away on a hunting trip. He left his son to watch the rabbit.

After the tiger had gone away, the rabbit said to the tiger's son, "The ox which your father is going to give me is marked with a white spot on his left ear and another on his right side, isn't he?"

"O, no," replied the tiger's son. "He is red all over with just a tiny white spot on his right ear."

The rabbit worked for a while longer and then he said, "The ox which your father is going to give me is kept by the river, isn't he?"

"Yes," replied the tiger's son.

The rabbit had made a plan to go and get the ox without waiting to finish his work. Just as he started off he saw the tiger returning. The tiger noticed that the rabbit had not worked so well when he was away. After that he stayed and watched the rabbit until the whole farm was cleared. Then the tiger gave the rabbit the ox as he had promised.

"You must kill this ox," he said to the rabbit, "in a place where there are neither flies nor mosquitoes."

The rabbit went away with the ox. After he had gone for some distance he thought he would kill him. He heard a cock, however, crowing in the distance and he knew that there must be a farmyard near. There would be flies of course. He went on farther and again he thought that he would kill the ox. The ground looked moist and damp and so did the leaves on the bushes. Since the rabbit thought there would be mosquitoes there he decided not to kill the ox. He went on and on and finally he came to a high place where there was a strong breeze blowing. "There are no mosquitoes here," he said to himself. "The place is so far removed from any habitation that there are no flies, either." He decided to kill the ox.

Just as he was ready to eat the ox, along came the tiger. "O, rabbit, you have been such a good friend of mine," said the tiger, "and now I am so very, very hungry that all my ribs show, as you yourself can see. Will you not be a good kind rabbit and give me a piece of your ox?"

The rabbit gave the tiger a piece of the ox. The tiger devoured it in the twinkling of an eye. Then he leaned back and said, "Is that all you are going to give me to eat?"

The tiger looked so big and savage that the rabbit did not dare refuse to give him any more of the ox. The tiger ate and ate and ate until he had devoured that entire ox. The rabbit had been able to get only a tiny morsel of it. He was very, very angry at the tiger.

One day not long after, the rabbit went to a place not far from the tiger's house and began cutting down big staves of wood. The tiger soon happened along and asked him what he was doing.

"I'm getting ready to build a stockade around myself," replied the rabbit. "Haven't you heard the orders?" The tiger said that he hadn't heard any orders.

"That is very strange," said the rabbit. "The order has gone forth that every beast shall fortify himself by building a stockade around himself. All the beasts are doing it."

The tiger became very much alarmed. "O, dear! O, dear! What shall I do," he cried. "I don't know how to build a stockade. I never could do it in the world. O, good rabbit! O, kind rabbit! You are such a very good friend of mine. Couldn't you, as a great favour, because of our long friendship, build a stockade about me before you build one around yourself?"

The rabbit replied that he could not think of risking his own life by building the tiger's fortifications first. Finally, however, he consented to do it.

The rabbit cut down great quantities of long sharp sticks. He set them firmly in the ground about the tiger. He fastened others securely over the top until the tiger was completely shut in by strong bars. Then he went away and left the tiger.

The tiger waited and waited for something to happen to show him the need of the fortifications. Nothing at all happened.

He got very hungry and thirsty. After a while, the monkey passed that way.

The tiger called out, "O, monkey, has the danger passed?"

The monkey did not know what danger the tiger meant, but he replied, "Yes."

Then the tiger said, "O, monkey, O, good, kind monkey, will you not please be so kind as to help me out of my stockade?"

"Let the one who got you in there help you out," replied the monkey and he went on his way.

Along came the goat and the tiger called out, "O, goat, has the danger passed?"

The goat did not know anything about any danger, but he replied, "Yes."

Then the tiger said, "O, goat, O, good kind goat, please be so kind as to help me out of my stockade."

"Let the one who got you in there help you out," replied the goat as he went on his way.

Along came the armadillo and the tiger called out, "O, armadillo, has the danger passed?"

The armadillo had not heard of any danger, but he replied that it had passed.

Then the tiger said, "O, armadillo, O, good, kind armadillo, you have always been such a good friend and neighbour. Please help me now to get out of my stockade."

"Let the one who got you in there help you out," replied the armadillo as he went on his way.

The tiger jumped and jumped with all his force at the top of the stockade, but he could not break through. He jumped and jumped with all his might at the front side of the stockade, but he could not break through. He thought that never in the world would he be able to break out. He rested for a little while and as he rested he thought. He thought how bright the sun was shining outside. He thought what good hunting there was in the jungle. He thought how cool the water was at the spring. Once more he jumped and jumped with all his might at the back side of the stockade. At last he broke through. He did not get through, however, without getting bad cuts on both his sides from the sharp edges of the staves. Until this day, the tiger has stripes on both his sides.

Arnomongo and Iput-Iput (The Ape and the Firefly)

ONE EVENING THE firefly was on his way to the house of a friend, and as he passed the ape's house, the latter asked him, "Mr. Firefly, why do you carry a light?" The firefly replied, "Because I am afraid of the mosquitoes." "Oh, then you are a coward, are you?" said the ape. "No, I am not," was the answer. "If you are not afraid," asked the ape, "why do you always carry a lantern?" "I carry a lantern so that when the mosquitoes come to bite me I can see them and defend myself," replied the firefly. Then the ape laughed aloud, and on the next day he told all his neighbours that the firefly carried a light at night because he was a coward.

When the firefly heard what the ape had said, he went to his house. It was night and the ape was asleep, but the firefly flashed his light into his face and awakened him. The firefly was very angry and said, "Why did you spread the report that I was a coward? If you wish to prove which of us is the braver, I will fight you on the plaza next Sunday evening."

The ape enquired, "Have you any companions?" "No," replied the firefly, "I will come alone." Then the ape laughed at the idea of such a little creature presuming to fight with him, but the firefly continued, "I shall be expecting you on the plaza about six o'clock next Sunday afternoon." The ape replied, "You had better bring someone to help you, as I shall bring my whole company, about a thousand apes, each as big as myself." This he said, thinking to frighten the strange little insect, who seemed to him to be crazy. But the firefly answered, "I shall not need any companions, but will come alone. Goodbye."

When the firefly had gone, the ape called together his company, and told them about the proposed fight. He ordered them to get each one a club about three feet long and to be on the plaza at six o'clock the next Sunday evening. His companions were greatly amazed, but as they were used to obeying their captain, they promised to be ready at the appointed time and place.

On Sunday evening, just before six o'clock, they assembled on the plaza, and found the firefly already waiting for them. Just then the church bells rang the Angelus, so the firefly proposed that they should all pray. Immediately after the prayer, the firefly signified that he was ready to begin. The ape had drawn up his company in line, with himself at the head. Suddenly the firefly lighted upon the ape's nose. The ape next in line struck at the firefly, but succeeded only in striking the captain such a terrible blow on the nose as to kill him. The firefly meanwhile, seeing the blow coming, had jumped upon the nose of the second ape, who was killed by the next in line just as the captain had been killed; and so on down the whole line, until there was but one ape left. He threw down his club and begged the firefly to spare him. The firefly graciously allowed him to live, but since that time the apes have been in mortal terror of the fireflies.

The Battle of the Crabs

ONE DAY THE land crabs had a meeting. One of them said, "What shall we do with the waves? They sing all the time so loudly that we cannot possibly sleep well at night." "Do you not think it would be well for all of us males to go down and fight them?" asked the eldest of the crabs. "Yes," all replied. "Well, tomorrow all the males must get ready to go."

The next day they started to go down to the sea. On the way they met the shrimp. "Where are you going, my friends?" asked the shrimp. The crabs answered, "We are going to fight the waves, because they will not let us sleep at night."

"I don't think you will win the battle," said the shrimp. "The waves are very strong, while your legs are so weak that your bodies bend almost to the ground when you walk," and he laughed.

The crabs were so angry at his scorn that they ran at the shrimp and pinched him until he promised to help them in the battle.

When they reached the shore, the crabs looked at the shrimp and said, "Your face is turned the wrong way, friend shrimp," and they laughed at him, for crabs are much like other people, and think they are the only ones who are right. "Are you ready to fight with the waves? What weapon have you?"

"My weapon," replied the shrimp, "is a spear on my head." Just then he saw a large wave coming, and ran away; but the crabs, who were all looking towards the shore, did not see it, and were killed.

The wives of the dead crabs wondered why their husbands did not come home. They thought the battle must be a long one, and decided to go down and help their husbands. As they reached the shore and entered the water to look for their husbands, the waves killed them.

A short time afterwards, thousands of little crabs, such as are now called fiddlers, were found near the shore. When these children were old enough to walk, the shrimp often visited them and related to them the sad fate of their parents. And so, if you will watch carefully the fiddlers, you will notice that they always seem ready to run back to the land, where their forefathers lived, and then, as they regain their courage, they rush down, as if about to fight the waves. But they always lack the courage to do so, and continually run back and forth. They live neither on dry land, as their ancestors did, nor in the sea, like the other crabs, but up on the beach, where the waves wash over them at high tide and try to dash them to pieces.

The Eagle and the Hen

ONE DAY THE eagle declared his love for the hen. He flew down to search for her, and when he had found her he said, "I wish you to be my mate."

The hen answered, "I am willing, but let me first grow wings like yours, so I can fly as high as you." The eagle replied, "I will do so, and as a sign of our betrothal I will give you this ring. Take good care of it until I come again."

The hen promised to do so, and the eagle flew away.

The next day the cock met the hen. When he saw the ring around her neck he was very much surprised and said, "Where did you get that ring? I think you are not true to me. Do you not remember your promise to be my mate? Throw away that ring." So she did.

At the end of a week the eagle came with beautiful feathers to dress the hen. When she saw him she became frightened and hid behind the door. The eagle entered, crying, "How are you, my dear hen? I am bringing you a beautiful dress," and he showed it to the hen. "But where is your ring? Why do you not wear it?" The hen could not at first answer, but after a little she tried to deceive the eagle, and said, "Oh, pardon me, sir! Yesterday as I was walking in the garden I met a large snake, and I was so frightened that I ran towards the house. When I reached it I found that I had lost the ring, and I looked everywhere for it; but alas! I have not yet found it."

The eagle looked keenly at the hen and said, "I would never have believed that you would behave so badly. I promise you that, whenever you have found my ring, I will come down again and take you for my mate. As a punishment for breaking your promise you shall always scratch the ground and look for the ring, and all your chickens that I find I will snatch away from you. That is all. Goodbye." Then he flew away.

And ever since, all the hens all over the world have been scratching to find the eagle's ring.

How the Lizards Got Their Markings

ONE DAY THE Chameleon (palas) and the Monitor lizard (ibid) were out in a deep forest together. They thought they would try scratching each other's backs to make pretty figures on them.

First the Chameleon said to the Monitor lizard, "You must scratch a nice pattern on my back."

So the Monitor went to work, and the Chameleon had a fine scratching. Monitor made a nice, even pattern on his back.

Then Monitor asked Chameleon for a scratching. But no sooner had Chameleon begun to work on Monitor's back than there came the sound of a dog barking. A man was hunting in the forest with his dog.

The sharp barks came nearer and nearer to the two lizards; and the Chameleon got such a scare that his fingers shook, and the pretty design he was making went all askew. Then he stopped short and ran away, leaving the Monitor with a very shabby marking on his back.

This is the reason that the monitor lizard is not so pretty as the chameleon.

The Living Head

THERE ONCE LIVED a man and his wife who had no children. They earnestly desired to have a son, so they prayed to their God, Diva, that he would give them a son, even if it were only a head.

Diva pitied them, and gave them a head for a son. Head, for that was his name, grew up, and gradually his father and mother ceased to think of his misfortune, and grew to love him very much.

One day Head saw the chief's daughter pass the house, and fell in love with her.

"Mother," he said, "I am in love with the chief's daughter and wish to marry her. Go now, I pray you, to the chief and ask him to give me his daughter to be my wife."

"Dear Head," answered his mother, "it is of no use to go on such an errand, the chief's daughter will surely not be willing to marry only a head." But Head insisted, so, in order to quiet him, his mother went to the chief and made known her son's desire. Of course she met with a refusal, and returned home and told Head the result of her errand.

Head went downstairs into the garden and began to sink into the ground.

"Head, come up," said his mother, "and let us eat."

"Sink! sink! sink!" cried Head.

"Head, come up and let us eat!" repeated his mother.

"Sink! sink! sink!" was Head's answer, and he continued to sink until he could no longer be seen. His mother tried in vain to take him out. After a while a tree sprang up just where Head had sunk, and in a short time it bore large, round fruit, almost as large as a child's head. This is the origin of the orange tree.

The Meeting of the Plants

ONCE UPON A time plants were able to talk as well as people, and to walk from place to place. One day King Molave, the strongest tree, who lived on a high mountain, called his subjects together for a general meeting.

Then every tree put itself in motion towards the designated spot, each doing its best to reach it first. But the buri palm was several days late, which made the king angry, and he cursed it in these terms:

"You must be punished for your negligence, and as king I pass upon you this sentence: You shall never see your descendants, for you shall die just as your seeds are ready to grow." And from that day the buri palms have always died without seeing their descendants.

The Spider and the Fly

MR. SPIDER WAS once in love with Miss Fly. Several times he declared his love, but was always repelled, for Miss Fly disliked his business.

One day, when she saw him coming, she closed the doors and windows of her house and made ready a pot of boiling water.

Mr. Spider called to be allowed to enter the house, but Miss Fly's only answer was to throw the boiling water at him.

"Well!" cried Mr. Spider, "I and my descendants shall be avenged upon you and yours. We will never give you a moment's peace."

Mr. Spider did not break his word, for to this day we see his hatred of the fly.

Why Dogs Wag Their Tails

ONCE UPON A time, there lived in a certain pueblo a rich man who had a dog and a cat. His only daughter, of whom he was very fond, was studying in a convent in a city several miles distant and it was his custom, about once a week, to send the dog and cat to take her a little present. The dog was so old that he had lost all his teeth, and so was unable to fight, but the cat was strong and very cunning, and so one could help the other, since the dog knew better how to find the way.

One day, the rich man wished to send a magic ring to his daughter, so he called the dog and the cat to him. To the cat he said, "You are very cunning and prudent. You may carry this magic ring to my daughter, but be sure to take very great care of it." To the dog he said, "You are to go with the cat to take a magic ring to my daughter. Take care not to lose the way, and see that no one molests the cat." Both animals promised to do their best and set out immediately.

On the way, they were obliged to cross a wide and deep river, over which there was no bridge, and as they were unable to find a boat, they determined to swim across it. The dog said to the cat, "Give me the magic ring." "Oh, no," replied the cat. "Did you not hear the master say just what each of us had to do?"

"Yes, but you are not very good at swimming, and may lose the ring, while I am strong and can take good care of it," answered the dog. The cat continued to refuse to disobey its master, until at last the dog threatened to kill it, and it was obliged to entrust the ring to the dog's keeping.

Then they began to swim across the river, which was so strong that they were about an hour in getting over, so that both became very tired and weak. Just before they came to the other side, the dog dropped the ring into the water, and it was impossible to find it. "Now," said the cat, "we had better go back home and tell our master that we have lost the ring." "Yes," answered the dog, "but I am very much afraid." So they turned back toward home, but as they drew near the house his fear so overcame him that he ran away and was never seen again.

The master was very much surprised to see the cat back so soon, and asked him, "Where is your companion?" The cat was at first afraid to answer. "Where is the dog?" asked the master again. "Oh, he ran away," replied the cat. "Ran away?" said the master. "What do you mean? Where is the ring?" "Oh, pardon me, my master," answered the cat. "Do not be angry, and I will tell you what has happened. When we reached the bank of the river, the dog asked me to give him the ring. This I refused many times, until at last he threatened to kill me if I did not give it to him, and I was obliged to do so. The river was very hard to cross, and on the way the dog dropped the ring into the water and we could not find it. I persuaded the dog to come back with me to tell you about it, but on the way he became so frightened that he ran away."

Then the master made a proclamation to the people, offering a reward to the one who should find his old dog and bring him to him. They could recognize the dog by his being old and having no teeth. The master also declared that when he had found the delinquent he would punish him by cutting off his tail. He ordered that the dogs all around the world should take part in the search, and so ever since that time, when one dog meets another he always asks, "Are you the old dog who lost the magic ring? If you are, your tail must be cut off." Then instantly, both show their teeth and wag their tails to mean no. Since that time, also, cats have been afraid of water, and will never swim across a river if it can be avoided.

The Monkey and the Turtle

ONE DAY, A Monkey met a Turtle on the road, and asked, "Where are you going?"

"I am going to find something to eat, for I have had no food for three whole days," said the Turtle.

"I too am hungry," said the Monkey, "and since we are both hungry, let us go together and hunt food for our stomachs' sake."

They soon became good friends and chatted along the way, so that the time passed quickly. Before they had gone far, the Monkey saw a large bunch of yellow bananas on a tree at a distance.

"Oh, what a good sight that is!" cried he. "Don't you see the bananas hanging on that banana tree? (pointing with his first finger toward the tree). They are fine! I can taste them already."

But the Turtle was short-sighted and could not see them. By and by they came near the tree, and then he saw them. The two friends were very glad. The mere sight of the ripe, yellow fruit seemed to assuage their hunger.

But the Turtle could not climb the tree, so he agreed that the Monkey should go up alone and should throw some of the fruit down to him. The Monkey was up in a flash; and, seating himself comfortably, he began to eat the finest of the fruit, and forgot to drop any down to the Turtle waiting below. The Turtle called for some, but the Monkey pretended not to hear. He ate even the peelings, and refused to drop a bit to his friend, who was patiently begging under the tree.

At last the Turtle became angry, very angry indeed, "so he thought he would revenge" (as my informant puts it). While the Monkey was having a good time, and filling his stomach, the Turtle gathered sharp, broken pieces of glass, and stuck them, one by one, all around the banana tree. Then he hid himself under a coconut shell not far away. This shell had a hole in the top to allow the air to enter. That was why the Turtle chose it for his hiding-place.

The Monkey could not eat all the bananas, for there were enough to last a good-sized family several days, "but he ate all what he can," and by and by came down the tree with great difficulty, for the glass was so sharp that it cut even the tough hand of the Monkey. He had a hard time, and his hands were cut in many places. The Turtle thought he had his revenge, and was not so angry as before.

But the Monkey was now very angry at the trick that had been played upon him, and began looking for the Turtle, intending to kill him. For some time he could not find his foe, and, being very tired, he sat down on the coconut shell nearby. His weariness increased his anger at the Turtle very much.

He sat on the shell for a long time, suffering from his wounds, and wondering where to find the Turtle – his former friend, but now his enemy. Because of the disturbance of the shell, the Turtle inside could not help making a noise. This the Monkey heard; and he was surprised, for he could not determine whence the sound came. At last he lifted his stool, and there found his foe the Turtle.

"Ha! Here you are!" he cried. "Pray now, for it is the end of your life."

He picked up the Turtle by the neck and carried him near the riverbank, where he meant to kill him. He took a mortar and pestle, and built a big fire, intending to pound him to powder or burn him to death. When everything was ready, he told the Turtle to choose whether he should die in the fire or be 'grounded' in the mortar. The Turtle begged for his life; but when he found it was in vain, he prayed to be thrown into the fire or ground in the mortar – anything except be thrown into the water. On hearing this, the Monkey picked the Turtle up in his bleeding fingers, and with all his might threw him into the middle of the stream.

Then the Turtle was very glad. He chuckled at his own wit, and laughed at the foolishness of the Monkey. He came up to the surface of the water and mocked at the Monkey, saying, "This is my home. The water is my home."

This made the Monkey so angry that he lost his self-possession entirely. He jumped into the middle of the river after the Turtle, and was drowned.

Since that day, monkeys and turtles have been bitter enemies.

Star Tales of the Aboriginal Australians

VENUS IN THE Summer evenings is a striking object in the western sky. Our Venus they call the Laughing Star, who is a man. He once said something very improper, and has been laughing at his joke ever since. As he scintillates you seem to see him grinning still at his Rabelais-like witticism, seeing which the aborigines say:

'He's a rude old man, that Laughing Star.'

The Milky Way is a warrambool, or water overflow; the stars are the fires, and the dusky haze the smoke from them, which spirits of the dead have lit on their journey across the sky. In their fires they are cooking the mussels they gather where they camp.

There is one old man up there who was once a great rainmaker, and when you see that he has turned round as the position of the Milky Way is altered, you may expect rain; he never moves except to make it.

A waving dark shadow that you will see along the same course is Kurreah, the crocodile.

To get to the Warrambool, the Wurrawilberoo, two dark spots in Scorpio, have to be passed. They are devils who try to catch the spirits of the dead, sometimes even coming to earth, when they animate whirlwinds and strike terror into the people. The old men try to keep them from racing through the camp by throwing their spears and boomerangs at them.

The Pleiades are seven sisters, as usual, the dimmed ones having been dulled because on earth Wurrunnah seized them and tried to melt the crystal off them at a fire; for, beautiful as they were with their long hair, they were ice-maidens. But he was unsuccessful beyond dulling their brightness, for the ice as it melted put out the fire. The two ice-maidens were miserable on earth with him, and eventually escaped by the aid of one of their 'multiplex totems,' the pine tree. Wurrunnah had told them to get him pine bark. Now the Meamei – Pleiades – belong to the Beewee totem, and so does the pine tree. They chopped the pine bark, and as they did so the tree telescoped itself to the sky where the five other Meamei were, whom they now joined, and with whom they have remained ever since. But they who were polluted by their enforced residence with the earth-man never shone again with the brightness of their sisters. This legend was told emphasizing the beauty of chastity.

Men had desired all the sisters when once they travelled on earth, but they kept themselves unspotted from the world, with the exception of the two Wurrunnah captured by stratagem.

Orion's Sword and Belt are the Berai-Berai – the boys – who best of all loved the Meamei, for whom they used to hunt, bringing their offerings to them; but the ice-maidens were obdurate and cold, disdaining lovers, as might be expected from their parentage. Their father was a rocky mountain, their mother an icy mountain stream. But when they were translated to the sky the Berai-Berai were inconsolable. They would not hunt, they would not eat, they pined away and died. The spirits pitied them and placed them in the sky within sound of the singing of the Meamei, and there they are happy. By day they hunt, and at night light their corroboree fires, and dance to the singing in the distance. Just to remind the earth-people of them, the Meamei drop down some ice in the winter, and they it is who make the winter thunderstorms.

Castor and Pollux, in some tribes, are two hunters of long ago.

Canopus is Womba, the Mad Star, the wonderful Weedah of long ago, who, on losing his loves, went mad, and was sent to the sky that they might not reach him; but they followed, and are travelling after him to this day, and after them the wizard Beereeun, their evil genius, who made the mirage on the plains in order to deceive them, that they and Weedah might be lured on by it and perish of thirst.

When they escaped him, Beereeun threw a barbed spear into the sky, and hooked one spear on to another until he made a ladder up which he climbed after them; and across the sky he is still pursuing them.

The Clouds of Magellan are the Bralgah, or Native Companions, mother and daughter, whom the Wurrawilberoo chased in order to kill and eat the mother and keep the daughter, who was the great dancer of the tribes. They almost caught her, but her tribe pursued them too quickly; when, determined that if they lost her so should her people, they chanted an incantation and changed her from Bralgah, the dancing-girl, to Bralgah, the dancing-bird, then left her to wander about the plains. They translated themselves on beefwood trees into the sky, and there they are still.

Gowargay, the featherless emu, is a debbil-debbil of waterholes; he drags people who bathe in his holes down and drowns them, but goes every night to his sky-camp, the Coalpit, a dark place by the Southern Cross, and there he crouches. Our Corvus, the crow, is the kangaroo.

The Southern Crown is Mullyan, the eagle-hawk. The Southern Cross was the first Minggah, or spirit tree a huge Yaraan, which was the medium for the translation of the first man who died on earth to the sky. The white cockatoos which used to roost in this tree when they saw it moving skywards followed it, and are following it still as Mouyi, the pointers. The other Yaraan trees wailed for the sadness that death brought into the world, weeping tears of blood. The red gum which crystallises down their trunks is the tears.

Some tribes say it was by a woman's fault that death came into the world.

This legend avers that at first the tribes were meant to live for ever. The women were told never to go near a certain hollow tree. The bees made a nest in this tree; the women coveted the honey, but the men forbade them to go near it. But at last, one woman determined to get that honey; chop went her tomahawk into that hollow trunk, and out flew a huge bat. This was the spirit of death which was now let free to roam the world, claiming all it could touch with its wings.

Of eclipses there are various accounts. Some say it is Yhi, the sun, the wanton woman, who has overtaken at last her enemy the moon, who scorned her love, and whom now she tries to kill, but the spirits intervene, dreading a return to a dark world. Some say the enemies have managed to get evil spirits into each other which are destroying them. The wirreenuns chant incantations to oust these spirits of evil, and when the eclipse is over claim a triumph of their magic.

Another account says that Yhi, the sun, after many lovers, tried to ensnare Bahloo, the moon; but he would have none of her, and so she chases him across the sky, telling the spirits who stand round the sky holding it up, that if they let him escape past them to earth, she will throw down the spirit who sits in the sky holding the ends of the Kurrajong ropes which they guard at the other end, and if that spirit falls, the earth will be hurled down into everlasting darkness.

So poor Bahloo, when he wants to get to earth and go on with the creation of baby girls, has to sneak down as an emu past the spirits, hurrying off as soon as the sun sinks down too.

Bahloo is a very important personage in legends.

When the blacks see a halo round the moon they say, 'Hullo! Going to be rain. Bahloo building a house to keep himself dry.'

When storms were threatening, some of the clouds have a netted sort of look, something like a mackerel sky, only with a dusky green tinge, they would say, 'See the old man with the net on his back; he's going to drop some hailstones.'

Meteors always mean death; should a trail follow them, the dead person has left a large family.

Comets are a spirit of evil supposed to drink up the rainclouds, so causing a drought; their tails being huge families all thirsty, so thirsty that they draw the river up into the clouds.

Every natural feature in any way pronounced has a mythical reason for its existence, every peculiarity in bird life, every peculiarity in the trees and stones. Besides there are many mythical bogies still at large, according to native lore, making the bush a gnome-land.

Even the winds carry a legend in their breath.

You hear people say they could have 'burst with rage,' but it is left to a black's legend to tell of a whole tribe bursting with rage, and so originating the winds.

There was once an invisible tribe called Mayrah. These people, men and women, though they talked and hunted with them, could never be seen by the other tribes, to whom were only visible their accoutrements for hunting. They would hear a woman's voice speak to them, see perhaps a goolay in mid-air and hear from it an invisible baby's cry; they would know then a Mayrah woman was there. Or a man would speak to them. Looking up, they would see a belt with weapons in it, a forehead band too, perhaps, but no waist nor forehead, a water vessel invisibly held: a man was there, an invisible Mayrah. One of these Mayrah men chummed with one of the Doolungaiyah tribe; he was a splendid mate, a great hunter, and all that was desirable, but for his invisibility. The Doolungaiyah longed to see him, and began to worry him on the subject, until at last the Mayrah became enraged, went to his tribe, and told them of the curiosity of the other tribes as to their bodily forms. The others became as furious as he was; they all burst with rage and rushed away roaring in six different directions, and ever since have only returned as formless wind to be heard but never seen. So savagely the Mayrah howled round the Doolungaiyah's camp that he burrowed into the sand to escape, and his tribe have burrowed ever since.

Three of the winds are masculine and three feminine. The Crow, according to legend, controls Gheeger Gheeger, and keeps her in a hollow log. The Eagle-hawk owns Gooroongoodilbaydilbay, and flies with her in the shape of high clouds. Yarragerh is a man, and he has for wives the Budtha, Bibbil and Bumble trees, and when he breathes on them they burst into new shoots, buds, flowers and fruits, telling the world that their lover Yarragerh, the spring, has come.

Douran Doura woos the Coolabah and Kurrajong, who flower after the hot north wind has kissed them.

The women winds have no power to make trees fruitful. They can but moan through them, or tear them in rage for the lovers they have stolen, whom they can only meet twice a year at the great corroboree of the winds, when they all come together, heard but never seen; for Mayrah, the winds, are invisible, as were the Mayrah, the tribe who in bursting gave them birth.

Yarragerh and Douran Doura are the most honoured winds as being the surest rain-bringers. In some of the blacks' songs Mayrah is sung of as the mother of Yarragerh, the spring, or as a woman kissed into life by Yarragerh, putting such warmth into her that she blows the winter away. But these are poetical licences, for Yarragerh is ordinarily a man who woos the trees as a spring wind until the flowers are born and the fruit formed, then back he goes to the heaven whence he came.

The Battle of the Giants

ONCE THE VOLCANOES Taranaki, Ruapehu, and Tongariro dwelled together. That was the time when Tongariro in her wonderful beauty had captured the fiery hearts of the two giants, so that their joy filled the heavens with majestic outbursts and covered the earth with their dark-glowing heart-blood of fiery lava and molten stones.

Softly then answered the gently ascending Steam-column of Tongariro, smiling and swaying, gold-bordered by the setting sun; smiling at both her suitors.

Ah, Tongariro was a woman!

Both, the straight and simple Taranaki and the rugged and strong Ruapehu, their cloud-piercing heads covered with spotless snow, or adorned in their passion-glowing lava-streams, were beloved by Tongariro; but the snows of the winter and the suns of the summer came and went from the first time, to the hundredth time, to the thousandth time, and still Tongariro was undecided whom she would prefer for a husband.

She became the sacred mountain of the Maori people; her beauty captured the hearts of all, so that she became the possessor of the highest tapu, and no foot dared walk upon her, and only the eyes of the new-born were directed towards her; and the eyes of the departing rested full love upon her beauty, whilst they wandered to the Reinga.

The eyes of generations upon generations of man.

Beautiful to behold from all the lands was the great love of the giants; now all covered with glittering snow, now hiding in the clouds and bursting forth, covered with strange and wonderful beauty; now girdling their bodies with clouds and lifting their endless heads into the golden heavens; and now again breaking forth into terrible passions, covering the earth with blackness.

Ah, Tongariro roused the passions of the giants: she made the volcanoes tremble! Their blood of fire and boiling stones shook them, the thundering of their voices, roaring insults at each other, made the earth tremble. Streams of lightning pierced the nights, and black smoke of deadly hate darkened the days, and the ears of man were filled with the roaring hate of the giants, and their wondering eyes beheld the beauty of Tongariro, smiling at both!

At last the two rivals decided to fight for Tongariro!

Now followed days of silence. The giants stood there grim and silent to the world, but they were gathering strength, and were melting stones in their insides, and lit terrible fires, their powerful weapons. So they stood silent and grim; the sun gilding their beautiful garments of snow, and Tongariro smiled at them with her graceful swaying column of steam; and the Maori people looked wonderingly upon the peaceful landscape.

Then a rolling grew into the nights, and rolling filled the days; louder and louder, night after night, day after day – a terrible groaning, damp and deep. Suddenly a crashing thunder shook the earth, and bursting forth from the mouth of Ruapehu a fiery mass of molten stones and black hate and fury fell upon Taranaki, covering him with a terrible coat of fire, whilst the flying winds howled and the melted snow-waters fled thundering down into the valleys.

A beautiful straight form gave the mass of fire and ashes to Taranaki – but he shook in terrible rage! He tore himself out of the ground, shaking the earth and breaking the lands asunder; he tried to fly at Ruapehu, to kill him with his weight. But Ruapehu made the water of his lake, high up in the snows, boil, and, hurling it down, it filled all the rends Taranaki had made in the earth, and burned all the inside of the earth and of Taranaki himself. He now, tearing the air with his roaring cries of pain and thundering howling of rage, threw a tremendous mass of stones at his enemy, and broke the highest cone, the loftiest peak of Ruapehu, so that his looks were not so majestic, and his reach not so far into the skies.

Ruapehu now, in deadly hate, swallowed his broken cone and melted it; he lit terrible fires in his inside, which spread to the lake Roto-aira, so that it rose and boiled, the steam covering all the world and blinding Taranaki. Then Ruapehu filled himself with the boiling water, and, throwing it out of his mouth down upon Taranaki, it filled all the crevices, and it lifted him, for he himself had loosened his bonds with the earth; and now, darkening day into night, he sent the molten mass of his swallowed cone against his enemy, so that he was compelled to retreat: blinded by steam, burned in his inside by the boiling water, and covered with the molten mass of the cone of Ruapehu he himself had broken.

He groaned, and rose, and tumbled, and shook himself; and he felt for a way to the sea to cool his burning pain; howling in unbearable pain he had to run, in order to get out of reach of Ruapehu, deeply hollowing his path through the lands. But his conqueror, Ruapehu, melting all his ice and snow, sent it as boiling water into this deep path, that his enemy might not come back again, for his strength also was exhausted.

On to the sea went Taranaki, and, when his pain had left him a little, he looked back at his conqueror, and saw how his three peaks were again covered with fresh snow, and how he was now the supreme lord over all the lands and the husband of Tongariro. They two were now the arikis over all the land; but it was waste now, and dead, for the terrible fight had killed all the people and the living beings all around. Once more a burst of black anger broke forth from Taranaki, and again it was answered by a wonderful swaying and smiling steam-column from Tongariro; and then he went and wandered along the coast till he had found a place for his sorrow. There he stands now, brooding on revenge.

"And my people know that one day he will come back in a straight line, to fight Ruapehu again; and none of my people will ever live or be buried in that lime; for one day he will come back to fight for Tongariro – who knows?"

But the path of Taranaki to the sea is now the Wanganui River.

The Origin of Kava

THIS IS THE story of how kava grew. It is said that there was once a chief called Loau, whose ancestors resided in Lifuka, and for whom the district of Haaloau in Lifuka is named. It is said that his dwelling had eight enclosures or fences and that a great number of people lived there.

Whilst Loau resided at Haamea, a man called Fevanga paid a visit to Loau. The name of Fevanga's wife was Fefafa. After residing some time with Loau, Fevanga told him that he would like to go to Eueiki to see his relatives and that he would soon return again. To this the chief agreed.

Fevanga went to the island of Eueiki and stopped there with his wife. They had a daughter who was a leper. Time went on and still Fevanga tarried in Eueiki. Loau missed Fevanga and finally decided to go to Eueiki himself, so he had his dependants prepare for the voyage. A large rowing canoe (*tafaanga*) was launched and away they went to Eueiki. They arrived there at dusk. Loau ordered that the canoe be carried to Fevanga's home and put close to a large *kape* plant (*Arum costatnm*), with the outrigger on top of the kape.

Fevanga came down to greet his visitors and they responded, saying: "Happy to see you in good health in this island." Loau sat down with his back to the big *kape*, whilst Fevanga searched for food. Fevanga's search was not fruitful, for Eueiki was suffering from famine at the time. Nevertheless, he fired his earth oven and at the same time suggested to Loau that, if he would not mind going down to the beach, he would find it cooler there. Fevanga was desirous that Loau should move in order that he might dig up the kape plant to roast.

After Loau had accommodatingly removed to the beach, Fevanga dug up the big *kape* plant and put it in the oven. He then killed his leperous daughter and roasted her together with the kape. Shortly after Loau and his men returned, the oven was opened, and the food set before Loau. Loau issued orders that the head of Fevanga's unfortunate daughter be cut off and buried in one place, while the body was to be buried in another place. Loau told Fevanga to take notice that two plants would grow from the head and that he was to care for them. Farewells were said and Loau returned to Tongatabu.

Fevanga remained in Eueiki to care for the plants, as it was his duty to take them to Loau in Haamea when they had reached maturity. They proved to be kava and sugar cane. He watched them carefully and, one day when they were nearly full grown, he saw a rat gnawing the kava. After eating the kava, the rat chewed the sugar cane. All the Tongan people drink the kava and eat the sugar cane, because the rat ate the kava first and then the sugar cane. Then Fevanga knew that the time had arrived to pull up the two plants and take them to Tongatabu for a meeting of the chiefs.

When Loau saw Fevanga approaching with the plants he cried: "This is the kava of Fevanga and Fefafa from Faimata. A single chief for the *olovaha* (i.e., the plain under side of the kava bowl which is towards the presiding chief at a kava party), and many for the *apaapa* (the place occupied by other chiefs at a kava party). Husk of the coconut for cleaning the kava root." A bowl was brought and a *matapule* directed a person from the *toua* (the place occupied in a kava party by the people as opposed to the aloft, the place of the chiefs) to make kava. Coconut husks were used to gather the pieces of kava in, as it was split. Then it was given to the people sitting in the toua to be chewed. After being chewed, it was placed in the bowl, mixed, and served. Directions were issued to chop the sugar cane, which was used as a relish (the yam, banana, or other food eaten at a kava drinking ceremony) with the kava.

The place where the kava grew is still to be seen in Eueiki even unto this day.

Death, the Afterlife & the Underworld

Introduction

SUMMONED DOWN TO the Underworld by the two Lords of Death – twin-brother deities – the twins Hunhun-Ahpu and Vukub-Hunahpu are challenged to a ballgame. The losers will die, the Lords declare. The young men can't compete, of course, and quickly lose once the playing starts and so are duly killed in sacrifice. Hunhun-Ahpu's head is hung in the branches of a barren tree, which promptly breaks out in flowers and fruit. An array of animal and spirit helpers bring the Hero Twins back to life, and ultimately enable them to overthrow the Lords of Death. Given fresh forms as the Sun and Moon, they preside from the sky over a new, more hopeful order in which humanity is born out of a head of maize. The story of 'A Journey to Xibalba' and of the sacrifice with which the twins brought the world to life is at the heart of the Maya's central mythic text, the *Popol Vuh*. Other cultures may not have seen the need to carry out industrial-scale human sacrifice as those of Mesoamerica did, but all have sensed that, in some way, death is key to life.

Pluto and the Underworld

AT THE BEGINNING of the world, before the gods came to dwell in Olympus, all the universe was in the hands of the Titans; and among these the greatest was Saturn – or Cronos, who wedded his sister Rhea (also called Cybele) and became the father of three sons and three daughters, Jupiter, Pluto, Neptune, Ceres, Vesta, and Juno. For many ages, Saturn and Rhea, having subdued all the opposing Titans, ruled over heaven and earth; but when the cruelty of Saturn drove his children into rebellion, there arose a mighty war in the universe, in which the sons and daughters of Saturn leagued against their father, who had called upon the other Titans for aid. After years of combat, the six brothers and sisters, helped by the Cyclops, defeated the allied Titans and imprisoned them in the black abyss of Tartarus – all except a few who had not joined in the war against the children of Saturn. Among those who were wise enough to accept the new sovereignty were Mnemosyne (Memory) and Themis, goddess of justice. Those descendants of the Titans who refused to acknowledge the supremacy of Jupiter were consigned to the centre of Mount Etna, as were the giants who constantly turned over and over, making Pluto fear for the safety of his realm. A few of the giants were spared: Atlas, whose punishment was to hold the heavens on his shoulders, and Prometheus and Epimetheus who had espoused the cause of Jupiter and so escaped the fate of the conquered Titans. When the children of Saturn found themselves masters of the world, they agreed to accept Jupiter as their ruler, on condition that the two other brothers be given a share in the universe. So a division was made whereby Pluto became king of the underworld – or Hades; Neptune took the dominion of the sea; and Jupiter, having married his sister, Juno, established his dwelling in Olympus as lord of heaven and earth.

The kingdom of Pluto was dreaded by all mortals, and its ruler inspired men with great fear. Though Pluto was known to visit the earth from time to time, no one wished to see his face, and each man dreaded the moment when he should be obliged to appear before the grim monarch of Hades, and be assigned a place among the innumerable dead. No temples were dedicated to Pluto, though altars were sometimes erected on which men burned sacrifices to this inexorable god while petitioning him to be merciful to the souls of the departed. The festivals held in his honour were celebrated only once in a hundred years, and on these occasions none but black animals were killed for the sacrifice.

The underworld, over which Pluto reigned, was deep in the heart of the earth; but there were several entrances to it, one being near Lake Avernus, where the mist rising from the waters was so foul that no bird could fly over it. The lake itself was in an extinct volcano near Vesuvius. It was very deep, and was surrounded by high banks covered with a thick forest. The first descent into Hades could be easily accomplished (*facilis descensus Averno*, says the poet Virgil); but no mortal was daring enough to venture far into the black depths, lest he should never again see the light of day.

At the portals of Hades sits the fierce three-headed dog Cerberus, who keeps all living things from entering the gate, and allows no spirit that has once been admitted to pass out again. From here a long dark pathway leads deeper into Hades, and is finally lost in the rivers that flow around Pluto's throne. The waters of the river Cocytus are salt, as they are made of the tears that stream forever from the eyes of those unhappy souls who are condemned to labour in Tartarus – that part of Hades that is the exclusive abode of the wicked. The Phlegethon River, which is always on fire, separates Tartarus from the rest of Hades, and wretched indeed is the soul that is forced to cross its seething waters. On the banks of the Acheron, a black and turbid river, stand the souls who come fresh from the sunlit earth; for all must pass this river and be brought before the judgment-throne of Pluto. There is no bridge over the murky stream, and the current is so swift that the boldest swimmer would not trust himself to its treacherous waters. The only way to cross is by the leaky, worm-eaten boat rowed by Charon, an aged ferryman who has plied his oar ever since the day that the curse of death first came upon the earth.

No spirit is allowed to enter the leaky craft until he has first paid Charon the fee of a small coin called the obolus. (During the funeral services, before the body is committed for burial, this coin is laid on the tongue of the dead, that the soul may have no trouble in passing to the throne of Pluto.) If any spirits cannot furnish the necessary money, they are ruthlessly pushed aside by the mercenary boatman and are required to wait a hundred years. At the end of this time, Charon grudgingly ferries them over the river free of charge. As the unstable boat can hold but few, there is always an eager group of spirits on the further bank, clamouring to be taken across the river; but Charon is never in a hurry, and repulses, sometimes with his oar, the pitiful crowd that waits his grim pleasure.

There is also in Hades the river Styx, by whose sacred waters the gods swear the most terrible of all oaths, and on the other side of Pluto's throne is the softly flowing Lethe, of which only those souls can drink who are to spend endless days of happiness in the Elysian Fields. As soon as those blessed spirits have tasted of the waters of Lethe, all regrets for friends that mourn completely vanish, and the joy and grief, and pleasure and pain of the soul's life on earth are forgotten. In the Elysian Fields there is no darkness such as fills the rest of Hades with its thick gloom; but a soft light spreads over the meadows where the spirits of the thrice-blessed wander. There are willows here, and stately silver poplars, and the 'meads of Asphodel' breathe out a faint perfume from their pale flowers.

The sighs and groans that rise by night and day from the black abyss of Tartarus do not reach the ears of those who dwell at peace in the Elysian Fields, and the sight of its painful torments is hid forever from their eyes.

Beside Pluto's throne sit the three Fates (also called Parcae), those deathless sisters who hold the threads of life and death in their hands. Clotho, the youngest, spins the thread; Lachesis, the second, twines into it the joys and sorrows, hopes and fears that make up human experience; and Atropos, the eldest sister, sits by with huge shears in her hand, waiting for the time when she may cut the slender thread.

Pluto and his queen Proserpina are seated side by side on a sable throne, ruling over the myriad souls that compose the vast kingdom of the dead. Perched on the back of the throne is the blinking owl, who loves this eternal darkness, and the black-winged raven that was once a bird of snowy plumage and the favourite messenger of Apollo. The raven fell from his high estate on account of some unwelcome tidings that he once brought to Apollo when that god was an ardent lover of the fair-haired Coronis. Believing that no one could supplant him in the maiden's affections, Apollo was happy in the thought of being beloved by so beautiful a mortal; but one day his snow-white raven flew in haste to Olympus to tell him that the maiden was listening to the wooing of another lover. Enraged at this duplicity, Apollo seized his bow and shot the faithless Coronis; but the moment that he saw her lying dead, he repented of his rash deed and vainly sought to restore her to life. Though skilled in the art of healing, Apollo could not save the maiden; and in his frenzied grief he cursed the unfortunate raven that had brought the evil tidings, and banished it forever from his sight.

Near Pluto's throne are seated the three judges of Hades (Minos, Rhadamanthus and Aeacus) who question all souls that are brought across the river. When they have learned every detail of the newcomer's past life, they deliver the cowering spirit into the hands of Themis, the blindfolded goddess of justice, who weighs impartially the good and bad deeds in her unerring scales. If the good outweighs the evil, the soul is led gently to the Elysian Fields; but if the bad overbalances the good, then the wretched spirit is driven to Tartarus, there to suffer for all its wrongdoings in the fires that burn forever and ever behind the brazen gates. To these gates the guilty one is urged by the three Furies, whose snaky hair shakes hideously as they ply their lashes to goad the shrinking soul to its place of torment. Sometimes they are joined by Nemesis, goddess of revenge, who hurries the doomed spirit over the fiery waters of the Phlegethon with her merciless whip, and sees that it follows no path but the one leading to the brazen gates of Tartarus.

As soon as the gates close on the newly admitted soul, there is a renewed clamour of voices, while heart-breaking sighs and groans mingle with the curses of those who in their misery dare to defy the gods. And beneath all the awful sounds that greet the listener's ears, there is an undertone of pitiful wailing like the sea's 'melancholy, long-withdrawing roar' that seems to come from millions of throats too feeble to utter a loud cry. The deepest sighs proceed from the Danaides – the beautiful daughters of Danaus, king of Argos – who must forever strive to fill a bottomless cask with water. They form a sad procession as, with their urns on their arms, they go down to the stream to begin their hopeless task, and then climb wearily up the steep bank to pour the water into the ever-empty cask. If they pause a moment, exhausted with fatigue, the whips of some avenging attendants of Pluto lash them again into action. Their punishment is severe, but the crime for which they are suffering was a dreadful one. The fifty daughters of Danaus were once pledged in marriage to the fifty sons of Aegyptus, brother of Danaus; but when the wedding was being celebrated, their father remembered the words of an ancient prophecy that said that he would die by the hand of his son-in-law. Fearing for his life, he confided to his daughters what the oracle had foretold, and gave them each a dagger, bidding them slay their husbands. On the evening of the wedding, when the sons of Aegyptus were heavy with wine, the new-made wives stole in upon them and killed them as they slept. Danaus then believed himself safe, until he learned that one of his daughters had spared her husband out of love for him. This son-in-law was eager to avenge his brothers' murder, and having sought out the wicked Danaus, fulfilled the prophecy by killing the king with the very dagger intended for his own death. The gods punished the cruel daughters – except Hypermnestra, who had saved her husband – by condemning them to labour in Tartarus at their impossible task.

Near the Danaides stands Tantalus, the father of Niobe, who on earth was a most inhuman and brutal king. He ill-treated his subjects, defied the gods, and dared to make his own will the religion of his kingdom. He boasted that the gods were not so omniscient as people were led to believe; and insulted the immortals by offering them at a banquet the flesh of his own son Pelops, believing that they would never learn the truth of this loathsome feast. But the gods were not deceived, and left the meal untouched – all except poor Ceres, who, still mourning over her daughter's detention in Hades, did not realize what was happening and bit off some of the lad's shoulder. When the gods restored Pelops to life, Ceres was very sorry for her carelessness and gave him a shoulder of ivory. The inhuman Tantalus was condemned to the torments of Tartarus, where he stands up to his chin in a clear stream. Though frenzied with thirst he can never drink of the water, for whenever he bends his head the stream recedes from his parched lips. Above him hangs a branch of delicious fruit; but when, tormented with hunger, he strives to grasp it, the branch eludes his eager fingers. Thus he stays, always 'tantalized' by the sight of food and drink he never can secure.

Not far from Tantalus is Salmoneus, also a king, who dared to challenge the gods by impersonating Jupiter. He made a huge bridge of brass, and drove heavily over it while he threw lighted torches among the people who were waiting below, hoping thus to frighten them into believing that he was the very ruler of the heavens who hurls the mighty thunderbolts. This insult to his divinity so angered Jupiter that he seized a real thunderbolt and soon dispatched the arrogant king. When Salmoneus came before the throne of Pluto, his fate was quickly decided, and he was driven to terrible Tartarus, where he sits under a huge rock that threatens every moment to fall and crush him beneath its weight.

Another unhappy king is Sisyphus, who, when ruler of Corinth, became a famous robber, and in the pride of his great wealth dared to set the gods at naught. Therefore, he was consigned to Tartarus, and his punishment is to roll an immense stone to the top of a steep hill. As soon as he reaches the summit, the rock slips from his aching arms and tumbles to the foot of the hill, and he must at once start on the hopeless task of pushing it up the long ascent again.

Beyond Sisyphus lies Tityus, a giant whose huge body covers nine acres of ground. He was condemned to the blackness of Tartarus because he dared to affront a goddess with his addresses, and so was doomed to suffer, like Prometheus, by being chained to a rock, while a vulture tears at his liver. Near him is Ixion, who was promised the hand of a certain maiden in marriage, on condition that he would give her father a large sum of money. Ixion agreed, but when the maiden became his wife, he refused to give the stipulated sum, in spite of her father's clamourous demands. At length, wearied by the old man's insistence, Ixion slew him; but the deed did not go unpunished, for the gods summoned him to appear before them and answer for his cruelty. Ixion pleaded his cause so well that Jupiter was about to dismiss him, when he saw the presumptuous mortal making love to Juno. This offense could not be overlooked, so Ixion was sent to Tartarus, where he was bound to an ever-revolving wheel of fire.

If anyone could follow the course of the gentle Lethe River, it would lead beyond the sunless realm of Pluto to a quiet and far-distant valley, where, in a soundless cave, live Somnus, the god of sleep, and his twin brother Mors, god of death. "Here the sun, whether rising or in his midcourse, or setting, can never come; and fogs, mingled with the dimness, form a strange twilight. No wakeful bird calls forth the morn, nor do watchful dogs disturb the brooding silence. No sound of wild beast or cattle, nor any noise of creaking bough, nor human voice, breaks in upon the perfect stillness, where mute Rest has her abode. Before the cave bloom abundant poppies and other sleep-producing herbs, which Night gathers, that she may distil their juice and scatter slumbers on the darkened earth. Within the cave is no door that could creak on rusty hinges, and no porter stands at the entrance of that inner room where, on a downy couch made of black ebony and draped with sable curtains, over which black plumes wave, lies Somnus, the god of sleep – Sleep, the repose of all things, gentlest of the deities from whom all care flies, the peace of mind who can sooth the hearts of men wearied with the toils of the day, and can refit them for labour."

Near Somnus sits Morpheus, one of his many sons, who watches over his slumbers and sees that no one shall break in upon his sleep. This god holds a vase in one hand, and with the other he shakes the nodding poppies that bring drowsiness and sleep. Sometimes he assumes varied forms in which he appears to men at night, and always he flies through the darkness with wings that make no noise. Around the couch of Somnus hover shadowy forms, the Dreams, which are as numerous as the forest leaves or the sands upon the seashore. In a distant corner of the room lurk the horrid Nightmares, which creep out of the cave to visit sleeping mortals, but are never led to earth by Mercury, as are the welcomed Dreams. Two gates lead out of the valley of sleep, one of horn and one of ivory.

Mors, god of death, occupies one of the rooms in the cave of sleep. He is a fearful-looking deity, cadaverous as a skeleton, and wrapped in a winding sheet. He holds an hourglass in one hand, and a sharp scythe in the other; and stands watching the sand run out of his glass that he may know when a human life is nearing its end. Then, as the last grains fall, he glides from the valley of sleep and stalks silently and unseen upon the earth, where he cuts down the unhappy mortal, who cannot even hear the rustle of his garments as he approaches. It is nothing to him whether the life he takes belongs to childhood or youth, for he mows them down as relentlessly as he does tottering old age. And to the rich he is as unsparing as to the poor.

The divinities who dwelt in the Cave of Sleep were distrusted by the ancients, and Mors was held in universal dread. No homage was ever offered to him, and no temples were dedicated in his honour; though sacrifices were sometimes made to ward off his dreaded coming. He was never represented in art except in a pleasing aspect, for although they believed him to have in reality the fearful appearance that tradition ascribed to him, yet the beauty-loving Greeks refused to have this kind of horror embodied in marble. So when Death appears in sculpture, it is usually with his brother Sleep, and both are represented as sleeping youths, whose heads are crowned with poppies or amaranths, and who hold inverted torches in their listless hands.

The Visit to the Dead

IN THIS PASSAGE from Homer's *The Odyssey*, Ulysses (the Roman name for Odysseus) recounts to the Phaeacians the tale of his journey to the Underworld, which he undertook in order to speak with the ghost of the prophet Teiresias regarding his journey homeward after the Trojan War.

"Then, when we had got down to the seashore, we drew our ship into the water and got her mast and sails into her; we also put the sheep on board and took our places, weeping and in great distress of mind. Circe, that great and cunning goddess, sent us a fair wind that blew dead aft and staid steadily with us keeping our sails all the time well filled; so we did whatever wanted doing to the ship's gear and let her go as the wind and helmsman headed her. All day long her sails were full as she held her course over the sea, but when the sun went down and darkness was over all the earth, we got into the deep waters of the river Oceanus, where lie the land and city of the Cimmerians who live enshrouded in mist and darkness which the rays of the sun never pierce neither at his rising nor as he goes down again out of the heavens, but the poor wretches live in one long melancholy night. When we got there we beached the ship, took the sheep out of her, and went along by the waters of Oceanus till we came to the place of which Circe had told us.

"Here Perimedes and Eurylochus held the victims, while I drew my sword and dug the trench a cubit each way. I made a drink-offering to all the dead, first with honey and milk, then with wine, and thirdly with water, and I sprinkled white barley meal over the whole, praying earnestly to the poor feckless ghosts, and promising them that when I got back to Ithaca I would sacrifice a barren heifer for them, the best I had, and would load the pyre with good things. I also particularly promised that Teiresias should have a black sheep to himself, the best in all my flocks. When I had prayed sufficiently to the dead, I cut the throats of the two sheep and let the blood run into the trench, whereon the ghosts came trooping up from Erebus – brides, young bachelors, old men worn out with toil, maids who had been crossed in love, and brave men who had been killed in battle, with their armour still smirched with blood; they came from every quarter and flitted round the trench with a strange kind of screaming sound that made me turn pale with fear. When I saw them coming I told the men to be quick and flay the carcasses of the two dead sheep and make burnt offerings of them, and at the same time to repeat prayers to Hades and to Proserpine; but I sat where I was with my sword drawn and would not let the poor feckless ghosts come near the blood till Teiresias should have answered my questions.

"The first ghost that came was that of my comrade Elpenor, for he had not yet been laid beneath the earth. We had left his body unwaked and unburied in Circe's house, for we had had too much else to do. I was very sorry for him, and cried when I saw him: 'Elpenor,' said I, 'how did you come down here into this gloom and darkness? You have got here on foot quicker than I have with my ship.'

"'Sir,' he answered with a groan, 'it was all bad luck, and my own unspeakable drunkenness. I was lying asleep on the top of Circe's house, and never thought of coming down again by the great staircase but fell right off the roof and broke my neck, so my soul came down to the house of Hades. And now I beseech you by all those whom you have left behind you, though they are not here, by your wife, by the father who brought you up when you were a child, and by Telemachus who is the one hope of your house, do what I shall now ask you. I know that when you leave this limbo you will again hold your ship for the Aeaean island. Do not go thence leaving me unwaked and unburied behind you, or I may bring heaven's anger upon you; but burn me with whatever armour I have, build a barrow for me on the seashore, that may tell people in days to come what a poor unlucky fellow I was, and plant over my grave the oar I used to row with when I was yet alive and with my messmates.' And I said, 'My poor fellow, I will do all that you have asked of me.'

"Thus, then, did we sit and hold sad talk with one another, I on the one side of the trench with my sword held over the blood, and the ghost of my comrade saying all this to me from the other side. Then came the ghost of my dead mother Anticlea, daughter to Autolycus. I had left her alive when I set out for Troy and was moved to tears when I saw her, but even so, for all my sorrow I would not let her come near the blood till I had asked my questions of Teiresias.

"Then came also the ghost of Theban Teiresias, with his golden sceptre in his hand. He knew me and said, 'Ulysses, noble son of Laertes, why, poor man, have you left the light of day and come down to visit the dead in this sad place? Stand back from the trench and withdraw your sword that I may drink of the blood and answer your questions truly.'

"So I drew back, and sheathed my sword, whereon when he had drank of the blood he began with his prophecy.

"'You want to know,' said he, 'about your return home, but heaven will make this hard for you. I do not think that you will escape the eye of Neptune, who still nurses his bitter grudge against you for having blinded his son. Still, after much suffering you may get home if you can restrain yourself and your companions when your ship reaches the Thrinacian island, where you will find the sheep and cattle belonging to the sun, who sees and gives ear to everything. If you leave these flocks unharmed and think of nothing but of getting home, you may yet after much hardship reach Ithaca; but if you harm them, then I forewarn you of the destruction both of your ship and of your men. Even though you may yourself escape, you will return in bad plight, after losing all your men, in another man's ship, and you will find trouble in your house, which will be overrun by high-handed people, who are devouring your substance under the pretext of paying court and making presents to your wife.

"'When you get home you will take your revenge on these suitors; and after you have killed them by force or fraud in your own house, you must take a well-made oar and carry it on and on, till you come to a country where the people have never heard of the sea and do not even mix salt with their food, nor do they know anything about ships, and oars that are as the wings of a ship. I will give you this certain token which cannot escape your notice. A wayfarer will meet you and will say it must be a winnowing shovel that you have got upon your shoulder; on this you must fix the oar in the ground and sacrifice a ram, a bull, and a boar to Neptune. Then go home and offer hecatombs to all the gods in heaven one after the other. As for yourself, death shall come to you from the sea, and your life shall ebb away very gently when you are full of years and peace of mind, and your people shall bless you. All that I have said will come true.'

"'This,' I answered, 'must be as it may please heaven, but tell me and tell me and tell me true, I see my poor mother's ghost close by us; she is sitting by the blood without saying a word, and though I am her own son she does not remember me and speak to me; tell me, Sir, how I can make her know me.'

"'That,' said he, 'I can soon do. Any ghost that you let taste of the blood will talk with you like a reasonable being, but if you do not let them have any blood they will go away again.'

"On this the ghost of Teiresias went back to the house of Hades, for his prophesyings had now been spoken, but I sat still where I was until my mother came up and tasted the blood. Then she knew me at once and spoke fondly to me, saying, 'My son, how did you come down to this abode of darkness while you are still alive? It is a hard thing for the living to see these places, for between us and them there are great and terrible waters, and there is Oceanus, which no man can cross on foot, but he must have a good ship to take him. Are you all this time trying to find your way home from Troy, and have you never yet got back to Ithaca nor seen your wife in your own house?'

"'Mother,' said I, 'I was forced to come here to consult the ghost of the Theban prophet Teiresias. I have never yet been near the Achaean land nor set foot on my native country, and I have had nothing but one long series of misfortunes from the very first day that I set out with Agamemnon for Ilius, the land of noble steeds, to fight the Trojans. But tell me, and tell me true, in what way did you die? Did you have a long illness, or did heaven vouchsafe you a gentle easy passage to eternity? Tell me also about my father, and the son whom I left behind me; is my property still in their hands, or has someone else got hold of it, who thinks that I shall not return to claim it? Tell me again what my wife intends doing, and in what mind she is; does she live with my son and guard my estate securely, or has she made the best match she could and married again?'

"My mother answered, 'Your wife still remains in your house, but she is in great distress of mind and spends her whole time in tears both night and day. No one as yet has got possession of your fine property, and Telemachus still holds your lands undisturbed. He has to entertain largely, as of course he must, considering his position as a magistrate, and how everyone invites him; your father remains at his old place in the country and never goes near the town. He has no comfortable bed nor bedding; in the winter he sleeps on the floor in front of the fire with the men and goes about all in rags, but in summer, when the warm weather comes on again, he lies out in the vineyard on a bed of vine leaves thrown any how upon the ground. He grieves continually about your never having come home, and suffers more and more as he grows older.

As for my own end it was in this wise: heaven did not take me swiftly and painlessly in my own house, nor was I attacked by any illness such as those that generally wear people out and kill them, but my longing to know what you were doing and the force of my affection for you – this it was that was the death of me.'

"Then I tried to find some way of embracing my poor mother's ghost. Thrice I sprang towards her and tried to clasp her in my arms, but each time she flitted from my embrace as it were a dream or phantom, and being touched to the quick I said to her, 'Mother, why do you not stay still when I would embrace you? If we could throw our arms around one another we might find sad comfort in the sharing of our sorrows even in the house of Hades; does Proserpine want to lay a still further load of grief upon me by mocking me with a phantom only?'

"'My son,' she answered, 'most ill-fated of all mankind, it is not Proserpine that is beguiling you, but all people are like this when they are dead. The sinews no longer hold the flesh and bones together; these perish in the fierceness of consuming fire as soon as life has left the body, and the soul flits away as though it were a dream. Now, however, go back to the light of day as soon as you can, and note all these things that you may tell them to your wife hereafter.'

"Thus did we converse, and anon Proserpine sent up the ghosts of the wives and daughters of all the most famous men. They gathered in crowds about the blood, and I considered how I might question them severally. In the end I deemed that it would be best to draw the keen blade that hung by my sturdy thigh, and keep them from all drinking the blood at once. So they came up one after the other, and each one as I questioned her told me her race and lineage.

"The first I saw was Tyro. She was daughter of Salmoneus and wife of Cretheus the son of Aeolus. She fell in love with the river Enipeus, who is much the most beautiful river in the whole world. Once when she was taking a walk by his side as usual, Neptune, disguised as her lover, lay with her at the mouth of the river, and a huge blue wave arched itself like a mountain over them to hide both woman and god, whereon he loosed her virgin girdle and laid her in a deep slumber. When the god had accomplished the deed of love, he took her hand in his own and said, 'Tyro, rejoice in all good will; the embraces of the gods are not fruitless, and you will have fine twins about this time twelve months. Take great care of them. I am Neptune, so now go home, but hold your tongue and do not tell anyone.'

"Then he dived under the sea, and she in due course bore Pelias and Neleus, who both of them served Jove with all their might. Pelias was a great breeder of sheep and lived in Iolcus, but the other lived in Pylos. The rest of her children were by Cretheus, namely, Aeson, Pheres, and Amythaon, who was a mighty warrior and charioteer.

"Next to her I saw Antiope, daughter to Asopus, who could boast of having slept in the arms of even Jove himself, and who bore him two sons Amphion and Zethus. These founded Thebes with its seven gates, and built a wall all round it; for strong though they were, they could not hold Thebes till they had walled it.

"Then I saw Alcmena, the wife of Amphitryon, who also bore to Jove indomitable Hercules; and Megara who was daughter to great King Creon, and married the redoubtable son of Amphitryon.

"I also saw fair Epicaste mother of King Oedipodes whose awful lot it was to marry her own son without suspecting it. He married her after having killed his father, but the gods proclaimed the whole story to the world; whereon he remained king of Thebes, in great grief for the spite the gods had borne him; but Epicaste went to the house of the mighty jailor Hades, having hanged herself for grief, and the avenging spirits haunted him as for an outraged mother – to his ruing bitterly thereafter.

"Then I saw Chloris, whom Neleus married for her beauty, having given priceless presents for her. She was youngest daughter to Amphion son of Iasus and king of Minyan Orchomenus, and was Queen in Pylos. She bore Nestor, Chromius, and Periclymenus, and she also bore that marvellously lovely woman Pero, who was wooed by all the country round; but Neleus would only give her to him who should raid the cattle of Iphicles from the grazing grounds of Phylace, and this was a hard task. The only man who would undertake to raid them was a certain excellent seer, but the will of heaven was against him, for the rangers of the cattle caught him and put him in prison; nevertheless, when a full year had passed and the same season came round again, Iphicles set him at liberty, after he had expounded all the oracles of heaven. Thus, then, was the will of Jove accomplished.

"And I saw Leda the wife of Tyndarus, who bore him two famous sons, Castor breaker of horses, and Pollux the mighty boxer. Both these heroes are lying under the earth, though they are still alive, for by a special dispensation of Jove, they die and come to life again, each one of them every other day throughout all time, and they have the rank of gods.

"After her I saw Iphimedeia wife of Aloeus who boasted the embrace of Neptune. She bore two sons Otus and Ephialtes, but both were short lived. They were the finest children that were ever born in this world, and the best looking, Orion only excepted; for at nine years old they were nine fathoms high, and measured nine cubits round the chest. They threatened to make war with the gods in Olympus, and tried to set Mount Ossa on the top of Mount Olympus, and Mount Pelion on the top of Ossa, that they might scale heaven itself, and they would have done it too if they had been grown up, but Apollo, son of Leto, killed both of them, before they had got so much as a sign of hair upon their cheeks or chin.

"Then I saw Phaedra, and Procris, and fair Ariadne daughter of the magician Minos, whom Theseus was carrying off from Crete to Athens, but he did not enjoy her, for before he could do so Diana killed her in the island of Dia on account of what Bacchus had said against her.

"I also saw Maera and Clymene and hateful Eriphyle, who sold her own husband for gold. But it would take me all night if I were to name every single one of the wives and daughters of heroes whom I saw, and it is time for me to go to bed, either on board ship with my crew, or here. As for my escort, heaven and yourselves will see to it."

Here he ended, and the guests sat all of them enthralled and speechless throughout the covered cloister. Then Arete said to them:

"What do you think of this man, O Phaeacians? Is he not tall and good-looking, and is he not clever? True, he is my own guest, but all of you share in the distinction. Do not be in a hurry to send him away, nor niggardly in the presents you make to one who is in such great need, for heaven has blessed all of you with great abundance."

Then spoke the aged hero Echeneus, who was one of the oldest men among them. "My friends," said he, "what our august queen has just said to us is both reasonable and to the purpose, therefore be persuaded by it; but the decision whether in word or deed rests ultimately with King Alcinous."

"The thing shall be done," exclaimed Alcinous, "as surely as I still live and reign over the Phaeacians. Our guest is indeed very anxious to get home, still we must persuade him to remain with us until tomorrow, by which time I shall be able to get together the whole sum that I mean to give him. As regards his escort it will be a matter for you all, and mine above all others as the chief person among you."

And Ulysses answered, "King Alcinous, if you were to bid me to stay here for a whole twelve months, and then speed me on my way, loaded with your noble gifts, I should obey you gladly and it would redound greatly to my advantage, for I should return fuller-handed to my own people, and should thus be more respected and beloved by all who see me when I get back to Ithaca."

"Ulysses," replied Alcinous, "not one of us who sees you has any idea that you are a charlatan or a swindler. I know there are many people going about who tell such plausible stories that it is very hard to see through them, but there is a style about your language which assures me of your good disposition. Moreover, you have told the story of your own misfortunes, and those of the Argives, as though you were a practiced bard; but tell me, and tell me true, whether you saw any of the mighty heroes who went to Troy at the same time with yourself, and perished there. The evenings are still at their longest, and it is not yet bedtime – go on, therefore, with your divine story, for I could stay here listening till tomorrow morning, so long as you will continue to tell us of your adventures."

"Alcinous," answered Ulysses, "there is a time for making speeches, and a time for going to bed; nevertheless, since you so desire, I will not refrain from telling you the still sadder tale of those of my comrades who did not fall fighting with the Trojans, but perished on their return, through the treachery of a wicked woman.

"When Proserpine had dismissed the female ghosts in all directions, the ghost of Agamemnon son of Atreus came sadly up to me, surrounded by those who had perished with him in the house of Aegisthus. As soon as he had tasted the blood, he knew me, and weeping bitterly stretched out his arms towards me to embrace me; but he had no strength nor substance anymore, and I too wept and pitied him as I beheld him. 'How did you come by your death,' said I, 'King Agamemnon? Did Neptune raise his winds and waves against you when you were at sea, or did your enemies make an end of you on the mainland when you were cattle-lifting or sheep-stealing, or while they were fighting in defence of their wives and city?'

"'Ulysses,' he answered, 'noble son of Laertes, I was not lost at sea in any storm of Neptune's raising, nor did my foes despatch me upon the mainland, but Aegisthus and my wicked wife were the death of me between them. He asked me to his house, feasted me, and then butchered me most miserably as though I were a fat beast in a slaughterhouse, while all around me my comrades were slain like sheep or pigs for the wedding breakfast, or picnic, or gorgeous banquet of some great nobleman. You must have seen numbers of men killed either in a general engagement, or in single combat, but you never saw anything so truly pitiable as the way in which we fell in that cloister, with the mixing bowl and the loaded tables lying all about, and the ground reeking with our blood. I heard Priam's daughter Cassandra scream as Clytemnestra killed her close beside me. I lay dying upon the earth with the sword in my body, and raised my hands to kill the slut of a murderess, but she slipped away from me; she would not even close my lips nor my eyes when I was dying, for there is nothing in this world so cruel and so shameless as a woman when she has fallen into such guilt as hers was. Fancy murdering her own husband! I thought I was going to be welcomed home by my children and my servants, but her abominable crime has brought disgrace on herself and all women who shall come after – even on the good ones.'

"And I said, 'In truth Jove has hated the house of Atreus from first to last in the matter of their women's counsels. See how many of us fell for Helen's sake, and now it seems that Clytemnestra hatched mischief against you too during your absence.'

"'Be sure, therefore,' continued Agamemnon, 'and not be too friendly even with your own wife. Do not tell her all that you know perfectly well yourself. Tell her a part only, and keep your own counsel about the rest. Not that your wife, Ulysses, is likely to murder you, for Penelope is a very admirable woman, and has an excellent nature. We left her a young bride with an infant at her breast when we set out for Troy. This child no doubt is now grown up happily to man's estate, and he and his father will have a joyful meeting and embrace one another as it is right they should do, whereas my wicked wife did not even allow me the happiness of looking upon my son, but killed me ere I could do so. Furthermore I say – and lay my saying to your heart – do not tell people when you are bringing your ship to Ithaca, but steal a march upon them, for after all this there is no trusting women. But now tell me, and tell me true, can you give me any news of my son Orestes? Is he in Orchomenus, or at Pylos, or is he at Sparta with Menelaus – for I presume that he is still living.'

"And I said, 'Agamemnon, why do you ask me? I do not know whether your son is alive or dead, and it is not right to talk when one does not know.'

"As we two sat weeping and talking thus sadly with one another, the ghost of Achilles came up to us with Patroclus, Antilochus, and Ajax who was the finest and goodliest man of all the Danaans after the son of Peleus. The fleet descendant of Aeacus knew me and spoke piteously, saying, 'Ulysses, noble son of Laertes, what deed of daring will you undertake next, that you venture down to the house of Hades among us silly dead, who are but the ghosts of them that can labour no more?'

"And I said, 'Achilles, son of Peleus, foremost champion of the Achaeans, I came to consult Teiresias, and see if he could advise me about my return home to Ithaca, for I have never yet been able to get near the Achaean land, nor to set foot in my own country, but have been in trouble all the time. As for you, Achilles, no one was ever yet so fortunate as you have been, nor ever will be, for you were adored by all us Argives as long as you were alive, and now that you are here you are a great prince among the dead. Do not, therefore, take it so much to heart even if you are dead.'

"'Say not a word,' he answered, 'in death's favour; I would rather be a paid servant in a poor man's house and be above ground than king of kings among the dead. But give me news about my son; is he gone to the wars and will he be a great soldier, or is this not so? Tell me also if you have heard anything about my father Peleus – does he still rule among the Myrmidons, or do they show him no respect throughout Hellas and Phthia now that he is old and his limbs fail him? Could I but stand by his side, in the light of day, with the same strength that I had when I killed the bravest of our foes upon the plain of Troy – could I but be as I then was and go even for a short time to my father's house, anyone who tried to do him violence or supersede him would soon rue it.'

"'I have heard nothing,' I answered, 'of Peleus, but I can tell you all about your son Neoptolemus, for I took him in my own ship from Scyros with the Achaeans. In our councils of war before Troy he was always first to speak, and his judgment was unerring. Nestor and I were the only two who could surpass him; and when it came to fighting on the plain of Troy, he would never remain with the body of his men, but would dash on far in front, foremost of them all in valour. Many a man did he kill in battle – I cannot name every single one of those whom he slew while fighting on the side of the Argives, but will only say how he killed that valiant hero Eurypylus son of Telephus, who was the handsomest man I ever saw except Memnon; many others also of the Ceteians fell around him by reason of a woman's bribes. Moreover, when all the bravest of the Argives went inside the horse that Epeus had made, and it was left to me to settle when we should either open the door of our ambuscade, or close it, though all the other leaders and chief men among the Danaans were drying their eyes and quaking in every limb, I never once saw him turn pale nor wipe a tear from his cheek; he was all the time urging me to break out from the horse – grasping the handle of his sword and his bronze-shod spear, and breathing fury against the foe. Yet when we had sacked the city of Priam he got his handsome share of the prize money and went on board (such is the fortune of war) without a wound upon him, neither from a thrown spear nor in close combat, for the rage of Mars is a matter of great chance.'

"When I had told him this, the ghost of Achilles strode off across a meadow full of asphodel, exulting over what I had said concerning the prowess of his son.

"The ghosts of other dead men stood near me and told me each his own melancholy tale; but that of Ajax son of Telamon alone held aloof – still angry with me for having won the cause in our dispute about the armour of Achilles. Thetis had offered it as a prize, but the Trojan prisoners and Minerva were the judges. Would that I had never gained the day in such a contest, for it cost the life of Ajax, who was foremost of all the Danaans after the son of Peleus, alike in stature and prowess.

"When I saw him I tried to pacify him and said, 'Ajax, will you not forget and forgive even in death, but must the judgment about that hateful armour still rankle with you? It cost us Argives dear enough to lose such a tower of strength as you were to us. We mourned you as much as we mourned Achilles son of Peleus himself, nor can the blame be laid on anything but on the spite which Jove bore against the Danaans, for it was this that made him counsel your destruction – come hither, therefore, bring your proud spirit into subjection, and hear what I can tell you.'

"He would not answer, but turned away to Erebus and to the other ghosts; nevertheless, I should have made him talk to me in spite of his being so angry, or I should have gone on talking to him, only that there were still others among the dead whom I desired to see.

"Then I saw Minos son of Jove with his golden sceptre in his hand sitting in judgment on the dead, and the ghosts were gathered sitting and standing round him in the spacious house of Hades, to learn his sentences upon them.

"After him I saw huge Orion in a meadow full of asphodel driving the ghosts of the wild beasts that he had killed upon the mountains, and he had a great bronze club in his hand, unbreakable for ever and ever.

"And I saw Tityus son of Gaia stretched upon the plain and covering some nine acres of ground. Two vultures on either side of him were digging their beaks into his liver, and he kept on trying to beat them off with his hands, but could not; for he had violated Jove's mistress Leto as she was going through Panopeus on her way to Pytho.

"I saw also the dreadful fate of Tantalus, who stood in a lake that reached his chin; he was dying to quench his thirst, but could never reach the water, for whenever the poor creature stooped to drink, it dried up and vanished, so that there was nothing but dry ground – parched by the spite of heaven. There were tall trees, moreover, that shed their fruit over his head – pears, pomegranates, apples, sweet figs and juicy olives, but whenever the poor creature stretched out his hand to take some, the wind tossed the branches back again to the clouds.

"And I saw Sisyphus at his endless task raising his prodigious stone with both his hands. With hands and feet he tried to roll it up to the top of the hill, but always, just before he could roll it over on to the other side, its weight would be too much for him, and the pitiless stone would come thundering down again on to the plain. Then he would begin trying to push it uphill again, and the sweat ran off him and the steam rose after him.

"After him I saw mighty Hercules, but it was his phantom only, for he is feasting ever with the immortal gods, and has lovely Hebe to wife, who is daughter of Jove and Juno. The ghosts were screaming round him like scared birds flying all whithers. He looked black as night with his bare bow in his hands and his arrow on the string, glaring around as though ever on the point of taking aim. About his breast there was a wondrous golden belt adorned in the most marvellous fashion with bears, wild boars, and lions with gleaming eyes; there was also war, battle, and death. The man who made that belt, do what he might, would never be able to make another like it. Hercules knew me at once when he saw me, and spoke piteously, saying, 'My poor Ulysses, noble son of Laertes, are you too leading the same sorry kind of life that I did when I was above ground? I was son of Jove, but I went through an infinity of suffering, for I became bondsman to one who was far beneath me – a low fellow who set me all manner of labours. He once sent me here to fetch the hellhound – for he did not think he could find anything harder for me than this, but I got the hound out of Hades and brought him to him, for Mercury and Minerva helped me.'

"On this Hercules went down again into the house of Hades, but I stayed where I was in case some other of the mighty dead should come to me. And I should have seen still other of them that are gone before, whom I would fain have seen – Theseus and Pirithous – glorious children of the gods, but so many thousands of ghosts came round me and uttered such appalling cries, that I was panic stricken lest Proserpine should send up from the house of Hades the head of that awful monster Gorgon. On this I hastened back to my ship and ordered my men to go on board at once and loose the hawsers; so they embarked and took their places, whereon the ship went down the stream of the river Oceanus."

The Story of Orpheus and Eurydice

THE DEEDS OF the immortal gods were told and sung at every fireside in Greece; and among these hero-tales there was none more popular than the story of how Apollo built for Neptune the famous wall of Troy. Many musicians would have been glad to perform a similar service for the mere fame that it would bring them, but they feared that the attempt to imitate Apollo would only result in failure and ridicule. So no mortal ever presumed to say that he could make rocks and stones obedient to the spell of his music.

The most famous of all musicians, except the one who played in the shining halls of Olympus, was Orpheus, son of Apollo and of the muse Calliope. When he was a mere child, his father gave him a lyre and taught him to play upon it; but Orpheus needed very little instruction, for as soon as he laid his hand upon the strings the wild beasts crept out of their lairs to crouch beside him; the trees on the mountainsides moved nearer so that they might listen; and the flowers sprang up in clusters all around him, unwilling to remain any longer asleep in the earth.

When Orpheus sought in marriage the golden-haired Eurydice, there were other suitors for her hand, but though they brought rich gifts, gathered out of many lands, they could not win the maiden's love, and she turned from them to bestow her hand upon Orpheus who had no way to woo her but with his music. On the wedding day, there was the usual mirth and feasting, but one event occurred that cast a gloom over the happiness of the newly married pair. When Hymen, god of marriage, came with his torch to bless the nuptial feast, the light that should have burned clear and pure began to smoke ominously, as if predicting future disaster.

This evil omen was fulfilled all too soon, for one day when Eurydice was walking in the meadow, she met the youth Aristaeus, who was so charmed with her beauty that he insisted upon staying beside her to pour his ardent speeches into her unwilling ears. To escape from these troublesome attentions, Eurydice started to run away, and as she ran she stepped on a poisonous snake, which quickly turned and bit her. She had barely time to reach her home before the poison had done its work, and Orpheus heard the sad story from her dying lips. As soon as Mercury had led away the soul of Eurydice, the bereaved husband hastened to the shining halls of Olympus, and throwing himself down before Jupiter's golden throne, he implored that great ruler of gods and men to give him back his wife. There was always pity in the hearts of the gods for those who die in flowering time, so Jupiter gave permission to Orpheus to go down into Hades and beg of Pluto the boon he craved.

It was a steep and perilous journey to the kingdom of the dead, and the road was one that no mortal foot had ever trod; but through his love for Eurydice, Orpheus forgot the dangers of the way, and when he spoke her name, the terrors of the darkness vanished. In his hand he held his lyre, and when he arrived at the gate of Hades, where the fierce three-headed dog Cerberus refused to let him pass, Orpheus stood still in the uncertain darkness and began to play. And as he played, the snarling of the dog ceased and the noise of its harsh breathing grew faint. Then Orpheus went on his way undisturbed, but still he played softly on his lyre, and the sounds floated far into the dismal interior of Hades, where the souls of the condemned labour forever at their tasks. Tantalus heard the music, and ceased to strive for a drop of the forbidden water; Ixion rested a moment beside his ever-revolving wheel; and Sisyphus stood listening, while the rock which he must roll through all eternity fell from his wearied arms. The daughters of Danaus laid down their urns beside the sieve into which they were forever pouring water, and as the mournful wailing of Orpheus's lyre told the story of his lost love, they wept then for a sorrow not their own. So plaintive, indeed, was the music, that all the shadowy forms that flitted endlessly by shed tears of sympathy for the player's grief, and even the cheeks of the Furies were wet.

When Orpheus came before the throne of Pluto, that relentless monarch repulsed him angrily as he attempted to plead his cause, and commanded him to depart. Then the son of Apollo began to play upon his lyre, and through his music he told the story of his loss, and besought the ruler of these myriad souls to give him the single one he craved. So wonderfully did Orpheus play that the hard heart of Pluto was touched with pity, and he consented to restore Eurydice to her husband on condition that as they went out together from the loathed country of the dead he should not once turn his head to look upon her. To this strange decree Orpheus gladly promised obedience; so Eurydice was summoned from among the million shadow-shapes that throng the silent halls of death. Pluto told her the condition on which her freedom was to be won, and then bade her follow her husband.

During all the wearisome journey back to earth, Orpheus never forgot the promise he had made, though he often longed to give just a hurried glance at the face of Eurydice to see whether it had lost its sadness. As they neared the spot where the first faint glimmerings of light filtered down into the impenetrable darkness, Orpheus thought he heard his wife calling, and he looked quickly around to find whether she was still following him. At that moment the slight form close behind him began to fade away, and a mournful voice – seemingly far in the distance – called to him a sad farewell.

He knew that no second chance would be given him to win his wife from Pluto's hold, even if he could again charm the three-headed Cerberus or persuade Charon, the grim ferryman, to take him across the river. So he went forlornly back to earth and lived in a forest cave far from the companionship of men. At first, there was only his lyre to share his solitude, but soon the forest creatures came to live beside him, and often sat listening to his music, looking exceedingly wise and sorrowful. Even in his sleepless hours, when he fancied he heard Eurydice calling, he was never quite alone, for the bat and owl and the things that love the darkness flitted about him, and he saw the glow-worms creep toward him out of the night-cold grass.

One day, a party of Bacchantes found him seated outside the cave, playing the mournful music that told of his lost love, and they bade him change the sad notes to something gay so that they might dance. But Orpheus was too wrapped up in his sorrow to play any strain of cheerful music, and he refused to do as they asked. The Bacchantes were half maddened by their festival days of drinking, and this refusal so enraged them that they fell upon the luckless musician and tore him to pieces. Then they threw his mangled body into the river, and as the head of Orpheus drifted down the stream, his lips murmured, again and again, "Eurydice," until the hills echoed the beloved name, and the rocks and trees and rivers repeated it in mournful chorus. Later on, the Muses gathered up his remains to give them honourable burial; and it is said that over Orpheus's grave the nightingale sings more sweetly than in any other spot in Greece.

Death and Burial of the Fjort

ONE OF MY cook's many fathers having died (this time, his real father), he came to me with tears in his eyes to ask me for a little rum to take to town, where he said his family were waiting for him. Some days previously the cook had told me that his father was suffering from the sleeping sickness, and was nearing his end, so that when I heard the cry of "Chibai-I" floating across the valley from a little town close to that in which the cook lived, I guessed who the dead one was, and was prepared to lose the cook's services for a certain number of days.

The death of the father of a family is always a very sad event, but the death of the father of a Fjort family seems to me to be peculiarly pathetic. His little village at once assumes a deserted appearance; his wives and sisters, stripped of their gay cloths, wander aimlessly around and about the silent corpse, crying and wringing their hands, their tears coursing down their cheeks along little channels washed in the thick coating of oil and ashes with which they have besmeared their dusky faces. Naked children, bereft for the time being of their mother's care, cry piteously; and the men, with a blue band of cloth (*ntanta mabundi*) tied tightly round their heads, sit apart and in silence, already wondering what evil person or fetish has caused them this overwhelming loss.

The first sharp burst of grief being over, loving bands shave and wash the body, and, if the family be rich enough, palm wine or rum is used instead of water. Then the heavy body is placed upon mats of rushes and covered with a cloth. After resting in this position for a day, the body is wrapped in long pieces of cloth and placed upon a kind of rack or framework bed, underneath which a hole has been dug to receive the water, etc, that comes from the corpse. A fire is lighted both at the head and foot of the rack, and the body is covered each day with the leaves of the Acaju, so that the smoke that hangs about it will keep off the flies. More cloth is from time to time wrapped around the body; but, unless there are many palavers which cannot be quickly settled, it is generally buried after two or three wrappings. The more important the person, the longer, of course, it takes to settle these palavers and their many complications; and as the body cannot be buried until they are settled, one can understand how the heirs of a great king sometimes come to give up the hope of burying their relation, and leave him unburied for years. On the other hand, the slave, however rich he may be, is quickly buried.

The family being all present, a day is appointed upon which the cause of the death shall be divined. Upon this day the family, and the family in which the deceased was brought up, collect what cloth they can and send it to some well-known Nganga, a long way off. The Nganga meets the messengers and describes to them exactly all the circumstances connected with the life, sickness and death of the deceased; and if they conclude that this information agrees with what they know to be the facts of the case, they place the cloth before him and beseech him to inform them the cause of their relation's death. This the Nganga sets himself to divine. After some delay he informs the relations (1) that the father has died because someone (perhaps now dead) knocked a certain nail into a certain fetish, with his death as the end in view, or (2) that so-and-so has bewitched him, or (3) that he died because his time had come.

The relations then go to the Nganga of the fetish or Nkissi mentioned, and ask him if he remembers so-and-so knocking a nail into it? And if so, will be kindly point out the nail to them? He may say yes. Then they will pay him to draw it out, so that the rest of the family may not die. Or the relations give the person indicated by the Nganga as having bewitched the dead man, the so-called Ndotchi (witch), a powdered bark, which he must swallow and vomit if he be really innocent. The bark named *Mbundu* is given to the man who owns to being a witch, but denies having killed the person in question. That of *Nkassa* is given to those who deny the charge of being witches altogether. The witches or other persons who, having taken the bark, do not vomit are either killed or die from the effects of the poison, and their bodies used to be burnt. Since civilized government have occupied the country a slight improvement has taken place, in that the relations of the witch are allowed to bury the body. If events turns out as divined by the Nganga, he retains the cloth given to him by the relations or their messengers: otherwise he must return it to the family, who take it to another Nganga.

While all this is going on, a carpenter is called in to build the coffin; and he is paid one fowl, one mat of rushes and one closely woven mat per day. Rum and a piece of blue cloth are given to him on the day he covers the case with red cloth. Palm wine, rum and cloth are given to him as payment on its completion. And now that all palavers are finished, and the coffin ready, the family are once more called together; and the prince of the land and strangers are invited to come and bear how all the palavers have been settled. A square in front of the shimbec containing the coffin is cleared of herbs and grass, and carefully swept; and here, during the whole night previous to the official meeting, women and children dance. Mats are placed immediately in front of the shimbec for the family and their fetishes (Poomba): the side opposite is prepared for the prince and his followers; and the other two sides are kept for those strangers and guests who care to come. At about three o'clock guns are fired off as a signal that all is ready. The family headed by their elder and spokesman then seat themselves ready to receive their guests. Then the guests glide into the village and make their way to the elder, present themselves, and then take their allotted seats.

When all are assembled, the elder addresses the two family fetishes held by two of the family. Pointing and shaking his hand at them, he tells them how the deceased died, and all the family has done to settle the matter; he tells them how they have allowed the father to be taken, and prays them to protect the rest of the family; and when he has finished his address, the two who hold the fetishes, or wooden figures, pick up a little earth and throw it on the beads of the fetishes, then, lifting them up, rub their heads in the earth in front of them.

Then the elder addresses the prince and his people, and the strangers who have come to bear how the deceased has died, and offers them each a drink. When they have finished drinking, he turns to the fetishes and tells them that they have allowed evil to overtake the deceased, but prays them to protect his guests from the same. Then the fetishes again have earth thrown at them, and their heads are once more rubbed in the earth.

And now the elder addresses the wives and tells them that their husband has been cruelly taken from them, and that they are now free to marry another; and then, turning to the fetishes, he trusts that they will guard the wives from the evil that killed their husband; and the fetishes are again dusted and rubbed in the earth.

On the occasion that I watched these proceedings, the elder got up and addressed me, telling me that my cook, who had served me so well and whom I had sent to town when he was sick, etc., etc., had now lost his father; and once more turning to his fetishes, the poor creatures were again made to kiss old mother earth, this time for my benefit.

If a witch has to undergo the bark test, rum is given to the prince, and he is told that if he hears that the Ndotchi has been killed he is to take no official notice of the fact.

Then the men dance all through the night; and the next day the body is placed in the coffin and buried. In KaCongo the coffin is much larger than that made in Loango; and it is placed upon a huge car on four or six solid wheels. This car remains over the grave, ornamented in different ways with stuffed animals and empty demijohns, animal boxes and other earthenware goods, in accordance with the wealth of the deceased. I can remember when slaves and wives were buried together with the prince; but this custom has now died out in Loango and KaCongo, and we only bear of its taking place far away inland.

The "fetish cbibinga" sometimes will not allow the corpse to close its eyes. This is a sure sign that the deceased is annoyed about something, and does not wish to be buried. In such a case no coffin is made, the body is wrapped in mats and placed in the woods near to an Nlomba tree. Should he be buried in the ordinary way, all the family would fall sick and die. Should his chimyumba (KaCongo *chimbindi*) appear to one of his family, that person would surely die. But others not of the family may see it and not die.

The deceased will often not rest quiet until his *nkulu* (soul? spirit?) is placed in the head of one of his relations, so that he can communicate with the family. This is done by the Nganga picking up some of the earth from the grave of the deceased, and, after mixing it with other medicine, placing it in either the born of an antelope (*lekorla*) or else a little tin box (*nkobbi*). Then seating himself upon a mat within a circle drawn in chalk on the ground, he shakes a little rattle (*nquanga*) at the patient, and goes through some form of incantation, until the patient trembles and cries out with the voice of the deceased, when they all know that the *nkulu* has taken up its residence in his head. The medicine and earth together with the *nkobbi* is called *nkulu mpemba*, and shows that the deceased died of some ordinary disease; but when the medicine and earth are put into the *lekorla* it shows that the deceased died of some sickness of the bead, and this is called *nkulu mabiali*.

The Fjort say the "shadow" ceases at the death of the person. I asked if that was because they kept the corpse in the shade; what if they put the corpse in the sun? The young man asked turned to his elderly aunt and re-asked her this question. "No," she said emphatically, "certainly not!"

The Twin Brothers

A CERTAIN WOMAN, after prolonged labour, gave birth to twins, both sons. And each one, as he was brought forth, came into this world with a valuable fetish, or charm. One the mother called Luemba, the other Mavungu. And they were almost full-grown at their birth, so that Mavungu, the first born, wished to start upon his travels.

Now about this time the daughter of Nzambi was ready for marriage. The tiger came and offered himself in marriage; but Nzambi told him that he must speak to her daughter himself, as she should only marry the man of her choice. Then the tiger went to the girl and asked her to marry him, but she refused him. And the gazelle, and the pig, and all created things that had breath, one after the other, asked the daughter in marriage; but she refused them all, saying that she did not love them; and they were all very sad.

Mavungu heard of this girl, and determined to marry her. And so he called upon his charm, and asked him to help him; and then he took some grass in his hands, and changed one blade of grass into a horn, another into a knife, another into a gun, and so on, until he was quite ready for the long journey.

Then he set out, and travelled and travelled, until at last hunger overcame him, when he asked his charm whether it was true that he was going to be allowed to starve. The charm hastened to place a sumptuous feast before him, and Mavuligu ate and was satisfied.

"Oh, charm!" Mavungu said, "are you going to leave these beautiful plates which I have used for the use of any commoner that may come along?" The charm immediately caused all to disappear.

Then Mavungu travelled and travelled, until at length he became very tired, and had to ask his charm to arrange a place for him where he might sleep. And the charm saw to his comfort, so that he passed a peaceful night.

And after many days' weary travelling he at length arrived at Nzambi's town. And Nzambi's daughter saw Mavungu and straightway fell in love with him, and ran to her mother and father and cried: "I have seen the man I love, and I shall die if I do not marry him."

Then Mavungu sought out Nzambi, and told her that he had come to marry her daughter.

"Go and see her first," said Nzambi,"and if she will have you, you may marry her."

And when Mavungu and the daughter of Nzambi saw each other, they ran towards each other and loved one another.

And they were led to a fine shimbec, and whilst all the people in the town danced and sang for gladness, Mavungu and the daughter of Nzambi slept there. And in the morning Mavungu noticed that the whole shimbec was crowded with mirrors, but that each mirror was covered so that the glass could not be seen. And he asked the daughter of Nzambi to uncover them, so that he might see himself in them. And she took him to one and uncovered it, and Mavungu immediately saw the perfect likeness of his native town. And she took him to another, and he there saw another town he knew; and thus she took him to all the mirrors save one, and this one she refused to let him see.

"Why will you not let me look into that mirror?" asked Mavungu.

"Because that is the picture, of the town whence no man that wanders there returns."

"Do let me see it!" urged Mavungu.

At last the daughter of Nzambi yielded, and Mavungu looked hard at the reflected image of that terrible place.

"I must go there," he said.

"Nay, you will never return. Please don't go!" pleaded the daughter of Nzambi.

"Have no fear!" answered Mavungu. "My charm will protect me."

The daughter of Nzambi cried very much, but could not move Mavungu from his purpose. Mavungu then left his newly married wife, mounted his horse and set off for the town from whence no man returns.

He travelled and travelled, until at last he came near to the town, when, meeting an old woman, he asked her for fire to light his pipe.

"Tie up your horse first, and come and fetch it."

Mavungu descended, and having tied his horse up very securely, he went to the woman for the fire; and when he had come near to her she killed him, so that he disappeared entirely.

Now Luemba wondered at the long absence of his brother Mavungu, and determined to follow him. So he took some grass, and by the aid of his fetish changed one blade into a horse, another into a knife, another into a gun, and so on, until he was fully prepared for his journey. Then he set out, and after some days' journeying arrived at Nzambi's town.

Nzambi rushed out to meet him, and, calling him Mavungu, embraced him.

"Nay," said Luemba, "my name is not Mavungu; I am his brother, Luemba."

"Nonsense!" answered Nzambi. "You are my son-in-law, Mavungu." And straightway a great feast was prepared. Nzambi's daughter danced for joy, and would not hear of his not being Mavungu. And Luemba was sorely troubled, and did not know what to do, as he was now sure that Nzambi's daughter was Mavungu's wife. And when night came, Nzambi's daughter would sleep in Luemba's shimbec; but he appealed to his charm, and it enclosed Nzambi's daughter in a room, and lifted her out of Luemba's room for the night, bringing her back in the early morning.

And Luemba's curiosity was aroused by the many closed mirrors that hung about the walls; so he asked Nzambi's daughter to let him look into them. And she showed him all excepting one; and this she told him was the one that reflected the town whence no man returns. Luemba insisted upon looking into this one; and when he had seen the terrible picture he knew that his brother was there.

Luemba determined to leave Nzambi's town for the town whence no man returns; and so after thanking them all for his kind reception, he set out. They all wept loudly, but were consoled by the fact that he had been there once already, and returned safely, so that he could of course return a second time. And Luemba travelled and travelled, until he also came to where the old woman was standing, and asked her for fire.

She told him to tie up his horse and come to her to fetch it, but. he tied his horse up only very lightly, and then fell upon the old woman and killed her.

Then he sought out his brother's bones and the bones of his horse, and put them together, and then touched them with his charm. And Mavungu and his horse came to life again. Then together they joined the bones of hundreds of people together and touched them with their charms, so that they all lived again. And then they set off with all their followers to Nzambi's town. And Luemba told Mavungu how he had been mistaken for him by his father-in-law and wife, and how by the help of his charm he had saved his wife from dishonour; and Mavungu thanked him, and said it was well.

Then a quarrel broke out between the two brothers about the followers. Mavungu said they were his, because he was the elder; but Luemba said that they belonged to him, because he had given Mavungu and them all life. Mavungu then fell upon Luemba and killed him; but his horse remained by his body. Mavungu went on his way to Nzambi's town, and was magnificently welcomed.

Now Luemba's horse took his charm and touched Luemba's body, so that he lived again. Then Luemba mounted his horse, and sought out his brother Mavungu and killed him.

And when the town had heard the palaver, they all said that Luemba had done quite rightly.

Sumerian Stories of the Netherworld

THE FOLLOWING THREE stories have been translated from ancient clay tablets, revealing a circular and almost musical style of expression which the anonymous scribe or scribes used in recording these ancient Sumerian tales of the afterlife and the spirit realm.

Inana's Descent to the Netherworld

From the great heaven she set her mind on the great below. From the great heaven the goddess set her mind on the great below. From the great heaven Inana set her mind on the great below. My mistress abandoned heaven, abandoned earth, and descended to the Underworld. Inana abandoned heaven, abandoned earth, and descended to the Underworld.

She abandoned the office of *en*, abandoned the office of *lagar*, and descended to the Underworld. She abandoned the E-ana in Unug, and descended to the Underworld. She abandoned the E-muc-kalama in Bad-tibira, and descended to the Underworld. She abandoned the Giguna in Zabalam, and descended to the Underworld. She abandoned the E-cara in Adab, and descended to the Underworld. She abandoned the Barag-dur-jara in Nibru, and descended to the Underworld. She abandoned the Hursaj-kalama in Kic, and descended to the Underworld. She abandoned the E-Ulmac in Agade, and descended to the Underworld. She abandoned the Ibgal in Umma, and descended to the Underworld. She abandoned the E-Dilmuna in Urim, and descended to the Underworld. She abandoned the Amac-e-kug in Kisiga, and descended to the Underworld. She abandoned the E-ecdam-kug in Jirsu, and descended to the Underworld. She abandoned the E-sig-mece-du in Isin, and descended to the Underworld. She abandoned the Anzagar in Akcak, and descended to the Underworld. She abandoned the Nijin-jar-kug in Curuppag, and descended to the Underworld. She abandoned the E-cag-hula in Kazallu, and descended to the Underworld.

She took the seven divine powers. She collected the divine powers and grasped them in her hand. With the good divine powers, she went on her way. She put a turban, headgear for the open country, on her head. She took a wig for her forehead. She hung small lapis lazuli beads around her neck.

She placed twin egg-shaped beads on her breast. She covered her body with a *pala* dress, the garment of ladyship. She placed mascara which is called "Let a man come, let him come" on her eyes. She pulled the pectoral which is called "Come, man, come" over her breast. She placed a golden ring on her hand. She held the lapis lazuli measuring rod and measuring line in her hand.

Inana travelled towards the Underworld. Her minister Nincubura travelled behind her.

Holy Inana said to Nincubura: "Come, my faithful minister of E-ana, my minister who speaks fair words, my escort who speaks trustworthy words.

"On this day I will descend to the Underworld. When I have arrived in the Underworld, make a lament for me on the ruin mounds. Beat the drum for me in the sanctuary. Make the rounds of the houses of the gods for me.

"Lacerate your eyes for me, lacerate your nose for me. Lacerate your ears for me, in public. In private, lacerate your buttocks for me. Like a pauper, clothe yourself in a single garment and all alone set your foot in the E-kur, the house of Enlil.

"When you have entered the E-kur, the house of Enlil, lament before Enlil: 'Father Enlil, don't let anyone kill your daughter in the Underworld. Don't let your precious metal be alloyed there with the dirt of the Underworld. Don't let your precious lapis lazuli be split there with the mason's stone. Don't let your boxwood be chopped up there with the carpenter's wood. Don't let young lady Inana be killed in the Underworld.'

"If Enlil does not help you in this matter, go to Urim. In the E-mud-kura at Urim, when you have entered the E-kic-nu-jal, the house of Nanna, lament before Nanna: 'Father Nanna, don't let anyone kill your daughter in the Underworld. Don't let your precious metal be alloyed there with the dirt of the Underworld. Don't let your precious lapis lazuli be split there with the mason's stone. Don't let your boxwood be chopped up there with the carpenter's wood. Don't let young lady Inana be killed in the Underworld.'

"And if Nanna does not help you in this matter, go to Eridug. In Eridug, when you have entered the house of Enki, lament before Enki: 'Father Enki, don't let anyone kill your daughter in the Underworld. Don't let your precious metal be alloyed there with the dirt of the Underworld. Don't let your precious lapis lazuli be split there with the mason's stone. Don't let your boxwood be chopped up there with the carpenter's wood. Don't let young lady Inana be killed in the Underworld.'

"Father Enki, the lord of great wisdom, knows about the life-giving plant and the life-giving water. He is the one who will restore me to life."

When Inana travelled on towards the Underworld, her minister Nincubura travelled on behind her. She said to her minister Nincubura: "Go now, my Nincubura, and pay attention. Don't neglect the instructions I gave you."

When Inana arrived at the palace Ganzer, she pushed aggressively on the door of the Underworld. She shouted aggressively at the gate of the Underworld: "Open up, doorman, open up. Open up, Neti, open up. I am all alone and I want to come in."

Neti, the chief doorman of the Underworld, answered holy Inana: "Who are you?"

"I am Inana going to the east."

"If you are Inana going to the east, why have you travelled to the land of no return? How did you set your heart on the road whose traveller never returns?"

Holy Inana answered him: "Because lord Gud-gal-ana, the husband of my elder sister holy Erec-ki-gala, has died; in order to have his funeral rites observed, she offers generous libations at his wake – that is the reason."

Neti, the chief doorman of the Underworld, answered holy Inana: "Stay here, Inana. I will speak to my mistress. I will speak to my mistress Erec-ki-gala and tell her what you have said."

Neti, the chief doorman of the Underworld, entered the house of his mistress Erec-ki-gala and said: "My mistress, there is a lone girl outside. It is Inana, your sister, and she has arrived at the palace Ganzer. She pushed aggressively on the door of the Underworld. She shouted aggressively at the gate of the Underworld. She has abandoned E-ana and has descended to the Underworld.

"She has taken the seven divine powers. She has collected the divine powers and grasped them in her hand. She has come on her way with all the good divine powers. She has put a turban, headgear for the open country, on her head. She has taken a wig for her forehead. She has hung small lapis lazuli beads around her neck.

"She has placed twin egg-shaped beads on her breast. She has covered her body with the *pala* dress of ladyship. She has placed mascara which is called "Let a man come" on her eyes. She has pulled the pectoral which is called "Come, man, come" over her breast. She has placed a golden ring on her hand. She is holding the lapis lazuli measuring rod and measuring line in her hand."

When she heard this, Erec-ki-gala slapped the side of her thigh. She bit her lip and took the words to heart. She said to Neti, her chief doorman: "Come Neti, my chief doorman of the Underworld, don't neglect the instructions I will give you. Let the seven gates of the Underworld be bolted. Then let each door of the palace Ganzer be opened separately. As for her, after she has entered, and crouched down and had her clothes removed, they will be carried away."

Neti, the chief doorman of the Underworld, paid attention to the instructions of his mistress. He bolted the seven gates of the Underworld. Then he opened each of the doors of the palace Ganzer separately. He said to holy Inana: "Come on, Inana, and enter."

And when Inana entered, the lapis lazuli measuring rod and measuring line were removed from her hand; when she entered the first gate, the turban, headgear for the open country, was removed from her head. "What is this?"

"Be satisfied, Inana, a divine power of the Underworld has been fulfilled. Inana, you must not open your mouth against the rites of the Underworld."

When she entered the second gate, the small lapis lazuli beads were removed from her neck. "What is this?"

"Be satisfied, Inana, a divine power of the Underworld has been fulfilled. Inana, you must not open your mouth against the rites of the Underworld."

When she entered the third gate, the twin egg-shaped beads were removed from her breast. "What is this?"

"Be satisfied, Inana, a divine power of the Underworld has been fulfilled. Inana, you must not open your mouth against the rites of the Underworld."

When she entered the fourth gate, the "Come, man, come" pectoral was removed from her breast. "What is this?"

"Be satisfied, Inana, a divine power of the Underworld has been fulfilled. Inana, you must not open your mouth against the rites of the Underworld."

When she entered the fifth gate, the golden ring was removed from her hand. "What is this?"

"Be satisfied, Inana, a divine power of the Underworld has been fulfilled. Inana, you must not open your mouth against the rites of the Underworld."

When she entered the sixth gate, the lapis lazuli measuring rod and measuring line were removed from her hand. "What is this?"

"Be satisfied, Inana, a divine power of the Underworld has been fulfilled. Inana, you must not open your mouth against the rites of the Underworld."

When she entered the seventh gate, the *pala* dress, the garment of ladyship, was removed from her body. "What is this?"

"Be satisfied, Inana, a divine power of the Underworld has been fulfilled. Inana, you must not open your mouth against the rites of the Underworld."

After she had crouched down and had her clothes removed, they were carried away. Then she made her sister Erec-ki-gala rise from her throne, and instead she sat on her throne. The Anuna, the seven judges, rendered their decision against her. They looked at her – it was the look of death. They spoke to her – it was the speech of anger. They shouted at her – it was the shout of heavy guilt. The afflicted woman was turned into a corpse. And the corpse was hung on a hook.

After three days and three nights had passed, her minister Nincubura, her minister who speaks fair words, her escort who speaks trustworthy words, carried out the instructions of her mistress.

She made a lament for her in her ruined (houses). She beat the drum for her in the sanctuaries. She made the rounds of the houses of the gods for her. She lacerated her eyes for her; she lacerated her nose. In private she lacerated her buttocks for her. Like a pauper, she clothed herself in a single garment, and all alone she set her foot in the E-kur, the house of Enlil.

When she had entered the E-kur, the house of Enlil, she lamented before Enlil: "Father Enlil, don't let anyone kill your daughter in the Underworld. Don't let your precious metal be alloyed there with the dirt of the Underworld. Don't let your precious lapis lazuli be split there with the mason's stone. Don't let your boxwood be chopped up there with the carpenter's wood. Don't let young lady Inana be killed in the Underworld."

In his rage father Enlil answered Nincubura: "My daughter craved the great heaven and she craved the great below as well. Inana craved the great heaven and she craved the great below as well. The divine powers of the Underworld are divine powers which should not be craved, for whoever gets them must remain in the Underworld. Who, having got to that place, could then expect to come up again?"

Thus father Enlil did not help in this matter, so she went to Urim. In the E-mud-kura at Urim, when she had entered the E-kic-nu-jal, the house of Nanna, she lamented before Nanna: "Father Nanna, don't let your daughter be killed in the Underworld. Don't let your precious metal be alloyed there with the dirt of the Underworld. Don't let your precious lapis lazuli be split there with the mason's stone. Don't let your boxwood be chopped up there with the carpenter's wood. Don't let young lady Inana be killed in the Underworld."

In his rage father Nanna answered Nincubura: "My daughter craved the great heaven and she craved the great below as well. Inana craved the great heaven and she craved the great below as well. The divine powers of the Underworld are divine powers which should not be craved, for whoever gets them must remain in the Underworld. Who, having got to that place, could then expect to come up again?"

Thus father Nanna did not help her in this matter, so she went to Eridug. In Eridug, when she had entered the house of Enki, she lamented before Enki: "Father Enki, don't let anyone kill your daughter in the Underworld. Don't let your precious metal be alloyed there with the dirt of the Underworld. Don't let your precious lapis lazuli be split there with the mason's stone. Don't let your boxwood be chopped up there with the carpenter's wood. Don't let young lady Inana be killed in the Underworld."

Father Enki answered Nincubura: "What has my daughter done? She has me worried. What has Inana done? She has me worried. What has the mistress of all the lands done? She has me worried. What has the hierodule of An done? She has me worried." Thus father Enki helped her in this matter. He removed some dirt from the tip of his fingernail and created the *kur-jara*. He removed some dirt from the tip of his other fingernail and created the *gala-tura*. To the *kur-jara* he gave the life-giving plant. To the *gala-tura* he gave the life-giving water.

Then father Enki spoke out to the *gala-tura* and the *kur-jara*: "Go and direct your steps to the Underworld. Flit past the door like flies. Slip through the door pivots like phantoms. The mother who gave birth, Erec-ki-gala, on account of her children, is lying there. Her holy shoulders are not covered by a linen cloth. Her breasts are not full like a *cagan* vessel. Her nails are like a pickaxe (?) upon her. The hair on her head is bunched up as if it were leeks.

"When she says, 'Oh my heart', you are to say, 'You are troubled, our mistress, oh your heart'. When she says, 'Oh my liver', you are to say, 'You are troubled, our mistress, oh your liver'. (She will then ask:) 'Who are you? Speaking to you from my heart to your heart, from my liver to your liver – if you are gods, let me talk with you; if you are mortals, may a destiny be decreed for you.' Make her swear this by heaven and earth...

"They will offer you a riverful of water – don't accept it. They will offer you a field with its grain – don't accept it. But say to her: 'Give us the corpse hanging on the hook.' (She will answer:) 'That is the corpse of your queen.' Say to her: 'Whether it is that of our king, whether it is that of our queen, give it to us.' She will give you the corpse hanging on the hook. One of you sprinkle on it the life-giving plant and the other the life-giving water. Thus let Inana arise."

The *gala-tura* and the *kur-jara* paid attention to the instructions of Enki. They flitted through the door like flies. They slipped through the door pivots like phantoms. The mother who gave birth, Erec-ki-gala, because of her children, was lying there. Her holy shoulders were not covered by a linen cloth. Her breasts were not full like a *cagan* vessel. Her nails were like a pickaxe (?) upon her. The hair on her head was bunched up as if it were leeks.

When she said, "Oh my heart", they said to her, "You are troubled, our mistress, oh your heart". When she said, "Oh my liver", they said to her, "You are troubled, our mistress, oh your liver."

(Then she asked:) "Who are you? I tell you from my heart to your heart, from my liver to your liver – if you are gods, I will talk with you; if you are mortals, may a destiny be decreed for you." They made her swear this by heaven and earth. They...

They were offered a river with its water – they did not accept it. They were offered a field with its grain – they did not accept it. They said to her: "Give us the corpse hanging on the hook."

Holy Erec-ki-gala answered the *gala-tura* and the *kur-jara*: "The corpse is that of your queen."

They said to her: "Whether it is that of our king or that of our queen, give it to us." They were given the corpse hanging on the hook. One of them sprinkled on it the life-giving plant and the other the life-giving water. And thus Inana arose.

Erec-ki-gala said to the *gala-tura* and the *kur-jara*: "Bring your queen...your...has been seized." Inana, because of Enki's instructions, was about to ascend from the Underworld.

But as Inana was about to ascend from the Underworld, the Anuna seized her. "Who has ever ascended from the Underworld, has ascended unscathed from the Underworld? If Inana is to ascend from the Underworld, let her provide a substitute for herself."

So when Inana left the Underworld, the one in front of her, though not a minister, held a sceptre in his hand; the one behind her, though not an escort, carried a mace at his hip, while the small demons, like a reed enclosure, and the big demons, like the reeds of a fence, restrained her on all sides.

Those who accompanied her, those who accompanied Inana, know no food, know no drink, eat no flour offering and drink no libation. They accept no pleasant gifts. They never enjoy the pleasures of the marital embrace, never have any sweet children to kiss. They tear away the wife from a man's embrace. They snatch the son from a man's knee. They make the bride leave the house of her father-in-law. They crush no bitter garlic. They eat no fish, they eat no leeks. They, it was, who accompanied Inana.

After Inana had ascended from the Underworld, Nincubura threw herself at her feet at the door of the Ganzer. She had sat in the dust and clothed herself in a filthy garment. The demons said to holy Inana: "Inana, proceed to your city; we will take her back."

Holy Inana answered the demons: "This is my minister of fair words, my escort of trustworthy words. She did not forget my instructions. She did not neglect the orders I gave her. She made a lament for me on the ruin mounds. She beat the drum for me in the sanctuaries. She made the rounds of the gods' houses for me. She lacerated her eyes for me, lacerated her nose for me. She lacerated her ears for me in public. In private, she lacerated her buttocks for me. Like a pauper, she clothed herself in a single garment.

"All alone she directed her steps to the E-kur, to the house of Enlil, and to Urim, to the house of Nanna, and to Eridug, to the house of Enki. She wept before Enki. She brought me back to life. How could I turn her over to you? Let us go on. Let us go on to the Sig-kur-caga in Umma."

At the Sig-kur-caga in Umma, Cara, in his own city, threw himself at her feet. He had sat in the dust and dressed himself in a filthy garment. The demons said to holy Inana: "Inana, proceed to your city, we will take him back."

Holy Inana answered the demons: "Cara is my singer, my manicurist and my hairdresser. How could I turn him over to you? Let us go on. Let us go on to the E-muc-kalama in Bad-tibira."

At the E-muc-kalama in Bad-tibira, Lulal, in his own city, threw himself at her feet. He had sat in the dust and clothed himself in a filthy garment. The demons said to holy Inana: "Inana, proceed to your city, we will take him back."

Holy Inana answered the demons: "Outstanding Lulal follows me at my right and my left. How could I turn him over to you? Let us go on. Let us go on to the great apple tree in the plain of Kulaba."

They followed her to the great apple tree in the plain of Kulaba. There was Dumuzid clothed in a magnificent garment and seated magnificently on a throne. The demons seized him there by his thighs. The seven of them poured the milk from his churns. The seven of them shook their heads like.... They would not let the shepherd play the pipe and flute before her (?).

She looked at him; it was the look of death. She spoke to him (?), it was the speech of anger. She shouted at him (?), it was the shout of heavy guilt: "How much longer? Take him away." Holy Inana gave Dumuzid the shepherd into their hands.

Those who had accompanied her, who had come for Dumuzid, know no food, know no drink, eat no flour offering, drink no libation. They never enjoy the pleasures of the marital embrace, never have any sweet children to kiss. They snatch the son from a man's knee. They make the bride leave the house of her father-in-law.

Dumuzid let out a wail and turned very pale. The lad raised his hands to heaven, to Utu: "Utu, you are my brother-in-law. I am your relation by marriage. I brought butter to your mother's house. I brought milk to Ningal's house. Turn my hands into snake's hands and turn my feet into snake's feet, so I can escape my demons, let them not keep hold of me."

Utu accepted his tears. Dumuzid's demons could not keep hold of him. Utu turned Dumuzid's hands into snake's hands. He turned his feet into snake's feet. Dumuzid escaped his demons. Like a *sajkal* snake he.... They seized...Holy Inana...her heart.

Holy Inana wept bitterly for her husband...

She tore at her hair like esparto grass; she ripped it out like esparto grass. "You wives who lie in your men's embrace, where is my precious husband? You children who lie in your men's embrace, where is my precious child? Where is my man? Where...? Where is my man? Where ...?"

A fly spoke to holy Inana: "If I show you where your man is, what will be my reward?" Holy Inana answered the fly: "If you show me where my man is, I will give you this gift: I will cover..."

The fly helped (?) holy Inana. The young lady Inana decreed the destiny of the fly: "In the beer-house and the tavern (?), may there...for you. You will live (?) like the sons of the wise." Now Inana decreed this fate and thus it came to be.

...was weeping. She came up to the sister (?) and...by the hand: "Now, alas, my.... You for half the year and your sister for half the year: when you are demanded, on that day you will stay, when your sister is demanded, on that day you will be released." Thus holy Inana gave Dumuzid as a substitute...

Holy Erec-ki-gala – sweet is your praise.

Ningishzida's Journey to the Netherworld

"Arise and get on board; arise, we are about to sail; arise and get on board!" – Woe, weep for the bright daylight, as the barge is steered away! – "I am a young man! Let me not be covered against my wishes by a cabin, as if with a blanket, as if with a blanket!"

Stretching out a hand to the barge, to the young man being steered away on the barge, stretching out a hand to my young man Damu being taken away on the barge, stretching out a hand to Ictaran of the bright visage being taken away on the barge, stretching out a hand to Alla, master of the battle-net, being taken away on the barge, stretching out a hand to Lugal-cud-e being taken away on the barge, stretching out a hand to Ninjiczida being taken away on the barge – his younger sister was crying in lament to him in the boat's cabin.

His older sister removed the cover (?) from the boat's cabin. "Let me sail away with you, let me sail away with you, brother, let me sail away with you."

She was crying a lament to him at the boat's bow: "Brother, let me sail away with you. Let me... for you in your boat's stern, brother, let me sail away with you. The *gudu* priest sits in the cabin at your boat's stern." She was crying a lament to him: "Let me sail away with you, my brother, let me sail away with you." [...]

The evil demon who was in their midst called out to Lugal-ki-suna: "Lugal-ki-suna, look at your sister!"

Having looked at his sister, Lugal-ki-suna said to her: "He sails with me, he sails with me. Why should you sail to the Underworld? Lady, the demon sails with me. Why should you sail to the Underworld? The thresher sails with me. Why should you sail to the Underworld? The man who has bound my hands sails with me. Why should you sail? The man who has tied my arms sails with me. Why should you sail?

"The river of the Netherworld produces no water, no water is drunk from it. Why should you sail? The fields of the Netherworld produce no grain, no flour is eaten from it. Why should you sail? The sheep of the Netherworld produce no wool, and no cloth is woven from it. Why should you sail? As for me, even if my mother digs as if for a canal, I shall not be able to drink the water meant for me. The waters of springtime will not be poured for me as they are for the tamarisks; I shall not sit in the shade intended for me. The dates I should bear like a date palm will not reveal (?) their beauty for me. I am a field threshed by my demon – you would scream at it. He has put manacles on my hands – you would scream at it. He has put a neck-stock on my neck – you would scream at it."

Ama-cilama (Ninjiczida's sister) said to Ninjiczida: "The ill-intentioned demon may accept something – there should be a limit to it for you. My brother, your demon may accept something, there should be a limit to it for you. For him let me...from my hand the...there should be a limit to it for you. For him let me...from my hand the...there should be a limit to it for you. For him let me...from my hips the dainty lapis lazuli beads, there should be a limit to it for you. For him let me...from my hips the...my lapis lazuli beads, there should be a limit to it for you.

"You are a beloved...there should be a limit to it for you. How they treat you, how they treat you! – there should be a limit to it for you. My brother, how they treat you, how haughtily they treat you! – there should be a limit to it for you. 'I am hungry, but the bread has slipped away from me!' – there should be a limit to it for you. 'I am thirsty, but the water has slipped away from me!' – there should be a limit to it for you."

The evil demon who was in their midst, the clever demon, that great demon who was in their midst, called out to the man at the boat's bow and to the man at the boat's stern: "Don't let the mooring stake be pulled out, don't let the mooring stake be pulled out, so that she may come on board to her brother, that this lady may come on board the barge."

When Ama-cilama had gone on board the barge, a cry approached the heavens, a cry approached the earth, that great demon set up an enveloping cry before him on the river: "Urim, at my cry to the heavens lock your houses, lock your houses, city, lock your houses! Shrine Urim, lock your houses, city, lock your houses! Against your lord who has left the *jipar*, city, lock your houses!" [...]

He...to the empty river, the rejoicing (?) river (addressing *Ama-cilama*): "You shall not draw near to this house...to the place of Ereckigala. My mother...out of her love." (addressing the demon) "As for you, you may be a great demon...your hand against the Netherworld's office of throne-bearer.

"My king will no longer shed tears in his eyes. The drum will...his joy in tears. Come! May the fowler utter a lament for you in his well-stocked house, lord, may he utter a lament for you. How he has been humiliated! May the young fisherman utter a lament for you in his well-stocked house, lord, may he utter a lament for you. How he has been humiliated! May the mother of the dead *gudu* priest utter a lament for you in her empty *jipar*, utter a lament for you, lord, may she utter a lament for you. How he has been humiliated! May the mother high priestess utter a lament for you who have left the *jipar*, lord, may she utter a lament for you. How he has been humiliated!

"My king, bathe with water your head that has rolled in the dust...in sandals your feet defiled from the defiled place." The king bathed with water his head that had rolled in the dust...in sandals his feet defiled from the defiled place. "Not drawing near to this house...your throne... to you, 'Sit down'. May your bed...to you, 'Lie down'." He ate food in his mouth, he drank choice wine.

Great holy one, Ereckigala, praising you is sweet.

The Death of Ur-Namma

...entire land...struck, the palace was devastated...panic spread rapidly among the dwellings of the black-headed people...abandoned places...in Sumer...the cities were destroyed in their entirety; the people were seized with panic. Evil came upon Urim and made the trustworthy shepherd pass away. It made Ur-Namma, the trustworthy shepherd, pass away; it made the trustworthy shepherd pass away.

Because An had altered his holy words completely...became empty, and because, deceitfully, Enlil had completely changed the fate he decreed, Ninmah began a lament in her.... Enki shut (?) the great door of Eridug. Nudimmud withdrew into his bedchamber and lay down fasting. At his zenith, Nanna frowned at the...words of An. Utu did not come forth in the sky, and the day was full of sorrow.

The mother, miserable because of her son, the mother of the king, holy Ninsun, was crying: "Oh my heart!" Because of the fate decreed for Ur-Namma, because it made the trustworthy shepherd pass away, she was weeping bitterly in the broad square, which is otherwise a place of entertainment. Sweet sleep did not come to the people whose happing...they passed their time in lamentation over the trustworthy shepherd who had been snatched away.

As the early flood was filling the canals, their canal-inspector was already silenced (?); the mottled barley grown on the arable lands, the life of the land, was inundated. To the farmer, the fertile fields planted (?) by him yielded little. Enkimdu, the lord of levees and ditches, took away the levees and ditches from Urim...

As the intelligence and...of the Land were lost, fine food became scarce. The plains did not grow lush grass anymore, they grew the grass of mourning. The cows...their...cattle-pen has been destroyed. The calves...their cows bleated bitterly.

The wise shepherd...does not give orders anymore...in battle and combat. The king, the advocate of Sumer, the ornament of the assembly, Ur-Namma, the advocate of Sumer, the ornament of the assembly, the leader of Sumer...lies sick. His hands which used to grasp cannot grasp anymore; he lies sick. His feet...cannot step anymore, he lies sick...

The trustworthy shepherd, king, the sword of Sumer, Ur-Namma, the king of the Land, was taken to the...house. He was taken to Urim; the king of the Land was brought into the... house. The proud one lay in his palace. Ur-Namma, he who was beloved by the troops, could not raise his neck anymore. The wise one...lay down; silence descended. As he, who was the vigour of the Land, had fallen, the Land became demolished like a mountain; like a cypress forest it was stripped, its appearance changed. As if he were a boxwood tree, they put axes against him in his joyous dwelling place. As if he were a sappy cedar tree, he was uprooted in the palace where he used to sleep (?). His spouse...resting place...was covered by a storm; it embraced it like a wife her sweetheart (?). His appointed time had arrived, and he passed away in his prime.

His (?) pleasing sacrifices were no longer accepted; they were treated as dirty (?). The Anuna gods refused his gifts. [...] Because of what Enlil ordered, there was no more rising up; his beloved men lost their wise one. Strangers turned into (?).... How iniquitously Ur-Namma was abandoned, like a broken jar! His...with grandeur like (?) thick clouds (?). He does not...anymore, and he does not reach out for...Ur-Namma, the son of Ninsun, was brought to Arali, the...of the Land, in his prime. The soldiers accompanying the king shed tears: their boat (*i.e.* Ur-Namma) was sunk in a land as foreign to them as Dilmun...was cut. It was stripped of the oars, punting poles and rudder which it had...its bolt was broken off... was put aside; it stood (?) in saltpetre. His donkeys were to be found with the king; they were buried with him. His donkeys were to be found with Ur-Namma; they were buried with him. As he crossed over the...of the Land, the Land was deprived of its ornament. The journey to the Netherworld is a desolate route. Because of the king, the chariots were covered over, the roads were thrown into disorder, no one could go up and down on them. Because of Ur-Namma, the chariots were covered over, the roads were thrown into disorder, no one could go up and down on them.

He presented gifts to the seven chief porters of the Netherworld. As the famous kings who had died and the dead *icib* priests, *lumah* priests, and *nindijir* priestesses, all chosen by extispicy, announced the king's coming to the people, a tumult arose in the Netherworld. As they announced Ur-Namma's coming to the people, a tumult arose in the Netherworld. The king slaughtered numerous bulls and sheep, Ur-Namma seated the people at a huge banquet. The food of the Netherworld is bitter, the water of the Netherworld is brackish. The trustworthy shepherd knew well the rites of the Netherworld, so the king presented the offerings of the Netherworld, Ur-Namma presented the offerings of the Netherworld: as many faultless bulls, faultless kids, and fattened sheep as could be brought.

To Nergal, the Enlil of the Netherworld, in his palace, the shepherd Ur-Namma offered a mace, a large bow with quiver and arrows, an artfully made...dagger, and a multi-coloured leather bag for wearing at the hip.

To Gilgamec, the king of the Netherworld, in his palace, the shepherd Ur-Namma offered a spear, a leather bag for a saddle-hook, a heavenly lion-headed *imitum* mace, a shield resting on the ground, a heroic weapon, and a battle-axe, an implement beloved of Ereckigala.

To Ereckigala, the mother of Ninazu, in her palace, the shepherd Ur-Namma offered a...which he filled with oil, a *cajan* bowl of perfect make, a heavy garment, a long-fleeced garment, a queenly *pala* robe...the divine powers of the Netherworld.

To Dumuzid, the beloved husband of Inana, in his palace, the shepherd Ur-Namma offered a...sheep...mountain...a lordly golden sceptre...a shining hand.

To Namtar, who decrees all the fates, in his palace, the shepherd Ur-Namma offered perfectly wrought jewellery, a golden ring cast (?) as a...barge, pure cornelian stone fit to be worn on the breasts of the gods.

To Hucbisag, the wife of Namtar, in her palace, the shepherd Ur-Namma offered a chest (?) with a lapis lazuli handle, containing (?) everything that is essential in the Underworld, a silver hair clasp adorned with lapis lazuli, and a comb of womanly fashion.

To the valiant warrior Ninjiczida, in his palace, the shepherd Ur-Namma offered a chariot with...wheels sparkling with gold...donkeys, thoroughbreds...donkeys with dappled thighs... followed...by a shepherd and a herdsman.

To Dimpimekug, who stands by his side, he gave a lapis lazuli seal hanging from a pin, and a gold and silver toggle-pin with a bison's head.

To his spouse, Ninazimua, the august scribe, denizen of Arali, in her palace, the shepherd Ur-Namma offered a headdress with the august ear-pieces (?) of a sage, made of alabaster, a...stylus, the hallmark of the scribe, a surveyor's gleaming line, and the measuring rod... [...]

After the king had presented properly the offerings of the Netherworld, after Ur-Namma had presented properly the offerings of the Netherworld, the...seated Ur-Namma on a great dais of the Netherworld and set up a dwelling place for him in the Netherworld. At the command of Ereckigala all the soldiers who had been killed by weapons and all the men who had been found guilty were given into the king's hands. Ur-Namma was...so with Gilgamec, his beloved brother, he will issue the judgments of the Netherworld and render the decisions of the Netherworld.

After seven days, ten days had passed, lamenting for Sumer overwhelmed my king, lamenting for Sumer overwhelmed Ur-Namma. My king's heart was full of tears, he...bitterly that he could not complete the wall of Urim; that he could no longer enjoy the new palace he had built; that he, the shepherd, could no longer...his household (?); that he could no longer bring pleasure to his wife with his embrace; that he could not bring up his sons on his knees; that he would never see in their prime the beauty of their little sisters who had not yet grown up.

The trustworthy shepherd...a heart-rending lament for himself: "I, who have been treated like this, served the gods well, set up chapels for them. I have created evident abundance for the Anuna gods. I have laid treasures on their beds strewn with fresh herbs. Yet no god stood by me and soothed my heart. Because of them, anything that could have been a favourable portent for me was as far away from me as the heavens, the.... What is my reward for my eagerness to serve during the days? My days have been finished for serving them sleeplessly during the night! Now, just as the rain pouring down from heaven cannot turn back, alas, nor can I turn back to brick-built Urim.

"Alas, my wife has become a widow (?)! She spends the days in tears and bitter laments. My strength has ebbed away.... The hand of fate...bitterly me, the hero. Like a wild bull...I cannot.... Like a mighty bull...Like an offshoot.... Like an ass.... I died...my...wife...She spends the days in tears and bitter laments. Her kind protective god has left her; her kind protective goddess does not care for her anymore. Ninsun no longer rests her august arm firmly on her head. Nanna, lord Acimbabbar, no longer leads (?) her by the hand. Enki, the lord of Eridug, does not.... Her...has been silenced (?), she can no longer answer. She is cast adrift like a boat in a raging storm; the mooring pole has not been strong enough for her. Like a wild ass lured (?) into a perilous pit she has been treated heavy-handedly. Like a lion fallen into a pitfall, a guard has been set up for her. Like a dog kept in a cage, she is silenced. Utu...does not pay heed to the cries, "Oh, my king," overwhelming her.

"My *tigi*, *adab*, flute and *zamzam* songs have been turned into laments because of me. The instruments of the house of music have been propped against the wall. Because I have been made to...on a heap of soil (?) instead of my throne whose beauty was endless; because I have been made to lie down in the open, desolate steppe instead of my bed, the sleeping place whose...was endless, alas, my wife and my children are in tears and wailing. My people whom I used to command (?) sing like lamentation and dirge singers because of her (?). While I was so treated, foremost Inana, the warlike lady, was not present at my verdict. Enlil had sent her as a messenger to all the foreign lands concerning very important matters."

When she had turned her gaze away from there, Inana humbly entered the shining E-kur, she…at Enlil's fierce brow. (Then Enlil said:) "Great lady of the E-ana, once someone has bowed down, he cannot…anymore; the trustworthy shepherd left E-ana, you cannot see him anymore." […] Then Inana, the fierce storm, the eldest child of Suen…made the heavens tremble, made the earth shake.

Inana destroyed cattle-pens, devastated sheepfolds, saying: "I want to hurl insults at An, the king of the gods. Who can change the matter, if Enlil elevates someone? Who can change the import of the august words uttered by An, the king? If there are divine ordinances imposed on the Land, but they are not observed, there will be no abundance at the gods' place of sunrise. My holy *jipar*, the shrine E-ana, has been barred up like (?) a mountain. If only my shepherd could enter before me in it in his prime – I will not enter it otherwise! If only my strong one could grow for me like grass and herbs in the desert. If only he could hold steady for me like a river boat at its calm mooring." This is how Inana…a lament over him…Lord Ninjiczida…Ur-Namma, my… who was killed…

Among tears and laments…decreed a fate for Ur-Namma: "Ur-Namma…your august name will be called upon. From the south to the uplands…the holy sceptre. Sumer…to your palace. The people will admire…the canals which you have dug, the…which you have…the large and grand arable tracts which you have…the reed-beds which you have drained, the wide barley fields which you…and the fortresses and settlements which you have…Ur-Namma, they will call upon…your name. Lord Nunamnir, surpassing…will drive away the evil spirits…"

After shepherd Ur-Namma…Nanna, lord Acimbabbar…Enki, the king of Eridug…devastated sheepfolds…holy…lion born on high…renders just judgments…lord Ninjiczida be praised! My king…among tears and laments…among tears and laments.

The Adventure of Setne Khamwas with the Mummies

AT ONE TIME there was a king named Usimares, l. h. s., and this king had a son named Setne Khamwas, and the foster-brother of Setne Khamwas was called Inarôs by name. And Setne Khamwas was well instructed in all things. He passed his time wandering about the necropolis of Memphis, to read there the books of the sacred writings and the books of the *Double House of Life*, and the writings that are carved on the stelae and on the walls of the temples; he knew the virtues of amulets and talismans, he understood how to compose them and to draw up powerful writings, for he was a magician who had no equal in the land of Egypt.

Now, one day, when he was walking in the open court of the temple of Ptah, reading the inscriptions, behold, a man of noble bearing who was there began to laugh. Setne said to him, "Wherefore dost thou laugh at me?" The noble said, "I do not laugh at thee, but can I refrain from laughing when thou dost decipher the writings here which possess no power? If thou desirest truly to read an efficacious writing, come with me. I will cause thee to go to the place where the book is that Thoth wrote with his own hand, and which will put thee immediately below the gods. The two formulae that are written there, if thou recites the first of them, thou shalt charm the heaven, the earth, the world of the night, the mountains, the waters; thou shalt understand what all the birds of heaven and the reptiles say, as many as there are. Thou shalt behold the fish, for a divine power will bring them to the surface of the water. If thou readest the second formula, even when thou art in the tomb, thou shalt resume the form thou hadst on earth; thou shalt also behold the sun rising in the heavens, and his cycle of gods, also the moon in the form that she has when she appears." Setne said, "By my life! Let it be told me what thou dost wish for, and I will do it for thee; but lead me to the place where the book is." The noble said to Setne, "The book in question is not mine, it is in the midst of the necropolis, in the tomb of Nenoferkephtah, son of the King Merenephthis, l. h. s. Beware indeed of taking this book from him, for he will make thee bring it back, a forked stick and a staff in thy hand, a lighted brazier on thy head." From the hour when the noble spake to Setne, he knew no longer in what part of the world he was; he went before the king, and he said before the king all the words that the noble had said to him. The king said to him, "What dost thou desire?" He said to the king, "Permit me to go down into the tomb of Nenoferkephtah, son of the King Merenphthis, l. h. s.; I will take Inarôs, my foster-brother, with me, and I shall bring back that book." He went to the necropolis of Memphis with Inarôs, his foster-brother. He spent three days and three nights searching among the tombs which are in the necropolis of Memphis, reading the stelae of the *Double House of Life*, reciting the inscriptions they bore. On the third day he recognized the place where Nenoferkephtah was laid. When they had recognized the place where Nenoferkephtah was laid, Setne recited a writing over him; a gap opened in the ground, and Setne went down to the place where the book was. [...]

When he entered, behold, it was as light as if the sun shone there, for the light came from the book and lighted all around. And Nenoferkephtah was not alone in the tomb, but his wife Ahuri, and Maîhêt his son, were with him; for though their bodies reposed at Coptos, their double was with him by virtue of the book of Thoth. And when Setne entered the tomb, Ahuri stood up and said to him, "Thou, who art thou?" He said, "I am Setne Khamwas, son of the King Usimares, l. h. s.; I am come to have that book of Thoth, that I perceive between thee and Nenoferkephtah. Give it me, for if not I will take it from thee by force." Ahuri said, "I pray thee, be not in haste, but listen first to all the misfortunes that came to me because of this book of which thou sayest, 'Let it be given to me.' Do not say that, for on account of it we were deprived of the time we had to remain on earth.

"I am named Ahuri, daughter of the King Merenephthis, l. h. s., and he whom thou seest here with me is my brother Nenoferkephtah. We were born of the same father and the same mother, and our parents had no other children than ourselves. When I was of age to marry, I was taken before the king at the time of diversion with he king; I was much adorned and I was considered beautiful. The king said, 'Behold, Ahuri, our daughter, is already grown, and the time has come to marry her. To whom shall we marry Ahuri, our daughter?' Now I loved Nenoferkephtah, my brother, exceedingly, and I desired no other husband than he. I told this to my mother; she went to find the King Merenephthis, she said to him, 'Ahuri, our daughter, loves Nenoferkephtah, her eldest brother; let us marry them one tot the other according to custom.' When the King had heard all the words that my mother had said, he said, 'Thou hast had but two children, and wouldest thou marry them one to the other? Would it not be better to marry Ahuri to the son of a general of infantry, and Nenoferkephtah to the daughter of another general of infantry?' She said, 'Dos thou wrangle with me? Even if I have no children after those two children, is it not the law to marry them one to the other? – I shall marry Nenoferkephttah to the daughter of a commander of troops, and Ahuri to the son of another commander of troops, and may this turn to good for our family.' As this was the time to make festival before Pharaoh, behold, one came to fetch me, one led me to the festival; I was very troubled, and I had no longer the manner of the previous day. Now Pharaoh said to me, 'Is it not thou who didst send me those foolish words, "Marry me to Nenoferkephtah my eldest brother"?' I said to him, 'Well, let me be married to the son of a general of infantry, and let Nenoferkephtah be married to the daughter of another general of infantry, and may this turn to good for our family.' I laughed, Pharaoh laughed. Pharaoh said to the major-domo of the royal house, 'Let Ahuri be taken to the house of Nenoferkephtah this very night; let all manner of fine presents be taken with her.' They took me as spouse to the house of Nenoferkephtah, and Pharaoh commanded that a great dowry of gold and silver should be taken to me, and all the servants of the royal house presented them to me. Nenoferkephtah spent a happy day with me; he received all the servants of the royal house, and he slept with me that very night, and he found me a virgin, and he knew me again and again, for each of us loved the other. And when the time of my monthly purifications was come, lo, I had no purifications to make. One went to announce it to Pharaoh, and his heart rejoiced greatly thereat, and he had all manner of precious things of the property of the royal house taken, and he had very beautiful gifts of gold, of silver, of fine linen, brought to me. And when the time came that I should be delivered, I brought forth this little child who is before thee. The name of Maîhêt was given him, and it was inscribed on the register of the *Double House of Life*.

And many days after that, Nenoferkephtah, my brother, seemed only to be on earth to walk about in the necropolis of Memphis, reading the writings that are in the tombs of the Pharaohs, and the stelae of the scribes of the *Double House of Life*, as well as the writings that are inscribed on them, for he was greatly interested in writings. After that there was a procession in honour of the god Ptah, and Nenoferkephtah entered the temple to pray. Now while he walked behind the procession, deciphering the writings that are on the chapels of the gods, an old man saw him and laughed. Nenoferkephtah said to him, 'Where fore dost thou laugh at me?' The priest said, 'I am not laughing at thee; but can I refrain from laughing when thou readest here writings that have no power? If thou verily desirest to read a writing, come to me. I will cause thee to go to a place where the book is that Thoth wrote with his hand himself, when he came here below with the gods. The two formulae that are written there, if thou recitest the first thou shalt charm the heavens, the earth, the world of the night, the mountains, the waters; thou shalt understand that which the birds of the heaven and the reptiles say, as many as they are; thou shalt see the fish of the deep, for a divine power will rest on the water above them. If thou readest the second formula, even after thou art in the tomb, thou shalt resume the form that thou hadst on earth; also thou shalt see the sun rising in the heavens, with his cycle of gods, and the moon in the form she has when she appears.' Nenoferkephtah said to the priest, 'By the life of the King, let me be told what good thing thou dost wish for, and I will cause it to be given to thee if thou wilt lead me to the place where the book is.' The priest said to Nenoferkephtah, 'If thou desirest that I should send thee to the place where the book is thou shalt give me a hundred pieces of silver for my burial, and thou shalt cause the two coffins of a wealthy priest to be made for me.' Nenoferkephtah called a page and commanded him that the hundred pieces of silver should be given to the priest, also he caused the two coffins to be made that the desired; in short, he did all that the priest had said. The priest said to Nenoferkephtah, 'The book in question is in the midst of the sea of Coptos in an iron coffer. The iron coffer is in a bronze coffer; the bronze coffer is in a coffer of cinnamon wood; the coffer of cinnamon wood is in a coffer of ivory and ebony; the coffer of ivory and ebony is in a coffer of silver; the coffer of silver is in a coffer of gold, and the book is in that. And there is a schene of reptiles round the coffer in which is the book, and there is an immortal serpent rolled round the coffer in question.'

"From the hour that the priest spoke to Nenoferkephtah he knew not in what part of the world he was. He came out of the temple; he spake with me of all that had happened to him; he said to me, 'I go to Coptos, I will bring back that book, and after that I will not again leave the country of the north.' But I rose up against the priest, saying, 'Beware of Amon for thyself, because of that which thou hast said to Nenoferkephtah; for thou hast brought me disputing, thou has brought me war; and the country of the Thebaid, I find it hostile to my happiness.' I raised my hand to Nenoferkephttah that they should not go to Coptos, but he did not listen to me; he went before Pharaoh, and he spake before Pharaoh all the words that the priest had said to him. Pharaoh said to him, 'What is the desire of thy heart?' He said to him, 'Let the royal cange be given to me fully equipped. I shall take Ahuri, my sister, and Maîhêt, her little child, to the south with me; I shall bring back the book, and I shall not leave this place again.' The cange fully equipped was given to him; we embarked on it, we made the voyage, we arrived at Coptos. When this was told to the priests of Isis of Coptos, and to the superior of the priests of Isis, behold they came down to us; they came without delay before Nenoferkephtah, and their wives came down before me. We disembarked, and we went to the temple of Isis, and of Harpocrates. Nenoferkephtah caused a bull to be brought, a goose, and wine; he presented an offering and a libation before Isis of Coptos, and Harpocrates. We were then conducted to a house which was very beautiful, and full of all manner of good things. Nenoferkephtah spent five days diverting himself with the priests of Isis of Coptos, while the wives of the priests of Isis of Coptos diverted themselves with me. When the morning of the following day came Nenoferkephtah caused a large quantity of pure wax to be brought before hum; he made of it a bark filled with its rowers and sailors, he recited a spell over them, he brought them to life, he gave them breath, he threw them into the water, he filled the royal cange with sand, he said farewell to me, he embarked, and I placed myself on the sea of Coptos, saying, 'I know what will happen to him.'

"He said, 'Rowers, row for me, to the place where the book is,' and they rowed for him, by night as by day. When he had arrived there in three days, he threw sand in front of him, and a chasm opened in the river. When he had found a schene of serpents, of scorpions, and of all manner of reptiles round the coffer where the book was, and when he had beheld an eternal serpent round the coffer itself, he recited a spell over the schene of serpents, scorpions, and reptiles who were round the coffer, and if rendered them motionless. He came to the place where the eternal serpent was; he attacked him, he slew him. The serpent came to life, and took his form again. He attacked the serpent a second time; he slew him. The serpent came to life again. He attacked the serpent a third time; he cut him in two pieces, he put sand between piece and piece; the serpent died, and he did not again take his previous form. Nenoferkephtah went to the place where the coffer was, and he recognized that it was an iron coffer. He opened it and he found a bronze coffer. He opened it and found a cinnamon-wood coffer. He opened it and found an ivory and ebony coffer. He opened it and found a silver coffer. He opened it and found a gold coffer. He opened it and found that the book was inside. He drew the book in question out of the gold coffer, and recited a formula of that which was written in it; he enchanted the heaven, the earth, the world of the night, the mountains, the waters; he understood all that was spoken by the birds of the heaven, the fish of the waters, the beasts of the mountain. He recited the other formula of the writing, and he beheld the sun as it mounted the sky with his cycle of gods, the moon rising, the stars in their form; he beheld the fish of the deep, for a divine force rested on the water above them. He recited a spell over the water, and it made it return to its former shape, he re-embarked; he said to the rowers, 'Row for me to the place where Ahuri is.' They rowed for him, by night as by day. When he arrived at the place where I was, in three days, he found me sitting near the sea of Coptos. I was not drinking nor eating; I was doing nothing in the world; I was like a person arrived at the *Good Dwelling*. I said to Nenoferkephtah, 'By the life of the King! Grant that I see this book for which you have taken all this trouble.' He put the book in my hand, I read one formula of the writing which was there; I enchanted the heaven, the earth, the world of the night, the mountains, the waters; I understood all that was spoken by the birds of the heaven, the fish of the deep, and the quadrupeds. I recited the other formula of the writing. I beheld the sun which appeared in the heaven with his cycle of gods, I beheld the moon rising. And all the stars of heaven in their form; I beheld the fish of the water, for there was a divine force which rested on the water above them. As I could not write, I said to Nenoferkephtah, my eldest brother, who was an accomplished scribe and a very learned man; he caused a piece of virgin papyrus to be brought, he wrote therein all the words that were in the book, he soaked it in beer, he dissolved the whole in water. When he saw that it had all dissolved, he drank, and he knew all that was in the writing.

"We returned to Coptos the same day, and we made merry before Isis of Coptos and Harpocrates. We embarked, we set off. We reached the north of Coptos, the distance of a schene. Now behold, Thoth had learnt all that had happened to Nenoferkephtah with regard to this book, and Thoth did not delay to plead before Râ, saying, 'Know that my right and my law are with Nenoferkephtah, son of the King Merenephthis, l. h. s. He has penetrated into my abode, he has pillaged it, he has taken my coffer with my book of incantations, he has slain my guardian who watched over the coffer.' One said to him, 'He is thine, he and all his, all of them.' One sent down a divine force from heaven saying, 'Nenoferkephtah shall not arrive safe and sound at Memphis, he and whoever is with him.' At this same hour Maîhêt, the young child, came out from under the awning of the cange of Pharaoh. He fell in the river, and while he praised Râ, all who were on board uttered a cry. Nenoferkephtah came out from below the cabin; he recited a spell over the child, and brought him up again, for there was a divine force which rested on the water above him. He recited a spell over him, he made him tell all that had happened to him, and the accusation that Thoth had brought before Râ. We returned to Coptos with him, we had him carried to the *Good Dwelling*, we waited to see that care was taken of him, we had him embalmed as beseemed a great one, we laid him in his coffin in the cemetery of Coptos. Nenoferkephtah, my brother, said, 'Let us go; do not let us delay to return until the king has heard what has happened to us, and his heart is troubled on this account.' We embarked, we parted, we were not long in arriving at the north of Coptos, the distance of a schene. At the place where the little child Maîhêt had tumbled into the river, I came out from below the awning of the cange of Pharaoh, I fell into the river, and while I praised Râ all who were on board uttered a cry. It was told to Nenoferkephtah, and he came out from below the awning of the cange of Pharaoh. He recited a spell over me, and he brought me up again, for there was a divine force which rested on the water above me. He took me out of the river, he read a spell over me, he made me tell all that had happened to me, and the accusation that Thoth had brought before Râ. He returned to Coptos with me, he had me carried to the *Good Dwelling*, he waited to see that care was taken of me, he had me embalmed as beseemed a very great personage, he had me laid in the tomb where Maîhêt, the little child, was already laid. He embarked, he set out, he was not long in arriving at the north of Coptos, the distance of a schene, at the place where we had fallen into the river. He communed with his heart, saying, 'Would it not be better to go to Coptos, and take up my abode with them? If, on the contrary, I return at once to Memphis, and Pharaoh questions me on the subject of his children, what could I say to him? Could I say thus to him: 'I took thy children with me to the nome of Thebes; I have killed them, and I live. I returned to Memphis still living.' He caused a piece of royal fine linen that belonged to him to be brought, he made of it a magic band, he tied the book with it, he put it on his breast, and fixed it there firmly. Neoferkephtah came out from below the awning of the cange of Pharaoh, he fell into the water, and while he praised Râ all who were on board uttered a cry, saying, 'Oh, what great mourning, what lamentable mourning! Is he not gone, the excellent scribe, the learned man who had no equal!'

"The cange of Pharaoh went on its way, before anyone in the world knew in what place Nenoferkephtah was. When it arrived at Memphis one informed Pharaoh, and Pharaoh came down in front of the cange. He was wearing a mourning cloak, and all the garrison of Memphis wore mourning cloaks, as well as the priests of Ptah, the high priest of Ptah, and all the people who surround Pharaoh. And lo! they beheld Nenoferkephtah, who was fixed on to the rudder-oars of the cange of Pharaoh by his knowledge as an excellent scribe. They raised him, they saw the book on his breast, and Pharaoh said, 'Let the book that is on his breast be taken away.' The couriers of Pharaoh, as well as the priests of Ptah and the high priest of Ptah, said before the king, 'Oh, our great lord – may he have the duration of Râ! – he is an excellent scribe and a very learned man, this Nenoferkephtah!' Pharaoh had him placed in the *Good Dwelling* for the space of sixteen days, clothed with stuffs for the space of thirty-five days, laid out for the space of seventy days, and then he was laid in his tomb among the *Dwellings of Repose*.

"I have told thee all the sorrows that came to us on account of this book, of which thou sayest, 'Let it be given me.' Thou hast no right to it; for, on account of it, the time we had to remain on the earth was taken from us."

Setne said, "Ahuri, give me that book that I see between thee and Nenoferkephtah; if not, I will take it from thee by force." Nenoferkephtah raised himself on the bed and said, "Art thou not Setne, to whom that woman has told all those misfortunes that thou hast not yet experienced? Art thou capable of obtaining this book by the power of an excellent scribe, or by thy skill in playing against me? Let us two play for it." Setne said, "Agreed." Then they brought the *board* before them, with its *dogs*, and they two played. Nenoferkephtah won a game from Setne; he recited his magic over him, he placed over him the playing-board which was before him, and he caused him to sink into the ground up to the legs. He did the same with the second game; he won from Setne, and he caused him to sink into the ground up to the waist. He did the same with the third game, and he caused Setne to sink into the ground up to the ears. After that, Setne attacked Nenoferkephtah with his hand; Setne called Inarôs, his foster-brother, saying, "Do not delay to go up on to the earth; tell all that has happened to me before Pharaoh; bring me the talismans of my father Ptah, as well as my books of magic." He went up without delay on the ground; he recounted before Pharaoh all that had happened to Setne, and Pharaoh said, "Take him the talismans of his father as well as his books of incantations." Inarôs went down without delay into the tomb; he placed the talismans on the body of Setne, and he at once rose to the earth. Setne stretched out his hand towards the book and seized it; and when Setne came up out of the tomb, the light went before him and darkness came behind him. Ahuri wept after him, saying, "Glory to thee, oh darkness! Glory to thee, oh light! All of it is departed, all that was in our tomb." Nenoferkephtah said to Ahuri, "Do not afflict thyself. I shall make him bring back this book in due time, a forked stick in his hand, a lighted brazier on his head." Setne went up out of the tomb, and he closed it behind him as it was before. Setne went before Pharaoh, and he recounted to Pharaoh all that had happened to him on account of the book. Pharaoh said to Setne, "Replace this book in the tomb of Nenoferkephtah, like a wise man; if not, he will force thee to take it back, a forked stick in thy hand, a lighted brazier on thy head." But Setne did not listen to him; he had no other occupation in the world than to spread out the roll and to read it, it mattered not to whom.

After that it happened one day, when Setne was walking on the forecourt of the temple of Ptah, he saw a woman, very beautiful, for there was no woman who equalled her in beauty; she had much gold upon her, and there were young girls who walked behind her, and with her were servants to the number of fifty-two. From the hour that Setne beheld her, he no longer knew the part of the world in which he was. Setne called his page, saying, "Do not delay to go to the place where that woman is and learn who she is." The young page made no delay in going to the place where the woman was. He addressed the maid-servant who walked behind her, and he questioned her, saying, "What person is that?" She said to him, "She is Tbubui, daughter of the prophet of Bastît, lady of Ankhutaûi, who now goes to make her prayer before Ptah, the great god." When the young man had returned to Setne, he recounted all the words that she had said to him without exception. Setne said to the young man, "Go and say thus to the maid-servant, 'Setne Khamwas, son of the Pharaoh Usimares, it is who sends me, saying, "I will give thee ten pieces of gold that thou mayest pass an hour with me. If there is necessity to have recourse to violence, he will do it, and he will take thee to a hidden place, where no one in the world will find thee." When the young man had returned to the place where Tbubui was, he addressed the maid-servant, and spake with her, but she exclaimed against his words, as though it were an insult to speak them. Tbubui said to the young man, "Cease to speak to that wretched girl; come and speak to me." The young man approached the place where Tbubui was; he said to her, "I will give thee ten pieces of gold if thou wilt pass an hour with Setne Khamwas, the son of Pharaoh Usimares. If there is necessity to have recourse to violence, he will do so, and will take thee to a hidden place where no one in the world will find thee." Tbubui said, "Go, say to Setne, 'I am a hierodule, I am no mean person; if thou dost desire to have thy pleasure of me, and no one in the world shall know it, and I shall not have acted like a woman of the streets.'" When the page had returned to Setne, he repeated to him all the words that she had said without exception, and he said, "Lo, I am satisfied." But all who were with Setne began to curse.

Setne caused a boat to be fetched, he embarked, and delayed not to arrive at Bubastis. He went to the west of the town, until he came to a house that was very high; it had a wall all around it, it had a garden on the north side, there was a flight of steps in front of it. Setne inquired, saying, "Whose is this house?" They said to him, "It is the house of Tbubui." Setne entered the grounds, and he marvelled at the pavilion situated in the garden while they told Tbubui; she came down, she took the hand of Setne, and she said to him, "By my life! The journey to the house of the priest of Bastît, lady of Ankhutaûi, at which thou art arrived, is very pleasant to me. Come up with me." Setne went up by the stairway of the house with Tbubui. He found the upper storey of the house sanded and powered with sand and powder of real lapis lazuli and real turquoise. There were several beds there, spread with stuffs of royal linen, and also many cups of gold on a stand. They filled a golden cup with wine, and placed it in the had of Setne, and Tbubui said to him, "Will it please thee to rest thyself?" He said to her, "That is not what I wish to do." They put scented wood on the fire, they brought perfumes of the kind that are supplied to Pharaoh, and Setne made a happy day with Tbubui, for he had never before seen her equal. Then Setne said to Tbubui, "Let us accomplish that for which we have come here." She said to him, "Thou shalt arrive at thy house, that where thou art. But for me, I am a hierodule, I am no mean person. If thou desirest to have thy pleasure of me, thou shall make me a contract of sustenance, and a contract of money on all the things and on all the goods that are thine." He said to her, "Let the scribe of the school be brought." He was brought immediately, and Setne caused to be made in favour of Tbubui a contract for maintenance, and he made her in writing a dowry of all his things, all the goods that were his. An hour passed; one came to say this to Setne, "Thy children are below." He said, "Let them be brought up." Tbubui arose, she put on a robe of fine linen and Setne beheld all her limbs through it, and his desire increased yet more than before. Setne said to Tbubui, "Let us accomplish now that for which I came." She said to him, "Thou shalt arrive at thy house, that where thou art. But for me, I am a hierodule, I am no mean person. If thou desirest to have thy pleasure of me, thou wilt cause thy children to subscribe to my writing, that they may not seek a quarrel with my children on the subject of thy possessions." Setne had his children fetched and made them subscribe to the writing. Setne said to Tbubui, "Let me now accomplish that for which I came." She said to him, "Thou shalt arrive at thy house, that where thou art. But for me, I am a hierodule, I am no mean person. If thou dost desire to have thy pleasure of me, thou shalt cause thy children to be slain, so that they may not seek a quarrel with my children on account of thy possessions." Setne said, "Let the crime be committed on them of which the desire has entered thy heart." She caused the children of Setne to be slain before him, she had them thrown out below the window, to the dogs and cats, and they ate their flesh, and he heard them while he was drinking with Tbubui. Setne said to Tbubui, "Let us accomplish that for which we have come here, for all that thou hast said before me has been done for thee." She said to him, "Come into this chamber." Setne entered the chamber, he lay down on a bed of ivory and ebony, in order that his love might be rewarded, and Tbubui lay down by the side of Setne. He stretched out his hand to touch her; she opened her mouth widely and uttered a loud cry.

When Setne came to himself he was in a place of a furnace without any clothing on his back. After an hour Setne perceived a very big man standing on a platform, with quite a number of attendants beneath his feet, for he had the semblance of a Pharaoh. Setne was about to raise himself, but he could not arise for shame, for he had no clothing on his back. This Pharaoh said, "Setne, what is the state in which you are?" He said, "It is Nenoferkephtah who has had all this done to me." This Pharaoh said, "Go to Memphis; thy children, lo! They wish for thee. Lo! they are standing before Pharaoh." Setne spake before this Pharaoh, "My great lord the king – mayest thou have the duration of Râ – how can I arrive at Memphis if I have no raiment in the world on my back?" This Pharaoh called a page who was standing near him and commanded him to give a garment to Setne. This Pharaoh said, "Setne, go to Memphis. Thy children, behold they live, behold they are standing before the king." Setne went to Memphis; he embraced his children with joy, because they were in life. Pharaoh said, "Is it not drunkenness that has caused thee to do all that?" Setne related all that had happened to him with Tbubui and Nenoferkephtah. Pharaoh said, "Setne, I have before come to thin aid, saying, 'They will slay thee, if thou dost not return that book to the place where thou didst take it for thyself, but thou hast not listened to me up to this hour.' Now take back the book to Nenoferkephtah, a forked staff in thy hand and a lighted brazier on thy head." Setne went out before Pharaoh, a fork and a staff in his hand and a lighted brazier on his head, and he descended into the tomb where Nenoferkephtah was. Ahuri said to him, "Setne, it is Ptah the great god who brings thee here safe and sound." Nenoferkephtah laughed, saying, "This is what I said to thee before." Setne began to talk with Nenoferkephtah, and he perceived that while they talked the sun was altogether in the tomb. Ahuri and Nenoferkephtah talked much with Setne. Setne said, "Nenoferkephtah, is it not something humiliating that thou askest?" Nenoferkephtah said, "Thou knowest this by knowledge, that Ahuri and Maîhêt, her child, are at Coptos, and also in this tomb, by the art of a skilful scribe. Let it be commanded to thee to take the trouble to go to Coptos and bring them hither."

Setne went up out of the tomb; he went before Pharaoh, he related before Pharaoh all that Nenoferkephtah had said to him. Pharaoh said, "Setne, go to Coptos and bring back Ahuri and Maîhêt her child." He said before Pharaoh, "Let the cange of Pharaoh and its crew be given me." The cange of Pharaoh and its crew were given him; he embarked, he started, he did not delay to arrive at Coptos. One told the priests of Isis, of Coptos, and the high priest of Isis; behold, they came down to him, they came down to the bank. He disembarked, he went to the temple of Isis of Coptos, and Harpocrates. He caused a bull, a goose, and some wine to be brought; he made a burnt offering and a libation before Isis of Coptos and Harpocrates. He went to the cemetery of Coptos with the priests of Isis and the high priest of Isis. They spent three days and three nights searching among the tombs that are in the necropolis of Coptos, moving the stelae of the scribes of the *Double House of Life*, deciphering the inscriptions on them; they did not find the chambers where Ahuri and Maîhêt her child reposed. Nenoferkephtah knew that they did not find the chambers where Ahuri and Maîhêt her child reposed. He manifested himself under the form of an old man, a priest very advanced in years, he presented himself before Setne.

Setne saw him; Setne said, "Thou seemest to be a man advanced in years, dost thou not know the house where Ahuri and Maîhêt her child repose?" The old man said to Setne, "The father of the father of my father said to the father of my father, 'The chambers where Ahuri and Maîhêt her child repose are below the southern corner of the house of the priest…'" Setne said to the old man, "Perchance the priest…hath injured thee, and therefore it is that thou wouldest destroy his house." The old man said to Setne, "Let a good watch be kept on me while the house of the priest…is destroyed, and if it happens that Ahuri and Maîhêt her child are not found under the southern corner of the house of the priest…let me be treated as a criminal." A good watch was kept over the old man; the chamber where Ahuri and Maîhêt her child reposed was found below the southern angle of the house of the priest…Setne caused these great personages to be carried to the cange of Pharaoh, and he then had the house of the priest…rebuilt as it was before. Nenoferkephtah made known to Setne that it was he who had come to Coptos, to discover for him the chamber where Ahuri and Maîhêt her child reposed.

Setne embarked on the cange of Pharaoh. He made the voyage, he did not delay to arrive at Memphis, and all the escort who were with him. One told Pharaoh, and Pharaoh came down before the cange of Pharaoh. He caused the great personages to be carried to the tomb where Nenoferkephtah was, and he had the upper chamber all sealed as before.

This complete writing, wherein is related the history of Setne Khamwas and Nenoferkephtah, also of Ahuri his wife and Maîhêt his son, has been written by the scribe Ziharpto, the year 5, in the month of Tybi.

The Death of Sigurd

IT HAPPENED ONE day that Brynhild, Gunnar's wife, now a Queen, was with Sigurd's wife, bathing in a river. Not often they were together. Brynhild was the haughtiest of women, and often she treated Gudrun with disdain. Now, as they were bathing together, Gudrun, shaking out her hair, cast some drops upon Brynhild. Brynhild went from Gudrun. And Sigurd's wife, not knowing that Brynhild had anger against her, went after her up the stream.

"Why dost thou go so far up the river, Brynhild?" Gudrun asked.

"So that thou mayst not shake thy hair over me," answered Brynhild.

Gudrun stood still while Brynhild went up the river like a creature who was made to be alone. "Why dost thou speak so to me, sister?" Gudrun cried.

She remembered that from the first Brynhild had been haughty with her, often speaking to her with harshness and bitterness. She did not know what cause Brynhild had for this.

It was because Brynhild had seen in Sigurd the one who had ridden through the fire for the first time, he who had awakened her by breaking the binding of her breastplate and so drawing out of her flesh the thorn of the Tree of Sleep. She had given him her love when she awakened on the world. But he, as she thought, had forgotten her easily, giving his love to this other maiden. Brynhild, with her Valkyrie's pride, was left with a mighty anger in her heart.

"Why dost thou speak so to me, Brynhild?" Gudrun asked.

"It would be ill indeed if drops from thy hair fell on one who is so much above thee, one who is King Gunnar's wife," Brynhild answered.

"Thou art married to a King, but not to one more valourous than my lord," Gudrun said.

"Gunnar is more valourous; why dost thou compare Sigurd with him?" Brynhild said.

"He slew the Dragon Fafnir, and won for himself Fafnir's hoard," said Gudrun.

"Gunnar rode through the ring of fire. Mayhap thou wilt tell us that Sigurd did the like," said Brynhild.

"Yea," said Gudrun, now made angry. "It was Sigurd and not Gunnar who rode through the ring of fire. He rode through it in Gunnar's shape, and he took the ring off thy finger – look, it is now on mine."

And Gudrun held out her hand on which was Andvari's ring. Then Brynhild knew, all at once, that what Gudrun said was true. It was Sigurd that rode through the ring of fire the second as well as the first time. It was he who had struggled with her, taking the ring off her hand and claiming her for a bride, not for himself but for another, and out of disdain.

Falsely had she been won. And she, one of Odin's Valkyries, had been wed to one who was not the bravest hero in the world, and she to whom untruth might not come had been deceived. She was silent now, and all the pride that was in her turned to hatred of Sigurd.

She went to Gunnar, her husband, and she told him that she was so deeply shamed that she could never be glad in his Hall again; that never would he see her drinking wine, nor embroidering with golden threads, and never would he hear her speaking words of kindness. And when she said this to him she rent the web she was weaving, and she wept aloud so that all in the hall heard her, and all marvelled to hear the proud Queen cry.

Then Sigurd came to her, and he offered in atonement the whole hoard of Fafnir. And he told her how forgetfulness of her had come upon him, and he begged her to forgive him for winning her in falseness. But she answered him, "Too late thou hast come to me, Sigurd. Now I have only a great anger in my heart."

When Gunnar came, she told him she would forgive him, and love him as she had not loved him before, if he would slay Sigurd. But Gunnar would not slay him, although Brynhild's passion moved him greatly, since Sigurd was a sworn brother of his.

Then she went to Högni and asked him to slay Sigurd, telling him that the whole of Fafnir's hoard would belong to the Nibelungs if Sigurd were slain. But Högni would not slay him, since Sigurd and he were sworn brothers.

There was one who had not sworn brotherhood with Sigurd. He was Guttorm, Gunnar's and Högni's half-brother. Brynhild went to Guttorm. He would not slay Sigurd, but Brynhild found that he was infirm of will and unsteady of thought. With Guttorm, then, she would work for the slaying of Sigurd. Her mind was fixed that he and she would no longer be in the world of men.

She made a dish of madness for Guttorm – serpent's venom and wolf's flesh mixed – and when he had eaten it Guttorm was crazed. Then did he listen to Brynhild's words. And she commanded him to go into the chamber where Sigurd slept and stab him through the body with a sword.

This Guttorm did. But Sigurd, before he gasped out his life, took Gram, his great sword, and flung it at Guttorm and cut him in twain.

And Brynhild, knowing what deed was done, went without and came to where Grani, Sigurd's proud horse, was standing. She stayed there with her arms across Grani's neck, the Valkyrie leaning across the horse that was born of Odin's horse. And Grani stood listening for some sound. He heard the cries of Gudrun over Sigurd, and then his heart burst and he died.

They bore Sigurd out of the Hall and Brynhild went beside where they placed him. She took a sword and put it through her own heart. Thus died Brynhild, who had been made a mortal woman for her disobedience to the will of Odin, and who was won to be a mortal's wife by a falseness.

They took Sigurd and his horse Grani, and his helmet and his golden war-gear and they left all on a great painted ship. They could not but leave Brynhild beside him, Brynhild with her wondrous hair and her stern and beautiful face. They left the two together and launched the ship on the sea. And when the ship was on the water they fired it, and Brynhild once again lay in the flames.

And so Sigurd and Brynhild went together to join Baldur and Nanna in Hela's habitation.

Gunnar and Högni came to dread the evil that was in the hoard. They took the gleaming and glittering mass and they brought it to the river along which, ages before, Hreidmar had his smithy and the Dwarf Andvari his cave. From a rock in the river, they cast the gold and jewels into the water and the hoard of Andvari sank for ever beneath the waves. Then the River Maidens had possession again of their treasure.

Frank Martin and the Fairies

MARTIN WAS A thin, pale man when I saw him, of a sickly look, and a constitution naturally feeble. His hair was a light auburn, his beard mostly unshaven, and his hands of a singular delicacy and whiteness, owing, I dare say, as much to the soft and easy nature of his employment as to his infirm health. In everything else he was as sensible, sober, and rational as any other man; but on the topic of fairies, the man's mania was peculiarly strong and immovable. Indeed, I remember that the expression of his eyes was singularly wild and hollow, and his long narrow temples sallow and emaciated.

Now, this man did not lead an unhappy life, nor did the malady he laboured under seem to be productive of either pain or terror to him, although one might be apt to imagine otherwise. On the contrary, he and the fairies maintained the most friendly intimacy, and their dialogues – which I fear were woefully one-sided ones – must have been a source of great pleasure to him, for they were conducted with much mirth and laughter, on his part at least.

"Well, Frank, when did you see the fairies?"

"Whist! there's two dozen of them in the shop (the weaving shop) this minute. There's a little ould fellow sittin' on the top of the sleys, an' all to be rocked while I'm weavin'. The sorrow's in them, but they're the greatest little skamers alive, so they are. See, there's another of them at my dressin' noggin. Go out o' that, you *shingawn*; or, bad cess to me, if you don't, but I'll lave you a mark. Ha! cut, you thief you!"

"Frank, aren't you afeard o' them?"

"Is it me! Arra, what ud' I be afeard o' them for? Sure they have no power over me."

"And why haven't they, Frank?"

"Because I was baptized against them."

"What do you mean by that?"

"Why, the priest that christened me was tould by my father, to put in the proper prayer against the fairies – an' a priest can't refuse it when he's asked – an' he did so. Begorra, it's well for me that he did – (let the tallow alone, you little glutton – see, there's a weeny thief o' them aitin' my tallow) – becaise, you see, it was their intention to make me king o' the fairies."

"Is it possible?"

"Devil a lie in it. Sure you may ax them, an' they'll tell you."

"What size are they, Frank?"

"Oh, little wee fellows, with green coats, an' the purtiest little shoes ever you seen. There's two of them – both ould acquaintances o' mine – runnin' along the yarn-beam. That ould fellow with the bob-wig is called Jim Jam, an' the other chap, with the three-cocked hat, is called Nickey Nick. Nickey plays the pipes. Nickey, give us a tune, or I'll malivogue you – come now, 'Lough Erne Shore.' Whist, now – listen!"

The poor fellow, though weaving as fast as he could all the time, yet bestowed every possible mark of attention to the music, and seemed to enjoy it as much as if it had been real.

But who can tell whether that which we look upon as a privation may not after all be a fountain of increased happiness, greater, perhaps, than any which we ourselves enjoy? I forget who the poet is who says –

> "Mysterious are thy laws;
> The vision's finer than the view;
> Her landscape Nature never drew
> So fair as Fancy draws."

Many a time, when a mere child, not more than six or seven years of age, have I gone as far as Frank's weaving-shop, in order, with a heart divided between curiosity and fear, to listen to his conversation with the good people. From morning till night his tongue was going almost as incessantly as his shuttle; and it was well known that at night, whenever he awoke out of his sleep, the first thing he did was to put out his hand, and push them, as it were, off his bed.

"Go out o' this, you thieves, you – go out o' this now, an' let me alone. Nickey, is this any time to be playing the pipes, and me wants to sleep? Go off, now – troth if yez do, you'll see what I'll give yez tomorrow. Sure I'll be makin' new dressin's; and if yez behave decently, maybe I'll lave yez the scrapin' o' the pot. There now. Och! poor things, they're dacent crathurs. Sure they're all gone, barrin' poor Red-cap, that doesn't like to lave me." And then the harmless monomaniac would fall back into what we trust was an innocent slumber.

About this time there was said to have occurred a very remarkable circumstance, which gave poor Frank a vast deal of importance among the neighbours. A man named Frank Thomas, the same in whose house Mickey M'Rorey held the first dance at which I ever saw him, as detailed in a former sketch; this man, I say, had a child sick, but of what complaint I cannot now remember, nor is it of any importance. One of the gables of Thomas's house was built against, or rather into, a Forth or Rath, called Towny, or properly Tonagh Forth. It was said to be haunted by the fairies, and what gave it a character peculiarly wild in my eyes was, that there were on the southern side of it two or three little green mounds, which were said to be the graves of unchristened children, over which it was considered dangerous and unlucky to pass.

At all events, the season was mid-summer; and one evening about dusk, during the illness of the child, the noise of a handsaw was heard upon the Forth. This was considered rather strange, and, after a little time, a few of those who were assembled at Frank Thomas's went to see who it could be that was sawing in such a place, or what they could be sawing at so late an hour, for everyone knew that nobody in the whole country about them would dare to cut down the few white-thorns that grew upon the Forth. On going to examine, however, judge of their surprise, when, after surrounding and searching the whole place, they could discover no trace of either saw or sawyer. In fact, with the exception of themselves, there was no one, either natural or supernatural, visible. They then returned to the house, and had scarcely sat down, when it was heard again within ten yards of them. Another examination of the premises took place, but with equal success. Now, however, while standing on the Forth, they heard the sawing in a little hollow, about a hundred and fifty yards below them, which was completely exposed to their view, but they could see nobody. A party of them immediately went down to ascertain, if possible, what this singular noise and invisible labour could mean; but on arriving at the spot, they heard the sawing, to which were now added hammering, and the driving of nails upon the Forth above, whilst those who stood on the Forth continued to hear it in the hollow. On comparing notes, they resolved to send down to Billy Nelson's for Frank Martin, a distance of only about eighty or ninety yards. He was soon on the spot, and without a moment's hesitation solved the enigma.

"'Tis the fairies," said he. "I see them, and busy crathurs they are."

"But what are they sawing, Frank?"

"They are makin' a child's coffin," he replied; "they have the body already made, an' they're now nailin' the lid together."

That night the child died, and the story goes that on the second evening afterwards, the carpenter who was called upon to make the coffin brought a table out from Thomas's house to the Forth, as a temporary bench; and, it is said, that the sawing and hammering necessary for the completion of his task were precisely the same which had been heard the evening but one before – neither more nor less. I remember the death of the child myself, and the making of its coffin, but I think the story of the supernatural carpenter was not heard in the village for some months after its interment.

Frank had every appearance of a hypochondriac about him. At the time I saw him, he might be about thirty-four years of age, but I do not think, from the debility of his frame and infirm health, that he has been alive for several years. He was an object of considerable interest and curiosity, and often have I been present when he was pointed out to strangers as "the man that could see the good people".

The Talking Head of Donn-Bo

THERE IS AN old tale told in Erin of a lovable and bright and handsome youth named Donn-bo, who was the best singer of 'Songs of Idleness' and the best teller of 'King Stories' in the world. He could tell a tale of each king who reigned in Erin, from the 'Tale of the Destruction of Dind Righ', when Cova Coelbre was killed, down to the kings who reigned in his own time.

On a night before a battle, the warriors said, "Make minstrelsy tonight for us, Donn-bo." But Donn-bo answered, "No word at all will come on my lips tonight; therefore, for this night let the King-buffoon of Ireland amuse you. But tomorrow, at this hour, in whatsoever place they and I shall be, I will make minstrelsy for the fighting men." For the warriors had said that unless Donn-bo would go with them on that hosting, not one of them would go.

The battle was past, and on the evening of the morrow at that same hour Donn-bo lay dead, his fair young body stretched across the body of the King of Ireland, for he had died in defending his chief. But his head had rolled away among a wisp of growing rushes by the waterside.

At the feasting of the army on that night a warrior said, "Where is Donn-bo, that he may make minstrelsy for us, as he promised us at this hour yesternight, and that he may tell us the 'King Stories of Erin'?"

A valiant champion of the men of Munster answered, "I will go over the battlefield and seek for him." He enquired among the living for Donn-bo, but he found him not, and then he searched hither and thither among the dead.

At last he came where the body of the King of Erin lay, and a young, fair corpse beside it. In all the air about there was the sound of minstrelsy, low and very sweet; dead bards and poets reciting in faint whispers old tales and poems to dead chiefs.

The wild, clear note of the battle-march, the *dord fiansa*, played by the drooping hands of slain warriors upon the points of broken spears, low like the echo of an echo, sounded in the clump of rushes hard by; and, above them all, a voice, faint and very still, that sang a song that was sweeter than the tunes of the whole world beside.

The voice that sang was the voice of the head of Donn-bo. The warrior stooped to pick up the head.

"Do not touch me," said the head, "for we are commanded by the King of the Plains of Heaven to make music tonight for our lord, the King of Erin, the shining one who lies dead beside us; and though all of us are lying dead likewise, no faintness or feebleness shall prevent us from obeying that command. Disturb me not."

"The hosts of Leinster are asking thee to make minstrelsy for them, as thou didst promise yesternight," said the messenger.

"When my minstrelsy here is done, I will go with thee," saith the head, "but only if Christ, the Son of God, in whose presence I now am, go with me, and if thou takest me to my body again."

"That shall be done, indeed," saith the messenger, and when it had ceased chanting for the King of Erin he carried away the head.

When the messenger came again amongst the warriors they stopped their feasting and gathered round him. "Hast thou brought anything from the battlefield?" they cried.

"I have brought the head of Donn-bo," said the man.

"Set it upon a pillar that we may see and hear it," cried they all; and they said, "It is no luck for thee to be like that, Donn-bo, and thou the most beautiful minstrel and the best in Erin. Make music, for the love of Jesus Christ, the Son of God. Amuse the Leinster men tonight as thou didst amuse thy lord a while ago."

Then Donn-bo turned his face to the wall, that the darkness might be around him, and he raised his melody in the quiet night; and the sound of that minstrelsy was so piteous and sad that the hosts sat weeping at the sound of it. Then was the head taken to his body, and the neck joined itself to the shoulders again, and Donn-bo was at rest.

This is the story of the 'Talking Head of Donn-bo'.

Departure of the Fairies

ON A SABBATH morning, all the inmates of a little hamlet had gone to church, except a herd-boy, and a little girl, his sister, who were lounging beside one of the cottages, when just as the shadow of the garden-dial had fallen on the line of noon, they saw a long cavalcade ascending out of the ravine, through the wooded hollow. It winded among the knolls and bushes, and, turning round the northern gable of the cottage, beside which the sole spectators of the scene were stationed, began to ascend the eminence towards the south. The horses were shaggy diminutive things, speckled dun and grey; the riders stunted, misgrown, ugly creatures, attired in antique jerkins of plaid, long grey cloaks, and little red caps, from under which their wild, uncombed locks shot out over their cheeks and foreheads.

The boy and his sister stood gazing in utter dismay and astonishment, as rider after rider, each more uncouth and dwarfish than the other which had preceded it, passed the cottage and disappeared among the brushwood, which at that period covered the hill, until at length the entire rout, except the last rider, who lingered a few yards behind the others, had gone by. "What are you, little manie? And where are ye going?" inquired the boy, his curiosity getting the better of his fears and his prudence. "Not of the race of Adam," said the creature, turning for a moment in its saddle. "The people of peace shall never more be seen in Scotland."

The Blacksmith's Stool

A LONG TIME ago, when Lord Jesus and the blessed St. Peter walked about together on earth, it happened one evening that they stopped at a blacksmith's cottage and asked for a night's lodging.

"You are welcome," the blacksmith said. "I am a poor man but whatever I have I will gladly share with you."

He threw down his hammer and led his guests into the kitchen. There he entertained them with a good supper and after they had eaten he said to them, "I see that you are tired from your day's journey. There is my bed. Lie down on it and sleep until morning."

"And where will you sleep?" St. Peter asked.

"I? Don't think of me," the blacksmith said. "I'll go out to the barn and sleep on the straw."

The next morning, he gave his guests a fine breakfast, and then sent them on their way with good wishes for their journey.

As they were leaving, St. Peter plucked Lord Jesus by the sleeve and whispered, "Master, aren't you going to reward this man? He is poor but yet has treated us most hospitably."

Lord Jesus answered Peter:

"The reward of this world is an empty reward. I was thinking to prepare him a place in heaven. However, I will grant him something now."

Then he turned to the blacksmith and said, "Ask what you will. Make three wishes and they will be fulfilled."

The blacksmith was overjoyed. For his first wish he said, "I should like to live for a hundred years and always be as strong and healthy as I am this moment."

Lord Jesus said, "Very well, that will be granted you. What is your second wish?"

The blacksmith thought for a moment. Then he said, "I wish that I may prosper in this world and always have as much as I need. May work in my shop always be as plentiful as it is today."

"This, too, will be granted you," Lord Jesus said. "Now for your third wish."

Our blacksmith thought and thought, unable at first to decide on a third wish. At last he said: "Grant that whoever sits on the stool where you sat last night at supper may be unable to get up until I release him."

St. Peter laughed at this, but Lord Jesus nodded and said, "This wish, too, will be fulfilled."

So they parted, Lord Jesus and blessed St. Peter going on their way, and the blacksmith returning home to his forge.

Things came to pass as Lord Jesus had promised they should. Work in plenty flowed into the blacksmith's shop. The years went by but they made no impression on the blacksmith. He was as young as ever and as vigorous. His friends grew old and one by one died. His children grew up, married, and had children of their own. These in turn grew up. The years brought youth and maturity and old age to them all. The blacksmith alone remained unchanged.

A hundred years is a long time, but at last even it runs out.

One night, as the blacksmith was putting away his tools, there came a knock at the door. The blacksmith stopped his singing to call out, "Who's there?"

"It is I, Death," a voice answered. "Open the door, blacksmith. Your time has come."

The blacksmith threw open the door.

"Welcome," he said to the woman standing there. "I'll be ready in a moment when I put away my tools." He smiled a little to himself. "Won't you sit down on this stool, dear lady, and rest you for a moment? You must be weary going to and fro over the earth."

Death, suspecting nothing, seated herself on the stool.

The blacksmith burst into a loud laugh.

"Now I have you, my lady! Stay where you are until I release you!"

Death tried to stand up but could not. She squirmed this way and that. She rattled her hollow bones. She gnashed her teeth. But do what she would she could not arise from the stool.

Chuckling and singing, the blacksmith left her there and went about his business.

But soon he found that chaining up Death had unexpected results. To begin with, he wanted at once to celebrate his escape with a feast. He had a hog which had been fattening for some time. He would slaughter this hog and chop it up into fine spicy sausages which his neighbors and friends would help him eat. The hams he would hang in the chimney to smoke.

But when he tried to slaughter the animal, the blow of his axe had no effect. He struck the hog on the head and, to be sure, it rolled over on the ground. But when he stopped to cut the throat, the creature jumped up and, with a grunt, went scampering off. Before the blacksmith could recover from his surprise, the hog had disappeared.

Next, he tried to kill a goose. He had a fat one which he had been stuffing for the village fair. "Since those sausages have escaped me," he said. "I'll have to be satisfied with roast goose."

But when he tried to cut the goose's throat, the knife drew no blood. In his surprise, he loosened his hold and the goose slipped from his hands and went cackling off after the hog.

"What's come over things today?" the blacksmith asked himself. "It seems I'm not to have sausage or roast goose. I suppose I'll have to be satisfied with a pair of pigeons."

He went out to the pigeon-house and caught two pigeons. He put them on the chopping-block and with one mighty blow of his ax cut off both their heads.

"There!" he cried in triumph. "I've got you!"

But even as he spoke the little severed heads returned to their bodies, the heads and bodies grew together as if nothing had happened, and cooing happily the two pigeons flew away.

Then at last, the truth flashed upon the blacksmith's mind. So long as he kept Death fastened to that stool, nothing could die! Of course not! So no more spicy sausages, no more smoked hams, no more roast goose – not even a broiled pigeon! The prospect was not a pleasing one, for the blacksmith loved good things to eat. But what could he do? Release Death? Never that! He would be her first victim! Well then, if he could have no fresh meat, he would have to be content to live on peas and porridge and wheaten cakes.

This actually was what he had to do and what everyone else had to do when their old provisions were exhausted.

Summer passed and winter followed. Then spring came, bringing new and unforeseen miseries. With the first breath of warm weather, all the pests and insects of the summer before revived, for not one of them had been killed by the winter cold. And the eggs they had laid all hatched out until the earth and the air and the water swarmed with living creatures. Birds and rats and grasshoppers, insects and bugs and vermin of every kind, covered the fields and ate up every green thing. The meadows looked as if a fire had swept them clean. The orchards were stripped bare of every leaf and blossom.

Such hordes of fish and frogs and water creatures filled the lakes and the rivers that the water was polluted and it was impossible for man to drink it.

Water and land alike were swarming with living creatures, not one of which could be killed. Even the air was thick with clouds of mosquitoes and gnats and flies.

Men and women walked about looking like tormented ghosts. They had no desire to live on but they had to live on for they could not die.

The blacksmith came at last to a realization of all the misery which his foolish wish was bringing upon the world.

"I see now," he said, "that God Almighty did well when He sent Death to the world. She has her work to do and I am wrong to hold her prisoner."

So he released Death from the stool and made no outcry when she put her bony fingers to his throat.

Solomon Cursed by His Mother

ONCE UPON A time the very wise Solomon, in a conversation with his mother, said that every woman on earth at the bottom of her heart was thoroughly bad. His mother scolded him very much, and said it was not true; and when he proved in some fashion that she, too, was like other women, she grew infuriated and cursed him, and said he was not to die until he had seen the depths of the sea and the heights of heaven.

When Solomon had reached a very great age, and became tired of life and this world, he bethought himself how he could break the spell of his mother's curse so that he might die. First of all he wrought a big iron box, big enough to allow him to sit inside. To the lid of the box he fastened an iron chain, long enough in his opinion to reach the bottom of the sea. Then he climbed into the box, and asked his wife to lock it, and to throw it into the sea, but to keep in her hands the end of the chain so that she might be able to pull it up again after the box and the chain had reached the bottom of the sea. Solomon's wife put the lid on, locked the box, and threw it into the sea. Whilst she was now holding in her hands the end of the chain, someone came and deceived her by telling her that the wise Solomon, together with his box, had been swallowed by a great fish already ever such a long time ago, and that she could do no better than let the chain drop and go home. She did so, and the heavy chain pressed the box with the wise Solomon inside firmly onto the bottom of the sea.

Some time after this event, the devils found the staff, cap, and stole of St. Johannes, and started a quarrel amongst themselves when dividing these things. At last they agreed to go to the wise Solomon, and he was to settle their differences. When they came to him at the bottom of the sea and told him what they wanted him to do, he said, "How can I decide your case here from within the box, where I cannot see either you or the object of your disputes? Carry me up to the surface and put me on the shore, and I will be your umpire." At once the devils carried him up in his box. As soon as the wise Solomon had got out, he took into his hands the things about which the devils were quarrelling just as if he was going to examine them and see what they were worth. All of a sudden he made the sign of the cross with the staff of the saint, and then the devils fled, so that all the things became his.

In this way the wise Solomon had beheld the bottom of the sea. Now he bethought himself how he might get a sight of the heights of heaven. For this purpose he caught two ostriches, starved them for a few days, and then he tied to their feet a big basket. Then he sat down in that basket, and in his hands he held on a long spit a roasted lamb just above the heads of the ostriches. Eager to seize the roasted lamb, up flew the ostriches, up and up, and they never stopped till the wise Solomon touched with his spit the vault of heaven. Then he turned his spit downwards, and thus the ostriches carried him again down to earth. And now that he had seen the depths of the sea and the heights of heaven, he could die at last.

The Voice of Death

ONCE UPON A time, something happened. If it had not happened, it would not be told.

There was once a man who prayed daily to God to grant him riches. One day, his numerous and frequent prayers found our Lord in the mood to listen to them. When the man had grown rich, he did not want to die, so he resolved to go from country to country and settle wherever he heard that the people lived forever. He prepared for his journey, told his wife his plan, and set off.

In every country he reached, he asked whether people ever died there, and went on at once if he was told that they did. At last, he arrived in a land where the inhabitants said they did not know what dying meant. The traveller, full of joy, asked:

"But are there not immense crowds of people here, if none of you die?"

"No, there are no immense crowds," was the reply, "for you see, every now and then somebody comes and calls one after another, and whoever follows him, never returns."

"And do people see the person who calls them?" asked the traveller.

"Why shouldn't they see him?" he was answered.

The man could not wonder enough at the stupidity of those who followed the person that called them, though they knew that they would be obliged to stay where he took them. Returning home, he collected all his property, and with his wife and children, went to settle in the country where people did not die but were called by a certain person and never came back.

He had, therefore, firmly resolved that neither he nor his family would ever follow anybody who called them, no matter who it might be.

So, after he had established himself and arranged all his business affairs, he advised his wife and all his family on no account to follow anyone who might call them, if, as he said, they did not want to die.

So they gave themselves up to pleasure, and in this way spent several years. One day, when they were all sitting comfortably in their house, his wife suddenly began to call:

"I'm coming, I'm coming!"

And she looked around the room for her fur jacket. Her husband instantly started up, seized her by the hand, and began to reproach her.

"So you don't heed my advice? Stay here, if you don't want to die."

"Don't you hear how he is calling me? I'll only see what he wants and come back at once."

And she struggled to escape from her husband's grasp and go.

He held her fast and managed to bolt all the doors in the room. When she saw that, she said:

"Let me alone, husband, I don't care about going now."

The man thought she had come to her senses and given up her crazy idea, but before long the wife rushed to the nearest door, hurriedly opened it, and ran out. Her husband followed, holding her by her fur sack and entreating her not to go, for she would never return. She let her hands fall, bent backward, then leaned a little forward and suddenly threw herself back, slipping off her sack and leaving it in her husband's grasp, who stood stock still staring after her as she rushed on, screaming with all her might:

"I'm coming, I'm coming."

When he could see her no longer, the husband collected his senses, went back to the house, and said:

"If you are mad and want to die, go in God's name, I can't help you; I've told you often enough that you must follow no one, no matter who called you."

Days passed, many days; weeks, months, years followed, and the peace of the man's household was not disturbed again.

But at last one morning, when he went to his barber's as usual to be shaved, just as he had the soap on his chin, and the shop was full of people, he began to shout:

"I won't come, do you hear, I won't come!"

The barber and his customers all stared in amazement. The man, looking toward the door, said again, "Take notice, once for all, that I won't come, and go away from there."

Afterward he cried:

"Go away, do you hear, if you want to get off with a whole skin, for I tell you a thousand times I won't come."

Then, as if someone was standing at the door constantly calling him, he grew angry and raved at the person for not leaving him in peace. At last, he sprang up and snatched the razor from the barber's hand, crying:

"Give it to me, that I may show him what it is to continually annoy people."

And he ran at full speed after the person who, he said, was calling him, but whom nobody else could see. The poor barber, who did not want to lose his razor, followed. The man ran, the barber pursued, till they passed beyond the city limits, and, just outside of the town, the man fell into a chasm from which he did not come out again, so he also, like all the rest, followed the voice that called him.

The barber, who returned home panting for breath, told everybody he met what had happened and so the belief spread through the country that the people who had gone away, and not returned, had fallen into that gulf, for until then no one had known what became of those who followed the person that summoned them.

When a throng set out to visit the scene of misfortune, to see the insatiable gulf which swallowed up all the people and yet never had enough, nothing was found; it looked as if, since the beginning of the world, nothing had been there except a broad plain, and from that time the population of the neighbourhood began to die like the human beings in the rest of the earth.

The Thirty-Three Places Sacred to Kwannon

WHEN THE GREAT Buddhist abbot of the eighth century, Tokudo Shonin, died, he was conducted into the presence of Emma-O, the Lord of the Dead. The castle in which Emma-O lived was resplendent with silver and gold, rosy pearls, and all manner of sparkling jewels. A light emanated from Emma-O too, and that dread God had a smile upon his face. He received the distinguished abbot with extreme courtesy, and thus addressed him:

"Tokudo Shonin, there are thirty-three places where Kwannon reveals her special favour, for behold she has, in her boundless love, divided herself into many bodies, so that he who cries for aid shall not cry in vain. Alas! men continue to go their evil ways, for they know not of these sacred shrines. They live their sordid lives and pass into Hell, a vast and countless number. Oh, how blind they are, how wayward, and how full of folly! If they were to make but a single pilgrimage to these thirty-three shrines sacred to our Lady of Mercy, a pure and wonderful light would shine from their feet, feet made spiritually strong to crush down all evil, to scatter the hundred and thirty-six hells into fragments. If, in spite of this pilgrimage, one should chance to fall into Hell, I will take his place and receive into myself all his suffering, for if this happened my tale of peace would be false, and I should indeed deserve to suffer. Here is a list of the thirty-and-three sacred shrines of Kwannon. Take it into the troubled world of men and women, and make known the everlasting mercy of Kwannon."

Tokudo, having carefully listened to all Emma-O had told him, replied: "You have honoured me with such a mission, but mortals are full of doubts and fears, and they would ask for some sign that what I tell them is indeed true."

Emma-O at once presented the abbot with his jewelled seal, and, bidding him farewell, sent him on his way accompanied by two attendants.

While these strange happenings were taking place in the Underworld the disciples of Tokudo perceived that though their master's body had lain for three days and nights the flesh had not grown cold. The devoted followers did not bury the body, believing that their master was not dead. And such was indeed the case, for eventually Tokudo awakened from his trance, and in his right hand he held the jewelled seal of Emma-O.

Tokudo lost no time in narrating his strange adventures, and when he had concluded his story he and his disciples set off on a pilgrimage to the thirty-three holy places over which the Goddess of Mercy presides.

Kwannon and the Deer

AN OLD HERMIT named Saion Zenji took up his abode on Mount Nariai in order that he might be able to gaze upon the beauty of Ama-no-Hashidate, a narrow fir-clad promontory dividing Lake Iwataki and Miyazu Bay. Ama-no-Hashidate is still regarded as one of the *Sankei*, or 'Three Great Sights', of Japan, and still Mount Nariai is considered the best spot from which to view this charming scene.

On Mount Nariai this gentle and holy recluse erected a little shrine to Kwannon not far from a solitary pine-tree. He spent his happy days in looking upon Ama-no-Hashidate and in chanting the Buddhist Scriptures, and his charming disposition and holy ways were much appreciated by the people who came to pray at the little shrine he had so lovingly erected for his own joy and for the joy of others.

The hermit's abode, delightful enough in mild and sunny weather, was dreary in the wintertime, for when it snowed the good old man was cut off from human intercourse. On one occasion the snow fell so heavily that it was piled up in some places to a height of twenty feet.

Day after day the severe weather continued, and at last the poor old hermit found that he had no food of any kind. Chancing to look out one morning, he saw that a deer was lying dead in the snow. As he gazed upon the poor creature, which had been frozen to death, he remembered that it was unlawful in the sight of Kwannon to eat the flesh of animals; but on thinking over the matter more carefully it seemed to him that he could do more good to his fellow creatures by partaking of this deer than by observing the strict letter of the law and allowing himself to starve in sight of plenty.

When Saion Zenji had come to this wise decision he went out and cut off a piece of venison, cooked it, and ate half, with many prayers of thanksgiving for his deliverance. The rest of the venison he left in his cooking-pot.

Eventually the snow melted, and several folk hastily wended their way from the neighbouring village, and ascended Mount Nariai, expecting to see that their good and much-loved hermit had forever passed away from this world. As they approached the shrine, however, they were rejoiced to hear the old man chanting, in a clear and ringing voice, the sacred Buddhist Scriptures.

The folk from the village gathered about the hermit while he narrated the story of his deliverance. When, out of curiosity, they chanced to peep into his cooking-pot, they saw, to their utter amazement, that it contained no venison, but a piece of wood covered with gold foil. Still wondering what it all meant, they looked upon the image of Kwannon in the little shrine, and found that a piece had been cut from her loins, and when they inserted the piece of wood the wound was healed. Then it was that the old hermit and the folk gathered about him realised that the deer had been none other than Kwannon, who, in her boundless love and tender mercy, had made a sacrifice of her own divine flesh.

Daikoku's Rat

ACCORDING TO A certain old legend, the Buddhist Gods grew jealous of Daikoku. They consulted together, and finally decided that they would get rid of the too popular Daikoku, to whom the Japanese offered prayers and incense. Emma-O, the Lord of the Dead, promised to send his most cunning and clever *oni*, Shiro, who, he said, would have no difficulty in conquering the God of Wealth. Shiro, guided by a sparrow, went to Daikoku's castle, but though he hunted high and low he could not find its owner. Finally Shiro discovered a large storehouse, in which he saw the God of Wealth seated. Daikoku called his Rat and bade him find out who it was who dared to disturb him. When the Rat saw Shiro he ran into the garden and brought back a branch of holly, with which he drove the *oni* away, and Daikoku remains to this day one of the most popular of the Japanese Gods. This incident is said to be the origin of the New Year's Eve charm, consisting of a holly leaf and a skewer, or a sprig of holly fixed in the lintel of the door of a house to prevent the return of the *oni*.

Ta-Hong

SIM HEUI-SU STUDIED as a young man at the feet of No Su-sin, who was sent as an exile to a distant island in the sea. Thither he followed his master and worked at the Sacred Books. He matriculated in 1570 and graduated in 1572. In 1589 he remonstrated with King Son-jo over the disorders of his reign, and was the means of quelling a great national disturbance; but he made a *faux pas* one day when he said laughingly to a friend –

> *"These sea-gull waves ride so high,*
> *Who can tame them?"*

Those who heard caught at this, and it became a source of unpopularity, as it indicated an unfavourable opinion of the Court.

In 1592, when the King made his escape to Eui-ju, before the invading Japanese army, he was the State's Chief Secretary, and after the return of the King he became Chief Justice. He resigned office, but the King refused to accept his resignation, saying, "I cannot do without you." He became chief of the *literati* and Special Adviser. Afterwards he became Minister of the Right, then of the Left, at which time he wrote out ten suggestions for His Majesty to follow. He saw the wrongs done around the King, and resigned office again and again, but was constantly recalled.

In 1608 Im Suk-yong, a young candidate writing for his matriculation, wrote an essay exposing the wrongs of the Court. Sim heard of this, and took the young man under his protection. The King, reading the essay, was furiously angry, and ordered the degradation of Im, but Sim said, "He is with me; I am behind what he wrote and approve; degrade me and not him," and so the King withdrew his displeasure. He was faithful of the faithful.

When he was old he went and lived in Tun-san in a little tumble-down hut, like the poorest of the *literati*. He called himself "Water-thunder Muddy-man," a name derived from the Book of Changes.

He died in 1622 at the age of seventy-four, and is recorded as one of Korea's great patriots.

The Story

Minister Sim Heui-su was, when young, handsome as polished marble, and white as the snow, rarely and beautifully formed. When eight years of age he was already an adept at the character, and a wonder in the eyes of his people. The boy's nickname was Soondong (the godlike one). From the passing of his first examination, step by step he advanced, till at last he became First Minister of the land. When old he was honoured as the most renowned of all ministers. At seventy he still held office, and one day, when occupied with the affairs of State, he suddenly said to those about him, "To-day is my last on earth, and my farewell wishes to you all are that you may prosper and do bravely and well."

His associates replied in wonder, "Your Excellency is still strong and hearty, and able for many years of work; why do you speak so?"

Sim laughingly made answer, "Our span of life is fixed. Why should I not know? We cannot pass the predestined limit. Please feel no regret. Use all your efforts to serve His Majesty the King, and make grateful acknowledgment of his many favours."

Thus he exhorted them, and took his departure. Every one wondered over this strange announcement. From that day on he returned no more, it being said that he was ailing.

There was at that time attached to the War Office a young secretary directly under Sim. Hearing that his master was ill, the young man went to pay his respects and to make inquiry. Sim called him into his private room, where all was quiet. Said he, "I am about to die, and this is a long farewell, so take good care of yourself, and do your part honourably."

The young man looked, and in Sim's eyes were tears. He said, "Your Excellency is still vigorous, and even though you are slightly ailing, there is surely no cause for anxiety. I am at a loss to understand your tears, and what you mean by saying that you are about to die. I would like to ask the reason."

Sim smiled and said, "I have never told any person, but since you ask and there is no longer cause for concealment, I shall tell you the whole story. When I was young certain things happened in my life that may make you smile.

"At about sixteen years of age I was said to be a handsome boy and fair to see. Once in Seoul, when a banquet was in progress and many dancing-girls and other representatives of good cheer were called, I went too, with a half-dozen comrades, to see. There was among the dancing-girls a young woman whose face was very beautiful. She was not like an earthly person, but like some angelic being. Inquiring as to her name, some of those seated near said it was Ta-hong (Flower-bud).

"When all was over and the guests had separated, I went home, but I thought of Ta-hong's pretty face, and recalled her repeatedly, over and over; seemingly I could not forget her. Ten days or so later I was returning from my teacher's house along the main street, carrying my books under my arm, when I suddenly met a pretty girl, who was beautifully dressed and riding a handsome horse. She alighted just in front of me, and to my surprise, taking my hand, said, 'Are you not Sim Heui-su?'

"In my astonishment I looked at her and saw that it was Ta-hong. I said, 'Yes, but how do you know me?' I was not married then, nor had I my hair done up, and as there were many people in the street looking on I was very much ashamed. Flower-bud, with a look of gladness in her face, said to her pony-boy, 'I have something to see to just now; you return and say to the master that I shall be present at the banquet to-morrow.' Then we went aside into a neighbouring house and sat down. She said, 'Did you not on such and such a day go to such and such a Minister's house and look on at the gathering?' I answered, 'Yes, I did.' 'I saw you,' said she, 'and to me your face was like a god's. I asked those present who you were, and they said your family name was Sim and your given-name Heui-su, and that your character and gifts were very superior. From that day on I longed to meet you, but as there was no possibility of this I could only think of you. Our meeting thus is surely of God's appointment.'

"I replied laughingly, 'I, too, felt just the same towards you.'

"Then Ta-hong said, 'We cannot meet here; let's go to my aunt's home in the next ward, where it's quiet, and talk there.' We went to the aunt's home. It was neat and clean and somewhat isolated, and apparently the aunt loved Flower-bud with all the devotion of a mother. From that day forth we plighted our troth together. Flower-bud had never had a lover; I was her first and only choice. She said, however, 'This plan of ours cannot be consummated to-day; let us separate for the present and make plans for our union in the future.' I asked her how we could do so, and she replied, 'I have sworn my soul to you, and it is decided for ever, but you have your parents to think of, and you have not yet had a wife chosen, so there will be no chance of their advising you to have a second wife as my social standing would require for me. As I reflect upon your ability and chances for promotion, I see you already a Minister of State. Let us separate just now, and I'll keep myself for you till the time when you win the first place at the Examination and have your three days of public rejoicing. Then we'll meet once more. Let us make a compact never to be broken. So then, until you have won your honours, do not think of me, please. Do not be anxious, either, lest I should be taken from you, for I have a plan by which to hide myself away in safety. Know that on the day when you win your honours we shall meet again.'

"On this we clasped hands and spoke our farewells as though we parted easily. Where she was going I did not ask, but simply came home with a distressed and burdened heart, feeling that I had lost everything. On my return I found that my parents, who had missed me, were in a terrible state of consternation, but so delighted were they at my safe return that they scarcely asked where I had been. I did not tell them either, but gave another excuse.

"At first I could not desist from thoughts of Ta-hong. After a long time only was I able to regain my composure. From that time forth with all my might I went at my lessons. Day and night I pegged away, not for the sake of the Examination, but for the sake of once more meeting her.

"In two years or so my parents appointed my marriage. I did not dare to refuse, had to accept, but had no heart in it, and no joy in their choice.

"My gift for study was very marked, and by diligence I grew to be superior to all my competitors. It was five years after my farewell to Ta-hong that I won my honours. I was still but a youngster, and all the world rejoiced in my success. But my joy was in the secret understanding that the time had come for me to meet Ta-hong. On the first day of my graduation honours I expected to meet her, but did not. The second day passed, but I saw nothing of her, and the third day was passing and no word had reached me. My heart was so disturbed that I found not the slightest joy in the honours of the occasion. Evening was falling, when my father said to me, 'I have a friend of my younger days, who now lives in Chang-eui ward, and you must go and call on him this evening before the three days are over,' and so, there being no help for it, I went to pay my call. As I was returning the sun had gone down and it was dark, and just as I was passing a high gateway, I heard the *Sillai* call. It was the home of an old Minister, a man whom I did not know, but he being a high noble there was nothing for me to do but to dismount and enter. Here I found the master himself, an old gentleman, who put me through my humble exercises, and then ordered me gently to come up and sit beside him. He talked to me very kindly, and entertained me with all sorts of refreshments. Then he lifted his glass and inquired, 'Would you like to meet a very beautiful person?' I did not know what he meant, and so asked, 'What beautiful person?' The old man said, 'The most beautiful in the world to you. She has long been a member of my household.' Then he ordered a servant to call her. When she came it was my lost Ta-hong. I was startled, delighted, surprised, and speechless almost. 'How do you come here?' I gasped.

"She laughed and said, 'Is this not within the three days of your public celebration, and according to the agreement by which we parted?'

"The old man said, 'She is a wonderful woman. Her thoughts are high and noble, and her history is quite unique. I will tell it to you. I am an old man of eighty, and my wife and I have had no children, but on a certain day this young girl came to us saying, "May I have the place of slave with you, to wait on you and do your bidding?"

"'In surprise I asked the reason for this strange request, and she said, "I am not running away from any master, so do not mistrust me."

"'Still, I did not wish to take her in, and told her so, but she begged so persuasively that I yielded and let her stay, appointed her work to do, and watched her behaviour. She became a slave of her own accord, and simply lived to please us, preparing our meals during the day, and caring for our rooms for the night; responding to calls; ever ready to do our bidding; faithful beyond compare. We feeble old folks, often ill, found her a source of comfort and cheer unheard of, making life perfect peace and joy. Her needle, too, was exceedingly skilful, and according to the seasons she prepared all that we needed. Naturally we loved and pitied her more than I can say. My wife thought more of her than ever mother did of a daughter. During the day she was always at hand, and at night she slept by her side. At one time I asked her quietly concerning her past history. She said she was originally the child of a free-man, but that her parents had died when she was very young, and, having no place to go to, an old woman of the village had taken her in and brought her up. "Being so young," said she, "I was safe from harm. At last I met a young master with whom I plighted a hundred years of troth, a beautiful boy, none was ever like him. I determined to meet him again, but only after he had won his honours in the arena. If I had remained at the home of the old mother I could not have kept myself safe, and preserved my honour; I would have been helpless; so I came here for safety and to serve you. It is a plan by which to hide myself for a year or so, and then when he wins I shall ask your leave to go."

"'I then asked who the person was with whom she had made this contract, and she told me your name. I am so old that I no longer think of taking wives and concubines, but she called herself my concubine so as to be safe, and thus the years have passed. We watched the Examination reports, but till this time your name was absent. Through it all she expressed not a single word of anxiety, but kept up heart saying that before long your name would appear. So confident was she that not a shadow of disappointment was in her face. This time on looking over the list I found your name, and told her. She heard it without any special manifestation of joy, saying she knew it would come. She also said, "When we parted I promised to meet him before the three days of public celebration were over, and now I must make good my promise." So she climbed to the upper pavilion to watch the public way. But this ward being somewhat remote she did not see you going by on the first day, nor on the second. This morning she went again, saying, "He will surely pass to-day"; and so it came about. She said, "He is coming; call him in."

"'I am an old man and have read much history, and have heard of many famous women. There are many examples of devotion that move the heart, but I never saw so faithful a life nor one so devoted to another. God taking note of this has brought all her purposes to pass. And now, not to let this moment of joy go by, you must stay with me to-night.'

"When I met Ta-hong I was most happy, especially as I heard of her years of faithfulness. As to the invitation I declined it, saying I could not think, even though we had so agreed, of taking away one who waited in attendance upon His Excellency. But the old man laughed, saying, 'She is not mine. I simply let her be called my concubine in name lest my nephews or some younger members of the clan should steal her away. She is first of all a faithful woman: I have not known her like before.'

"The old man then had the horse sent back and the servants, also a letter to my parents saying that I would stay the night. He ordered the servants to prepare a room, to put in beautiful screens and embroidered matting, to hang up lights and to decorate as for a bridegroom. Thus he celebrated our meeting.

"Next morning I bade good-bye, and went and told my parents all about my meeting with Ta-hong and what had happened. They gave consent that I should have her, and she was brought and made a member of our family, really my only wife.

"Her life and behaviour being beyond that of the ordinary, in serving those above her and in helping those below, she fulfilled all the requirements of the ancient code. Her work, too, was faithfully done, and her gifts in the way of music and chess were most exceptional. I loved her as I never can tell.

"A little later I went as magistrate to Keumsan county in Chulla Province, and Ta-hong went with me. We were there for two years. She declined our too frequent happy times together, saying that it interfered with efficiency and duty. One day, all unexpectedly, she came to me and requested that we should have a little quiet time, with no others present, as she had something special to tell me. I asked her what it was, and she said to me, 'I am going to die, for my span of life is finished; so let us be glad once more and forget all the sorrows of the world.' I wondered when I heard this. I could not think it true, and asked her how she could tell beforehand that she was going to die. She said, 'I know, there is no mistake about it.'

"In four or five days she fell ill, but not seriously, and yet a day or two later she died. She said to me when dying, 'Our life is ordered, God decides it all. While I lived I gave myself to you, and you most kindly responded in return. I have no regrets. As I die I ask only that my body be buried where it may rest by the side of my master when he passes away, so that when we meet in the regions beyond I shall be with you once again.' When she had so said she died.

"Her face was beautiful, not like the face of the dead, but like the face of the living. I was plunged into deepest grief, prepared her body with my own hands for burial. Our custom is that when a second wife dies she is not buried with the family, but I made some excuse and had her interred in our family site in the county of Ko-yang. I did so to carry out her wishes. When I came as far as Keum-chang on my sad journey, I wrote a verse –

> 'O beautiful Bud, of the beautiful Flower,
> We bear thy form on the willow bier;
> Whither has gone thy sweet perfumed soul?
> The rains fall on us
> To tell us of thy tears and of thy faithful way.'

"I wrote this as a love tribute to my faithful Ta-hong. After her death, whenever anything serious was to happen in my home, she always came to tell me beforehand, and never was there a mistake in her announcements. For several years it has continued thus, till a few days ago she appeared in a dream saying, 'Master, the time of your departure has come, and we are to meet again. I am now making ready for your glad reception.'

"For this reason I have bidden all my associates farewell. Last night she came once more and said to me, 'To-morrow is your day.' We wept together in the dream as we met and talked. In the morning, when I awoke, marks of tears were still upon my cheeks. This is not because I fear to die, but because I have seen my Ta-hong. Now that you have asked me I have told you all. Tell it to no one." So Sim died, as was foretold, on the day following. Strange, indeed!

The King of Yom-Na (Hell)

PAK CHOM WAS one of the Royal Censors, and died in the Japanese War of 1592.

The Story

In Yon-nan County, Whang-hai Province, there was a certain literary graduate whose name I have forgotten. He fell ill one day and remained in his room, leaning helplessly against his arm-rest. Suddenly several spirit soldiers appeared to him, saying, "The Governor of the lower hell has ordered your arrest," so they bound him with a chain about his neck, and led him away. They journeyed for many hundreds of miles, and at last reached a place that had a very high wall. The spirits then took him within the walls and went on for a long distance.

There was within this enclosure a great structure whose height reached to heaven. They arrived at the gate, and the spirits who had him in hand led him in, and when they entered the inner courtyard they laid him down on his face.

Glancing up he saw what looked like a king seated on a throne; grouped about him on each side were attendant officers. There were also scores of secretaries and soldiers going and coming on pressing errands. The King's appearance was most terrible, and his commands such as to fill one with awe. The graduate felt the perspiration break out on his back, and he dared not look up. In a little a secretary came forward, stood in front of the raised dais to transmit commands, and the King asked, "Where do you come from? What is your name? How old are you? What do you do for a living? Tell me the truth now, and no dissembling."

The scholar, frightened to death, replied, "My clan name is So-and-so, and my given name is So-and-so. I am so old, and I have lived for several generations at Yon-nan, Whang-hai Province. I am stupid and ill-equipped by nature, so have not done anything special. I have heard all my life that if you say your beads with love and pity in your heart you will escape hell, and so have given my time to calling on the Buddha, and dispensing alms."

The secretary, hearing this, went at once and reported it to the King. After some time he came back with a message, saying, "Come up closer to the steps, for you are not the person intended. It happens that you bear the same name and you have thus been wrongly arrested. You may go now."

The scholar joined his hands and made a deep bow. Again the secretary transmitted a message from the King, saying, "My house, when on earth, was in such a place in such and such a ward of Seoul. When you go back I want to send a message by you. My coming here is long, and the outer coat I wear is worn to shreds. Ask my people to send me a new outer coat. If you do so I shall be greatly obliged, so see that you do not forget."

The scholar said, "Your Majesty's message given me thus direct I shall pass on without fail, but the ways of the two worlds, the dark world and the light, are so different that when I give the message the hearers will say I am talking nonsense. True, I'll give it just as you have commanded, but what about it if they refuse to listen? I ought to have some evidence as proof to help me out."

The King made answer, "Your words are true, very true. This will help you: When I was on earth," said he, "one of my head buttons that I wore had a broken edge, and I hid it in the third volume of the Book of History. I alone know of it, no one else in the world. If you give this as a proof they will listen."

The scholar replied, "That will be satisfactory, but again, how shall I do in case they make the new coat?"

The reply was, "Prepare a sacrifice, offer the coat by fire, and it will reach me."

He then bade good-bye, and the King sent with him two soldier guards. He asked the soldiers, as they came out, who the one seated on the throne was. "He is the King of Hades," said they; "his surname is Pak and his given name is Oo."

They arrived at the bank of a river, and the two soldiers pushed him into the water. He awoke with a start, and found that he had been dead for three days.

When he recovered from his sickness he came up to Seoul, searched out the house indicated, and made careful inquiry as to the name, finding that it was no other than Pak Oo. Pak Oo had two sons, who at that time had graduated and were holding office. The graduate wanted to see the sons of this King of Hades, but the gatekeeper would not let him in. Therefore he stood before the red gate waiting helplessly till the sun went down. Then came out from the inner quarters of the house an old servant, to whom he earnestly made petition that he might see the master. On being thus requested, the servant returned and reported it to the master, who, a little later, ordered him in. On entering, he saw two gentlemen who seemed to be chiefs. They had him sit down, and then questioned him as to who he was and what he had to say.

He replied, "I am a student living in Yon-nan County, Whang-hai Province. On such and such a day I died and went into the other world, where your honorable father gave me such and such a commission."

The two listened for a little and then, without waiting to hear all that he had to say, grew very angry and began to scold him, saying, "How dare such a scarecrow as you come into our house and say such things as these? This is stuff and nonsense that you talk. Pitch him out," they shouted to the servants.

He, however, called back saying, "I have a proof; listen. If it fails, why then, pitch me out."

One of the two said, "What possible proof can you have?" Then the scholar told with great exactness and care the story of the head button.

The two, in astonishment over this, had the book taken down and examined, and sure enough in Vol. III of the Book of History was the button referred to. Not a single particular had failed. It proved to be a button that they had missed after the death of their father, and that they had searched for in vain.

Accepting the message now as true, they all entered upon a period of mourning.

The women of the family also called in the scholar and asked him specially of what he had seen. So they made the outer coat, chose a day, and offered it by fire before the ancestral altar. Three days after the sacrifice the scholar dreamed, and the family of Pak dreamed too, that the King of Hades had come and given to each one of them his thanks for the coat. They long kept the scholar at their home, treating him with great respect, and became his firm friends for ever after.

Pak Oo was a great-grandson of Minister Pak Chom. While he held office he was honest and just and was highly honoured by the people. When he was Mayor of Hai-ju there arose a dispute between him and the Governor, which proved also that Pak was the honest man.

When I was at Hai-ju, Choi Yu-chom, a graduate, told me this story.

* * *

Note: The head button is the insignia of rank, and is consequently a valuable heirloom in a Korean home.

Hong's Experiences in Hades

HONG NAI-POM WAS a military graduate who was born in the year ad 1561, and lived in the city of Pyeng-yang. He passed his examination in the year 1603, and in the year 1637 attained to the Third Degree. He was 82 in the year 1643, and his son Sonn memorialized the King asking that his father be given rank appropriate to his age. At that time a certain Han Hong-kil was chief of the Royal Secretaries, and he refused to pass on the request to his Majesty; but in the year 1644, when the Crown Prince was returning from his exile in China, he came by way of Pyeng-yang. Sonn took advantage of this to present the same request to the Crown Prince.

His Highness received it, and had it brought to the notice of the King. In consequence, Hong received the rank of Second Degree.

On receiving it he said, "This year I shall die," and a little later he died.

In the year 1594, Hong fell ill of typhus fever, and after ten days of suffering, died. They prepared his body for burial, and placed it in a coffin. Then the friends and relatives left, and his wife remained alone in charge. Of a sudden the body turned itself and fell with a thud to the ground. The woman, frightened, fainted away, and the other members of the family came rushing to her help. From this time on the body resumed its functions, and Hong lived.

Said he, "In my dream I went to a certain region, a place of great fear where many persons were standing around, and awful ogres, some of them wearing bulls' heads, and some with faces of wild beasts. They crowded about and jumped and pounced toward me in all directions. A scribe robed in black sat on a platform and addressed me, saying, 'There are three religions on earth, Confucianism, Buddhism and Taoism. According to Buddhism, you know that heaven and hell are places that decide between man's good and evil deeds. You have ever been a blasphemer of the Buddha, and a denier of a future life, acting always as though you knew everything, blustering and storming. You are now to be sent to hell, and ten thousand kalpas[1] will not see you out of it.'

"Then two or three constables carrying spears came and took me off. I screamed, 'You are wrong, I am innocently condemned.' Just at that moment a certain Buddha, with a face of shining gold, came smiling toward me, and said, 'There is truly a mistake somewhere; this man must attain to the age of eighty-three and become an officer of the Second Degree ere he dies.' Then addressing me he asked, 'How is it that you have come here? The order was that a certain Hong of Chon-ju be arrested and brought, not you; but now that you have come, look about the place before you go, and tell the world afterwards of what you have seen.'

"The guards, on hearing this, took me in hand and brought me first to a prison-house, where a sign was posted up, marked, 'Stirrers up of Strife.' I saw in this prison a great brazier-shaped pit, built of stones and filled with fire. Flames arose and forked tongues. The stirrers up of strife were taken and made to sit close before it. I then saw one infernal guard take a long rod of iron, heat it red-hot, and put out the eyes of the guilty ones. I saw also that the offenders were hung up like dried fish. The guides who accompanied me, said, 'While these were on earth they did not love their brethren, but looked at others as enemies. They scoffed at the laws of God and sought only selfish gain, so they are punished.'

"The next hell was marked, 'Liars.' In that hell I saw an iron pillar of several yards in height, and great stones placed before it. The offenders were called up, and made to kneel before the pillar. Then I saw an executioner take a knife and drive a hole through the tongues of the offenders, pass an iron chain through each, and hang them to the pillar so that they dangled by their tongues several feet from the ground. A stone was then taken and tied to each culprit's feet. The stones thus bearing down, and the chains being fast to the pillar, their tongues were pulled out a foot or more, and their eyes rolled in their sockets. Their agonies were appalling. The guides again said, 'These offenders when on earth used their tongues skilfully to tell lies and to separate friend from friend, and so they are punished.'

"The next hell had inscribed on it, 'Deceivers.' I saw in it many scores of people. There were ogres that cut the flesh from their bodies, and fed it to starving demons. These ate and ate, and the flesh was cut and cut till only the bones remained. When the winds of hell blew, flesh returned to them; then metal snakes and copper dogs crowded in to bite them and suck their blood. Their screams of pain made the earth to tremble. The guides said to me, 'When these offenders were on earth they held high office, and while they pretended to be true and good they received bribes in secret and were doers of all evil. As Ministers of State they ate the fat of the land and sucked the blood of the people, and yet advertised themselves as benefactors and were highly applauded. While in reality they lived as thieves, they pretended to be holy, as Confucius and Mencius are holy. They were deceivers of the world, and robbers, and so are punished thus.'

"The guides then said, 'It is not necessary that you see all the hells.' They said to one another, 'Let's take him yonder and show him;' so they went some distance to the south-east. There was a great house with a sign painted thus, 'The Home of the Blessed.' As I looked, there were beautiful haloes encircling it, and clouds of glory. There were hundreds of priests in cassock and surplice. Some carried fresh-blown lotus flowers; some were seated like the Buddha; some were reading prayers.

"The guides said, 'These when on earth kept the faith, and with undivided hearts served the Buddha, and so have escaped the Eight Sorrows and the Ten Punishments, and are now in the home of the happy, which is called heaven.' When we had seen all these things we returned.

"The golden-faced Buddha said to me, 'Not many on earth believe in the Buddha, and few know of heaven and hell. What do you think of it?'

"I bowed low and thanked him.

"Then the black-coated scribe said, 'I am sending this man away; see him safely off.' The spirit soldiers took me with them, and while on the way I awakened with a start, and found that I had been dead for four days."

Hong's mind was filled with pride on this account, and he frequently boasted of it. His age and Second Degree of rank came about just as the Buddha had predicted.

His experience, alas! was used as a means to deceive people, for the Superior Man does not talk of these strange and wonderful things.

Yi Tan, a Chinaman of the Song Kingdom, used to say, "If there is no heaven, there is no heaven, but if there is one, the Superior Man alone can attain to it. If there is no hell, there is no hell, but if there is one the bad man must inherit it."

If we examine Hong's story, while it looks like a yarn to deceive the world, it really is a story to arouse one to right action. I, Im Bang, have recorded it like Toi-chi, saying, "Don't find fault with the story, but learn its lesson."

*　*　*

Note: Kalpa means a Buddhistic age.

The Daughter of the Sun: Origin of Death

THE SUN LIVED on the other side of the sky vault, but her daughter lived in the middle of the sky, directly above the earth, and every day as the Sun was climbing along the sky arch to the west, she used to stop at her daughter's house for dinner.

Now, the Sun hated the people on the earth, because they could never look straight at her without screwing up their faces. She said to her brother, the Moon, "My grandchildren are ugly;

they grin all over their faces when they look at me." But the Moon said, "I like my younger brothers; I think they are very handsome" – because they always smiled pleasantly when they saw him in the sky at night, for his rays were milder.

The Sun was jealous and planned to kill all the people, so every day when she got near her daughter's house she sent down such sultry rays that there was a great fever and the people died by hundreds, until everyone had lost some friend and there was fear that no one would be left. They went for help to the Little Men, who said the only way to save themselves was to kill the Sun.

The Little Men made medicine and changed two men to snakes, the Spreading-adder and the Copperhead, and sent them to watch near the door of the daughter of the Sun to bite the old Sun when she came next day. They went together and hid near the house until the Sun came, but when the Spreading-adder was about to spring, the bright light blinded him and he could only spit out yellow slime, as he does to this day when he tries to bite. She called him a nasty thing and went by into the house, and the Copperhead crawled off without trying to do anything.

So the people still died from the heat, and they went to the Little Men a second time for help. The Little Men made medicine again and changed one man into the great Uktena and another into the Rattlesnake and sent them to watch near the house and kill the old Sun when she came for dinner. They made the Uktena very large, with horns on his head, and everyone thought he would be sure to do the work, but the Rattlesnake was so quick and eager that he got ahead and coiled up just outside the house, and when the Sun's daughter opened the door to look out for her mother, he sprang up and bit her and she fell dead in the doorway. He forgot to wait for the old Sun, but went back to the people, and the Uktena was so very angry that he went back, too. Since then we pray to the rattlesnake and do not kill him, because he is kind and never tries to bite if we do not disturb him. The Uktena grew angrier all the time and very dangerous, so that if he even looked at a man, that man's family would die. After a long time, the people held a council and decided that he was too dangerous to be with them, so they sent him up to Gălûñ'lătĭ, and he is there now. The Spreading-adder, the Copperhead, the Rattlesnake, and the Uktena were all men.

When the Sun found her daughter dead, she went into the house and grieved, and the people did not die anymore, but now the world was dark all the time, because the Sun would not come out. They went again to the Little Men, and these told them that if they wanted the Sun to come out again they must bring back her daughter from Tsûsginâ'ĭ, the Ghost country, in Usûñhi'yĭ, the Darkening land in the west. They chose seven men to go, and gave each a sourwood rod, a hand-breadth long. The Little Men told them they must take a box with them, and when they got to Tsûsginâ'ĭ they would find all the ghosts at a dance. They must stand outside the circle, and when the young woman passed in the dance they must strike her with the rods and she would fall to the ground. Then they must put her into the box and bring her back to her mother, but they must be very sure not to open the box, even a little way, until they were home again.

They took the rods and a box and travelled seven days to the west until they came to the Darkening land. There were a great many people there, and they were having a dance just as if they were at home in the settlements. The young woman was in the outside circle, and as she swung around to where the seven men were standing, one struck her with his rod and she turned her head and saw him. As she came around the second time, another touched her with his rod, and then another and another, until at the seventh round she fell out of the ring, and they put her into the box and closed the lid fast. The other ghosts seemed never to notice what had happened.

They took up the box and started home toward the east. In a little while, the girl came to life again and begged to be let out of the box, but they made no answer and went on. Soon, she called again and said she was hungry, but still they made no answer and went on. After another while, she spoke again and called for a drink and pleaded so that it was very hard to listen to her, but the men who carried the box said nothing and still went on. When at last they were very near home, she called again and begged them to raise the lid just a little, because she was smothering. They were afraid she was really dying now, so they lifted the lid a little to give her air, but as they did so there was a fluttering sound inside and something flew past them into the thicket and they heard a Redbird cry, "*kwish! kwish! kwish!*" in the bushes. They shut down the lid and went on again to the settlements, but when they got there and opened the box it was empty.

So we know the Redbird is the daughter of the Sun, and if the men had kept the box closed, as the Little Men told them to do, they would have brought her home safely, and we could bring back our other friends also from the Ghost country, but now when they die we can never bring them back.

The Sun had been glad when they started to the Ghost country, but when they came back without her daughter she grieved and cried, "My daughter, my daughter," and wept until her tears made a flood upon the earth, and the people were afraid the world would be drowned. They held another council, and sent their handsomest young men and women to amuse her so that she would stop crying. They danced before the Sun and sang their best songs, but for a long time she kept her face covered and paid no attention, until at last the drummer suddenly changed the song, when she lifted up her face, and was so pleased at the sight that she forgot her grief and smiled.

How Glooskap Left the World

NOW GLOOSKAP HAD freed the world from all the mighty monsters of an early time: the giants wandered no longer in the wilderness; the *cullo* terrified man no more, as it spread its wings like the cloud between him and the sun; the dreadful Chenoo of the North devoured him not; no evil beasts, devils, or serpents were to be found near his home. And the Master had, moreover, taught men the arts which made them happier; but they were not grateful to him, and though they worshiped him they were not the less wicked.

Now, when the ways of men and beasts waxed evil, they greatly vexed Glooskap, and at length he could no longer endure them, and he made a rich feast by the shore of the great Lake Minas. All the beasts came to it, and when the feast was over he got into a great canoe, and the beasts looked after him till they saw him no more. And after they ceased to see him, they still heard his voice as he sang; but the sounds grew fainter and fainter in the distance, and at last they wholly died away; and then deep silence fell on them all, and a great marvel came to pass, and the beasts, who had till now spoken but one language, were no longer able to understand each other, and they fled away, each his own way, and never again have they met together in council. Until the day when Glooskap shall return to restore the Golden Age, and make men and animals dwell once more together in amity and peace, all Nature mourns. And tradition says that on his departure from Acadia the Great Snowy Owl retired to the deep forests, to return no more until he could come to welcome Glooskap; and in those sylvan depths the owls even yet repeat to the night *Koo-koo-skoos!* which is to say in the Indian tongue, 'Oh, I am sorry! Oh, I am sorry!' And the Loons, who had been the huntsmen of Glooskap, go restlessly up and down through the world, seeking vainly for their master, whom they cannot find, and wailing sadly because they find him not.

But ere the Master went away from life, or ceased to wander in the ways of men, he bade it be made known by the Loons, his faithful messengers, that before his departure years would pass, and that whoever would seek him might have one wish granted, whatever that wish might be. Now, though the journey was long and the trials were terrible which those must endure who would find Glooskap, there were still many men who adventured them.

Now ye shall hear who some of these were and what happened to them. And this is the first tale as it was told me in the tent of John Gabriel, the Passamaquoddy.

When all men had heard that Glooskap would grant a wish to anyone who would come to him, three Indians resolved to try this thing; and one was a Maliseet from St. John, and the other two were Penobscots from Old Town. And the path was long and the way was hard, and they suffered much, and they were seven years on it ere they came to him. But while they were yet three months' journey from his dwelling, they heard the barking of his dogs, and as they drew nearer, day by day, it was louder. And so, after great trials, they found the lord of men and beasts, and he made them welcome and entertained them.

But, ere they went, he asked them what they wanted. And the eldest, who was an honest, simple man, and of but little account among his people, because he was a bad hunter, asked that he might excel in the killing and catching of game. Then the Master gave him a flute, or the magic pipe, which pleases every ear, and has the power of persuading every animal to follow him who plays it. And he thanked the lord, and left.

Now the second Indian, being asked what he would have, replied, "The love of many women." And when Glooskap asked how many, he said, "I care not how many; so that there are but enough of them, and more than enough." At hearing this, the Master seemed displeased, but, smiling anon, he gave him a bag which was tightly tied, and told him not to open it until he had reached his home. So he thanked the lord, and left.

Now the third Indian was a gay and handsome, but foolish, young fellow, whose whole heart was set on making people laugh, and on winning a welcome at every merry-making. And he, being asked what he would have or what he chiefly wanted, said that it would please him most to be able to make a certain quaint and marvellous sound or noise, which was frequent in those primitive times among all the Wabanaki, and which it is said may even yet be heard in a few sequestered wigwams far in the wilderness, away from men; there being still here and there a deep magician, or man of mystery, who knows the art of producing it. And the property of this wondrous sound is such that they who hear it must needs burst into a laugh; whence it is the cause that the men of these our modern times are so sorrowful, since that sound is no more heard in the land. And to him Glooskap was also affable, sending Marten into the woods to seek a certain mystical and magic root, which when eaten would make the miracle the young man sought. But he warned him not to touch the root ere he got to his home, or it would be the worse for him. And so he kindly thanked the lord, and left.

It had taken seven years to come, but seven days were all that was required to tread the path returning to their home, that is, for him who got there. Only one of all the three beheld his lodge again. This was the hunter, who, with his pipe in his pocket, and not a care in his heart, trudged through the woods, satisfied that so long as he should live, there would always be venison in the larder.

But he who loved women, and had never won even a wife, was filled with anxious wishfulness. And he had not gone very far into the woods before he opened the bag. And there flew out by hundreds, like white doves, swarming all about him, beautiful girls, with black burning eyes and flowing hair. And, wild with passion, the winsome witches threw their arms about him, and kissed him as he responded to their embraces; but they came ever more and more, wilder and more passionate. And he bade them give way, but they would not, and he sought to escape, but he could not; and so panting, crying for breath, smothered, he perished. And those who came that way found him dead, but what became of the girls no man knows.

Now, the third went merrily onward alone, when all at once it flashed upon his mind that Glooskap had given him a present, and, without the least heed to the injunction that he was to wait till he had reached his home, drew out the root and ate it; and scarce had he done this ere he realized that he possessed the power of uttering the weird and mystic sound to absolute perfection. And as it rang o'er many a hill and dale, and woke the echoes of the distant hills, until it was answered by the solemn owl, he felt that it was indeed wonderful. So he walked on gayly, trumpeting as he went, over hill and vale, happy as a bird.

But by and by he began to weary of himself. Seeing a deer he drew an arrow and stealing silently to the game was just about to shoot, when despite himself, the wild, unearthly sound broke forth like a demon's warble. The deer bounded away, and the young man cursed! And when he reached Old Town, half dead with hunger, he was worth little to make laughter, though the honest Indians at first did not fail to do so, and thereby somewhat cheered his heart. But as the days went on they wearied of him, and, life becoming a burden, he went into the woods and slew himself. And the evil spirit of the night air even Bumole, or Pamola, from whom came the gift, swooped down from the clouds and bore him away to 'Lahmkekqu', the dwelling place of darkness, and he was no more heard of among men.

The Funeral Fire

FOR SEVERAL NIGHTS after the interment of a Chippewa a fire is kept burning upon the grave. This fire is lit in the evening, and carefully supplied with small sticks of dry wood, to keep up a bright but small fire. It is kept burning for several hours, generally until the usual hour of retiring to rest, and then suffered to go out. The fire is renewed for four nights, and sometimes for longer. The person who performs this pious office is generally a near relative of the deceased, or one who has been long intimate with him. The following tale is related as showing the origin of the custom.

A small war party of Chippewas encountered their enemies upon an open plain, where a severe battle was fought. Their leader was a brave and distinguished warrior, but he never acted with greater bravery, or more distinguished himself by personal prowess, than on this occasion. After turning the tide of battle against his enemies, while shouting for victory, he received an arrow in his breast, and fell upon the plain. No warrior thus killed is ever buried, and according to ancient custom, the chief was placed in a sitting posture upon the field, his back supported by a tree, and his face turned towards the direction in which his enemies had fled. His headdress and equipment were accurately adjusted as if he were living, and his bow leaned against his shoulder. In this posture his companions left him. That he was dead appeared evident to all, but a strange thing had happened. Although deprived of speech and motion, the chief heard distinctly all that was said by his friends. He heard them lament his death without having the power to contradict it, and he felt their touch as they adjusted his posture, without having the power to reciprocate it. His anguish, when he felt himself thus abandoned, was extreme, and his wish to follow his friends on their return home so completely filled his mind, as he saw them one after another take leave of him and depart, that with a terrible effort he arose and followed them. His form, however, was invisible to them, and this aroused in him surprise, disappointment, and rage, which by turns took possession of him. He followed their track, however, with great diligence. Wherever they went he went, when they walked he walked, when they ran he ran, when they encamped he stopped with them, when they slept he slept, when they awoke he awoke. In short, he mingled in all their labours and toils, but he was excluded from all their sources of refreshment, except that of sleeping, and from the pleasures of participating in their conversation, for all that he said received no notice.

"Is it possible," he cried, "that you do not see me, that you do not hear me, that you do not understand me? Will you suffer me to bleed to death without offering to stanch my wounds? Will you permit me to starve while you eat around me? Have those whom I have so often led to war so soon forgotten me? Is there no one who recollects me, or who will offer me a morsel of food in my distress?"

Thus he continued to upbraid his friends at every stage of the journey, but no one seemed to hear his words. If his voice was heard at all, it was mistaken for the rustling of the leaves in the wind.

At length the returning party reached their village, and their women and children came out, according to custom, to welcome their return and proclaim their praises.

"Kumaudjeewug! Kumaudjeewug! Kumaudjeewug! they have met, fought, and conquered!" was shouted by every mouth, and the words resounded through the most distant parts of the village. Those who had lost friends came eagerly to inquire their fate, and to know whether they had died like men. The aged father consoled himself for the loss of his son with the reflection that he had fallen manfully, and the widow half forgot her sorrow amid the praises that were uttered of the bravery of her husband. The hearts of the youths glowed with martial ardour as they heard these flattering praises, and the children joined in the shouts, of which they scarcely knew the meaning. Amidst all this uproar and bustle no one seemed conscious of the presence of the warrior-chief. He heard many inquiries made respecting his fate. He heard his companions tell how he had fought, conquered, and fallen, pierced by an arrow through his breast, and how he had been left behind among the slain on the field of battle.

"It is not true," declared the angry chief, "that I was killed and left upon the field! I am here. I live; I move; see me; touch me. I shall again raise my spear in battle, and take my place in the feast."

Nobody, however, seemed conscious of his presence, and his voice was mistaken for the whispering of the wind.

He now walked to his own lodge, and there he found his wife tearing her hair and lamenting over his fate. He endeavoured to undeceive her, but she, like the others, appeared to be insensible of his presence, and not to hear his voice. She sat in a despairing manner, with her head reclining on her hands. The chief asked her to bind up his wounds, but she made no reply. He placed his mouth close to her ear and shouted:

"I am hungry, give me some food!"

The wife thought she heard a buzzing in her ear, and remarked it to one who sat by. The enraged husband now summoning all his strength, struck her a blow on the forehead. His wife raised her hand to her head, and said to her friend:

"I feel a slight shooting pain in my head."

Foiled thus in every attempt to make himself known, the warrior-chief began to reflect upon what he had heard in his youth, to the effect that the spirit was sometimes permitted to leave the body and wander about. He concluded that possibly his body might have remained upon the field of battle, while his spirit only accompanied his returning friends. He determined to return to the field, although it was four days' journey away. He accordingly set out upon his way. For three days he pursued his way without meeting anything uncommon; but on the fourth, towards evening, as he came to the skirts of the battlefield, he saw a fire in the path before him. He walked to one side to avoid stepping into it, but the fire also changed its position, and was still before him. He then went in another direction, but the mysterious fire still crossed his path, and seemed to bar his entrance to the scene of the conflict. In short, whichever way he took, the fire was still before him – no expedient seemed to avail him.

"Thou demon!" he exclaimed at length, "why dost thou bar my approach to the field of battle? Knowest thou not that I am a spirit also, and that I seek again to enter my body? Dost thou presume that I shall return without effecting my object? Know that I have never been defeated by the enemies of my nation, and will not be defeated by thee!"

So saying, he made a sudden effort and jumped through the flame. No sooner had he done so than he found himself sitting on the ground, with his back supported by a tree, his bow leaning against his shoulder, all his warlike dress and arms upon his body, just as they had been left by his friends on the day of battle. Looking up he beheld a large canicu, or war eagle, sitting in the tree above his head. He immediately recognised this bird to be the same as he had once dreamt of in his youth – the one he had chosen as his guardian spirit, or personal manito. This eagle had carefully watched his body and prevented other ravenous birds from touching it.

The chief got up and stood upon his feet, but he felt himself weak and much exhausted. The blood upon his wound had stanched itself, and he now bound it up. He possessed a knowledge of such roots as have healing properties, and these he carefully sought in the woods. Having found some, he pounded some of them between stones and applied them externally. Others he chewed and swallowed. In a short time he found himself so much recovered as to be able to commence his journey, but he suffered greatly from hunger, not seeing any large animals that he might kill. However, he succeeded in killing some small birds with his bow and arrow, and these he roasted before a fire at night.

In this way he sustained himself until he came to a river that separated his wife and friends from him. He stood upon the bank and gave that peculiar whoop which is a signal of the return of a friend. The sound was immediately heard, and a canoe was despatched to bring him over, and in a short time, amidst the shouts of his friends and relations, who thronged from every side to see the arrival, the warrior-chief was landed.

When the first wild bursts of wonder and joy had subsided, and some degree of quiet had been restored to the village, he related to his people the account of his adventures. He concluded his narrative by telling them that it is pleasing to the spirit of a deceased person to have a fire built upon the grave for four nights after his burial; that it is four days' journey to the land appointed for the residence of the spirits; that in its journey thither the spirit stands in need of a fire every night at the place of its encampment; and that if the friends kindle this fire upon the spot where the body is laid, the spirit has the benefit of its light and warmth on its path, while if the friends neglect to do this, the spirit is subjected to the irksome task of making its own fire each night.

Retrospection

IT WAS EVENING in the bad-lands, and the red sun had slipped behind the far-off hills. The sundown breeze bent the grasses in the coulées and curled tiny dust-clouds on the barren knolls. Down in a gulch a clear, cool creek dallied its way toward the Missouri, where its water, bitter as gall, would be lost in the great stream. Here, where Nature forbids man to work his will, and where the she wolf dens and kills to feed her litter, an aged Indian stood near the scattered bones of two great buffalo-bulls. Time had bleached the skulls and whitened the old warrior's hair, but in the solitude he spoke to the bones as to a boyhood friend:

"Ho! Buffalo, the years are long since you died, and your tribe, like mine, was even then shrinking fast, but you did not know it; would not believe it; though the signs did not lie. My father and his father knew your people, and when one night you went away, we thought you did but hide and would soon come back. The snows have come and gone many times since then, and still your people stay away. The young-men say that the great herds have gone to the Sand Hills, and that my father still has meat. They have told me that the white man, in his greed, has killed – and not for meat – all the Buffalo that our people knew. They have said that the great herds that made the ground tremble as they ran were slain in a few short years by those who needed not. Can this be true, when ever since there was a world, our people killed your kind, and still left herds that grew in numbers until they often blocked the rivers when they passed? Our people killed your kind that they themselves might live, but never did they go to war against you. Tell me, do your people hide. or are the young-men speaking truth, and have your people gone with mine to Sand Hill shadows to come back no more?"

"Ho! red man – my people all have gone. The young-men tell the truth and all my tribe have gone to feed among the shadow-hills, and your father still has meat. My people suffer from his arrows and his lance, yet there the herds increase as they did here, until the white man came and made his war upon us without cause or need. I was one of the last to die, and with my brother here fled to this forbidding country that I might hide; but one day when the snow was on the world, a white murderer followed on our trail, and with his noisy weapon sent our spirits to join the great shadow-herds. Meat? No, he took no meat, but from our quivering flesh he tore away the robes that Napa gave to make us warm, and left us for the Wolves.

That night they came, and quarrelling, fighting, snapping 'mong themselves, left but our bones to greet the morning sun.

These bones the Coyotes and the weaker ones did drag and scrape, and scrape again, until the last of flesh or muscle disappeared. Then the winds came and sang – and all was done."

The Visit to the Dead

A TACHI HAD a fine wife who died and was buried. Her husband went to her grave and dug a hole near it. There he stayed watching, not eating, using only tobacco. After two nights, he saw that she came up, brushed the earth off herself, and started to go to the island of the dead. The man tried to seize her but could not hold her. She went southeast and he followed her. Whenever he tried to hold her she escaped. He kept trying to seize her, however, and delayed her. At daybreak she stopped. He stayed there, but could not see her. When it began to be dark the woman got up again and went on. She turned westward and crossed Tulare Lake (or its inlet). At daybreak, the man again tried to seize her but could not hold her. She stayed in that place during the day. The man remained in the same place, but again he could not see her. There was a good trail there, and he could see the footprints of his dead friends and relatives. In the evening his wife got up again and went on.

They came to a river which flows westward toward San Luis Obispo, the river of the Tulamni (the description fits the Santa Maria, but the Tulamni are in the Tulare drainage, on and about Buena Vista lake). There the man caught up with his wife and there they stayed all day. He still had had nothing to eat. In the evening, she went on again, now northward. Then, somewhere to the west of the Tachi country, he caught up with her once more and they spent the day there. In the evening, the woman got up and they went on northward, across the San Joaquin river, to the north or east of it. Again he overtook his wife. Then she said, "What are you going to do? I am nothing now. How can you get my body back? Do you think you shall be able to do it?" He said, "I think so." She said, "I think not. I am going to a different kind of a place now."

From daybreak on that man stayed there. In the evening the woman started once more and went down along the river, but he overtook her again. She did not talk to him. Then they stayed all day, and at night went on again. Now they were close to the island of the dead. It was joined to the land by a rising and falling bridge called ch'eleli. Under this bridge a river ran swiftly. The dead passed over this. When they were on the bridge, a bird suddenly fluttered up beside them and frightened them. Many fell off into the river, where they turned into fish. Now the chief of the dead said, "Somebody has come." They told him, "There are two. One of them is alive; he stinks." The chief said, "Do not let him cross."

When the woman came on the island, he asked her, "You have a companion?" And she told him, "Yes, my husband." He asked her, "Is he coming here?" She said, "I do not know. He is alive." They asked the man, "Do you want to come to this country?" He said, "Yes." Then they told him, "Wait. I will see the chief." They told the chief, "He says that he wants to come to this country. We think he does not tell the truth." "Well, let him come across." Now they intended to frighten him off the bridge. They said, "Come on. The chief says you can cross." Then the bird (kacha) flew up and tried to scare him, but did not make him fall off the bridge into the water. So they brought him before the chief. The chief said, "This is a bad country. You should not have come. We have only your wife's soul (ilit). She has left her bones with her body. I do not think we can give her back to you."

In the evening, they danced. It was a round dance and they shouted. The chief said to the man, "Look at your wife in the middle of the crowd. Tomorrow you will see no one."

Now the man stayed there three days. Then the chief said to some of the people, "Bring that woman. Her husband wants to talk to her." They brought the woman to him. He asked her, "Is this your husband?" She said, "Yes." He asked her, "Do you think you will go back to him?"

She said, "I do not think so. What do you wish?" The chief said, "I think not. You must stay here. You cannot go back. You are worthless now." Then he said to the man, "Do you want to sleep with your wife?" He said, "Yes, for a while. I want to sleep with her and talk with her." Then he was allowed to sleep with her that night and they talked together.

At daybreak the woman was vanished and he was sleeping next to a fallen oak. The chief said to him, "Get up. It is late." He opened his eyes and saw an oak instead of his wife. The chief said, "You see that we cannot make your wife as she was. She is no good now. It is best that you go back. You have a good country there." But the man said, "No, I will stay."

The chief told him, "No, do not. Come back here whenever you like, but go back now." Nevertheless, the man stayed there six days. Then he said, "I am going back." Then in the morning he started to go home. The chief told him, "When you arrive, hide yourself. Then, after six days, emerge and make a dance."

Now the man returned. He told his parents, "Make me a small house. In six days I will come out and dance." Now he stayed there five days. Then his friends began to know that he had come back. "Our relative has come back," they all said. Now the man was in too much of a hurry. After five days he came out. In the evening, he began to dance and danced all night, telling what he saw. In the morning, when he had stopped dancing, he went to bathe. Then a rattlesnake bit him. He died. So he went back to the island. He is there now.

It is through him that the people know how it is there. Every two days, the island becomes full. Then the chief gathers the people. "You must swim," he says. The people stop dancing and bathe. Then the bird frightens them, and some turn to fish, and some to ducks; only a few come out of the water again as people. In this way, room is made when the island is too full. The name of the chief there is Kandjidji.

Qalagánguasê, Who Passed to the Land of Ghosts

THERE WAS ONCE a boy whose name was Qalagánguasê; his parents lived at a place where the tides were strong. And one day they ate seaweed, and died of it. Then there was only one sister to look after Qalagánguasê, but it was not long before she also died, and then there were only strangers to look after him.

Qalagánguasê was without strength, the lower part of his body was dead, and one day when the others had gone out hunting, he was left alone in the house. He was sitting there, quite alone, when suddenly he heard a sound. Now he was afraid, and with great pains he managed to drag himself out of the house into the one beside it, and here he found a hiding-place behind the skin hangings. And while he was in hiding there, he heard a noise again, and in walked a ghost.

"Ai! There are people here!"

The ghost went over to the water tub and drank, emptying the dipper twice.

"Thanks for the drink which I, thirsty one, received," said the ghost. "Thus I was wont to drink when I lived on earth." And then it went out.

Now the boy heard his fellow villagers coming up and gathering outside the house, and then they began to crawl in through the passageway.

"Qalagánguasê is not here," they said, when they came inside.

"Yes, he is," said the boy. "I hid in here because a ghost came in. It drank from the water tub there."

And when they went to look at the water tub, they saw that something had been drinking from it.

Then some time after, it happened again that the people were all out hunting, and Qalagánguasê alone in the place. And there he sat in the house all alone, when suddenly the walls and frame of the house began to shake, and next moment a crowd of ghosts came tumbling into the house, one after the other, and the last was one whom he knew, for it was his sister, who had died but a little time before.

And now the ghosts sat about on the floor and began playing; they wrestled, and told stories, and laughed all the time.

At first Qalagánguasê was afraid of them, but at last he found it a pleasant thing to make the night pass. And not until the villagers could be heard returning did they hasten away.

"Now mind you do not tell tales," said the ghost, "for if you do as we say, then you will gain strength again, and there will be nothing you cannot do." And one by one they tumbled out of the passageway. Only Qalagánguasê's sister could hardly get out, and that was because her brother had been minding her little child, and his touch stayed her. And the hunters were coming back, and quite close, when she slipped out. One could just see the shadow of a pair of feet.

"What was that," said one. "It looked like a pair of feet vanishing away."

"Listen, and I will tell you," said Qalagánguasê, who already felt his strength returning. "The house has been full of people, and they made the night pass pleasantly for me, and now, they say, I am to grow strong again."

But hardly had the boy said these words, when the strength slowly began to leave him.

"Qalagánguasê is to be challenged to a singing contest," he heard them say, as he lay there. And then they tied the boy to the frame post and let him swing backwards and forwards, as he tried to beat the drum. After that, they all made ready, and set out for their singing contest, and left the lame boy behind in the house all alone. And there he lay all alone, when his mother, who had died long since, came in with his father.

"Why are you here alone?" they asked.

"I am lame," said the boy, "and when the others went off to a singing contest, they left me behind."

"Come away with us," said his father and mother.

"It is better so, perhaps," said the boy.

And so they led him out, and bore him away to the land of ghosts, and so Qalagánguasê became a ghost.

And it is said that Qalagánguasê became a woman when they changed him to a ghost. But his fellow villagers never saw him again.

The Land of the Dead

A YOUNG WOMAN on the Lower Yukon died. When she died she went to sleep for a while. Then someone shook her arm and said, "Get up. Do not sleep. You are dead." Then she saw she was in her grave box and the shade of her grandfather was shaking her. Then she went with her grandfather back to the village, but the country she knew had disappeared. In its place was a strange village which reached as far as the eye could see.

As she entered the village, the old man told her to go into one of the houses. As soon as she entered it, a woman picked up a stick of wood and raised it to strike her. The woman said, "What do you want here?"

So the young woman ran out, crying to her grandfather. He said, "This is the village of the dog shades. Now you see how living dogs feel when beaten by people."

They came to another village. Here she saw a man lying on the ground with grass growing up through his joints. He could move, but he could not rise. The grandfather said this shade was punished for pulling up and chewing grass stems when he was on earth. Then the grandfather suddenly disappeared.

The girl followed a trail to another village, but she came to a swift river. This river was made up of the tears of people who on earth weep for the dead. When the girl saw she could not cross the river, she began to weep. At once a mass of straw floated down the river to her. Upon this, as a bridge, she crossed the stream. Before she reached the village, the shades smelled her. They crowded around her, saying, "Who is she? Where does she come from?" They looked for the totem marks on her clothing.

Someone said, "Where is she? Where is she?" and her grandfather came toward her. He led her into a house nearby and there was her grandmother. The old woman asked her if she was thirsty. The girl looked about and saw only one water vessel made like those of her own village. This had in it their own Yukon water. It had been given them at the festival of the dead by the girl's father. The other tubs had only the water of the village of the shades. The old woman gave the girl a piece of deer fat. This, too, had been given at the festival of the dead. Then the grandmother explained that the guide had been the grandfather because the last person thought of by a dying person hurries away to show the road to the new shade. Thoughts are heard in the land of the shades.

The Return of the Dead Wife

ONCE UPON A time, there lived in Alaska a chief of the Tlingit tribe who had one son. When the boy grew to be a man, he saw a girl who seemed to him prettier and cleverer than any other girl of the tribe, and his heart went out to her, and he told his father. Then the chief spoke to the father and the mother of the girl, and they agreed to give her to the young man for a wife. So the two were married, and for a few months all went well with them and they were very happy.

But one day, the husband came home from hunting and found his wife sitting crouched over the fire – her eyes dull and her head heavy.

"You are ill," he said, "I will go for the shaman," but the girl answered:

"No, not now. I will sleep, and in the morning the pains will have gone from me."

But in the morning she was dead, and the young man grieved bitterly and would eat nothing, and he lay awake all that night thinking of his wife, and the next night also.

"Perhaps if I went out into the forest and walked till I was tired, I might sleep and forget my pain," thought he. But, after all, he could not bear to leave the house while his dead wife was in it, so he waited till her body was taken away that evening for burial. Then, very early next morning, he put on his leggings and set off into the forest and walked through that day and the following night. Sunrise on the second morning found him in a wide valley covered with thick trees. Before him stretched a plain which had once been full of water, but it was now dried up.

He paused for a moment and looked about him, and as he looked he seemed to hear voices speaking a long way off. But he could see nobody, and walked on again till he beheld a light shining through the branches of the trees and noticed a flat stone on the edge of a lake. Here the road stopped; for it was the death road along which he had come, though he did not know it.

The lake was narrow, and on the other side were houses and people going in and out of them.

"Come over and fetch me," he shouted, but nobody heard him, though he cried till he was hoarse.

"It is very odd that nobody hears me," whispered the youth after he had shouted for some time longer; and at that minute a person standing at the door of one of the houses across the lake cried out:

"Someone is shouting," for they could hear him when he whispered, but not when he made a great noise.

"It is somebody who has come from dreamland," continued the voice. "Let a canoe go and bring him over." So a canoe shot out from the shore, and the young man got into it and was paddled across, and as soon as he stepped out he saw his dead wife.

Joy rushed into his heart at the sight of her; her eyes were red as though she had been crying; and he held out his hands. As he did so the people in the house said to him:

"You must have come from far; sit down, and we will give you food," and they spread food before him, at which he felt glad, for he was hungry.

"Don't eat that," whispered his wife. "If you do, you will never get back again"; and he listened to her and did not eat it.

Then his wife said again:

"It is not good for you to stay here. Let us depart at once," and they hastened to the edge of the water and got into the canoe, which is called the Ghost's Canoe, and is the only one on the lake. They were soon across and they landed at the flat stone where the young man had stood when he was shouting, and the name of that stone is the Ghost's Rock. Down they went along the road that he had come, and on the second night they reached the youth's house.

"Stay here," he said, "and I will go in and tell my father." So he entered and said to his father:

"I have brought my wife back."

"Well, why don't you bring her in?" asked the chief, and he took a fur robe and laid it on top of a mat for her to sit on. After that, the young man led his wife into the house, but the people inside could not see her enter, but only her husband; yet when he came quite close, they noticed a deep shadow behind him. The young man bade his wife sit down on the mat they had prepared for her, and a robe of marten skins was placed over her shoulders, and it hung upon her as if she had been a real woman and not a ghost. Then they put food before her, and, as she ate, they beheld her arms, and the spoon moving up and down. But the shadow of her hands they did not see, and it seemed strange to them.

Now from henceforth, the young man and his wife always went everywhere together; whether he was hunting or fishing, the shadow always followed him, and he begged to have his bed made where they had first seated themselves, instead of in the room where he had slept before. And this the people in the house did gladly, for joy at having him back.

In the day, if they happened not to be away hunting or fishing, the wife was so quiet that no one would have guessed she was there, but during the night she would play games with her husband and talk to him, so that the others could hear her voice. At her first coming, the chief felt silent and awkward, but after a while he grew accustomed to her and would pretend to be angry and called out, "You had better get up now, after keeping everyone awake all night with your games," and they could hear the shadow laugh in answer, and knew it was the laugh of the dead woman.

Thus things went on for some time, and they might have gone on longer, had not a cousin of the dead girl's, who had wanted to marry her before she married the chief's son, become jealous when he found that her husband had brought her back from across the lake. And he spied upon her, and listened to her when she was talking, hoping for a chance to work her some ill. At last the chance came, as it commonly does, and it was in this wise:

Night after night the jealous man had hidden himself at the head of the bed, and had stolen away unperceived in the morning without having heard anything to help his wicked plans. He was beginning to think he must try something else, when one evening the girl suddenly said to her husband that she was tired of being a shadow, and was going to show herself in the body that she used to have, and meant to keep it always. The husband was glad in his soul at her words, and then proposed that they should get up and play a game as usual; and, while they were playing, the man behind the curtains peeped through. As he did so, a noise as of a rattling of bones rang through the house, and when the people came running, they found the husband dead and the shadow gone, for the ghosts of both had sped back to Ghostland.

A Journey to Xibalba

MYSTERY VEILS THE commencement of the Second Book of the *Popol Vuh,* the sacred narrative text of the K'iche' Maya people. The theme is the birth and family of Hun-Ahpu and Xbalanque, and the scribe intimates that only half is to be told concerning the history of their father. Xpiyacoc and Xmucane, the father and mother deities, had two sons, Hunhun-Ahpu and Vukub-Hunahpu, the first being, so far as can be gathered, a bi-sexual personage. He had by a wife, Xbakiyalo, two sons, Hunbatz and Hunchouen, men full of wisdom and artistic genius. All of them were addicted to the recreation of dicing and playing at ball, and a spectator of their pastimes was Voc, the messenger of Hurakan. Xbakiyalo having died, Hunhun-Ahpu and

Vukub-Hunahpu, leaving the former's sons behind, played a game of ball, which in its progress took them into the vicinity of the realm of Xibalba (the Underworld). This reached the ears of the monarchs of that place, Hun-Came and Vukub-Came, who, after consulting their counsellors, challenged the strangers to a game of ball, with the object of defeating and disgracing them.

For this purpose, they dispatched four messengers in the shape of owls. The brothers accepted the challenge, after a touching farewell with their mother Xmucane, and their sons and nephews, and followed the feathered heralds down the steep incline to Xibalba from the playground at Ninxor Carchah. After an ominous crossing over a river of blood, they came to the residence of the kings of Xibalba, where they underwent the mortification of mistaking two wooden figures for the monarchs. Invited to sit on the seat of honour, they discovered it to be a red-hot stone, and the contortions which resulted from their successful trick caused unbounded merriment among the Xibalbans. Then they were thrust into the House of Gloom, where they were sacrificed and buried. The head of Hunhun-Ahpu was, however, suspended from a tree, which speedily became covered with gourds, from which it was almost impossible to distinguish the bloody trophy. All in Xibalba were forbidden the fruit of that tree.

But one person in Xibalba had resolved to disobey the mandate. This was the virgin princess Xquiq (Blood), the daughter of Cuchumaquiq, who went unattended to the spot. Standing under the branches, gazing at the fruit, the maiden stretched out her hand, and the head of Hunhun-Ahpu spat into the palm. The spittle caused her to conceive, and she returned home, being assured by the head of the hero-god that no harm should result to her. This thing was done by order of Hurakan, the Heart of Heaven. In six months' time her father became aware of her condition, and despite her protestations, the royal messengers of Xibalba, the owls, received orders to kill her and return with her heart in a vase. She, however, escaped by bribing the owls with splendid promises for the future to spare her and substitute for her heart the coagulated sap of the bloodwort.

In her extremity, Xquiq went for protection to the home of Xmucane, who now looked after the young Hunbatz and Hunchouen. Xmucane would not at first believe her tale. But Xquiq appealed to the gods, and performed a miracle by gathering a basket of maize where no maize grew, and thus gained her confidence.

Shortly afterwards, Xquiq became the mother of twin boys, the heroes of the First Book, Hun-Ahpu, and Xbalanque. These did not find favour in the eyes of Xmucane, their grandmother. Their infantile cries aroused the wrath of this venerable person, and she vented it upon them by turning them out of doors. They speedily took to an outdoor life, however, and became mighty hunters, and expert in the use of their blowpipes, with which they shot birds and other small game. The ill-treatment which they received from Hunbatz and Hunchouen caused them at last to retaliate, and those who had made their lives miserable were punished by being transformed by the divine children into apes. The venerable Xmucane, filled with grief at the metamorphosis and flight of her ill-starred grandsons, who had made her home joyous with their singing and flute-playing, was told that she would be permitted to behold their faces once more if she could do so without losing her gravity, but their antics and grimaces caused her such merriment that on three separate occasions she was unable to restrain her laughter and the men-monkeys appeared no more. Hun-Ahpu and Xbalanque now became expert musicians, and one of their favourite airs was that of 'Hun-Ahpu qoy', the 'monkey of Hun-Ahpu'.

The divine twins were now old enough to undertake labour in the field, and their first task was the clearing of a milpa or maize plantation. They were possessed of magic tools, which had the merit of working themselves in the absence of the young hunters at the chase, and those they found a capital substitute for their own directing presence upon the first day. Returning at night from hunting, they smeared their faces and hands with dirt so that Xmucane might be deceived into imagining that they had been hard at work in the maize field. But during the night, the wild beasts met and replaced all the roots and shrubs which the brothers – or rather their magic tools – had removed. The twins resolved to watch for them on the ensuing night, but despite all their efforts the animals succeeded in making good their escape, save one, the rat, which was caught in a handkerchief. The rabbit and deer lost their tails in getting away. The rat, in gratitude that they had spared its life, told them of the glorious deeds of their great fathers and uncles, their games at ball, and of the existence of a set of implements necessary to play the game which they had left in the house. They discovered these, and went to play in the ball-ground of their fathers.

It was not long, however, until Hun-Came and Vukub-Came, the princes of Xibalba, heard them at play, and decided to lure them to the Underworld as they had lured their fathers. Messengers were despatched to the house of Xmucane, who, filled with alarm, despatched a louse to carry the message to her grandsons. The louse, wishing to ensure greater speed to reach the brothers, consented to be swallowed by a toad, the toad by a serpent, and the serpent by the great bird Voc. The other animals duly liberated one another; but despite his utmost efforts, the toad could not get rid of the louse, who had played him a trick by lodging in his gums, and had not been swallowed at all. The message, however, was duly delivered, and the players returned home to take leave of their grandmother and mother. Before their departure, they each planted a cane in the middle of the house, which was to acquaint those they left behind with their welfare, since it would wither if any fatal circumstance befell them.

Pursuing the route their fathers had followed, they passed the river of blood and the river Papuhya. But they sent an animal called Xan as *avant courier* with orders to prick all the Xibalbans with a hair from Hun-Ahpu's leg, thus discovering those of the dwellers in the Underworld who were made of wood – those whom their fathers had unwittingly bowed to as men – and also learning the names of the others by their inquiries and explanations when pricked. Thus they did not salute the mannikins on their arrival at the Xibalban court, nor did they sit upon the red-hot stone. They even passed scatheless through the first ordeal of the House of Gloom. The Xibalbans were furious, and their wrath was by no means allayed when they found themselves beaten at the game of ball to which they had challenged the brothers. Then Hun-Came and Vukub-Came ordered the twins to bring them four bouquets of flowers, asking the guards of the royal gardens to watch most carefully, and committed Hun-Ahpu and Xbalanque to the 'House of Lances' – the second ordeal – where the lancers were directed to kill them. The brothers, however, had at their beck and call a swarm of ants, which entered the royal gardens on the first errand, and they succeeded in bribing the lancers. The Xibalbans, white with fury, ordered that the owls, the guardians of the gardens, should have their lips split, and otherwise showed their anger at their third defeat.

Then came the third ordeal in the 'House of Cold'. Here the heroes escaped death by freezing by being warmed with burning pinecones. In the fourth and fifth ordeals they were equally lucky, for they passed a night each in the 'House of Tigers' and the 'House of Fire' without injury. But at the sixth ordeal, misfortune overtook them in the 'House of Bats', Hun-Ahpu's head being cut off by Camazotz, 'Ruler of Bats', who suddenly appeared from above.

The beheading of Hun-Ahpu does not, however, appear to have terminated fatally, but owing to the unintelligible nature of the text at this juncture, it is impossible to ascertain in what manner he was cured of such a lethal wound. This episode is followed by an assemblage of all the animals, and another contest at ball-playing, after which the brothers emerged uninjured from all the ordeals of the Xibalbans.

But in order to further astound their 'hosts', Hun-Ahpu and Xbalanque confided to two sorcerers named Xulu and Pacaw that the Xibalbans had failed because the animals were not on their side, and directing them what to do with their bones, they stretched themselves upon a funeral pile and died together. Their bones were beaten to powder and thrown into the river, where they sank, and were transformed into young men. On the fifth day, they reappeared like men-fish, and on the sixth in the form of ragged old men, dancing, burning and restoring houses, killing and restoring each other to life, with other wonders. The princes of Xibalba, hearing of their skill, requested them to exhibit their magical powers, which they did by burning the royal palace and restoring it, killing and resuscitating the king's dog, and cutting a man in pieces, and bringing him to life again. The monarchs of Xibalba, anxious to experience the novel sensation of a temporary death, requested to be slain and resuscitated. They were speedily killed, but the brothers refrained from resuscitating their arch-enemies.

Announcing their real names, the brothers proceeded to punish the princes of Xibalba. The game of ball was forbidden them, they were to perform menial tasks, and only the beasts of the forest were they to hold in vassalage. They appear after this to achieve a species of doubtful distinction as plutonic deities or demons. They are described as warlike, ugly as owls, inspiring evil and discord. Their faces were painted black and white to show their faithless nature.

Xmucane, waiting at home for the brothers, was alternately filled with joy and grief as the canes grew green and withered, according to the varying fortunes of her grandsons. These young men were busied at Xibalba with paying fitting funeral honours to their father and uncle, who now mounted to heaven and became the Sun and Moon, whilst the four hundred youths slain by Zipacna became the stars. Thus concludes the Second Book.

The Boat that Went to Pulotu

THIS IS THE story of the gods that went to Pulotu (the unseen world, the land of the departed) in a boat. There was one god whose name was Plaveatoke (Slippery Eel), another whose name was Fakafuumaka (Like-a-Big Stone), another whose name was Haelefeke (Octopus-Comes, or Walking-Octopus), and the last one's name was Lohi (Lie). These four embarked in their boat and paddled away with the intention of journeying to Pulotu.

As they were passing a part of the coast not far from their starting point a goddess named Faimalie (Take-Care or Perform-Fortunately) was standing on the beach. She called to them; 'Why are you coming here and where are you going?' The gods in the boat told her that they were going to Pulotu. Then the goddess cried: 'Come here and we will all go together.'

Then the gods in the boat said: 'We tell you that the boat is overloaded.' But Faimalie persisted, saying: 'I will go too and sit on the outrigger, or else bail the water from the boat.' The four gods in the boat held a consultation. 'What is the use of this old woman coming with us? But it might be as well to ask old Faimalie, who is very anxious to come, of what use she would be.' So the gods in the boat called out: 'Of what use would you be, old woman, you who are so anxious to accompany us?' Faimalie at once replied: 'Let me go with you. I will be of some little use.' The gods in the boat, becoming impatient, cried: 'Come then. We will go together.' They continued their voyage towards Pulotu after getting Faimalie aboard. There were thus five of them altogether and they exulted in their own strength.

At last they reached Pulotu and dragged their boat up on the beach. Then they went to the house of Hikuleo (Watching Tail), who was out at the time and hid there. When the people of Pulotu came down to the beach, they saw the boat and asked one another: 'Whose boat is this? Perhaps it is a boat from the world.'

So they guessed until they were tired. Then someone suggested that as the boat was there its crew must be somewhere about, especially because the boat smelt as if people from the world had been in it. Several suggested: 'Well, let us search and perhaps we will find them.' So they searched and searched, but could not discover them anywhere. Then they went and told Flikuleo: 'There is a boat on the beach. We think it is a boat from the world, but we cannot find her people, or even their whereabouts.'

Their inability to find the five gods from the world is not remarkable, for the five had transformed themselves and hidden most effectually. One of them had transformed himself into a small insect and had entered one of the big posts that supported the roof. From this vantage point he was quietly watching the people of Pulotu as they searched for him and his companions. Others had gone into the ground. One was hidden in the big cross beam of the house, but Fakafuumaka (Like-a-Big-Stone) simply lay down in the doorway. When the people were searching, they paid no attention to him, saying, 'It is only a big stone.' Thus he escaped.

Hikuleo then addressed the people, saying, 'So you are tired of searching for the gods from the World. Then go, someone and tell the Haama–takikila (Those of the Piercing Eyes) to come and see what they can do. They came and glared until their eyes were nearly falling out, but were unable to find the intruders. Then they told Hikuleo: 'We have looked and looked until our eyes are sore, but we have to admit defeat.' So saying, they departed.

Then the gods that were in hiding breathed audibly in mockery of the Haamatakikila who had been looking for them so earnestly. Hearing the breathing, the people of Pulotu exclaimed at once, 'The gods must be hiding here, for they are breathing to mock us, because we cannot find them.' Again they searched but without success, until some one said, 'Let us go and get the Haafakanamunamu (Those of the Keen Scent), so that they can smell out the gods from the world, for we are tired of searching and Those of the Piercing Eyes were unable to find them.' So they called out, saying, 'Come, ye of the Keen Scent.'

Those of the Keen Scent came and smelt and sniffed in every direction, until they were tired. Then they departed, as they were unable to find the gods from the world. Again the gods in hiding breathed loudly in derision. The people of Pulotu were tired of asking each other whence the breathing came, so they called to the Guessers to come and guess and perhaps thus be able to find the hiding places of the gods from the world. The Guessers came and guessed until they were tired, but not a bit wiser as to the whereabouts of the lurking gods. Being tired of guessing they went away. Whereupon, the people of Pulotu told Those-of-the-Sharp–Ears (Faahingatelingaongo) to try. They came and listened and listened until they were weary. Then they departed.

Thereat Hikuleo said, 'Come you and lift up my palanquin. I will go and examine into these things and into the gods that seem almighty. There are people in Pulotu that are supposed to know everything and yet they are weary. In fact, we are all weary. Where is there a greater chief, or one that can compare with me? Yet we are tired of searching for these gods from the world.'

Addressing the gods from the world, who were in hiding, Hikuleo said: 'Show yourselves to us that we may meet, for we cannot find you.' So the gods of the world showed themselves and each one spoke from his hiding place. 'It is I, Haveatoke (Slippery Eel).' Then another spoke from his hiding place: 'It is I, Fakafuumaka (Like a Big Stone).' Again, another spoke from his place of concealment: 'It is I, Haelefeke (Octopus Comes).' Then another, from his hiding place, called out: 'It is I, the Lie (Lohi).' The last one then spoke and said: 'It is I, Faimalie (Take Care).' That is how the five gods from the world introduced themselves to Hikuleo and the people of Pulotu.

Thus they met Hikuleo and the people of Pulotu and these were heard to remark: 'These gods from the world are most wonderful on account of their power. We grew weary of searching for them.' Hikuleo then said: 'Several of you go and get me a very large piece of kava and we will drink kava with the gods from the world.'

A great concourse of people went away to bring in the kava. They cut down twenty coconut trees to carry it on, so immense was the piece of kava which they brought. Some compared it with a country, so large was it. They brought the kava to Hikuleo and to the gods from the world, who returned thanks for the huge kava that had been brought to them. They remarked that they themselves were only fools and commoners (*tua*).

Hikuleo then spoke to the gods from the world: 'Listen to what I have to say to you, gods who have come from the world. We will drink this kava that has been brought, but if you do not drink so as to finish it, you will be murdered, for you are only common gods who have been stopping all the time in the world. You suddenly drift into Pulotu. But is it permissible for gods who are but commoners and fools to come to Pulotu?'

The kava was cut in small pieces and chewed until it was soft; then the bowl was brought and placed ready to mix the kava. It was an enormous bowl. Some compared it with a huge open space, whilst others said it was as large as all of Haapai. The kava was then mixed and was like the sea, so enormous was the bowl.

Then the gods from the world wept, being frightened, for they were not much accustomed to kava drinking. Hikuleo addressed them sternly: 'If the kava is not finished, we will kill you.' Haveatoke, one of the gods from the world cried. Fakafuumaka, another of the mundane gods, wept also. Then another one of them, Haelefeke, likewise cried. Lohi also began to shed tears and all the four gods from the world wept together. Only the old woman, the goddess Faimalie, with a flat nose, sat quiet. She was the only god that did not weep, but sat silent while the other four lamented.

The kava was next strained and, when it was clear, it was dealt out to Haveatoke to drink first. Pie drained the cup, but it made him drunk. Again the cup was filled and brought to Fakafuumaka. He drank to the dregs and also became drunk. Again the kava was served, this time to Haelefeke and with the same effect. Once more the cup was passed and Lohi became drunk. In fact, the whole four became drunk. Faimalie, who had not had her kava, now spoke, addressing her four companions: 'How do you feel? Cannot you endure more kava? Will you be carried away by a little kava?' the four of them replied: 'We cannot possibly drink any more. Our stomachs are full and we are drunk.'

Then said Faimalie, rating her companions: 'To be sure, you did not want to take me on board. I have come because I almost compelled you to take me. You told me to remain behind, because the boat was overloaded. I was of no use anyhow, you said. But I told you that I would come and that I had a little use, even if I came only to bail the boat.

'Now you are not able to drink the kava. If I had not come, but remained behind, would you have been able to drink this kava? As it is, you are drunk. This kava is enough to make us afraid, because we cannot drink it and we will be killed very shortly.'

Then Hikuleo interrupted and ordered silence. She now said to Faimalie: 'What is it, old woman, that you are talking about? Has no kava been brought to you to drink? What does it mean?'

Faimalie replied, saying to Hikuleo in a respectful manner: 'Do not trouble. I will run and drink my kava from the bowl.' Then Faimalie stood up in order to go and drink from the great bowl the kava that had not been served to her. Bending down she drank from the middle of the bowl. She drank and drank until the kava was finished. Then she swallowed the bowl and ate the fiber strainer and the stalks of the kava. Next she ate the twenty coconut trees on which the kava had been brought. She swallowed the whole lot together with the pulverized root of the kava from which the infusion had been made. All of these did Faimalie swallow, and nothing was left.

This made Hikuleo and all of the people of Pulotu very angry and they said: 'Dear me, this boat that has come from the world is very cheeky.' Then Hikuleo commanded the people of Pulotu: 'Go and make known to all of the people in Pulotu that every man has to prepare an oven of yams, breadfruit, taro and other things. Furthermore, every man is to bring a roast pig. Thus we will pay our respects to this boat and the gods from the world.' So all of Pulotu worked at their ovens and roasted pigs, an oven and a pig to each man. The cooked food was brought to the gods from the world to show the respect of the people of Pulotu. Then Hikuleo said: 'Come and eat this. If it is not all eaten, you will be killed.'

Haveatoke, Fakafuumaka, Haelefeke, and Lohi, the whole four of them, began to weep, but Faimalie did not cry; she remained quiet. The four cried when they saw the enormous size of the pile of food. But how about eating it? That thought was what made them weep, because if the food was not finished they would be murdered.

Faimalie, the old woman with the flat nose, asked: 'What are you crying about?' The four told her: 'We are crying because our feast will not be entirely eaten. There are so many baskets of food and pigs that they are piled up almost to the sky. How are we to eat them?' Faimalie replied: 'You four come and eat first, you Haveatoke, you Fakafuumaka, you Haelefeke, and you Lohi. Is there anything you can do?' she inquired scathingly. 'You eat one basket of food and one pig. What there is left leave to me. I will go and see what I can do.' The four responded, saying: 'Very well, Faimalie. You wait a little. We will eat first and you eat afterwards, for we fear that we cannot finish the food and that we will be killed stone dead.' Faimalie's only response was: 'You eat.'

So the four started to eat, but were not able to finish even one pig. One yam each and a small piece of pork were all they were able to eat, and then they were full, surfeited in fact. Then they said to Faimalie: 'We are finished and cannot eat any more, as we are full and surfeited.' Then Faimalie, the old woman with the flat nose, replied: 'The reason you gave for not wanting to bring me from the world was that I was of no use and had better remain behind. Yet were it not for me you would have been murdered in the kava drinking a short time ago. Wait a little and I will go and eat.'

Faimalie started to eat. She ate first all the yams and pigs and they were finished. Then she ate the leaves that had covered the ovens; after that the ropes that were used to carry the baskets and the sticks by which the baskets were carried. In fact, she ate everything and nothing remained.

This made Hikuleo and all the chiefs in Pulotu very angry and they said: 'Really, this boat, that has come from the world, is exceedingly cheeky. But let us find something that they will not be able to do.' Then Hikuleo said: 'Tell Haveatoke, Fakafuumaka, Haelefeke, Lohi, and Faimalie to come here, or at least one of them that is clever in any sport. We will hold a sports competition, but we will wait until our sportsmen go along. The sport that will be tried first,' said Hikuleo addressing the five gods from the world, 'is surf riding. If some one of you cannot ride the surf, you will all be killed.'

Upon hearing this the five gods from the world held a consultation, inquiring: 'Which one of us is clever in each particular sport? If we are weak in surf riding, we will be killed. Hikuleo and the chiefs of Pulotu have selected something in which we are not accomplished. If we fail we will die. The gods of Pulotu are boasting that surf riding is the sport in which they are strong.' Thus the gods from the world kept inquiring who was the cleverest in surf riding.

Then spoke Faimalie, the old woman who ate so much, saying: 'I will not be of any use, because I cannot go into the water on account of my sickness. My nose is bad and that is why I cannot go surf riding and indulge in similar sports which require diving about in the sea.' Then spoke Haveatoke (Slippery Eel), saying: 'Leave it to me. I will go and ride the surf, for that is what I can do well.'

So the two contestants, the god from Pulotu and the god from the world, went down to the sea and swam, while Hikuleo and the people of Pulotu sat and watched to see who would be first in the surf riding. The two gods rode the boiling surf. The people of Pulotu began to breathe freely, for they felt that their champion would win. They roundly abused and ridiculed the gods from the world, because they felt happy in the thought that Pulotu would be victorious in the surf riding. The two contestants dived into the surf, rose together, came in abreast, and lay on the sand. They went out again, while the people of Pulotu increased their ridicule, for they were light-hearted to think that they would be the stronger in the sport of surf riding. Again the champions went out and returned together, and so again and again they went. Suddenly, however, Haveatoke, the god from the world, made a jump at the god from Pulotu, bit the back of his neck, and killed him at once. Then he went ashore and claimed the victory and the gods of Pulotu were once more beaten.

This defeat of Pulotu made Hikuleo very angry and she said that there was no one of any use in Pulotu, for they had not been victorious in any contest. However, Hikuleo decided to have another contest and she said to the gods from the world: 'We have an expert diver. If there is one of you that can hold his breath a long time, let him come and pit himself against our man, who is long winded.' Then the gods from the world held a conference. There was not one that was used to diving or that was long winded, and if they were beaten in the contest they would be murdered. Old Faimalie said: 'I am not any use in diving, so you four settle the matter of that sport among yourselves.' Then one of them, Fakafuumaaka (Like a Big Stone), volunteered and said, 'Leave it to me to go. I will dive with the Pulotu champion.'

Fakafuumaaka went at once with the Pulotu diver and they dived and remained at the bottom. Meanwhile Hikuleo and all the people of Pulotu, together with the crew of the boat from the world, Haveatoke, Haelefeke, Lohi, and Faimalie, watched the diving to see who would come to the end of his breath first and rise to the surface to breathe.

So the two contestants dived and dived and remained at the bottom of the sea. For one night they dived and for two nights they dived and then they remained at the bottom of the sea for ten nights. At last a month had passed and still they were down on the bottom of the sea and neither was so short winded that he had to rise to the surface. So there they remained, when lo, the Pulotu diver's breath gave out and he made as if to go up to the surface to breathe. When Fakafuumaaka perceived that his rival wanted to go up for breath, he rushed him and jumped on his head and neck and held him, in order to prevent his rising to the surface to save his life. Fakafuumaaka caught him in his arms and held him until he was dead. When the victor knew that his Pulotu rival was dead and his flesh had become rotten and stinking in the sea, he then went up to the surface of the sea, having thus killed the Pulotu diver.

This defeat of the Pulotu champion angered Hikuleo and the Pulotu chiefs very much and they said: 'There is nothing good here. This small boat with only a few people has arrived and is able to overcome us. Let us choose something else.' 'But,' inquired Hikuleo, 'what other sports still remain that we can use to try conclusions with this vessel and the gods from the world?'

Then replied several Pulotu people: 'There are plenty more sports, but they are only games. We have exhausted our difficult sports, such as surf riding and diving, in which we lost two of our number. There is not one difficult sport left.'

'There remains yet one thing, our big tree,' said Hikuleo. It was a *vi* tree (*Spondias dulcis*) of enormous size, so large, in fact, that it nearly filled the whole of Pulotu with its branches, trunk, and fruit. Hikuleo continued, addressing the visitors: 'Gods from the world, which one of you is clever enough to catch and pluck the fruit which you must eat?'

Haveatoke, Fakafuumaka, Haelefeke, Lohi, and Faimalie discussed the matter and said: 'Who can catch all the fruit of that huge *vi* tree? It looks exceedingly difficult.' They were afraid and in their fright they said to themselves: 'This is too much, but if we are not able to accomplish it, we are sure to be murdered.' They thought about and discussed the matter, because Hikuleo had said to them: 'When plucking the vi only one person may come to catch the fruit. If any falls to the ground, you gods of the world will be slain. If you catch all the fruit, you will be allowed to live, for this is the last trial in Pulotu. However, when you have plucked and caught all the fruit, you must eat it so that none remains. If it is not all finished, you will be killed.'

So they held consultation together, did the gods of the world, almost weeping, because they thought they would be unable to catch all the fruit without one falling to the ground. Then said one god, Haelefeke by name: 'Leave it to me. I will catch all of the fruit of the *vi* tree, so that not one shall fall to the ground.'

Haelefeke came forward and lay his head on the roots of the tree, face upwards. Then he put some of his tentacles up so that they held the branches in one direction, but still his tentacles went up and along the branches until all were encompassed. By this means he would be able to catch and pluck all of the fruit, so that none should fall to the ground, otherwise the five gods from the world would be slain. Then he shook the tree to make the fruit fall, but not one touched the ground, for all were caught by Haelefeke. Once more Pulotu was beaten.

Great was Pulotu's wrath and Hikuleo said: 'Come now, and eat the fruit of the *vi*. If you do not finish it, you will be killed. Understand, this is absolutely the last of your trials.' Haveatoke, Fakafuumaka, Haelefeke, and Lohi commenced to eat, but they soon wearied for they were not great eaters. They said to Faimalie: 'Faimalie, you come and eat, for we ourselves do not care for the vi fruit. We are tired of it and besides we are full and our stomachs have turned against it. If you love us, then come.' And continued the gods to Faimalie: 'You come and finish the vi, for this is the last of Hikuleo's petty tyranny to us. If we are able to accomplish this feat of eating all the fruit, then we will be able to return to the world alive.' Faimalie obligingly came and finished all the fruit, then ate all the leaves, so that not one remained. Then she ate the branches and finished by devouring the whole trunk of the huge tree.

This annoyed Hikuleo and all of the chiefs of Pulotu exceedingly, so that they drove away the boat of the gods of the world and Hikuleo addressed them thus: 'Get back to the world. Do not dare to come here again and pretend to be important and to play tricks. You came, you low born ones. But where did you come from? The world. That is the place of the low commoners. Get ye hence.'

The gods from the world departed, but Faimalie came away with something, a yam she had swallowed. She buried it beneath a fire and when she lifted it out, she found that it was burnt on one side but quite raw on the other. Taking it up she put it out of sight. Another god, Lohi, stole some taro from Pulotu and hid it about his person. That was the beginning of taro in Tonga. He planted it in his island of Eua. All taro started in Eua, for it was stolen from Pulotu by Lohi.

Besides the yam, Faimalie also stole the fish known as the *o*. When Faimalie came back, she gave birth to the yam in the bush and that portion of the bush is known as Koloi. It is in the part of the country called Haamotuku. Faimalie went to dwell in the bush so that she might give birth. After she was delivered, the yam was called *kahokaho*. It is amongst the finest and best of yams, fit for chiefs. There are also the *manange* and *levei* and that is all of the chiefs' yams. There are a great many other sorts of yams. There are plenty of white yams, as well as purple yams, but the origin of these particular yams is in the one brought by Faimalie, as also the fish, and the taro brought by Lohi. But the yams known as the *tuaata* and the *nguata* are different. These were early yams, for they fell from the sky on to the island of Ata (near Tongatabu). Then there is the yam *heketala*, that was brought from heaven to Ilaheva and Ahoeitu by an old woman called Vaepopua. These were the earliest yams in Tonga. Faimalie came afterwards from Pulotu with the different sorts of yams and in giving birth leaned her back against a tree known as the *masikoka*. The place was called 'The Resting Place.'

This is the conclusion of the tale of the boat belonging to the gods called Haveatoke, Fakafuumaka, Haelefeke, and Lohi. The vessel came from Eua and went to Pulotu. Only four were going, but an old woman stood on the beach at the end of the island. It was she who called to the boat that there might be five persons to go to Pulotu. This is the end of the tale of the gods that went to Pulotu, their challenge, and their strength, and of the overcoming of Plikuleo and all the people of Pulotu.

The Burial of Te Heu-Heu on Tongariro

DREAMILY IS NGAWAI staring into the embers, whilst the pale new morning is crawling through the spaces between the fern-stems which form the walls of the mountain-whare (hut).

Cold and pale at first appear the long stripes painted over the floor, till they change slowly into warmer and more glowing colours, lighting up the calabashes, the nets, the paddles, and the mats, which hang on the walls smoke-blackened under the raupo roof. The stripes of daylight are able, too, to light up Ngawai's eyes, which stare into the nearly burnt-out embers. More fiery glow the stripes, and suddenly they flood the whare with wonderful golden light: it is pure gold, through which, like music, the blue smoke ascends to the roof. Now the Sunshine pours in at the door, and with it the wonderful picture of the mountain-lake, reflecting the mountain giants, to the astonished eye. And in all the beautiful world life commences again with laughter and happiness – the laughter and happiness of the parting day.

Slowly is the sun wandering his way in the skies; up to the height of midday he wanders; the shades grow longer, and Rangi-o-mohio, a very old woman, the daughter of the famous Rangatira Te Heu-heu, is still relating:

'Listen: A great procession is ascending with much noise and shouting and frolic the barren wilderness around the stone-body of Tongariro – a great procession of Tohungas, warriors, women, and children.

Ah, Iwikau the Rangatira is leader, and they carry the bones of Te Heu-heu, my father. – Ah, Te Heu-heu, he was my father! Ah, with his bones we wander and crawl and climb over the lonely wilderness. Ah, he was the Rangatira over the lands – but, my son, look upon the greatest Rangatira of all the lands: look upon the Tongariro-tapu!'

Ngawai listens to the narrative of the old Rangi-o-mohio whilst her eyes are gazing upon the sacred Tongariro. The moon has risen over the lake, and a fine silvery gleam is glittering upon the snow of the mountain, which is sending its beautiful column of silver high up into the skies. Then once more Ngawai looks sorrowfully back, and goes on her way to her people in the distant pa.

This is Rangi-a-mohio's story:

Iwikau, the brother of the dead Rangatira Te Heu-heu, and chief now over the tribe of the Ngati-tu-wharetoa, is the leader of a large procession of sorrowing, weeping people of the tribe. The four greatest warriors of the tribe carried the carved box which contained the bones of Te Heu-heu; it was painted red, and adorned with white albatross-feathers.

The whole tribe had decided to give their dead Rangatira the mightiest burial-ground in all Ao-tea-roa – the crater of Tongariro-tapu!

Truly, the mountain Tongariro shall swallow the bones of the Rangatira, that they never may fall in the hands of man – perhaps enemies.

The sharp-edged coke-rocks cut the feet of the bearers, and the sulphur in the air is the deadliest foe to frolic – and what can be properly done without frolic in Maoriland? The feet of the bearers begin to bleed, the incantations of the Tohungas grow weaker; less overbearing, too, become the songs of defiance which Iwikau is shouting to the gods: silence and ghostly fright fall upon the multitude.

Deeper now are the precipices, steeper the rocks, and hellish the sulphurous fumes; but high above still towers the crater, the summit of Tongariro, the mighty grave of the Rangatira! The sacred mountain shall swallow the bones of the sacred chief – as the base of the mountain, in a frightful landslip, has swallowed his life!

Great is the conception, and bravely they try to carry it into effect beneath the mighty column of steam and sulphur which Tongariro is streaming out and which the heaven is pressing down again upon the people, in wrathful defiance of its sanctity.

Distant thunder rolls, shaking the ground, and the sulphur-fumes press fiercely beneath the broadening steam-column. Hard and heavy breathe the bearers; terror at the temerity of the undertaking, which violates the sacredness of the mountain, grows in the heart of their leader.

The vast world stretches all around, and the people who surround the dead Rangatira seem tiny and powerless as the mountain defends his sacred crater with mighty bursts of steam and smoke and rolling thunder and suffocating fumes. Overawed by terror the strength of the bearers fails: they let fall their burden upon a rock; the hearts of the bravest are trembling.

The sanctity of Tongariro-tapu cannot be violated; no, not even by the sacred bones of the Rangatira; and fear grows overpowering beneath the still high-towering, angry crater-summit.

None dares touch the remains of Te Heu-heu again; one and all let them be where they are, upon the rock, overtowered and defended by the majestic summit, with its rolling, thundering, steaming crater – and down they tumble, down, down, helter skelter, in wild and fearful fright they run, a shouting, shrieking body of men, possessed by overpowering terror of the sacred giant. Down, down.

But high up in the sacred regions of Tongariro lie bleaching the bones of the greatest Rangatira of the mountain people –

Maui Pomare, M.D., the grandson of a famous chief, gave me, at parting, this lament composed by the wife of his ancestor:

'Behold! far off, the bright evening star
Rises – our guardian in the dark,
A gleam of light across my lonely way.
Belov'd, wer't thou the Evening Star,
Thou wouldst not, fixed, so far from me remain.
Let once again thy spirit wander back,
To soothe my slumbers on my restless couch,
And whisper in my dreams sweet words of love.
Oh! cruel Death, to damp that beauteous brow
With Night's cold softly falling dews.
Rau-i-ru, Keeper of Celestial Gates,
There comes to thee a lovely bride
Borne from me on Death's swollen tide.
Belov'd, thy wandering spirit now hath passed
By pendant roots of clinging vine
To Spirit Land, where never foot of man
Hath trod – whence none can e'er return –
Paths to the Gods which I not yet have seen.
Belov'd, if any of that host of Heaven
Dare ask of thee thy birth or rank,
Say thou art of that great tribe
Who, sacred, sprang from loins of Gods.
As stands lone Kapiti, a sea-girt isle,
And Tararua's solitary range,
So I to-day stand lonely midst my grief.
My bird with sacred wings hath flown away
Far from my ken, to Spirit Land.
I would I were a Kawau, resolute
To dive into the inmost depths of time,
To reappear at my beloved's side
Amidst the throng upon the further shore.
Belov'd, I soon will join thee there!
I come! Await me at the gates!
My spirit frets; how slow is time.'

How Milu Became the King of Ghosts

LONO WAS A chief living on the western side of the island Hawaii. He had a very red skin and strange-looking eyes. His choice of occupation was farming. This man had never been sick. One time he was digging with the oo, a long sharp-pointed stick or spade. A man passed and admired him. The people said, 'Lono has never been sick.' The man said, 'He will be sick.'

Lono was talking about that man and at the same time struck his oo down with force and cut his foot. He shed much blood, and fainted, falling to the ground. A man took a pig, went after the stranger, and let the pig go, which ran to this man. The stranger was Kamaka, a god of healing. He turned and went back at the call of the messenger, taking some popolo fruit and leaves in his cloak. When he came to the injured man he asked for salt, which he pounded into the fruit and leaves and placed in coco cloth and bound it on the wound, leaving it a long time. Then he went away.

As he journeyed on he heard heavy breathing, and turning saw Lono, who said, 'You have helped me, and so I have left my lands in the care of my friends, directing them what to do, and have hastened after you to learn how to heal other people.'

The god said, 'Lono, open your mouth!' This Lono did, and the god spat in his mouth, so that the saliva could be taken into every part of Lono's body. Thus a part of the god became a part of Lono, and he became very skilful in the use of all healing remedies. He learned about the various diseases and the medicines needed for each. The god and Lono walked together, Lono receiving new lessons along the way, passing through the districts of Kau, Puna, Hilo, and then to Hamakua.

The god said, 'It is not right for us to stay together. You can never accomplish anything by staying with me. You must go to a separate place and give yourself up to healing people.'

Lono turned aside to dwell in Waimanu and Waipio Valleys and there began to practise healing, becoming very noted, while the god Kamaka made his home at Ku-kui-haele.

This god did not tell the other gods of the medicines that he had taught Lono. One of the other gods, Kalae, was trying to find some way to kill Milu, and was always making him sick. Milu, chief of Waipio, heard of the skill of Lono. Some had been sick even to death, and Lono had healed them. Therefore Milu sent a messenger to Lono who responded at once, came and slapped Milu all over the body, and said: 'You are not ill. Obey me and you shall be well.'

Then he healed him from all the sickness inside the body caused by Kalae. But there was danger from outside, so he said: 'You must build a ti-leaf house and dwell there quietly for some time, letting your disease rest. If a company should come by the house making sport, with a great noise, do not go out, because when you go they will come up and get you for your death. Do not open the ti leaves and look out. The day you do this you shall die.'

Some time passed and the chief remained in the house, but one day there was the confused noise of many people talking and shouting around his house. He did not forget the command of Lono. Two birds were sporting in a wonderful way in the sky above the forest. This continued all day until it was dark.

Then another long time passed and again Waipio was full of resounding noises. A great bird appeared in the sky resplendent in all kinds of feathers, swaying from side to side over the valley, from the top of one precipice across to the top of another, in grand flights passing over the heads of the people, who shouted until the valley re-echoed with the sound.

Milu became tired of that great noise and could not patiently obey his physician, so he pushed aside some of the ti leaves of his house and looked out upon the bird. That was the time when the bird swept down upon the house, thrusting a claw under Milu's arm, tearing out his liver. Lono saw this and ran after the bird, but it flew swiftly to a deep pit in the lava on one side of the valley and dashed inside, leaving blood spread on the stones. Lono came, saw the blood, took it and wrapped it in a piece of tapa cloth and returned to the place where the chief lay almost dead. He poured some medicine into the wound and pushed the tapa and blood inside. Milu was soon healed.

The place where the bird hid with the liver of Milu is called to this day Ke-ake-o-Milu ('The liver of Milu'). When this death had passed away he felt very well, even as before his trouble.

Then Lono told him that another death threatened him and would soon appear. He must dwell in quietness.

For some time Milu was living in peace and quiet after this trouble. Then one day the surf of Waipio became very high, rushing from far out even to the sand, and the people entered into the sport of surf-riding with great joy and loud shouts. This noise continued day by day, and Milu was impatient of the restraint and forgot the words of Lono. He went out to bathe in the surf.

When he came to the place of the wonderful surf he let the first and second waves go by, and as the third came near he launched himself upon it while the people along the beach shouted uproariously. He went out again into deeper water, and again came in, letting the first and second waves go first. As he came to the shore the first and second waves were hurled back from the shore in a great mass against the wave upon which he was riding. The two great masses of water struck and pounded Milu, whirling and crowding him down, while the surf-board was caught in the raging, struggling waters and thrown out toward the shore. Milu was completely lost in the deep water.

The people cried: 'Milu is dead! The chief is dead!' The god Kalae thought he had killed Milu, so he with the other poison-gods went on a journey to Mauna Loa. Kapo and Pua, the poison-gods, or gods of death, of the island Maui, found them as they passed, and joined the company. They discovered a forest on Molokai, and there as kupua spirits, or ghost bodies, entered into the trees of that forest, so the trees became the kupua bodies. They were the medicinal or poison qualities in the trees.

Lono remained in Waipio Valley, becoming the ancestor and teacher of all the good healing priests of Hawaii, but Milu became the ruler of the Underworld, the place where the spirits of the dead had their home after they were driven away from the land of the living. Many people came to him from time to time.

He established ghostly sports like those which his subjects had enjoyed before death. They played the game kilu with polished cocoanut shells, spinning them over a smooth surface to strike a post set up in the centre. He taught konane, a game commonly called 'Hawaiian checkers,' but more like the Japanese game of 'Go.' He permitted them to gamble, betting all the kinds of property found in ghost-land. They boxed and wrestled; they leaped from precipices into ghostly swimming-pools; they feasted and fought, sometimes attempting to slay each other. Thus they lived the ghost life as they had lived on earth. Sometimes the ruler was forgotten and the ancient Hawaiians called the Underworld by his name – Milu. The New Zealanders frequently gave their Underworld the name 'Miru.' They also supposed that the ghosts feasted and sported as they had done while living.

Maluae and the Underworld

THIS IS A story from Manoa Valley, back of Honolulu. In the upper end of the valley, at the foot of the highest mountains on the island Oahu, lived Maluae. He was a farmer, and had chosen this land because rain fell abundantly on the mountains, and the streams brought down fine soil from the decaying forests and disintegrating rocks, fertilizing his plants.

Here he cultivated bananas and taro and sweet potatoes. His bananas grew rapidly by the sides of the brooks, and yielded large bunches of fruit from their tree-like stems; his taro filled small walled-in pools, growing in the water like water-lilies, until the roots were matured, when the plants were pulled up and the roots boiled and prepared for food; his sweet potatoes – a vegetable known among the ancient New Zealanders as ku-maru, and supposed to have come from Hawaii – were planted on the drier uplands.

Thus he had plenty of food continually growing, and ripening from time to time. Whenever he gathered any of his food products he brought a part to his family temple and placed it on an altar before the gods Kane and Kanaloa, then he took the rest to his home for his family to eat.

He had a boy whom he dearly loved, whose name was Kaa-lii (rolling chief). This boy was a careless, rollicking child.

One day the boy was tired and hungry. He passed by the temple of the gods and saw bananas, ripe and sweet, on the little platform before the gods. He took these bananas and ate them all.

The gods looked down on the altar expecting to find food, but it was all gone and there was nothing for them. They were very angry, and ran out after the boy. They caught him eating the bananas, and killed him. The body they left lying under the trees, and taking out his ghost threw it into the Underworld.

The father toiled hour after hour cultivating his food plants, and when wearied returned to his home. On the way he met the two gods. They told him how his boy had robbed them of their sacrifices and how they had punished him. They said, "We have sent his ghost body to the lowest regions of the Underworld,"

The father was very sorrowful and heavy hearted as he went on his way to his desolate home. He searched for the body of his boy, and at last found it. He saw too that the story of the gods was true, for partly eaten bananas filled the mouth, which was set in death.

He wrapped the body very carefully in kapa cloth made from the bark of trees. He carried it into his rest-house and laid it on the sleeping-mat. After a time he lay down beside the body, refusing all food, and planning to die with his boy. He thought if he could escape from his own body he would be able to go down where the ghost of his boy had been sent. If he could find that ghost he hoped to take it to the other part of the Underworld, where they could be happy together.

He placed no offerings on the altar of the gods. No prayers were chanted. The afternoon and evening passed slowly. The gods waited for their worshipper, but he came not. They looked down on the altar of sacrifice, but there was nothing for them.

The night passed and the following day. The father lay by the side of his son, neither eating nor drinking, and longing only for death. The house was tightly closed.

Then the gods talked together, and Kane said: "Maluae eats no food, he prepares no awa to drink, and there is no water by him. He is near the door of the Underworld. If he should die, we would be to blame."

Kanaloa said: "He has been a good man, but now we do not hear any prayers. We are losing our worshipper. We in quick anger killed his son. Was this the right reward? He has called us morning and evening in his worship. He has provided fish and fruits and vegetables for our altars. He has always prepared awa from the juice of the yellow awa root for us to drink. We have not paid him well for his care."

Then they decided to go and give life to the father, and permit him to take his ghost body and go down into Po, the dark land, to bring back the ghost of the boy. So they went to Maluae and told him they were sorry for what they had done.

The father was very weak from hunger, and longing for death, and could scarcely listen to them.

When Kane said, "Have you love for your child?" the father whispered: "Yes. My love is without end." "Can you go down into the dark land and get that spirit and put it back in the body which lies here?"

"No," the father said, "no, I can only die and go to live with him and make him happier by taking him to a better place."

Then the gods said, "We will give you the power to go after your boy and we will help you to escape the dangers of the land of ghosts."

Then the father, stirred by hope, rose up and took food and drink. Soon he was strong enough to go on his journey.

The gods gave him a ghost body and also prepared a hollow stick like bamboo, in which they put food, battle-weapons, and a piece of burning lava for fire.

Not far from Honolulu is a beautiful modern estate with fine roads, lakes, running brooks, and interesting valleys extending back into the mountain range. This is called by the very ancient name Moanalua (two lakes). Near the seacoast of this estate was one of the most noted ghost localities of the islands. The ghosts after wandering over the island Oahu would come to this place to find a way into their real home, the Underworld, or, as the Hawaiians usually called it, Po.

Here was a ghostly breadfruit-tree named Lei-walo, possibly meaning 'the eight wreaths' or 'the eighth wreath' – the last wreath of leaves from the land of the living which would meet the eyes of the dying.

The ghosts would leap or fly or climb into the branches of this tree, trying to find a rotten branch upon which they could sit until it broke and threw them into the dark sea below.

Maluae climbed up the breadfruit-tree. He found a branch upon which some ghosts were sitting waiting for it to fall. His weight was so much greater than theirs that the branch broke at once, and down they all fell into the land of Po.

He needed merely to taste the food in his hollow cane to have new life and strength. This he had done when he climbed the tree; thus he had been able to push past the fabled guardians of the pathway of the ghosts in the Upper-world. As he entered the Underworld he again tasted the food of the gods and he felt himself growing stronger and stronger.

He took a magic war-club and a spear out of the cane given by the gods. Ghostly warriors tried to hinder his entrance into the different districts of the dark land. The spirits of dead chiefs challenged him when he passed their homes. Battle after battle was fought. His magic club struck the warriors down, and his spear tossed them aside.

Sometimes he was warmly greeted and aided by ghosts of kindly spirit. Thus he went from place to place, searching for his boy, finding him at last, as the Hawaiians quaintly expressed it, 'down in the papa-ku' (the established foundation of Po), choking and suffocating from the bananas of ghost-land which he was compelled to continually force into his mouth.

The father caught the spirit of the boy and started back toward the Upper-world, but the ghosts surrounded him. They tried to catch him and take the spirit away from him. Again the father partook of the food of the gods. Once more he wielded his war-club, but the hosts of enemies were too great. Multitudes arose on all sides, crushing him by their overwhelming numbers.

At last he raised his magic hollow cane and took the last portion of food. Then he poured out the portion of burning lava which the gods had placed inside. It fell upon the dry floor of the Underworld. The flames dashed into the trees and the shrubs of ghost-land. Fire-holes opened in the floor and streams of lava burst out.

Backward fled the multitudes of spirits. The father thrust the spirit of the boy quickly into the empty magic cane and rushed swiftly up to his home-land. He brought the spirit to the body lying in the rest-house and forced it to find again its living home.

Afterward the father and the boy took food to the altars of the gods, and chanted the accustomed prayers heartily and loyally all the rest of their lives.

A Visit to the King of Ghosts

WHEN ANY PERSON lay in an unconscious state, it was supposed by the ancient Hawaiians that death had taken possession of the body and opened the door for the spirit to depart. Sometimes if the body lay like one asleep the spirit was supposed to return to its old home. One of the Hawaiian legends weaves their deep-rooted faith in the spirit-world into the expressions of one who seemed to be permitted to visit that ghost-land and its king. This legend belonged to the island of Maui and the region near the village Lahaina. Thus was the story told:

Ka-ilio-hae (the wild dog) had been sick for days and at last sank into a state of unconsciousness. The spirit of life crept out of the body and finally departed from the left eye into a corner of the house, buzzing like an insect. Then he stopped and looked back over the body he had left. It appeared to him like a massive mountain. The eyes were deep caves, into which the ghost looked. Then the spirit became afraid and went outside and rested on the roof of the house.

The people began to wail loudly and the ghost fled from the noise to a cocoanut-tree and perched like a bird in the branches. Soon he felt the impulse of the spirit-land moving him away from his old home. So he leaped from tree to tree and flew from place to place wandering toward Kekaa, the place from which the ghosts leave the island of Maui for their home in the permanent spirit-land – the Underworld.

As he came near this doorway to the spirit-world he met the ghost of a sister who had died long before, and to whom was given the power of sometimes turning a ghost back to its body again. She was an aumakua-ho-ola (a spirit making alive). She called to Ka-ilio-hae and told him to come to her house and dwell for a time. But she warned him that when her husband was at home he must not yield to any invitation from him to enter their house, nor could he partake of any of the food which her husband might urge him to eat. The home and the food would be only the shadows of real things, and would destroy his power of becoming alive again.

The sister said, "When my husband comes to eat the food of the spirits and to sleep the sleep of ghosts, then I will go with you and you shall see all the spirit-land of our island and see the king of ghosts."

The ghost-sister led Ka-ilio-hae into the place of whirlwinds, a hill where he heard the voices of many spirits planning to enjoy all the sports of their former life. He listened with delight and drew near to the multitude of happy spirits. Some were making ready to go down to the sea for the hee-nalu (surf-riding).

Others were already rolling the ulu-maika (the round stone discs for rolling along the ground). Some were engaged in the mokomoko, or umauma (boxing), and the kulakulai (wrestling), and the honuhonu (pulling with hands), and the loulou (pulling with hooked fingers), and other athletic sports.

Some of the spirits were already grouped in the shade of trees, playing the gambling games in which they had delighted when alive. There was the stone konane-board (somewhat like checkers), and the puepue-one (a small sand mound in which was concealed some object), and the puhenehene (the hidden stone under piles of kapa), and the many other trials of skill which permitted betting.

Then in another place crowds were gathered around the hulas (the many forms of dancing). These sports were all in the open air and seemed to be full of interest.

There was a strange quality which fettered every new-born ghost: he could only go in the direction into which he was pushed by the hand of some stronger power. If the guardian of a ghost struck it on one side, it would move off in the direction indicated by the blow or the push until spirit strength and experience came and he could go alone. The newcomer desired to join in these games and started to go, but the sister slapped him on the breast and drove him away. These were shadow games into which those who entered could never go back to the substantial things of life.

Then there was a large grass house inside which many ghosts were making merry. The visitor wanted to join this great company, but the sister knew that, if he once was engulfed by this crowd of spirits in this shadow-land, her brother could never escape.

The crowds of players would seize him like a whirlwind and he would be unable to know the way he came in or the way out. Ka-ilio-hae tried to slip away from his sister, but he could not turn readily. He was still a very awkward ghost, and his sister slapped him back in the way in which she wanted him to go.

An island which was supposed to float on the ocean as one of the homes of the aumakuas (the ghosts of the ancestors) had the same characteristics. The ghosts (aumakuas) lived on the shadows of all that belonged to the earth-life.

It was said that a canoe with a party of young people landed on this island of dreams and for some time enjoyed the food and fruits and sports, but after returning to their homes could not receive the nourishment of the food of their former lives, and soon died.

The legends taught that no ghost passing out of the body could return unless it made the life of the aumakuas tabu to itself.

Soon the sister led her brother to a great field, stone walled, in which were such fine grass houses as were built only for chiefs of the highest rank. There she pointed to a narrow passage-way into which she told her brother he must enter by himself.

"This," she said, "is the home of Walia, the high chief of the ghosts living in this place. You must go to him. Listen to all he says to you. Say little. Return quickly. There will be three watchmen guarding this passage. The first will ask you, 'What is the fruit of your heart?' You will answer, 'Walia.' Then he will let you enter the passage.

"Inside the walls of the narrow way will be the second watchman. He will ask why you come; again answer, 'Walia,' and pass by him.

"At the end of the entrance the third guardian stands holding a raised spear ready to strike. Call to him, 'Ka-make-loa'. This is the name of his spear. Then he will ask what you want, and you must reply, 'To see the chief,' and he will let you pass.

"Then again when you stand at the door of the great house you will see two heads bending together in the way so that you cannot enter or see the king and his queen. If these heads can catch a spirit coming to see the king without knowing the proper incantations, they will throw that ghost into the Po-Milu. Watch therefore and remember all that is told you.

"When you see these heads, point your hands straight before you between them and open your arms, pushing these guards off on each side, then the ala-nui will be open for you – and you can enter.

"You will see kahilis moving over the chiefs. The king will awake and call, 'Why does this traveller come?' You will reply quickly, 'He comes to see the Divine One.' When this is said no injury will come to you. Listen and remember and you will be alive again."

Ka-ilio-hae did as he was told with the three watchmen, and each one stepped back, saying, 'Noa' (the tabu is lifted), and he pushed by. At the door he shoved the two heads to the side and entered the chief's house to the Ka-ikuwai (the middle), falling on his hands and knees. The servants were waving the kahilis this way and that. There was motion, but no noise.

The chief awoke, looked at Ka-ilio-hae, and said: "Aloha, stranger, come near. Who is the high chief of your land?"

Then Ka-ilio-hae gave the name of his king, and the genealogy from ancient times of the chiefs dead and in the spirit-world.

The queen of ghosts arose, and the kneeling spirit saw one more beautiful than any woman in all the island, and he fell on his face before her.

The king told him to go back and enter his body and tell his people about troubles near at hand.

While he was before the king twice he heard messengers call to the people that the sports were all over; any one not heeding would be thrown into the darkest place of the home of the ghosts when the third call had been sounded.

The sister was troubled, for she knew that at the third call the stone walls around the king's houses would close and her brother would be held fast forever in the spirit-land, so she uttered her incantations and passed the guard. Softly she called. Her brother reluctantly came. She seized him and pushed him outside.

Then they heard the third call, and met the multitude of ghosts coming inland from their sports in the sea, and other multitudes hastening homeward from their work and sports on the land.

They met a beautiful young woman who called to them to come to her home, and pointed to a point of rock where many birds were resting.

The sister struck her brother and forced him down to the seaside where she had her home and her responsibility, for she was one of the guardians of the entrance to the spirit-world.

She knew well what must be done to restore the spirit to the body, so she told her brother they must at once obey the command of the king; but the brother had seen the delights of the life of the aumakuas and wanted to stay. He tried to slip away and hide, but his sister held him fast and compelled him to go along the beach to his old home and his waiting body.

When they came to the place where the body lay she found a hole in the corner of the house and pushed the spirit through.

When he saw the body he was very much afraid and tried to escape, but the sister caught him and pushed him inside the foot up to the knee.

He did not like the smell of the body and tried to rush back, but she pushed him inside again and held the foot fast and shook him and made him go to the head.

The family heard a little sound in the mouth and saw breath moving the breast, then they knew that he was alive again. They warmed the body and gave a little food. When strength returned he told his family all about his wonderful journey into the land of ghosts.

Biographies & Text Sources

The stories in this book derive from a multitude of original sources, often from the nineteenth century and often based on the writer's first-hand accounts of tales narrated to them by native people, while others are their own retellings of traditional tales. Authors, works and contributors to this book include:

Dr. Karl E. H. Seigfried
Foreword
Dr. Karl E. H. Seigfried is a writer and educator on mythology and religion. His work on Norse mythology, Hindu mythology, medieval literature and modern Paganism has been widely published. He has served as President of Interfaith Dialogue at University of Chicago and taught at Carthage College, Cherry Hill Seminary, Illinois Institute of Technology, Loyola University Chicago and Newberry Library. He holds degrees in religion, literature and music from University of Chicago Divinity School, University of Texas at Austin, University of Wisconsin–Madison and University of California San Diego.

Hartley Burr Alexander
The Creation Story of the Four Suns
Hartley Burr Alexander (1873–1939) was a philosopher, author, scholar, educator, iconographer and poet. Born in Nebraska to a Methodist family, Alexander came to distrust Christianity and developed an interest in First Peoples of the Americas, their religions and their spirituality. He attended the University of Nebraska, after which he earned a graduate degree at the University of Pennsylvania and a doctorate at Columbia University. Alexander wrote prolifically on the subjects of Native American philosophy, lore, mythology and art. One of his best-known works is the poem 'To a Child's Moccasin (Found at Wounded Knee)', which stood in stark contrast to the prevailing negative views and treatment of Native Americans by the US government and American society of the time.

Emilie Kip Baker
Pluto and the Underworld; The Story of Orpheus and Eurydice
Emilie Kip Baker (1873–1951) was an American author and a significant figure in the realm of education and literature of her time. Taking a scholarly approach to her retellings of ancient myths and stories, her work gained popularity among both academics and ordinary readers alike. She is the author of the popular collection *Stories of Old Greece and Rome* (1913), as well as *Stories from Northern Myths* (1914).

Im Bang and Yi Ryuk
Ta-Hong; The King of Yom-Na (Hell); Hong's Experiences in Hades
Im Bang (1640–1724) was a Korean author who wrote traditional stories capturing Korea's folklore and culture. He is best known for his stories that appear in *Korean Folk Tales: Imps, Ghosts, and Fairies* (1913), a classical collection which also features works by fellow Korean author Yi Ryuk (1438–1498). Bang's stories in the collection include 'A Story of the Fox' and 'A Visit from the Shades'. The stories by Ryuk include 'The "Old Buddha"', 'The Senses' and 'Faithful Mo'.

Clara Kern Bayliss
Arnomongo and Iput-Iput; The Battle of the Crabs; The Eagle and the Hen; How the Lizards Got Their Markings; The Living Head; The Meeting of the Plants; The Spider and the Fly; Why Dogs Wag Their Tails; The Monkey and the Turtle
Clara Kern Bayliss (1848–1948) was an American author and educator, born on her family's farm in Michigan. Bayliss was the first woman to graduate from Michigan's Hillsdale College in 1871, where she also earned her master's degree in 1874. She was the head of the Education Committee of the Illinois Congress of Mothers, and was vice president of the Illinois State Teachers Association. Her published works include *Philippine Folk-Tales; In Brook and Bayou: or, Life in the Still Waters* (1897); and *A Treasury of Eskimo Tales* (1922).

W.H.I. Bleek
The Girl of the Early Race, Who Made Stars
Wilhelm Heinrich Immanuel Bleek (1827–75) was a German linguist and philologist. He participated in projects in Niger and Natal before becoming Sir George Grey's official interpreter, cataloguer and curator. Bleek conducted research and contributed to publications, collecting examples of African literature from missionaries and travellers. He wrote regularly for the newspaper *Het Volksblad*, and published his *A Comparative Grammar of South African Languages* in two parts in 1862 and 1869. Together with Lucy Lloyd, he met and interviewed members of the San people in order to research and record linguistic, anthropological, ethnographic and cultural information, leading to 'The Bleek and Lloyd Archive' of |Xam and !Kung texts. Examples from this were collated into a printed book called *Specimens of Bushman Folklore* (1911).

Samuel Butler
The Visit to the Dead
Samuel Butler (1835–1902) was born in Nottinghamshire, England. He was a novelist, essayist and critic. His most famous works include *The Way of All Flesh*, an autobiographical novel largely considered his magnum opus, and *Erewhon*, a utopian satire of the mentality and lifestyles embraced by Victorian England. The chapters of *Erewhon* that make up 'The Book of the Machines' were adapted from articles he submitted to *The Press*, which posited that machines might undergo evolution in a similar way to humans.

William Carleton
Frank Martin and the Fairies
William Carleton (1845–1912) was an American poet, born in Michigan. Growing up in a rural setting in Lenawee County, he attended Hillsdale College, where he graduated in 1869. He went on to become a newspaper journalist in Hillsdale, and later an editor of the *Detroit Weekly Tribune*, as well as a poet. One of his best-known poems is 'Betsey and I Are Out', first printed in the *Toledo Blade*, and reprinted by *Harper's Weekly*. Another poem, 'Over the Hill to the Poor House', earned him a level of literary renown.

Padraic Colum
Tales of Ragnarok; The Death of Sigurd
Padraic Colum (1881–1972) was born in County Longford, Ireland. He wrote prolifically as a poet, biographer, novelist, playwright, dramatist, children's book author and folklore collector.

A prominent figure in the late nineteenth-century Irish Literary Revival, Colum developed connections with numerous well-known Irish writers, including James Joyce and W.B. Yeats. His first book, a poetry collection entitled *Wild Earth*, was published in 1907. Later living in the US, Colum ventured into prose fiction and children's books, and taught at Columbia University and CCNY.

Margaret Compton
The Coyote or Prairie Wolf
Margaret Compton (1852–1903) was an American author. With a strong interest in Native American cultures and folklore traditions, she published several works on the subject. Her book *American Indian Fairy Tales* (1907) collects a number of Native American stories. Her short fiction includes the stories 'How Mad Buffalo Fought the Thunder-Bird' (1895), 'Snowbird and the Water-Tiger' (1895), and 'The Adventures of Living Statue' (1895).

Jeremiah Curtin
The Winning of Halai Auna at the House of Tuina
Jeremiah Curtin (1835–1906) was a Detroit-born ethnographer and folklorist. While much of his work would focus on collecting myths and folktales from around the world, Curtin would also be renowned for his translations of works by Polish author Henryk Sienkiewicz. Between 1883 and 1891, Curtin's interests would focus closer to home when he worked as a field researcher recording the myths and customs of Native American people, which would later result in the publication of the book *Creation Myths of Primitive America* (1898).

F. Hadland Davis
Izanagi and Izanami; Benten and the Dragon; The Thirty-Three Places Sacred to Kwannon; Kwannon and the Deer; Daikoku's Rat
Frederick Hadland Davis was a writer and historian – author of *The Land of the Yellow Spring and Other Japanese Stories* (1910) and *The Persian Mystics* (1908 and 1920). His books describe these cultures to the western world and tell stories of ghosts, creation, mystical creatures and more. He is best known for his book *Myths and Legends of Japan* (1912).

Elphinstone Dayrell
Why the Sun and the Moon Live in the Sky; Why the Moon Waxes and Wanes
Elphinstone Dayrell (1869–1917) collected his tales after hearing many first-hand from the Efik and Ibibio peoples of Southeastern Nigeria when he was District Commissioner of South Nigeria. His collections of folklore include *Folk Stories from Southern Nigeria* (1910) and *Ikom Folk Stories from Southern Nigeria*, the latter published by the Royal Anthropological Institute of Great Britain and Ireland in 1913.

Richard Edward Dennett
Why Some Men Are White and Others Black; The Fight Between the Two Fetishes; Lifuma and Chimpukela; Why the Crocodile Does Not Eat the Hen; Death and Burial of the Fjort; The Twin Brothers
Richard Edward Dennett was an English trader who operated in the present-day Republic of Congo during the early twentieth century. His publications, which had an influence on the sociological and anthropological research of West African cultures at the time, include *Notes on the Folklore of the Fjort* (1898) and *My Yoruba Alphabet* (1916).

W. Dittmer
Tane – The Creation of Nature; The Creation of the Stars; The Creation of Hawaiki; The Battle of the Giants; Ngawai: The Burial of Te Heu-Heu on Tongariro

Primarily an artist, Wilhelm Dittmer (1866–1909) came from Hamburg, Germany, but worked in New Zealand from 1898 to 1905. In that time, he became fascinated by the life and lore of the country's indigenous people; he travelled through the islands, collecting their stories, soaking up their culture and absorbing their artistic traditions. On returning home to Hamburg, he published *Te Tohunga*, a wonderful compilation of Maori mythology, richly illustrated in the art nouveau style.

Roland Burrage Dixon
The Making of Daylight

A renowned American anthropologist, Roland Barrage (1875–1934) was a student of Franz Uri Boas who would go on to carve his own distinct path in his chosen field of expertise. A graduate and later professor at Harvard University, much of Dixon's work regarding Native American people was conducted in northeastern California and the Sierra Nevada, focusing on the Maidu and Chimariko tribes. His work was published as *Achomawi and Atsugewi Tales* (1908), while he also edited *Achomawi Myths* (1909), a collection of stories previously recorded by Jeremiah Curtin.

Constance Goddard DuBois
The Story of the Creation; San Luiseño Creation Myth

Born in Zanesville, Ohio, in 1869, Constance Godard DuBois was the author of six novels and a self-taught ethnographer. DuBois devoted a significant portion of her life to the study of Native American people in California, writing articles that revealed much about their lives, customs, traditions and myths, and working to preserve their way of life. Her work on Native Americans was published as *The Mythology of the Diegueños* (1901) and *The Dawn of the World: Myths and Weird Tales Told by the Miwok Indians of California* (1904–06). She died in 1934.

Elsie Spicer Eells
How Night Came; How the Brazilian Beetles Got Their Gorgeous Coats; How the Rabbit Lost His Tail; How the Tiger Got His Stripes

Elsie Spicer Eells (1880–1963) was an American author and researcher of folklore. She travelled widely throughout her life, leading to her publication of several short story collections which were based on oral traditions from Brazil, the Azores and other regions. She lived in Brazil for three years, and visited numerous other countries as a researcher for The Hispanic Society of America. Her works include *Fairy Tales from Brazil* (1917), *Tales of Giants from Brazil* (1918), and *The Islands of Magic: Legends, Folk and Fairy Tales from the Azores* (1922).

Parker Fillmore
The Blacksmith's Stool: The Story of a Man Who Found that Death Was Necessary

Parker Fillmore (1878–1944) was an American author born in Cincinnati, Ohio. Upon taking a job as a teacher in the Philippines, Fillmore was given no textbooks to teach his students English, and so he crafted his own stories for this purpose, launching his career in writing. Returning to the US and moving to a primarily Czech neighbourhood in New York City, he gained a great passion for the Czechoslovakian folklore that his neighbours shared with him. This led to his publication of several collections of these stories including *Czechoslovak Fairy Tales* (1919) and *The Shoemaker's Apron* (1920).

James S. Gale
Ta-Hong; The King of Yom-Na (Hell); Hong's Experiences in Hades
James S. Gale (1863–1937) was a translator and Presbyterian missionary. Born in Ontario, Canada, he studied arts at the University of Toronto. Following his studies, he became a missionary for the university's YMCA and moved to Korea in 1888, where he taught English at the Christian School in Pusan. He is known for his translation of the collection *Korean Folk Tales: Imps, Ghosts, and Fairies* (1913) by Im Bang and Yi Ryuk. He was also a member of a board that worked to translate the Bible into Korean.

Edward Winslow Gifford
The First Tui Tonga; The Origin of Kava and Sugar Cane; The Boat that Went to Pulotu
Edward Winslow Gifford (1887–1959) was an anthropologist, ethnographer and author born in Oakland, California. Fascinated with the indigenous peoples of California, Gifford focused much of his career on ethnography of the state's many tribes. He became an assistant curator at the Museum of Anthropology, within the University of California, Berkeley, and later joined the Bayard Dominic Expedition of 1920. During this expedition, he conducted anthropological and archaeological surveys of the indigenous Polynesian people of Tonga. In 1945, he became a professor of anthropology at Berkeley, and he rose to the position of director at the Museum of Anthropology.

Pliny Earle Goddard
The Origin of Corn and Deer
Pliny Earle Goddard (1869–1928) was a linguist and ethnologist whose early work was dedicated to writing about the lives and customs of Native American tribes in northwestern California. Goddard would later move to New York to take up a curatorship at the American Museum of Natural History, where he would work alongside famed anthropologist Franz Uri Boas and further his work by studying tribes as far afield as Alaska and Canada. Goddard wrote extensively on Native Americans in a number of books such as *Jicarilla Apache Texts* (1911) and *Indians of the Northwest Coast* (1924).

George Grey
The Children of Heaven and Earth; The Discovery of New Zealand; The Voyage to New Zealand; The Art of Netting Learned by Kahukura from the Fairies
George Grey (1812–1898) was barely born when his father fell in the Peninsular War: a scion of Britain's imperial ascendancy he was born to serve. And so he did – as a soldier; as an explorer in Western Australia; and as colonial governor of South Australia and of New Zealand. Grey's loyalty was always to the Crown – he took a tough line with local insurrections – but he also had an eager interest in the folklore of the Pacific peoples.

Elizabeth W. Grierson
Assipattle and the Mester Stoorworm
Elizabeth Grierson (1869–1943) was born on a farm near Hawick, in the Scottish Borders. Throughout the course of her life she published more than thirty books, many of which covered Scottish fairy tales and folklore. In addition to these, she also published travel

guides to the cities of Edinburgh, Scotland, and Florence, Italy. Her best-known works are her collections *The Scottish Fairy Book* (1910) and *Children's Tales from Scottish Ballads* (1906).

William Elliot Griffis
How the Cymry Land Became Inhabited; The Great Red Dragon of Wales; The Wonderful Alpine Horn; The Story of the Fleur-de-Lys; Prince Sandalwood, the Father of Korea; Why the Stork Loves Holland
Born in Philadelphia in 1843, William Elliot Griffis served as a corporal in the American Civil War, and later graduated from Rutgers University in 1869. In 1870, Griffis went to Japan and became Superintendent of Education in the province of Echizen. Throughout the 1870s, Griffis taught at several subsequent institutions and wrote for numerous newspapers and magazines. His works include the collections *Japanese Fairy Tales, Korean Fairy Tales, Belgian Fairy Tales*, and *Swiss Fairy Tales*. He died in Florida in 1928.

H.A. Guerber
Chaos and Nyx; The Egg Myth; The Titans; Birth of Zeus; The Giants' War; Pandora; Prometheus; The Great Deluge
Hélène Adeline Guerber (1859–1929) was an American author whose work focused mainly on retellings of myths and folklore for adult audiences. She was born in Michigan and was educated in Paris. She published more than two dozen books throughout her life, including *Myths of Greece and Rome* (1908), *Legends of the Rhine* (1905) and *The Book of the Epic* (1913).

Lafcadio Hearn
The Tradition of the Tea-Plant
Patrick Lafcadio Hearn (1850–1904, also known as Koizumi Yakumo) was a journalist and writer whose wandering life led him eventually to find a home in Japan, which would prove to be his true inspiration. He wrote about the country and, especially, its legends and ghost stories. His books about Japan include *Japanese Fairy Tales* (1898) and *In Ghostly Japan* (1899). His intriguing *Some Chinese Ghosts* (1887) retells Chinese ghost stories through a Japanese lens, aided by his writerly artistry.

Homer
The Visit to the Dead
Little is known for certain about the life of Homer, the Greek poet credited as the author of the great epics *The Iliad* and *The Odyssey*, although he is believed to have been born sometime between the twelfth and eighth centuries BCE. *The Odyssey* describes the trials of the hero Odysseus on his journey home to Ithaca following the Trojan War. It has had a huge influence on Western literature, inspiring extensive translations, poems, plays and novels.

Eleanor Hull
The Talking Head of Donn-Bo
Eleanor Hull (1860–1935) was an English author, journalist and scholar of Old Irish. Born in Manchester, her family relocated to Dublin, Ireland, when she was a child. Hull attended Alexandra College, Dublin from 1877 to 1882, and later took up Celtic studies in London. In 1915, she was elected president of the Irish Literary Society. She was also a co-founder of the Irish

Texts Society. Her published works include *The Cuchullin Saga in Irish Literature* (1898), *The Northmen in Britain* (1913) and *A History of Ireland and Her People* (1931).

James Athearn Jones
The Mother of the World; The Origin of Women; The Fall of the Lenape
Born in Massachusetts in 1790, James Athearn Jones would go on to work as a lawyer and editor. It is for his work collecting Native American legends that he is best remembered, however, beginning in 1820 with *Traditions of the North American Indians, or Tales of an Indian Camp*, which featured stories told to him by an Indian woman of the Gayhead tribe who was employed as his nurse. Jones would write three volumes in the *Traditions of the North American Indians* series prior to his death in 1853.

Katharine Berry Judson
How the World Was Made; Osage Creation Story; Spider's Creation; The Creation of the World; Omaha Sacred Legend; The Legend of the Peace Pipes; The Raven Myth; The Flood and the Rainbow; The Creation of Man and the Flood; The Flood; The First Fire; Origin of Strawberries; Legend of the Corn; The Origin of the Tides; The Land of the Dead
Born in Poughkeepsie, New York, in 1871, Katherine Berry Judson was the author of numerous books, including the novel *When the Forests Are Ablaze* and several works of non-fiction. She is perhaps best remembered for her series of *Myths and Legends* books, published between 1910 and 1917, which collected folk tales and myths of Native American people from across the North American continent. She died in 1929.

Thomas Keightley
Origin of Tiis Lake; Departure of the Fairies
Thomas Keightley (1789–1872) was an Irish author, primarily of mythological and folkloric works. Born in Newtown, County Kildare, he attended Trinity College Dublin but left without completing his law studies. He moved to London in 1824 to pursue a literary career. Keightley helped pioneer the modern study of folklore, working as a 'comparativist' collector to draw connections between stories and traditions across various cultures. His two volumes of *The Fairy Mythology* were published in 1828, and they quickly gained popularity among folklore researchers and literary figures. His other works include *The Mythology of Ancient Greece and Italy for the Use of School* (1831) and *Tales and Popular Fictions* (1834).

Mite Kremnitz
The Voice of Death
Mite Kremnitz (1852–1916) was a German author who was born Marie von Bardeleben. Growing up in London and Berlin, she later moved to Bucharest in 1875. Becoming good friends with Queen Elisabeth of Wied, also a writer, the two published a number of novels and a drama together. Publishing her own works under the pen names Mite Kremnitz and George Allan, she produced several books including *Roumanian Fairy Tales* (1885) and *Rumänische Dichtungen* ('Romanian Poems', 1881).

A.L. Kroeber
The Visit to the Dead
A.L. Kroeber (1876–1960) was an American cultural anthropologist. Born in New Jersey, Kroeber grew up immersed in an intellectual and bilingual atmosphere as a descendant of German

immigrants. After receiving his PhD in Anthropology at Columbia University in 1901, he went on to become the first professor in the Department of Anthropology at the University of California, Berkeley. He was the father of acclaimed author Ursula K. Le Guin. His works include *Indian Myths of South Central California* (1907) and *The Religion of the Indians of California* (1907).

Ignácz Kúnos
The Creation
Ignácz Kúnos (1860–1945) was a Hungarian linguist, author and Turkologist. He was a prominent scholar of Turkish folk literature and dialectology. Having studied linguistics at Budapest University and spent five years studying the Turkish language and culture in Constantinople (now Istanbul), he became professor of Turkish philology at Budapest University in 1890. He later worked as a professor at various other institutions and established the Department of Folkloristics at Istanbul University in 1925. His folktale collections include *Turkish Fairy Tales and Folk Tales* (1896) and *Forty-Four Turkish Fairy Tales* (1914).

Gertrude Landa
The Giant of the Flood
Gertrude Landa (1892–1941) was a journalist and writer often referred to simply by her pseudonym Aunt Naomi. Landa wrote a number of plays and novels with her husband, the writer Myer Jack Landa, and published a collection of classic tales and folklore stories in the book *Jewish Fairy Tales and Legends* (1919).

Andrew Lang and Nora Lang
The Return of the Dead Wife
Scottish writer and critic Andrew Lang (1844–1912) was born and raised in Selkirk. In 1875, he married Leonora 'Nora' Blanche Alleyne (1851–1933), who would become his collaborator on many works. Although Lang worked variously as a historian, journalist, poet and anthropologist, his greatest legacy has been his works on folklore, mythology and religion. Among these are the *Fairy Books*, 25 volumes of folk and fairy tales Lang published with his wife, including *The Arabian Nights Entertainments* (1898), their adaptation of the *One Thousand Nights and a Night* folk tales. While many volumes in the series list Lang alone as the editor, it was in fact Nora who translated and adapted these works. Lang later acknowledged his wife's significant contribution in the preface to *The Lilac Fairy Book* (1910), crediting almost all of the series to 'the work of Mrs. Lang', and later volumes also listed her as an author.

Charles Godfrey Leland
Origin of the Black Snakes; How Glooskap Left the World
Charles Godfrey Leland (1824–1903) was a qualified lawyer, journalist and civil war veteran whose various interests saw him travel widely and write about many topics. Perhaps most notably, Leland's keen fascination with folklore would lead him to write many books on the subject, covering everything from pagan and Aryan traditions, to studies of Gypsies; his work on Native American tales was published in 1884 as *The Algonquin Legends of New England*.

Frank Bird Linderman
Retrospection
Born in Ohio in 1869, Frank Bird Linderman moved to Montana at the age of 16, where he found himself living among the Salish and Kootenai tribes. Thereafter a lifelong supporter of Native

American peoples, Linderman campaigned tirelessly for the preservation of their culture and way of life, and was instrumental in the establishment of the Rocky Boy Reservation for the Ojibwe and Cree people in 1916. Among his most famous works was *Indian Why Stories: Sparks from War Eagle's Lodge-Fire* (1905). He would continue to write about Native Americans right up until his death in 1938.

L.C. Lloyd
The Girl of the Early Race, Who Made Stars
Lucy Catherine Lloyd (1834–1914) worked with W.H.I. Bleek to create 'The Bleek and Lloyd Archive' of |Xam and !Kung texts, which led to *Specimens of Bushman Folklore* (1911), which she edited. When the first |Xam speakers arrived to live with them at their house in Mowbray, she became responsible for recording two thirds of the texts collected, and continued the work alone after Bleek's death, assuming the curatorship of the Grey Collection and maintaining her own research. Lucy also played an important role in the founding of both the South African Folklore Society and, in 1879, the *Folklore Journal*. In 1913, Lloyd became the first woman in South Africa to receive an Honorary Doctorate from the University of the Cape of Good Hope in recognition of her contribution to research.

Logan Marshall
The Good King Arthur; The Sack of Troy
Logan Marshall was the pen name of Logan Howard-Smith (born in 1883). He was an American author born in Philadelphia, Pennsylvania. Marshall graduated from the University of Pennsylvania in 1905, following which he became an assistant editor at the publishing firm The John C. Winston Co. There he both edited and authored a great number of books under his pen name. His most well-known of these was *The Sinking of the Titanic and Great Sea Disasters* (1912), which grew hugely popular due to massive public interest in the tragedy.

Frederick H. Martens
How the Five Ancients Became Men
Frederick H. Martens (1874–1932) was an American translator and music journalist. His translation work mainly consisted of books for children, and he worked several times with the author Clara Stroebe to translate her collections of stories and fairy tales into English. Martens was the translator of Stroebe's *The Norwegian Fairy Book* (1922) and *The Swedish Fairy Book* (1921). He also translated Elsie Spicer Eells' *The Brazilian Fairy Book* (1926) and R. Wilhelm's *The Chinese Fairy Book* (1921). His original works include *Violin Mastery* (1919) and a number of newspaper and magazine articles.

Gaston C. Maspero
The Adventure of Setne Khamwas with the Mummies
Gaston C. Maspero (1846–1916) was a French Egyptologist, widely regarded as the most preeminent of his day. Born in Paris, he showed an early interest in history and Egyptology following a visit to the Louvre's Egyptian galleries as a teen. He taught the Egyptian language as a professor at the Collège de France. In 1880, he led an archaeological expedition in Egypt, which evolved into the Institut Français d'Archéologie Orientale. Among his many contributions to Egyptology were his translations of the Egyptian *Book of the Dead* and his work *Histoire ancienne des peuples de l'Orient classique* (1895–1897).

Washington Matthews
The Navajo Origin Legend: The Story of the Emergence
Washington Matthews (1843–1905) was an Irish ethnographer, linguist and surgeon in the United States Army. He is best known for his studies of Native American peoples, particularly the Navajo people. Born in Killiney near Dublin, Ireland, Matthews and his family moved to the United States after his mother's death. Spending most of his childhood in Wisconsin and Iowa, he later graduated from the University of Iowa with a degree in medicine in 1864. He volunteered as a surgeon for the Union Army in the American Civil War, after which he was posted at Fort Union in Montana. There he developed a strong interest in Native American cultures, and he spent much of his life studying the Navajo. He published a number of works on them including *The Mountain Chant: A Navajo Ceremony* (1877), *Navaho Legends* (1897) and *Navaho Myths, Prayers and Songs* (1907).

Clinton Hart Merriam
O-wel'-lin the Rock Giant
Clinton Hart Merriam (1855–1942) was a zoologist, naturalist and doctor who conducted a number of expeditions to the American West in the latter half of the nineteenth century. Reliant on the knowledge of Native American guides in his surveys, Merriam would in later years become fascinated by their culture and abandon his zoological work to study the tribes of California, hoping to preserve their knowledge, language, customs and mythology before they were lost forever. This would lead to the publication of his book *The Dawn of the World: Myths and Weird Tales Told by the Miwok Indians of California* (1910).

James Mooney
The Deluge; Origin of Disease and Medicine; Origin of the Pleiades and the Pine; The Daughter of the Sun: Origin of Death
James Mooney (1861–1921) was an American ethnographer, born in Richmond, Indiana, and the son of Irish Catholic immigrants. He was a pioneer in the emerging field of ethnography, becoming a self-taught scholar in Native American cultures. Much of his knowledge he gained first-hand during his long stays with various tribes, including the Cherokee. Mooney worked with the Bureau of American Ethnology in compiling the names of tribes across the country. He studied Native American groups in the southeast and the Great Plains, and he conducted studies on the Ghost Dance. His published works include *The Sacred Formulas of the Cherokees* (1891), and *Myths of the Cherokee* (1900).

Maximilian A. Mügge
Why the Sole of Man's Foot Is Flat; Solomon Cursed by His Mother
Maximilian A. Mügge (b. 1878) was an author and translator. He is best known for his book *Serbian Folk Songs, Fairy Tales and Proverbs* (1916). His other published works include *Friedrich Nietzsche, His Life and Work* (1908) and *Heinrich von Treitschke* (1915). He was also a translator; one such work he translated was *Early Greek Philosophy and Other Essays* (1911) by Friedrich Wilhelm Nietzsche.

Robert H. Nassau
Origins of the Ivory Trade; Why Mosquitoes Buzz; Origin of the Elephant; The Magic Drum; Leopard's Hunting Companions; Is the Bat a Bird or a Beast?; Dog, and His Human Speech
Robert H. Nassau (1835–1921) was an American presbyterian missionary who spent four decades in Africa. He was born in Pennsylvania. He studied at Princeton Theological Seminary from 1856

to 1859, then earned a medical degree from Pennsylvania Medical School in 1861. Becoming a missionary for the Presbyterian Board of Foreign Missions, Nassau was first posted to the island of Corisco, in Equatorial Guinea. He would go on to participate in missions in a number of places, including Benita and Belambla. His published works include *Where Animals Talk: West Africa Folk Lore Tales* (1900) and *Fetichism in West Africa* (1904).

K. Langloh Parker
Star Tales of the Aboriginal Australians
K. Langloh Parker (1856–1940) was the pen name of Catherine Eliza Somerville Stow, an Australian author and ethnographer. Living in northern New South Wales, she was introduced to the culture of the Yuwaalaraay people and developed a strong affinity. Her work mainly involved the recording of the Yuwaalaraay's stories and mythology. Although her accounts are considered the most accurate and comprehensive of their time, they nonetheless reflect European views on the Aboriginal peoples of Australia and present their stories through a Western colonialist lens.

Norman Hinsdale Pitman
How Footbinding Started; The Golden Beetle, or Why the Dog Hates the Cat
Norman Hinsdale Pitman (1876–1925) was an author and educator, born in Lamont, Michigan. His works include *The Lady Elect: A Chinese Romance* (1913), *A Chinese Wonder Book* (1919), *Chinese Fairy Tales* (1924) and *Dragon Lure: A Romance of Peking* (1925).

Knud Rasmussen
Qalagánguasê, Who Passed to the Land of Ghosts
Knud Rasmussen (1879–1933) was a Greenlandic-Danish anthropologist and polar explorer. Born in Jacobshavn, Greenland, Rasmussen grew up among the Kalaallit, an Inuit ethnic group, from whom he learned their language and culture. Rasmussen was an early pioneer of what became Inuit Studies, or Greenlandic and Arctic Studies. He was also the first European to cross the Northwest Passage on a dog sled. His published works include *Eskimo Folk-Tales* (1921) and *The People of the Polar North* (1908).

Henry Rowe Schoolcraft
Ojeeg Annung, or The Summer-Maker; Peboan and Seegwun; Nezhik-e-wä-wä-sun, or The Lone Lightning; Opeechee, or The Origin of the Robin; Mon-daw-min, or The Origin of Indian Corn; The Star Family, or Celestial Sisters; Mishemokwa, or The Origin of the Small Black Bear
Henry Rowe Schoolcraft (1793–1865) devoted a significant portion of his life to interactions with Native American people. In 1822, he served as an Indian agent for the US government covering Michigan, Wisconsin and Minnesota, before later marrying Jane Johnston, who was herself the daughter of an Ojibwa war chief. From his wife, Schoolcraft would learn the Ojibwa language and much about their history and way of life. He would go on to write extensively about the Native American people, with works including *The Myth of Hiawatha, and other Oral Legends, Mythologic and Allegoric, of the North American Indians* (1856) and a comprehensive six-volume series titled *Historical and Statistical Information Respecting the History, Condition, and Prospects of the Indian Tribes of the United States* that was published between 1851 and 1857.

Lewis Spence
Creation Story of the Mixtecs; A Story of the Rise and Fall of the Toltecs; The Mexican Noah; Tezcatlipoca, Overthrower of the Toltecs; Tezcatlipoca Deceives the Toltecs; A Journey to Xibalba

James Lewis Thomas Chalmers Spence (1874–1955) was a scholar of Scottish, Mexican and Central American folklore, as well as that of Brittany, Spain and the Rhine. He was also a poet, journalist, author, editor and nationalist who founded the party that would become the Scottish National Party. He was a Fellow of the Royal Anthropological Institute of Great Britain and Ireland, and vice president of the Scottish Anthropological and Folklore Society.

Henry M. Stanley
The Goat, The Lion, and the Serpent; The City of the Elephants
"Dr Livingstone, I presume?" Welshman Sir Henry Morton Stanley (1841–1904) is probably most famous for a line he may or may not have uttered, on encountering the missionary and explorer he had been sent to locate in Africa. He was also an ex-soldier who fought for the Confederate Army, the Union Army and the Union Navy before becoming a journalist and explorer of central Africa. He joined Livingstone in the search for the source of the Nile and worked for King Leopold II of Belgium in the latter's mission to conquer the Congo basin. His works include *How I Found Livingstone* (1872), *Through the Dark Continent* (1878), *The Congo and the Founding of Its Free State* (1885), *In Darkest Africa* (1890) and *My Dark Companions* (1893).

E.T.C. Werner
The Five Spirits of the Plague
Edward Theodore Chalmers Werner (1864–1954) was a sinologist specialising in Chinese superstition, myths and magic. He worked as a British diplomat in China during the final imperial dynasty, working his way up to British Consul-General in 1911. Being posted to all four corners of China encouraged Werner's interest in the mythological culture of the land, and after retirement he was able to concentrate on his sinological studies, of which *Myths & Legends of China* (1922) was one result.

W.D. Westervelt
How Milu Became the King of Ghosts; Maluae and the Underworld; A Visit to the King of Ghosts
W.D. Westervelt (1849–1939) was an American author and pastor. He settled in Hawaii in 1899 and served as the Corresponding Secretary for the Hawaiian Historical Society beginning in 1908. His enormous interest in Hawaiian mythology and culture led him to publish numerous articles and books on the subject. His best-known works include *Legends of Gods and Ghosts (Hawaiian Mythology)* (1915), *Legends of Old Honolulu* (1915), and *Hawaiian Legends of Volcanoes* (1916). He is considered one of the foremost authorities on Hawaiian folklore in English.

R. Wilhelm
How the Five Ancients Became Men
R. Wilhelm (1873–1930) was a German sinologist, theologian and missionary. He was born in Stuttgart and attended the University of Frankfurt. Wilhelm lived in China for 25 years and was fluent in both spoken and written Chinese. He is best known for his translation of the *I Ching*, which is considered one of the best translations, and for his translation of Chinese philosophical works into German.

FLAME TREE PUBLISHING
Epic, Dark, Thrilling & Gothic

New & Classic Writing

Flame Tree's Gothic Fantasy books offer a carefully curated series of new titles, each with combinations of original and classic writing:

A Dying Planet • African Ghost • Agents & Spies • Alien Invasion • Alternate History
American Gothic • Asian Ghost • Black Sci-Fi • Bodies in the Library • Chilling Crime
Chilling Ghost • Chilling Horror • Christmas Gothic • Compelling Science Fiction • Cosy Crime
Crime & Mystery • Detective Mysteries • Detective Thrillers • Dystopia Utopia • Endless Apocalypse
Epic Fantasy • First Peoples Shared Stories • Footsteps in the Dark • Haunted House
Heroic Fantasy • Hidden Realms • Immigrant Sci-Fi • Learning to be Human
Lost Atlantis • Lost Souls • Lost Worlds • Lovecraft Mythos • Moon Falling • Murder Mayhem
Pirates & Ghosts • Robots & AI • Robots Past & Future • Science Fiction • Shadows on the Water
Spirits & Ghouls Strange Lands • Sun Rising • Supernatural Horror • Swords & Steam
Terrifying Ghosts • Time Travel • Urban Crime • Weird Horror • Were Wolf

Also, new companion titles offer rich collections of classic fiction, myths and tales in the gothic fantasy tradition:

Charles Dickens Supernatural • George Orwell Visions of Dystopia • H.G. Wells • Lovecraft
Sherlock Holmes • Edgar Allan Poe • Bram Stoker Horror Stories • Mary Shelley Horror Stories
Sheridan Le Fanu Horror Stories • M.R. James Ghost Stories • Algernon Blackwood Horror Stories
Arthur Machen Horror Stories • William Hope Hodgson Horror Stories • Robert Louis Stevenson
The Age of Queen Victoria • Alice's Adventures in Wonderland • The Wonderful Wizard of Oz
King Arthur & The Knights of the Round Table • Ramayana • The Odyssey and the Iliad • The Aeneid
The Divine Comedy • Paradise Lost • The Decameron • One Thousand and One Arabian Nights
Moby Dick • Don Quixote • Hans Christian Andersen Fairy Tales • Brothers Grimm Fairy Tales
Babylon & Sumer Myths & Tales • Persian Myths & Tales • African Myths & Tales
Greek Myths & Tales • Norse Myths & Tales • Chinese Myths & Tales • Japanese Myths & Tales
Native American Myths & Tales • Aztec Myths & Tales • Egyptian Myths & Tales • Viking Folk & Fairy Tales
Celtic Myths & Tales • Irish Fairy Tales • Scottish Folk & Fairy Tales • Heroes & Heroines Myths & Tales
Quests & Journeys Myths & Tales • Gods & Monsters Myths & Tales • Titans & Giants Myths & Tales
Beasts & Creatures Myths & Tales • Witches, Wizards, Seers & Healers Myths & Tales
Origins & Endings Myths & Tales • Prophecies & Oracles Myths & Tales

Available from all good bookstores, worldwide, and online at
flametreepublishing.com

See our new fiction imprint
FLAME TREE PRESS | FICTION WITHOUT FRONTIERS
New and original writing in Horror, Crime, SF and Fantasy

And join our monthly newsletter with offers and more stories:
FLAME TREE FICTION NEWSLETTER
flametreepress.com

For our books, calendars, blog
and latest special offers please see:
flametreepublishing.com